Praise for 'Crossing the Water'

coming of age novel with a difference... 'Crossing the Water'
gins against the backdrop of the Irish civil war when two boys are
ight in an incident which will change their lives forever. They take
fferent paths, but their lives remain linked in distinctive ways as a
e of friendship and conflict, loyalty and emigration, love and war
folds. The novel spans three continents (Europe, America and
'·) and three decades (1919-1946) during which the central
ters and their families experience the joys of life but also
e with the realities of separation, trauma and loss.
background as a clinical psychologist informs his descriptions
the problems that befall his characters and their resilience
coping methods. However, what makes this an exceptionally
rable novel is his empathy for his characters and his thoughtful
elling ... a masterpiece."

sor Alan Carr, University College Dublin

ibes the journey of two Irish lads from the trouble torn Ireland
1920s to the end of the Second World War; plus, the decisions
must make in loyalty and love. A great read for book groups."

eth Taylor, Librarian

About the author

ilkinson spent twenty years helping people to cope with
trauma, ill health and other dilemmas. In that career, he
etaphors, stories and poems to communicate truths to and
s patients, and also when teaching others.

oauced two editions of a standard text and was known as a
who had an ability to sum up the heart of the matter in
ex situations. This was very useful with patients, but often got
o a lot of trouble with colleagues and managers...

vel has its roots in stories handed down within his own
Irish) family.

Crossing the water

Ian Wilkinson

MAKRI PRESS

First published in Great Britain by Makri press 2014
This paperback edition published by Makri press 2014
Darlington, UK
Web: Makripress.com
Email: makripress@btinternet.com

Copyright © Ian Wilkinson 2014

A CIP catalogue record for this book is available from the
British library

ISBN 978-0-9928485-0-7

Cover design by Angela Carrington at The Bigger Picture ©
www.thisisthebiggerpicture.co.uk

Printed in the UK by CPI Anthony Rowe Ltd

Crossing the Water
One: September 1919

The cool, damp ground along the leafy green corridor shivers, stirred by running footsteps, as a young black-haired boy bursts through a curtain of leaves. He turns his run into a flying leap, stamping on a flat stone with a satisfying slap as he passes, which in turn fires a cluster of birds into the patchwork blue and white sky. The boy glances up, slows, and inclines his head sideways, listening to a voice that peals like a church bell, "Fons, hang on now, Fons, hang on a while ..." He dances from one foot to the other, his arms outstretched like wings, as if the sheer joy of running will help him fly. Reluctantly, he conjures the run into one final leap and skids to a halt, arms waving. A partly-chewed apple slips out of one hand and drops away; narrowing his eyes at the betrayal, he takes his revenge with a solid, satisfying kick, pitching it into the bushes by the side of the lane. He sighs, and turns. His pursuer - an older, lanky, fair-haired boy - lopes into view and slows to a walk, dropping the volume but raising the pitch of his voice. Fons listens not to the words but to the insistent tone; "Wouldn't ye wait, one tiny little minute?"

Fons shrugs and grins, watching his companion lift his arm to fill his mouth with apple, munching hard as if satisfying his belly before they both come into public view on the main road. Smelling the skin and the juices, Fons sniffs loudly, shakes his head in impatience, and glances back at the hedgerow. "Aw, c'mon, Pat..."

The older boy chews on, more slowly if anything, as if considering the whining urgency in Fons' plea carefully, yet fixing the younger boy still with his eyes to make him wait. Eventually, Pat spits out the core and nods. "No need to hurry, now - they'll all still be at Mass. The both of us will be for it, anyhow."

At the end of the narrow lane, Fons peers round the hedgerow and stares down the main road leading to the bridge, half dazzled by the bright dappled sunlight. A large open motorcar waits, facing up the slope. Fons sees an arm hanging out, fingers drumming, and a newspaper. He hesitates until Pat whispers, "C'mon, those fellas won't be anyone we know." They meander down the hill, trying to look casual but nudging one another in silent dares to ask for a ride. Fons has only ever ridden in a pony and trap; he longs to sit in those shiny leather seats, but also feels acutely aware of his ill-fitting old boots, the holes at the elbows of his shirt, and the dirt covering his shins and knees. In any event, the men occupying the front seats hold cigarettes in front of their faces, frowning through their fingers. They pull up the collars of their coats, draw on their cigarettes, and look away. One even jerks his thumb down the road towards the town, "Away with ye now."

September 1919

The boys saunter past, Fons rolling his eyes as soon as the men are behind him. Pat nods and murmurs, "The two of them look like they found a penny, then lost a five pound note".

Down on the long, cobbled and hump-backed bridge, standing just out from the riverbank, Fons notices a gawky red-haired youth, a couple of years older than Pat. As they stroll down the hill, the youth leans back on his elbows against the side of the bridge. He glances in their direction twice, the lump in his throat bobbing up and down, before turning to glance across the Blackwater River towards the town. Then he stares at them again, as if he recognises them.

"Who's that?" whispers Fons.

"That's no one we know. He's fishing with his Da, see?"

Fons sees that behind the youth, a dark, unshaven man holds a fishing rod, gazing across the water. Abruptly, the man nudges the coppertop and gestures at a kitbag, which the boy pulls closer to their feet. As they stroll past, Fons catches the coppertop's eye and nods; the boy does look vaguely familiar. The youth drops his eyes, gives a slight shake of his head, and turns away. Fons looks at the fisherman's rod. It doesn't seem to have a line attached, so he stops, looks again, and scratches his head. But now they both have their backs to him, and Fons doesn't know what to say to them. He stares at the empty rod for a while longer, then shrugs and walks on. They must be waiting for someone else, he thinks.

Meanwhile Pat has moved on, twenty yards ahead; Fons dawdles along, feeling the pleasure of the sun warming his face and limbs. He becomes aware of bells ringing from Christ Church, the steady repeated notes signalling the end of the service. He thinks, that means we have about half an hour before Mass ends at St Patrick's. Hopefully, we can avoid Brother Daniel and his stick for the rest of the day, God willing. As Fons approaches the rise in the centre of the bridge, a British soldier hurrying away from Christ Church jogs past in the other direction, his pack and rifle slung across his back. Fons speeds up a little, thinking to tell Pat about the daft fisherman, the one without a line, who surely must be a Kerry man. As he tops the rise in the middle of the bridge, he sees more soldiers wandering down from the church onto the far end of the bridge, smiling and laughing now that they have the rest of the day to relax. Two others pass him, lost in thought, strolling in silent companionship.

Within his own reverie, Fons feels an urge to catch up with his friend; his impatience feels like music, suddenly growing louder, matched by a sudden sound of raised voices in the distance, shouting and imploring. Just as this penetrates his daydreaming, Fons feels a large hand grasp him between his shoulders, thrusting him forward and down. As his chest and face hit the cobblestones they seem to make a deafening noise, a crack like a gun. He feels pain inside his

2

nose, his chin, and his chest, and something whizzes past. He tries to take a breath but the air has been knocked out of him; he hears a gasp, but has no sense that it belongs to him. Something heavy flops across him; slowly, it seems, like a blanket. A deep voice gasps a command, "Keep still, son. Don't move."

Fons can't breathe but he manages to lift up his head up, to stare ahead. He watches with awful fascination, as if in a dream. Pat stands motionless on one side of the bridge, frozen. Near him, a British soldier fumbles frantically with his kit, swinging his pack and rifle off his back; he drops to one knee, preparing to adopt a firing position. Beyond this, two men sprinting this way both start to scream, "Put the bloody gun down, Tommy", in unison. The first man brandishes a revolver as he runs; the second hesitates, moves to the side, and raises a shotgun to his shoulder. The soldier raises his rifle, fumbles with the bolt for a second, curses, and then abruptly ducks into a position behind Pat, using the boy as a shield. While the soldier works the rifle bolt, the two Volunteers scream at Pat, "Get out the fucking way...you...get down."

Pat suddenly seems to wake up and tries to move aside, but in one movement the soldier wraps an arm around Pat's neck and with the other swings his rifle around Pat's side. He yells triumphantly, pointing the rifle at the two Volunteers. "Alright, boys, you two put *your* fucking guns down."

While the two men hesitate, Irish voices shout encouragement from the far end of the bridge; Fons glimpses other soldiers holding their hands over their heads while men in a motley assortment of raincoats wrench rifles from their backs. Another voice behind him barks out, "Put your fucking gun down, Tommy, before the boy gets hurt."

Fons watches a dark patch appear on Pat's trousers, fluid running down the bare leg below, sparkling in the sun, while revolver and rifle point at each other with his friend in the middle. Fons suddenly feels his own fear and wants to scream out too, to tell the soldier to let Pat go, to leave him alone, and to tell the Volunteers not to shoot, but he has no voice, he's trapped in silence. That silence explodes as the rifle crashes and a lump of stone splatters out of the bridge behind the man with the shotgun. The revolver cracks twice in response, but Fons has already shut his eyes to pray for Pat. He hears curses from every direction, then more footsteps approaching. He still can't breathe, and feels dizzy. The voice on top of him speaks again; "Denny, behind you."

Fons opens his eyes. His prayer seems to have worked. He sees the British soldier turn and look back over his shoulder. He seems to look through Fons, a hard, aggressive look boring past into the air behind him. The soldier releases his grip on Pat, grasps his rifle two-handed, and swings it round, working the bolt. Pat staggers; Fons feels pain as he bites his own lip. A deafening crash above his head seems to fling the soldier backwards, spraying blood into the air; a flailing arm and leg collide with Pat, who wobbles like a skittle before he also falls. Pat lies still while Fons hears a strange ringing in his ears. As this dies away, replaced by a wailing noise, Fons watches the two Volunteers walk forward. The first picks up the discarded rifle and slings it over his shoulder, half-grinning, half-grimacing. Fons realises that the wailing, the crying in terror, comes from Pat; relief floods through him. The second Volunteer helps a blood-splattered, sniffling Pat to his feet; the two of them both look down at the wounded man with horrified expressions. His legs kick like a swimmer as he lies prone, coughing and choking.

Fons hears a low moan; at last the weight above him is lifted away, so that air fills his own lungs. He too finds himself hauled to his feet. Now he sees, lying on his back, another British soldier - the man who pushed him to the ground, the man who took a bullet and then fell on top of him. He's bleeding from his shoulder and grimacing in pain, but his eyes seek out Fons' gaze, eager both to see and be seen; for a long second the man regards the boy, before he attempts a smile and winks. Fons manages a slight nod of his head. The man grunts and closes his eyes, satisfied.

He senses Pat behind him and turns as a broad hand descends onto each of their shoulders. Looking up, his mouth drops open as he sees the face of the fisherman. "Fuck off home now, boys. But just ye remember, ye don't know anyone and ye didn't see anything, did ye now?"

*   *   *

Fons perches on his toes to twist a stick of willow into the narrow gap, manipulating it upwards and across, aiming to dislodge the stay that holds the upper, smaller part of the window fast. Twice it slips, and twice his tongue slips back into his mouth as he frowns. On his third attempt, the stay capitulates, flipping off its rusty metal pin; Fons works his fingers into the gap, pushing it open. "Pat," he urges, half-whispering, half-triumphant, "C'mon, give us a hand."

Pat grunts and glances up from a squatting position, his back against the wall. Even bathed in bright sunshine, he seems to be shivering with cold, hugging his arms around himself as if it were a December night. He's not spoken a word while they scuttled through the alleys all the way from the bridge. Reluctantly, he pushes himself upright without moving his arms, steps forward, and stares blankly at Fons.

Close up, Fons sees the mess splattered all over Pat's shirt and trousers clearly. What he was hoping was mud and dirt is revealed to be spatters of blood; all over Pat's face too - and in his hair. "Are ye all right, Pat?" Pat blinks, shaking his head sideways at first, and then nods. Fons looks away and down, feeling a sense of confusion; he watches himself twisting his foot, as if he were crushing a wasp. "Are ye sure?"

Pat nods again, tight-lipped, and suddenly his eyes fill with tears. He speaks in an urgent whisper, "For the love of Jesus, Fons, leave it alone. That English bastard almost got me my death. Will you not let me forget it?"

Fons feels the heat glow in his face. He nods in acquiescence, though his eyes are still drawn to the spots of blood all over Pat. Catching a warning look in Pat's eye, he swallows and points behind his friend. "That seat; push it closer, will ye?"

Pat's eyes swivel slowly around and rest upon the ancient garden seat, carefully placed in the centre of the yard where the sun has most chance of falling. He blinks twice and then walks over to it. Fons sees that he looks puzzled, as if he can't work out how to do it without the use of his arms. Then, reluctantly, he drops one hand onto it, drags it over to Fons, averts his eyes, and then slides back down against the wall, shivering ferociously and hugging himself again.

Fons studies the older boy for a moment; then he pushes one arm into the upper window as he clambers up onto the seat. He levers the gap fully open and squirms his head and upper body into it, pulling himself up until he feels the frame under his ribs. He rocks forward, balancing on his stomach, his feet waving behind him; he stretches one arm down, fishing for the lever that holds the bottom part of the window shut. This bit is easy; his index finger hooks the end, lifts it off the pin, and drops it to one side. Now he rocks and slides his torso back out, gently bringing his feet down, careful that his knees don't hit the glass. Finally, he bangs the inside sill twice with his fist to unstick it. He slips out and down, opening the lower window wide, looking at Pat for approval. The older boy nods but frowns again, seemingly reluctant to move.

"C'mon, then," Fons grasps Pat's hands - limp and surprisingly cool - and pulls until his friend jerks into motion; he guides Pat toward the open window and helps him through. He looks around and scratches his head, then decides to push the garden seat back to its original position. When Fons clambers through, he discovers a smear of clotted blood on the window frame; he carefully wipes it off with his sleeve as he heaves himself up. Once inside, his eyes are drawn to a large, half-dried clot on Pat's face. He reaches out to wipe it but Pat jerks his arm up, batting his hand away, so that Fons only succeeds in creating a large red smear. Pat gives him a daggers look, and squats on his haunches again, shivering. Fons decides to leave the cleaning up for later.

He glances around the square, whitewashed pantry, gazing up at the highest shelves, wondering what could be up there, out of reach. Opposite the window, a door leads through a passage to the kitchen. Fons looks to Pat expectantly; when Pat shrugs, Fons steps over and tries the handle. It turns, but the door won't budge. "It must be bolted; no way through, from here."

Pat shrugs. Fons looks around the shelves, opens the breadbin and takes out some stale pieces, small ones that won't be missed. He offers some to Pat, who shakes his head. Fons munches, considering whether to go back out of the window. "What d' ye think, Pat?" He tries to catch Pat's eye, then nudges his friend with his elbow. "Pat? What will we do?"

For a moment, Pat seems to wake up again and look around, realising where he is. He swallows and then speaks in a flat whisper. "Sure, it's Sunday. They'll be going for tea and biscuits at the church hall with Father O'Connor after Mass. Then they'll all be traipsing back here for the quiet time, the bible stories and the playtime. What we need is to hide ourselves, keep out of Brother Daniel's way. Otherwise, he'll tullock us. We should be waiting till he goes away after supper. Then we have to sweet talk Sister Rose, tell her I wanted to show you where my uncle used to live. So we might as well hide in here till suppertime."

Fons follows his gaze. Two man-sized wicker baskets, one for potatoes and the other for onions, sit in the far corner, each with an old blanket thrown over the top. Fons pulls the two baskets forward to create a space behind. The boys squeeze into this space, pull the blankets over their heads, and settle down to wait.

*   *   *

"Fretting won't bring them back, Sister Rose. They'll turn up eventually, and I'll tan their backsides when they do - especially that little pestilence, Gilligan. That boy's a terrible influence on Patrick Mahon."

"Well, I wouldn't be worrying but you saw the soldiers for yourself. They didn't seem like wasps out of their nest just for the air, did they?"

Brother Daniel abandons the inspection of his fingernails; sometimes Sister Rose surprises him with her wit. "Yes, indeed, they surely did seem like wasps today." The image came back to him; as they'd crossed the town square, walking the column of children back from Mass, a British lorry had roared up the hill past them, squealing to a halt in front of the pub. Soldiers had jumped off, swinging rifles with their bayonets fixed, and run inside. As the children from St Joseph's home filed past, men had been pulled through the door and made to sit on the ground outside, amidst a cacophony of shouts and insults. The landlord, a Home Rule sympathiser, had been pushed against the wall with a pistol in his back. "Something has gone off, that's for sure. *The boys* have been up to something."

"Well, you can go down and find out what, before supper. And have a look for *our* boys when you go. I'll take the reading today."

"Surely, Sister Rose." They sit in silence for a while. For Brother Daniel, stillness and silence feel comfortable. His ungainly body prefers rest; his mind enjoys losing itself in his own thoughts, which often calm him far more than prayer. He thinks about young Mahon, brought here to St Joseph's after his mother died; Brother Daniel can still remember how that situation had felt in his own life. So he had felt sympathy for the boy, initially. During the first days in his schoolroom, Patrick Mahon had also shown that he was truly a bright lad; he could read fluently, and even understand a little Latin. The dead mother had taught him, apparently. So Brother Daniel had begun to think that this boy could be worth saving, that he too might be guided into God's service, even as early as that first week. That Sunday, Daniel had led the children into church as usual. Singing was one of the few pleasures that Daniel could enjoy without guilt. He wished he could have been talented enough to be a singer himself, or perhaps a choirmaster, but he recognised his own limitations. Nonetheless, he enjoyed hearing his own voice hold a note, showing how well it might be done, each Sunday. Most of the boys sang badly, if at all, though a couple of the girls could hold a note.

That particular Sunday, after the opening bar of the first hymn Daniel had stopped, open-mouthed, to listen. Patrick Mahon's voice seemed to be everywhere, echoing from the four walls, forming and reforming harmonies with its own echoes, floating around the rafters. All around him, people were turning to look, nudging, pointing, and nodding in appreciation. No one in Fermoy had heard the like of it before. As they filed back outside, Sister Rose had whispered in his ear, summing it up. "The boy's face is uncommonly like an angel, uncommonly so. Then he opens his mouth and you want to know where the good Lord has hidden his wings, you surely do."

Daniel nods to himself, remembering that voice soaring like an angel through the rafters of their own little church, right here in Fermoy. As he had sat there listening, the idea dawned - he could do something special for this boy. His friend in Dublin would help him, the choirmaster at the pro-cathedral. Daniel would talk to the father, who would surely be grateful for such an opportunity. So when the reply from his friend had finally arrived Daniel had been unable to stop himself, ripping it open as soon as he had it in his hands. At first, he frowned at the contents...

Dear (Brother) Daniel,

It was such a pleasant surprise to hear from you, after these long years. Of course I recall our times together at Belvedere, and with pleasure too, at the memories.

*Regarding the boy you mentioned to me, I'm afraid he is
already too old for the pro-cathedral choir, and we do keep strictly
to our limits. I could certainly find him a place in a local school, but
without the choral training I guess that's missing the boat.*

*This all depends on the boy's family, of course, but the 'other'
(Church of Ireland) cathedral has a choir for boys of his age and
older. That's not as bad as it sounds. This choir is run as part of a
mixed faith school, which has its own separate quarters and proper
pastoral support for the catholic boarders, and there are many of
them. They also have scholarships and suchlike to encourage our
bright lads from the country. If his singing is as good as you say,
they'll surely take him. Provided the boy's faith will stand this little
test, it'll give him the chance to sing in a truly beautiful old church-
just a shame that Henry VIII stole it away from us! But it's also
supposed to be a good school, one of the best in Dublin for science
and mathematics. I do know the choirmaster, so I can put in a good
word if you wish.*

Well, that'll be all for now.

Best wishes, your old friend, Edward Martyn

Daniel decided not to mention the mixed faith business to Sister
Rose. Events had proved him right about the father; the man seemed
grateful and excited about such a grand opportunity for his son. The
only problem was that the boy himself was still resisting the idea.
Patrick Mahon kept insisting that he didn't want to go to Dublin,
further away from his home. He'd been especially difficult this last
week, so much so that Daniel had almost lost his temper. But he
really did not want to do that with *this* boy – he sensed that he
needed to encourage his God given talent, rather than beat the devil
out of him. Daniel frowns, suddenly wondering if the boy had
skipped Mass deliberately to provoke him. No, it surely couldn't be
that. It was the Gilligan boy, for sure. That boy did have the devil in
him; it would be him who had tempted young Mahon astray...

He hears a cough, and looks up. She looks at him, expectantly,
"Well, we'd better get on..."

"Indeed, Sister Rose, we had indeed."

* * *

After her bible reading, Sister Rose goes to her room at the top
of the house to still her mind and pray. By nature a worrier, it is only
prayer that calms her, if the truth were told. Especially today - she
fears for the two boys, for their safety; and not just for today, for she
feels in her heart that these next few years are going to be violent
times as all these boys grow into young men. She feels a need to pray
for all the soldiers and the Volunteers, "*the boys*", who are growing in
number, drawing in many local young men. Fighting has started in

the cities; she fears it will happen here too. They have already started to kill each other and that is a terrible tragedy, as well as a sin. She wants to pray for young Gilligan also. He is indeed a difficult child; only his mother visits, and that rarely, with her working on the liners. The boy himself seems immune to discipline, unable to withstand any temptation. In fact it seems like the more he is corrected, the more determined he is to go his own way. She tried reasoning with him yesterday only to meet a brick wall, as he stubbornly repeated, "You're not my Ma, you're not my Ma..." She wonders if he might indeed become a criminal, as Brother Daniel predicts. She sighs, thinking about Daniel's hands, solid and strong, a farmer's hands. She prays often enough for him, too. He can appear devout, God bless him, and she knows he's well meaning, but he possesses no patience at all. She knows the older boys need the strap to keep them in line, but sometimes, well ...

Her mind will not stop its restless movement; after a while, she stands and walks over to her window. She often looks over the town from this little watchtower, trying to enjoy some moments of solitude before she makes her way back down to the world below. Amidst the descending gloom she makes out a glow in the distance, down by the river. A bonfire? Someone must be shooting pigeons, too, by the noise; on a Sunday, too, what is the world coming to? She notices Brother Daniel scurrying back up the hill alone. What is the man doing? What on earth is he in such a hurry for? She shuts her eyes and tries to calm herself; the bang of the front door interrupts her efforts. She shakes her head, mutters her contrition, and prepares herself for the world below.

*   *   *

Daniel pushes the heavy oak door and peers into the gloomy darkness known as the day room. The sound of giggling emanates from a cluster of girls surrounding the fireplace, then ceases abruptly. Two of the older boys, sprawled prone across the bare floorboards, glance up; seeing his expression, they avert their gaze. A foot nudges another boy, who shifts his position to mask a cluster of marbles dotted across the threadbare rug in the centre of the room. Daniel growls, "Sister Rose? Where will she be?" Shrugs and blank faces answer him; he scowls and pulls the door to. Yet as he turns away, candlelight descends the stairs. He forces a smile, "There you are."

She withholds her reply until she faces him. "Of course, but why are you back so soon? Could you not find them? I'm just about to give the rest of them their supper and put them to bed."

Her sharp tone causes Daniel to restrain himself, not least from blasphemous thoughts. He takes a deep breath, "To be frank, Sister, I did not have the great expectation of finding those two. They'll turn up when the Good Lord wants them to be found. But there's a fierce old mess brewing out there, tonight."

"Surely you ..." As he wonders what acerbic comment she has just bitten off in mid-air, she lifts the candle to examine his expression. "Go on, Brother Daniel..."

"The British garrison is making a riot, so they are. Something happened this morning at Christ Church; one or two soldiers got themselves shot. At least one got his death, and some others got wounds."

"Dear God, no... not in the church?"

"Yes, yes. Well, just outside the church, and on the bridge, anyway."

"What a dreadful thing, have *the boys* lost their senses?"

Daniel sighs and scratches his head. "They did it for the rifles, so they did. *The boys* need the guns, Sister Rose. So they tried to take the guns away from the soldiers when they least expected it. But that's only the half of it... remember this morning, the soldiers raiding the pub on our way back from Mass? Well, they were looking for information. And they probably beat it out of anyone they found in there. So now the British lads have come out of camp and they're looking for their revenge. They've taken the Coughlan and Malone boys away, and torched both of the family homes. Most of the houses down by the river are getting smashed. You can hear the noise out in the street. I heard shooting, too."

"That's why you came back?"

"Yes."

"But *our* boys are out there, somewhere. Maybe caught up in it?" Her voice rises, insistent, then pleading; it is only this that stops his anger carrying him off. Is she calling him a coward?

He rubs his forehead. "I hardly think so. *They'll* be hiding somewhere. Listen, I had to come back here. If the garrison come up here on the rampage, I need to be here, to talk some sense into them. But listen..." he pauses for a moment, frowning. Should he tell her? "...they might have seen what happened, this morning. Father O'Connor says there were two young boys on the bridge, witnesses. The British are looking for them. It sounds like it might be our boys."

Sister Rose's expression, normally so implacable, now takes on the form of a silent scream. At that exact moment they hear a muffled wail, followed by a metallic clang, from the direction of the kitchen.

* * *

Fons feels Pat nudge his ribs and whisper, "Someone's in the kitchen". Before he can reply he hears the scraping of a bolt being pulled, the squeak of a door. Slow, heavy footsteps enter the pantry and the faint flickering of a candle penetrates the blanket. Abruptly, the heavy blanket is pulled away; he sees the face of the cook, Mrs O'Leary, staring down at Pat, her eyes widening. She screams, and the pan she has brought with her drops onto the stone floor with a loud clang...

Fons stands up to face her, pulling Pat up with him, "We're alright, Mrs, we're alright." He repeats this until Mrs O'Leary stops screaming, waits for a few seconds, then picks up the metal pan and tries to push it back into her hand; but she's too busy inspecting Pat, her eyes widening in horror at the blood smeared over his face. He pulls at her arm, trying to get her attention. Suddenly Sister Rose and Brother Daniel appear, Sister Rose also reaching out hesitantly towards Pat's blood-splattered face, "God forgive them, what have they done to you?"

Pat shakes his head from one side to another, silently, as a large tear forms in one eye and slowly runs down his face. His lips move, but no sound emerges. "He's alright, Sister Rose. It's not his blood." No one replies, but Fons sees that his words have some impact; Brother Daniel shifts his position to get a better view of Pat, and this seems to break the spell that has them all paralysed.

Daniel puts his hand on Sister Rose's shoulder. "Take the boy into the kitchen, clean him up and see where he's hurt. I'll take Gilligan upstairs and find out what's happened. Mrs O'Leary, you can give out the supper to the others."

Fons feels a large hand grasp the back of his shirt and push him down the gloomy passage, emerging into the musty warmth of the kitchen. His eyes are drawn to the black range, the boiling kettle, and the washing hung to dry above it. They stop and wait. Fons turns his head and watches Sister Rose enter, leading Pat to the kitchen sink. Sister Rose looks as if she wants to embrace Pat but she can't bring herself to do that, to risk messing up her white robe. He notices Brother Daniel watching her, a half-smile on his face, before the man glances down and frowns at Fons. Fons has a bad feeling about this, but he feels frozen, powerless. Daniel nods at the cook, and then Fons feels his shirt being grasped again as he is lifted and pushed out of the kitchen, his feet scurrying to keep up. Halfway along the corridor Daniel releases his shirt, but a large hand takes a firm grip on his ear instead. Fons finds himself being pulled up the stairs by his ear, less carefully now, once they move out of earshot of the others. He tries not to cry out, but he can't help whimpering. At the top of the stairs, he has to duck and twist, following the hand that pulls him towards Brother Daniel's office. At last, the grip on his ear is released. Fons looks on through a watery blur; he sees Daniel stand his candle on the ledge, unlock and open the door, then pick up the candle again. A hand clamps onto his collar, and Fons feels himself propelled face down towards a battered old desk, glimpsing a foot kicking the door shut behind them. He senses the candle being carefully placed somewhere above him while he is pulled across the desk, face hanging over the edge, his collar still gripped tightly. He sees the other hand pick up a long stick and wave it, testing its weight and balance, as a silence grows in the room. Fons watches the stick waving in front of his eyes, a stout piece of polished cane. He can't take his eyes from it.

"So where did you go this morning?"

"To find the apples, sir, please sir, just to get the apples..."

Fons knows what will happen. He still hopes, though, that by telling the truth he can stop it happening. This is what Daniel has told them repeatedly; if they confess, they won't be punished.

"Go on, what else, boy? Where did you steal these apples?"

"From the orchard at the big empty house... no one wants them, sir, it's not like stealing, they're falling off the trees, no-one wants them..." Daniel laughs and Fons realises, he doesn't care where the apples came from.

Daniel waits a few seconds before waving the cane again in front of Fons eyes. "What else? Where did all the blood come from?"

"The two of us were stuck on the bridge, sir - it was a soldier. There was a lot of shouting first, so there was, but he wouldn't give up his gun and he ...he got Pat in front of him and then they all started shooting...and then the soldier fella got shot and he fell into Pat, sir... that's how Pat got all that blood on him, sir..." Fons senses Daniel nodding, thoughtfully, and for a moment he feels hopeful. Maybe this time he won't get hit.

"What were you doing? You've got some blood on your clothes too."

"Me self, sir? Well, I was knocked down onto the ground too, sir - another soldier fell on top of me and he kept me down. He got himself a wound too."

"Did he now? And why on earth did you hide, after all that? Why didn't you bring yourselves here to get cleaned up?"

Fons knows too well that if he admits that they were avoiding Daniel, waiting until he left, he'll just be madder still. "I dunno, sir." Daniel laughs again, and Fons feels his stomach clenching in fear. Daniel waves the stick gently, and sighs. Fons feels his own hope dangling there, balancing in the air with the stick, just out of reach. Daniel waits a little longer, taps the stick on the side of the desk below Fons' nose, and stares into the distance as if considering his sentence. In the background, far away, Fons hears shouting, a shot, the sound of breaking glass; but none of that really registers, nothing can stop him staring at that length of cane.

"Well, Gilligan, at least you haven't lied about everything this time. You have made a confession of sorts..." Fons looks up, eagerly, but he cannot see any mercy on Brother Daniel's face, no matter how hard he tries.

"I did sir, I told you the truth, I swear to God..."

Daniel laughs. "Ah, but you only told me part of the truth, Gilligan; only part of it. You missed out the most important bit. Didn't you?"

Fons feels panic. "Did I, sir? Maybe I did... but I'm a bit thick, sir, I am too..."

"Oh you're not stupid, Gilligan, I know that. Come on, boy, what did you miss out?" Fons can't think; he can only hear his heart beating. He feels Daniel's hand on his back again, pushing his face down into the desk. "What did you miss out, boy?"

Suddenly, he knows. "I missed Mass, sorry sir, sorry...forgive me, please..."

"That's right, Gilligan, you skipped Mass and you don't even realise the sin of it. And you think it's all right to steal, even when the owner's not there. But that's still a sin, as you well know. Lastly, you tell me you don't know why you hid. Do you think I'm stupid, Gilligan? So that's lying, too. So three times you've sinned, and you couldn't even confess when you had the chance..."

"I meant to, really sir, I tried, I'm sorry..." Fons is looking for the stick now but it's gone, and he wants to wee and he hears the cane whistle through the air and hears a smack and then the pain hits his bum and he hears himself yelp like a dog...

Daniel chants to himself rhythmically, working to beat the devil out of this child, as the cane whistles down upon the boy's buttocks, legs, and back.

"Right...now...this...is...for...Mass...this...is...for...stealing...and... this...is...for...lying....and...this...is...for...being...an...evil...evil...little... bastard...an...evil...little... bastard..."

These, and other sounds of the outside world, fade from Fons' perception; his own cries seem to break the surface from a deep pool of pain and then thrash the air like the arms of a drowning man.

* * *

Two: September 1919

"Patrick? Patrick Mahon? Come along now…" She stands at the foot
of the stairs, calling up from an empty, echoing hallway, stroking the
crucifix around her neck as if it were a magic lamp. Where on earth
has that boy got to? Since the day of the shooting, he's like a
lighthouse in a bog. She sighs, places her shopping basket down by
the stairs, and goes to look in the day room, finding it empty. The
other children are all in school; she and Daniel have allowed Pat to
stay in the house for nearly two weeks, after Father O'Connor
whispered in their ear that the British soldiers were looking for a fair-
haired boy. In Fermoy, he stands out like a nun at the races, God
bless him; especially now that he carries a nervous twitch in his
cheek and dark rims under his eyes. According to the other boys, his
sleep is all over the place. He won't tell her about his nightmares,
though; he just clams up and looks tearful, whenever she asks.

She sighs with exasperation and climbs the stairs, shaking her
head. As she passes the linen cupboard, heading for the boys'
bedroom, she detects a faint noise; something musical and distant?
She stops, and waits. After a long pause, the sounds begin again. She
puts her ear to the cupboard door and hears a distinct humming. The
boy has taken to doing this in bed, or in quiet corners, as if he wants
to ignore the world but needs something to keep his mind occupied.
She opens the door. Pat, seated on the floor, stares up at her,
swallows, and lapses into silence.

"Well now, what on earth is the meaning of this, Patrick
Mahon?"

"It's Handel's Messiah, Sister."

"I know *that*, Patrick, but do you plan to keep me waiting at the
front door the whole day?"

"I forgot, Sister."

"Well, I'm reminding you now. You're suddenly after turning as
slow as a wet week, Patrick, which is not your usual character at all, is
it? I can't be chasing you all over the house every time I need you,
now can I?"

The boy stares at the floor until she finishes, then glances up.
For a second she seems to see something malevolent in his eyes
before he looks away. "You can't, Sister."

"I want you to carry the shopping basket for me today,
remember?"

Pat sniffles and gives one quick nod, his eyes averted,
clambering to his feet slowly. Sister Rose rests one arm across his
shoulder, pointing the way with the other arm. She watches him
move, sensing the reluctance in his puppet-like motions, his body

14

half hesitating before moving mechanically, as if against his will. She follows behind like a gentle, silent sheepdog, herding him down the stairs. In the hallway, she bends to pick up the basket. His eyes widen at the sight of it; he seems prompted to make one last effort to grasp his own strings again; "Sister, aren't there soldiers all over the town? I won't be meeting any soldiers, I will not. I'm staying in the house, so I am."

She purses her lips at his tone of voice, at the pleading tone she has heard from children so many times before. "We'll be fine, Patrick, there won't be any soldiers today. But just in case, you can put this woollen hat on, so you'll be safe in your disguise, won't you?" He glances up, blinking as he examines the dark knitted hat she is offering him. He frowns, as if he doesn't understand. She shakes her head in exasperation, moves closer. "It will cover your fair hair, Patrick. Then if there are soldiers, they won't know you from Adam, will they?" He stands, passive and mute, while she fits the hat upon his head. "There. Come on, now," she murmurs into his ear, as she slips her arm across his shoulder and opens the door. Once again, his body moves like a puppet, following her will rather than his, out of the door and down the path. Sister Rose smiles her satisfaction, feeling some pride in this skill that God has given her to help in her vocation; something she knows marks her out, so that others say, "You have a way with those children, Sister, you surely do..."

Just as she thinks this, as if to punish her for the sin of pride, Pat ducks down to one side and flops onto the ground. He hisses, "I'm not taking the chance, Sister, thanks all the same."

She forces herself to smile at him, bending down as far as her dignity allows. "Come along now, Patrick, I need you to carry this basket. We won't go anywhere near any soldiers, I promise. And they won't be bothering you when you're helping me, will they now?" His only reaction is to start humming, quietly. The problem is, she knows, with him sitting on the ground and looking away, refusing to make eye contact, she can't seem to make a connection. She taps him on the shoulder gently, trying to nudge him forward and upward, but he continues to ignore her. Her smile slowly fades while she tries to think, her world narrowing into this task. Part of her has an urge to sit down beside him and put an arm right around him, but the ground is wet and she cannot risk muddying her best cassock. Have patience, she tells herself, that's the trick. "Patrick, come on, I really do need your help today." She waits a few seconds and then shifts position, trying to make eye contact with him. "Patrick, by all the Saints, come along now please. It's not as if you're sickening for anything; besides, the time has surely come to put your feet outside the gate."

Pat puts his hands over where his ears would be if the hat were not covering them already; he begins to rock backwards and forwards, humming loudly. Despite her best efforts, Sister Rose cannot bring herself to smile again. This situation is stretching her patience to its limit; perhaps that's the problem, she thinks, I've let the whole thing drag on too long. "For pity's sake, Patrick, you are full thirteen years old. So please stop yourself behaving like a three year old." He shuts his eyes, ignoring her, continuing to rock and hum. She feels the last of her patience slipping away – it feels as if she is losing sight of her own world, as if this boy's world grows far too large all around her. She tells herself that, if nothing else works, she is physically stronger than this boy. So she bends down, grasps him under his arms, and pulls him up into a standing position, feeling his body go slack as she takes his weight. "Up you come."

Pat does not resist at first, although she notices a half-smile play upon his face; as if he enjoys the limpness, the sensation of being carried like an infant. The thought needles her as she carries his body the last few steps to the gate. When she reaches the gate, she drops him. To her satisfaction, the boy allows his legs to work, to stop himself falling over. He stands, passively waiting. Perhaps he's accepted her persuasion, at last. As she reaches to open the gate, he ducks and tries to twist away from her; but she too has kept herself alert and grasps his collar with her other hand. His head jerks around, his mouth spitting out the words, "Get off me."

"Don't you talk to me like that, Patrick Mahon, after all I've done for you. Now you stop this nonsense at once."

"I'm not going."

"We'll see about that." She starts to pull him bodily through the gate. He yelps and begins to pull back, unsuccessfully at first, but then hooks an arm around the gatepost, gripping one hand with the other; she can't budge him. Patiently, she starts to unpick his fingers, but now he begins to emit a loud noise, something between whining and screaming. She slaps his shoulder, more in emphasis than in retribution, "Be quiet, will you." The noise doubles in volume and she slaps him again, harder. It trebles. She can't believe that she is hearing this, from this boy, of all of them. She can feel her own temper rising now, and hears herself blaspheming; *damn this boy.* Did she say that or just think it? She makes one last effort to detach him from the gate; slowly, she frees his hands from each other, and wrenches him away. She has both her arms around him now. The noise stops for second; then he fills his lungs, and it begins again. She turns him around, to face her. "Stop this nonsense, now." The raw anger in his face shocks her, reminding her of nightmares in which she sees the devil. She feels a stab of fear, tries to think. She has to get control of this boy somehow, for his own good. Perhaps a shock is what he needs. She slaps him hard, in the face, more in desperation than in hope. Instantly he slaps her back, also full in the face.

She feels stunned, paralysed, and releases her grasp. He turns and dashes back up the path, disappearing into the house while she gazes after him, the shame of her failure descending upon her. For a minute or so, she feels as if a curtain has fallen around her. The sounds of her own sobbing and gasping fill her world until her breathing gradually slows. She notices the shopping basket abandoned on the path; gradually she feels her surroundings return to fill her world again. She hears voices, turns to see a man and two women watching her from across the road. They must have seen everything. Although they nod at her sympathetically, she feels her neck flush with blood. She still has the urge to cry; but she shuts her eyes for a moment, collects herself, and retrieves the basket. She wipes her eyes and forces herself to walk down the street toward the shops, resisting a powerful urge to run away, to follow the boy into the house.

Returning from the shops, she makes no effort to find Patrick. Brother Daniel can sort the boy out – he often says how he wants to help him. Well, let him try. She goes to her room, to pray.

*   *   *

Pat lies hugging his knees, curled up under a blanket on his bed. Perhaps two hours have passed, he thinks. He hums to himself quietly, trying to keep his mind occupied, to keep it moving steadily, flowing down familiar channels. He doesn't want it to flood again, for those feelings of terror to swell and rise around him until he can't breathe, the fear overwhelming and drowning him. That is exactly what seems to happen whenever he allows the memory of that day to force itself back into his mind; or whenever he sleeps, since he dreams of nothing else. He can't remember feeling fear like this before, plus it seems to be getting worse. It isn't just the soldiers that terrify him – he's starting to worry that the Volunteers will think he's a traitor when the soldiers do find him, whatever he says or doesn't say. If the soldiers don't hurt him, the Volunteers will accuse him of helping the British. He can't win. And someone is bound to tell everyone how he pissed himself that day, and then everyone will laugh at him. An image of the sun glinting on the river, the moment just before it all happened, pushes into his mind. He quickly shakes his head and hums louder to shut the image out. He wants to go home, back to the farm. That brings another memory, also painful, but without the same terror; so he lets this one into his head.

He pictures himself standing on the doorstep of St Joseph's for the first time. It must have been two months after his mother's death;

he remembers thinking about the breakfast that his mother had not cooked and he had not eaten, that morning. He missed many things about her, especially her beautiful singing. But every morning the grumbling of his stomach proclaimed a potent and aching reminder of her death; the memory of her warm, fresh soda bread. That was what had preoccupied him while his father and two older brothers arranged themselves around him. Three men cap in hand, all trying to explain something to a nun who stood before them, smiling and nodding politely. Pat hadn't really understood why they had come into the town, at first; it wasn't a market day and they hadn't brought anything from the farm to sell. But as he stood there, it gradually dawned upon him that it was something to do with him, and something to do with this place and the nun, and whatever they were saying.

He'd not listened while his father told the nun about the farm, the family, and his mother's death; that was nothing new, and he didn't like to be reminded of the last part. But suddenly his father's words caught his attention, "...My wife, she taught the boy to read herself, God love her, and he took to it real quick... he can read the newspaper to us, or even a book. On the Holy Book, Sister, he's a bright lad, he's worth educating for sure, he can make something of himself..."

The deep voice of his older brother Ernest added a chorus, "It's a hard life on the farm, Sister, and there's no school close by. Me brother and me self, we're used to it, we're bigger an' stronger and anyways, we don't have his brains. But Pat's still young, and he's made of different stuff...the farming wouldn't suit him, it surely would not..."

His other brother, Sean, had cleared his throat, and Pat felt a big hand, squeezing his shoulder. "The other thing, Sister, he was awful close to our Ma, and he's just a young lad. He needs a woman's touch, to be sure, as you will appreciate yourself..." Pat had a distinct impression that they were all explaining this to him, as well as to the nun.

As he stared at the floor, confused by his own emotions, he heard a female voice; "What about you, Patrick? Would you like to look around and see?" He shuffled forward reluctantly, unwilling to speak. His initial feeling was hurt, that his own family were pushing him out, but he knew he couldn't show that. His father and brothers sounded too imploring, too pleading as they willed him to understand. When he finally looked up from the floor, the nun stepped forward and took his hand, "My name is Sister Rose, Patrick." She led him inside, speaking softly and gently like his mother, and showed him around a large house, much bigger than his father's farm. The first thing he liked was the smell, a strong clean smell of soap, prominent in the large dormitory where all the beds seemed to have clean white sheets. The second thing he liked was the kitchen; he could smell the bread, baking. The third thing was the shelf of books in the hallway. Last, she showed him the dayroom, where other children stared at him blankly; except for one small, dark-haired boy who looked up from a game of marbles, stuck out his tongue for a second, winked at him, and grinned. The idea of being with other children of his own age was new to him, but he decided maybe that wasn't such a bad idea, either.

Even so, the final part of that memory still hurts. His father and brothers stood awkwardly around him, aware of their betrayal, before they abandoned him. "We'd better be going now, Pat. We'll be coming to see you on market days, after the selling. Take care, now." They each hugged him once before he had to watch them all walk away. Sean turned to have the last word, "See you, boyo." Ernie turned too, waved, and nodded his head. His father, though, didn't even look back.

Suddenly, a noise drags him back to his bed as he hears the sound of footsteps coming up the stairs and along the corridor. He hums a bit louder. A door opens, and the footsteps approach and then stop. He stops humming and waits.

The blanket over his head whisks away; Pat blinks in the sudden light. He sees Brother Daniel's face looking down on him and his heart skips a beat. Fons has told him what Daniel did to him; a tale whispered across the bedroom in the middle of the night. Pat has been expecting the same punishment ever since. Did Sister Rose persuade Brother Daniel to wait? If so, she's probably changed her mind now... he feels an urge to pee, and his body shivers. But when he looks up again, Daniel's expression does not seem hostile. Rather, he appears curious, as if Pat were a puzzle that he can't work out. Eventually, he nods. "Come along, Patrick. You and I need to talk."

Pat nods in return, but he feels a lump growing in his throat. He expects to be manhandled; to his surprise, a large hand simply grasps both his feet and sweeps them over the side of the bed. His legs follow automatically, so that his body pivots, slowly pushing itself upright. He can feel Daniel's eyes boring through him, making him move as he walks through the doorway and along the corridor towards the office. He stands to one side, thinking *let's get it over with*, while Daniel unlocks the door. But instead of being pushed across the desk, he's invited to perch on a stool while Brother Daniel sinks into an armchair in the corner.

The man stares at him, sighs, and then tips his bulk forward, his elbows resting on his knees. "You're mighty scared, aren't you?"

Dropping his eyes, Pat nods. "Scared of the soldiers?" He nods again. "Well, you're not crazy. They are looking for you, as we all know. And that is why we've let you stay inside the house all this time. They probably just want to ask you questions, but you never know with the British. The real worry is they might be thinking you were a lookout." He pauses, while Pat thinks about that. "And what else is giving you this fear - the Volunteers?" Almost imperceptibly, Pat feels himself nod. "The *boys* will not be any trouble as long as they think you've kept your mouth shut. But if the British find you, and then the *boys* think you've blabbed, then..." Brother Daniel shakes his head and shrugs, leaving uncertainty dangling in the air like bait on a hook. In the long silence that follows, Pat beats away his memories of the bridge - but he can't prevent the terror of the unknown rising in his chest and throat. It's not fair; he still seems to be caught in the middle, just in a different way, now. Why can't they just leave him alone?

Brother Daniel clears his throat; Pat hears the tone of his voice change. The note of warning, of doom, has vanished. "But to my way of thinking this can be solved easily." Pat looks up, feeling puzzled but hopeful. "Do you remember the school I told you about - the one with the choir, in Dublin?" Pat swallows, and begins to understand where all this might be leading. "You will be completely safe there, Patrick, safer than any place around these parts. The soldiers there will not be looking for you. Dublin is a world away from here, Patrick, and like as not you will also feel completely different there. You'll be able to go outside there, without any of this fear. And you'll enjoy the teaching there, the singing in the choir, and the city itself. It'll open your eyes to a whole new world, boy. And by the time the school holidays come, all the soldiers here will have forgotten all about you. So will the Volunteers, for that matter. But you have to go now."

Pat blinks several times as he absorbs this, feels the frown on his own face gradually lessening. He sneaks a look up at Daniel, who nods at him. "I've explained it all to your father; he wants you to go. I can even get some money from the church so that your father can take you all the way there on the railway. How about that?"

Pat looks up into Daniel's face. He can see far too much satisfaction there, which Pat resents, but he knows that it makes no sense to resist him. At least I'll get away from him too, he thinks. He nods, and then it occurs to him... "What about Fons?"

Brother Daniel snorts and leans back in his chair. He grins, looks up at the ceiling, and then back at the boy. "Oh, don't you worry about Gilligan. The British won't get their hands on him. I'll take care of young Gilligan, I promise you that."

* * *

Years later, Pat would think of his journey to Dublin as the end of his childhood. Sister Rose wakes him before dawn; her anxious face looms over him, one hand shaking his shoulder, the other raising a candle high above the bed. He stumbles after her to the bathroom, where clothes are thrust into his hands. He washes and dresses in a daze, then stumbles down the stairs; he finds her waiting in the hallway, fingering her rosary beads. She smiles, hands him sandwiches wrapped in brown paper, and leads him toward the door. He hears a murmur of familiar voices outside (his father and Ernest) and feels a leap of joy in his heart. But the same heart also lurches with the knowledge that he is leaving St Joseph's for good, sneaking out in the dark of early morning. He feels a sudden panic, an impossible desire to go back and wake Fons and the others. He stops and turns to face her, wordlessly trying to plead for a proper farewell. She seems to understand, for she hugs him and whispers in his ear, "Sure, 'tis a terrible grief on all of us, Patrick. We'll miss our singer too - but you must sing for all of us, in Dublin. Beannacht De, child, Beannacht De." And very gently, she pushes him through the door.

Outside in the street, Pat stares up at his father's veined hands, grasping the reins; he climbs up into the trap between his brother and father. The door of St Joseph's shuts behind him while a distant orange glow slowly grows in the east. His father clicks his tongue and shakes the reins. No one speaks. Pat listens to the clip-clop of the pony and the rumble of the wheels as they move out of the town, the world slowly taking shape around them. He watches birds stretch their wings, flapping warmth into their blood and cold, crisp air into their lungs, and listens to the burst of the dawn chorus. He sits hunched between his father and brother, feeling the motion of their breathing, protected once again by their physical bulk, by their warmth pressing on both sides.

They call at the farm to eat their breakfast and collect Sean, who has been milking the cows. Pat walks methodically around the grey stone house one last time, fixing it in his mind, searching for traces of his mother, which he finds on the bookshelves and in the kitchen. He warms his hands on the stove and strokes the arms of the wooden rocking chair, a silent farewell harmony in his head. When they leave, Sean stretches out in the back of the trap, using Pat's pigskin travelling case as a pillow. Along the road to Mallow, Pat feels Sean nudging his back occasionally. Soon Ernest begins to point at the girls and the motorcars, to catch his eye and wink. At the railway station, the brothers stand there flanking him while his father buys the tickets to Dublin. They tell him what a grand place Dublin will be and instruct him on the places where he must obtain postcards to send home. Later, in Dublin, his memory will fail him; he will only remember their arms around his shoulders. His father emerges, nodding. Sean announces, "Well, Ernest, we'd better be off now, back to the farm. The cattle won't be herding themselves today, will they, Pat?" And with one wave and one last backward look each, his brothers stride out of his life.

The railway carriage seems almost new, the wooden seats polished and the back cushions as yet unspoiled, moving even his father to comment how grand it is. People surge on and off the crowded train in every town, yet nobody sits in the two seats behind them. At first Pat feels embarrassed, thinking it must be because of the smell of the dung from the farmyard, ingrained in his father's boots. But that smell is common among their fellow travellers, and much worse, so it can't be that. He also keeps imagining that someone is humming a tune behind him throughout that journey. He turns around to look and each time, finds the seat is empty. Later, he realises that the tune is one of his mother's favourite songs; but at the time, he has no sense of her presence.

Nevertheless, he does feel as if he is slowly being reborn on that journey. He sees no soldiers in Mallow, or on the train; eventually, he realises that his constant companions - that constant gnawing, twisting fear in his guts and the lurking panic, waiting to pounce - have been left behind. At first he sits hunched up, noticing only his own discomfort. He gradually registers his father's solid presence, taking comfort from that, although he knows the journey will end with their separation. This thought makes Pat blink back a tear; he glances sideways hoping for an acknowledgement, but finds his father studying the other passengers intently. His father's curiosity about them (and apparent indifference to himself) feels like a slap that forces Pat to breathe and look outside of himself. Sitting next to the window, he rubs the fog of condensation away and begins to look outside at the world flashing by. New sights, towns and villages pass by, roads and rivers and hills. It dawns upon him that this will truly be a new start, and by the same token he is leaving behind the sources and reminders of grief and terror. Towards the end of the journey, Pat's nose is glued to the window while he tells his father to look at this, or that.

Dublin is quite a sight, in more ways than one. Pat has never seen so many houses or people or cars before. He sees soldiers among the crowds, but this shock passes quickly and his instinctive urge to run dies away. He will be anonymous here among these crowds; in any case, these are different soldiers. He feels surprise and relief that he can escape, after all. As they walk down toward the city centre, he notices boarded up windows and smashed up buildings. "What's all that, Da? Is it the Germans?"

His Da stops and glances around them. "Didn't you hear about the Rising, son?"

"They wouldn't ever tell us any news at St Joseph's, Da, especially about the war. Terrible evil, they called it."

His father nods, and lowers his voice. "And so it is. But you know *the boys*?" Pat nods. "Well, in Dublin *the boys* had themselves an armed rising against the government, back in 1916. They didn't just want Home Rule, they wanted a proper fight with the British army. And they got one, a big fight, and of course they got a bloody nose. Those houses, they've been shelled. And see those marks around the windows up there? Them's bullet holes, Pat."

"What happened to them, Da?"

His father sighs. "They surrendered, of course. The poor foolish lads had no chance. But the worst of it was, the government shot the leaders in cold blood." He spits; something his father rarely does, and looks sideways at Pat. "The authorities are after making a rod for their own back, I reckon. But you and your brothers should stay out of it, you hear?" Pat nods.

Suddenly they were back in among the crowds, his father shouldering the pigskin case while Pat follows in his wake. They stop to ask directions from a match seller, an ex-soldier wrapped in his greatcoat. Pinned to his chest are medals and a scrawled sign reading, "Gassed and blind, please help". Much to Pat's surprise, the blind man has no problem telling his father precisely what to look out for. He sees his father silently slip a silver three pence into the greatcoat pocket as they leave.

Ten minutes later, father and son stand staring through two massive iron gates, set into a high wall, behind which they see a large empty courtyard and a huge grey stone building, decorated with stern-looking stone angels. His father gives a low whistle of appreciation and catches his eye. Pat nods; he thinks how out of place his father looks and feels a moment of panic. Looking up, he notices a boy waving his arm from one of the second floor windows, pointing to the right. It takes a long moment to realise that he is waving at them; Pat looks along the wall and notices the wooden cover of a gatekeepers hut.

A white-haired, be-whiskered gatekeeper slowly escorts them around the back, limping and grimacing all the way. Pat catches an enticing glimpse of playing fields populated by boys chasing each other. Eventually, they reach a small white door marked "Catholic boarders' entrance". Inside, the gatekeeper gestures for his father to leave the pigskin case in a hallway next to some stairs. Then he turns to Pat, conspiratorially. "Come with me, boy." Pat follows him down a narrow corridor into a much grander one, all the way to a shiny polished oak door which creaks slowly open while the old man peers in. The old man turns, smiles, and waves Pat forward into the room. The smell of polished wood and leather assaults his nose; the boy sees columns of tall dark oak shelving, stretching to the ceiling. He gapes at the rows of books. An arm pushes him forward until he picks out and inspects two samples, well-thumbed copies of "Treasure Island" and "Ivanhoe".

He hears a polite cough, and looks up to see his father waiting by the door. The gatekeeper winks at him, before limping ahead of them down yet another corridor. He delivers them into the hands of an earnest, rotund matron, whose ample seat occupies an armchair behind a large desk, within an office smelling of disinfectant. She looks them up and down. "You do realise, Mr Mahon, just how lucky your son is, to have this chance?"

His father sends Pat a warning glance. "I do, Sister, I do."

"He's the singer, is he? Well, he'll have to show he can do the schoolwork too, or we'll be sending for you to take him back. We'll have no slackers here. It's not just famous for the choir, you know. Some boys come to learn the history, and others the science; for these, too, it's the best school in Dublin."

His father nods, "So I've been told."

She stands. "Have you the money, then, for the first term?"

"I have." His father passes her an envelope, which she tears open, carefully counting the notes and coins. Pat feels a wave of shock at the sight of it, even a faint sickness. He watches the Matron's intent face while she finishes counting and locks it away in a steel box. She glances down at him from a greatly superior position. Pat looks away, towards his father. In later years, what Pat will remember most from that day is the pleading look that his father gives him at that moment, silently begging him not to mess this up, imploring him not to waste all the hard work that has bought that money.

And then, all too quickly, his father too was gone from his life.

* * *

Three: October-November 1919

Fons stops, leans against the wall, and takes a deep breath; so far, so good. He glances back along the lane to check that no one is following him. Scratching his head, he peeps around the corner, studying the occupants of the street. Three pairs of old men pass the time of day outside their doorsteps, leaning against the wall or sitting on stools. One man taps a clay pipe meaningfully with his index finger, hoping for a refill; his companion shrugs. Two apron-clad women stand in the road, arms folded. "Mercy, what good is a grand morning like this when you have our good kettle, Mrs Kelly, and himself as dry as a parched bone, waiting for his tea..."

"But it was himself who gave it to us, Mrs Leary, and him saying this was an old one that he had just replaced with a copper kettle from the fair..."

"God love him, Mrs Kelly, he has no sense, for the new one is half of the size, and besides, he was only after lending it, not giving it away..."

Fons frowns, steps into the street, and saunters slowly down the shady side, hoping to make himself invisible; he whistles to himself quietly, avoiding eye contact. One of the old men stares at him; otherwise, it seems to work. As he moves down the long, gentle slope towards the river and the bridge, his heart quickens. He hears muted, discordant singing from Christ Church, growing louder. Somehow the familiar tune he hears calms him; he starts to hum it. Two armed soldiers standing outside stare at him as he approaches, then turn away to continue their conversation. This causes his face to flush with heat as he remembers - they might recognise him - so he quickly crosses the road, his heart hammering like an anvil. He quickens his pace and hurries past towards the bridge, praying that the soldiers won't follow or call him back. Their gaze seems to bore into his back while a lump forms in his throat. Halfway across the river he lets out a deep sigh, his eyes beginning to scan the cobbles, searching for proof that the whole fine mess here was not all some strange dream of his own imagining. The stones have all been scrubbed clean, but he can still see bullet marks in the wall of the bridge. Glancing to the east, he also notices the blackened shells of burned out houses further along the waterfront.

The lump in his throat disappears when he crosses the water. As he leaves the town behind Fons bursts into a run, smelling the wet vegetation along the hedgerows; a heady mix of relief, joy and excitement flows through his veins. He enters the little lane enclosed by trees, heading for the orchard next to the big house. Clambering onto a wall from an adjacent tree, he peers over. The trees have been stripped, but a few apples and pears, mostly windfalls, remain. He drops down, collects the best of these and adds them to a sack that he pulls out from under his woollen jumper, and clambers out, slinging the sack over his shoulder. Retracing his steps to the road, he begins his journey. He knows the direction from here, but how long will it take? Can he remember his way?

By late afternoon, Fons thinks he is somewhere near. The route he's followed, travelling upstream and looking down on the valley from the south side, then re-crossing the river via a narrow bridge, seems familiar. He's had to guess once or twice at junctions, but the lie of the land seems especially familiar here, down this stretch of road, or rather boreen; the surface roughly made, flat stones laid on clay, rutted with recent cart-tracks and hoof marks. He spots a large tree with twin stems, its tall branches inhabited by rooks; his heart leaps. Not far now, he thinks. He hears a horse approaching, clip-clop, clip-clop. Spotting a gap in the hedgerow, he crawls through into the field, noticing that it contains potatoes, and ducks down to wait. Ever so slowly, the sound grows, accompanied by the rumble of a cart. Fons watches a pile of hay rumble past, glimpsing the top of a cloth cap. He's glad that he chose a Sunday; the fields and roads have been mostly empty.

Finally, just as darkness is gathering, just when he thinks he must have gone wrong again, he turns a corner and sees a small thatched cottage about a hundred yards off the boreen; tears spring to his eyes. He breaks into a run for a moment, until his aching legs remind him how far he's walked. He notices a lack of smoke emerging from the chimney; the lump in his throat appears again. Closer still, he sees that planks have been nailed across the shutters on the windows. He runs to the door and hammers on it with his fists, shouting at the solid door, appealing to the stones and the thatch, pleading with the still, damp air, "Ma, Ma, it's me, Fons..."

When his shouting and hammering finally drowns, sinking below the silence, Fons wipes the tears from his cheeks and tries to think. They must have been telling the truth, after all. She must be away working on the boats again, like before he was born. He recalls that first day, standing on the steps of St Josephs, his mother talking to the lady in the black clothes and strange hat, and himself wondering whether this lady really was his mother's sister, because it was news to him. Watching his mother shrug when Sister Rose asked about his father, he could sense at that moment a change in attitude from the woman in black, suddenly looking down on his mother (though remaining polite to her face). Somehow he could also feel his mother's hidden shame, and feel it becoming his own. Soon, he sensed, this lady would be saying bad things about his mother, after she'd gone. The worst thing about this memory, he could never remember his mother saying goodbye, the moment of her leaving; and somehow that always brought the blackest shame of all.

He remembers something else, though; an image from when he was even smaller, watching his mother. So he walks around the back, to the other door, and hunts around, moving slowly down the path to the vegetable patch, where he sees a short piece of cane protruding from the ground. He digs his hands into the earth beneath it, grasping the edge of something solid. He pulls up a small pot, and tips the contents out. Something rattles, and a large iron key flops out of a piece of sailcloth, landing on the pile of earth.

He returns to the door and struggles with the lock. Finally, it surrenders, giving one last rusty shriek before it turns. The darkness inside smells musty, damp, but underneath there is a trace of something else; smoky peat fires, and perhaps (or is it just his memory?) the soapy, sweet smell of his mother. Out of one pocket, Fons carefully pulls out a small box of matches, and from the other, half a candle. He hopes there are more candles inside. Maybe his mother left some food somewhere, just in case. Maybe she will come back soon, if he prays hard enough.

*   *   *

Fons wakes up with a start. A shaft of light penetrates the gloom; it comes from a small hole in the ceiling above him. He rolls over, still expecting to hear Sister Rose; instead, he feels sackcloth under his neck and cheek, lumpy stone and earthen floor under his body. He remembers where he is, and blinks twice. Then he hears a voice, coming from outside the cottage. "It's a lonesome place, and still boarded up, all right."

It's a boy's voice, he realises; just then, a girl speaks. "Well, Da was only saying he smelt smoke on the wind last night, and that could've come from anywhere over this way; tinkers, maybe." He hears someone pushing at the front door, trying to turn the handle, and feels a shock of panic. After a pause, something thumps the door. A kick of frustration, Fons decides; very carefully, he unwraps himself from the blankets that he acquired the day before, a strong musk of horse assaulting his nose. The girl's voice continues, "Anyway, I can't smell any smoke here." Within the cottage, Fons also sniffs the air, feeling more panic as he inhales the distinct scent of last night's fire. Having found these blankets in an empty stable at the manor house nearby, he used them to gather as much dead wood as he could carry, from the wood surrounding the demesne. They and the fire had kept him warm for the first time since he'd arrived.

The other voice speaks. "There's something; but maybe that's only the turf at old Ryan's farm, on the wind. We'll take a look at the door to the garden, round at the back." Fons pads quickly and quietly to the back door, the soles of his feet protesting at the cold, and gently twists the heavy bolt up and across, sliding into its socket with a small squeak of protest. The voices approach.

"There, you see, Michael, it's all boarded up on this side too."

"It is, but didn't you hear something? I hope it's not tinkers, making themselves at home."

"Ah well, it might be a small tinker with whiskers and a long tail, probably." Someone pushes against the back door, and thumps it twice. "Leave it alone, Michael. Mrs Gilligan won't thank you for kicking her doors, if she comes back. And Da will skin you alive, if I tell him."

"You won't."

"I might."

"No, you won't, Mary. Or I'll tell him what you told me about Mrs Doyle."

"Whist now, an' come on." The voices retrace their way around to the front and begin to fade away. Fons pads over to his bedding and tips the hay out from the sack, hoping it will dry a little. He pulls his boots on, slings the sack over one shoulder and tiptoes to the back door, sliding open the bolt as quietly as he can. Slipping through the door, he inserts the key on the outside and struggles vainly with it. Scanning the ground nearby, he picks up a stick, inserts this through the hole in the key handle, and levers the key. The lock clicks.

He peers around the corner of the cottage. A boy and girl can be seen walking away up the boreen; he watches them until they clamber over a gap in the hedgerow and disappear. They must be the Conlon children, he thinks, from the nearest farm. The boy must be about his own age, skinny like him, but the girl looks more like Pat's age. She has long, dark hair, too, something he likes, and her figure looks womanly already. Does he know them? Not really, he thinks, though he does remember their mother...a memory of Mrs Conlon picking him up, fussing and smiling, has stuck in his mind. Maybe he should follow them? Dare he speak to them? They might know when his mother was coming back. He could always pretend to be staying in the village...

This thought reminds him, he needs to buy more matches and some bread, maybe. His stomach is aching with hunger, and he is sick of apples and pears. Last night, he cooked potatoes on the fire; he could do that again, but sure, he'll have to be careful. He thrusts his hands deep into his pocket and counts his money, again. He has one silver three pence, two pennies and a farthing, the result of selling his precious marble collection. That should be enough, he hopes.

A dog stands guard outside the village shop; a strange misshapen hound, its black coat splashed with tufts of white fur, the front legs exceeding the hind legs by two inches, so that it stands permanently at attention, ready to leap. As he approaches the shop, Fons steers his way carefully around it. The dog follows him, growling all the while and pulling at the rope which ties it to the wall. As Fons reaches the door, the dog retreats a step and then attempts a frustrated leap forward, ending with a throttled howl.

Fons edges into the gloomy interior of the shop, sniffing cabbage and stale tobacco. He hears a chesty cough and discovers a tall, stooping man with wispy grey hair leaning over the counter to inspect him. "Don't you mind Danu; her bark's a lot worse than her bite. Mind you, she takes a little nip from a stranger now and then." Fons swallows, and nods. "So I wouldn't get too close, not before she knows you. Where is it you've come from, anyways?"

Fons blinks. "Mrs Conlon sent me. I'm her nephew." The man nods, considering this. "She wants me to get some matches."

"Does she now?" A sharper tone; Fons realises his mistake.

"Well, mainly she's wanting a loaf of bread; but she asked me to get some matches too, if you could spare some."

The man frowns, but he bends down and pulls a round loaf of soda bread from under the counter, then slowly wraps it in a sheet of newspaper. A long, bony hand stretches up to a high shelf and removes a box of matches. He tips it from one side to the other, as if checking the contents, as he studies Fons. "And how are your cousins?"

Despite himself, Fons turns crimson while he tries to think. "Grand. They're both grand, especially...especially...Mary."

The man nods, and gestures for Fons to open his bag. "Tell your aunt that Mr Finnegan says she's welcome. That'll be three pence ha'penny." His goods safely claimed, Fons unclutches his fist, inspects the contents, and hands over four pence. The shopkeeper pauses, waiting to see if the boy expects change; he sighs, and then hands the ha'penny down. Fons backs out of the door so hurriedly that he almost forgets the dog behind him until he hears the growl.

Halfway back to the cottage, his stomach can't wait any longer. Fons flops by the hedgerow and wolfs down a quarter of the loaf before forcing himself to stop; aware not only of the wonderful taste but also his need to make this bread last. This dilemma absorbs him so much that he only glances up when he hears, far too close for comfort, the sound of creaking pedals and gasping breath. A bright red face and a large uniformed body slowly rise into view, nearing the brow of the hill upon which he sits. Fons feels a shock; his mouth drops open in horror. He blinks and observes that this overweight policeman is puffing hard, swaying from side to side; the eyes of authority are glued to the ground below him. Fons sinks silently into the long grass. Should he try to crawl through the hedge into the field? Probably better to lie completely still, he thinks; he should be difficult to spot here. But to his utter horror, he hears the man dismount just before he reaches the spot where Fons is hiding. Now Fons wants to run; yet he feels frozen, pinned like a butterfly. Through a veil of grass he watches the policeman stand a while to catch his breath, pull out a handkerchief and wipe his brow, all the while staring absently into the distance. Then he farts; a long, loud, rippling, bubbling fart, before commencing a gentle, rolling walk, pushing the bike onto and over the brow of the hill. Fons watches the beetroot face pass by, oblivious to all but the hill; he forces himself to count to ten, then to twenty. He rolls silently onto his back while the grass around him gradually begins to shake; desperately he stuffs his hands into his mouth while the tears roll silently down his cheeks.

*   *   *

Mary sits on the bank of the stream, half watching her brother and half picking at some dry grass stalks. Michael stands above the stream, legs splayed between two flat stones, lips pressed together and brow furrowed, looking down into the water. He holds the fishing net a few inches under the surface, his hands grasping the long wooden handle tightly as he impersonates a statue. Mary watches him wobble slightly, and smiles. "Keep still."

Michael frowns and mutters, "Whist."

Mary sighs. Her attention drifts; she studies the struggles of a black beetle attempting to move something three times its size. Hearing a splash, she looks up to see Michael flailing the air with one arm, his body arching, the net momentarily free of the water. As she opens her mouth, Michael jams the net back down into the water and regains his balance, "Be careful, Michael..."

He sticks out his tongue; she thinks about reminding him of the last time he fell in. A large bush at the top of the opposite bank suddenly twitches; another boy emerges from behind it, a lop-sided grin announcing the magic of his entrance, "Did ya catch the fish, then?" She studies the dark, unkempt hair and worn, dirty clothes, wondering if he's a tinker boy; although he talks like a local.

"Well, I did, but it got away again. The fish must have moved just before I did."

The mysterious boy nods at Michael's reply then looks to her, expectantly. Part of a woman's job, she remembers her mother telling her, is to make the introductions; to pour the drinks. "I'm Mary Conlon," she announces, "and that's my brother Michael." She shifts the tone of her voice upward just a little for her brother's name, expressing a hint of contempt.

The stranger boy flashes a wide grin at her. "I'm Fons," he replies, his face flushed, "Fons Gilligan". He turns toward Michael, "I'm staying at me Ma's cottage; but don't tell anyone, it's a secret, please." It seems to be understood that Mary need not be asked, that he trusts her already.

Michael nods as if secrets were an everyday event. He steps sideways and jumps onto the rock nearest the bank, looking across at Mary, the triumph on his face. "See?" He turns back to Fons, "I had a doubt the place was empty."

Fons ignores this and points at the net. "Can I have a go?"

Mary sighs, loudly. *Boys,* she thinks; but she watches the way Fons removes his boots and crouches on a large stone under a tree to hide his shape from the fish, and sees how patient he is, ignoring the tiddlers, waiting for a fat trout to appear, then manoeuvring the net so slowly that she really can't tell if it's getting any closer. Is it? Michael nudges her elbow; she nudges back, and puts her finger to her lips. She jumps as an explosion of movement sprays upward with a rushing noise like a waterfall; a silver brown shape flies into the air, half-in and half-out of the net, surrounded by drops of water catching the sun. The boy's foot plunges momentarily into the water and out as the net reaches its highest point; the trout tips slowly, drunkenly over the lip of the net, which chases it downwards, but only toward a plop in the water, then bubbles and widening ripples.

"Jesus... that one truly did jump out of the net," Fons announces. "Mind, I'll be needing someone to teach me how to cook a fish when I do catch one."

"You surely had that one, for a little minute," consoles Michael.

Mary teases Fons for a while with her silence, before telling him, "Our Ma often wraps the fish in a cabbage leaf, and then she lets it cook a while in the embers." She remembers something else and pulls a face. "Mind, you have to be cutting out all the guts first, or it'll make you bad. And they're disgusting. Ugh." Fons nods at her, signalling gratitude, and then crouches down again while the other two watch him.

Half an hour later Mary announces, "We'll have to be getting back now." Seeing the disappointment on Fons' face, she adds, "Maybe we'll come back later."

He starts to climb towards them, then stops, tilts his head, and lifts the net. "Can I have a loan of this? If I catch a couple, you can have one." Mary shrugs; Michael nods. As they turn to leave, Fons clears his throat. "You will give me your promise not to blather? I really want to surprise me ma." She turns and sees a face set with anxiety; then hears desperation in the hoarse whisper that follows.

"Sure, if they drag me back to St Joseph's, I'll get a terrible beating."

She turns to face him, examining his expression. "Will you now?"

"I will, I swear."

His steady gaze convinces her. "Well, in that case, we won't be blathering."

He sighs with relief, "Thanks." He frowns. "And I also thought, if you have plenty in your house, could you spare me a candle?"

That night, as it gets dark, Fons flicks round pebbles across the floor, playing against himself with black and white stones. He waits until dark and then makes a fire with the sticks he collected the day before, losing himself in the light and warmth. He thinks, they must have forgotten about me by now. But then, maybe his mother has done the same? To distract himself, he gets up and brings over the tin plate to examine the fish by the fire. Not so large, but there are two of them, and he's done what Mary told him. As the fire dies down he rakes the remaining embers flat, carefully places a large potato on one side, wraps the fish in leaves from the garden and puts them on the other side. He settles down to wait, listening for the hissing sounds that will tell him something is cooked.

*   *   *

Half a mile away, Sarah Conlon snuffs out the candle and climbs into bed, listening to the owl for a moment before snuggling up to the warmth of her husband's back. She rubs his shoulder gently, feeling the hard muscles and bone loosening under her touch. "Ernie?"

"Be careful, now, Sarah Conlon, or you'll set me off."

She slaps his shoulder and smiles to herself, "Oh, behave yourself." She pauses, listening; she hears nothing from the children in the attic above. "What was it the constable was wanting, when he took himself over the field yesterday?"

He turns his head slightly, but makes that characteristic noise, half-grunt, half-sigh, telling her he's tired. "You don't miss much, Sarah Conlon, and I meant to tell you, anyway. He was enquiring for Alice Gilligan's boy, as the lad's run away from St Joseph's. Can't say as I blame him; but the constable is wanting us to keep an eye out in case he comes here, looking for his mother. But for meself, I'll be betting that he'll be back there in Fermoy by now." He settles his head back into the pillow and then hears her humming a little tune to herself. Ernie sighs; this is her way of telling him that she has something on her mind. "What is it?"

"Finnegan said something odd to me at the shop today."

"He's an odd man, that's for sure."

"Whist, now, and listen; he asked if my nephew was still staying with us. I stood there wondering what sort of humbug he was meaning until he started to tell the tale. Some young boy has been in his shop buying matches and bread, telling Finnegan he was staying with us; a boy with a dark mess of hair, Michael's age. I remember little Fons, with his hair as black as coal."

She pauses to let this sink in, and feels him shift his arm, rubbing the stubble on his chin before he speaks. "Maybe; I did take myself another look at Alice's cottage, and it's a sad state, but the doors and windows are locked up. Though it may be that the boy has known where Alice hides the key; and that would be a mystery to me. And I smelled smoke on the wind a couple of nights, from that direction. And again, someone's been taking potatoes from the west field, by the stream. My first thought would be it was tinkers, though I never saw them."

He feels a squeeze on his shoulder, and listens. "Don't be saying anything to the children, but a few things have gone missing - just a couple of candles and scraps of food, nothing much." He feels her breath on his ear as she whispers, "So I think we've got a terror of a mouse, one with two legs, somewhere near."

He chuckles, "Aye, it sounds like we have." He feels her arm slip over his waist as she snuggles up again. "You be keeping your eyes peeled; I'll be having a word with the constable next time I pass that way. That'll be soon enough."

Four days later, Fons returns from the wood at the desmesne, carrying fuel for his fire. There's a chill in the evening air these nights as the autumn prepares to depart. He hurries along, thinking about Pat and the bridge. The bundle he carries in his arms blocks his view of the ground. As he hurries along the boreen towards his cottage he passes over cycle tracks and footprints, oblivious. When he turns the corner, round to the back of the cottage, he stops. A black bicycle leans next to the back door. The bundle slips from his grasp, his stomach churns, and he blinks twice. He hears a step behind him and turns to meet a black uniform looming above him. Two large outstretched arms grasp his shoulders. He looks up at the cap badge, a crown above the harp.

"And you'll be young Master Gilligan, won't you?"

* * *

Two weeks later, Sarah Conlon finishes her preparation, dusts the loaves with flour and carefully places them in the oven. She allows herself a little rest, sitting down with a deep sigh. Less than half a minute later, though, she stands, goes over to the narrow window and peers out into the yard. Something is up with Mary, she's sure; perhaps her bleeding has started in earnest, she thinks, or maybe the business with that boy has upset her more than she thought. She's been distracted and forgetful ever since, and the last few days she's been prone to make excuses to go outside 'for some air'. The girl hates the cold normally, and the last few mornings have seen frost whitening the ground. This time, Michael went too; where have those children got to, anyway?

She sighs and goes over to pour herself some tea from the pot hanging above the hearth. It's black, well stewed; just how she likes it. As she takes a sip from the cup, she hears the door latch slide up and turns to watch the children entering. They seem to be sneaking around these days as if they are hiding from her, instead of rushing about like they used to; she never thought she'd miss their shouting and banging, but she does. "Where've you been? It's time to feed the hens, both of you, and then there's the cow to milk, Mary."

Mary's face flushes but she stays silent. Michael pipes up, "Sorry, Ma. We've just been down by the stream looking for mushrooms. Can we have some bread first?"

"Again? You two must have hollow legs." Sarah shakes her head but she turns and walks into the pantry, unwraps what is left, and cuts two thin slices. She lifts the lid off the butter pot and smears a little on; then sighs, and adds a little more. She hears a giggle, turns, and discovers the children behind her. "Come on now, out of here. Eat this and then go and do your jobs." Back in the kitchen, Mary takes one bite from her slice and then turns her back on her mother. Sarah wants to tell her daughter not to be so rude, but she bites her tongue and turns away to pour cold water from the jug into a large basin.

"I'm just going to get me woolly hat..."

Sarah follows her to the inner door and calls out, "Don't you be dropping crumbs up there. I've just swept this house..." She moves back to the hearth, unhooks the hot water pot, and takes it to the basin, mixing the cold and hot water. She replaces the pot over the fire and lathers the water with soap. She inspects the pile of washing and picks out one of her husband's shirts. Then she notices Michael, still watching her, waiting. She goes back to the inner door and calls out, "Come on, Mary, will ya? Are you still dreaming, girl?" She stands a while, waiting. Looking through into their neat little house, she sees into the parlour to the stepladder that goes up into the attic under the thatch, the children's room. Mary appears, wearing her hat; but not from those steps - she appears through the small door below that leads into her parents' bedroom. Sarah folds her arms. "What the devil have you been doing in our room?"

Mary turns bright red, averts her eyes, "I...I just wanted to use the mirror, to see my hat..."

"In heaven's name, what sort of festival is happening in your head these last few days? I've been thinking my daughter has lost her senses, maybe." Sarah waits by the door, unsure whether to slap her daughter or embrace her. She wants to give her a shake, if only to get through to her. Mary walks towards her, stubbornly keeping her head down, saying nothing, and silently tries to push past her mother. Sarah reaches out, grabs her arm, and steps across to block her path.

"Let me go..." Mary is suddenly shouting, pushing past her, and Sarah is so shocked she steps aside for an instant, as she registers something hard under Mary's dress.

"Wait. What have you got there? Come back here, *now*." That last word explodes out of Sarah's mouth, forcing Mary to stop and turn. The girl's eyes begin to brim with tears. Her mother reaches across, her hands invading Mary's dress, wrenching the folds apart, her anger causing her to violate her daughter's privacy. "What's this? God a mercy! Iodine? A piece of bacon? And why in heaven stuff your bread up under your skirt? For pity's sake girl, what are you up to?"

Mary's face turns crimson; she sniffles and studies the floor during a long pause. Then she lifts her head up and wipes her eyes. "Come along with me, Ma, and you'll see."

"You can't..." Sarah jumps, turns toward the sound of Michael's shout, sees him glaring.

"We have to..."

"But we promised..."

"Come on, Michael, it's no use, we have to tell Ma. Come on, Ma."

Sarah follows her daughter out into the yard, her son trailing behind. Mary leads them all into the barn, around the side of the stacks of hay, to the far corner. She pulls up the corner of a tarpaulin. "Come on out, Fons, it's alright."

Sarah watches a boy crawl out, moving stiffly; he looks up, and then steps back, wincing.

Mary reaches out and takes his hand, "I'm sorry, Fons, we had to tell her. This is me Ma."

"Please don't send me back."

"She won't. But you have to *show* her, Fons."

The boy gives Mary a pleading look, then drops his eyes and bends forward. Mary gently turns him around and carefully pulls the woollen sweater over his head. Sarah hears the boy whimper, and steps forward. She helps Mary loosen the shirt, and lifts a corner, revealing a mass of purple and orange bruises. She tries to pull it further, but sees that darker patches of the shirt are stuck to his back with blood.

"Holy Mother of God...Jesus a mercy... what sort of devil would do this to a child?" Sarah Conlon has never sworn in front of her children, but on this day it takes a powerful effort to stop herself. She turns Fons around gently, "Who did this to you?"

Mary speaks for him, "The Brother in charge at St Joseph's. That's why he ran away, Ma. And that's why we were helping him. He's a good lad, Ma; he's got a good heart."

Sarah swallows, suddenly calm. She pulls her daughter to her, filled with a new respect for her, and embraces her. "I'll talk to your father." Looking down, she sees Mary smiling, trying to catch Michael's eye. She releases her daughter with one arm and takes hold of Fons' hand, wary of touching his body. "We'll be writing to your mother, Fons, through the shipping company. Meanwhile you'll be staying here, and we'll sort something out with her." She feels Michael's body arrive, trying to join in the circle. "Sure, the house will feel a bit crowded, but we'll manage."

*　　*　　*

Boys stream through the vestry door in twos and threes, leaping out into freedom, their feet splashing pebbles about wherever they land, skidding in triumph as they turn and run. Choir practice is over; the rest of this fine spring weekend is theirs (barring worship on Sunday, of course). Some meet parents; others rush the other way along a path and through a wooden gate, across the playing field towards the buildings at the back of the school. Halfway across this field Pat changes course, slowly diverging from his companions. At the far edge of the field two boys glance up from the ball they're kicking to and fro. "Hey, Mahon, where are you headed for? Don't you want to play football?"

Pat turns and grins at the sight of his two new friends; they both stand hands on hips, frowning and gazing at him. Carr and McDermott seem uncannily like a mirror reflection of each other; not so much in looks as in behaviour. They both have a swagger, a confidence that he envies. City boys, he thinks; but despite their differences, they both seem to like him. "Maybe later; I want to have a look at that bike of yours first, Carr. See if I can fix it."

The boy on the left tilts his head quizzically, pulling a face. "It's badly pranged, I told you; bent in all the wrong places." Pat considers this, but shrugs. "Though if you can fix it, you can borrow it whenever you like - fair enough?" Pat smiles and nods; Carr's great fun, but he's spoilt. His family will buy him another bicycle eventually, but this one is almost new so he can't ask for another one just yet; giving Pat a window of opportunity. Carr gives him a shrewd but respectful look, before he turns away and boots the ball. "Best of luck, then..."

"See you later." Pat hurries around towards the front of the school, entering a small courtyard and opening a stable door. His eyes scan a dozen bicycles of various ages, leaning against the sides of empty stalls. He frowns until his gaze is drawn to a faint gleam in the darkest corner, where a new machine lies across a heap of old harnesses. Making a careful inspection, he shakes his head. The front wheel and handlebars point in different directions; the wheel seems jammed fast against the mudguard. The chain feels very loose, though it looks intact. The back wheel sticks too; Pat nods thoughtfully, tracing the route of the brake lever mechanism, and then pulls each part until he finds the problem. He's always had an instinct for spotting faults with the farm machinery, even if his brothers' muscles had to do the fixing. Next, he looks around the stable carefully, scratching his head. No matter how hard he looks, he can't see any tools.

Pat reads the name on the first door, grimaces, and quickly moves on to the second. 'Daniel O'Brien, Science master.' This sounds more promising, he thinks, though he still hesitates. Are these staff residences out of bounds to him? Will he get into trouble? In for a penny...he bites his lip and knocks. As the footsteps approach, he crosses his fingers behind his back. The door opens, revealing a bespectacled man about thirty, newspaper folded over one arm. The man sighs and looks him up and down, "Good Lord. What's your name again, boy?"

"Mahon, sir; I'm in three alpha."

"And what on earth are you doing here, Mahon?"

"Well, sir, I thought with yourself being the science teacher I should ask for your help. I need some tools, sir."

"Tools?"

"Tools it is, sir, for a bicycle. I want to fix a bicycle for my friend, sir."

O'Brien rubs his chin, examining Pat's expression carefully. He looks away, seemingly deep in thought. "And why on earth can't your friend fix it himself?"

Pat thinks quickly. "He has no tools either, sir. But he said I could use it if I fix it."

Mr O'Brien nods sagely. "Aha." He takes out a pipe, "Show me."

An hour later, Pat glances up; O'Brien sits on a stool on his own doorstep, his pipe clamped between his teeth, apparently browsing the last page of his newspaper. Pat knows that he's being observed; the way that he's tried to tackle the faults with the bicycle has been studied. Yet until this moment, O'Brien has offered no comments or assistance. Finally, he speaks, "Has someone taught you how to do this, Mahon?"

Pat's frown of concentration relaxes; he places his index finger on a spot on the wheel rim and looks up again. "They have not, sir. But I like machines."

"Do you? And why is that?"

He shrugs. "I don't know, sir. I always did have a liking for them."

"Well, you've fixed most of this one, haven't you?"

"I have sir, almost there I'd say."

"But this last bit is tricky, isn't it? Do you want me to give you a hint?"

Pat nods; O'Brien grins. He stands up and walks over to the boy. "This bit is easier if we flip the bike over. In fact, with bicycles, most things are easier to fix this way up. See how it balances on the seat and handlebars? Now, how are you going to stop this wheel jamming against the mudguard?"

Pat frowns and reaches out, touching and pointing as he talks. "Well, sir, this is the place where it sticks. The wheel can't move down so somehow we have to move this up. Maybe if we can straighten these..."

"Good lad. But how; what with?"

"I don't know, sir. I don't know what tool you might use for that."

O'Brien laughs. "Ah well, that's where you'll need my help." He leans over the bicycle, pushing inward with both arms, grunting as he heaves at the supporting forks. "Hmmm... that should do it - brute force and ignorance, Mahon; the mechanic's last resort." He sighs, and flips the wheel with his index finger. It spins, ticking gently.

"Do you think they'll send me back, sir? I mean... is my work good enough?" The question rocks O'Brien back on his heels; he straightens up and removes the pipe from his mouth. "What brought you here, boy? Singing, or is it the learning?"

"Singing, sir, that's not a problem, sir."

"Well, your science is basic, but you've got potential. You're some way behind, but from what I've seen today you can catch up. No, if you can sing too I doubt they'll send you back, Mahon." Pat feels his whole body relaxing at this, all his hidden tension draining away. Mr O'Brien also seems to relax; he yawns, stretches his arms, and looks sideways at Pat. "Tell you what, with you a singer, do you want to see my latest machine? And hear something magical from it?"

Pat really wants to go for a bike ride, but he can't refuse the offer. He follows O'Brien back into his apartment where, in a small front parlour, his teacher instructs him to sit down and shut his eyes. He listens to movement within the room, the sound of metal parts fitting together, and a winding noise; a faint rustle of paper, Mr O'Brien humming. Suddenly, out of nowhere, he hears a brass band in the room, blasting out the opening bars of "It's a long way to Tipperary..."

Pat almost jumps out of his chair; his eyes jerk open in astonishment, but all he sees is a small wooden box with a large horn protruding upwards. He blinks rapidly while his mouth falls open. Meanwhile a voice begins to sing the words; he can actually make out the sound of boots marching. He notices Mr O'Brien laughing silently to himself, holding his sides and rocking backwards and forwards with mirth. Pat ignores this, shuts his eyes again and listens, carried away to another place where a brass band plays, soldiers march, and someone sings in a near-perfect pitch. At the end, he opens his eyes.

"Like it? This machine's called a phonograph, or a Victor talking machine. That was John McCormack. Do you want to hear more?"

Pat nods. This time, he hears stringed instruments with the same near-perfect voice, singing a familiar song, one that his mother taught him. He screws his eyes tightly shut, partly to stop the prospect of tears, and listens; gradually, his breathing returns to normal as he follows the slow dance of the notes and wonders at the perfection of the voice. It's like his idea of what he might hear sitting with his mother, in heaven. He opens his eyes.

"The first song was recorded for the British soldiers. The second was not; I think secretly Mr McCormack meant that for our Volunteers. A Dublin shopkeeper called Napper Tandy wrote that one; I prefer the second song, don't you?"

Pat nods. "I do too, by a mile."

"Good lad. Finally, I'll play you a special one. If you want to be a singer, listen to this." Mr O'Brien lovingly places another disc on the machine. "This is Enrico Caruso at the Metropolitan opera house in New York, singing from an Italian opera called Il Travatore. Maybe one day you'll be able to sing it. If you are exceptionally good, one day you might sing at the Metropolitan too..."

Pat watches, fascinated. Mr O'Brien drops an arm with a small, needle-like point onto the disc. He sees how it turns, moving the arm inwards. Then he hears an orchestra and a voice, truly a perfect pitch voice, and also richer, more expressive; he's instantly transported to another world...

*   *   *

Pat stretches out his maturing, gangly frame in the old armchair; eyes closed, he sings quietly to himself, tapping a rhythm with his fingers on the arms of the chair. Like his body, his mind has settled into the comforts of this place; a decent bed, good food, unlimited books, and new friendships. During the last year, he's also fed and grown on the stimulation of Dublin, stretching his mind and growing his confidence. After a long and tedious summer back on the family farm, anxiously avoiding the town, his return has made him realise how comfortable he feels here. He allows that comfort to flood through his body, and then brings his mind back to the music in his head. He tries to imagine the costumes of the pearl fishermen, singing their duet of eternal friendship, having been deadly rivals in love for the beautiful Leila. He pictures a simple stage, a background of nets and boats within a grand and large theatre. It takes no effort to imagine the music; he can recall every note of the soaring melody and much of the orchestra accompanying it, which he hears echoing in his mind. He's listened to O'Brien's recording of Caruso and Ancona performing this duet many times. It's his gift, he knows, to be able to do this; to have a memory that can store music effortlessly. What he really needs, he thinks, is a score, so he can read and understand the words. The voices rise and swell toward the final crescendo; he becomes dimly aware of footsteps approaching, accompanied by a sense of the familiar. Frowning, he tries to ignore the cajoling banter that begins to insinuate into the song, despite his best effort. A howl of recognition bursts his concentration, scattering the orchestra and chorus back into the hidden corners of his dreaming theatre. "*Here* he is, skulking in the boarder's common, as usual."

Keeping his eyes firmly shut, Pat shakes his head in exasperation. "Carr. I suppose the football team is finally taking itself seriously, if they made a decision to dispense with *your* flat feet. After years of wondering whether it's possible to ignore your undoubted enthusiasm, they were after deciding to win a game for a change, I suppose?" He hears a snort, accompanied by a chuckle. "And that must be you, McDermott. Nothing better to do, I suppose. Has Sister Bernadette finally abandoned the impossible task of trying to save your soul?" He opens one eye in time to see McDermott's already ruddy complexion turn crimson.

Carr flops into the armchair opposite and sighs. "You can talk, Mahon. I seem to remember the first time that woman ever came to take our class, I'd say the hormone level in the room doubled, and *you* couldn't keep your eyes off her, either. Slavering at the mouth like the rest of us. I'll bet your body went to attention so fast, it damn near kicked the desk over." McDermott looks relieved, shoots a sly grin at Pat, then pulls up a wooden chair and sits on backwards, resting his chin on his folded arms.

Pat shakes his head and looks up, as if to heaven. "You have a filthy mind, Carr. But I do confess she is uncommonly *unlike* your average nun. Even swaddled in her penguin suit, I don't have to be a scientific genius to spot *her* femininity. And unlike those of our dear classmates who want to follow a saintly path into the church, I have no intention of keeping my own body unemployed forever."

"You can dream; but please remind me not to introduce you to my sister."

"You already have, Carr, but sadly the poor girl looks far too much like you, God help her. And you surely are a cunning devil, McDermott, to try and get the buxom Sister on her own by seeking spiritual advice. The problem is, though, with herself not being familiar with the habits you seek, she's unlikely to give you the guidance that you really want, is she?"

McDermott chortles, "Come on, Mahon. You know fine well what a grand and a rare thing it is just to pass the time of day with a woman, in this place."

Pat nods, "He's not so dumb, after all, is he?" With a bitter tone, he adds, "It's certainly better than fighting off assistant choirmasters who covet your arse." He regrets the remark instantly, knowing it will be used against him.

Carr raises his eyebrows, "Ah well, you see, I for one never did quite understand the attractions of the choir - has old Harry finally managed to lift your shirt, then?"

Pat shakes his head, feeling the heat in his cheeks. Mostly, he enjoys this bantering game, but sometimes it goes too far. "God forbid. To be fair, the old divil would never try it on with me. He knows I would knock him over."

Carr nods as if deep in thought. "Yes. For sure, he knows you're a *farm* boy, with great big boots. He only goes for the girly types, the ones unlikely to object." He waves a hand, as if dismissing the subject. "Anyway, I prefer the scientific view of the world. While the two of you do all your singing and praying, I'll simply follow Mr Darwin's theory and evolve..."

"Ah, we have a name for that species, in Cork." Pat studies the ceiling, waiting for a reply before he plays his next card.

"Oh, go on then, you Cork culchie; tell me."

Pat winks at McDermott, "Back at home we know them as Dublin Jackeens, you spot them by their English accent and their façade of superiority; like a monkey in a suit." McDermott blinks in surprise, shrugs nervously and glances over at Carr; he gives a baleful smile. Pat wonders if he has gone too far but waits for the inevitable riposte from Carr, who loves these verbal duels.

"Careful now, Mahon; remember, according to Darwin we're *all* closely related to monkeys. That must be true even here in Dublin, but at least we are *civilised* monkeys. Down there in Cork, alas, due to the agricultural habits, everyone's related to the *same* monkey. And he knows most of his sisters far too well." Pat shakes his head but cannot suppress a grin, while Carr catches their companion's eye. "I suppose you believe that even Cork monkeys like Mahon have souls, don't you, McDermott?"

"Well, I'm a simple soul myself, Carr. Mr Darwin may have the right ideas as a scientist, but that doesn't say much to me about God, in my opinion. That's a different matter entirely. So unless he's already sold his soul to old Nick in exchange for one of those gramophone things, he probably has one hidden away somewhere. Hidden away; a bit like God, really."

Pat snorts, "Hidden away? God? Look closely at the European war, I'd say. If there was a God, he's surely been sleeping as sound as the corpse at a wake, the last few years." He remembers Carr's brother; so he quickly adds, "Any road, we should think ourselves lucky on that score."

Carr stares at him for a moment. "We should, it would've been us next. Still, at least it was a proper war. What do we get instead? Murder gangs on the streets. Even my father doesn't want me in the army now. It'll get nasty, he says; not a proper job for a soldier. But who else will do it?" McDermott shakes his head sadly and looks at the floor. Pat sighs and closes his eyes for a moment; to his horror, a vision intrudes, his boyish self on the bridge looking down the barrel of a gun. He opens his eyes and blinks twice, wondering for a second if he could possibly tell McDermott and Carr all about *that*, and its aftermath. He decides no, they would never understand. Their parents are part of the Dublin establishment; they have no idea what it's been like in the countryside.

"Someone will have to sort these bloody Shinners out; bet you wish you were back in Cork, Mahon, must be peace and quiet down there."

Pat nods, looking away. "Sure, it's a riot, midnight in the graveyard."

During the long silence that follows, Carr begins to tap his feet alternately, slowly at first, then faster and faster, until at the end of his mock drum roll he pushes himself up onto his feet, "Anyway, let's go into town and see what Grafton Street has to offer; how about it, you two?"

McDermott lets out a whoop of approval, but Pat shakes his head. "Sorry lads, not today, I've got to see O'Brien about my science homework."

Carr shakes his head sadly, "Tough luck, old chap. See you later..."

Pat watches them leave then stretches out again for an hour, transporting himself back to his own musical heaven, hearing the sounds and imagining the scenes in the Metropolitan Opera House in New York. When four o'clock approaches he yawns, rubs his eyes, stands up and stretches his limbs. Then he sets off, humming quietly to himself in anticipation.

The entrance to O'Brien's home stands ajar and he hears voices within; deep, anxious tones. He taps lightly on the door; the voices stop. He calls out, "Hello?"

Steps approach; O'Brien half opens the door. "Ah, it's you." He glances outside, up and down the street. "I'd forgotten; never mind, you'd better come in, you might be able to help." He waves Pat inside. "Come through, I'd like you to meet a friend of mine." In the tiny kitchen, Pat meets the gaze of a very tall, well-built man in a long dark coat. "Mick, this is one of my lads, Pat Mahon; from Cork, by the way." Pat takes the outstretched hand and tries not to wince when it crushes his own. "He comes to listen to my gramophone; I've been teaching him a bit of Irish history, the sort you don't read in books. He's a good lad. More to the point, he may be able to lend you a bicycle. If you do that, Pat, I'll let you listen to my latest Caruso. I've got some coffee, too."

Pat looks at Mick. The blue-grey eyes twinkle and the large face creases into a smile. "Oh, that would be just grand, Pat. I find myself in a bit of a fix today, do you know? Got to meet my dear little sister away on the other side of town, and I'll never make it on foot. Will you help me out and get that bike for me now?" Pat swallows and nods, entranced. "Off you go, then. Oh, and keep your eyes peeled; let us know if you see anything unusual." The big man taps his nose.

When Pat returns, wheeling the bicycle, they both wait on the doorstep. The big man has changed into one of O'Brien's coats, shorter and a lighter colour. It fits quite badly, the sleeves riding up his long arms, though that is not so unusual in this city of ill-fitting clothes. Pat also notices his enormous boots, and wonders what size they must be. The two men look at him expectantly until he remembers, "I... I didn't see anything queer, nothing at all."

The two men exchange glances; O'Brien nods, and Mick gives him a broad smile. "I'll be off, then. I'll get the bike back to yourself in a couple of days, Pat."

The big man swings the bicycle onto the path and leaps into the saddle, suddenly agile, though something bangs against the crossbar as he swings his torso across it. The seat is as high as it will go, for Pat is tall himself, but the big man still looks hunched up, his legs too bent as he pedals away, throwing a half-wave behind him.

*   *   *

Pat watches air blast from the horses' nostrils and form a freezing mist before merging with the steam rising from their necks as they trot; the vapours trail like a cloak before vanishing into the horses' wake. He sniffs the aroma of musky sweat that will linger in the early morning air behind them. The hooves beat a steady, insistent rhythm, the wheels rattling steadily on the road while bumps and dips provide a lyric of irregular creaks and groans, voiced by the seats and springs of the ancient trap. Every half mile or so his father slows the horses while they pick their way around a fallen tree or by-pass a damaged bridge over a stream, finding a route through adjacent fields. His father seems to know these detours by heart, even when the obstacle looks new. "Sure, *the boys* have been at work all over the county," his father explains. "They'll never get rid of the British troops entirely, but this sure as hell slows them up, when they're after making a raid."

Pat nods, "You've changed your tune, Da."

"I have, I surely have. It was the blowing up of the creamery that did it, Pat. Before that I was thinking we should not be taking any notice, even when they burned the houses of *the boys*. I was thinking, *the boys* were after bringing that trouble on themselves and on their own families. But then the peelers burned the creameries with the government's blessing, all over the county. They chose their lot and declared war on all of us, that day. Not a farming man around these parts will help the bloody peelers now." He leans out and spits for emphasis.

"Was that when Sean joined *the boys*?"

His father sighs and slows the horses to a halt while he considers his reply. "It is, Pat. He wanted to go before, but he waited until he had my blessing. Ernie's not a man for fighting, so himself and myself will run the farm. But you listen to me now, Patrick. The devil knows what will happen in the long run, but I will say one more thing to you now before you come of age. One son is enough, God help me, to be risking his neck against all the forces of the Crown; and you have a gift that is not to be squandered. You got from your mother your brains and the gift of your voice; herself would've burst with pride to see how far it's taken you. So don't you be thinking of following Sean, whatever else you might do, you hear me?"

The idea comes as a shock to Pat; his face flushes. "I won't, Da, I won't." But deep down, he feels a tug of shame at the ease of his acquiescence. Since he returned home for Christmas to find his brother absent, Sean has become his hero. Whenever he reads about the troubles in the newspapers, or the nationalist leaflets given to him by O'Brien, his feelings stir, drawn to reports of government brutality and the actions of the protestant gangs in Ulster. It seems a curious thought that he might become a soldier, after what was done to him by a soldier on that bridge. Until today it was unthinkable, and yet the idea attracts him, to fight back. For once, he allows himself to examine the memory of that day. It pains him still, and moves him to anger and shame. But yes, he thinks, it won't be long now before I am old enough to fight back...and what would that mean for me; an end to the shame? He looks up to see his father, apparently waiting for him to speak again.

"How are *the boys* doing, round here, Da?"

His father nods again, considering his reply before delivering it. "Not so bad. *The boys* have the country in their pocket now. The Crown has the towns, with the garrisons, but it's a queer sort of government when the peelers have to travel with an escort of soldiers in armoured cars. You know *the boys* are after burning the big houses?"

"I heard that."

"Well, the priests will still be talking about it till Judgement Day, but that has surely made the peelers think twice about firing the homes of *the boys*. Two can play at any game, so they can."

"What will happen next, Da?"

"To my way of the thinking, Pat, the peelers can't win the country back, and *the boys* will never take the towns against an army. That's why this truce has been agreed. There will have to be a heap of talking, in the end." Pat nods, wondering what Carr and his father will be making of all this.

After another mile, his father stops and lets the horses drink from a roadside trough while he and Pat chew bread and cheese. His father coughs and clears his throat as Pat swallows his last mouthful. He turns to give his full attention, suspecting that some great revelation is likely. He watches his father's eyes lift from the ground and settle on him like a great paw.

"Is it alright for you, in Dublin?"

Pat feels surprise initially; then he realises his father has never actually asked him this question before. "It is, Da; it's grand. It was terrible strange at first but I've got used to it now. I enjoy the learning, as well as the singing."

"Ah..." His father expresses a world of emotion in one little noise, Pat thinks, as he listens to his father's voice rise, hit a steady note, and fall away to a low rumble, his head nodding slowly. The eyes leave him for a second and when they return, they look misty. "It was your mother..." He struggles with his words and Pat resists his urge to break in, to demand, what about her? Another long pause... "I promised your mother, you know, on her deathbed, that you would be going to school. So I'm glad it's befitting you. She'd be happy about that, so she would."

Pat feels his own tears spring up. He nods and bows his head, feels a large arm enfold him. He allows himself to be comforted, allows the tears to run down his cheeks. He manages to gasp, "That's grand, thanks, Da." At the back of his mind, another voice whispers, "Why didn't you tell me, back then, when you first sent me away?" But he cannot bring himself to ask this question.

Two miles further on his father slows the trap and points across a field. "Here we are now. Look, you can see the farm just along that boreen. I'll be back here an hour before dark."

Pat steps down, watches his father turn the trap. "See you later, Da. And thanks..."

His footsteps slither across the tops of pebbles and stones buried in the boreen, the surface still slippery with melting frost, as he watches a bird appear from the edge of the thatched farmhouse roof, flutter up to the chimney to warm itself, and warble an off-tune greeting to the world. Entering the yard, he steps around patches of fresh dung, still steaming, and approaches a flaking, olive green door. A familiar voice behind him cuts across his thoughts, sharp, eager, reminding him of orchards and anticipation; "Pat...halloo..."

Pat swings around and sees through the open barn door; a pitchfork falling, abandoned, into the hay, as Fons rushes towards him. Instantly recognisable, his friend is now larger, heavier, his pubescent figure filling out evenly with muscles, in contrast to Pat's purely vertical growth. That must be the farm work, thinks Pat. Fons brakes abruptly to a halt in front of Pat, his arms flailing the air, undecided whether to embrace, to clasp an arm, or shake a hand. The eager, boyish expression changes into a shy smile as he looks up and down, uncertain. "Fons Gilligan, you're a sight for sore eyes. Look at all the muscles on you now."

Fons grins happily, nods, and holds his head on one side, looking his friend up and down. "You too, you must be growing taller than all of your teachers now."

Pat laughs, "Too right. The trouble is, Fons, down here in County Cork I do nothing but crack my head on the doorways."

Behind them, the door unlatches and opens, a girl's face appearing, round-eyed. Behind her, a woman's voice calls. "Come along now, Alfonsus; ask your friend in and offer him a cup of tea after his journey." Inside the house, Pat finds the Conlon family shy of talk, although he can't help but wolf down several of the biscuits proffered with his tea, and the girl's mother seems pleased that he does. Pat also feels shy and confused, unsure how to address them, wondering if the children are cousins to Fons, and he can't quite work out how to ask.

Eventually the father speaks. "Well, I'll be getting back to work. Fons, why don't you show your friend around, you'll be wanting to catch up with each other." He stands and slaps Michael on his back, "You can be helping me out a bit, Michael, and joining them after." The girl gives her mother an appealing look but receives a silent refusal.

Back in the yard, Fons nods back down the lane, "I'll show you me Ma's house first." His face now furrows; Pat feels awkward, suddenly wondering why he has gone to all this trouble, just to see this particular boy again; perhaps they have nothing left in common. No more is said until they reach a small, abandoned cottage, its tiny windows boarded up. The thatch is old, in dire need of replacement. Fons turns, his body announcing that this is the place.

Pat scratches his head. "Where is she?"

"Who?"

"Your Ma, Fons." Suddenly, he remembers something, "Is she still on the ships?" Fons seems to flinch, tears springing into his eyes.

Pat feels a moment of panic, thinking Jesus, please - she can't be dead, can she?

Fons twists his foot in the dirt. "She is; that's where she is." Pat hears pain embedded in the flat, exhausted tone. After a pause, his friend's voice drags itself upward and climbs the scales again towards a note of hope. "But she's writing to me every month, and she'll be coming to visit whenever she can. Only that means travelling the length of Ireland, since the liners are not putting in at Queenstown any more. She'll be coming back and living here one day, when she's saved enough of her wages to fix the old place up. I'll be able to help her when I'm older." His foot is still working, twisting a round pebble free of the earth, which he flips onto flat ground, and studies it. He toys with it for second, before sending it spinning away with a decisive kick.

Fons' tone sounds a little hollow to Pat. Maybe he doesn't quite believe what he is saying, against the reality of the decaying cottage? A hollow sensation grows in Pat's own stomach; he feels shame for his own clumsiness, sorrow for his friend, and surprise at his own realisation that sudden, complete loss might be kinder than a long, slow, teasing absence. He swallows and mutters, "I'm sorry for your trouble, Fons. It must be a divil of a wait. "

His friend lifts his head and stares back at him proudly, as if suddenly strengthened by the unburying of his secret doubt. "Ah well, things could be worse. At least I got away from St. Joseph's and that fat culchie Daniel. And the Conlons are grand."

"Who are they, exactly?"

"Neighbours...just neighbours." Fons grins. "You'll like Mary. Well, you should, she's more your age and her smile will light up a wet bog. And what about you, Pat? What the divil is a Choir school, anyhow? Will you become a priest?"

Pat explodes with laughter, "Jesus, no way, Fons. Brother Daniel put me off that nonsense for life. No, the school is a good one for learning, and it has a special choir that sings in the cathedral. I like the singing, and it's lucky for me that I did. That's how they let me go to the school. I want to be a scientist or an engineer; maybe I'd want to get away across the water, and start a new life over there."

"Across the big water?"

"Yes, the big one; the country's a terrible mess thanks to the English. It's getting worse, not better; I won't stay here unless we kick them out. I won't live my life under the heel of their boots."

"Fair enough."

"I hate them, you know; the English soldiers."

Fons says nothing, but he shoots a sideways look at Pat. "Da Conlon thinks they'll be gone soon, anyway. He thinks any truce will be the end for them."

"Does he now?"

Fons grins, "Ask anyone round these parts. They've lost control, with all their soldiers."

Pat nods, and then jerks his head back down the lane. "Ah well, but you can show me this farm now, Fons."

"I will, I'll give you the grand tour. What's Dublin like, anyhow?"

As the day passes Pat finds himself studying Fons and the Conlon family with renewed interest, comparing his own new life to that of his friend. The buried guilt harboured after leaving Fons behind in St Joseph's ebbs away. He relaxes so much that he sings for an hour to the Conlon family after lunch, around the fireside. Even Fons is astonished by his voice, lost for words.

Mary's face flushes when he leaves. She swallows, seems to take her courage in her hands, and tells him, "You must come back again, and see us. You'll always be welcome here."

Pat nods, understanding her tone and, for once, lost for words. She's a sweet and pretty girl, he thinks; if ever I come back to Cork. As he walks down the lane toward the trap waiting on the road, his mind fills with all the changes happening here in the country; *the boys*, his brother the hero, his father's revelations, and Fons' new life. He thinks how pleased Mr O'Brien will be, to hear how much support there is for *the boys* among the ordinary people. The country is shaking itself free, he thinks. He feels elated and liberated in his own self too; suddenly regarding himself as almost an adult, who will soon be able to lead his own life. I can leave all this too, he thinks; if I wish, and never come back... I can free myself too, if I wish. It feels such a powerful and intoxicating idea, echoing around in his mind.

*   *   *

"I've had enough of all this swotting. Fancy a game of chess, Mahon? Pit your clever Fenian brain against a stupid Jackeen?"

Pat frowns for a second; he sighs, marks his place by folding a corner of the page, and claps his book shut. "Come on, then."

Carr pulls out a battered board and then sets out some fine, if rather ancient, ebony and ivory pieces. "You can have the first move. That seems rather appropriate in the current political circumstances."

Pat laughs, "You're after changing your tune. A year ago, you told me the government were just toying with the Shinners. Only a matter of time before they were all rounded up, you said."

Carr's face flushes slightly; he looks up and meets Pat's eye. "Well, I really did think that, but so did all the newspapers, if you remember. That was before my dad told me what was really going on. Like everyone at the Castle, he'd been putting a brave face on for a long time."

"So when did he tell you that?" Pat moves a pawn.

Carr moves one of his. "Just before the last summer holidays, when he knew a cease-fire was on the cards. He decided he had to tell us how bad things were, anyway, to prepare us." He watches Pat move another pawn. "Your usual opening, Mahon; you really must try a new one."

"It usually works. I thought you were quiet when you first came back. What did your Da say? Preparing you for what?" Carr moves a piece, and Pat responds.

"It used to work, you mean. Look, Mahon, as you know my father's a senior civil servant at the Castle. Apart from anything else, he thought the murder gangs might make him a target. For a long time, he didn't tell us. They probably would have, without this cease-fire. Maybe not just him; he was also worried about my mother, my sisters and me too. I nearly didn't come back here. He would've sent us all to England last summer if there hadn't been a cease-fire. Maybe he still will, or maybe we'll be driven out anyway." Carr moves his knight.

"Jesus. You kept all that quiet." Pat moves another pawn, forming a line, moving forward.

"Don't look so surprised; look, if the fighting starts up again, he will send us away. And if the truce and the treaty hold, there'll be a new government soon, a kind of Home Rule. If that happens, then he may not have a job for very long. The new leaders may want a clean sweep. Don't get me wrong; we don't want to leave Ireland, it's our home too. But we may be driven out for taking the wrong side. That's what he was preparing us for." Carr moves a bishop.

"Sorry, Carr, I rubbed your nose in it. I didn't realise, I swear."

His friend sighs. "Apology accepted; your move."

Pat moves a piece. He feels distracted, upset for his friend, despite his own convictions. (In Ireland, how many poor families have lost their homes? The Carrs have money, at least.) Still, this feels too close to home, despite all that rhetoric about the price to be paid. "So what does your Da think about the Treaty, now?"

"He thinks anything that stops the fighting and lets us get back to normal is a good thing. He was upset at first when those negotiations were going on in London. Nobody here knew what was going on. And when the Treaty was signed, he said it felt like a defeat and a betrayal, and we would all have to leave. But now he thinks if it holds it may be for the best, if everyone can live with it. Your move, by the way. And what does a good Fenian like you think about it all? What's going on with these mutineers? They've won, but they seem to be the ones who want to carry on fighting."

"They haven't won, that's the point."

"What do you mean?"

"Most of *the boys* are Republicans. That means they fought for a Republic in all of Ireland, not just for Home Rule in the south. They won't accept being a part of the British Empire in any way, especially not with partition."

"But you have to make some compromises when you sign a peace treaty. You can't have it all your own way. Their own representatives signed the agreement and their own parliament voted to accept it. Like it or not, they have to go with the majority vote, surely? And what about the majority in Ulster?"

Pat sighs. "My understanding is that the delegates to London didn't have the authority to sign that treaty. De Valera, the president of the Dail, rejected it immediately. He could have arrested the delegates for exceeding their authority, but I guess he was too afraid of Collins. So he allowed it to go to a vote in the Dail. The Republican view is that Collins and the others then lied to the Dail; they claimed the army supported the Treaty because they had no ammunition left to fight. In fact, most of the army wanted to fight on. If the Dail had been told the truth, they would have rejected that Treaty too, for sure. As for Ulster, you might as well say every small garrison town in Ireland will remain English, and the Liverpool slums will become part of Ireland."

"Shit; that all sounds like a real can of worms."

"I'll agree with you there."

"How do you know about all this, Mahon?"

Pat shrugs. "My brothers know plenty of Volunteers, so they tell me what *the boys* are thinking. But it's easy enough, even here in Dublin. Go down and read the Republican pamphlets they hand out on Grafton Street. The problem is the newspapers and clergy are still in the pockets of the British, of the old order. That's why you don't read it in the newspapers."

"Look, I can see the logic, but it still sounds like an argument over spilt milk. It's done now surely, mistakes have been made and have to be lived with."

"Maybe the jug is falling off the table, but a quick pair of hands can still catch it. That's why the mutineers, as you call them, have taken over the Four Courts, to set up an army headquarters that truly represents the army. They did hold an army convention, you know."

"I thought the Dail had prohibited that."

"They held it anyway."

"Shit. So they've gone against their own parliament."

"Only because they had to..."

Carr snorts, "And if the Dail prohibited it, surely that means only the mutineers attended this conference, and the rest of the army didn't, presumably?"

"Maybe..."

"It's a bloody mess, Mahon, whichever way you look at it. At least the English knew how to organise things. It strikes me the only thing we Irish can organise is a pot still." He moves his queen. "Check-mate, by the way."

* * *

"Time to stop; now."

Pat looks up along the row of desks, his pen hovering in the air, hoping to scribble one last idea down. But the headmaster seems to be staring straight at him; Pat feels his cheeks flush, puts his pen down, and blows on the page to dry the ink. Around him the room slowly comes back to life; ancient oak legs first groan at the weight of boys shifting, then scrape the floor when they stand. He and Carr look to each other for confirmation; Carr shrugs, signals "middling" with his hand, and Pat nods. They file in a slow snake towards the exit, each boy turning his head in pensive farewell to the exam paper as he passes out of the door.

"One down, eight to go."

Carr nods with a rueful grin. "Sure, countdown at the last chance saloon. I'll miss this damn place; God knows why." He thrusts his hands deeper into his pockets and looks around. "Well, see you later. My father's meeting me outside."

Pat watches him go before heading in the opposite direction to the boys' boarding house, chewing his lip thoughtfully. An hour later, after a meal of bread and soup, he slips around the corner to O'Brien's house. His teacher is more than usually preoccupied writing a long letter, though he allows Pat to listen to his favourite Caruso pieces while he completes it. Pat simply feels relief that he does not have to talk about the exams; he slips into his customary reverie.

As the music fades away, leaving only a faint hiss and rhythmic knocking, Pat feels his foot being nudged. "Wake up, young man. I won't have you wearing out my precious needle listening to nothing."

"Sorry, sir."

Pat feels O'Brien's eyes upon him while he lifts the arm and handles the disc like the precious jewel that it is. The teacher nods his approval. "In return, you can do me a big favour."

Pat shrugs, sliding the disc into its inner sleeve, "Surely."

"You can deliver a letter for me, by hand. You know where the Four Courts are, I presume?"

Pat looks up, his eyes widening, and slowly straightens. "The Republican Headquarters?"

"Correct. I want you to take this and deliver it in person to the Director of Organisation. Can you remember that? And don't let anyone mess you around; make sure it gets into his hands." He studies Pat's face. "It's important; I can trust you, can't I?"

Pat nods and starts to open his mouth; O'Brien shushes him. "Away with you now. One other thing - when you come back, make sure you're not followed. If you are, take a little detour and lose him in the back lanes. Slip into a yard and run through to the front of a house. Here, take this." He hands Pat a thin, grubby, stained raincoat. "That'll help you blend in." The coat smells of dog, tobacco, and sweat. Pat puts it on, feeling faintly ridiculous, overdressed on a warm summer evening. O'Brien accompanies him to the door and studies his progress all the way to the corner, filling his pipe, his eyes narrow and thoughtful.

Away from the school, the Dublin streets at first feel alive, bustling, the pleasure of peace jostling with eager hope and expectation. Couples of all ages walk arm in arm, enjoying the last sunshine of the day. Pat feels caught up by the carefree mood, listening to buskers singing for coins and to the calls of the street-sellers offering flowers, fruits and toffees. But when he nears the Liffey the crowds thin out and the mournful sounds of scavenging seagulls replace human voices. Crossing the river, two men also in dingy raincoats on the opposite side of the bridge study his progress. He turns his face away, looking up river, watching the breeze pattern the water. The dome of the Four Courts looms up above him, just to the right of the bridge. He glances past the dome towards the main Court entrance facing the Liffey, noticing the sandbags piled in front of the gate. He resists an urge to turn in that way and continues further along the street, reasoning that there must be another entrance, conscious of eyes burning into his back. He passes another, smaller gate, behind which two sentries in shirt sleeves, rifles slung over their backs, are sharing a cigarette. They glance at him but he mooches past to the next street, then turns right, keeping his eyes downcast, forcing himself not to stare at a car parked further up the road.

Down this street, he finds another gate, the tradesman's entrance; the barrier down, sandbags piled on either side. But there's a gap to one side; Pat stops, and hails the makeshift sentry-box. "Hallo, *a chara*. I have a message for the Director of Organisation."

A gap-toothed face dotted with stubble appears. "Do you indeed? And who would you be?"

"Nobody; I'm... just a messenger. But it's important, I have to deliver it in person."

The man studies him for a few seconds, coughs, and spits. Then he turns and speaks to his companion. "Con, go and fetch Paddy." He turns back, "You - put your hands on your head and step this way." Pat obeys. "Now turn around." Strong hands almost unbalance him, checking to see if he has anything hidden under his clothes.

After a while, the other sentry returns with a tall, blue-eyed officer in a captain's uniform. They seem amused; Pat feels himself blush, they obviously think it's a huge joke. Nonetheless the officer listens and then invites him to follow. He strides into a large inner courtyard, walking past an armoured car parked there, its machine gun trained on the front entrance. They head left towards a large building opposite the dome; the double doors are decorated with a single sheet of paper marked 'HQ.' Up to the second floor they go, along a corridor, before the officer raps softly on another door. "Ernie, wake up. It's Paddy O'Brien. You have a visitor."

Standing on one side, Pat hears movement while the officer waits, grinning. After about thirty seconds the door appears to fling itself open. Captain O'Brien, his face expressionless, invites Pat to enter the semi-darkness first. In the gloom, a tall stick-thin figure in shirtsleeves sits on a chair, pulling on a riding boot. "Jesus, Paddy, what the hell is it now? I was up all night last night. I just put my head down." Pat notices the blanket strewn across a row of chairs.

He hears a cough behind him. "It's a messenger, Ernie, specifically for you."

"Christ. Draw the bloody curtains, will you, Paddy?" A few seconds later, Pat finds himself studied by bleary, red-rimmed eyes under a mess of tousled red hair. This must be the famous O'Malley, he thinks. The face is incredibly youthful for someone so important. He pulls out his letter and hands it over. "Who's this from?"

Pat shrugs at first, unsure of what to say. But as the eyes bore into him, he panics, afraid that the message might not be read; "O'Brien...Mr. O'Brien."

"Is this a joke? *That's* O'Brien, behind you."

"A different O'Brien, sir."

"Sweet Jesus, Paddy, have you got a damn brother?" Pat does not see the response; he watches O'Malley tear open the envelope and begin to read. After a while, O'Malley nods and glances up. "Actually, Paddy, you might say that we *all* have brothers out there. You can go, now. Not you, boy." Pat waits while he reads every page carefully. "There's no response, but please thank Mr O'Brien for his consideration. You're not a Dublin lad, are you?"

"I am not, sir. I'm a Cork man."

"Good. I assume you are a Republican?"

Pat's chest swells. "I am, sir."

The eyes glint and look away. "Well, it's a hard road." He looks up, and the tone of his voice softens; "But I should warn you, if you really want a Republic, you may have to fight for it, and soon." He sighs. "I'll show you out, now."

At the gate Pat takes off his coat, turns it inside out, and puts it over his arm. Crossing the bridge, the two men waiting there stare hard at him. When he looks back after a couple of hundred yards, they haven't moved; he sighs with relief. He walks slowly, thinking hard, and by the time he nears the school gates dusk has fallen. Almost home; then something alerts him, a light tapping rhythm. He realises with a jolt that this rhythm has been following him for some time. It's a woman, he sees, glancing back as he crosses the road, walking past the school gates. He's gone too far to detour into the slums now; he feels his heart juddering. Then he sees the cathedral spire.

Inside the great church figures are dotted randomly throughout, heads hidden, bowed in prayer as whispered pleas echo upwards. Pat knows the layout too well, so that he moves swiftly and silently to one side, hiding behind the first giant column of stone on the left. He hears the door swing open and shut; the tapping steps move forward and then stop. He waits a long while, preparing to sneak a glance, before he hears the steps moving carefully down the centre aisle. Pat moves backwards slowly, drops down, and then crawls on his hands and knees, keeping out of sight behind the rearmost wooden bench. Nearing the door, he peeks down the centre aisle. She's halfway down, scanning from one side to the other. He stands, lifts the heavy latch quietly and slips out, running on the grass next to the path into the gathering gloom. Where the second path leads off toward the school, he ducks along it for thirty yards, slips off the path and hides behind a thick bush, counting slowly. No one follows.

*   *   *

The boys cluster outside the café, chattering. The last exam has come and gone; Carr's father has promised to buy everyone cream teas, enticing them all with visions of hot scones, loaded with butter and jam, topped with thick yellow cream. Only Pat seems to notice the lorry filled with khaki uniforms, motoring past down the wide street. A minute later a motor-bike roars past in a hurry, leading two more lorries. Five minutes later, three more pass by in a leisurely fashion, accompanied by an armoured car.

Pat feels a tap on his shoulder; Carr whispers in his ear, "What do you make of that?"

"I think that would be the uniform of the Free State army. They're won't be British, for sure, and most of the Republican soldiers don't wear uniforms. It's probably just a show of force."

"Impressive. I suppose I could always join up, next year. That would prove I was Irish, wouldn't it?" Pat laughs and listens to his stomach rumble.

"There are better ways, but I suppose it would. Let's go in, anyway, now you're here."

Inside the cafe, the tables have been pushed together in preparation for the banquet and covered with cutlery, napkins, plates, glasses, large jugs of ginger beer and fruitcake. The boys jostle into position; the excited chatter begins again, talk of the summer to come for the day boys, perhaps a holiday or a visit to relatives in the country. For the boarders, the yearning to return home mingles with the sadness of farewells. Carr sits quietly, watching the others boys. Pat nudges his arm, "What will you do?"

A wry grin breaks across his face as he meets Pat's gaze. "I told you - join the new army, when I'm old enough." After a pause, he winks. "It would have to be over my father's dead body, I suspect. We're going to London next week until things are settled. I may even be sent to some college full of toffee-nosed English boys; I expect I'll hate it." At that moment, a loud cheer heralds the arrival of the scones and butter.

"Nonsense, you'll fit in perfectly."

Carr looks up to the heavens. "You've no idea, do you, Mahon?"

A second cheer greets the jam and cream, setting off a good-natured free-for-all. Pat works efficiently; soon two scones sit sliced on his plate while he spreads the butter, one eye on the progress of the jam dish. "About what?"

"About being piggy in the middle..."

Carr's voice fades away, as do all the voices; this void is filled by the sound echoing down the street, the distant rat-tat-tat of machine gun fire. For five seconds nobody moves; then Pat reaches for the jam and the spell is broken. His heart is juddering, but he spoons jam onto his plate while whispers of curiosity break out around him. He looks at Carr. Whatever was it Carr just said to him? It's vanished from his mind. "You were saying?"

Carr shakes his head, murmurs, "No matter," and points toward the window. Pat follows his eyes and watches a man in civilian clothes, rifle slung over his shoulder, stroll past the café. After a pause two more walk past, followed by a column of about twenty men. Something is going on, for sure; Pat shovels a scone into his mouth. "What do you reckon is going on, Fenian?"

Pat shrugs, chewing rapidly. The café bell tinkles, and a tall man with grey hair and two pistols stuck in a belt surveys the party. The café owner appears, patting his hair nervously. "Can I help you, sir?"

"You may. This building is hereby occupied by the fourth battalion, Dublin volunteers, Republican Army." He turns towards the boys. "Sorry, lads, you'll all have to be on your way now. It's not safe here. Just go home, the lot of you."

Carr watches Pat stuff his pockets with scones. The other boys stand up, whispering to each other. Carr dumps butter into a napkin and passes it to Pat. "Here, Mahon, you'll need that. Good luck, and wish me luck across the bloody water. Trust the IRA to ruin a farewell party, eh?" As the room empties, the two boys stare at each other for a long moment, before a messy and incomplete grasping of hands, slippery with butter and sticky with jam, causes them both to part with a memory of shared, silent hysterics.

By the time Pat reaches O'Brien's flat, the regular crash and explosion of artillery has begun to echo across the city. The front door stands half-open, so he calls out, "Hello?"

"Come in, and shut the door would you?" He follows the voice, and finds the teacher packing a small suitcase in his front room.

"What's going on?"

O'Brien looks up and barks an angry laugh. "Christ knows. Listen, I think that noise is the Free State army attacking the Four Courts. I only wish it were the British, and not the Staters. We..." He hesitates.

"We what?"

A grim smile; "If the British had attacked the Courts, we could have united the army. Now, we'll never heal the split."

"Who's we?"

O'Brien reddens slightly and looks away, "The Republican movement, of course."

He slumps onto the bed, rubs his hands through his hair and looks to the heavens. "It's now or never; this is the moment in history we've been waiting for. But we've all been paralysed by indecision; De Valera against the Treaty, Mick Collins with it because he signed it, thinking it was the best we'd get. The Dail couldn't decide between them, and now the army too has split down the middle."

"The man I lent me bike to... that was Mick Collins, wasn't it? I recognised his face in the newspapers after the Treaty was signed."

O'Brien nods and meets Pat's eye. "It was. I wondered if you would work that one out."

"Well, I'm not daft. A fella who knows Mick Collins, and sends messages to the Four Courts, and works at a school where half the boys' fathers work at the Castle. A useful place to hear gossip, I'd say."

O'Brien's face stays frozen at first; then his eyebrows lift, and a half smile begins to play upon his lips. "I'd say so."

"And when I gave Colonel O'Malley your letter, he made a crack about himself having lots of brothers out there. So maybe he was talking about the 'Brotherhood', maybe."

O'Brien smiles, watching Pat intently, "Ah well, I wouldn't know anything about that, Pat. I'm just a poor schoolteacher."

"Surely, I understand that. But like anyone else, sir, you can be guessing at what's going on, now can't you?"

O'Brien looks at the floor and chews his lip for a few moments; then looks up. "Well, I'm not normally a guessing man, Pat, but you've been a mighty help, so I will. But you must promise not to breathe a word of me or my guessing, even to your family." Pat nods. "Do you swear? On whatever is most precious to you?"

Pat nods, his face intent, "I swear, on... on the memory of my mother."

O'Brien nods. "All right; well, I'd be guessing that the brotherhood was also split and paralysed by indecision. That's been the nub of it, these last six months. In the past, there was always a clear direction. I would also guess that the army was always the key – and I mean our army, the Irish Republican Army. Whichever way the army would go, the country would follow in the end. The Staters think they can be as devious as the British, beat them at their own game; take an inch now and grab a mile later. The Republicans think they must win everything now, or not at all. Well, that was fine, when it was only politicians arguing. But now the army is split asunder and fighting itself because of that damned Treaty. Damn Mick Collins, for giving that order."

"You think he ordered the attack?"

"Who else? He should've waited, let the British do it. I'd guess that the message you took to O'Malley, maybe it was in the hope that O'Malley could persuade the IRA to attack the British garrison. That would have forced their hand. But the army too was probably paralysed by indecision; and now the idiots are fighting each other and we all have to take sides."

"So what now?"

"The army is still the key. The Staters may be strong here in Dublin, but the bulk of the army elsewhere are Republicans. It's now or never, and I'm going to join the rest. If they can be persuaded to move quickly, they can take Dublin in no time at all. I can't stay here, anyway. Mick Collins knows who I am and where my sympathies lie. Once they've dealt with the Four Courts, they'll come for the likes of me."

"What about me?"

"What do you mean?"

Pat glances at the gramophone, frowns, and puts on his most determined expression. "I mean I want to fight too."

"You're not old enough."

"It's only a year. And if you want to go to the country, come down to Cork with me. It's solid Republican, and my brother's one of *the boys* there. He can take you to his commander. Anyway, surely I can be a runner or something? You said it yourself, it's now or never, this is the moment in history the country's been waiting for. You said I've been a mighty help already. And I want to be part of this too." Pat expects his teacher to argue, to refuse him; he doesn't, he just looks away. Encouraged by his silence, Pat plays his final card. "In the end, you can't stop me, so we might as well leave together."

*   *   *

Five: 1922

Pat feels an overwhelming sense of confusion and puzzlement; he can't understand why he finds himself back at St Joseph's, the other children staring at him, making him feel that he has outgrown his body like some kind of awkward, lumbering giant. Waiting in the hallway with the others, a raw mix of hope and anticipation stirs his chest. It dawns upon him that they are preparing to sing for some special kind of concert, which will take place at the big house with the apple orchard. The location puzzles him; he runs upstairs and then down again, searching for Fons, anxious to ask him if someone is living there again; but Fons is nowhere to be seen. Has he run away again, unable to face his own part in this performance? Pat fervently hopes that he has merely gone on ahead, because now he remembers that Fons has all the music sheets for the performance. Christ in heaven... Pat realises that he has absolutely no idea what they are supposed to sing; he frowns, wondering what to do. Perhaps he should tell someone, maybe Sister Rose? No, he thinks, he can't risk Brother Daniel finding out; God alone knows what he might do to Fons. So; what should he do? He feels someone shaking his shoulder and turns, hoping it might be Fons, but it isn't. Some stranger is shaking him, somewhere else, wrenching his weary body back to reality...

He wakes, feeling a stab of pain in his back, an aching stiffness in his neck and arm, and a rough voice grating in his ear. "Wake up, boyo; this is the length of my road." He opens his eyes. An unshaven, lumpy face grins at him, displaying several blackened and rotten teeth.

He remembers the face, the delivery van. "Where are we?"

"It's Mallow, so it is. See – there's your post office, large as life." On his other side, he hears O'Brien yank the handle and push the van door, hinges squealing in protest as it opens. He watches O'Brien gingerly descend, yawn, and carefully stretch his limbs. Pat picks up his case, nods at the driver, and clambers down onto the cobbles, blinking in the watery evening sunlight.

"Jesus Christ. What a journey."

"That's the truth. So this is Mallow; where do we find your brother's friends?"

"Our farm's about seven miles east of here. We should maybe have a look in the pubs, see if there's any fella who can give us a lift home or get a message to my father. Then we can rest up at home while my brother gets a message to *the boys*." Pat notices his own voice, the tone sounding distinctly flat with a note of truculence. I must be really tired, he thinks; and hungry too, he remembers, feeling the emptiness within his gut.

O'Brien shakes his head, scratches it, and stares moodily at the ground. "You can do that if you wish. But what if your brother's not there?" He kicks a pebble away. "I'm damned if I'm going to waste another minute. I've got to find the area commander as soon as possible. God knows what's happening across the country, but here is where our support is strongest. On my life, the best chance for a Republic is for the southern army to move on Dublin now, without delay, before the Staters get themselves organised. Every day the army waits, the chances of victory slip away. That would be exactly why the Staters stopped the trains running, to give themselves more time."

"We still need to find my brother first."

"We do not, I'll bet my life on it. We just need to find someone who knows someone, in one of these pubs."

A couple of hours later, Pat jerks awake again, just in time to stop himself falling sideways. He feels a bony back shift against his own. Pupil and teacher sit back to back, using Pat's pigskin suitcase as a seat, by a deserted crossroads. Pat grunts in frustration; he feels an urge to tell O'Brien that no one here in County Cork knows him from Adam, and who is going to be bothered listening to a fussy little science teacher, anyway? He turns and pulls a face at him behind his back, then squints at his companion with one eye. "That fella in the pub was probably pulling your leg, anyway. I didn't like the look of him. It'll be dark soon - we should head back into Mallow."

"Maybe; we'll give it ten minutes more."

Pat nods, sits back, and sighs with relief. His thoughts drift while he listens to a cuckoo in the distance. He's about to ask if the ten minutes are up when he hears footsteps from one of the side roads. Two men emerge, one tall, carrying a rifle. O'Brien stands up, smiling, "At last..."

The rifle lifts, pointing at his chest. "Hands up; you too, boyo. Brendan, check them." The second, smaller man moves around behind them and inspects their pockets, removing O'Brien's revolver plus a small box of bullets.

"Looky here, Dinny. He brought me a pistol."

"Look, there's no need for this..." The short man steps forward and kicks O'Brien between his legs. Pat watches his body crumple, doubled up in agony; he feels suddenly wide awake. "We'll be the judge of that. You Tans are so fucking stupid. Same pattern every time, some local lad brings along a Jackeen officer. We've been expecting you, soon as the fighting started in Dublin. Still, you'll be giving us a bit of target practice. Now, start walking." He jerks his head to indicate the road they have just emerged from.

Pat looks down at his suitcase; "What about...?"

"Leave it." A wolfish grin crosses the tall man's face. "You won't be needing that, boyo, where you're going." Tramping in single file down the side road, Pat's shock turns to disbelief; he wonders if he's still dreaming. Of course he's not, he tells himself, feeling a growing sense of fear, and glances back at the rifle behind him. The sight of it prompts a sudden flashback; a rifle thrust out in front of him, the sensation of being held by the throat, voices shouting all around. He feels a long banished but familiar panic rising within him; he quickly shakes his head to rid himself of the memory, brushing his throat with his own hand as if to brush the phantom arm away. He glances back at O'Brien's face. To Pat's surprise, he seems quite calm; he even catches Pat's eye and gives a little shrug. He must think they can talk their way out of this. His apparent confidence helps Pat to calm down. After ten minutes, they turn down a track; after another ten minutes, a pathway through a wood leads into several meadows. Half an hour later, they stumble out of the deepening gloom into a deserted shell of a barn.

"Sit down there; in the middle, where we can see both of ye." The earthen floor feels damp and cold, but at least they can rest, back to back, while their captors produce an oil lamp and then light a fire in one corner. Brendan disappears for a while and then returns with a small bottle. He takes a swig and throws it to his companion. "Maybe we will just shoot them now and get it over with. What you think, Dinny?"

O'Brien clears his throat, about to speak. Pat elbows him hard in the ribs and speaks up himself. He senses that his local accent will be safer. "Listen, a chara, this is God's truth I'm telling you. My name is Pat Mahon and my brother Sean is one of your Mallow *boys*. Himself here sounds like a Jackeen, sure; but that's because he's a schoolteacher from Dublin. And I swear on my mother's grave he's a Republican. I brought him down here because he has important information for your commander." The short man looks at his revolver and walks over to Pat, places the gun against his forehead and very slowly pulls the trigger. The barrel revolves and suddenly Pat feels, rather than hears, a shuddering impact as the hammer clicks. His mind and body have completely frozen; it takes him several long moments to realise that the gun did not fire.

"Shut it, boyo. Next time, I'll put a bullet in the chamber." Pat feels an irresistible urge to pee, images suddenly crowding into his head, transporting him back to the bridge in Fermoy; he feels the arm choking his throat again and hears the voices shouting, sees the pistol waving, and then steadying... he wants to cry, feels a spurt of warmth trickling down his leg. He sobs.

Suddenly, the taller man looms above him. "Leave the boy alone, Brendan; we don't know for certain they're spies just yet. He might really be Sean's brother. You OK, lad?"

Pat nods, and whispers, "I need a piss. Please."

Two hours later, he needs another. The fire's dying down now; Brendan's bottle is empty and he's clearly bored. He sits, spinning the revolver chamber, watching them and waiting. Pat can see that Dinny has nodded off; he hopes Brendan hasn't noticed. But Brendan catches his eye meaningfully, mimes sleep, and starts to feed bullets into the chambers. Pat feels O'Brien's body tensing up behind him. He's kept his mouth shut recently, and Pat silently prays for him to keep it that way. Should he try and call out, to wake Dinny? He can't decide. He feels paralysed by fear. Brendan slowly stands up, stretches quietly, and clips the drum back into the revolver. He starts to move towards them. Behind him, Pat can feel O'Brien's body, trembling along with his own. He looks up to see Brendan's face, hard and cruel, staring down at him as he plays with the revolver.

Pat begins to sing, softly at first, then slowly raising the volume until, by the end of the song, the full power of his voice resounds into the night;

"Oh, list to the strains of a poor Irish harper
And scorn not the strings from his old withered hand
But remember these fingers could once move more sharper
To raise up the memory of his dear native land...

At wake or at fair I would twirl my shillelagh
And trip through the jigs with my brogues bound with straw
And all the pretty maidens from the village and the valley
Loved the bold Phelim Brady, the bard of Armagh...

And when sergeant Death in his cold arms shall embrace me
Oh lull me to sleep with sweet Erin Go Bragh
By the side of my Kathleen, my young wife, then place me
And forget Phelim Brady, the bard of Armagh."

Brendan lowers the gun and taps his leg with it, "Well, I'll be the Holy Mother's uncle, Dinny; did you ever hear singing like that?"

Pat sees that Dinny is now awake, alert, watching Brendan carefully. "Never, but once at the big fair in Cork. Mind you, Sean Mahon was after telling me once, it comes to mind now, his brother Patrick is a singer."

"Did he now? Well, maybe we won't shoot them yet; not the singer, anyway." He looks down at Pat, walks over to the fire, and adds some sticks. "Sing us *the garden where the praties grow,* then."

When Pat begins to sing again, Brendan joins in with such a hoarse and tuneless voice that Pat falters for a second. He feels a sort of numb horror, and has to stifle a terrible urge to laugh before he manages to carry on with the song. Dinny watches; he looks up to the sky, but says nothing. At the end of the song, silence descends for a long minute. Pat stays quiet; Brendan has enjoyed the song, and Pat does not wish to break his mood. From out of the darkness, a third voice rings out, "*Pray let me tell my story, O...*" a burly, squat figure, rifle slung over his back, and a grizzled face covered by grey stubble, appears in the open doorway. His voice is surprisingly deep and true; even Brendan laughs, nodding at the newcomer.

"Can we shoot them yet, Mickey?"

"We cannot, the Captain wants them at headquarters."

Brendan's face falls into a scowl, "Ah, Jesus wept. Can't we just say they tried to run?"

Pat watches the other man consider this carefully; feeling his urge to pee becoming irresistible, he gives in to it. "I suppose that will be what happened last time, is it?" The newcomer gives Brendan a long stare, shakes his head, and glances at Dinny - who shrugs and looks away. "The Captain will skin us alive, Brendan. We need to know exactly what they know, so that *we* can be staying one step ahead of *them*. *That's* the only reason we've beaten the Tans, so far. Same applies to these Staters." He emphasises the last word, and spits onto O'Brien's feet. Pat nudges him with his elbow, and feels a response; they both keep their mouths shut.

Stumbling through the darkness for another hour, Pat feels increasingly unreal, that he has stepped into a waking nightmare. He feels so dead on his feet that he constantly stumbles and falters, jerking awake repeatedly whenever he almost falls. Every so often, the column stops dead, so that Pat stumbles into O'Brien. The first time this happens, Pat curses, but O'Brien shushes him and whispers, "Stay quiet. Don't react." He shivers, wondering if Brendan really is that crazy. Is he still trying to engineer an excuse to shoot them?

Eventually a small farmhouse looms up before them; waiting outside, his urge to pee returns. Before he can utilise the darkness, the door opens and a gun barrel prods his back. Inside, an oil lamp hangs from a beam above a grey haired man clad in a leather jacket. He glances up to inspect them, stony faced, from behind a small desk. They stand, waiting. "Tell me exactly who you are and why you're here. And no bullshit or it may be the last story you ever tell." O'Brien speaks first, then Pat. The Captain questions both of them with growing interest for half an hour. At the end, appearing more relaxed, he tips his chair back and tells them, "Well, if you are not who you say you are, you are certainly well-informed. How on earth did you get yourselves down here?"

"It was pretty chaotic; it took us over five days. The Staters have stopped the trains. We caught local buses where we could, and begged lifts with farmers or delivery vans. Getting out of Dublin was the worst part. We had to turn back twice and then walk cross country to avoid the checkpoints."

"Did you see any fighting on the way?"

"No. We saw a few convoys of Stater troops around Carlow, and further south we passed small groups of Republicans, but there didn't seem to be a pattern to any of the movements. It looked like chaos." Pat sees the Captain give a wry smile, shake his head, and chuckle to himself. O'Brien clears his throat and then continues, "If you want my opinion, Captain, the army needs to move fast. The Staters are weak now - if the Southern Army command moved its troops up together and took Dublin, it would be all over. But the longer we leave it, the stronger they'll become."

The Captain stares back at him, pushes his cap up, and scratches his forehead. Pat hears a clock ticking somewhere in another room. "You may well be right about that, too, Mr O'Brien. The trouble is, you see, there's no proper command structure yet. We all knew what the old one was, when we were united, but who's in charge now? We're still after finding out just who's on our side, you see. And even then, you see, that's a different kind of war you're talking about. We wouldn't know how to fight an open war, even if we had the weapons. That worries me, for sure." O'Brien blinks; Pat watches him silently mumble a curse. His eyes stare down at the floor, the body slowly slumping downward, as if deflating, while he finally allows himself to feel fatigue. "You should be glad we're not rushing into anything, Mr O'Brien, right now. If we had of been in a hurry, we might've had to shoot you. And we still might, if the boy's not who he says he is." He pauses; when they don't react, he nods at Mickey, behind them. "Take them up now."

Led upstairs at gunpoint and pushed into a small, empty room, Pat puts his own back to the wall and slides to the floor in silence as the door is locked and darkness engulfs them. He hears O'Brien do the same and listens to their breathing slowly steadying. Neither says a word. Mickey returns briefly, throwing a blanket to each of them. "The Captain has sent for your brother. You'd better hope he comes." The door shuts again, leaving them fumbling to share the narrow space in the darkness. They both lie down on the floor, too tired to speak. Pat remembers the wetness in his trousers and feels a rush of shame. He hears O'Brien begin to snore, so he staggers to his feet again and strips the trousers off. He attempts to squeeze out what moisture he can and dries himself with the blanket. He shivers. This is stupid, he thinks, who cares about a bit of piss. He dresses again, wraps himself in the blanket, and lies down. The blanket smells strongly of horse; by the morning, he hopes, no one will notice the other smell. He surrenders to sleep.

*   *   *

He becomes aware of the light growing; he tries to ignore it, drifting along somewhere between sleep and the cold hard floor upon which he squirms, trying to find a position in which his bones do not ache. He jerks awake when someone hammers upon the door; a key turns and the door pushes open against his legs. As he rubs the sleep from his eyes his brother's voice sings out, "Well, well, little brother, what is yourself doing here?"

Pat sits up, blinking, blinded by a shaft of light. "Sean, thank the Lord. Tell these culchies who I am or the idiots will be murdering us." He feels an elbow in the ribs, from O'Brien.

Looking up, he sees the Captain standing beside Sean, his face expressionless. "Ah well, that will not be necessary now, in your case. Maybe, I'm hoping, we won't ever have to do it again. But if it does come to another fight, it might happen to those who pretend to be something else than they are. Any road, you should go back to your family. Take a few days rest and think about it. Then, if you want to come back and join us, you can. Mister O'Brien, I think we should try to get you up to Tipperary to see General Lynch. I'll see if I can organise a car for you." He turns and leaves.

Pat dresses quickly, self-conscious, wondering if Sean can see or smell the damp on his trousers, also hoping that his teacher will not be too ashamed of him. As he leaves, O'Brien reaches out to grasp his arm, "Wait. Thank you for that singing, Pat. That was very clever thinking. And I'm sorry for involving you in this..."

"Don't be." Pat hears anger in his own response; the last thing he wants is sympathy. "I'm part of it and proud to be."

O'Brien meets his eye, colours a little, and nods, "Surely. In that case, Pat, take care - but when this is all over please go back and finish your schooling. You have it in you to be an engineer. This country will need some rebuilding." Pat's surprise takes away his power of speech, though he feels a flush of pleasure and pumps O'Brien's hand.

Sean has brought the pony and trap; on their way home, they retrieve Pat's suitcase. Someone has opened it and stolen all the socks and underwear. Sean grins ruefully, and comments, "Probably Brendan. He's a light-fingered magpie, that one." He rubs his chin and glances across at Pat. "What are ye thinking to do, anyhow? The Captain said something about yourself wanting to join the fight against the Staters."

"That I do." Sean frowns and looks at the floor. "What's up? Don't ye want me to join ye?"

Sean shrugs; his brow furrows. "Well, the first thing is, Pat, ye won't be joining *me*..." He looks up and holds Pat's gaze. "I'll fight the Tans again if we need to, but I'm not taking up arms against fellow Irishmen. There's a few of us feel that way. Ye should think hard about that." Pat swallows, the lump in his throat bobbing up and down. "And then there's Da. I know he can't stop ye, but Da won't like it, will he? Himself and Ernie have all their hopes pinned on yourself finishing your education. Ye must know how hard they've worked, to send ye to that school. It'll break Da's heart if ye waste all that, it surely will...so just ye be thinking hard, before ye make up your mind."

Pat hears the tone of disapproval loud and clear; he lapses into a silence, behind which arguments rage like a maniacal opera within his aching head. Eventually, he reaches over and pats Sean's arm. "Thanks for the warning, Sean. I can see where ye stand, and that's fine by me. I'm not sure if I can do the same. But if I do fight I'll go back to school later, like Mr O'Brien says."

Sean nods thoughtfully, but his brow furrows again. "That may be your intention, Pat, God love you, but fighting can change a man, in more ways than one. And how long will this last? Look, forget all about it for a few days and then decide."

Pat feels a sliver of doubt amidst overwhelming disappointment. He'd been so sure that Sean of all people would understand. And how would waiting help? Then, he thinks, maybe it is better to leave this topic alone for now; so he nods his agreement.

As the pony and trap rattles into the farmyard, Ernie and his father emerge from the barn. "God love you, here he is..."

"Look, Ernie, he's taller than you already..." The two men slap him on the back and shoulder; Pat can see curiosity in their faces. He pumps their hands, waiting for the inevitable questions, wondering how to explain what has happened, and how much to tell them.

His father asks, "So how was the journey? And what did *the boys* want with you?"

While he considers his reply, Sean speaks for him. "It was all a bit of a misunderstanding, Da. Pat had come down with a Dublin man, one of his teachers, and *the boys* didn't like the look of him. They're a bit suspicious of any stranger right now, so they are. They wanted me to vouch for Pat, so he could vouch for the teacher."

"That's a fine thing, Sean, when a stranger can't show his face in Mallow."

"There's been fighting in Dublin, Da."

"God help us, is it the Tans again?"

"It is not, Da. I wish it were. It is what I feared, Collins and the Free State against those of *the boys* who will not abide with the treaty."

"Well in that case, Pat came home from Dublin just in time, Sean, didn't he?"

Sean laughs and catches Pat's eye. "I reckon he did, Da."

"And what happened to your friend, Pat?"

"He's fine, Da. He had to go on to Tipperary. Maybe he'll come and visit another time."

"Well, he'll be very welcome here."

The next morning Pat dresses in his Sunday best for mass. His father and brothers wait by the pony and trap; Ernie and his father take their usual places on the front seat while Sean climbs into the back. Pat moves to sit between them, but finds the gap that he used to occupy has somehow disappeared. "Jesus, you two have been growing sideways while I grew taller."

His father glances at him a little sharply, but Ernie chuckles. "I've been learning myself how to cook, Patrick; didn't you notice the fresh bread this morning?"

"That was you, Ernie?"

"None other, so I've earned this big seat; ye can get yourself in the back with Sean, boyo."

In church, Pat finds himself dozing off at odd moments, giving in to the remnants of his fatigue. When it comes to the sermon Pat hopes to doze a little more. He switches off his mind, and settles back in his seat; but after the first five minutes, he suddenly finds himself listening, almost against his will...

"...these are the great sins of modern times; this fighting of wars, the murder of our fellow men. We have all seen the horror of the European war, the tragic loss of hundreds of thousands of decent men on both sides. That was a sin visited on us not by the common soldiers, but by the Kaiser's government. The lifeblood of decent Irishmen lies in Flanders and beyond; God knows little good has come of that. We've also seen Irishmen fighting injustice and oppression here in our own land, and that was a terrible fight against the villainy of the cruel and murderous Tans. Those men who fought honestly and clean will be excused by God. Those who resorted to cold-blooded murder will have to answer to God for their sin. And now; those of you who will have the newspapers, you'll know that the fighting has started again. But let's be clear what kind of fighting this is. These fighters are arrogant men who do not accept the will of the people; your will, since you, the people, voted for peace. These men who are fighting, they drape themselves in the flag of Ireland, but they are fighting the elected government of Ireland. They are hypocrites; they want to destroy the new Irish government and the new peace with the British Crown, so that they can continue to rob banks and take whatever they need. They're no better than thieves who want the country to bend to their will. They're led by those who organised the murder gangs, not by those who fought cleanly..."

At this last insult, Pat jerks upright and is about to stand up and leave when Sean grasps his arm firmly and whispers in his ear, "Don't be a fool; if you show yourself here you're telling every Free State supporter in the area who you are." That, at least, is good advice; he nods at Sean and stays in his seat.

"...The hand of God will be against those who are fighting on for fighting's sake. You, the people, should have nothing to do with them; you should not offer food, shelter, or aid. This is not a struggle against a foreign oppressor but a rebellion against our own government by outlaws and criminals who want power for themselves..."

Pat grits his teeth, internally raging for the rest of the sermon. After hearing it he will not sing another word. Yet outside, afterwards, the congregation greet each other as if nothing has happened. How could they listen to that and act as if nothing has been said?

Only after they return home does his father speak; "Seemed a bit tough on *the boys* today".

Sean nods, glancing at Ernie, "He was, so he was."

Ernie nods, "A bit harsh."

Pat explodes, "A bit harsh? How could we all listen to that nonsense? It's bad enough that the British fill the newspapers with that sort of rubbish, but when our own church sells out and takes their side...all we Republicans want is what the army fought for in the first place. And if that makes me an outlaw and a rebel, so be it."

Ernie holds up his hand, "Wait just a minute, Pat, calm down, will you?"

"I will not calm down, not for anyone. Ye all want me to sell out too, and I'm not going to. If we don't fight for a Republic now, there'll never be one, don't ye see?"

He feels Sean grasp his arm, squeezing hard, "Will ye listen to me for a second, Pat? I don't give two monkeys about Father O'Donnell and his like. They were slow enough to get behind *the boys* in the first place during the Tan war. It was only when they began to lose the donations to their bloody plate that they stopped telling us the Tans were the law. But I'll say one thing more - the only reason *the boys* beat the Tans was that all the people were with them. This time, if *the boys* fight the Staters, a good half of the people won't be behind them. Some will be for them, like you, some against, like the Staters and all their kin, and some will be neutral like myself; and many more will be just plain sick of the fighting, like all those whose houses have been burned already. So *the boys* can't ever win, even if they are right. Think on that, before you volunteer."

Pat hears a door shut, turns, and realises his father has just left the room. He looks from the face of one brother to the other, while he swears to himself under his breath. He has a horrible feeling Sean is right, though he knows that won't make any difference to his decision. He's given his word already.

* * *

Pat shifts uncomfortably upon his thin horsehair mattress, unable to sleep. Men sigh and snore in the room around him, a curious rhythmic chorus for his restless thoughts. Half of him still wonders what on earth he is doing here, while the other half compels him to believe that he must do this to become a man; to do his duty and help make his country one united Republic. He sighs and pictures himself singing patriotic songs to a sleeping army. At last, he drifts off into a shallow doze. Suddenly, an arm shakes him roughly awake; the sound of a bell clangs outside while men shout and curse in the dark around him, "Get up, lads, it's the alarm..."

"Jesus, it must be a raid..." He stumbles to his feet, but immediately steps on another man's foot. He hears a loud curse before his shoulder thumps into something solid, bumping him backwards. He hears another curse, and the clatter of something falling over. He reaches for his trousers, only to find that some other person has already got hold of them; for a few seconds, they both tug furiously for possession. Pat loses. He shouts into the dark, "Those are my trousers." He waits, realising the man in possession is trying to put them on; after another curse his trousers are flung back to him by unseen hands. He gets one leg into them before another body barges into him, knocking him back down onto his mattress.

A door opens nearby; someone outside in the distance shouts, "Cavalry", followed by the crack of a pistol shot.

Another voice nearby cries, "Feck it, where's the bloody candles?" Pat pulls on his trousers and buttons them up, then stands up and feels around for his woollen sweater. It's gone. Finally, someone appears with a lit candle.

"Outside, now, and bring your weapons." Someone has left a rifle against a wall, so Pat picks it up and follows the voice outside into the farmyard, feeling his way along the wall to a thorny hedge that borders the field to the south. His eyes are just beginning to adjust when the moon abruptly vanishes behind a thick cloud. The sound of drumming horse hooves seems to be amplified all around them. Someone whispers, "Is that the Stater cavalry?"

"How the feck should I know..."

They cower by the hedge in silence until they hear someone

whistling. "What's that?"

"That's Brendan, I reckon. He's a way with horses."

The whistle repeats several times; they hear a gruff voice, murmuring endearments repeatedly. After a minute of this, the pitch of the voice raises, as if surprised. After another twenty seconds of silence they hear a man laughing. When the laughing stops, Brendan's voice calls out, "It's alright, Captain. It's the full gang of racehorses from Wilson's farm; some eejit must have left the gate open and so they took their exercise in this fairy moonlight. The horses will be after coming down by the stream and then brought on to your land by the smell of hay in your meadow, I'll bet. Whose is the sentry business tonight, anyways?"

"It's Keane." A chorus of curses greets the sentry's name.

"From now on, lads, I reckon himself will be known as 'Cavalry Keane'".

*   *   *

Six weeks later, Pat resists the urge to call the nickname out loud as his eyes light upon the owner's back. He brings up the rear of a dozen Mallow *boys*; somehow he's still clinging on to his rifle after the night of the horses. Ask no questions, he thinks; tell no lies.

"Dinny, where are we going?"

The man ahead of him considers this for a full minute before making his reply. "That would be a mystery to me too, Pat. But it will be something out of the usual, because a motorcar brought a message to the Captain from the Brigade commander this morning. I reckon we're meeting up with the other groups, so we are, or why would we be tramping through the countryside for three hours? Maybe we're going to move up on Cork tonight."

"If that's the case, Dinny, we're headed the wrong way."

"Ah well, maybe we're taking a little diversion first to join the others."

Pat grunts and shakes his head in despair. "While we wander round in circles in the countryside, the Staters are whittling away at the south, getting control of the towns."

Dinny turns his head to stare back at him for a second, as if surprised by Pat's tone of voice, and walks on. Pat follows, waiting for his reply. "We can't risk a daylight battle for the city. Didn't you know the Staters contrived to sneak a ship down to Queenstown harbour?"

"Did they now? So what?"

Dinny laughs, "So what? So what? I'll tell you so what, boyo. The ship was filled with infantry, armoured cars and artillery. That is exactly why the city of Cork is in Stater hands and why we can't fight them in an open battle by day. Ye wouldn't find that rifle much use against artillery shells, now would ye?"

Pat's mouth falls open. So that's why the Republicans seem so powerless. He chews his lower lip, thinking that the war is panning out exactly as O'Brien feared. Paralysed by caution, our commanders are slipping back into the familiar pattern of guerrilla fighting, using the countryside as a base. But this time, he thinks, half the people are against us, so we spend most of the time moving our hideouts, splitting into smaller and smaller groups. Pat curses to himself. Maybe Sean's going to be proved right, but I'm not giving up just yet. So I'll tramp on and on across this bloody heath with the others, he tells himself.

As the summer evening approaches, the silence is suddenly broken by the crackle of rifle fire, followed by bursts of machine gun fire, coming from the other side of a narrow, elevated ridge that runs parallel to their path. Two thirds of the men run back towards a gap in the ridge, where a farm track meanders its way up and over and down the other side. Pat and the rest head straight up the slope, aiming for the nearest point of the crest, eager to see what is happening on the other side. Reaching the highest point, Pat flings himself down. Half way down the slope below him, he sees a lane bordered by wispy hedges. Down in the valley, a road runs parallel with the lane and enters a small, scattered village. He sees men running along the lane, stopping occasionally to fire at vehicles down on the road; including an armoured car. A classic ambush, he thinks; and we have the higher ground. He stands up, pulls the rifle off his back, and starts to run down the slope towards the lane. He gets about halfway there before the machine gun on the car starts firing. Fear suddenly grips him, so that he flings himself to the ground. As he lies there he realises he probably isn't the target, but he feels horribly exposed on this hill; his stomach begins to tighten and revolve. The machine gun stops; someone yells that it's jammed. Men down in the lane begin moving again. He tries to stand up again, wondering what to do, but his limbs will only let him crouch. He wants to run, but his legs are frozen. Far down below on the road, a man stands up and puts a rifle to his shoulder. Christ, Pat thinks, he's aiming at me. He's sure of it. He wants to move, but nothing works. A rifle cracks, and the man falls. Shit, he thinks, that could have been me. A strong hand grabs his shoulder, pulls him up and propels him forward, his limbs responding at last.

"Get yourself some cover, boyo." It's Brendan; for once, he's glad to see him. "Follow me." His body is relieved of responsibility, happy to be told what to do, as he follows Brendan down. From the lane, they peer through a hedge down at the road below, fire two or three poorly aimed shots into the distance towards the armoured car and then, it's suddenly over - the order to retreat is passed along. They sprint back along the lane to where it splits and follow the fork away, back over the rise, and head for home.

It's not until two days later that they realise what they have done that day. "Collins; by Christ... take a look here, in this newspaper. Someone shot Michael Collins in that poxy village."

"Ah, fuck a Tan's daughter. Not Collins. I know he signed the fucking treaty, but..."

"Well, that won't have been one of our *boys*; we never got near enough to shoot anybody. The only thing we could of hit was bloody rabbits; must've been one of the Bandon *boys*."

After a long silence, he hears Brendan's voice. "Maybe that was Collins, the one that damn near shot yourself, do ye think, Pat?" The burst of laughter makes Pat cringe. "Ye was a bloody good decoy on that hill, for sure, boyo." He'd been hoping that no one else had noticed those events; a hot flush of shame rushes into his face. He finds himself thinking, fervently, I hope that isn't how it happened; I don't want to be part of history, in that way. The idea shocks him, and something about it alarms him.

After a long silence, Dinny puts it into words. "Christ, lads, don't you see? There will surely be hell to pay, now. There'll be no quarter at all. Whatever you do, don't anyone ever be boasting that we were there, that day."

*　　*　　*

Fons strides across the farmyard to unlatch the gate that leads into the lane, heaves it upward and drags it across, taking care not to strain the tired hinges. A sharp-faced collie watches him eagerly, waiting outside the cowhouse; inside, the animals begin to voice their anticipation. The dog, too, yelps at him to hurry. He grunts and pauses, wrapping the ends of his trousers inside his socks to stop the bitter December wind chilling his calves. "Just ye wait a minute, Boxer..."

Positioning himself to one side of the half-door, he yanks the metal bolt free and quickly steps back. The cows burst through, the leaders trotting eagerly toward the lane. After pushing the door shut again, he jogs after them. Ahead of him, Boxer yelps encouragement, though the cows do not seem to need any. By the time he reaches the gate into the field, two of the younger animals have already forced their way through a gap in the hedge while the rest crowd at the gate, lowing impatiently. He fumbles with the rope fastening the gate, his fingers numb; a low growl makes him turn. A tall figure wrapped in a greatcoat and balaclava ambles towards him down the lane, the face erupting into a grin. The voice too seems familiar, confident, "Hello there, Farmer Gilligan..."

"Pat?" At a loss for words, Fons feels his face redden with pleasure and embarrassment. "Ah, sure, this is one of me jobs..."

"And well ye look the part, Fons Gilligan. Go on then, finish with the herd."

Fons nods and lifts the gate, rapidly walking it open, grinning from ear to ear with pride while the cows push their way past him, and then walks it back shut. Boxer looks from one to the other, studying their faces, and yelps. He wags his tail, hesitantly. Fons catches Pat's eye, nodding at the dog, "Yourself is a rare beast. That one doesn't often take to new people; his name's Boxer."

Pat shrugs, "Well, I'm glad he sees me as an exception. Better a lick than a bite."

Fons rubs his hands together, "Well, will we go up to the house?"

"Why not?" Pat scratches his head. "Maybe later, we can go over to your Ma's cottage?"

"Surely." Fons feels his curiosity waken while they stroll side by side. "What brings ye to this neck of the woods, anyway? Have ye finished with that fancy school yet?"

"For the moment; let's just say I came back home for a while. I'll tell you the tale later. What about yourself? Have ye taken any more schooling?"

"Oh, ye know fine well the schooling never suited me; I spent more time dodging the Christian brothers than listening to them. They gave up on me in the end, but Mary's taught me to read. I like to be reading the newspapers, and Mary says I've a talent for numbers."

"And how is the lovely Mary?"

"Go on. She's like a sister and a Ma to me."

Pat chuckles and whispers, "I know that, Fons. I wasn't thinking about *ye* and her."

The two stride on while Fons considers this idea carefully. When they turn into the yard, Fons reaches across and taps his friend's arm. "Be nice to her, Pat. She liked your singing last time. She's already a bit sweet on ye."

"Is she indeed?" Pat's tone of voice seems a mite too cheery for Fons' liking. Ah well, he thinks, I've said my piece.

As they open the door, Mrs Conlon's greeting seems to hint in the same direction. "Good Lord; Mary, come and see who it is. It's the singer, so it is..."

Hearing this enthusiasm, Fons feels a small flush of envy. Pat turns and winks at him; he shakes his head and pulls a face in response, then privately sends a wry look to the heavens. He's always accepted that Pat is the elder, the one more skilled with words and song. So, deferring to Pat has always seemed the natural way of things, the price he pays for the friendship of an older boy. His own natural shyness also makes Fons a good listener, a keen observer; a role he adopts during the reintroductions and chatter that accompanies their tea and biscuits. Fons feels every inch the farm boy as he listens to Pat's descriptions of Dublin. Pat seems to have an instinct for what the women like to hear; the Grafton street shops with their silks and fancy cakes, the cathedral, the grand houses and gardens... he also adopts an easy manner as he tells of these sights, with himself in the position of a naïve outsider; as if in their shoes.

After a while, they extricate themselves with a promise to return (and another from Pat to sing, later). As they walk over to the empty cottage, Pat begins to quiz him about the farm, the routine, and the neighbours. Fons finds himself wondering if Pat is now planning to come courting. He's not sure how he feels about that, but he goes along with the conversation, anyway.

"So, not many people come past here, then?"

"They don't but rarely - we're between the villages here. I hid in my Ma's cottage when I first came here. I ran away from St Joseph's."

"Did you now? What about your Ma? Does she visit?"

Fons looks down and shuffles his feet. "She's visited a couple of times. She sends money to Da Conlon every month. She might come back home in a while, but there's no work here now." He looks up and watches Pat nod to himself, thoughtfully.

"And what do the Conlon's think about the troubles? Which side are they on?"

"Oh, we're all thinking it's a terrible mess, and best stayed out of. There's little gained by fighting our own, either way. That's what most of the farmers think, round here."

Pat nods again, apparently studying the cottage. "I'm needing a place to stay, Fons. I'm with the Mallow *boys*, so I am. The Stater troops are after raiding our headquarters again. We moved to a dug out, but they have the local knowledge too and they'll soon find us again, so we've split up. They know who some of us are, and they watch the homes and likely hideouts. The devil take them, the Staters... did ye know, they're threatening to shoot anyone harbouring us, or holding weapons?" Fons frowns, shaking his head in disbelief; he recalls, Pat's brother was also one of *the boys*. He's also about to comment that the threats don't seem right, when Pat adds, "So, I can't stay with me family. This place would be grand, though, with it being empty. They couldn't blame anyone if I was staying here. I'll be telling them nobody knew, not even yourself, if they catch me. Don't tell the Conlons that I'm with *the boys*, it's safer for them that way. I might be here a night or two, but they can think I'm just come for the day."

Fons realises that the purpose of Pat's questioning had nothing to do with Mary; he feels a small flush of relief. He bites his lip while he considers and then nods his agreement; he can't refuse his friend. "Sure, you're welcome." The truth is, Fons realises, he feels envious that Pat is old enough to be part of it all, whichever side he's on. Fons has a hankering to be a soldier himself; though he is mighty surprised that Pat has become one, after the business on the bridge. Then again, it's no surprise which side Pat has chosen, after what happened to him. "Ye got a lot of boldness, I'll say that. As for the cottage, the roof leaks a bit, but we patched most of it up. Better not burn a fire in daylight, but ye can at night, the chimney's sound." He looks at Pat sideways, and whistles. "Christ, I'd never thought of *ye* joining *the boys*. What in God's name made ye do that?"

Pat shrugs, "Oh, it seemed a good idea at the time. Me brother fought the Tans, these last few years. I just wanted to be a good Republican too. But the daft thing is, Fons, he's neutral now. He thinks the fighting won't last much longer. I'm starting to think he's right. When I'm sure there's no more chance of winning, I'll go back to school. Me Da's wrote and told them I've got myself a broken leg, for now."

Fons nods and feels some relief that Pat isn't a die-hard, for even he knows that *the boys* are losing this war. He watches Pat stride over to an overgrown patch of nettles in the corner and reach carefully down into the dying leaves, emerging with a battered suitcase and a long object carefully wrapped in an oilskin. "Well, Fons, how do we get into this place?"

Fons stares at the oilskin. "Is that your rifle? Will ye show it to me?"

*   *   *

The footsteps approach eagerly; in Pat's mind, they run like notes up and down a scale of desire as they circle the cottage and then pause, before her voice sings out in a half-whisper, half-chime, "Patrick; Patrick, it's me, Mary..."

He opens the door, throws her his best smile, and grasps her waist as she moves past him. She counters with her elbow, nudging his arm to make him shut the door, before brushing his lips with her own, teasing him. "Let me put this down first; I brought you some food." He releases her waist, but grasps the thick hem of her skirt and lets her pull him across the room, now teasing her. She places her burden on the table and swings back to him.

"You're impossible. Wait a minute now, we have to talk."

"Talk away." He pulls her towards him, and joins his hands behind her back.

She places her hands on his shoulders and looks up, studying his eyes. "My mother knows something's going on, I'm sure of it. They'll find out soon enough. And what are you going to do then? Have you made your mind up yet?"

"Oh, Mary, you temptress..."

She giggles, then frowns; "What do you mean, Pat Mahon?"

He shakes his head, pulls a wry face. "I mean you're tempting me to give up the cause and abandon the Republic, all for a sweet girl who smells like honey..."

She slaps his shoulder, "That's not what I meant, and you know it."

He sighs, feigning a look of devastation. "The trouble is, there's some truth in my joking. I should've made contact with the others yesterday." He stares down at the floor, listening to the whole tone and timbre of his own voice changing. "The simple truth is, Mary, I'm a terrible lousy soldier and I think this war is damn near lost. You're my first girl, and you're lovely. I'm thinking of giving it up. But that's where it gets complicated; that will also mean going back to school in Dublin and leaving you here."

"I never know when you're serious, or not."

Their eyes meet; "Never more serious."

"In that case, you should go back tomorrow. I'd rather have you safe, and then when you come back later, we can be properly together."

He rubs her back, gently. "Another week."

"No, you fool, that's too long. Go back to your home and your school now. Well, not right now; tomorrow."

Now? Pat wants to stay here forever, as long as no one bothers him here. He also has a hope that what Mary also means is, *I can't resist you that long*. That is what makes him want to stay longer. If it were not for Mary, he suspects, he would already have given up the fight.

"A few more days; every day with you is worth a lifetime."

Pat watches a tear forming on her cheek, and reaches out for her, to kiss it away. They hold each other for a long time in silence, before they lie down together. They do not have the nerve to undress, but she allows him to loosen her clothes, to allow his hands some access. He knows that she likes to be stroked, especially down her back, which is all she will normally allow. Pat kisses her lips and face as his hands gradually extend their movements, for the first time meeting no resistance or attempts to delay him. He fondles her breasts, outside and then inside her clothes, reaching a little further each time, cautiously listening to her breathing as it increases in depth and speed. It feels to him as if he is playing a tune upon her body, andante - instinctively, he guesses that patience is the key. He listens to the rhythm of her sighs and uses it to guide his own movements, slowly drawing a melody out of her, a slow aria, using gentle circles of touch upon her body. He can feel his own desire and curiosity rising as he slowly shifts his caresses below her breasts, gradually reaching her stomach and below, stroking her soft skin gently, carefully. At first, much to his surprise, he meets no resistance. All the while, her breathing and sighs continue to rise gently and rhythmically around him. But at some moment when his fingertips cross a boundary, she takes one enormous sigh and pulls his hand away.

He stops and lies still, conscious of the invasive position of his hand, still inside her clothes, embarrassed now by the awkward proximity of their bodies. He feels intrigued by the smell of her body, elated by the strength of her reaction, but unsure whether he has upset or displeased her. Self-conscious again, he notices his own desire.

Just as he wonders whether she can feel it too, and what she must be thinking about his hardness and size, she reaches down and touches the outside of his trousers, exploring the shape of his masculinity. After a moment of shock, he realises that she too is curious, and hears her giggle. He feels torn between his mounting desire, his lust to enter her *properly*, and his concern for her. He has to ask; he whispers in her ear, "Mary... come on... can't we do it properly now?"

She pushes him away, looks him in the eye, and shakes her head. "Not yet. This will be sin enough for us, now..." He feels a stab of resentment, frustration, but as if in compensation she cuddles back in, kissing his neck and shoulder. After her previous passivity, her actions excite him wildly, his own melody rushing ahead far too fast, far too allegro, it seems to him later. His body responds instinctively and he starts to push himself hard against her, the sensation of her wet mouth on his neck sending acute spasms of pleasure through his body. He strokes her back with one hand, reaching for her breast with the other. His mind fills with the scent of her, the feel of her soft flesh, her breathing, her mouth, as he moves against her. He wonders what it will be like, to really be inside her properly; as soon as his imagination connects with this idea, all the sensations of her body surround and fill his mind, so that his desire rushes to a finale, rising like an orchestral crescendo around and within him, until he hears his own gasping reach a final, plaintive note.

They rest together in silence after this, hugging their own thoughts. Pat feels half embarrassed at his loss of control, half elated with the pleasure of it; the mess and discomfort balanced by the sense that his body does work, after all. Is she upset? Shocked? But she made it happen, didn't she, so surely she can't be too shocked? Besides, she's a farm girl, she must know about these things. A part of him also feels deeply at ease, at peace with the world, he realises, for the first time since his mother died. This closeness, this physical intimacy with a woman, is what that lonely part of him needs. Whatever Mary feels, he hopes it is something alike to this, as he lets himself drift away into a state of contentment.

Suddenly, a hammering at the door jerks him back, setting his heart off to echo, bringing a panic to his brain. They both leap to their feet, Mary hastily fastening and rearranging her clothes. Pat stares with horror at the rifle leaning by the door.

A fist pounds the door again. "Open up, I know you're in there."

He knows the voice, but in his anxiety he can't recognise it. He crosses the floor silently and returns with the rifle, slips it under the mattress, and whispers in her ear, "You've only just found me here, today, whoever it is." She nods, although her expression tells Pat that she thinks that no one will ever believe her. They walk over to the door. Mary stands back a couple of paces and Pat opens it a sliver, peering out through the crack.

Brendan stands outside, lips pursed in a silent whistle. "Come on, boyo, there's a job for you." Pat lets the door open. Brendan grins slyly, looking at Mary. "If you're not too busy, that is."

Mary swallows, flushes bright red, and looks at the floor. "I'll be getting back to the farm, now." She looks up, her eyes pleading with him. "Be careful, Pat."

"I will." Brendan steps aside, grinning, and watches her go.

Once she's out of sight, he winks at Pat. "I wouldn't mind a piece of that little arse myself. No, I surely wouldn't." He looks at Pat, raising an eyebrow.

For a moment, Pat feels too shocked to respond. Then he feels anger, rising. "Watch your mouth; she's a decent girl."

Brendan studies him carefully. Pat feels a stab of fear, thinking that Brendan will give him a bloody nose for his trouble. But Brendan merely smirks and taps his nose, "Ah well, boyo, to be sure she's a grand girl; and no doubt being a *country* girl she is all too impressed by your fine manners and education. And I'm sure she was a *decent* girl once, but certainly not today. I've been watching this place all afternoon, and I've been *listening* too. You're both entitled to your fun. But if you are telling me you were teaching her to sing, then that's a song I'd like to hear myself sometime, I surely would. But don't you worry, your little secret's safe with me."

He grins again and spits onto Pat's boot. "Anyway, boyo, go and be getting your gun. We've got work to do, so we have."

* * *

An hour later, Pat trudges along behind Brendan, following a rough path that climbs from the riverbank up to an abandoned cottage, hidden from the land around it by a small copse of blackthorn and willow. The evening light fades around them; Dinny's hideout has a safe, isolated feel, but his roof is in a bad state, half of it collapsed. He stands waiting at the door and waves them both in, slapping each on the back in welcome.

After a quick sup of tea and bread to warm them, the three men tramp away from the river into a deepening gloom and a steadily increasing drizzle, across meadows and fields, then along dark lanes for an hour and a half. The wind drops, but the damp of the night seems to seep through their boots and into their bones. Eventually they join a road and approach the lights of a prosperous looking farm. Two hundred yards before the farm entrance, Brendan puts up his hand, and gestures them all under the shelter of a tree. He takes out a cigarette, lights it, and points at the farm. "That's the place, Fitzgerald's."

Pat stares at it and swallows, a knot growing in his stomach. His doubts mix with a feeling of puzzlement. "What are we thinking to do here?"

Brendan draws on his cigarette, looking each of them in the eye, enjoying the suspense. Dinny slaps and rubs his hands together, trying to warm them, and gestures at Brendan to share his smoke. "Pass it over. Where's the others? Will they be meeting us here?"

"We're it, boys. It's a tit for tat, Dinny, like we did for the Tans. I'll tell you why. The Staters raided the Captain's farm last week; he wasn't there but he'd left a store of rifles in the barn, buried in the ground. For some reason his father also had a pistol hidden in the house. They found the rifles first, then the pistol. The silly old fool told them it was his own, and they shot him – right there, in front of his wife. When she went to pick up the gun, they shot her too. The next day, they were after claiming they resisted arrest. The Captain reckons it was a message to the rest of us."

"Oh, sweet Jesus; his Da was a lovely man."

Brendan hands the cigarette to Dinny, and then places a fatherly hand on Pat's shoulder. Pat feels the contact with shock and unease, which spreads through him, his heart hammering as he waits for Brendan to speak. The big hand squeezes Pat's shoulder and Brendan leans his face forward, emphasising the force of his instructions. Pat smells sour breath and stale tobacco. "So, we're going to send them a message back. You'll be thinking there's no sense in this, and you might be right, but it has to be done. It's dirty work, and we don't expect you to take the leading part, boyo; Dinny and I'll take care of that. We'll go in the front door while you watch the back of the house. Just don't let anyone out of that door. We need time to get away, so we do. So make sure your rifle's loaded with the safety off. If your man is at home, he'll be carrying a gun."

Pat feels some relief at first, then a rising sense of panic, and hears the crack in his own voice when he asks, "Who are they?"

Brendan turns aside and spits. "Some Stater Major; but even if himself is not at home, there'll be a guard." He takes the cigarette back from Dinny, sucks one last drag out of it, tosses it aside, and fishes his pistol from his belt. He fills the chambers with bullets, while Dinny does likewise. "Go on, boyo, check your weapon; you know the drill by now."

A wild, unkempt hedge borders the road; from here they creep along, keeping their heads down, towards a boreen on the other side of the house. Right in front of the house, Brendan holds up his hand just before a small gate. Pat peeks through a gap in the hedge, seeing a path leading through a neat rose garden to the front door. He feels the hand on his shoulder again, and listens to the hoarsely whispered command. "You'll have to go down that boreen, boyo. There's a gate down there that leads to the back of the house and the barns." Pat stares at a window, at gleaming firelight showing through half drawn curtains. It seems unreal, so ordinary and peaceful. "Right, Pat, we'll be going up to the front door now, and getting ready. When I signal, you take yourself round the back. Get yourself as close to the back door as ye can without disturbing anyone. Quietly does it, and listen out for the dogs. We'll count to a hundred and then go in. Remember now, just stop anyone from leaving. Shoot if ye have to; but try not to make a noise before you hear us going in." Pat nods.

Dinny carefully pushes the gate half open. The two older men then run, surprisingly quickly and quietly, down the path and station themselves on either side of the door. Brendan gestures at him; the time to play his part has arrived. Pat swallows, stumbles in a crouch along to the boreen entrance, and turns along it. The earth feels soft underfoot; he sees the glint of puddles and slows his pace to avoid making a splash. His heart hammers like a drum; to his ears, his footsteps sound like those of an elephant, and he can hear his own voice whispering almost imperceptibly, "Shit, shit, shit, shit..." He moves out of sight from the front of the house. There are no windows down this side of the house, so he jerks upright at last, watching his legs stepping hesitantly forward. One of his thigh muscles is twitching uncontrollably. He feels that he is moving like a puppet again, as he reaches the gate to the backyard. It's much darker here in this corner. How does this blessed gate open? He fumbles around, exploring with one hand for what seems an eternity, until he realises he's found a hinge. The fastening must be at the other end. How much time has passed? When did he stop counting? He decides to slip over the gate, since it is long and low, low enough to hop over. Much to his surprise his body executes this manoeuvre without a problem, even with the rifle in his hands. Then he fumbles along the back wall of the house until suddenly a door opens, flooding the yard with light from inside the kitchen. A boy of about thirteen steps into the yard holding a bucket of slops, probably food for the pigs, Pat realises. He lifts the rifle. The boy notices the movement and turns. The boy's jaw drops open, his eyes and mouth round, and he drops the bucket. Somewhere across the yard, a dog barks, and others join in. Someone calls from inside the house, telling the boy to shut the door. Pat and the boy stare at each other, his own uncertainty mirrored in the boy. Pat doesn't know what to say. He looks a bit like me, he thinks, but with red hair, like the boy on the bridge...

A door bangs inside the house; the dogs bark, more urgently. Two shots ring out from the house, then two more. The boy glances back at the open door, turns sideways and runs into the darkness towards the outbuildings. Pat watches him go curiously, listening to his own heartbeat and breathing, but otherwise does not react. His footsteps disappear and Pat lowers his rifle, relieved that the possibility of killing the boy has gone. He hears another shot, and after a pause, another. He kicks out at the slop bucket, sending it flying into the darkness, and forces himself to move into the house. A fire dances beneath a large black pot of soup in the empty kitchen. He walks past this into a hallway lit by a bare electric bulb. At the far end, he sees a man in uniform lying slumped face down. Dinny's head pokes around out of a doorway. He comments, "It's Pat," and disappears.

He steps forward and looks into the room. Dinny now stands over another man, apparently checking his pockets. This man lies on his back staring vacantly upward, wounds in his chest and face, his arms outstretched, a poker fallen out of one hand. A pool of blood from the back of his bald head seeps out over the carpet. Behind him, Brendan stands patiently over a woman who cowers in a corner, coughing blood and holding up her hands, as if to stop a bullet with them. Brendan waits, silently, until her will weakens and she drops her hands and looks away. The revolver crashes and Pat watches for a second more, then rushes outside to vomit. I have no stomach for this, he thinks, no stomach at all, while his guts empty and convulse. He tries to fix upon this idea, his lack of stomach, which seems oddly reassuring in the face of the reality around him. He uses it as a curtain, to block out the new and old images that press upon his imagination.

As they hurry away, Pat wonders if he should mention the boy. He decides not to; they would just think him even more of a fool. "Did you have to kill the woman?" he asks Brendan.

Brendan ignores him. Dinny glances up and replies, "Sure, we might have left her alone, but we live too close, Pat. She knows our faces."

Pat nods. It gnaws at him, then, and all the way home. He knows the boy's face, from the church, and the boy must know his, too. Even if the boy doesn't know his name, he will remember something. They will work it out soon enough, he realises. He suddenly feels exhausted. God help me, what have they done? What have *we* done, he thinks, what has Brendan brought me into, mixing up this mess up with my life? They will know who I am for sure, in good time. Then I'll be a wanted man, and all that means. He feels his hopes and dreams for the future slowly draining out of him, washing away in the cold February rain, as sure as if someone has blown a hole in his own chest. I'll have one more night at home, he thinks, with my brothers and my father, while I can.

*   *   *

Two days later, a pensive Pat trudges back down the lane to his cottage hideout, having said his farewells to his father and brothers. He's not slept much, despite his exhaustion. Earlier that day, he'd told Sean the gist of what happened. The image of his brother's face, opening with shock and then crumpling with disappointment, has stuck in his mind. His fists clenched, Sean had muttered, "Jesus, what a crock of shit. I told ye..." and then bitten his tongue. After a long silence, he added, "Sure, but there's no blessing in being right, little brother. I did warn you, fighting will change a man's life. So, what'll you do now?"

"I'll lie low for a while, maybe try and find O'Brien. The main thought in my mind is that I need a plan, and I must not run without one."

Sean nodded, "That at least is sounding like good sense."

"I'll have to leave here; I've risked enough these two nights. Can ye do me a favour, Sean?"

"Surely, Pat, whatever you ask."

"Will ye break the news to Da and Ernie after I've left?"

"I will." As soon as this was promised, Pat had felt an immediate urge to flee; the one thing he cannot face is his father's disappointment. Sean seemed to sense this, too. "Ye'd better be off then. No sense in giving the hounds a sniff before they start. It might be best to slip away without a fuss." Pat had nodded his relief at this, mixed with a bitter dose of shame.

He approaches the cottage from the fields, so dog-tired that he doesn't notice the smell of smoke and the light in the window until he reaches the door. He feels a rush of panic, fearing 'they' might have come for him already; then he realises, there's nothing to connect him with this place, even if the Free State authorities have realised his identity. He tiptoes around to the door and presses his ear to it. He hears a murmur of voices inside, and one of them sounds like Fons. He scratches his head, thinking. Then he retrieves the oilskin from its hiding place in the undergrowth, wraps his rifle in it and hides it away. He hesitates, then goes back and taps on the door lightly. Steps run to the door, which flings itself open to reveal that familiar, boyish grin. The sight has never felt as welcoming as it does now. "Pat! Where've you been? Guess what – my Ma's here, come and meet her." Fons grasps his arm and pulls him into the cottage. A slim, dark, youthful looking woman rises from her seat by the fire in the kitchen, meeting his gaze steadily, as if waiting for him to speak.

He feels shock at her appearance; a small, girlish body with narrow hips, accented by a frame of dark hair around a bird-like face. "Pleased to meet you, I'm sure, er – Mrs Gilligan."

"Call me Alice. So you're the singer, the famous Patrick."

"Oh... not so famous, I hope." He manages a smile at the floor, then sneaks another look.

"I suppose you expected some old harpy." Pat blushes. "Anyway,

I should thank you for being such a good friend to Fons. It has been a precious gift for him, you know, that you have kept in touch." Pat looks up again, noticing her tired smile and the little lines around her eyes. This seems like the first positive thing he has heard or felt all day. He doesn't know what to say; he just nods and listens. "I was very young when I had Fons. His father didn't hang around, if you know what I mean, but I was lucky enough to get work on the liners. I know it was hard for Fons, but I've seen far too much poverty in my life, so I have. My only regret is that I didn't think of the Conlon's in the first place. But then, he wouldn't have met you, would he?"

"I suppose not." Pat rubs his aching shoulder; an image of that day on the bridge intrudes for a second until he shuts it out.

"You must be cold, come sit by the fire. Fons, bring that box over. Patrick, you sit on this stool. You must be hungry too...some bread and cheese?"

Pat sinks onto his haunches, dazed with relief at the notion that he might still be welcome somewhere. Alice moves to the other side of the cottage, into the corner used as a pantry, and sets to work. Fons pulls up an upturned wooden box marked 'Mitchell's', sits down beside him, and smiles sheepishly.

Pat whispers, "Does she know I was staying here?" Fons nods. "Does she know why?"

Fons nods again; "She's a clever woman, Pat. She'd have found out. Don't worry, she can keep a secret."

Pat groans silently; then he thinks, what the hell, everyone will know soon enough. He pushes these thoughts away when Fons' mother returns with his supper. It's hard to think of her as 'Alice', somehow. He eats ravenously, despite his worries. Watching Fons and his mother while he eats, he can see a strong bond between them, despite their separation. They are comfortable with each other. He feels a pang of jealousy, then a rush of it, as he realises this kind of normal life may be gone forever, for him. He feels a wish to be a snail, to retreat into his shell, and sing to himself. He has listened to the sound of the sea in shells; I will need a hard shell, he thinks.

"You look tired, Patrick. If you want to sleep, you and Fons are in the other room. I'll make up a bed for myself here by the fire. I've brought a trunk full of things for the cottage. We'll fix it up eventually, won't we, Fons?"

On a makeshift mattress, Pat sleeps fitfully, his exhaustion fighting his terror. He wakes frequently, disturbed by dreams of the bridge and the slaughter at Fitzgerald's farm. As the light begins to creep through the window, he hears the sound of the fire being raked out and rekindled, while he tosses and turns. He hears someone pouring water and pulls himself quietly upright, shaking the sleep out of his head. Looking toward the doorway into the other room, half-draped with an old sheet, he catches a glimpse of naked legs and a half turned back; feels a shock of desire. Fons' mother is washing herself in the kitchen. She has the body of a young girl, he thinks, far more so than the voluptuous Mary. He forces himself to lie down again, ashamed of his sudden lust, especially with Fons sleeping peacefully beside him. Christ, what is he going to do about Mary, anyway? What about himself? Make a run for it? Where to? He tries to make himself think like O'Brien. He has to a have a plan; but no inspiration comes, and his mind jumps from one question to another without answers.

Fons' mother interrupts this reverie when she enters, now fully dressed, with two mugs of steaming tea. She kneels down and hands him one. "We'll talk properly later," she whispers conspiratorially, "but no guns in the cottage or the garden. Hide it somewhere else, understand?"

Pat nods, "Surely."

She examines his expression and gives him a rueful smile. Then, she turns away from him to reach over and ruffle Fons' head, "Rise and shine, son of mine." Pat can smell soap mixed with her body odour; not sweet like Mary, but peppery. Fons stretches and yawns. "There's hot water in the kitchen. I'll walk over to the farm for some eggs. Remember what I said, Patrick."

Most of that day, Pat feels disconnected and distracted; he drifts away into solitude, as if preparing himself, already slipping away from the life he knows. He wonders if, once caught, he would be shot or hanged. He spends most of the day avoiding people, going for walks, making excuses, racking his brains for ideas; the only practical plan he can think of is to go to Limerick to find O'Brien somehow, ask for his help, and then what? Would O'Brien send him back to Dublin, to some friend of his? That was risky, but better than staying here.

On his third return to the cottage, Fons grins and tells him, "Mary was here. She'll see you later. We're all going over there for supper."

So Pat cannot avoid one last supper at the Conlon farm, which has the intention of a celebratory farewell for Fons and his mother. A few days ago, he would have jumped at it. Now, he dreads it. From the moment he enters, he feels the weight of Mary's expectant gaze upon him; yet he cannot respond or even find his tongue. He mutters brief answers in conversation, unable to think of anything worthwhile to say, even on subjects upon which he has opinions. The problem is that his mind keeps jumping, switching haphazardly between the conversations around him, imagined or half-baked schemes of escape, and visions of being caught, imprisoned, or worse.

"Pat, are you going deaf?" He stares blankly at Mrs Conlon. "Mary was asking you if you would like to sing…"

He gulps, "Of course." Looking around, he sees that it's too late to prevent a tearful look in Mary's eyes. What on earth can he tell her, anyway?

He sings a repertoire of Irish songs he has learned from his childhood and from the recordings of John McCormack. His singing is flat, and his timing jumps about like a fish on a line, but no one else seems to notice. He finds himself performing to a sea of smiling faces while he feels increasingly numb, frozen, unable to respond to their good humour. Nevertheless, he copes until the moment when Fons mischievously asks him to sing "a song for *the boys*". Abruptly he feels a deluge of panic that makes him choke up and gasp like a fish for air. The others crowd round, concerned, offering advice…

"Have some water…"

"Is it the sore throat? We have some pastilles…"

Pat pushes past everyone to the door, muttering, "I need some air…" He turns in the doorway, noticing a sea of concerned faces; except for Alice, who sits apparently unmoved, studying him. "Sorry, I don't feel well. I'll see you tomorrow, Mary." He catches a look of fright and pain on Mary's face as he turns away. He shuts the door, quietly, and leans forward, arms on his knees to catch his breath, fighting the urge to vomit. After a minute, he walks away as fast as he can and stumbles back to the cottage, his mind a turmoil. He feels an urge to leave now, to flee before it's all too late.

When Alice returns to the cottage, Pat is sitting, still undecided, staring into the remains of the fire. At first she says nothing and patiently rekindles the fire. She stands over him, warming her hands, while he gradually becomes aware of her presence. After a while, he sighs.

Her response is to reach down and take one of his hands and press it between her own. "What on earth is the matter? Come on, laddie, you've had something on your mind all day. Fons knows it and so do I. Is it to do with Mary?" He shakes his head. "What is it then? Is it *the boys*? Are you wanting to pack it in?" He nods. "Thank the sweet Lord. You're too young to be wasting your life, believe me. Don't you dare feel bad about that, Patrick. A man's not a coward if he has the sense not to die for nothing. I wouldn't let Fons throw his life away in *this* stupid fight." Her tone is so vehement and angry that it pulls him out of his torpor.

He looks up to see her observing him, a smile slowly creeping out of the corner of her mouth. He clears his throat and speaks. For the first time all that day, his voice finally sounds like his own. "It's not just that. I've done something terrible." He considers this statement carefully, and then corrects it. "Truth is; some of the other *boys* did the deed. But I helped – I was the lookout. It was murder, so it was; revenge, tit for tat, but murder all the same. The real trouble is, someone saw me. The Staters know it was me, or they will soon, once they work it out. I'll be a marked man."

He looks up again. Her pale, thin face has coloured, but she meets his eyes. "You are a deep one, Patrick Mahon. So what will you do?" He shrugs. "Have you nowhere to go?"

"No. Maybe I might as well die fighting. They'll shoot me or hang me, anyway."

She doesn't so much drop his hand as throw it back at him; then she glares at him, her lips pursed. "No you bloody won't, Patrick Mahon. No friend of my son is going to chuck his life away as if it was nothing. I'll tell you what we'll do. I'm going back to my ship tomorrow. First, we'll get you to Queenstown. Then we'll get you onto a boat somehow; any boat, to get you away from here. I've got my husband's old pay book somewhere, so you can be Francis Gilligan if anyone stops us. We'll get you across the water somehow, even if we have to stuff you in my case. After that, you'll have to make your own way. But you have a brain, and you may not have thought of this, but you can always sing for your supper. You'll be fine."

The feeling of being verbally slapped slowly fades, and a sudden urge to laugh seizes him, though he dare not upset her. "Are you serious?"

She shakes her head impatiently, and glares down at him. "Are you not?"

"God's truth I am – it feels like a curse, what's been done, but what I've told you is as true as the grass is green and the sea wet." He thinks for a moment. "And God bless you for those ideas. They sound better than anything I've been thinking of, or could be doing on my own. But won't it be a risk for you?"

"I'll be the judge of that. You had better tell me exactly what happened, and when, so I know what the risks are, exactly..."

When Fons returns to the cottage, half an hour later, Pat has finished his tale. He watches Alice take Fons aside and whisper instructions in his ear; Fons glances at Pat, his eyes widening. Pat shrugs in acknowledgement. Fons nods back at him; then he takes a message back to the Conlon farm before returning to help his mother pack.

*   *   *

His dreams take him on long and complicated journeys that night, travelling across Europe and America. Wherever he goes a constant anxiety accompanies him. Everywhere he travels, he carries a small green bag that contains something most precious, more precious than any of his possessions; in his dream, he cannot even bear to open the bag, in case it turns out to be empty. He also has brief meetings with many of those he has left behind, such as his brothers and father, who somehow manage to be in two places at once; and such unlikely places. He finds Sean serving at the counter of a post office, and his father in a London street. He meets Mary in a church, in the confession box, somewhere in America. There's no priest, however, and no confession; only hurried kisses and hugs, and an urgent desire to sin most properly, before she leaves him alone inside the box, where he waits for someone else. This scene remains bright in his mind for some time, only fading as the sound of splashing water and a growing light in the sky accompany an unwelcome, dawning sense of reality. He resists the urge to sit up, to sneak another look at the woman washing in the next room, making himself wait until she brings him tea, as he knows she will. Listening to Fons' peaceful breathing, he feels envious.

She nods an acknowledgement when she sees that he's awake, and whispers, "Have you got your baptismal certificate with you? Anything like that?"

"I have, in my case; along with some school certificates."

"Good. Quench your thirst with this and then get them out for me to see while you wash."

Pat nods and takes the tea. When he is ready, he calls her through and gives her the papers. She points with her finger at his baptismal certificate. "I thought so. Look, we can alter this – so you can change your name to *Mac*Mahon – and here, we can change your date of birth easily. It's a common trick on the boats and it's usually enough to throw the authorities off the scent. All we need is some indigo ink. We can buy that in Cork. Then you can use something like to your own name later, and maybe your certificates too, but only after you've crossed the water. You'll have to use my husband's papers now."

"Thanks."

"Now, you should pack what you can into this canvas bag; you can't take the case. I'll make some breakfast." Pat is about to open his mouth when he remembers; the case has his name stamped into the leather.

As dawn rises, Da Conlon meets them with his horse and trap. Pat is given an old tweed jacket to wear and a cap to cover his fair hair; together with a pipe, the outfit seems to put years on him. Alice also hands him a battered cardboard booklet. "Remember, from now on you are Frank Gilligan. You have to be that person, Patrick

Mahon, do you understand?"

He nods, suddenly aware of his responsibility to her. "Don't you worry, I'll be fine." He meets her eye. "I won't let you down." He forces a smile. "We'll make a lovely couple, don't you worry."

She studies his expression, her eyes narrow; an enigmatic smile passes across her face as she turns away. "Let's hope so." She turns back, "One other thing. Fons will explain to Mary; but you'd better write to her yourself, young man, if there's any kindness in that heart." She taps his chest to emphasise, then turns away from him to say her farewell to Fons. "Goodbye, my precious son and sunshine. Don't worry, I'll take care of your friend." Pat notices a playful wink as Fons clings to her one last time. "It'll soon pass, son. I'll see you next time we dock at Queenstown."

As they set out on the road, she whispers in his ear, "Put your arm around me; try to act like a protective husband. Then, even if they are looking for you, they won't see you. Do you understand?" He nods and tentatively puts one arm around her, catching a look of surprised disapproval from Da Conlon.

Alice sees it too. "It's only acting, Michael. The boy's got my husband's papers, so he has to play the role or the peelers might be bothering with us. You know what's at stake here."

The older man nods, reddens, and bites his lip. After a while, he gives Pat a lop-sided grin and tells him, "I'll be terrible surprised if the peelers work that fast, anyway. It normally takes them a week before they put any word about the district."

Alice nods in response; then drops her voice to a whisper for Pat's benefit. "Think of this as a ticket away from this stupid civil war. You'll be escaping the whole sorry mess soon, and then you'll be across the water with a new life."

He sits, conscious of an underlying terror but reassured by her confidence. He remembers a similar journey, years earlier, with his father. That journey, after all, took him to another life in Dublin. The thought, so solid, reassures him. Then, he suddenly realises that on this present journey, Alice is acting as his parent; she has taken his mother's role. He feels a flood of emotions; grief, longing, gratitude and warmth. Mostly, he feels his lost love for his mother, as if she were there, after all. When this recedes he feels, inside his long arm, a small, delicate frame; and yet marvels at how her tiny body seems to contain such inner strength and courage.

In Fermoy, they disembark to catch the Queenstown bus. Pat embraces and thanks Da Conlon, who nods, touches his cap, and announces, "The priest's luck and a safe road to both of you. Fons will be fine with us, Alice." He turns to Pat, takes off his cap, and examines it. "Now, you will be writing to us and letting us know how you are, won't you?" Pat nods. The older man touches his arm. "And when you are next singing of home, you will remember us, I hope?" His dark eyes meet Pat's for a long moment before he leaves the question unanswered, climbing into the trap and leaving without a backward glance, while Pat fights back his tears.

Alice waits until he is out of sight and then takes Pat's arm. "Come along now, young man. It's a hard farewell, God knows, but it could be a lot harder, couldn't it? Think of all the poor souls driven away by the famine, leaving nothing but graves behind, with not a penny in their pockets."

Approaching the port, their battered old bus, largely empty, approaches a roadblock manned by Free State troops. Pat has an immediate urge to hide under his seat and to piss his pants. Then he feels Alice laying her head on his shoulder, pretending to sleep; so he too feigns a doze. Through half-closed eyes he watches soldiers stare curiously, as they slow; their officer steps forward with raised arm. The bus groans to a stop while Pat and Alice feign shock as if rudely awoken, almost toppling forward off the seat. The officer steps up into the aisle and stares at each of the occupants in turn. Pat realises he's the only male of fighting age on the bus.

"Where are you two going this fine morning?" Pat swallows, his mind a blank.

"If it's all the same with your good self, Captain, I'm working on the liners, and my husband here on any boat that needs a crew." Her tone is one of enforced patience.

The Captain grunts and looks them up and down. Pat feels the thumping in his heart and swallows, discovering that his mouth is as dry as a bone. But the man doffs his cap at Alice, steps down and waves the bus through without another word. Pat takes a deep, deep breath, his pulse gradually slowing as they pull further away.

They exit the bus by the harbour side. "Before we do anything else, we should catch our breath and take some tea in that café over there, how about that?" He nods. In the café, they sit in silence for a long while, Pat staring out of the window towards the water. He guesses that Alice's thoughts will be of Fons, of leaving her son again. He tries to think of something to say, but words fail him. When she finishes her tea, she catches his eye. "You wait here with the bags while I go to my ship and see what time we're sailing. Have another tea."

She returns an hour later, her face expressionless. "They're still working on the ship's engines. We sail tomorrow." She flashes him a grin. "And that's not all. Two of the junior stewards have buggered off to join the army. If we hurry back right now one of those jobs is yours. After that, we'll need to find somewhere to stay tonight, and then we'll find you some ink and any other things we need." Pat gazes at her in total awe.

That evening, their preparations done, they eat a fish supper and drink a farewell to Ireland in a cosy inn by the waterside. She drinks a whiskey, and he a pint of stout. Gradually, the tension in his body begins to ease away and the tiredness begins to fill his bones. He yawns.

She nudges him deftly and raises her glass. "Slainte; and how will your sea legs be, Mr Gilligan?"

"I have no idea. Look, Alice..." the name rolls off his tongue, now, he realises, as she tilts her head, waiting. "I don't know how to thank you. You've saved my life, for sure."

"Accepted; but I have my own motives. Fons has had a very hard time, and I surely didn't want him to lose his best friend too. You can thank me by keeping in touch with him, wherever you go. Agreed?"

He nods, "I swear I will. You know, you're not really such a bad mother, are you?"

At this, tears spring into her eyes, which dart away. Pat realises his own clumsiness far too late, with a shock, as he sees the impact of his words upon her face. He reaches out, trying to take her hand, "Forgive me, I didn't mean it like that."

She brushes his hand away and turns away from him; he grasps her arm. "Look, God's truth, I think you're amazing, truly amazing...whatever other people might say or think. Fons is proud of you and he is right to be that way."

She sniffs and nods, but will not look at him, speaking to the wall, "The truth is painful sometimes, isn't it, soldier boy? I'm not a good mother, but maybe I'm not such a bad one either, am I?" She glances around briefly and wipes her eyes. "And while I think on it, I wasn't a bad wife either, short and sweet though the experience was. Well, Pat the singer, now you can buy me one more drink and then we had both better get some rest. It's an early start in the morning."

When he returns from the bar, she tosses her whiskey back, still avoiding his eyes, sniffs, and walks out. He curses to himself, forced to leave most of his own drink on the table, and follows ten yards behind her, listening to the heels of her shoes tapping a determined rhythm on the cobbles. She doesn't look back, increasing his sense of shame. At the door to the boarding house, she raps the knocker and then turns to face him. "Don't you be saying a word; just play your part and take my arm when we go up the stairs." He nods, feeling more shame at the reminder of what she is doing for him.

The door opens and the landlady peers out, eyeing them up and down. "So it's yourselves at last." She steps aside, and hands Alice a candle as she enters. "Breakfast is at seven, mind."

Alice smiles back at her evenly, "That will suit us very nicely. Good evening, Mrs Flynn." She lifts the candle and rests her other arm lightly on Pat's while they climb the creaking stairs together, their movements suddenly awkward and stiff. Her arm promptly withdraws when they reach the landing above. She leads the way across a threadbare rug to room number three. The room had seemed adequate when they inspected it; now it feels bare, unwelcoming. A double bed on a cast iron frame stands opposite a wooden dresser upon which sit a cracked mirror, an enamel bowl of cold water, and half a bar of soap. Two rickety chairs stand either side of the bed, under which sits a large chamber pot. Alice moves to one side of the bed, by the empty fireplace, and places the candle on the mantelpiece above the hearth. Pat moves to the other side, stares out of the window into the night, and then sinks onto the chair. He rests his head on his hands, trying to think of something to say, and shuts his eyes.

He hears movement; then, in front of him, the sound of the curtains being pulled across. He opens his eyes to see her bare feet on the floorboards; a pillow is thrust into his lap. He watches her move back around to her side, extracting a nightgown from her bag. She throws him a determined glance. "Turn around."

He turns his chair to the wall, the act bringing back the memory of a familiar classroom ritual. He clears his throat. "I'm terrible sorry that I have been such a glorious dunce, Alice. The stupid part is, God's truth, I was truly wanting to say to you how grateful I am, how much I owe you, how..." He runs out of words and stares at the wall, noticing a series of vertical cracks and spots of mildew. He hears her moving, but she does not reply. "And I am truly, truly jealous of Fons. That's all I can really say. Isn't that what matters, about you and him? Don't you think?"

Her movement stops; he can sense her carefully considering his words. He hears a deep sigh, followed by the sound of her blowing her nose into a handkerchief. "You have a damned fine way of showing it, is all I can say." He hears her move into the bed. When she next speaks, the hard edge has gone from her voice. "You'd better get ready; it'll be a long day tomorrow." He turns to see her watching him, the blanket pulled up to her chin. She makes no effort to look away, a glint of mischief showing as she punishes him with her eyes.

He takes off his boots and jacket, hesitates, and then drops the pillow down onto the floor. From his canvas bag, he carefully pulls out an embroidered quilt, which he lays down by the pillow.

"Was that your mother's work?"

"It was, God rest her soul. It's all I have of her now." Not true, he realises, and corrects himself. "Well, I also have all the songs she used to sing to me. That was her best gift; I just wish I could sing them back to her, sometimes." He can hear a sharp note of anger in his own voice, which catches him by surprise.

"She left you all alone, didn't she?"

"I never thought of it like that, but I suppose she did." His voice is thick now, the emotions dense within it. He looks up to find her studying him carefully in her watchful way.

"Well, maybe that explains a little about you, Patrick Mahon. You like to be mothered, and God knows there are not enough men in the world that manage to be charming about that. But deep inside you're still destroyed and hurting, and so you'll be hurtful sometimes to girls, without meaning to."

"Will I?" That particular thought is no comfort to Pat.

"Sometimes; not always... put the candle out and come into the bed, Patrick. You'll freeze on that floor. Put the quilt over the bed and take your socks and trousers off. But keep your shirt and drawers on." Pat does as he is told, feeling relief that he seems to be forgiven at last. He climbs into his side of the bed gingerly, wary of any contact.

"Thanks, Alice; goodnight."

"Goodnight, Pat. Sleep well."

He does sleep soundly at first. He dreams of Mary, of a farewell party where he sings. But the occasion seems rather like his own wake, for he can only observe and sing; he cannot take a drink or join in the conversations. Then he dreams of his childhood, of the time when his mother used to take him for walks, carry him in her arms, and sing to him. He feels comfortable, safe, and for a while it is Mary that holds him, and he is not a child any more. He tries to stay in this dream, to hold onto it, but slowly he drifts back to reality, realising gradually that the body he has wrapped himself against and around is not Mary or his mother, at all.

He dare not move at first, terrified of rousing her anger again. He lies there wondering what to do. And then she moves, shifting the back of her head against his chest, and sighs. He can feel her breathing, slow and warm, and smell her hair. She shifts again, turning her body and drawing up her knees, shaping herself into the space that his arms and legs enclose. He begins to sense that she's not asleep even before she speaks.

"It's all right, Pat, I won't bite. I can't sleep either, if you want the truth. Women have needs too, you know, even old women like me." He starts to say something, but she moves again and her finger presses on his lips to silence him. "I thought I'd forgotten about all this. But it's so nice to be held in a man's arms." She sighs and moves again, slipping an arm around his waist, giving him a playful squeeze.

The relief he feels allows his mind to relax, though he cradles her gingerly, still wary of movement. But now he can allow himself to feel the reality of her body, mysteriously lithe yet soft under her nightgown, her warm breath upon his chest, and the earthy smell and fine threads of her hair upon his face. His body will not relax; without thinking, he starts to stroke her hair.

"You can kiss me if you want to."

He feels surprise and pleasure, though he still hesitates. "Are you sure?"

"Well, I wouldn't be asking you otherwise. I told you, Pat Mahon, that women have needs too. And God knows, it's been a long time since I've lain in a bed with a handsome boy. Is it such a terrible idea, to give me a kiss?"

"It is not, I swear; it is a wonderful idea to me."

He feels a finger, drawing a shape upon his chest. "But don't misunderstand me. I am not in love with you, and I don't want you to be in love with me. That would be too messy. I know you're sweet on Mary, and that would have been fine for both of you. But you've left that little treasure behind you, just like I left mine." She undoes a button on his shirt, and then another. "So think of this as an act of kindness, Pat Mahon, for the both of us. I'll be kind to you tonight because you've got a long road ahead of you, and feeling like a man when you set off on that road will not be doing you any harm. And you can be kind to me because I need some comfort too, tonight, and I want to remember what it feels like to be woman again. So how does that sound to you?"

Pat considers this carefully, feels a smile break out upon his face. "It sounds like Caruso."

"Like what?"

"Enrico Caruso. He's a singer, Alice. A very great singer, so he is."

He hears a giggle, a sudden girlish sound, and then feels her wriggling around, and he realises she is pulling the nightdress over her head. "Well then, you can sing away, but quietly, now. Sing me a song with that fine young body of yours, soldier boy."

He reaches out, finding a body that is both girl and woman - her breasts small but somehow more pronounced. Where Mary had been soft, receptive, but passive, Alice is lithe, active, teasing with approach and retreat, constantly surprising him. They play together in his mind, that night, like violins; a duet rapidly increasing in speed, chasing each other in turn up and down the scales, with heartbeats for drums, sighs as cymbals, and a long plaintive note to finish the tune. In his later years, he will realise it was probably a short and frantic melody without finesse. But he will think of it often, that first time, during all the rest of his days.

The day that follows feels so hectic that Pat has little time to reflect upon anything; even upon that music, or his departure from his homeland. Only after midnight does he go up onto the deck of the ship and look back across the water, along the silvery wake that trails behind them, and realise that he has missed his chance to take one last look at Ireland.

*   *   *

Seven: 1924-1927

Fons throws all of his weight onto the new growth, wrestling with nature; he pulls and twists it into submission. Weaving the end of the branch through one gap in the hedge, he pulls it back out from another and watches Michael tie it down. Then he examines the green smudges covering his forearm and sucks a deep scratch clean, the aroma of crushed leaves and sap filling his nose. Watching Da Conlon swing his sledgehammer down, rooting a stake deep into the earth, he feels the shocks through the soles of his feet. Da lays the hammer down, straightens and stretches his back, rubbing the muscles at the base of his spine with both hands. He turns to examine their work; Fons hears a muttered, "Between you, as able as any man" and feels a flush of pride. Da picks up another stake from the pile and returns to the gap he's intent on plugging, preparing a framework for the lads to weave.

In the distance, a voice seems to float on the breeze. Da turns and stares at the far side of the field, where his 'little nightingale' stands on her toes at a gate, waving her arms. "Da, Da... there's a letter arrived for Fons; it's come from across the water..."

The boys watch Da expectantly. He shouts back, "Tell your Ma we'll take some tea soon. We'll just be finishing along this side, first." His daughter waves an acknowledgement, her eagerness apparent in her quick movements as she turns and runs out of view; Da scratches his head and nibbles his lip. "Come on, boys; work up one more lather and the job will be done."

Back in the house, Mary fidgets, her eyes fluttering repeatedly to the letter standing tucked between her father's tobacco tin and a bottle of metal polish on the high mantelpiece above the fire. It seems an eternity to wait, on top of the ones already passed, hours stretching into days, days into weeks, weeks into a month, almost two; and now each singe minute seems to last a year...

Eventually the door bursts open. Fons enters, his quick eyes darting around the room. Her mother starts to rise from her chair but Mary is too quick for her, snatching up the letter and running to thrust the precious offering into his hand, leaving her own hands clasped as if in prayer, her eyes examining his face. He looks at the envelope, hesitating. "Go on, then," she whispers.

Her father, framed in the threshold, clears his throat, steps towards Fons, and nods at him. "So whose is the writing? Would that be your Ma's hand?" Fons looks up at him and nods. "Well, will we just see if they're both fine? You can be reading the rest of it later, by yourself, if you like, but there's some of us here dying of impatience." He smiles and inclines his head towards Mary.

Fons nods and tears the envelope open, reading the first page while his audience waits. Mary herself remains still, as if frozen, though the deep red heat flushing through her face and neck seems to melt a tear, which trickles down unnoticed by all except her mother. Both women watch Fons' lips moving while he reads, each trying to decipher the silent words forming and passing away. Ma Conlon silently moves to her daughter's side, just in case. Fons clears his throat, "They're both fine. They got away from Cork without any problem, and me Ma got Pat a job on the liner. He'll write later, and he sends his love."

"Thank the Lord," whispers Ma Conlon, hugging her daughter.

Fons folds the pages back together and puts the letter away, trying not to feel the glare of Mary's eyes upon his face. "Is that all?" she whispers, incredulous at his action.

Fons shrugs, avoiding her eyes. "That's the important part. I'll read the rest and tell you all about it later. Where's that tea? I'm parched." Mary wrestles free from her mother's grasp, and runs up to the room in the attic. Her parents watch her leave but make no comment.

Later, alone at last, Fons settles himself on the old tree stump in the cottage garden, pulls out the letter and reads every word carefully; especially the final page, written in a different hand.

Dear Fons, your mother is truly a remarkable woman, and I surely owe her my life. When we first met, I felt sorry for you; now, I feel envious. My own mother was wonderful too, but she's gone forever. I miss you all terribly, especially my own family and Mary, but I do know that I am a wanted man in Ireland from some newspapers that followed us across the water. I may not ever be able to return, so I think it's best if I don't write to Mary. For her sake, she needs to forget me and find someone else. It'll be hard for her, I know, but surely that will be the best in the long run. Please go to see my family and tell them I am safe; but take care, the authorities will be watching the farm. Tell them if I had known what the others would do, I would never have gone along. My brother Sean will understand, I think, but it will be hard on my father. Tell them I am truly sorry for the trouble I must have caused them. The authorities will have spies in the post office, I'm sure. If they want to send me a message or a letter, tell them to pass it through to you, and you can send it inside a letter to your Ma. You should, I suppose, destroy my letters once you've read them, to be safe. The work is hard but it passes the days, and New York makes Dublin seem but a village. Let me know how they all are.

Your friend; a chara, Pat.

* * *

The red sun fades and slowly sinks below the horizon while he strides evenly along the boreen towards home, in no hurry now that he has filled the bag on his back. He hears a crow in the distance, smiles, and begins to whistle to himself. Another year older tomorrow, he thinks, and things have turned out alright. His mother will be here for her next visit, soon. Bursting through the back door of the farm, he unslings the shotgun from his back, stowing it within a battered ottoman, and then throws a canvas bag to Mary, nodding, "Tomorrow's supper."

Da Conlon looks up from his seat by the fire and taps his pipe on the hearth. "How many did ye get?"

"Three." He grins. "Ye told me not to waste shot."

"So I did, and I'm sure ye did not. Well, I'm just glad the troubles is over, ye would be far too good a soldier. Wouldn't he just, Mary?"

Fons flushes with pleasure while Mary's eyes dart from her father's face to his. She sighs, deep in thought, before she replies. "He's got a great eye all right, but I'd rather he used his head. He's got a gift for numbers, Da. Those maths books...the ones that Pat left behind..." During these moments of hesitation, Fons senses a raft of images cramming into her mind, as if Pat himself was stepping through a door, "...they're way beyond me, but Fons has a gift for it."

"Only when *you* read it out and help him work out what it means..." interjects Michael.

"True, but we have a dictionary. And Fons is getting the hang of reading Da's newspapers." Da stares at him for a moment, but Fons merely shrugs and shakes his head; he doesn't want to sit at a desk, he just likes solving the practical puzzles in the books.

Later that night, lying on the large mattress in the attic room with Michael, a curtain dividing the space, he listens to Michael and Mary breathing. He can hear Da and Ma too, talking down below, though he only catches the odd word. He suspects they'll be fretting about Mary again. He hopes it's not about him; the older he gets, the more he feels like a cuckoo in the nest.

A whispered voice, the tone rising in a heartfelt appeal, slips through the curtain dividing the room. "Fons, are you awake?"

He hesitates, wondering whether to ignore her; he hopes it's not going to be about Pat again. "Maybe I am. What is it?"

"Do you really want to be a soldier?"

Fons considers this carefully. No one has ever asked him this question, or anything like it. "I think I would."

"Why is that? You know, after all that's happened... doesn't it scare you?" Fons feels his forehead knit as he considers. He hears Michael emit a fake snore and Mary shush him impatiently, before she insists, "Well?"

"I don't know. It might if there was still a war on, I suppose. But I think all that's finished now. I like the outdoor life. It's good here, but I want to be able to look after myself. Soldiers are good at that." He can't quite bring himself to tell her about the bridge, the soldier who saved his life. "An' like my Ma, I want to see a bit of the world."

"What about the mathematics?"

"I couldn't add up numbers in an office, Mary; it'd bore me silly. But numbers are useful to soldiers, too, you know, with guns and other stuff." In the silence that follows, he thinks about Michael. Everyone assumes he'll take over the farm from his father, but nobody has asked Michael what he wants, either; and Mary? He's wary of asking, in case it sets her off about Pat; but in the end, he's too curious. "What about you, Mary?"

He hears a pause, and then a sniffle. "Oh, I wouldn't really know. I always thought I'd just get married and have children like Ma, but I don't know... I can't..." Fons hears her voice crack apart, and he senses that she's struggling to push Pat out of her mind again. He can almost feel his friend's presence, standing there between them. Then her voice starts up again, her wistful tone slowly steadying itself. "I can't imagine how it can be that simple, any more. And I'm not even sure if it's what I want now. The hard thing is, Fons, I love this place too much. My home, I mean, here in Cork. I can't imagine going away and I can't imagine ever wanting to." Then Fons hears a new quality in her voice, a note of grim determination, as if she is wiping her tears away. "But then most of the young men leave this place; they have to, for work. And even if Pat himself did write to me I can't see what I would do. I don't want to leave this place. He can't come back, and I don't want to leave. And that might apply to nearly any man."

He listens, discomforted by the pain he hears in her voice, but too curious to interrupt.

She sniffles at length, and changes her tone again. "I'll not be a bloody nun, anyway, if that's what you might be worried about. And I'm not too keen on getting married to some old farmer, either. So I suppose that means working in a shop, round here. It's not such a bed of roses for us girls, you know."

Fons chuckles, feeling most relieved by the determination in her voice. "I'm sure it is not. But if I know you, Mary, you'll be running the shop by the end of a year..."

When Michael and Mary awake the next day, Fons' bed is already empty. They shrug and dress in their Sunday best, their parents fussing over their outfits. No one mentions Fons' absence. Da and Sarah Conlon gave up trying to encourage, bribe, entice, beg or force Fons to accompany them to mass years ago. It was simply too much hard work; as it was with the village school after he turned twelve. They were lucky if he lasted part of a day; despite the fact that the Christian Brother in charge there was a decent man, by all accounts. The Conlons have wisdom enough to know that Fons has his reasons to avoid the Christian brothers and, by association, priests; and since otherwise he's respectful, honest, helpful and hard-working, they've decided to turn a blind eye.

Most Sundays, Fons takes himself on a long walk or cycle ride, testing his endurance. This day, he cycles west through Mallow, then south along a track up into the Boggeragh mountains, carrying a fishing net tied around what looks like a long bag of spare rods. Where the track ends, he hides the bike in the undergrowth and walks up a valley through some woods, emerging on the edge of a deserted plateau, carrying the bag. He takes out a sheet of paper from his pocket and unfolds it, then pins it to a tree; it has a red circle painted upon it.

He walks three hundred paces from the tree. Out of the bag, he first removes his decoy – a fishing rod. Reverently, he then slides out Pat's rifle and ammunition, and loads the weapon. He has only nine rounds; assuming the ammunition still works. He settles down on the ground, sights, and shoots. He fires four shots first, and then goes to check the target. Not bad, he thinks. Should he save the rest? He can hardly use this to shoot rabbits, can he? For all that the civil war's over, it's still illegal to possess a military weapon like this. What the hell... he fires all his ammunition, sending it away into the target while he tries to get a good feel of the gun, a sense of connection.

Folding the target up into his pocket, he wonders if he dare show it to Da Conlon. Maybe when he's old enough to join up, that'll be the moment, he thinks. He checks that the rifle is empty, repacks the bag, and retraces his steps down the valley.

* * *

It feels not so much like a dream as a jumble of memories, tipped out from deep in his mind. An unknown face looms over him as he lies on his back, a helpless infant. Holding his mother's hand, he waits on a strange doorstep. Then, escaping through the back door, the other boy pulls his arm and they run for the garden gate together, giggling; the wonderful thrill of freedom courses through his body. Now standing at the front of a class, he feels trapped again; he holds out one hand while he sucks the fingers of the other, trying to make the stinging stop. He escapes again and finds himself lying out in the sun, listening to the sound of birdsong. He turns his body and suddenly the sounds change. Now, he hears the sound of steady breathing in the darkness; his own and two others, both asleep. He can tell them apart; Mary's breathing is slower, more regular. He savours the sound and smell of their companionship, infusing the air around him. Outside, the cock crows; for the third time, he realises. He hears movement in the room below; dim light slowly begins to appear through the thatch above his head. He sits up and pulls on his underwear, tiptoes to the door and slips through. He descends the stairs and heads for to the kitchen to wash.

At the breakfast table, Sarah Conlon asks him, "Well young man, will you be ready for this momentous day?"

Fons looks at her expression and sees concern; he nods, "I think I am, Ma Conlon. I hope it will be today, but only the Lord knows what time she'll show her face."

"If all goes well, I reckon sometime in the afternoon. It'll also depend on how much she brings with her this time. Did she mention anything in her letter?"

"She did not; but the cottage is almost ready, in my eyes. I can't imagine what else we could be wanting. The whole place is clean and tidy and I'm after leaving a fire on, to dry it out, the last two days."

Ma smiles and glances at Mary. "What you think is clean, Fons, may not quite look that way to a female eye. Mary will give you a hand this morning; Michael can help Da."

Two hours later, at the cottage, Mary finishes in the other room and comes to inspect the kitchen floor. Fons looks on hopefully, bucket in hand. "It'll do; I'm not sure it would get past my mother, but she's not here, is she?"

Fons grins and wipes his brow in mock relief. "It'll be time for a cuppa tea, then."

The two of them sit staring thoughtfully at the peat fire, each cupping their hands around a new enamel mug, their bodies mirroring each other's posture. Each glances up occasionally, waiting for the other to speak. Eventually, Fons clears his throat; at the exact same moment, Mary asks, "Do you...do you think she'll like it here?"

"I was wondering about that meself. I think she will; she always tells how much she misses home. What do ye think?"

"Visiting is one thing and settling down again another, but it's a good little house. And she will have you for company, Fons. If you were not here, I imagine it would be much harder for her to come back and live here alone. We will miss you at our house, Fons. I will, for sure. You understand me better than my brother does."

His face reddens and he bites his lip. "Ye'll be glad of the extra space, though."

She looks up and shakes her head. "It's Michael who'll have the extra space, not me. No, I'll miss you. I hope I won't be losing you, like I lost Pat. Will you still be helping on the farm? I asked me Ma and she said she wasn't sure..."

"Not as much; your Da says he can't afford to pay me, except in kind. When I stayed with you, I could work for my keep. Now I'll just come and help now and then; whenever he needs it."

She bites her lip. "You make sure you do that, Fons Gilligan, and make sure we feed you when you do. And come and visit me whenever you like. You might find it a bit strange here in this cottage."

He laughs. "I will, too." He stares into the fire a while, his brow working at a little furrow and then straightening. "You know I waited so long for this, but now, well..."

"You wish you were younger?"

He nods forcefully, and emits a deep sigh. "Yes. That's it. I still want her here at home, but now that time has come I'm not a child anymore. I need to be finding my own way."

"Like Pat?"

"Don't be stupid," he growls, and then, catching her expression, he softens his voice. "Pat can't come back even if he wanted to. If things had been different, he would have finished his schooling and then come back here. But the troubles were like the famine, for him. He had to go, or it was the end for him."

Now she furrows her brow; "I never thought of it in that way. You're right, though. The trouble is I'm one of these people that feels rooted in the land here, with my family and you. I feel as if a part of me would wither away if I left. Not that I've ever been asked..." She bites her lip.

Fons allows another long pause while he watches her chew her lip; then he shrugs. "You've said it yourself; it would be an impossible choice now, let alone then. Sure, don't torture yourself with the idea. Pat knew it was over. He decided what was for the best, for both of you."

"Did he now?" She wipes her cheek.

"He did. And it can't be undone, what he did at the Fitzgerald's farm, or what he decided."

"He might have asked me about it." Fons does not reply; after a long pause she wipes her face again. "So what about you, Fons Gilligan; are you rooted here, or are you going to be a bird on the wing too?"

"When he writes about America, it sounds a queer place to me. I want to see a bit of the world, though. It doesn't matter to me where, it can be the rest of Ireland for all I care."

She blinks, and then stares into the fire for an age. Then she speaks; her tone flat, a statement rather than a question, "You'll leave us all behind."

He shrugs, and whispers, "Maybe."

She puts the mug down, gets to her feet, and stands over him, embracing him, and kisses his cheek. Then she leaves, quickly; probably, he thinks, to spare him the sight of her grief.

* * *

Mary takes a deep breath and knocks at the cottage door, hoping that Fons will be alone; but when the door opens, Alice's eyes meet her own. She blinks and forces a smile. "Good morning, Mrs Gilligan."

"Good morning." Alice beckons her in, turns, and calls out, "Fons... here's Mary, from the farm." Mary swallows another morsel of disappointment; secretly, she longs for a more personal term of identification, a term that reflects how she *feels* (like a sister to Fons) although her intuition tells her that Alice may never acknowledge *that*. "Come in, child." She murmurs her thanks as she steps past, feeling her cheeks blush faintly. She has turned nineteen, after all.

Fons sits by the fireside cleaning his boots, and waves her over. "You're looking grand this morning, Mary. Will ye be going to the village shop today, by any chance?"

A smile breaks out on her face at that, and she shakes her head in mock exasperation. "I might. It depends what *you* might be wanting."

Fons chuckles, "Well, Ma tells me she wants some sugar. I'll pay you for it, and if you take the trouble to bring it for me, I might just find a spare rabbit for you. Sit ye down a minute, anyway. How is everyone?"

Mary smiles at his lop-sided grin. "Oh, they're all grand. I suppose a rabbit makes a fair bargain, anyway. But Da would like you to help Michael with the ditches next week."

"That's fine with me."

As Mary settles herself onto a stool, Alice calls out, "Be careful, Mary, he'll have you darning his socks next. And that's a job I wouldn't wish on anyone. I don't know how you do it, Fons; every time you promise to go shopping for me, someone else does it for you."

They all pass the time together for half an hour; Alice mostly listening while she washes clothes in a large tub. For a long time, Mary avoids asking the topic most on her mind. She knows she should wait until the next time she can catch Fons alone, but eventually she can't stop herself. "Have you heard from Pat recently?"

Fons nods, thoughtfully. "We had a letter the other day. He's doing fine. He's still working as a steward on one of the big ships between New York and Southampton. They moved him up to second class. He must be getting better, eh Ma?"

Alice shakes her head, and sucks her teeth. "About time..." She sighs and looks sideways at Mary. "He's bright enough, Mary, we all know that; probably far too clever to be a steward, if the truth were told. But he shouldn't take the job for granted."

"What do you mean?"

Alice picks up the shirt she has been scrubbing and inspects it in the light from the window. "I mean his heart really isn't in it, being a steward. He knows what to do all right, but sometimes he goes through the motions. I expect he wishes he'd stayed on to finish his education." She gives Mary a hard look. "And he should have, don't you think?" Mary feels confused; this isn't quite what she wanted to hear. She nods. "Anyways, he's had to grow up too fast. You do realise that, don't you?" Mary nods again; she feels uncertain where this is leading, but it doesn't bode well. "The trouble is, Mary, he's not a boy anymore. He was always far too handsome for his own good; and if he didn't know it before, he certainly does now."

Mary stiffens at the implication; there's no mistaking it. She feels herself blushing and notices a pink tinge in Alice's cheeks, too. It must be something terrible to embarrass Fons' mother so much, she thinks. Her voice trembling, she asks, "How do you mean?"

Alice sighs and turns to look at her. "I mean, my dear, he's grown up to be a womaniser. I know you won't thank me for telling you, but you'd better know the truth. His mind isn't on his job because he's thinking of the girls all the time. It's a common problem on the liners. That's why Fons doesn't want to show you his letters. There's a different girl in every one."

Mary feels paralysed for a long moment; she looks away, trying to beat her feelings down before they overwhelm her. She stands. "I'm sorry...to hear that...I'd better go back now..." Fons takes her by the arm, guides her gently to the door, and walks her home. She's glad of his company, though neither speaks a word.

*   *   *

When he returns he asks his mother, "Did you have to tell her that?"

Alice looks at him. "I understand her more than you think, son. Sometimes you have to be cruel to be kind."

Fons goes back to the fire and sits for a while, waiting until he feels calm again. "Have you thought about what I said?"

Alice nods, leaves her washing, and sits by him next to the fire. "If you want to be a soldier, Fons, I'll not stop you. I don't think there'll be another war, not after this last one. Not for a long while, anyway. And soldiering is a good job in peacetime, if you like it. But if you want to see the world, you'd be better joining the British army. In

Ireland all you'll see is the Curragh; with the British, you could go anywhere. It's better paid, too."

"You wouldn't mind?"

She laughs, "I'd be a hypocrite if I did. After all, I worked for them. Look, when I was a girl, I grew up in Fermoy. It's a garrison town. We never hated them then; they were our bread and butter. There's good and bad soldiers in every army."

Fons nods. "I know, Ma. You know that time on the bridge? When I was a boy?" She turns and meets his eye. "I think one of the soldiers saved my life."

"Ah... well, I should think that makes a bit of a difference, don't you?"

He nods, feeling a weight lift off his chest.

Six months later, Fons stands statuesque, staring straight ahead without blinking. He knows he must ignore the eyes that stare into his own, three inches in front of his nose. He can smell the man's bad breath along with the pungent odour of carbolic soap.

"And where might you be from, Private?"

"County Cork, sir."

The Sergeant emits a groan expressing disgust and revulsion, and sniffs the air. He walks a slow circuit around Fons, staring down at his boots, as if expecting them to be covered in shit. "So, which particular bog did you spring from, Private Paddy?"

"Fermoy, sir." Fons knows this is probably the wrong answer, but he also knows it's usually better to reply quickly, even so.

The Sergeant bellows into Fons' left ear at close range; "Fermoy? Fermoy? You horrible, ignorant little man." He moves into view and thrusts his face up at Fons, so that the peak of his cap makes intermittent contact with Fons' eyelashes while he continues to talk. This forces Fons to blink repeatedly – though he does manage to keep his head still. "I asked you which bog you sprang from, you little fucker, and I don't mean your mother's cunt, or the name of the nearest God-forsaken town. So which bog did you spring from, you horrible little turd?" Fons frowns but stays silent. One wrong answer is permissible; two are usually a very bad move. Plus, he has no idea what the required answer is. "Shall we start with something very simple, Private? What's your name?"

"Private Gilligan, sir."

"When your sergeant asks you a question, Gilligan, you're supposed to bloody answer it, aren't you, you horrible little bog insect?"

"I am, sir."

The Sergeant groans again in disgust, shakes his head and steps away. "I am? I am? God help us, don't you speak English, Gilligan?"

"I do, sir."

The Sergeant groans again and then raps the side of Fons' head with pointed knuckles, emphasising each word, while he roars, "No you bloody don't, you horrible bog insect." After a pause for dramatic effect, he steps away and continues, "Let me demonstrate." He walks over to a man two places to Fons' right, so that Fons hears the following:

"Private McAllinden, isn't it?"

"Yes, sir."

"Can you speak English, Private McAllinden?"

"Yes, sir."

"Can you speak French?"

"No, sir."

"Are you, or are you not, a bog dweller?"

"Yes, sir."

"And which bog do you come from?"

"Ulster, sir."

After a pause, the sergeant's face reappears. "Right, Gilligan, do you catch my drift?"

"I'm not sure I do, sir."

The sergeant turns puce and then slowly nods. Fons senses that he is being studied to see if his ignorance is feigned or genuine. "It's bleeding obvious that you don't, Gilligan, so you can spend your next leave cleaning the toilet block. I'll give you one more chance, Gilligan, you little cretin, otherwise you'll be cleaning toilets till Christmas. Let me demonstrate the English language to you once again." He disappears from view, and Fons hears the following conversation with the man directly behind him:

"Private O'Rourke?"

"Yes, sir."

"Are you a bog dweller, O'Rourke?"

"No, sir."

"What are you, Private O'Rourke?"

"London Irish, sir. Camden town."

"So what are you, O'Rourke?"

"I'm slum scum, sir."

"But can you speak English, O'Rourke?"

"Yes, sir."

The sergeant's face reappears, along with his bad breath. "Right, Gilligan. Think very, very hard before you answer this. Do you speak English?"

Fons bites his tongue, forcing himself to use the affirmative in the English way; "Yes, sir."

"Hallelujah. Do you speak French?"

"I... no, sir."

"Hmmm; I think you are finally beginning to understand. You see, no matter how stupid you are, a bog hopper like you only needs three words of English; yes, no, and sir. Three types of Irish guardsmen, each needing three words; do you understand?"

"Yes, sir."

"So which bog did you spring from, Gilligan?"

"An Irish bog, sir. Ireland."

"That's right, Gilligan. You are from the God-forsaken bog, aren't you?"

"Yes, sir."

"That's correct, Gilligan, God forsaken. There are three types of Irish guards, the northern bog hoppers, the slum scum and the God-forsaken bog hoppers, who are particularly good at cleaning toilets. Now that you've learned English like the others, you and me will get on like a house on fire, won't we?"

"Yes, sir."

*   *   *

"Stand at ease...dismiss..." Fons allows himself a sigh of relief and turns to walk away from the parade ground with the others. He has taken three paces when the voice cuts through him again, "Gilligan, you horrible little man. *You* can come back here now."

Oh Christ, he thinks, what have I done now? He stops, comes to attention, stamps his foot, turns and marches back to the Sergeant in double quick time, stops and salutes. The Sergeant is grinning at him; usually, this means big trouble.

"Well, well, you horrible little bog hopper. I've spent the last four months licking you into shape, teaching you the importance of spotless hygiene in the shit-house, which by the way looks like it needs a really good clean this weekend..." The Sergeant disappears from view while he circuits Fons, inspecting his kit from every angle, "...and how do you reward me, Gilligan?"

"I don't know, sir."

"No, you really don't know, do you, Gilligan?"

"No, sir."

"Well, you horrible little bog hopper, it must be all your practice shooting the fucking horseflies in your godforsaken bog. Because for some strange reason that I cannot, for the life of me, understand, you keep hitting the bull's-eye on the shooting range, don't you?"

The memory brings a flush of pleasure to Fons' face. "I do; yes, sir."

The Sergeant frowns. "Well, lucky for you Gilligan or you'd be scrubbing those fucking toilets again." In the pause that follows, it dawns upon Fons that he is not going to be punished this time.

"You're going to escape that pleasure because you've been selected for other duties, Gilligan." The Sergeant grins wickedly, "You will report to Captain McManus at 1700 sharp, this evening. As you may or may not know, Captain McManus is in charge of the regimental shooting team. He will be putting you through your paces tomorrow to see just how well you can shoot. A word of advice, Gilligan..."

"Yes, sir?"

"Make sure you shoot well, you horrible little man, because you are representing my platoon. If you're any good, you may also be representing the regiment. You don't want to come back to cleaning toilets all day long, do you, Gilligan?" The Sergeant winks.

Fons mouth almost drops open before he recovers and salutes, "No, sir, I do not."

"On your bike, Gilligan, off you go."

* * *

Four months later, Fons sits waiting his turn on a long bench. An assortment of uniforms surrounds him; each man carries a standard issue Lee-Enfield rifle. Most look nervous - biting lips, fidgeting or glancing at the men at the front of the queue; others stare into space, affectionately stroking the rifle stock and barrel. In the distance, the crack of rifle fire holds every man's attention.

"Next..." Two men rise to their feet in unison, and exit the door.

Fons feels a nudge on his arm as he shuffles sideways along the bench. He turns to see a long, lop-sided face breaking into a grin, "First time at Bisley?"

Fons nods, glad to break the tension. "It is." He examines the other man's cap badge.

"Durham Light Infantry, Albert's the name. And you'll be Paddy, no doubt."

They shake hands. "Paddy will do, Albert." He's given up telling people his real name. They all call him Paddy, even within his own platoon. They chat for a while; though he can't concentrate, his mind too busy listening, watching the queue shrink until he and Albert are next. When his mind drifts back to what Albert is saying, he realises that Albert's giving him advice. "...don't worry too much about the time on the snap shots, it always seems longer here, it's best to make sure you get the bull every time..."

This is very bad advice; in fact, the opposite of what Captain McManus has drilled into the team. He lifts his eyes to examine Albert's face; at that moment the other man glances away, grinning to himself. Clever bastard, Fons thinks.

A voice calls from the door, "Next..."

They rise; Fons tries to keep a straight face and a neutral voice as he whispers, "Thanks for the advice. And good luck, Albert." He thinks, up yours.

He feels his heart thumping against the inside of his chest, seeming to do so ever faster while a stony-faced corporal escorts them for what seems like miles. The noise of shooting grows and then ceases just before they reach a firing trench with two shooting positions. The corporal hands them each a cloth bag containing twenty rounds. "Four rounds each target, deliberate fire, thirty seconds per target." Fons loads four rounds and lays out the rest on a sandbag next to his firing position. In the distance, a yellow flag waves. "Ready." Fons waits for what seems an age before he sees the red flag and hears, "Fire at will."

He sets his sights for three hundred yards and settles the gun into his shoulder, waiting for his first target to appear. The figure of a charging man flips up into view. Four hundred yards, he thinks, and quickly screws the sight down a notch. He swallows and blinks; his throat feels dry and his left leg is shaking. But once he begins to fire, he forgets his discomfort. Apart from the first shot, it feels good. He's already re-loaded by the time the second target pops up at one hundred yards, forcing him to re-adjust his sights carefully. It's a much smaller target, the head only, and he wants bull's-eyes, between the eyes. After that it becomes a routine; five hundred yards, three hundred and two hundred to finish. He has plenty of time to aim during this round. At the end, he shoulders the rifle and waits for the order to leave.

After another period of queuing, Fons and Albert arrive at the second firing station. The first part of round two - shooting from a standing position - is his personal weakness. He doesn't like the time limits either, come to that. "Five rounds upright, rapid fire, five hundred yards." He adjusts his sights. "Ready." The gun snuggles into his shoulder, waiting. "Fire..."

He gets three rounds off perfectly; then the bolt slips in his hand as he pushes the fourth into the chamber. A small slip, but he loses his focus on the target; he has to take deliberate aim again while time runs out, before he can shoot. One more, he thinks; come on. He gets the last shot away at the very moment the target drops out of sight. I hope that one got there in time, he thinks.

"Five rounds kneeling; snap shooting, random distances." This is the tricky one, he thinks. He reloads, sets the sights for three hundred and then goes down on one knee, resting his elbow on the other. "Ready." The gun snuggles into his shoulder. "Fire..."

The first target pops up, obligingly, at three hundred yards. He shoots and it drops away. During the long pause that follows, he sights under the range and waits. The next one pops up very close; he moves his body, lifting the rifle in one movement; the target appears in the sights. Aim below, a little bit more, he thinks; his rifle crashes. It registers, while he works the bolt - the other man's rifle is firing earlier. Albert is getting his shots away first. Hope he misses, he thinks. The next one is far away; aim high, a little more...fire. For once, his snap shooting falls into a steady rhythm; target up, find the bull, and fire just before the target drops. He's using the time well.

After that, five rapid shots from the prone position feel like a piece of cake. Normally his rapid fire feels clumsy in that position; his body making an awkward roll as he shifts onto one elbow to use the bolt action between shots. McManus has tried to get him to stay fixed on one elbow, but that doesn't work for Fons. Today, though, he's in a steady rhythm. The round finishes with five more snap shots from any firing position, which for most means prone. He gets all his shots away, much to his relief. He sighs and rubs his head.

Fons counts over a hundred soldiers taking part when the competitors sit down to a buffet lunch. Tables are separated by rank, though they all use the same mess room. The atmosphere is tense; no one speaks except to ask for food, salt and pepper. The food tastes very good; straight from the officer's mess, thinks Fons. He helps himself to sausages and potato plus a delicious creamy trifle, adding ice cream on top of it. After this, he's sharing a woodbine with another man when he sees Captain McManus approaching, a glint in his eye. He gives the cigarette away, steps forward, and salutes.

"At ease, man; we're not on the parade ground here."

"No, sir, we are not, thank the good Lord."

"Do you want to know how you are doing, Gilligan?"

"I suppose I do, sir, indeed yes I do."

McManus smiles and shakes his head, "You Irish; never use one word when you can use half a dozen, eh?"

"That would be us, alright, so it would."

"Well, you are in the silver medal position, Gilligan, going into the final round."

"Second place? Jesus, that's a pleasant surprise if I ever had one."

McManus frowns. "No, no, that's not how it works. You're not in second place. Didn't I explain this? The silver medal is awarded to the top man after the first two rounds. That's you. You've definitely got silver, whatever happens. The gold medal is then awarded to the top man after the final round. That could be you too, though it's unusual to win both. You might, if you can run fast enough. I hope you had a light lunch." Fons doesn't want to reply to the last remark; he'd forgotten that instruction. So he just shrugs.

An hour later, his stomach still feels too full. He can still taste the trifle and ice cream as he and Albert move to the starting position. "Fifteen rounds each." The corporal hands over two bags and steps back. "You must fire three rounds each from five firing stations, using any firing position. You must hit the target with each shot but you can earn extra points for speed of completion of the course. You may load your weapon only at the firing stations, not before. The watch will start on my whistle, and stop when you cross the red line beyond the final firing station. Understood?"

"Yes, Corporal." The two men glance at each other's faces.

"Make ready."

Fons plants his feet, ready to sprint, and looks down the course. A white line separating the left from the right shooter leads down a gentle slope towards a series of sandbag walls marking the firing stations. The path looks churned up, a little muddy; he'll have to be a bit careful of that. In the distance, two red flags mark the target area.

The whistle blasts; Fons runs like the wind. At the first station, he arrives just ahead of Albert, loads three rounds and flings himself down into the prone position. His breathing feels fast but under control, so he shoots rapidly, keeping his focus as he works the bolt. Albert's shots and his own seem to be almost synchronised. After his final shot he adjusts the sight, ready for the next station. Pushing himself up, he curses. Albert has fired from a kneeling position; this has gained him a couple of yards. Fons moves quicker over the ground, though, and soon overtakes him.

He arrives at station two five yards ahead of his rival. This time, Fons adopts the kneeling position too. Not so accurate; but probably a risk worth taking for the time points. His breathing feels heavier now, though; he has to take a long deep breath to steady himself. Albert seems to have no such problem; his shots crash out fractionally before Fons. Once again, Fons has to make up a few yards of ground as they race against each other and the clock. Albert lopes along, a long-legged easy style that Fons recognises, his breathing smooth and steady. He's a long distance runner, thinks Fons. He's not going to slow down. On the other hand, he's not that quick, he tells himself.

At station three, he's managed to get ahead of Albert again; he takes two deep breaths while he loads. He gets three shots away quickly and leaves with his lead just intact. But now his legs are beginning to tire and his lungs just can't suck enough air in. He can hear and feel Albert behind him, gaining ground.

He puts in a final sprint and slides, almost falls, into a kneeling position. He loads two rounds but the third slips through his fingers for a second, before he catches it and fumbles it home. He tries to sight, but has to take another couple of deep breaths to steady himself. He can't understand why Albert hasn't fired yet. His focus returns, his sights are steady. Two shots ring out almost in unison; twice, and then again a third time. They set off together, both men gritting their teeth. For a while Albert gains the lead, but Fons finds a second wind and gradually overhauls him. Albert seems to slip for a moment, and Fons feels something hit his leg. It occurs to him that Albert has either kicked or thrown some mud at him, though he can't quite believe his senses, it seems such a pointless thing to do.

He's still puzzling over this as they both arrive, gasping, at the final firing station. He kneels, empties the bag, and loads his rifle, taking four deep breaths before holding his breath and raising the rifle to sight the target. Something's wrong; he stares, uncomprehending, for a moment. A lump of mud has lodged in the sight. Damn him, he thinks, he threw that mud at my gun. Albert's rifle crashes once as Fons frantically cleans his gun sight, and then again before he can take aim. His first shot coincides with Albert's last. He hears footsteps moving away; in his desperation to keep up, he shoots his last round too quickly, and feels sure it misses the target completely. He swallows, pushes himself up and runs the last fifty yards to cross the red line.

Albert is waiting for him; Fons gives him the hard stare. The other man shrugs and grins. "All's fair in love and war, Paddy; better luck next time."

He resists the urge to punch the smile off Albert's face, though it takes a lot of effort. He suddenly feels sick, feeling the bile rising in his throat. He turns around and walks away, so that he can vomit in peace. It must be the company I keep, he thinks.

*   *   *

Eight: 1928

That familiar smell, an autumn afternoon rich with the scent of new mown hay and cow dung, unlocks an attic of memories. Staring over the fields towards a line of trees marking the stream, he sees himself straddling rocks as he catches his first fish, the other children watching. He recalls his first impressions of their house, the smallness of it; a cosy nest of safety. He stands hands on hips at the junction of road and boreen, feeling once again the hesitation of his nine year old self, how his hopes had crumbled at the door of an empty cottage. Dark times, he thinks, remembering the fat policeman. But this path had been the right road to travel, for all that.

Today, he thinks, I have some stories to tell. He can sniff turf-smoke on the wind, and shoulders the khaki kit bag again, grinning with anticipation. He has the best part of a week's leave and he's going to make damn sure he savours every moment. Approaching the cottage, he steps onto his toes and eases the bag gently down to one side of the door. Placing his ear on the door, he hears someone singing to themselves inside, a clear female voice, though he doesn't recognise the tune. He drums the door with his knuckles, rapping out the bars from the chorus of "Wild Rover".

When the door opens he has a quick glimpse of his mother's round eyes before she screams and leaps upon him, hanging off his shoulders as he swings her round and round. He remembers, *once I used to hang from her shoulders...*

"That's enough, now, put me down, put me down. Let me look at you. My God, Fons Gilligan, you get taller every day. But they've cut off your lovely dark hair. You're looking grand, though, so you are. Fit to run the length of the county."

"I should hope so, Ma, they make us do that every other day."

"I'll bet they do. Come in, come in; sit yourself down. Leave the bag there for now... tell me what it's like in London while I get you some tea."

"Well, I don't see a lot of the city, Ma. I mainly see the whitewash on the barracks walls, most of the days."

"You must have been out a few times; it's been nearly a year."

"I suppose. There was one time I got to the museum, sure; that was a wonder - all these giant statues and things from all over the world. I swear, Ma, I was walking all day and still never saw the half of it. I'd have to go back a dozen times if I'm wanting to take it all in."

"And what about some fun? Have you not been dancing and charming some young girls in your handsome uniform?" Fons feels his face blush, and shakes his head. "Why not? Sure, you've turned into a good looking man."

He feels the heat in his ears, now. "Aw, Ma, you're biased. And anyway, they don't have the same kind of dancing in London. At least, not that I know of..."

"They must have..."

Fons scratches his head and grins. "Maybe, but some of our lads will take you to other places, Ma, and you can lose all your pay awful quick that way..." Now, he watches her blush. "Mind you, I did get myself to the music hall one night. Now, that was the best night out I had. More often, I just go for a quiet drink with the lads; that suits me fine. Oh, and I did get to see the Arsenal play one Saturday too. That was an experience. I never saw so many people together at one time - and when they scored, the roar was just like a cannon."

"What about the sights?"

"Oh, the Tower and such?" She nods. "After a while you get so used to them, you don't pay much attention. Except maybe when I was standing guard at the Palace..."

"You didn't."

"I did so. It's our regiment's turn this year."

"What was it like?"

"Grand. Well, the Palace is grand, but you don't see much of it, standing like a statue for hours on end."

Alice hands him his tea, shaking her head as she inspects her son. She looks sceptical, as if she thinks he's hiding things from her. "Well, you've got your father's looks, and he had no problems with the girls, I can tell you." Fons pulls a face, but his ears prick up. "Well, I have to tell you that I found out what happened to him. I always thought he'd gone up north for work; he had relatives up there in Belfast. It turns out he had, and later he helped the Volunteers in the north during the troubles. He was braver than I thought, Fons; you must have got that off him. Then he ended up in Dublin after the Treaty; it was there he got the flu in 1921. That was what killed him. Maybe he would have turned up, otherwise. I'm sorry, Fons, sorry you'll never meet him."

Fons feels stirred up, though he's not sure why. He's never asked much about his father, preferring the idea that if his father didn't want to stay around, Fons didn't want to know him. Now he feels relieved to hear something about him, though he also has a sense of being cheated. After a long silence, he shakes his head, "I'm more sorry for him, Ma; I can't remember anything about him, so there's nothing for me to miss."

His mother moves closer and kisses the top of his head. "He would've been proud of you, anyway." She sniffs, "Lord knows, we might never have found out at all, if Sean and I hadn't met up. For that, I needed to know if I was free to marry again. So, God rest his soul, his death makes me a respectable woman again."

"I did wonder about that, Ma, when you told me your plans. I couldn't picture you as a bigamist, I surely could not." She blushes at this, looks away, and wipes a tear from her eye. He bites his lip. "So tell me about your fancy man."

"Oh, there's not much to tell. After you left I had to take Pat's letters over there, like you used to do. Sean and I started talking and that was it. He's a good man, a kind one, and he listens to me. He can talk about himself, too. That's rarer than you think, Fons. He's sweet on me, too."

"What about you, Ma?"

She blushes and nods; he can see the schoolgirl in her, at that moment. "I wouldn't marry a man I didn't care for. But it's a practical romance, too. He'll look after me, and I'll bring a woman's touch back to that farm."

Fons laughs, "I'm sure you will, Ma, God help them." They both laugh long and hard, as the tension seeps out of the room. "What news of the prodigal son, anyway?"

"Pat? We think he's coming, but he'll have to be careful. The Fitzgerald family have not forgotten or forgiven, and the other brothers are well connected. If they hear about the wedding, they'll be watching out for him. He's still a wanted man, here. We were thinking he'd better stay here with you when he arrives; I'll go to the farm."

"Is that not bad luck, before the ceremony?"

"That is an old wives tale." She winks at her son. "Sean won't be complaining, I dare say, and I reckon it would be much worse luck for Pat if he was seen at the farm. On the day itself, we'll play it by ear."

"I'll look out for him."

"I'm sure you will. And when do I get to see this uniform of yours, soldier boy?"

"I've got some pictures for you. When do I get to see your wedding dress?"

"When do I get to see your uniform?"

Fons can't stop grinning. "Maybe later..."

* * *

He takes long and careful steps into the farmyard, avoiding the dung, watching his feet. The creak of a door opening makes him look up; Mary has lost her youthful pink cheeks, but her slimmer face contrasts well with a shapely figure. She looks handsome rather than beautiful, he thinks; she also has the same look of determination, of constancy and reliability, as her mother.

He walks over and hugs her, whispering in her ear, "Hello there, sister of mine."

At this, her embrace tightens; her head drops on his shoulder in a moment of benediction. "That's true. Thanks for all your letters, Fons, they have been a great comfort. They let me see another world, but they also show me it's not a bed of roses. Come in; my mother's gone to put on her best - she saw you coming - and the lads are out in the fields."

"How are they?"

"Da has some trouble with his knees, but Michael is grand, and the two of them work well as a team. Ma's the same as ever, she's baked your favourites for you."

"I thought I could smell biscuits."

"So tell me about this medal you won. Have you brought it?"

He fishes in his pocket. "It was for the rifle shooting at a place called Bisley. The King's silver medal for marksmanship, see? It just seemed to come natural to me."

"I do see, Fons, and so do all the poor orphaned rabbits in these parts."

He grins, thinks for a second, and then places the medal into her hand. "You keep it for me, Mary. It'll be safer here, for sure. I was going to let my Ma keep it, but she's got other things on her mind right now."

For a moment, her serenity is disturbed. Her eyes dart from the medal to his face and back, while she stammers, "I couldn't... are you sure?"

"I am; it's some compensation for not being here."

She hugs him again, "You're a wonderful man, no matter what your Sergeant thinks." She breaks away, holding the medal to her chest. "And what about this wedding; what do you think?"

He shrugs, "I'm happy for her, as long as she's happy. He sounds a decent man - a steady sort of fella, the brother; not like Pat." He examines her expression, but it remains constant. "I mean, you know..."

"I know what you mean, Fons. He's been a good friend to both of us, but we both know he's got itchy feet and a character that always wants to run before it can walk."

Fons laughs, though he notes a slight change of tone in her voice. "You can still hit the nail on the head, Mary, for sure. You got him down to a tee."

"More's the pity..." To Fons' relief, she smiles. "Will he be turning up, like the bad penny he is?"

"Your guess is as good as mine; if he does, he'll be with me at the cottage, keeping his head down. Would you be wanting to see him?"

She sighs, nibbling her lip. "I'd feel worse avoiding him, than seeing him." She looks down at the floor for a second and then raises her head proudly, as a little smile breaks across her features. "You haven't heard my latest news, have you?" He waits, patiently, while she teases him with a long silence. "I've got myself a job, Fons, up in Cork. It's shop work, but it's in one of the big fancy stores. I start next week. So it's my turn to see a bit of the world; I'll be in lodgings there from next week."

Sarah Conlon hears a yelp of delight as she enters the room, just in time to witness Fons throwing her daughter up into the air.

* * *

The high-pitched whining increases as the driver shifts gears and climbs the hill; Pat pulls the front of his cap down to shade his eyes from the setting sun. He cocks his ear and frowns. "Did you know you're running on just the three cylinders?"

The driver looks at him sharply, then displays a crooked grin. "Is that what it is? Sure, I thought it was Riley's petrol, watered down."

"If that was what it was, we wouldn't be going far. That would stop you dead. Your cylinder needs fixing in the long run, but don't worry, the motor will run a while yet." They both lapse into silence. Pat feels grateful, thinking that he doesn't want to have this man know his business, just in case, and he doesn't want to lie. He reached Cork that morning on the Liverpool ferry (unofficially, thanks to a member of the crew he knows) and then asked around for a lift in the pubs by the docks. The old country, he thinks, watching the fields pass by. So peaceful now, at dusk; he thinks of the ghosts that must be wandering these parts, and shivers. I must be mad, he thinks. Well, I'd be crazy to miss my brother's wedding, too; especially when his bride has saved my skin. Half an hour later, he raps on the dashboard, and points ahead. "You'll see a big oak tree in a couple of hundred yards and then a boreen on the left; just drop me there." He listens as the engine coasts, with a faint whine of the transmission, as they slow.

"Here?"

"This is the place; well, a million thanks, and a safe road to you."

"And to you..."

He steps out of the car with a small bag, shutting the door carefully. He watches it disappear, letting his eyes adjust to the darkness. He feels a curious sensation, a pressure on his right shoulder; he rubs the spot, puzzled. Then, he realises it's a memory of tramping along, the weight of a heavy rifle slung over his shoulder. He puffs out his breath in a long sigh and shakes his head. Come on, he thinks. Closing his eyes, he sees an image of himself running, but where to? Anywhere but here, he thinks; but what I really need is a good night's sleep. Come on, he tells himself, two days, and then you can let this go again, and go back to your new life. He lifts his cap and smoothes his hair, replaces the cap, and picks up his bag.

When the silhouette of the cottage looms up out of the darkness he stops again, as more memories come flooding back. Leaving... it was all such a rush, he realises. I never had enough time to say goodbye to the old places properly, here or my father's farm. I never said goodbye to Mary at all; at least I could write to Fons. And Dublin, the school; he wonders, whatever became of O'Brien? He knows things were tough for the Republicans who fell into the hands of the Free State authorities; Kilmainham gaol for most, if they were lucky. That thought, in turn, brings back memories of a cold wet night in the rain, Brendan and Dinny sharing a cigarette. He blocks the stream of memories at this point, telling himself yes, that's the reason my life is as it is, but I need to put it out of my mind. But then, maybe that's what this trip is about for me - one last chance to say goodbye. Yes, he thinks, that will do.

He taps gently on the door and waits. Footsteps (male, he thinks) approach; the door swings open to reveal Fons - who looks puzzled for a second, then grins. "Well hello there, stranger. I see you've dyed your hair."

"A fella can't be too careful round here, in my boots."

Fons pokes his head out, scanning the night. "You can't indeed, who knows when a government badger will pass by?" He laughs; Pat feels himself enveloped in a bear hug.

"Good to see you, Fons." He slaps his friend's back and feels himself released; they both step back to inspect each other. He still looks down on Fons, but now only by an inch or two; and his own wiriness contrasts with solid muscle on a broader frame. He looks like a soldier in a way I never did, he thinks. The days of me ordering him around have long gone.

"And you, Pat. Get yourself inside. Me Ma's gone over to your family farm today, so we got the place to ourselves."

"Have we indeed?" Pat feels half disappointed, half pleased. Both Mary and Alice tend to haunt his fantasies... and another part of him knows he can say things to Fons that he can tell no one else. Fons knows him as he is, warts and all; they have no need to pretend to each other. He nods and grins, "Well, we've got a lot of catching up to do." Pat rummages in his bag as they settle by the fire; he pulls out a bottle of whiskey. "We'll have a little nightcap, Fons; one of the advantages of working on the boats."

"I'll not be refusing. How is the work now? Have you worked your way into first-class yet?"

Pat picks up a rag and drapes it over his arm. "Of course, sir; one moment, sir..." He performs a stately walk into the kitchen and returns with two cups. He pours a measure into one of them. "Would you like ice, sir?"

"I would, my good man, but *that* would be a bloody miracle in these parts."

"It would indeed, sir. In that case, we'll take it as it comes." He bows and sits down next to Fons, "Slainte." He watches Fons savour the taste. "Not bad, is it? This is the one your brigadiers will drink - cases of it, probably. But to answer your question, Fons, I'm not stewarding any more. I persuaded them to let me sing; it pays better and it's far less like hard work. For me it's fun, and it's a grand way to get to know the girls. So, I've fallen on my feet - and sometimes, these days, on someone else's sweet little feet..."

Fons shakes his head, "Christ, that's typical of you, Pat. I envy you *that*."

Pat hears the note of raw emotion in Fons' voice, but he ignores it. "What, my ability to jump out of a frying pan?"

"Ye know what I mean, with the girls." Fons shakes his head again, and shuts his eyes for a moment. "You, Pat Mahon, have the ability to land not in the fire, but in an armchair by the fire." His eyes open and lift to meet Pat's gaze. "And then, some pretty girl will come in with a plate of supper for you." A familiar wry grin slowly appears and spreads across Fons' face. "And more; whereas most of the time, I can't even get up the courage to talk to a girl."

"I'm just lucky that way, Fons. I think I just got off to a good start." And I won't be telling you about that, he thinks. "Really; you'll be fine, once you get started. Believe me."

"I hope so. God knows, I wish it would happen soon. Let's drink to that, will we?"

*   *   *

Pat dreams of his mother for the first time in years. He finds himself sitting alone on a foreign mountain, somewhere overseas with a warm climate. In the distance below him he sees a harbour full of ships; the sight of which makes him wonder what his shipmates are doing. Probably all in bars or lying in the sun, he thinks. Suddenly conscious of his own solitude, he finds himself thinking about his mother in order to invoke a comforting presence, someone whose memory comforts him. But suddenly she is not just in his mind, but sitting before him, holding his hand. Her physical presence brings him an amazing, enormous rush of relief and joy - he sits there, speechless, trying to fix this moment in his mind, only half-aware that he truly is in dreamland. He savours the moment and the feelings for as long as he can; eventually, the dream moves on, becomes a long journey working on the boat, not as a steward but as a stoker in the engine room. The ship docks in Dublin, where he is due to sing in the cathedral in his mother's honour. He plans to sing a selection of his favourite arias, accompanied by the orchestra from the liner. Peering out at the audience from behind the curtain, hoping to see his mother again, he sees Carr and his other classmates in the front row; behind them, a mass of soldiers. On one side of the hall, Republicans, on the other, British uniforms; worn by Staters, he wonders? This will be trouble...

Looking up at the white ceiling, he blinks. The light seems very bright; he must have slept in. At last, he thinks, a decent night's sleep. He rubs his eyes and sits up, looking around. Fons must be up and away. He listens to the birds singing outside. Then, he hears a light tapping on the back door. Was that what woke him? He scratches his head and shouts, "I'll be there in a minute." He pulls on his shirt and trousers, his instinct somehow telling him it will be Mary at the door.

She looks better than he remembers, regarding him calmly but with an open expression, neither hurt nor hostile. He swallows, lost for words.

"Are you going to leave me standing out here, Pat the singer?"

He can't help but laugh at her bluntness. "I am not, but forgive me, at this time in the morning I'm half asleep. Come in, Mary." He shrugs, "On the liners, I'm working until dawn sometimes."

"Well, I hear you and Fons were working hard on a whiskey bottle last night."

He laughs again, surprised but not displeased by this new Mary. "We were, but not excessively so; I'm hoping a good half of it is left. And I haven't slept so well for years." He follows her into the kitchen, noticing and remembering her warm, clean scent. "You're looking grand, Mary; the same you, but more of a woman."

"Older, you mean?"

"And wiser, maybe; more...more confident, for sure."

She turns and looks him in the eye. "Maybe on the surface - bolder, maybe, at saying what I mean. I suppose I realised there's no point in sitting there feeling sorry for myself, that I had to decide what was possible." She looks him up and down. "Well, considering the hours you keep, you don't look so bad either. And how are you keeping, Pat Mahon?"

"I'm fine..."

"Really, Pat... I mean, how are you coping with being away; away from everyone?"

He swallows, and meets her eyes. Dark, he thinks, and very determined. He shrugs, "It's hard. But it's what I have to do; there's no use in crying over spilt milk. I just have to make a new life for myself."

"I know, but do you miss the old life?"

He's taken aback by her directness; yet it also hurts, that she should need to be told. "Of course I do, Mary. I miss my family, my home, my friends, and I miss you. But I can't turn the clock back."

"You didn't miss me enough to write to me."

"I couldn't offer you anything, Mary; we had no future together."

"You decided that without asking me. I would like to have had a choice, Pat. If I had said I would come with you, what would you have done?"

He sighs; it feels like she is probing her own wound as well as his, and he wants no part of it. "I really don't know."

"What would you do now?"

The question puzzles him; for a long moment, he can't understand what she's asking, or why. Then, he suddenly realises what she means. Here she is, real and alive, here, in this room; no longer a memory of loss, no longer a ghost from his past. He sucks in a deep sigh. Welling up within him, much to his surprise, he feels his own aversion to the prospect of constriction. The feeling overwhelms the attraction he feels for her. He feels fear; a fear of constriction that he knows he could not live with. He shakes his head to himself and then meets her eyes with his own. "I'm sorry, Mary, but I don't love you, not enough to take you with me. It's gone; I'm sorry."

She nods, and he realises, that was what she expected. So much for dreams, he thinks.

* * *

He shades his eyes from the setting sun as the lorry slowly groans to a halt opposite the church, the red-faced driver next to him virtually standing on his brakes. Exchanging a knowing glance, he and Fons both climb down into the street, muttering their thanks. Fons waves the driver off, Pat grimacing and shaking his head at the grinding of the gears. "The town doesn't look like it's changed much, does it? And neither has the driving in these parts."

Fons looks up and down the street. "Not much that I can tell. One or two shops have changed hands and there's a new petrol pump down beside Murphy's. Otherwise, the old place looks just the same. I was thinking someone might have fixed up a few of the burned out houses, but not a sign of that."

"Probably there won't be any need for it. Since the soldiers left, the town's been shrinking; I'll be putting money on that."

"Did you want to go looking around?"

Pat can't help but glance back towards the bridge, and allows himself a wry grin. "We've crossed the Blackwater once today, and that's just about the only thing worth seeing. And the last time we went looking for apples, Fons, we got more than we bargained for, didn't we?" He sees a flash of surprise before Fons grins and releases a deep, throaty chuckle, a bass drumming that emanates from his abdomen. (His own laughter seems hollow and tinny, by comparison, he thinks.) "Well, where's the quietest bar in Fermoy, Fons?"

"Ah." His friend rubs his hands together, staring down at the ground while he thinks. "I reckon John Cannon's bar would be the one. It's not the smallest, but it was always used by the lads from the east side of town. No one from Mallow direction will be drinking there."

"Then lead the way to this unknown paradise, Mr Livingstone." He follows in Fons' wake up the slope, away from the river. Laughter's a great cure for the nerves, he thinks. That Sunday changed our lives, but at least we can still laugh about it. He wonders whether Fons thinks about it much, making a mental note to ask him. He watches a fat middle-aged man slowly waddling down the hill towards them, carrying a briefcase; something about him seems vaguely familiar. The man slows to a halt as Fons approaches, perhaps expecting the younger man to step aside. But Fons marches straight at the man as if he hasn't seen him, forcing the older man to step off the pavement. As he passes, Fons dips his shoulder and leans into him, barging the man half off his feet; he staggers and drops his case, issuing a wail of inarticulate surrender. Papers spill out. The fat man turns, his eyes wide and mouth open, full of fear and incomprehension; Pat recognises the face of Brother Daniel. They both stare at Fons who stands, hands on hips, a wicked grin on his face. As his own recognition dawns, the fat man raises his arms, as if to protect himself, or even in surrender, Pat cannot tell. Fons says nothing and simply stares. His face reddening, the fat man eventually lowers his arms and bends down, shuffling his papers back into the case.

Pat steps forward without a word, takes Fons' arm and leads him away. As his own shock dissipates he feels something else growing within him, as the distance grows. After fifty yards, Fons inclines his head towards a side street. Around the corner, they both lean against the wall and explode with laughter. "Jesus, Fons, what did you do that for?"

"I couldn't..." (Fons wipes tears from his face) "...honest to God, I couldn't help myself, Pat. I just saw who it was, and bang..." He bangs his fist against the wall to illustrate. "Oh good Lord, I never enjoyed a shoulder charge so much... did you see the look on the old bastard's face?"

Pat too cannot stop his own laughter; he has to force his words out between a sequence of giggles. "I did... I did..." He bends double, clutching his sides, the image of the fat man's face causing him physical pain. "He damn near... shit... himself..." He can't speak any more, other than muted soprano squeaking. After another minute of helpless silence, he sees Fons straighten up, and manages to do so himself. "Come on," is all he can trust himself to say.

Entering the pub, a couple of elderly men watch from one corner. Otherwise, the place is empty. The two of them exchange pleasantries with the landlord and sit for a while, staring at a couple of pints of stout, waiting for their involuntary grins to subside. Pat dips his finger and tastes the head. Nothing like it, he thinks.

"So much for keeping our heads down. Sorry, Pat."

"He had it coming. Bumping into someone is hardly a criminal act. And he didn't recognise me, I'm sure of that - though I think he caught on with your good self. "

"As long as he doesn't put in a bad word with Father O'Connor before tomorrow - that would be my only worry."

"He won't have any knowledge of the wedding. Even if he did, he's a coward, he'll be steering well clear of you and your family." Pat sees a look of relief cross his friend's face and taps the table. "You're a tough looking fella, now, Fons. But you did give me old heart a bit of exercise for a minute or two. Just being back here in this town makes me feel like a boy again, so it does. I didn't recognise him, I swear, he's so fat now, until you bumped him into the road. And then I near jumped out of my skin. But Jesus, it was funny after the event. You laid a ghost there, Fons."

"Let's drink to that."

"Slainte." He takes a long pull, surprised at his own thirst, before he speaks again, lowering his voice. "Mind you, I'm glad they're not getting married in Mallow. That would be Fitzgerald territory; I couldn't ever show my face there."

"Well, you're right to be careful. Will you come to the church?"

"I think I'd better not. If anyone will be looking for me, it will be at the church. My brother understands – he told me to wait back at the hall for them coming along afterward. There's a storeroom in the back; I'll wait in there and come out when Sean thinks it's safe. I'll sorry not to see it, but there you go."

Fons grins. "You will indeed. Did you know I'll be giving my mother away?"

Pat nods, ruefully. "Of course you will; I'll be sorry to miss that, Fons."

"It'll be a bit special for me."

"It will, for sure. But I'm glad the reception is in the old church hall, too. You remember the time we sneaked out the back of it, when Sister Rose dozed off?"

"I do, I do."

"Well, there's another experience that might be useful if I have to do it again tomorrow."

"Let's hope it won't come to that. Does it worry you?"

Pat sighs. "Seriously?" He watches Fons nod. "There's hardly a moment goes by when I'm not worried, Fons. I'm constantly looking over my shoulder, even on the boats. I've got false papers, but that's what they are; false. It would only take one culchie to recognise me and tip the nod to the guard. They'd come after me, for sure. And now I'm singing again, for the love of God, I'm up in front of people every night. Now, I know there's hardly a rush of Cork farmers in first class on the liners, but you never know. Some spotty little steward might recognise me. So maybe after this little trip I'll try and settle across the big water, well away from all of them."

Fons nods again and swallows, his Adam's apple bobbing. "Jesus. I hadn't really thought that much about it, Pat. You might be wise, I reckon. Keep in touch, though, I'll be coming to see you out there one day." Fons looks down at the glasses, now nearly empty. "I'll get us another."

Pat thinks to himself, I'm glad I came. I wouldn't have admitted that stuff to anyone else. It's funny how you discover things you didn't know about yourself, with friends. Yes, he thinks, I'll settle in America. Just as Fons returns with two more pints, the front door creaks. Pat glances up and sees another familiar face entering the pub; his heart sinks. He whispers to Fons, "Don't look around, but there's a fella come in that I'd rather avoid."

Fons stiffens. "Who is it?"

"No one you know. Don't worry, Fons, he's not going to turn me in. He was one of the Mallow *boys* himself...oh Christ, he's seen me."

Fons takes a pull at his pint. "Do you want to drink up?"

"We'll make this the last one, but take your time. If he comes over, play dumb; don't rile him whatever you do. And don't tell him anything about yourself, he's not a fella I'd trust with a farthing." Pat looks down and inspects his nails, tries to think of a neutral topic of conversation. A few minutes later, a shadow falls across the table. Pat glances up to see Brendan's eyes examining his own.

"Well, well. How are you, boyo?"

"Grand, Brendan; and yourself?"

"Keeping me nose clean, boyo." He glances at Fons. "Are you going to introduce me to your friend, boyo?"

Pat sighs; Fons shifts in his seat, staring up at Brendan. "I will. Fons, this is Brendan. Brendan, this is Fons, a lad I know from years back."

Brendan nods at Fons, pulls up a chair, and sets his own drink down. "I was wondering if you'd come to your brother's wedding. You have the nerve, I'll say that for you." At that moment Fons excuses himself, perhaps deliberately letting them speak in private. Brendan pulls out a cigarette and lights it without offering the packet. "Mind you, I wish you didn't have the nerve. After all, it might concern me, too."

"It wouldn't, Brendan. I would never talk about my friends, never."

Brendan nods. "Well, I'm glad I ran into you, today, boyo. I'd heard a whisper they'll be watching the church tomorrow, so if I was you, I wouldn't be going as the best man."

Pat considers his reply carefully. "I won't be at the church, Brendan, but thanks for the warning. Where did you hear this whisper?"

Brendan taps his nose. "I know a guard. He and I were in the army together." He grins, displaying yellow incisors stained with nicotine. "After you left us, boyo, I decided the game was up. So I took out some insurance. I went over to Limerick and joined the Free State army."

Typical, thinks Pat. "And Dinny?"

"He carried on the fight, all the way to Kilmainham. He might be out now, but he's not shown his face down here."

"I'll be careful, Brendan."

"You better be, boyo. Just to be sure, though, I'll help you keep an eye out for any trouble that might be going. Me and a couple of the *boys* will be outside the church hall just in case, as your insurance. If you need us to get ye out of there, just send your friend out for us."

For once, Pat feels something positive towards Brendan. I loathe the man, he thinks, but if you need someone to sort out a spot of trouble, that's when you pick him. "Thanks, Brendan."

"How did ye get down here, anyways?"

Pat's instinct still screams at him, anything but the truth. "I came down by car from Dublin with Fons. The same fella will be taking us back on Monday."

Brendan draws on his cigarette and considers this. "And after that?"

"We both work in London, Brendan. It's a good place to disappear."

Brendan nods. "So it is, so it is." He smiles, looks almost relaxed, and nods again. "One more thing, boyo?"

Pat meets his eye and sighs, "What is it, Brendan?"

"Will that girl be there tomorrow, the one you were sweet on?"

Pat knows she will be, but he shrugs. "I doubt it. She's not with me anymore, Brendan. That's been over awhile now."

He sees a flash of yellow incisors again. "That's a crying shame for you, boyo. But every cloud has a silver lining, so they say."

*   *   *

He hates waiting at the best of times - but the inside of this storeroom, with its blank whitewashed walls, reminds him far too much of a prison cell. He thinks, I should have brought myself a newspaper, or a book. He's passed some time helping set up the tables and chairs; he told the charlady that he's a protestant, so he cannot go to the church. She shook her head in sympathy for the poor devil he must be. He takes another careful look outside - nobody seems to be hanging around; not yet, at any rate, thank God. He sighs. He feels like a boy again, skipping church. And look what good that did me, he thinks. And then, it strikes him; Christ, this room even looks like the bloody pantry at St Joseph's. Then he realises, today is the first time he has been able to think about that day without feeling a surge of panic. He takes a deep breath. Here we are again, he thinks; Fons and me, years later, returning to the same old places, maybe for the last time. He looks again at the whitewashed walls; God forbid. Should I take another little walk, or sit it out?

He feels a shock as his body jerks awake, and realises he's been dozing in the chair - a sailor's catnap. The sound of heavy footsteps creaking down the small corridor outside has woken him. Pat stands up; half-expectant, half-fearful. Too heavy for Sean, he thinks. As the door opens, the first things that he sees are a large shiny black boot and a bright red uniform. He struggles to make sense of that while the panic rises in his throat; he looks up and sees an enormous black bearskin helmet duck under the entrance and rise again, revealing one of the widest grins he's ever seen. It takes him several seconds before the perception falls into place.

"Jesus, Mary, mother of God! What the devil are you doing, Fons? You scared the shit out of me in that outfit."

Fons laughs, embraces him, and slaps his back. "Sorry, Pat, I couldn't resist getting here first. It was a grand ceremony, Pat, what with her wedding dress and my uniform. You should have seen me Ma's face, it was a picture."

Pat swallows. He still feels confused, unsure how to respond. "I wish I'd been there, Fons, I'd like to have seen all the faces. Forgive me that I am not exactly jumping for joy, but the sight of a uniform is something I wanted to avoid today. At least it's not..." He stops mid-sentence, as a thought begins to take shape.

Fons, still beaming with pride, winks at him. "Your brother was a bit taken aback too. He said he wished he'd known; he would have liked to have been able to warn his friends..."

Pat swallows. "Christ, Fons, that's a *British* uniform." He reaches out and grasps his friend's arm, squeezing for emphasis. "Don't you see? All his friends were all with *the boys*, spent the best part of their youth fighting the Tans... "

Fons' smile slowly dies on his face, an awkward awareness slowly suffusing and reddening his cheeks. "Surely that's past, Pat; they know I'm Irish..."

Pat shakes his head and bites his lip. He wants to bite his tongue, but he can feel his own anger stirring. Why didn't you tell me, he thinks, you idiot? "They'll never forgive the British for what went on here, Fons. And that uniform is just exactly like a red rag to a bull, whoever is wearing it. Did you bring any other clothes with you today?"

Fons swallows and then nods. "I did so. I didn't want to risk getting food spilt on the uniform. I got a jumper and some trousers in my kitbag."

"Thank the devil for *that* foresight. Go and get them, quickly now, and get this fancy dress off your back." He sighs, allowing his friend a glimpse of a rueful smile. "The devil only knows how the bastards conquered such a great empire in those bloody monkey suits."

"They put them on good Irish lads, Pat. That's how they did it."

"Get on with you, now, I'll go and have a chat with my brother about it. By the by, did you happen to see anyone hanging around outside, when you came in?"

"I did not; it was as quiet as a graveyard out there."

He watches Fons exit, thinking, thank God that Brendan and his friends didn't witness that one; I hope they weren't at the church. But then, it's not in Brendan's interests to cause trouble, he tells himself, as he follows Fons out the door. Outside in the hall he sees women loading the tables with plates of bread, an enormous ham, potatoes, peas pudding, cheeses, butter, and dishes of homemade pickles. His brother stands on one side, looking serious, in conversation with two men. He breaks off as soon as he sees Pat and waves him over. Pat leans over his brother to embrace him, feeling the wiry hardness of him, the sweet farm smell mixed with soap and a hint of whiskey.

"Congratulations, brother of mine. You got yourself a good woman there..."

A shy grin slips across his brother's face. "That I do know, Pat; that I do know." He grasps Pat by the shoulders. "And thanks for coming, Pat. I know it wasn't easy." Pat nods and shrugs. Sean turns back to the others. "Brian, this is my brother Pat. Pat, this is Brian and Dan Murphy. They know what the score is and they'll help if need be."

The two men both nod at Pat; the older brother offers his hand first. "I was on the wrong side myself; we've had to smuggle people away, before now." He nods at his companion, "My brother, Dan." Pat shakes their hands, feeling a surge of gratitude.

"I hope I won't be needing help but God bless you, lads, for offering."

Sean slaps his back. "Mind you, brother, right now I'm more worried about your daft friend."

"Fons? I've told him to get changed. He didn't know what he was doing, Sean; he was just a kid back then. And now he's a big kid wanting to show off for his mother."

Sean looks up the heavens. "God save us, he's a bloody Irishman. Has he no sense?" He lowers his voice. "If only he'd a had the wit to mention it to me or his mother beforehand, we would've told him. As it is, if he steps outside the door half the room will follow him outside, looking for a fight. And that's just me *friends*. I hope the wrong bunch of lads doesn't hear about it, or it'll be him we'll be smuggling away." He shakes his head. "But we'll cross that bog when it rains. Come on, Pat, let's go find Da and open some of the beer."

Pat has been dreading this moment; he's already seen how much older his father looks, a man broken by hard work and grief. From what Sean has told him, the brothers do most of the work now. While Sean and Ernie have replied to his letters, his father has not. It feels to him that his father can hardly bear to look at him, crushed by the weight of his disappointment. So Pat stands on one side, watching his brothers attend to his father, noticing the pride filling his father's eyes as he embraces Sean, listening to them talk of how the house will change with a woman's touch. He feels like a ghost already, he thinks, outside of everything. At that moment, he feels an arm slip through his own and recognises her scent. He feels his face flush with his own embarrassment at the strength of his response, when she whispers in his ear, "Come on, face up."

She pulls him forward and speaks gently to his father. "Well, Da Mahon, here is your prodigal son, and you must enjoy his company while you can, because he can't stay."

A buzz of conversation continues around them, while Pat feels himself at the centre of a small bubble of silence. His father looks up first at Alice, then reluctantly at Pat, as if searching for someone he once knew. He grunts and then speaks. "Your brother has married a clever woman. The prodigal son... my Lord, that's exactly what *he* is... what *you* are. Except that, in the bible story, I suppose, Sean would be the jealous one. But here today, Pat, you and me are the jealous ones, aren't we? And why not?" His father turns back to the others and raises his glass. "To all my sons, but mainly to the one with all the good sense, especially the sense to find this woman..."

Pat raises his glass, numbly, and joins in the toast. After the shock of being spoken to so directly, he feels a little relief and then disappointment as he realises his father has turned his back on him once again. Is that all he will say? Ah well, he thinks, maybe that's for the best. His father might say much more in anger and regret it later. Pat bends down and whispers in Alice's ear, "Nice try. But go to your husband. I'll go and find your son." She meets his eye and nods.

Pat walks away from his family, only to find Brian beckoning him over. "Put your ears on you, Pat. There's a can of sour milk brewing out there, with a few unwanted guests. I think it's your soldier friend they're after; there's a fella there with a tricolour wrapped around him. But I've sent Dan out to have a quiet word."

Pat nods, "Fine, I'll better find Fons and warn him."

When he returns with Fons, most of the guests have started to fill plates with food. Dan stands waiting for them. "Someone's put the word out there's a British soldier wearing his uniform in here." He gives Fons a hard look. "I told them he's long gone but they didn't want to believe me. I wouldn't worry about most of them, but there's a couple I didn't like the look of." That'll be Brendan and his mate, Pat thinks. Brian scratches his head. "Any other day, we'd be asking the guard to move them on."

"Not today."

"Maybe we should think about getting you out of here?"

"How many are there?"

"Six or seven at the moment, but more could be coming."

Pat sighs. "We'll have to go, Fons. We'll grab a quick bite to eat and then we'll vanish out the back while the darkness is falling. Then Dan can bring the guard along to keep the peace."

Fons stares back; then nods. "I'll just say goodbye to Ma."

Pat watches him go, knowing he should say his own farewells. He doesn't, though; telling himself to be practical, he grabs his food first. Chewing on an enormous sandwich, he moves toward one of the small windows at the front of the building and peers carefully out into the growing dusk. The small grassy area in front of the hall is deserted, but two groups of men stand by the roadside, either side of the entrance. That's Brendan, he thinks, looking at the smaller group. As he watches, two more men join the other group. He moves away, cursing to himself. What on earth was Fons thinking of? What on earth am I doing here, anyway? It's not like they rolled out the red carpet, he thinks, looking at his father. He shakes his head and grabs another sandwich.

Fons, it seems to Pat ten minutes later, eats far too slowly. Maybe he's just reluctant to go, but at least he's got his bag ready. He feels a tap on his shoulder; Brian whispers, "There's a fella called

Brendan wants a word. Should I let him in?"

"Oh, Christ, I suppose so. I'll move nearer the door. Fons, wait here."

For once, Brendan looks flustered. "Listen, boyo, you'd better be on your way. Some nonsense about a British soldier, but I can't hold them much longer. I said I'd come in and see for meself; is it true, Pat?"

Pat doesn't blink. "Look around you. You know nonsense is the father of rumour, Brendan, in this town."

That yellow smile again, as he slaps Pat's arm and turns away. But as Brendan exits the door, Dan re-enters. He grasps Pat's arm and propels him towards the rear of the building, to where Fons is waiting. "I went down to look for the guard and there's no one there. It looks like he's made himself scarce. There's talk out there of another bunch of lads on their way; it could be the Fitzgerald brothers and their friends."

"Oh Christ...this is just what they wanted."

Dan nods, looks at Fons, but speaks to Pat. "Get him out *now*."

The last word is accompanied by a loud crash, followed by the sound of broken glass falling, as a brick bounces twice on the wooden floor before sliding to a stop by Dan's foot, somehow missing everyone in the hall. After a moment's pause, most of the men move toward the door, while the women move away from the windows.

Fons slaps his arm, "Come on, Pat; quickly..." and runs. Pat takes one look back at his brother, who grimaces a farewell, and follows Fons down the corridor, past the storeroom into a bare kitchen area lit by a candle. Fons pushes the window above the sink open, throws his bag out, and then squeezes himself through. Pat blows the candle out and then follows, scraping his ankle on the edge of the window. He curses quietly and hears Fons whisper, "That window's got smaller, so help me God."

Pat blinks as his eyes adjust to the darkness and looks around the enclosed yard. "So it has, Fons, but fortunately for us, so has the bloody wall." He joins his hands to receive Fons' boot, and heaves him up onto the top of the wall, his bicep giving him a sharp pain as he does so. Fons straddles the wall, drops his kitbag over and then leans back to grasp Pat by the arms. Pat puts a foot out against the wall and finds himself lifted up. From a sitting position on top of the wall, he watches as Fons drops down the other side, admiring his friend's agility. An outburst of cursing floats over the rooftop, both male and female voices. It's ruined their wedding day, he thinks, as he too drops down into the overgrown garden. A bed of nettles, he thinks, in more ways than one.

"Which way, Pat?"

"Down to the end, quietly now." As he speaks he hears another crash of glass, or crockery, behind him; he can't pick out the individual voices anymore, just a grumbling chorus of insults, rising towards a roar. Jesus wept; what's going on back there? They pick their way to the end of the ramshackle garden only to find another wall, much higher.

Fons whispers, "Didn't we go through into the next garden?"

"So we did." He remembers; there was only a wooden fence at the side, not so high, easy to climb. They feel their way to it, and find a gap where it has rotted and squeeze through. At the far side of this adjoining garden, they reach a low wooden fence. Beyond that, a road; across the road, the school playing fields, surrounded by trees, part of an adjoining wood. And more woods behind these, by the college. Perfect, he thinks. "Come on." He places his foot on the first bar of the fence and steps up onto it, only to feel a soft splintering and a cracking noise as the whole fence collapses while he falls bodily through it. As Fons picks him up, he hears a shout somewhere nearby; he can't make out the words. He dusts himself off and points across the road. "We'll run for those trees, Fons. We should get well away from here and then decide what next. Follow me."

He sets off across the road, loping in a half run, half walk. He turns to glance to his right, and then hears a shout from the other direction, "There he goes, lads..." As he reaches the trees, he turns to see Fons running after him, the kitbag across his shoulder spelling out his identity. Oh Christ, he thinks. He hears a crack, and then the echo of the pistol shot from the school buildings. The noise seems to pin him to the ground, his limbs won't move. He feels stuck in time, or rather, between times. Fons shakes him, pushes him forward. His body feels static, reluctant, resisting; but at the sound of a second shot, his limbs jerk back into action. "This way, Fons," he gasps, no longer bothering to whisper, and heads into the thickest part of the wood. He hears Fons crashing along behind him at first. After a couple of hundred yards, he stops. Where's Fons? He hears shouts behind them and someone or something rustling in the trees nearby. Funny how he is the leader again, he thinks, just like when we were boys. The noise comes closer; in the darkness, he makes out a figure staring at him. Pat keeps quiet, hoping the man is not pointing a gun.

"Is that you, Pat?" The whisper sounds like a firecracker.

"Jesus, I hope so, Fons."

"I fell over, Pat, went sprawling. I lost the kitbag. You got to help me find it."

Pat listens carefully before replying. He can hear movement, but some distance away. Nevertheless, it takes an effort not to shout at Fons. "For the love of God, Fons, they'll kill us if they catch us. Forget the bloody bag."

"It's me uniform, Pat... they'll kill me if I go back without it."

He listens again; moving this way, Pat thinks. "You can replace a uniform, Fons, but you can't replace the man that wears it. Follow me, but quietly." With that, he turns on his heels and sets off at a right angle to the way they've come, stepping slowly and carefully. He hears footsteps behind him and feels relief plus a tinge of guilt. Bloody uniform, he thinks. Good riddance. He wonders who they were after; him, or me, or the both of us? They emerge into a dark lane behind a row of terraced houses; following it, they criss-cross more back lanes, heading east. By now, they seem to be alone. Near the edge of town, Pat gestures towards a big house, and breaks the silence. "You remember that place?"

"I do, Pat, I do. Look, there's a light on, someone must be living there again."

"So there is." He stops to look, while Fons walks on ahead. "Hang on a moment, Fons. Do you see what I see?"

Silently, Fons reappears at his shoulder. Illuminated by the light from the porch, two bicycles rest against the front of the house. "We'll take the back road, shall we?"

* * *

They ride past cottages where lights glow in the windows, though they pass nothing on this road except for two men walking near Bridebridge. They both ride at a leisurely pace, wary of being thrown off by a pothole, conserving energy. Once across the river Bride the long, slow ascent takes its toll, so that they stop to catch their breath for ten minutes at the summit. Neither man speaks.

Heading across the plateau towards the valley leading to Midleton, a bright half-moon emerges behind them, allowing them to cycle flat out. The moon seems to follows them, dipping in and out of white fluffy clouds. Pat can't help but think how beautiful the scenery is, despite all the clutter in his mind. The road gently curves through partially wooded slopes, looking down on farms where the land has been cleared, gradually descending from the flat hills into the valley. When they freewheel down the final steep slope towards the Owennacurra River, silver moonlight illuminates the junctions of hills, valley and town, glinting off the bends in the river. One last look at the old country, he thinks; suddenly his bike hits a rut, jerking him back to reality.

Down in the valley they double back to cross the river, avoiding the centre of Midleton and the main road, taking the quieter route through Carrigtohill. By the time they join the main Queenstown road, even this road seems deserted. Pat watches Fons pedalling steadily ahead of him. Jesus, he thinks, what a mess; he hasn't said a word since we left Fermoy. Poor sod, probably just dawning on him what a disaster he's made of his mother's wedding. I hope Sean will forgive him. He wonders whether he should offer Fons money to help replace the uniform, or let him learn that lesson for himself.

As they cycle across Foaty Island (only the Irish would call a peninsula this, he thinks) Pat can see the outlines of the Martello tower and of Belvelly castle in the distance, across the mudflats. They seem to have been cycling for hours; his legs feel exhausted. It must be late, judging by all the quietness. So far, the roads have all been open, no sign of any guard. Maybe whatever happened in Fermoy has kept them all occupied. The moonlight dims and disappears; he turns, looks back and then shouts to Fons. They look back together; black clouds are rolling down towards the coast.

"It'll be raining soon."

"Looks like it."

"We'll get ourselves across the Belvelly Bridge, at least. We can shelter in the castle ruins. Then it's only a couple of miles into Queenstown in the morning." Fons acknowledges with a grunt. Pat re-mounts and pedals on, wondering about his friend's state of mind; time for that later, he thinks. As the dim outline of the long, hump-backed bridge appears, just discernable against the oily black of the mudflats, he feels the first spots of rain, rising to a patter by the time he turns onto the bridge. He puts his head down, bumps his way over the cobbles to the apex of the bridge, then relaxes, allowing the bike to bump its way down the slope. Nearly there, he thinks, just a short ride in the morning.

Something moves, though, in the darkness ahead; suddenly a light blinds him, playing on his face so that he instinctively brakes, shutting his eyes and hoping he can stop. He hears Fons cursing, using his boots to skid to a halt behind him. When he opens his eyes again he sees a makeshift roadblock, two men holding large torches and two others with rifles. Army, he thinks. Jesus, I hope this is routine. Deep inside, he suspects it's not.

"It's a queer time of night to be riding your bicycle, lads."

Pat adopts an easy going tone. "We're off to Queenstown but we had a couple of punctures. I'm a seaman looking for work; my friend here's a soldier like you, lads. Look at his boots."

One of the torches dips and inspects Fons' boots. Pat feels hopeful. "Let's see your papers."

They hand over their documents to a tall man wrapped in an oilskin cape. As he inspects them with his torch, Pat crosses his fingers. The man does nod, as if to imply he's happy with the papers, but he doesn't hand them back. Pat watches him walk over to one of his companions and whisper in his ear. The other man speaks in a stage whisper; "That's right, any single man under 30 to see the Captain." His heart sinks. Oh, Jesus, please. So near, yet so far.

The tall man returns. "Follow me, lads. Our captain wants a little word with ye."

They wheel their bikes a hundred yards up the road, Pat glancing casually behind only to see a soldier with a rifle bringing up the rear. They reach a long, low cottage, light glowing from tiny windows, entering a room furnished with a large table and one chair, whitewash peeling off the walls, smelling of urine. Someone's peed in the old fireplace, thinks Pat. After a short pause, the door to the next room opens and a face under a peaked cap inspects them. Pat feels an enormous shock of recognition, then a wave of panic. *He knows me, he knows who I am.*

"All right Sergeant, I'll take it from here." The Captain sits down behind the table and fishes his revolver out, placing it next to his hand. His eyes inspect both of them, and then he glances at the Sergeant. "You can wait in the kitchen, Sergeant." He nods at the pistol. "I'll be fine. Go and warm yourself by the fire." The Sergeant grins and disappears. Pat finds himself praying that he hasn't been recognised, unlikely as that seems. The Captain fishes in his hip pocket, pulls out cigarettes and matches, and lights one. He takes a pull and leans back in his chair, studying first Fons and then Pat. "So who's your friend, Mahon - another Fenian on the run?" Pat flushes, unsure how to respond. Is it worth feigning ignorance? Probably not, he admits to himself.

"He's too young for that. He's just a lad from Fermoy I've known since we were boys. Strangely enough, he's a soldier in the British army. Irish guards, isn't it, Fons?" He sees Fons come to attention out of the corner of his eye.

"Well, I often heard you could tell a man by the company he keeps; in your case, obviously not. It might have been a good cover if some culchie hadn't started a riot in Fermoy this evening." Pat ignores this, though he hears an intake of breath from Fons. "Tell me what happened at the Fitzgerald farm that night." The question seems to drop out of the air, like a boxer's blow to the kidneys; Pat struggles to understand, his mind racing. "Tell me what happened. I've got all night."

He knows all about it. After the shock of understanding, Pat takes a deep breath, trying to calm himself. Oh well, he thinks, I might as well. He swallows, his throat suddenly dry, trying to keep the panic out of his voice. "There were three of us. It was tit for tat, for the killing of our commander's parents. They'd been shot the week before on some pretext. I was told that much beforehand, though I didn't really understand what it would mean in practice. I was supposed to be the lookout. It may or may not surprise you, but I was a bloody useless soldier. I was supposed to stop anyone leaving the back door. As the other two went in the front, this young lad stepped out the back. He took one look at me and ran. I didn't shoot him; I couldn't. So I let him go, and he must have recognised me. That's how your people know I was involved."

"Go on."

"That's all there was to it for me. The other two did all the killing."

"How convenient." Pat watches the other man's expression shifting from disbelief to scepticism. "You know, I've been dreading this moment. I was stupid enough to mention I knew you, so they sent me down here to help. They knew all about your brother's wedding. You were stupid to imagine you could come back for that." He shakes his head. "I'm sorry, but what you did at that farm was vile."

He hears a cough and then hears Fons ask, "Permission to speak, sir?" The Captain nods. "I was there when he came back that night, the night of the murders." Pat winces at the word; though it's true, he thinks. "I remember him being awful upset, sir. He threw up and looked terrible, and then he told me and my mother exactly what he told you just now." That's not how I remember it, thinks Pat; but he keeps that thought to himself. "He'd been hiding out in an old cottage near where we lived, you see, Captain. I can tell you lots about him, sir, like he's a hell of a singer; but I'll be betting he was an awful lousy soldier, like he says."

For the first time, Pat sees a familiar smile cross Captain Carr's face. His old school friend looks from one face to the other, and laughs. "He's not so dumb, your culchie friend. Where've you been all this time, Mahon?"

Pat stiffens. "Out of the country, working."

"What as?"

"Anything I can turn my hand to."

Captain Carr shakes his head. "What a waste."

Pat looks up and responds without thinking. "You too, Carr; you joined the army, after all."

Carr picks up the revolver, and spins the chamber while he considers this. "Yes. I thought it was the best way to show that my family were truly Irish after it was all settled. Not that that helped my father." He rests the gun on the table, but keeps his grip on it. "And now I have to show my loyalty to my country by turning in my old school friend, who happens to be a murderer. Jesus, Mahon, it really turns out to be a shitty job, being a soldier, doesn't it?"

Pat suddenly wants to cry, all his tension released, as he thinks *it's over*. But he simply nods, blinks the tears back, and looks at the floor, wanting it to swallow him up.

Carr slowly climbs to his feet and shrugs, his posture most unmilitary. Pat hears the sudden softness in his voice before he understands the words. "Well, it turns out we're not so different, Mahon. I've just realised I'm a lousy soldier, too." Pat watches him holster his revolver and walk to the door. "Sergeant!" He turns back and puts his fingers to his lips. Pat blinks back his tears, and nods. "Send them on their way, Sergeant. They're just two idiots who drank too much at a wedding and missed their bloody bus."

*   *   *

The great mechanical beast howls out a long blast of steam, as if mourning the departing night. As the rhythmic clatter slows, he feels the carriage lurch sporadically; buildings reveal themselves, looming up out of the grey light of dawn. Moving to the door, he pulls the window down and thrusts his head out to douse himself with morning air. His head clear at last, he watches the engine hiss slowly to a halt, cloaking its arrival with clouds of steam and smoke that swirl along the empty platform. Releasing his grip on the doorway, he drops, skips briefly and then steps out in long even strides along the platform, dropping his ticket into the inspector's hand at the barrier. The other passengers emerge slowly, yawning and stretching, as if emerging from a collective chrysalis.

Fons pauses, sucking in a few deep breaths to calm his jangling nerves, when he emerges onto the silent street. The air tastes fresher here, outside the station, though not much; he sniffs burned rubber and exhaust fumes, plus a pungent aroma of stale urine drifting from the end of an alley. He sighs and watches a vendor push a laden cart of fruit towards a street corner. Another man emerges from behind a stationary lorry and half throws, half drops a bundle of newspapers in front of a boarded hut nearby; two others push carts loaded with more bundles towards him, heading into the station. A tram rounds a bend in the distance, heading in his direction. Jogging across the road, he times his movement carefully, hopping onto it as it slows for the stop. Most of the seats are empty. He flops down by a window, watching the world waken around him.

No matter how he tries to keep them out, thoughts about his uniform crowd into his head. In theory, he can replace it; but that will take time and money. He might borrow the money, he hopes, from Captain McManus. Time is another matter; the tailoring and fitting takes an age, and has to be done by the official regimental suppliers. Unless another soldier with a similar build happens to be sick or about to go on leave, he's up shit creek without a paddle. Please God, someone he knows; or he'll be scrubbing toilets for a year, if he's lucky. Maybe they'll transfer me to the Catering Corps, he thinks, ruefully. He suspects that this is quite possible. In the Guards regiments, your dress uniform is particularly precious, part of the mystique; you simply don't lose it. He sighs and stands up, weaving toward the exit while the tram corners, passes a bicycle, and gradually, jerkily decelerates. He leaps off at the next junction, just before the stop; he needs to bide his time, maybe sit and have a think in the park before heading for Wellington Barracks.

A couple of hours later, the sentry outside the regimental

headquarters colours slightly, nods at him, and moves aside. Must know me, or of me, through the shooting team, Fons assumes. He enters the building, hearing a distant chatter of typewriters, and follows a series of threadbare rugs down a familiar corridor. Pausing outside the Captain's door, he inclines his head towards it. He detects a faint scratching of pen on ink. He takes a deep breath and raps upon the door. Despite his effort to restrain himself, the result sounds deafening.

By contrast, the reply sounds neutral, muffled, and reassuringly familiar, "Come in." He opens the door, moves through as rapidly as he can, pulls it shut, and comes to attention in front of the desk. "What can... good Lord, what on earth are you doing here, Gilligan?" The Captain's tone seems to be one of extreme surprise.

This reaction puzzles him for a second, though Fons has little option but to press on. "Well, sir, I've just got back from a spot of leave, and..."

"So I understand." The interruption is delivered with a tone of dry detachment. Fons glances up to examine the Captain's facial expression and sees a hybrid of wry humour and deep concern. The latter should be reassuring; for a moment Fons wonders why the Captain knows about his leave. He swallows and looks down.

"Well you see, sir, I got myself into a spot of bother..." The Captain grunts in acknowledgement, apparently inviting him to continue, "...so, I was wondering if I might be able to ask you for some help, sir." Fons pauses to look up, hoping for an encouraging sign. What he sees this time, however, is not uplifting. The Captain's mouth has turned down, settling into a grimace as if he has toothache; his eyes are narrowed, as if he is thinking hard. His own desperation forces the next words out; too quickly, he fears. "I just need to borrow some money for a new uniform, sir. I will pay you back for sure in a couple of months..." Fons feels the shame burning across his face, hearing the pleading tone in his voice.

After a long pause, the Captain slowly shakes his head and bites his lip. Then he looks up and meets Fons' gaze with his own. The tone of voice is not unkind, perhaps even friendly, but the eyes are like steel. "Replacing your uniform is the least of your worries, Gilligan. I gather that you haven't been reading the newspapers on your way back from Ireland?"

The question shocks him, before the dread of what he does not know begins to churn in his gut. Is it to do with Pat? Have they caught him? Or worse, could it be his mother, or Sean? Surely the fighting could not have been that bad, after a wedding? He shakes his head; his mouth suddenly dry, his voice too thick, "I...I did not, sir."

"Look, if it had just been losing your uniform I would have

helped you. But it's how you lost it. You're a damned good soldier, Gilligan, and I don't want to lose you. But you've broken Queen's Regulations. I assume you were told not to wear your uniform in the Irish Free State?"

Fons swallows. "I was, sir, but this was my mother's wedding..."

The Captain's voice explodes in irritation, "Dammit, man, that's the whole point." Fons watches him take a deep breath; he shuts his own mouth firmly, grits his teeth. No excuses, he should have known that. "If you had worn it in the privacy of her home you might have got away with it. But wearing it at a wedding? Jesus wept, Gilligan; how could you be so stupid?" Fons stays silent, feeling the hot flush in his face. He blinks rapidly and swallows, trying to stop the tears forming, during a long pause. "You're young, I suppose. That's no excuse, though - and I'm afraid you will learn a hard lesson from this, Gilligan. I hope for your sake you never do anything so stupid again. You've broken Queen's Regs and you've done it in such a way that you've been splashed over all the newspapers in Ireland. That would have been bad enough - we couldn't very well have ignored that, could we?" Fons shakes his head, unable to speak. He feels as if he is eight years old again, splayed across a desk, hoping for mercy. "You might just have stayed in the regiment if that was all. But certain Irish politicians have stirred up their government. So you, Private Gilligan, have become a diplomatic incident. The Irish government is making an issue of it. And since our government remains very, very keen to keep its hands on the western treaty ports, I don't fancy your chances much at your court martial."

Fons feels his mouth falling open as he takes an involuntary step backwards. He swallows. "Court martial? What...what do you mean, sir?"

"I mean, Gilligan, that in order to appease the Irish you will almost certainly be made an example of. You are most likely facing a dishonourable discharge and probably a couple of years in a military prison too. I'm truly sorry; but from what the Colonel has already told me, I don't think there's anything I can do to prevent that."

"Jesus." The news stuns him, at first; the idea that his army career is over, that the army doesn't want him anymore. It's all he's ever wanted, and it's gone. An image of prison bars passes in front of him; he realises that he and Pat have a lot in common, once again.

The Captain's voice interrupts his thoughts, the tone sinking to a quiet whisper. "I'm going to tell you something else, off the record, Gilligan, and you can forget it as soon as you hear it. These diplomatic rows can lose their impetus after a while. If they find you in a couple of years, they may not punish you so severely. You'll never get back in the regiment, but you may spend a lot less time pacing up and down a cell. Think about your options on the way back to your barracks. Do you catch my drift?"

Fons nods, "I do, sir." He glances over his shoulder, at the door.

"Sorry to lose you. Now, officially, I'm ordering you to go and report back immediately to your barracks. That's all, Gilligan."

He looks up, meets the Captain's eyes, and salutes him. "Goodbye, sir."

"Goodbye, Gilligan". The captain shakes his head, and waves him away.

*   *   *

Fons dreams of his foster home again, of the first great feast that Ma Conlon presented to him. He smells a great plate of buttery potatoes, bacon and cabbage; the very definition of heaven to a small and hungry boy. Mary carries two plates of this divine banquet, one for him and one for Michael. Those smells rise up, invading his nose so that his self-control surrenders and he rushes to the table to pick up his knife and fork, salivating helplessly. Yet Mary withholds the food, scolding him about his dirty hands, telling him to go and wash off the muck. He forces a smile and summons enough goodwill to obey her, taking a jug of water outside to wash. But as soon as he steps out into the farmyard, the cold air hits him like a brick in the face. Instantly he feels a dull aching pain seeping deep into all his bones, his marrow seeming to turn to ice, numbness spreading through his muscles as all the heat vanishes from his body. He can literally feel his body seizing up with cold; he turns back to the door, only to discover that someone has locked him out. In desperation, he hammers on the door, but no one answers...

He groans and turns his body as the dream dissolves and recedes, abruptly feeling the harsh stabbing reality of aching bones upon the flagstones beneath him. Despite numerous blankets that he hugs around himself and a thin bed of straw, his body feels as stiff and cold as a corpse. At least the straw smells clean and dry, he thinks, but the air temperature must have plummeted overnight - he watches his breath turning to frost where it hits a shaft of light from gaps around the door. He takes a deep breath, steeling himself, then throws off the blankets and leaps to his feet, rubbing his hands and massaging his body through a grubby woollen vest and long johns. Throwing on another layer of clothes, he ventures outside and splashes his face and hands from a butt of icy rainwater. Firelight glows from the kitchen window; the farmer's wife must be up already to feed the chickens and bake the bread. Returning to the cowhouse (they call it a byre here, he reminds himself) he begins to roll his blankets into a tight cylinder using a canvas belt. He hears a cough from the doorway, and turns. The farmer, a grizzled old man in worn and patched tweeds under a dirty cap, watches him pack for a while before speaking. "Now then, lad. Ist thaa aah reet?"

Fons stops to think for a moment. These hill dialects are unlike anything he's ever heard in London. On the other hand, they don't seem to mind his Irish way of speaking, either. "I'm grand, Billy, top of the morning to yourself. I'll just be packing me bags and then I'll be on me way; unless you'll have some more jobs for me?"

Billy shakes his head, removes his cap, scratches his head, and then replaces the cap. He pulls out a pipe from his hip pocket and rummages for his tobacco. Fons sighs, and returns to his packing. "Ast thaa minded thaa way?"

Fons considers this carefully, and then guesses at the meaning of it. "Originally, I was thinking of going to Scotland. An Irishman like myself might feel more at home there. But I'd say the weather's turning a bit, so maybe not so far. What's the best direction to find work in these parts?" He turns and watches Billy tap his tobacco into place.

"Wark?" The man shakes his head, frowning. "Aah wuddent mind." The tone seems final, but after a pause he looks sideways at Fons and gives a little shrug. "Still, some greaves still givin' leed i'n't next valley north. An thaa's a good strang lad."

"Greaves?"

The farmer smiles, strikes a match, and carefully watches the flame settle and grow. "Greaves is mines, leed mines." He smiles again and winks. "Lead." He sucks on the pipe, puffing repeatedly until it catches. "Greave's an old word, lad. Hole i'n't ground, see?" Fons catches his breath; the idea does not appeal to him. Billy watches his expression and puffs a rich blast of tobacco odour over him. "Aye, it's daggy, door wark. But sometimes them greavers needs lads to help back on't farm." Fons nods his appreciation at this idea and stands up, ready to shake Billy's hand in farewell. "Anyhows, Jennie sez cum get thaa bait afore thaa gan. An tak this brass for thaa trouble. Them windows thaa fixed good an proper, lad." Billy reaches out and drops two half-crowns into Fons' hand, pats his arm, puffs out another cloud of smoke, and turns to leave. Fons stammers his thanks and follows his host, his stomach singing with anticipation.

Two hours later the long slow climb out of the valley, carrying everything he owns on his back, begins to exercise his muscles. He keeps to the centre of the narrow road, avoiding the rutted and muddy edges. Every half mile he stops to catch his breath, turning to admire the views behind him. Farther north, the way he's heading, the sky looks dark and threatening. For an hour he sees no one on the road; then a tramp passes, heading in the opposite direction, his hair and beard unkempt, matted and prematurely grey. His clothes consist of successive bundles of rags, one layer upon another. Fons stops, waiting to greet him; the man avoids his eyes and hurries past, a pungent body odour trailing in his wake. The long stride and watchful, grim expression convince Fons that this is a veteran of the Great War, unable to settle back into normal life. He's met a few like him on the road. He shivers, crossing his fingers, hoping he'll not end up like that.

Soon, the road flattens out onto the top of the moors, his journey stretching away into the distance across a desolate, empty wilderness. Long poles are driven into the roadside at intervals, like small telegraph poles, though they carry no wire. The wind whistles and moans in his ears; he can feel it biting through his clothes.

Half an hour later he passes a shepherd driving his flock in the other direction, aided by two dogs. The first flakes of snow begin to hit him as they meet. The man points at the sky ahead of Fons, "Thaa'll be plowtherin, soon, mind."

Fons lets this one pass, shrugs, and asks, "How far to the next valley?"

The man nods, looks him up and down, and speaks again. "Four or five miles; but thaa can shelter at Bollihope if thaa needs to." Fons shrugs again, unsure what he means; the shepherd points at the sky again. "A fair lashing of snow, I'd say. Best get a move on if you're gannin' right over."

Fons nods his understanding, touches his cap, and quickens his pace. His body has begun to shiver even when he's walking; the effort would normally keep him warm. Must be the wind, he thinks. The snow doesn't settle on the ground at first, though it does whip into his eyes and sting his ears, despite his cap. After a mile or so, he reaches a crest; squinting through a gathering whiteness, the road descends only to a small, unpopulated dip between two high moors. He makes out some old buildings down by a tiny stream, and what looks like winding gear. He marches on, head down, gritting his teeth, until the buildings loom closer, revealing boarded up doors and windows, land fenced off with rusted, barbed wire. The ancient and battered sign announces, "*Bollihope mine. CLOSED until further notice, by order of the Weardale Lead Mining Company. KEEP OUT.*" One small building on the opposite side of the road is accessible, its door hanging half open. He pokes his head inside but instantly recoils, smelling a mixture of smoke, animal musk and human excrement. This makeshift bothy must be what the shepherd was referring to; it seems the tramp has just spent several nights here.

The sky now begins to darken rapidly, though Fons knows it's only mid-afternoon. He munches the last of his bread in the lee of the bothy, rubbing his hands and stamping his feet until he can feel them again. Then he sets off up the hill towards the last leg of his journey. The first waves of thick snow begin to hit him well before he tops the rise. Once he does, the rising wind seems to whip the driving snow into his face with malicious glee. His shivering becomes intense again. The sheer strength of the wind ensures that the snow takes a while to settle on the ground, but once it does, Fons suddenly realises what the wooden poles are for. Without them, he wouldn't be able to see the direction of the road. He'd be lost in a dim white wilderness.

He struggles on, the wind rising until it howls across the moor, gradually realising that he is in real physical danger. The dim light, coupled with a constant blur of white motion, begin to play tricks on his eyesight. The blizzard whips the snow into a white maelstrom, so that the marker poles disappear from view almost as soon as he passes them. When darkness falls, this will be impossible, he realises; he has no torch. If he doesn't get off this moor before dark, he may never get off it. He takes a mental bearing at each pole and scrapes the ground with his heel constantly, to check that he's still on the road, trying to keep his sense of direction. Every so often he stumbles onto uneven ground which tells him he has left the road, so that he has to retrace his steps and adjust his direction of travel. As his feet begin to lose their sensations, he finds it harder to tell what surface he is walking on. His progress becomes painfully slow, snail-like. He forces himself to focus on his task, not to wander away from the road. Stumbling on, he tries to make himself count each pole that he passes; after a while he finds he has lost count and has to start again.

The wind seems to be dying down a little, or is it that he has simply stopped shivering? He's not sure; his body feels like it's floating, or falling; he feels a terrible urge to lie down, to pause and take a little rest. He turns away from the wind to wipe his eyes, and then turns back. In doing so, he suddenly realises that the road itself is sloping down ahead of him. It's almost dark, but please, God, he thinks, make this go down into the valley. He struggles on and the incline becomes steeper. He falls at one point, laughing to himself, falling into the valley at last. It seems a great joke. His laughter fades away as he stumbles on, somehow keeping to the road, searching for the next pole without success. Where is it? Has he lost the road, gone into a field? Abruptly he collides with an obstacle. It's a wall, he realises, brushing the deep snow away. For a moment he panics and then realises that if a stone wall borders the roadside, maybe that's why the poles have disappeared. He stumbles on. He can't work out whether it's dark, or not. He wants to lie down, now. Why not? Just for a minute.

Out of the snow flurries, he sees movement; a light, and a dog. It barks at him, then sniffs him and licks his hand. He recognises it, thinking, "It's Boxer, I'd know that dog anywhere. Has he come to find me? Am I back in Ireland?" A strong hand grasps his shoulder and turns him around. It's Da Conlon, though he looks different - shorter and slimmer, a younger face. The man with the light beckons to him - he doesn't understand, and stands there, floating in the snow. The man grasps his arm and half pulls, half drags him along, following a light raised in his other hand. Fons sees a building emerge out of the whirling snow, a stable of some kind; he finds himself pushed inside. A large cow turns its head curiously. Fons unhooks his pack from his shoulders and drops it on the floor. The cow lows a welcome and sniffs him. The door shuts. Fons puts his arms around the beast in the darkness, feeling its warmth, savouring the body heat that seems to glow from within the cow, his hands tingling in response, the warmth seeping into his own exhausted body. The cow shifts its position but does not move away. It lowers its head and munches a mouthful of hay, while Fons drapes himself over the animal, bathing in its body heat. He falls asleep where he stands.

Someone is shaking, then slapping, his shoulder. Reluctantly, Fons opens his eyes and sees that the man with the light has returned. He tries to concentrate on what the man is saying; something about a house, a fire. The man takes his arm again and places it over his shoulder, as if to support him. Fons manages to mumble a response, "S'all right. I'll be walking myself now." He extracts his arm and wobbles a little as the man looks him up and down.

"Suit yourself, lad; but follow close behind me." He moves toward the door; after a short pause, Fons follows him. The man sighs, reaches out to the wall, and takes a short length of rope off a rusty nail. "Tell you what, hold on to this." Fons takes hold of the rope. His fingers are still numb, so he wraps it around his hand twice. "Good lad. You're Irish, aren't you?" Fons nods. "Well, follow me, Paddy." Fons focuses on keeping his feet and counting the steps from the byre to the house - fifty-six. Not so far, he thinks, as he shuffles into an entrance porch, then through that into a large kitchen. The door shuts behind him and he looks up.

A fire blazes inside a large cast-iron range, heat glowing out of the opened door. He can feel it on his face all the way across the room. He blinks, and notices his audience. To one side of the range, a woman sits in a wooden armchair, her delicate face framed by long dark hair. She looks heavily pregnant; Madonna framed by three daughters. The youngest, sitting on her knee, sucks her thumb. The other two sit on patchwork mats on the flagstone floor, backs resting against the legs of her chair, either side of their mother. The eldest girl has dark, straight hair; the middle one reddish brown waves (like her father) while the youngest has a mop of fair curls. The mother and eldest girl dart quick glances at him, anxiously, before looking away. The youngest child stares at him, solemn and curious. But the middle child smiles at him warmly and returns his gaze; he swallows, remembers his manners, and takes off his cap. She blushes and looks away into the fire.

"This is my family, Paddy. What's your real name, anyway?"

"Paddy will do, sir; Paddy Reilly." The name pops out of his head automatically. Reilly was his mother's maiden name, he remembers.

"Call me Gilly, lad. I'm Gilbert Hardy - this is my wife, Violet. And these three terrors are Grace, Maggie and June." He points each out, in turn.

"Dad..." The two older girls echo a tone of gentle admonishment, as if used to being teased.

"Sorry I had to put you in the byre first, but I had to make sure the girls were decent." He points at the washing hanging from the beams above the range to dry, and winks. Grace looks to the heavens while Maggie blushes again. Gilly rubs his hands and takes two chairs from the scrubbed deal table in the corner, bringing them both near the fire. He catches a glance from his wife, and seats himself between Fons and the family, gesturing for Fons to take the other chair. Fons sits and bathes in the warmth, staring into the fire. "It's a good job for you, Paddy, I was out bringing the sheep down." Fons nods and rubs his hands together, feeling some sensation at last. "I lost one, see? We were looking for her, me and the dogs."

Fons feels his body beginning to shiver at last, as it rediscovers itself. He remembers his manners again. "Ah, thanks be to God that you *were* out there, Mr Hardy."

"Gilly, lad, call me Gilly."

Fons feels his feet beginning to tingle; the bones in his arms ache with sharp, sudden pains. He hugs them into his body. A thought occurs to him. "Did you find her?"

Gilly smiles, ruefully, "Nay, lad. We found you instead." He looks at the girls and winks. "Paddy can be our lost sheep tonight, eh, Maggie?" She blushes and looks away, but she can't help grinning. "And what brought you across the seas and over the moors today, then, Paddy?"

Fons realises how curious they must be, knowing how few people must pass this way. "A feller in the last valley told me there might be work over here - on the farms, or maybe in the mines. I was a farm boy in Ireland, Mr...I mean, Gilly...and I'm good with all the animals, so I am. I can shift loads like any man, and I can turn my hand to fixing things."

Gilly nods and looks at him sideways, "Can you now?" He shakes his head, and pulls a pipe out of his pocket, inspects it, and begins to clean it. "But work, over here? The only mines still going are small ones, families picking over what the companies have shut down. My father has one, and there's only one reason he makes it pay - me and my brothers working for free, before we marry." He smiles and looks across at Violet. "That is the best thing I ever did, anyhow." He looks back to Fons. "This is a poor valley, mostly tenant farmers to the church commissioners." The tone of his voice hardens. "And those buggers don't know the meaning of Christian charity. Squeeze the blood out of a stone, they would, and then serve it up as dinner."

"Is that from yourself too, Gilly?"

Gilly takes a suck out of his pipe to test it, and smiles again. "Thank the Lord, no. I rent this place, Cowburn farm, from the Bonville family. They're the only decent landlords in these parts; Violet's father used to work for Henry Bonville." He nods at the fire. "So I can afford coal. And I have some other irons in the fire." Fons is tempted to ask what, but he waits, watching Gilly ponder. "You might have wandered into the one farm that might use you. As you can see, Violet is in no condition to work right now. The girls help when they can, but I do need a bit of help around the farm; that would free me up for my other schemes. I'll give you a trial for a few days, Paddy. I can't afford to pay you proper wages, but if you prove yourself you can stay here and eat, and have a bit of pocket money over the winter. That'll be worth losing a sheep for. How does that sound?"

"At this particular moment it sounds like a grand bit of meadow, Mr Hardy."

*   *   *

By the time that first snowfall has thawed, Fons hopes that he has already proved his usefulness with the animals. He's also spent half a day fixing various leaks in the guttering. He needs somewhere to stay for the winter; and though the girls and their mother are wary of him, no one seems to resent his presence. He desperately wants to stay; it gives him a lump in his throat when he thinks about it. Why does he feel so strongly? Perhaps, he reasons, the emotional shock of leaving the army, plus the physical shock of the blizzard, have left him needing a bolt-hole.

Gilly interrupts his thoughts, calling him into the barn. Fons feels curiosity, surprise and then excitement as they haul back a tarpaulin to reveal a black Austin 7, sitting there in all its glory. It's a small box of a car, a tourer with a canvas roof, but it's still a car. "There you are, lad. That's my chariot. Five years old."

Fons strokes the bonnet, admiring the front lights. "How did you come by this, Gilly?"

Gilly grins. "I got it off old man Bonville. He bought it for his gamekeeper, Dick Peart. But Dick hated it; he was always a motorbike man. Hardly used it; it was him that told me it was sitting doing nowt in a shed. Now, I had a good bike, a Triumph. So I persuaded Bonville to let Dick swap it for my Triumph, and everyone's happy."

"Where do you go with it? Do you take the family out?"

Gilly hands him the cranking lever, "Crank her up and I'll show you."

Gilly sits behind the wheel while Fons turns the handle. Four times the engine coughs and dies, before it starts. The engine bumps and stutters, then ticks over into a steady rattle while Gilly warms it up. He notices Gilly laughing; "What's up, Gilly?"

"Get in, Paddy. You can give me a hand today."

Fons does as he's told. "Where are we going?"

"First a little tour of the dale. This is my other business, Paddy. It's why I went after the car. First we'll go and take some orders form the local shops and one or two farms. Then we'll drive north up to Newcastle for the day. You see, with my father having the mine, I can buy from the wholesalers in Newcastle. The farmers need seeds, wire and tools. As for the shops, the delivery lorries come once a week, but things get missed or forgotten. And then there's items that has to be got from a specialist shop in the city. So there's always room for an independent trader to fill the gaps and make a bit of money on the side."

They drive down into the valley to a ford; but the river's still in spate, the water far too surging and deep for the little car. Gilly shrugs and drives upstream a quarter of a mile to cross a bridge, and then back downstream to the village. In the largest shop, Gilly receives a list of items and scrutinises it. He nods; they return to the car. Fons goes around to the front of the car with the crank, only to hear the motor start by itself. He looks up in surprise to see Gilly rolling forward with laughter, hugging the steering wheel. "Get back in, Paddy. You should have seen the look on your face. I was just testing your strength, lad. Even when the battery's flat, I usually just roll it down the hill." He looks at Fons and winks. "Don't worry, Paddy, I played the same trick on Violet when we first got the car. She chased me all round the yard with that crank."

Fons feels his confusion give way to a rueful smile; the image of Violet chasing her husband makes him chuckle for the first time in weeks. It's a good sign, to be teased, he thinks. As they drive away he asks, "Gilly?"

"Yes, lad?

"How would it be that you and Violet don't have the same way of talking as all the others round here?"

"Whast thaa mean, bonny lad?" Gilly grins at his own parody and scratches the side of his head. "Well, that's mainly Violet. Her family are what we call parlour people; better-off farmers, or skilled tradesmen. In the pubs, they go in the parlour. My family are kitchen people, or were, until my dad got the mine after the company shut it. So I can speak both ways. But Violet wants the girls to speak without the Weardale twang. She's right, mind, it makes a difference."

"It certainly does, Gilly. I didn't have a clue what the lads in that shop were saying."

Gilly nods. "A professor came up here from the university collecting old words. He told me the dialect comes mainly from old English and the Old Norse language, from the Vikings. When the sheep farmers count their sheep, you know what they say?" Fons shrugs. "Yan, tan, tetherin; that's one, two, three, in Viking. Most of the lads will ask for yan or tan beers in the pubs, too."

"I'll try to remember that, when I get the chance."

Gilly looks at him and grins again. "Maybe later; what brought you to England, Paddy?"

Fons colours a little while he decides what to say. A version of the truth, but not all of it, he thinks. "I came for work. I was raised on a farm but it wasn't my own family. So I had to go looking for work and there isn't much in Ireland."

"Where are your parents?"

"My mother's alive. I never knew my father, but she's married again." After a pause, he adds, "Oh, he's a decent feller. But where I come from, if you cross the water, they don't give you such a welcome if you go back."

"Because of the Black and Tans?"

"You know about that?"

"A little; I've heard fellers talking that were in the army back then. There was some that didn't much like what they were doing over there. And others that enjoyed it, God knows why. But when did you last see your mother?"

Fons colours again. "Not so long, as it happens. And I've sent her postcards to let her know I was fine." A thought occurs to him. "Maybe I'll be writing to her, now, if I can use your address?"

"Of course you can." Fons feels a surge of relief; apparently, he's passed the test, for now. Gilly too seems satisfied with this information: at least, he doesn't ask for more.

A little further down the road, Fons dares to ask, "How long until the baby's due?"

"A couple of months," Gilly answers matter-of-factly, but his expression seems troubled.

"Are you worried?"

Gilly looks across at him, surprised, but then nods. "Yes and no. We love the girls, but Violet... well, she's not herself, afterwards. After a baby's born, I mean. It was bad, last time, it went on for months. Maybe she'll be all right this time. If not, you'll be running the farm for a while, Paddy. She does most of that when she's well; I do the heavy work and keep my businesses ticking over. So maybe you came along at the right time for us."

Later, in a Newcastle warehouse, Gilly picks out a large roll of wire and hands it to Fons to carry. "Wait a second, Gilly; how much did the feller need?"

"Two hundred and eighty yards, he said."

"I thought so. Look, it's cheaper to buy him three small rolls."

Gilly turns back, looks at the prices, and frowns with the effort while he calculates the costs. Eventually, he nods. "Did you just work that out in your head, Paddy?"

Fons grins. "I did so. I write like a snail, but numbers is a gift I have."

Gilly shakes his head. "Well, well, Paddy the abacus. Better put the big one back then, hadn't you?" It turns out to be a long day; by the time they make the deliveries, darkness has fallen. Violet has prepared them a good supper, cold ham and buttery potatoes with cabbage, which they eat with a great appetite. This place reminds me of home, he realises, as he drifts off to sleep.

Two days later, a short, slim figure appears by his side while he fixes a hinge on a chicken coop, watching him intently. "Hallo, Paddy."

"Good morning, Maggie."

"I'm sorry about your daddy, Paddy."

"What's that?"

Maggie sighs, "I heard my dad telling my mammy that your daddy died."

Fons looks up and sees a serious look of concern on her face. He swallows; to his surprise, he feels a lump in his throat. "He did, Maggie. But it was a long time ago now, and I never really knew him."

Maggie nods, chewing her lip. "Is your mummy all right?"

He considers this. "I think so, Maggie. She was fine the last time I saw her."

Maggie nods. "When are going to see her next?"

He takes a deep intake of breath, and shakes his head. This child has an uncanny knack of asking difficult questions. "Well, it's a long way across the water."

"The sea?"

"That's right. And the thing is, Maggie, between you and me, I did something stupid last time I saw her. So I need to wait a while before I go back, and let everyone forget about it. But don't you worry, she'll be fine. She's a lovely woman, like your mammy."

"Is she?" Maggie considers this carefully, and then she leans closer, her voice dropping to a whisper. "My mammy gets very sad sometimes. That's when she won't talk to anyone. It's like she's not there." Maggie bites her lip one more time, and looks at him. "That's when Grace and I have to look after June."

He nods, unsure how to respond. She turns and skips away, as if her statement is quite enough for one day.

*   *   *

"Come on girls, come and get your breakfast. Grace, Maggie, you're back to school today." Gilly shouts from the bottom of the stairs, holding a pan of porridge in one hand and stirring it with the other. He takes it to the table and ladles out three good portions. A clatter of short, quick steps precedes Maggie's arrival, followed by Grace, who prises a reluctant June from around her neck and places her in one of the chairs. She watches her father butter bread for sandwiches and then asks, "Is mum alright?" Maggie looks up from blowing on a spoonful of her porridge.

"She's worn out, Grace, that's all; just having a rest."

The back door opens and Fons enters, carrying a can of milk, fresh from the cow. At the sight of him, Maggie elbows Grace, who in turn blushes and then kicks her sister's leg under the table, before they chorus, "Good morning, Paddy."

Fons smiles and winks at them, dropping into his Irish lilt. "Top of the morning to you too, girls; and here is the milk, nice and creamy." Grace takes the milk jug first and pours generously into June's bowl; she mixes it well while Maggie helps herself.

"Did you milk the cow, Paddy?" Maggie's voice has an air of innocence, but she looks at Grace, who studiously ignores her, while she speaks.

"I did."

"Do you like milking the cow, Paddy?"

At this, Fons hears a snort of suppressed laughter from Gilly, and sees Grace give her sister a daggers look, before Gilly intervenes. "Come on girls, leave Paddy alone and eat your breakfast. Or the pair of you will be milking every morning."

"Can we have a lift today, Dad?"

"No, it's a fine morning and I've got a lot to do today. I'm taking June over to Auntie Ettie's first, while you go to school, so your mum can rest. And that's in the other direction."

The girls exchange glances; Grace shrugs. June claps her hands, looking pleased, and announces, "June go see Aunty Ettie..."

Fons sits and drinks his tea, watching the girls finish their breakfast and ready themselves for school. He can't help but compare the two families who have rescued him. They have a lot in common – it seems to him that this part of England is more like County Cork than any other part of England that he's seen. The way of life is simple, traditional, based on small tenant farms. The outer form of the religion may be different, but the various chapels and churches of the dale seem to permeate the lives of the ordinary people, just as Catholicism does in Ireland. The chapels seem to organise most of the social events, the sports and recreations. Maggie, for instance, confided that she goes to a certain Sunday school because they have the best summer outings; Gilly told him that he and Violet met at a church-sponsored dance. Plus, the families themselves; like the Conlons, the Hardy family are self-educated, aspiring, with a spirit of independence. The only difference he sees is that in Ireland, the women were at the centre of the family; the real decision-makers, as well as the heart, while the men were only the muscle. Here, it seems that Violet's problems have thrust Gilly to the heart of everything, leaving him holding his wife and children together, physically and emotionally, while he also schemes to keep the wolf from the door. He needs me to be the muscle here, Fons thinks, until Violet's well again. As the days pass, Fons feels his respect for Gilly grow.

The girls interrupt his reverie when they kiss their father goodbye. Standing at the door with her sister, Maggie steals a sly look at Fons, and asks her father, "Dad?"

"Yes, baby Margaret?"

She looks up at the sky, but then assumes an innocent expression. "Grace wanted to know if she should kiss Paddy goodbye...I think she should."

Her sister's face turns bright red; "Maggie! I never did!"

For a brief moment Gilly looks surprised; then he informs her, in a dry tone, "Ask him yourself, girls. I dare say he wouldn't mind too much."

"Dad!" Grace adopts an expression of humiliated horror, turns her back on both of them, and runs out of the door. Maggie catches Fons' eye, blows a kiss, giggles, and follows her. Gilly stands watching them, holding June in his arms and shaking his head ruefully, until he shuts the door. The screams of laughter and recrimination gradually fade.

"Women!" He looks over at Fons. "Take it as a compliment, Paddy. They wouldn't tease you if they didn't like you."

Fons gets up and puts his jacket and scarf on, ready to go. "Don't you worry, Gilly, I know that. They're sharp as needles, though, your girls. They make me feel awful slow."

"You'll get used to them. They got their brains from Violet." He speaks to June, who sits in his arms, sucking her thumb. "Come on, little one. We'll get you wrapped up and take you to your aunt." He walks towards the stairs, then stops and turns. "One other thing, Paddy..."

"Surely..."

"...after you've fed the stock, keep an eye out for Violet. Don't be away too long..."

"I won't, Gilly; she must be near her time, is she?"

Gilly nods and puffs air out of his cheeks, "Aye, that she is."

It takes Fons an hour and a half to carry extra hay down to the lower pastures, for the sheep, in three trips. Then he feeds the cow, the pig and the chickens, collects the eggs. In the house, all seems quiet. He works for a while longer in the yard and then goes in to make some tea. He sees no sign of Violet. She often stays in her room upstairs, "resting" as Gilly terms it; retreating from the world, it seems to Fons. Usually, she emerges from time to time, speaking little, but her eyes taking everything in, as if to check that the world is still there. Fons considers Gilly's words that morning, "...*keep an eye out.*" He decides that this implies more than waiting, so he shouts up the stairs, "Mrs Hardy, would you like some tea?" No response. He repeats the call, but the silence stretches into a minute, more. He sighs and mounts the stairs, reluctantly. The stairs normally mark the limit of his acceptance in the family, the privacy boundary he does not normally cross.

He knocks on the bedroom door. No answer. "Are you all right, Mrs Hardy?" Silence; Fons bites his lips, and presses the latch slowly. "I'm coming in, Mrs Hardy, just to make sure you're all right." He pushes the door open. The room is empty, everything tidy, her nightdress neatly folded on the bed. He exhales slowly, and then mutters to himself, "Well, I'll be damned." He remembers the dogs barking half an hour ago, while he was collecting the eggs. He thought nothing of it, then, but that must have been Violet on her way out, he realises. He frowns. It's winter; the ground has thawed after a series of heavy frosts, but it's still wet and muddy. She likes to walk in the summer, Gilly has told him that, but surely she can't have gone far today? He puts his thick coat on, noticing that she has only taken a light one, and goes outside to take a look. He circuits the farm, checking all the buildings, before scanning the hills and fields nearby; nothing. What would Gilly have him do? He knows the answer instantly, almost hearing Gilly's voice in his head, "*Find her.*"

He goes to the dogs and lets the bitch, Nellie, off her chain. "Where's Violet, Nellie?" Nellie's ears stand to attention as she stares at Fons. She barks twice and turns away, running across the yard towards the path up the hill, stops and looks back. Fons follows her. Climbing the hill, Fons has his doubts. Why on earth should she walk this way? Surely at this time of year she would head down the hill to the riverside walk, across the footbridge into the town? But Nellie seems determined to bring him this way, and refuses to turn back when he calls her. She has a scent of something, Fons realises. I hope to God it's Violet, he thinks. They cross the last stonewall and continue to climb a barely discernible path toward the moors. Suddenly Nellie barks; a couple of surviving grouse break cover and flap loudly away, their alarm call causing his heart to judder. He scans the edge of the moor, but sees nothing. Maybe it was the birds, after all. But Nellie continues to bark; she pauses for a moment to look at him, then turns and barks again. He follows the direction her body points.

An old quarry, he realises. Of course, that's where this path leads. He can see the top edge from here, and scans it carefully. No movement. Then, Christ have mercy, the perception hits him. That dark shape near the top is a human figure sitting on a ledge. She is perched atop a lethal drop, all for sake of a fine view down the valley. Well, that explains her wandering, he thinks. But I'd better make sure she gets down this bloody hill in one piece.

At the edge of the quarry, Fons tells Nellie to stay. The collie whines but sits obediently, as if relieved, her job done. Fons decides to make his approach obvious; he waves at the figure on the ledge several times as he walks across the quarry floor. He sees no gesture of response, though when he looks again her hands seem to have moved from her lap into a crossed position across her chest. She wears a long skirt and boots with her light coat buttoned up to her neck.

The approach to the ledge entails climbing a steep path that zigzags up to the side of the quarry face, and then a tricky traversing of the ledge itself, which narrows dangerously at three points, before widening into a central platform where Violet sits, a hundred feet above the quarry floor below. As he makes his way slowly along the ledge, Fons watches her carefully. She does not move. He speaks gently to her when he comes within earshot, "Hallo, Mrs Hardy. It's a lovely view from up here." He detects a faint nod. Encouraged, he moves nearer, wondering what to say next. Instinctively, he also sits down on the ledge, a couple of yards to one side of her. Then he blurts out, "Are... are you all right, Mrs Hardy?"

Her head jerks round, as if he has poked her with a sharp stick.

Her eyes flash, and she seems to glare at him for a long moment, before her expression changes to one of puzzlement. She blinks and shakes her head, as if awakening from a dream. "Oh...it's you."

"It is indeed, it's me, Mrs Hardy."

She forces a smile, and her voice whispers, "Call me Violet. You're Mr Reilly, aren't you?"

"I am, please call me Paddy."

"The girls have told me about you." She looks away, back to the view over the valley, and lapses into silence. After a minute, she continues. "I'm all right, Paddy. It's just sometimes I just can't move. I can't do anything, some days. I thought it might help if I came here. This is my favourite place; but I... I couldn't do anything here, either." She looks down at her stomach, and moves her arms down across her belly, cradling the child within. "She wouldn't let me."

Fons blinks, he wonders what to say. Eventually, he asks, "Are sure it's a girl?"

Violet flashes him a secretive, feminine smile, "Quite sure, Paddy. I want to call her Rose." In that moment of private revelation, Fons suddenly sees the healthy woman inside her, the one Gilly loves. This impression is short-lived. Violet looks away, moans suddenly, and leans forward, almost over the edge. Fons scrabbles to his feet, his heart lurching, trying to keep his voice calm. "We'd better get you back home, Violet."

She takes a couple of deep breaths and looks up at him. "I can't move, Paddy. It's started."

He stares at her, at her legs dangling over the edge, and catches a glimpse of fluid trickling into her boots. He gulps. Then he tells himself, it's just like the animals. I've seen them give birth often enough, and carried them to safety. "You can move, Violet, just hang on to me, and we'll move in between times. How often are your pains coming?"

She looks away and shrugs, "Now and then."

"Come on then, we can get a fair way in that time." She nods, but does not move. Fons steps behind her, reaches down, puts his wrists under her armpits, and pulls her up to her feet and away from the edge. Her upper frame feels light to the touch initially, but lifting all of her dead weight, inert, strains his muscles. Yet she does not resist, or complain. In fact, after a moment she takes a deep breath and takes up her own weight on her legs. Then, she turns to embrace him for a moment. "Gilly was right about you," she whispers.

Fons feels his cheeks burn and bites his lip. "Tell me later; now, you just keep holding tight onto my arm and take one step at a time. When you feel it's time to stop, tell me."

Together, they inch their way along the ledge, Fons leading the way. As luck would have it, a contraction occurs at the final narrow point, without warning. Violet gasps and leans forward, pulling his arm down. Fons also feels a sudden push in his back, sending his front foot sliding onto wet rock. For a moment, they seem to be tumbling over the edge together, about to go spinning into the air. But that same sliding foot slams into a raised step just as his free hand somehow grabs a dry piece of outcrop. He stiffens this arm, pulling both their bodies towards the cliff face, while his rear leg bends to drop him into a half-kneeling position, slowing and turning their momentum. She hangs over his back, almost double, for a long moment. Then he turns carefully, stands up, and holds her against the rock face. She gasps for air while she recovers. Eventually, she nods at him. He counts to thirty before he asks her to move again, steadying his own nerves. When she does move, the last part of the descent seems easy, by comparison. After a slow walk down to level ground, she has another contraction. By the time they reach the first stone wall, another. The interval seems to be shortening rapidly by the time they reach the farm. Nellie barks continuously in the yard, as if demanding a reward, while Fons half carries Violet upstairs to her room.

She clings to him when he turns to go. "Don't leave me..." It is the plea of a child, delivered in a child's voice. He loosens her hands, gently.

When he replies, he can almost hear Da Conlon in his own voice. "I'll be coming back soon, Violet. I have to go to get the midwife, as you well know; Gilly would kill me if I don't. You have a while yet, so don't you worry."

She looks hurt, but nods. As he reaches the door, she speaks again, "Wait...you won't tell Gilly, will you...about the quarry?" He examines her face; tearful, but also alive, determined.

"I won't be telling him if you don't want me to." He hurries down the stairs, puts water to heat on the range, then looks for the paper with the midwife's address, written out for him by Gilly. Then he runs to the barn and pulls a small tarpaulin away from the bicycle. It'll be fun going down the hill, he thinks, but hell coming back up.

The midwife seems like calmness personified, thank the Lord. She knows Mrs Hardy well, thank you very much, and will be along as soon as she has got ready. No, she has her own bicycle, thank you very much. He cycles back immediately, allowing himself to push the bicycle up the steepest gradient. He drops the bicycle outside the door and rushes inside.

Maggie stands by the range, bringing water to boil. "Hello, Paddy. It's OK, Grace is upstairs with mum. Do you want some tea?"

He thinks, is it that time already? It must be; after all, it's getting dark, and school must be over. He sucks air into his lungs, and sighs, "I'd love a sup of tea, baby Margaret."

She sticks out a tongue at him while he flops into a chair, feeling his body calming down at last. Let the women take over now, he tells himself.

* * *

Every couple of weeks, that winter, Fons returns to Ireland in his dreams. This time, he and Pat run down a country lane in some kind of race that will end outside Pat's school gates in Dublin; where they will each be awarded some kind of certificate. He's not sure exactly what his own certificate will be, but he does understand its importance. At first, things seem to be going smoothly - but when they stop for a short rest, Pat tells him that they're lost, and asks if he has brought the map. Fons shrugs and tells Pat he hasn't, why should he? At that very moment, they hear a shot in the distance, and start to run again. Something bad is happening. Now the other runners are chasing after them, intending to harm them; they both have to run for their lives. After a long chase, Pat draws well ahead; Fons can hear footsteps gaining on him from behind. He knows it's the other soldier from Bisley, his rival, the long distance runner, with his rifle. He begins to feel the clutch of fear at his stomach. Then, suddenly, he's back in his mother's home, watching her shut the door, and he knows that he and Pat are safe at last. He falls into bed, exhausted...

He rolls over and blinks his eyes in the early morning light, considering the dream as it recedes. This place, here, has become like a home; that is what he feels and understands, lying here at this moment. But now, the new Hardy baby is thriving, Violet is recovering, and spring has arrived. Part of him still feels reluctant to leave, but another part of him wants to see more of the world, to find out what he might be capable of. Gilly has made a great impression on him; given him the confidence that an ordinary man can make something of himself, outside of the army. As for Ireland, he's finally written home and received letters in return. His mother seemed to be overjoyed to hear from him, though she did not answer his questions about the aftermath of the wedding. Mary had also replied, telling him the evening had been a terrible disaster, but without elaboration. He would dearly love to see his mother again, but his instincts tell him not to go yet. I can't go back to Ireland without some success to offset that night, he thinks; I can't be nothing more than a fool.

He sits up and scratches his head; no point in just lying there. He swings his legs over and stands up, looking out of the window into the light of dawn. He slips his boots on and steps out into the yard in his underwear, to wash himself in a bucket of rainwater, sneaking a glance up at one of the upstairs windows. Some mornings those curtains twitch, so that he knows one of the girls is watching him, much to his (and probably their) amusement. This morning the water feels cool but not cold. The air too is almost warm, with that promise of early summer; another clear sky. Back in the small storeroom adjoining the kitchen, he folds up his bedding and the camp bed. In the kitchen, he builds up the fire in the kitchen range and fills the kettle. He can hear movement up above, already.

Gilly appears first, as usual. He goes to shave in the yard with some of the hot water; afterwards he encourages Fons to do the same, handing him the razor, shaving bowl, and strop. Thinking it may be his last chance for a while, Fons takes them. By the time he returns to the kitchen, Gilly hands him an enamel mug of tea. It's far too weak, as usual, but Fons drinks it anyway. Weak tea, he thinks; the curse of the English.

"We'll have some bacon this morning," Gilly tells him.

"It's not Sunday, Gilly."

"It's not Saturday either, but we both need a good breakfast today." He winks. "You for your journey and me to keep you company."

Fons reddens with pleasure, "Well, you have things to celebrate too."

Gilly slurps his tea while he considers this. "I suppose I do. For a start, Violet's feeling better. She's feeding Rose, but she'll be down soon." He nods to himself. "A whole lot better, in fact." He pauses, as if considering how to phrase his next statement. "I think it's the idea of us getting a smaller farm; it seems like a weight off her shoulders."

"I'm sure it is, Gilly. I don't know how she managed this place with three children. So with four to look after..."

Gilly shrugs, as if to say, that can't be changed. "It helps that Rose is an easy baby. But this is just what it was like the last time, as I recall, after June was born. Once the baby was a few months old she slowly got back to her old self. You could have stayed longer, though, Paddy. I would have found you something, there's always someone needs extra help in the summer."

"That's a real grand offer, Gilly, but I want to see what the country's like down in Kent. And they say the fruit pickers there get some decent money. Speaking of which, did you get a decent price for the stock?"

"Not bad. The lamb prices were a bit low, but I got a good price for the ewes." He stares at Fons, one eyebrow half raised, as if daring him to ask, what about my share?

Fons ignores this. By now, he knows Gilly's ways; that he will wait until the last minute, as he walks away, and then call him back. At least, he hopes so. "So, where is the new place, again?"

"It's called Chesters - a small holding above Westgate - a good solid house, on the south-facing side of the valley, with a nice kitchen garden and just enough land to feed a few livestock. I've got my eye on the shop in that village, you see; that's coming up for lease. When the girls are older they can help to run that."

"Sounds grand, I'll be terrible sorry not to see it."

Gilly looks up at him. "You'll see it, Paddy, when you come back here for the winter."

Fons opens his mouth to say no, he won't, and then shuts it again without saying anything. He feels a deep flush of embarrassment on his face. He'd assumed that, with the farm and the main flock gone, there would be no place for him; but he clearly heard the expectation in the other man's voice. He stammers, not sure what to say. "But Gilly, you won't be needing me there... now that Violet will be fine..."

Gilly fixes him with a steely glare. "You just listen to me, lad. I know you're a man who wants to make his own way, but this is not about that. This is different. You've been a part of this family for the last six months. Violet told me what happened the day Rose was born." Fons' mouth drops open, silently. "Aye, she did. Wanted to tell me herself, she did. And more credit for you, for not breathing a word of it. Plus, my girls think of you like a cousin. So don't tell me you won't be coming back, or I'll be coming after you to fetch you back myself. Understand?" Fons nods. "When you come back, I'll find you something to do, don't you worry. Here." He pushes an envelope across the table. "A little something to tide you over until you reach Kent and earn some wages. And I've put you a railway ticket as far as Darlington in there. You should be able to get a lift south from there on the Great North Road. But don't hang about in that area, there's an army base at Catterick. Too many soldiers thereabouts - someone might recognise you."

Fons blushes even redder. How on earth did Gilly guess his secret?

Gilly points at Fons' feet, "If I were you, I'd buy yourself some new footwear on your way." He winks, "I was in the army too, you know, in 1918. Recognise those bloody boots anywhere."

*   *   *

Ten: 1929-32

"Come on, Danby; just give me what's owing in dollars."

"Can't do it, Pat; it's against regulations. You signed on for four return journeys; I can't pay you off here." The assistant purser scratches his head, avoiding Pat's eyes. "The best I can do is to give you an advance on wages, half of what's owed you. Sorry, but that's all I can do. But at least if you change your mind, you can just come aboard again before we sail..." He squints up sideways at Pat, watching his reaction.

Able seamen might threaten or even attack Danby at this point, feeling that he was cheating them personally. Pat knows better; and besides, Danby's a big lump of a man. He shakes his head and sighs, "Jesus wept. The cunning bastards that run *this* company saw me coming and going, didn't they? Go on then."

As he emerges onto the deck the late afternoon sun, sinking towards its own reflection in the Hudson River, blinds him. An autumn chill in the air prompts him to remove the thick woollen sweater tied around his waist and pull it over his head. Meanwhile, a small army of stevedores replenishes supplies for the kitchen and bars; the passengers have long disembarked. Gulls wheel over his head, screaming to be fed; a cleaner tips a bucket of waste over the side. Pausing again at the top of a gangplank, he kisses his fingertips and strokes the teak railing encircling the outer deck of the liner. "Farewell, Old Reliable." Facing an uncertain future, he feels a faint twist of anxiety in his gut and adds, "You got me this far, but I'm sick of being your flunky." Thinking of one passenger in particular, he mutters "Ye fat old cow..." Being a singer had its advantages, but you couldn't risk upsetting the rich ones; they could be vicious if you didn't give them what they wanted. He shakes her image out of his head, only for it to be replaced by the man who had recognised him on the second night of this voyage. "Mahon, isn't it? We were at the same school, old chap. You were a couple of years ahead of me. In the choir, weren't you? Obviously, came in useful, didn't it..." The voice and the put-down had seemed far, far too English, though his face had been familiar. Pat had been too shocked to deny it, anyway. Now, he couldn't risk staying on the boat. Maybe you did me a favour, he thinks, whoever you were.

He turns to examine the city before him. Beyond the pink granite facades fronting the Chelsea dock, skyscrapers tower over wide streets, along which ant-like figures scurry. A good place to disappear, he thinks. He shoulders his kitbag and tucks the wooden box under his arm; he's not going anywhere without his phonograph. He heads south and east, towards the docks on the east river and the seaman's mission, where he plans to hole up for a few days and get his bearings.

At first he crosses broad avenues of flowing traffic, mingling with crowds of well-dressed workers; cheerful faces look forward to the company of wives and friends, emitting a collective low murmur of satisfaction. They seem oblivious of his presence; their mood is infectious. Next, he passes flattened areas where giant frameworks reach up to the sky, dots of men riding high above on girders, cowboys in the sky. Anything seems possible, here. But after this the streets gradually narrow and the light darkens while he walks on away from the sinking sun. Soon the streets seem to press in from all sides, not so much filled as littered with humanity, shadows of men who shuffle rather than stride, eyeing him sideways, examining his burden. Pale children stand on street corners, watchful as he passes, appealing with their eyes. The hum of traffic sounds distant here; the rattle of a nearby tram seems to shatter the silence. He begins to glance behind, whenever he crosses a street. At last, the streets widen again; the smell of the river begins to replace the acrid smells of the tenement streets, blowing the stink of poverty away. He smells baking, passes an area of shops and cheap diners, his stomach grumbling when he fails to stop. He turns a corner, emerging at last into an open square facing the river, a concrete wharf visible beyond a ramshackle collection of small warehouses. The seaman's mission looms up to his left, a run-down old building that he knows is freezing in winter; but tolerable now, in the autumn.

A group of large, thick set men cluster by the entrance, hands in pockets. One wears a black fedora, the rest are bare headed. Beyond them, planks have been nailed across the front doors. Only then does Pat notice the scorch marks above some of the windows. Looking up, he sees that part of the roof has also gone. As he approaches, the men turn to stare with a cold curiosity. He keeps his voice neutral, trying to make his Irish lilt less obvious. "When was the fire?"

The eyes look him up and down for a long moment; fedora man spits out a stream of tobacco juice, shrugs, and flashes a humourless grin. "Some time ago, sailor boy."

"Is there another mission round here?"

The men other shrug and exchange glances. One inclines his head at the man in the hat, who nods, giving him permission to reply. "Try Brooklyn - the ferry's that way."

A third voice adds, "Beat it, sailor boy. This ain't your neighbourhood no more."

Pat shrugs and walks away. Crossing a road, he glances behind him only to discover that two of the men seem to be following him. He increases his pace, keeping close to the river but avoiding the alleys and shadows. Even the river's swirling depths seem menacing now as he remembers his earlier thought; "*A perfect place to disappear.*" Ahead of him he notices a second group standing under a gaslight outside an old warehouse; short, stocky men with peaked cloth caps. Two hold long sticks. Pat stops, hesitating, his nerves jangling. Behind him, his followers do the same. He waits. As he watches, a small thin man approaches the group with caps; he seems to be welcomed and directed inside. He glances back. His followers have begun to edge closer. Pat sighs, and moves toward the men with caps. A tall man steps forward and thrusts a leaflet towards his hand, "Welcome, brother. Are you hungry?" The eyes seem curious, but not unfriendly.

Pat nods, "That I am." He takes the leaflet.

"Well, you've come to the right place. This here is Freedom Hall. We're having ourselves a meeting tonight. Free bread and soup to all comers - all you have to do is listen to our message."

"Sounds grand to me."

The man looks at Pat's bag and glances up the street. "Sailor?"

"I am."

"You'll be safe from those monkeys inside."

Pat looks back at his followers. "Who are they?"

The man chews for a second and regards him. "Just arrived?" Pat nods. "Let's just say they're the crew that run the docks here - ten per cent of everything, plus the bootlegging. Rumour has it they burnt the mission down for the real estate. You'll understand if you listen to Red Cat."

Pat wonders if he's heard right. "Who?"

The man grins, "Red Cat. Her full name's Catherine Daley, from Boston." Inside the hall, fifty or sixty men have scattered themselves sparsely among makeshift rows of chairs. At the back, smells of boiling vegetables emanate from behind a metal screen. Two large red banners dominate the stage. One shows part of a globe, with the letters IWW above, separated by stars. On the other, a ships wheel surrounds the globe and a hand reaches up, holding a hook. Pat twists his head to read, around the wheel, "Marine Workers Industrial Union." He takes a seat and settles down to wait.

The first speaker's rhetoric about the working class struggle sounds depressingly familiar, albeit a different perspective, to Pat. Almost as idealistic as the Republicans, he thinks. He begins to doze until a female voice breaks in, "So, who gives a fuck about you guys? Really, who gives a fuck about you?"

A low murmur punctures the long silence that follows, before a voice cries out, "You can care. Anytime you want, Cat." A burst of laughter erupts, echoed by other ribald cries.

The flame haired woman on the stage nods in appreciation. "You think the employers care about you? You think the ILA cares? You think those sluggers taking their ten per cent care? No, you ain't that dumb, are you? No, you aint. But *they* think you're dumb. *They* think you're so dumb you'll queue up to work, and work like a slave, and then pay the sluggers a cut for the privilege. *They* think you're so dumb you'll pay them to let them walk all over you. How dumb is that? So this is my message to you. Wise up, boys. Join the union. The only guy who gives a fuck about you is the guy working with you. That's the guy who lifts the load with you, and the other guys on the crane who stop the load from flattening you, or the guys who keep your ship afloat. You look after each other. That's just the way it works. That's the way it's always worked." The murmurs of approval grow. "So join the union. Spread the word. Get enough real union guys on the waterfront and the sluggers go home."

"Sounds like a great idea, Cat, but the last two longshoremen joined your Union, they ended up floating in the East River."

"I ain't saying it's easy; at some point there'll be fighting, but we ain't ready yet. Your problem in this city is that since prohibition, the ILA has gotten into bed with the mobs. The ten per cent men run that union now. It's rotten to the core. We all know who runs the ILA here in New York, and it ain't the boy scouts. So my advice to you longshoremen here is join us but keep your heads down, wait till we got more guys. We got close on a hundred others on this part of the waterfront now; not enough, but heading in the right direction. Those two boys in the river got pushy and tried to take on the sluggers all by themselves. Thought they were tough guys, thought if they took a lead others would follow. Well, that was dumb because Unions don't work that way. Everyone has to act together. So those boys got isolated, caught on their own, picked off. Unions work when everyone waits for the right moment to act, all together. If those boys had bided their time with the others they'd a' been alright."

After all the speeches are done, the other listeners rush to the back for a bowl of soup and a chunk of bread. Pat resists his groaning stomach and heads up onto the stage. "It's a long time since I heard someone who wasn't singing, hold an audience like that."

The woman looks up and examines him. "You Irish?" He nods. "You have to be, with a line like that; just off the boat, Irish?"

"That I am..."

"So what are you here for, Irish?"

Pat scratches his head, "Oh, a few things - a little conversation, the benefit of your local knowledge, maybe some advice about work. Right now, maybe you can keep an eye on my stuff while I grab some of that soup?"

She grins. "Long as you get me a bowl too, Irish."

While they eat, he studies her more carefully. At close quarters her hair is a darker red than it seems from a distance. A bundle of curls frame an oval face, with striking steel-grey eyes prominent above a button nose. She's not beautiful, but close-up she seems younger and far more feminine; rounded curves under those blue dungarees and tough manner. "You been doing this a while, Cat?"

"Long enough, Irish. My dad was a Union man before the war, organised the longshoremen on the west coast. They killed him in 1918; made out it was an accident. Mother brought me back to Boston hoping I'd leave it behind, but I never could."

"Who killed him?"

"Shit, don't you know anything, Irish?"

"I only just arrived, Red."

She bites her lip and looks at him, sideways. "I suppose you did. Well, Irish, here's a bit of potted American history. If you're a Union man it sticks a bull's-eye on your head. If the government don't lock you up, or the law don't shoot you, then the bosses' hired thugs will break your bones." Pat almost flinches, wondering which of these befell her father; he resists the urge to ask and simply nods. "You jump ship, Irish?"

"In a way; I was a singer on the liners. I thought I'd try my luck ashore."

"What do you sing?"

"Opera, mainly, plus traditional songs; you know the Irish, the old favourites."

"Jeez. Not much call for that onshore, Irish. Jazz is the stuff here."

"I'm good with machines. I could fix engines, sure, with a bit of experience. I always liked to hang around the engine room and watch the boys work."

"But I guess from that you ain't got no experience yet? Jeez, you don't need advice, you need a miracle." She looks at his gear. "What's in the box?"

"Enrico Caruso, in a manner of speaking."

She grins, "I hope so, Irish, since he's been dead a while now. What's your name, anyways? Your real name?"

Pat laughs, shaking his head. "You aint so dumb yourself. Call me Pat... that'll do."

"You been a Republican, Pat? In Ireland?" Her eyes are wide, concerned pools.

"I might have been once, Red Cat."

She nods, "Maybe you should come back up to Boston with me. There's a bunch of Irish boys who all look after their own, up there."

He looks at her face and sees that she's not joking.

"That's a grand offer, but I left all that behind me. I want to see what I can do here, first. If I get stuck, I could always come find you."

"Maybe you could, at that. I'm not hard to find."

Staring at the sudden softness in her face, Pat feels a surge of desire. "Is there anywhere we could get a drink round here?"

"Jeez, Irish, you are just off the boat." He stares at her, puzzled, until she mouths the word at him, silently - *prohibition.* "I know a few speakeasies in Boston. Not round here. I wouldn't exactly be welcome in this part of town."

He slaps his forehead with his palm, but then taps his nose. "There's one good thing about just being off a boat, Cat."

"What's that?"

"I took a bottle of good Irish whisky off that liner, in my kitbag."

"You're kidding me."

"I'm not."

"In that case, Pat, I'll take you back where I'm staying. If you can stand the idea, that is."

"Oh, I can stand that one all right. I might even sing for you."

She leans over, and whispers in his ear. "I was thinking more of a duet, sailor boy."

* * *

He wakes early, disturbed by the sound of deliveries in the street below. He listens to her breathing for a while, reluctant to move in the cramped, creaky bed; her rounded softness reminds him of what might have been, with Mary. Between the whiskey and their duet, it had been quite a night; he drifts back to sleep, resting against her back. When next he opens his eyes, she's turned to face him, watching intently. "Rise and shine, sailor boy," she whispers.

He examines her eyes; in the morning light, flecks of pale blue mix with grey. "At this time of the morning, I can rise all right, but shining might be a different matter." He reaches down to stroke her hips, more in hope than expectation.

She nods and blushes, "No sense in rushing, I guess." Her hand moves to his waist. "I can do the shining, if you do the rising." She pulls him closer, her lips kissing his neck, sending a shudder of desire through him, while her leg slips across his hip.

Afterwards, he drifts back into sleep again, waking only when she presents him with a cup of coffee, standing above him in her dungarees. He sits up. "Thanks for everything, acushla. You're a cut above the average woman."

"I'm different, is what you mean. I ain't no bible thumper like most of your Irish girls."

"It's not just that..."

"You mean I ain't no shrinking violet? I know what I like, and I ain't afraid to have it." She laughs and sips her coffee. "You may like it now, but after a couple of days most men can't handle it. First they tell me I'm not ladylike and later they're out the door because I'm too much of a whore. So if you do come up to Boston, you better think about that." Her voice is harsh, but Pat sees a softer look in those eyes.

"I'll give it some thought, Catherine Daley."

She goes over to the window, staring out at the street below, apparently deep in thought while she drinks. "It goes with the territory. You really believe in the class struggle, you realise the bible just keeps people in their place. So you gotta ditch all that nonsense. Marriage too, that's just to keep the woman in her place. You realise you got one life, and you gotta do something with it. You got one life and you realise it don't last forever, especially in this line of work. So you might as well enjoy it."

"I wouldn't argue with any of that. But I don't have your courage, Cat. I realised that a long time ago. I'm no good at sticking my head above the parapet."

She turns and looks at him. "At least you don't kid yourself. But promise me one thing. When you get yourself a job, join the union."

"I will, surely. Got any other ideas for me?"

She scratches her head. "Not in this city. No call for your kind of singing except on the liners. Other jobs; well, don't bother with the waterfront, those jobs are all sewn up. You have to know people."

"So where should I start?"

"Look, I'll ask Johny if you can use this room for a couple of days. Johny Lewis, he runs the union here, this is his apartment. You can ask him about work." She turns away, staring out of the window; then adds, in a doubtful tone, "Tell you what, I know a guy who might know someone. He's Italian and he likes opera, so maybe if there's anything, he'll know about it. Freddy Manzini; he also fixes small boats, but he's strictly a one-man operation. You'll probably find him down on the quayside at the tip of lower Manhattan, among the boats there. He might just know someone."

"Would he be a Union man too?"

She laughs, "No, not at all." She looks embarrassed. "He's useful, though. He knows a lot of people. Fixes up all kind of boats, tells me things."

"An old flame?"

She smiles, shakes her head, and drains her cup. "Once upon a time; he's taken now, anyhow." Pat raises his eyebrows but doesn't comment. "Look, Irish, I gotta catch my train back to Boston. You'd better get dressed." She leans across him, her lips brushing his with a light, teasing farewell; she strides to the door, where she gives him one last grin. "Remember what I said, now..." As the door closes, he feels an urge to go after her. On the liners he used women for their bodies. The possibility of something more never seemed realistic. Onshore that will change, he realises. Things could be more lasting. Though perhaps not wise, he reflects, to chase a human whirlwind.

Later that day, every dock that he passes seems to have its own minders. Usually a couple of men stand by each entrance, checking every person going in and out. On the larger docks a black car sits nearby, filled with muscular men. So as Pat walks along the waterfront, he quietly sings to himself to keep his mood upbeat. He's prepared himself for this task by listening to Caruso, trying to absorb the voice of his hero and let the spirit of the man fill his senses, imagining himself as the great man entering the stage.

At dock 109, two men in sharp suits step across his path at the entrance to the dock. "Can we help? What's your business here, sir?" Their manner is firm, but polite. A result of all the rich guys with private boats on this pier, Pat thinks. He forces a smile.

"I'm hoping to see a man about some opera. His name's Freddy Manzini." He lifts his arms to demonstrate that he's not hiding anything.

One gives him a curious look; the other nods and points, "Sure, buddy. You'll find Freddy on that pier at the far end, working on a launch."

Pat strolls on, taking his time, until he reaches a boat whose engine hatches sit wide open. He hears muffled hammering from inside. The deserted foredeck consists of highly polished wood, its new brass rails gleaming. Pat stands, waiting patiently, whistling to himself. After a while, a balding head emerges, glances around quickly, and disappears. Pat hears grunting, and then muted curses. The face reappears, briefly glowers at him, and vanishes again. Pat scratches his head. Things are not going as he'd hoped, but what the hell. He remembers a night in Ireland, the first time he heard this song. He stands tall and shuts his eyes, thinking himself into the part, and opens his mouth. His voice hits the first note perfectly, and he holds it a moment too long, announcing his presence. Then he moves into the song, his voice rolling across the water, carrying a great wave of astonishment, of wonder, at a woman unlike any other... "*Donna non vidi mai...*"

As his voice rises further, in homage to her beauty, the head pops up again, an expression of puzzlement slowly dissolving into a rueful smile. Pat's voice, meanwhile, rolls out the rich Italian lyrics, caressing the words of the aria, telling how the very name of this woman caresses his soul. His voice, unaccompanied, stays true and rises through the final verse, building slowly to a soaring climax as he begs that such sweet thoughts should never end. When he stops, a solitary cheer erupts from somewhere in the distance. He opens his eyes, and the bald-headed man speaks. "You got my attention, Enrico. I take it you like to sing."

"I've always had a song in me, sure. Are you Mr Manzini?" The stocky, swarthy man nods. "After crossing the water, Mr Manzini, I could do with some help to find work."

"Work?" the man snorts. "When I first saw you up there, I thought you was some kind of shake-down. Well, not so far off."

Pat shrugs. "Red Cat told me you might help."

"Did she now? You been misinformed." The scowl returns, perhaps a reaction to her name, Pat thinks.

He holds up his hands as if in surrender. "Look, I just want advice. I just got off the boat; advice about New York, about opera, about how I can find work."

Manzini turns away; he sighs, and turns back. "How is she?"

Pat sees the longing in his face. "She's good; she sends her best."

"Does she now?" Manzini chews his lip. "Look, feller, I run an amateur opera company. That's all. Only the rich pay for opera here. That's another world entirely. You gotta be trained at one of the fancy music schools. As for the entertainment business, the speak easies all want nigger music. And as for work in general, this city's a bitch. What d'ya do, apart from sing?"

"I'm good with machines, with engines. Maybe I can give you a hand with that." Pat points into the boat.

Manzini laughs, his voice incredulous, "You know marine engines?"

Pat resists the urge to be too truthful. "I've worked on ships, mainly steam liners, but I spent a lot of time in those engine rooms. And I read a lot about other types of engine."

The eyes dart up and down, taking in his appearance. "You read, do you? Your hands don't exactly look like an engineer's." He glances back down into the boat. "Shit, you know anything about diesel engines?"

"A little." Pat adds, grudgingly, "Mostly stuff I've read."

"Well, this little baby's misbehaving. Trouble is most of my customers have gas engines. Small boats here, they don't want economy, they want speed. Mostly, they want to impress the girls and out-run other boats, if ya know what I mean. So diesels, I hate, they ain't so familiar. I'll make you a deal. You fix this baby for me, I'll help you. Meanwhile, I'm gonna go eat." Pat watches him clamber up to the pier. He unbuttons his boiler suit, hands it to Pat, points at a bucket of dirty rags, and walks away.

"Got any kerosene?"

"With the tools, down below."

Six hours later, the engine splutters, coughs twice, and dies. Freddy Manzini shakes his head in exasperation. Pat bites his lip and crosses his fingers. "Give that glowplug more time. Give it a good long burst. I'll put a bit more kerosene into the mix for the governor."

Freddy grunts, "Not too much, don't blow her, this baby's expensive."

Pat frowns. The torch is so dim, so he can't see how much is going in anyway. He stops, adds a bit more, wipes his brow, clips the cover back on, and moves away. "Ready." The engine splutters, coughs, makes three enormous bangs, shaking the boat and giving Pat a momentary urge to pee. It coughs again, fires, stutters, gives one almighty shake and then fires again, starting to turn over erratically, the whole boat shuddering.

"One cylinder." They both listen, hoping. More coughing, a second loud bang, and the engine runs faster, with less juddering. "Two."

"Two and a half, maybe."

"Throttle it up a little."

The engine responds slowly but surely and then bursts into life with a roar, settling into a deep throbbing hum. Freddy whoops and slaps Pat on the back so hard it hurts. "Fantastic. Now you can call me Freddy; I will call you Ricky. You sing like Enrico, and you make this boat sing too."

"Luck of the Irish."

"I watched you work. Slow, but you got method. Anyhow you can come home with me, clean up, eat with us tonight, and we'll talk. Meet my family. My wife, she sings soprano in our group." He grins. "You should sing her that song, she'll be tickled pink. We need a good tenor."

After the night before and this, the most testing of days, the evening that follows feels even more extraordinary to Pat; dream-like, events upon a stage. His fatigue, the alien environment and his own feeling of dislocation overwhelm him. The district of Little Italy seems like a pantomime scene, filled with larger than life characters. The smell of authentic Italian food in the Manzini apartment ushers in a family drama; while he inhales the aroma, a dutiful son and daughter, aged about 7 and 9 years old, politely greet their father in Italian. Somehow, he expects Freddy's wife to be made in the same image as the man himself; a short stocky mama. So when a beautiful, slim young woman with black hair appears, he assumes this is another daughter. "My wife, Paula." Pat's surprise literally takes his breath and his speech away. He offers a hand, unsure if even this is appropriate, while Freddy makes elaborate, slightly grandiose gestures at him from behind his wife, confusing Pat completely. She stares back at him curiously, a half smile indicating her amusement at his shyness. Freddy slaps his shoulder, leans across and whispers in his ear, "Sing, maestro."

Comedy, again; somewhat thrown, Pat obeys. But now his singing is not his best, perhaps because he is far too distracted by the high colour and dimples in Paula's blushing face. The scene becomes even more unreal as a neighbour starts up a terrific banging on the wall, only for Freddy to retaliate, shouting that the man is a philistine, ordering Pat to continue...

Later, the meal tastes wonderful; but Pat has never eaten spaghetti before, so that his efforts cause much embarrassment and great hilarity for the children. He accepts this with good grace, even hamming it up a little, conscious of Paula's eyes upon him, hoping this won't offend her. After the meal, Freddy takes him on one side and offers him work as an apprentice engineer. Relief floods through him; he finally relaxes while he walks back through the darkened streets to his borrowed room. When he wakes the next morning, he pinches himself to make sure that he's not dreaming.

* * *

On the deck of the great liner, the chorus sings the drinking song from La Traviata. The heavy sea rises and falls in regular musical swells, the bows lifting and falling along with the massed voices of the chorus. At the end of each verse, the ship cuts downward into the waves just as the chorus knock their pewter jugs together. By the end of the song, Pat realises that he has been singing, drinking and toasting with Fons, who slaps him on the back and then gestures for Pat to follow. Fons leads Pat down into the ship, descending into a deep, dark well by means of a rope ladder, holding a large flaming torch. They enter a long passage leading to the engine rooms, where Fons has some kind of surprise in store for him. Pat has seen the great steam engines, the mighty cylinders and giant pistons driving this ship many times, but he feigns ignorance to please Fons. His friend winks, and tells him to follow into the coal storage hold. Much to Pat's surprise, the hold contains no coal; only a herd of cows. All this time, Fons has been tending them, deep in the bowels of the ship...

Footsteps clatter in the room above his own. Pat groans, yawns, and opens his eyes, shaking the images of the dream from his head. He must write to Fons, he thinks, now that he feels settled here. Only six months, yet he feels at home, enjoying his new routine. Six days a week working, tinkering with engines of all types; he's fallen on his feet all right. For most men here, work of any kind is difficult to come by. Sundays, like today, he spends resting and singing. From the quiet outside, he knows it's still early. He rolls over and shuts his eyes. Lying in his bed, his thoughts inevitably turn to Freddy's wife, remembering their first meeting. She must have thought him such a fool. He thinks about Paula far too much, but he can't help himself. Does she still laugh at his dumb clumsiness? Or perhaps the song he'd sung to her at Freddy's insistence was one of her favourites, because that evening seems to have had some effect on her, too. He feels sure that she reacts to him, ever since. Was his singing so awful, that night? Or was she embarrassed by the meaning of the song, from a stranger? She seems to avoid meeting his eyes, her colour intensifies; she seems flustered, distracted. The real problem is he can't stop thinking about *her*.

She must have been half Freddy's age, when they married, he thinks. And now, even more galling, Freddy seems to take her for granted. He never talks about her, except in domestic terms, as a cook or as the person who mends his clothes. He never mentions her beauty, her talents for singing and dressmaking (her clothes are modelled on the latest fashions) or her sharp wit. Freddy's no slouch, but when the headlines had screamed about the Wall Street crash, shortly after his arrival, it was Paula who had explained what it would mean, correctly predicting later events to him and Freddy. Another thing Pat suspects; Freddy's involvement with Red Cat must have happened after he was married, not before, judging by the ages of the children. He remembers how each of them had seemed embarrassed at the mention of the other's name. How on earth did that happen? It's none of his business, but it intrigues him.

What makes the situation even more awkward is that Freddy persistently tries to match him up with Anna. Paula's sister seems, in his eyes, a very pale imitation. A few years younger, slightly plump, diffident, she appears dim and innocent to the point of naivety. After his experiences on the liners, Pat finds this combination tedious in the extreme. Freddy seems unable to grasp this and persists in bringing them together. Of course, Paula is always there, watching. To Pat, it feels as if Freddy is rubbing his nose in the situation. Look what a woman I've got; you can't have anyone like her, but I'll give you her sister...

He sits up and runs his hands through his hair, groans to himself, and holds his head in his hands for a moment. Jesus, he tells himself, I have to stop thinking like this. I can't afford to upset this man or his wife. I've finally fallen into a decent new life and I depend upon them for it. I even get to sing properly, for once in my life... and today is Sunday, rehearsal day. He frowns. Of all the operas the group could have chosen, of course, it had to be Carmen. The capricious temptress... played by Paula herself. He shakes his head and mutters to himself, "So what on God's own earth could possibly be better for a lovesick Irishman already in purgatory, than playing the part of Don Jose, is that not exactly what I am needing?" He sighs, and forces himself up to wash and dress.

Two hours later, he stands next to Paula at one side of the stage, waiting to rehearse his part while the director fusses around the chorus. Pat shuts his eyes, trying to imagine the action.

"I've never seen you look so nervous, Ricky."

He opens his eyes and sees genuine concern in her face. "Ah well, I'm not worried about the singing. The acting, though, that would be a different thing entirely. This scene in particular... "

"But it's a wonderful scene..."

"It depends which part you play."

She smiles at that. "Yes, I know, Carmen is a wonderful part for a woman. You can be all the things that you are not supposed to be in normal life, someone who lives only for the moment."

"It suits you." The words are out of his mouth before he can stop them.

She looks away, her face flushed. "Perhaps..."

"What I mean is; you play her brilliantly, Paula. This feller Don Jose, I really struggle with him. I can see that he's a weak character; he can't stand up to her. He falls for her and she leads him into all sorts of trouble. He struggles against it, fighting with his conscience. He can never make his mind up, so he always ends up giving in to his feelings for her, one way or another. But I can't see such a weak character killing anyone, let alone her."

"You English, you miss the point..." He's about to remind her he's Irish, when he sees her grin. "It's all about his passion, Ricky. He can't fight it. When he finally does decide he wants her, it's too late; but his passion is so strong that he kills her rather than give her up."

"Maybe you have to be Italian to understand that."

She looks him in the eye. "Maybe, but you don't need to be Italian to feel it, or to act it. In this scene, just let your passion go, Ricky."

Now, it is his turn to look away, his face hot, unable to meet her eye. He clears his throat. "Where's Freddy today?"

She shrugs, "Oh, you know Freddy. If he misses the early mass he feels he has to take the kids later. He's kind of traditional that way. Then he has to take them to his mother's. He'll be along soon." She avoids his eyes; before he can ask more, the rehearsal begins.

Pat does his best with the singing, but can't hide his discomfort when he has to pretend to kill Paula with the knife; so much so, the director comes over to confront him. "Come on, Ricky, you act like you are an assassin, as if you do not care who you are killing. You should act this scene as if you are already in hell. This woman is everything you have ever desired, you simply cannot bear the idea of her in another man's arms; this is hell. She laughs in your face; this is also hell. So you must stop it. And when you stick the knife in her, act as if the blade is entering your own heart, as well as hers."

Feeling a hot flush in his cheeks, Pat turns back to Paula. She shrugs and taps his chest with her finger, "He's right. Try to feel that passion for her, in here."

Staring into her eyes, it seems she is teasing him, just as the real Carmen would. He cannot stop himself. "Jesus Christ, Paula, that's a feeling I won't ever have to pretend."

Initially he sees a look of puzzlement, and then understanding dawns in her eyes; perhaps satisfaction, too. She stares back into his eyes for a long moment, as if searching for confirmation, and then looks away while her face colours a deep red. After a slight pause, she steps to his side and squeezes his arm. She breathes the words softly into his ear, the sensation of her warm breath teasing his ears, "Me, too, Ricky; me, too."

*   *   *

Pat dreams of Dublin; he and Carr, somehow older, push their way into a raucous bar, searching for girls. There's plenty of choice; the trouble is Carr's far too fussy. He's not at all interested in the blowsy girls who frequent the sailors' bars. He whispers, "I want classy women."

Pat sighs and reluctantly takes Carr to the Gaiety theatre; here, backstage, they meet Paula and her sister Anna. Somehow, the two girls are both appearing there in a production of Madame Butterfly. Freddy, apparently, has gone back to America. Pat tries to catch Paula's eye; he secretly hopes that he can pair Carr off with Anna so that he and Paula can finally be alone together. But this plan backfires spectacularly; Carr seems immediately attracted to Paula, and ignores Anna. Worse still, as usual Carr has lots of money and knows how to use it. He lavishes gifts upon Paula, buying her flowers, perfume, and diamond ear-rings. At first Pat watches helplessly, then he takes Carr aside to explain his feelings; Carr shakes his head, unmoved. He has power as well as money, since Pat knows that he dare not oppose him. If he does, Carr will simply have him arrested and thrown into prison. So once again, Pat must watch Paula with another man. He must watch the object of his desire being dangled in front of him, close enough to touch, but unable to act...

He jerks awake; at least it is Sunday, today, at last. He sighs. This day has become sacred to him because of Paula. Their whispered conversations during rehearsals, plus their operatic performances together, have become the most precious time that he has. That acknowledgement of their mutual attraction has never been spoken of again; but in his own mind it is always there, an understanding between them. In one way this feels like torture, his ever-present desire for her, unfulfilled. In another way, the knowledge that she also feels something sustains him. He copes with his frustration by telling himself there can be no possibility of fulfilment, that Paula is so immersed within her family and the culture of little Italy that there never will be an opportunity for them to be alone together, even if she really wanted that... which he doubts. She might like to play Carmen, but she wouldn't really wish to be like her in reality. He smiles at the thought and pulls himself upright, rubbing the sleep from his face. The situation makes him feel more alive, that's for sure. The fact that he can experience a real feeling of closeness and friendship with a woman reassures him, in a way. And he can still have some fun on the side...

He turns his thoughts back to their latest production; La Traviata, the fallen woman. Freddy always casts Paula as the female lead; she may not be the best soprano, but she can act. Pat also suspects that he enjoys showing her off in this situation, where he can take some credit for her performance. Pat's excellent voice has given him the role of Alfredo, Violetta's lover, while Freddy (who often takes the older male parts) plays the Baron. So in drama, as in real life, they play out a curious triangle upon the stage. Pat shakes his head and reaches for his trousers. He whistles to himself while he shaves.

A rat-tat-tat from his front door interrupts him. He assumes it's the woman in the rooms above again, wanting to borrow a dollar, and ignores it. The rapping repeats three times, insistently, before he hears a loud whisper, "Alfredo... Alfredo..." For a long moment he stands, frozen in surprise, staring at his reflection in his shaving mirror, half of his chin still soaped and unshaven. He takes a deep breath, places the razor by the bowl of water, pulls a vest over his head, and goes to the door. She must have been leaning against the door listening, because she almost falls into the room when he opens it, before recovering herself and giving him a wry smile, perhaps amused by his appearance. His first thought is to ask her what she is doing here, but that doesn't seem very welcoming, so he says nothing. Behind her, footsteps sound from the stairwell. She glances behind her, gives him an impatient look, and pushes past him, into his room. "Shut the door." The urgency of her whisper brings him to his senses; her hand and his own push the door shut together.

"Sorry. I was just surprised... I didn't expect ...I mean..."

"You didn't think I would come to you?" Her eyes search his face for a response as she continues. "You forget, I have Italian blood, and I have thought a long, long time about this. Maybe you thought I was some perfect little wife. But Freddy is the traditional one, not me. I am the modern one, and I can't live without passion." She looks down, grasps his arm, and gives it a gentle shake. "But maybe you only like the idea of me, not the reality."

A note of despair in her voice acts like a slap in the face. Suddenly he can smell her hair, feel her hands gripping his arm, and see the curve of her neck. He brings his free arm around her, encircling her, nestling her head on his shoulder. "Jesus, Paula, it's more than just the idea of you that I'm liking." He inhales the scent of her deep into his lungs. "Just to be standing here holding you is a bloody miracle. But how on earth did you get away..."

"He thinks I'm at my mother's. Freddy doesn't like my family so much, you see, we're not religious. We are like your Irish rebels - your Republicans."

He chuckles to himself, "Holy mother of Satan, we do have something in common." She punches him, gently, but giggles, while he whispers, "More than you think."

"I know." He feels her sigh, and then feels her hand moving into his vest, around his back, and up. His spine tingles. She really does want him, he realises, and not at some distant point in the future. He feels a pang of doubt, his shock keeping him paralysed for a moment. Then he kisses her neck, watches her body shiver. He hears her whisper, "Amami, amami, Alfredo. Come on Alfredo, Ricky, Pat; whoever you are."

Her coat drops to the floor while she wipes soap from his face and nibbles at his neck. He starts to pull at her clothes, initially hesitant and curious; then, as his surprise dissolves, more urgently. She lifts her arms, helps him remove her blouse. He starts to move her toward the bedroom; they circle each other silently, a clumsy dance, fumbling and pulling at each other's clothes, leaving a trail of garments across the floor. Having waited so long, his urgency overwhelms him. He touches the warmth of her skin, feels her tremble in response, hears and feels her short gasping breaths upon him, kisses her soft, wet mouth; he stuffs his senses full with her as a starving man will cram his mouth with food. She seems equally impatient, pushing one of his hands down into her undergarments, inviting him to feel her readiness. They circle each other again and again, hands fumbling with buttons, pushing skirts and pants down, feet kicking them away. At the bed, he pushes her knickers down over her hips. She wriggles, steps out of them, and falls backwards, pulling him onto her. He reaches down to guide himself into her only to discover that, despite his mental arousal, he's not ready physically. He feels a sharp pang of anxiety, a fear of disappointing her. Yet he cannot stop; he feels obliged to force himself into her clumsily, his desire for her overriding his senses. His mental desire slowly hardens into a physical need as he moves inside her; carefully at first, then thrusting into her mechanically, watching her breasts rising as she breathes deeply, occasionally moaning, her eyes closed, her hands encouraging his own hands to roam everywhere across her body; into her ears, her mouth. For a while he enjoys watching her, watching his dreams coming true; suddenly, he feels acutely detached and self-conscious, as if looking down on himself, his desire ebbing away, the awful thought growing and persisting that he is failing her as a lover; she'll be disappointed, she'll laugh at him. Yet she saves him from this fear, and from the humiliation of impotence, when she suddenly gasps in surprise and climaxes, her eyes opening wide and holding onto his gaze with her own, reaching out for him with her eyes. Her body convulses as she lifts her legs high and wide, reigniting his own urgent arousal, so that now he pushes into her roughly, brutally, grunting like a beast, using her splayed body as he might use any woman for his own need until he finishes at last, more with relief than pleasure, and falls across her.

Lying there in silence, his head turns away as he tastes acute disappointment; sharp, bitter, like lemon on a wound. He tells himself not to admit these feelings to her; what could he say? After a while he feels her begin to stroke his hair. "Don't worry; cara mia. It will be much better next time. We were both far too impatient, and a little scared."

"You think so?" That does make sense of it, he thinks.

"Of course; we're both scared of what we are doing. And I am not a good lover, Ricky. I have very little experience. In fact, as far as real passion goes I am a virgin. You must remember that. You have much more experience. You must teach me... if you want to."

"So there will be a next time?"

She laughs. "Go and finish your shave. I'll make some coffee. Next time I go to visit my mother we should do it very, very slowly."

Her wisdom takes his breath away; how lucky he is, he thinks, to meet a woman who understands so much. He feels movement down below, in anticipation, and remembers the love duet between Alfredo and Violetta. Next time, I'll put that music on the phonograph before we start...

* * *

Each Sunday that she lies there in his arms, in his bed, he feels a peculiar mixture of conflicting emotions; completely at peace, healed, and filled with inner calm, but also alert, alive, and wary. On this particular morning, something makes him try to savour these feelings, to fix them in his mind. Yet, inevitably, his mind turns to the day's rehearsal, which has abruptly taken on an added importance. The Metropolitan Opera Company, suffering from the effects of the depression, has announced that it will offer its facilities to the best three amateur opera productions in the city. Eleven amateur groups are competing for this prize; three nights performing at the Met with all expenses paid, plus the use of all their facilities. The Met will pocket any profit from ticket sales, of course, but like many others Pat would sell his soul just for the chance to sing there, if he wasn't trampled to death in the rush. Christ, if only. Well, we have as good a chance as anyone, he tells himself. He grins. The chemistry between him and Paula can't do any harm, either. He kisses her back and strokes her hip until she turns over to face him.

"Do you think we can win it, Paula?"

"Of course we can. But that won't make any difference to the two of us. If anything, it might spoil things, all those other women hearing you sing. That might spoil everything."

"It won't, Paula, I promise. You know everything we do together works like a dream, on the stage and off of it. That won't ever change. And if I sing there for three nights, so do you. You'll be a star, too."

She sighs. "I know. It frightens me, all those faces watching us. On the other hand, it would be good to have it on your application for citizenship. That would help a lot."

"I hadn't thought of that."

"Only don't get involved with Freddy's friends and their games down at the docks. Keep your nose clean. A steady job and no trouble, that's what they want to see from immigrants."

"Which friends are those, the rich guys with the fancy boats?"

"You know what I mean, Ricky; the ones who control the waterfront. Freddy has to deal with them, but he's gotten far too friendly for his own good. He's started to go out on the town with them. If you were Italian, he'd have asked you along already. But if he does, don't go. And if some rich guy asks you to help with a boat trip, don't bother."

"I know, Paula. I'm not as dumb as I appear. Truth is I had my fingers burned in Ireland. So I don't play with fire here. My line is, I just fix boats, I can't sail them; ain't got a clue." He grins, while he thinks about her words. "I used to feel so jealous of him, being at home with you."

"Then don't be jealous, Ricky. If he's there, he's not there."

"What's that mean?"

She shrugs and bites her lip. "I told you, he's religious."

"So?"

She sighs. "We don't want any more kids. Unlike you, he's a Catholic who does what he's told. So you got no cause to be jealous."

Pat scratches his head. "Jesus, he's crazy."

"Not that crazy. His shirts smell of cheap perfume whenever he comes in late from those nights on the town, sometimes not until the morning."

"Christ. And he thinks he's religious?"

She buries her head in his chest, and then bangs it against him. "You know the score. He needs the confession box to wipe his slate clean each week. That's how it works."

Pat thinks about this for a long time. "We'll run away, when I've got my citizenship."

She shakes her head slowly, emphatically. "A nice dream, cara mia, but that is all it can be. I could never leave my children."

"We could take them with us."

Her voice rises now in exasperation. "You know they wouldn't come. They adore him."

"Maybe when your children are older..."

Now her voice is angry, spitting the words at him. "No. Don't talk about it. How can you possibly understand? You don't have children. You don't know him or his friends. They would find us." She pushes him away, turning away from him. "You torture me. I can't go on like this. You don't know what it's like, waiting for him to come home, wishing he was you every night, pretending I am happy to the children. I'm afraid I will end up hating my children, and I won't let myself do that."

He kisses her back. "I'm sorry, Paula. It'll get easier. Something will change, in time."

"No, it won't." She gets up out of the bed, and starts to dress. "I have decided, we have to stop now or it will make me crazy." He's too stunned to reply; he simply watches her, his emotions in turmoil. Does she mean it? How could she? Why now? This involves him, too. Surely he has a right to try to change her mind? Before he can say a word, she anticipates his intention. "Ricky, I will see you at the rehearsal. But listen to me. If you love me, you must do this for me. We must be... as if this never happened, like friends, like... professional singers. If you love me, don't ever speak of it to me, you will just be torturing me. My mind is made up. Promise me, if you love me."

"Jesus Christ, Paula..." More than anything, he wants to tell her that he really does love her; to tell her properly. Yet now, he can't even do that, can he? She stares at him, waiting. Her eyes give nothing away, her look hard and demanding. Maybe she needs time, he thinks. He will have to be patient. He nods. "All right."

She waits for a second, seems to decide this is enough, and walks to the door without looking back. He watches the door shut and then slowly puts his head in his hands, as if to check that his head is still there, resting on his shoulders.

*   *   *

Another year older, but not much wiser; Pat stands just offstage, watching the females of the chorus. My God, he thinks, they are nailing it tonight, no trouble. And he has to admit, Freddy's decision to stick with La Traviata for a second season, to keep polishing every aspect of their performance, has worked a treat. Dressed as gipsy singers, their golden earrings and bracelets offset by sensual scarlet and blue, the young Italian-American girls look and sound positively ravishing. A wealthy high society party is in full swing; he taps his feet while the chorus, the entertainers, sing. He nods in admiration as the men enter with a flourish, dressed as bullfighters (the silk provided by Freddy's waterfront friends). As their song builds to a climax, he clears his throat and prepares to enter the stage. Now the gambling begins, and his stomach makes one final flip as he enters.

The guests and dispersing entertainers sing his name in welcome, Alfredo, Alfredo. In the glare of the lights, he smiles and sings his reply, showing that he is a friend to them all; then he steps back to take a seat at the gambling table, flipping a deck of cards from one hand to the other (a trick he learned on the liners). The game begins; in front of him, other guests take centre stage as the musical mood darkens, heralding the entrance of his lover Violetta with the powerful Baron Douphol who now possesses her. He pointedly turns his back on them; the Baron forbids Violetta to speak to him. As a result, she sings her distress aloud. Her voice, trembling with emotion, feels like a hot needle in a wound. He grimaces in pain, not entirely in role. But it's also very easy to feel that this serves the bitch right for the way she's treated him, just as Alfredo feels. So he pretends to ignore her while throwing his cards down with a flourish as he wins, repeatedly. He sings a line about returning happily to the country to spend his winnings, putting on a rustic accent which produces a ripple of laughter in the audience. He can't speak Italian fluently yet, but he can certainly sing it well enough.

The party's hostess pointedly asks Alfredo if he will do this alone. Oh no, he sings, summoning his cockiest Irish manner, I'll go back with the woman who was with me before, until she ran away. Pat delivers this line without even a glance at his lover or his rival, adding to the insult. Only when Violetta wails her despair aloud does he glance at Paula and see the depth of her colour in her blush. It's a sweet moment, for Alfredo and for Pat.

The Baron responds by challenging Alfredo in the card game, trying to use his wealth as a weapon. Pat has come to enjoy this interlude intensely; he's always felt that Freddy has somehow bought Paula when she was too young to know better. So as he plays cards with the Baron on the stage he tells himself, one day I am bound to win her back from you, just as I will win this theatrical game today. As Alfredo defies the laws of chance, winning everything the Baron bets, Pat sings his triumph aloud as if it were only to be expected, laughing at the Baron's cards, holding up his own, glorying in his triumph as the director instructed. (His Irish reticence about such exuberance soon gave way to the intense pleasure of humiliating his rival; fantasy perhaps, but it feels wonderful.) Violetta wails again in discomfort, calling for God's mercy; he turns his back on her and taunts the Baron until he threatens revenge.

The card game ends abruptly with a call for supper; Pat leaves the stage with the rest of the cast and then turns to watch from just behind the curtain. Violetta takes centre stage, singing like a siren tonight, he thinks. No acting is required. He feels just like Alfredo, genuinely unable to resist her call. He sucks in a deep breath as he steps back onto the stage, close enough to touch her; they both stare into each other's eyes, wary of each other's pain. This scene still feels raw with emotion, every time they play it. She sings that his life is in danger; her breath, warm upon his face, almost makes him forget where he is. He turns away, turns back, and asks if she thinks he is a coward. Now she turns away, denying this; he demands to know what she is afraid of. She turns back and sings that the Baron frightens her. Now he turns away for a moment before turning back to confront her again, boasting that he will kill the Baron. She turns, walks away, turns back, and turns away. Their postural dance has evolved, Pat realises, because they cannot bear to look in each other's eyes while they play this scene. Her voice rises to a crescendo, screaming at him - what really frightens her is the idea that the Baron may kill him. He runs after her, seizing his advantage by grasping her hand, and in his most perfect, plaintive Italian, he sings to her that he will go, if only she swears that she will come with him. He sings this twice, a small invention of their director. As the audience applaud, the tears trickle down her face, real tears; but she shakes her head, turns away, refuses.

He summons the fury buried within him and taunts her again, echoing her refusal in a tone of pure contempt. In desperation to make him leave, she tells him she loves the Baron. He knows this is a lie, but he feels too angry now. This is his own special moment of pure drama and he has learned to savour it. He summons the rest of the cast back onto the stage and sings to them of his debt to Violetta;

but just when he seems to be singing her praises he turns to her, calling on everyone to witness the fact he has paid her back, and flings all the money he's won at her feet. This is the ultimate insult, highlighting that she is a courtesan, who can be bought and sold by her patrons. (In Pat's mind, not so far from the truth; Paula has refused love to return to her comfortable cocoon with Freddy, his money and his gangster friends.) On stage, she covers her eyes, cries out and falls, as if dying of shame. When the scene ends, the tumultuous applause fills their ears. Pat glances at Paula and winks; she looks away. Freddy silently mouths, "Bravo".

After the final curtain call, his feelings still churning inside him, he feels a sudden and complete exhaustion. Finding a quiet corner, he lies down upon the floor, trying to relax and calm himself. Half of him feels like jumping for joy; the other half wants to crawl away, weep, and pick up a girl in some dark speakeasy. He shuts his eyes. The next thing he feels is a shoe nudging his leg. "Wake up, maestro."

He opens one eye and grunts, "We nailed it, Freddy."

"We sure did, Ricky." The grin on Freddy's face is wider than usual.

"What's up?"

Freddy glances around. "I just got through speaking with the guys from the Met. They were here tonight."

"Were they now? I'd say they picked a grand evening to come."

"Too right, buddy. They just gave me the wink; very professional this year, that was the gist of it. Liked the whole tone of the production, whatever that means. Also told me the tenor's Italian accent and his acting have gone up a few notches."

"Very reassuring; but have we won?"

"Officially, they can't say yet."

"Unofficially?"

"It's a shoe in."

"No kidding?"

"Cross my heart, Ricky, on the bones of the saints. They loved it."

Pat sits up. "Jesus wept." He can't think of anything to say.

"One other thing?"

"Sure, Freddy."

"Do me a favour and walk Paula back to the apartment. It ain't so safe, this time of night. One of my best customers is here; he wants to take me out to celebrate."

Pat looks up at him, trying to stay expressionless. It might be a test, he thinks. "Sure, I was thinking of taking a stroll uptown tonight, it's on my way."

He walks a pace or two behind Paula; at first, the warm spring evening brings a pleasant breeze that plays with her hair, tempting him to reach out and do the same. He bites his lip, and looks around, checking they are alone. "Do you think he's watching us?"

She laughs, "Not now. But someone will be around when I get home. He'll check when I got in and when you leave."

He can't resist, "That's a crying shame."

She does not respond immediately; to his relief, he hears no anger in her voice when she does. "He does get a bit jealous, these days. I think too many people see how we are on the stage."

Again, he can't resist. "As if we're meant to be together, you mean?"

"I tell him it's because you were a professional singer, and I can also act. I keep telling him, that's just Ricky and me being professional."

"A professional idiot, maybe."

"You're not the idiot."

He hears that longed for softness, in her voice. "What do you mean?"

"Did you mean it, when you said shame?"

"Just now? Of course I meant it."

"You should find yourself a woman who can give you what you need."

He thinks carefully, resists the urge to make a joke. "Look, I know it doesn't make great sense for me either. But I tried looking for someone else and I just can't do it. I know it's not the right thing to do, but I still want you, Paula, no one else. I don't regret a minute of the time we had together, not one. Believe me; I've done far worse things in my life, things that I do regret - but not this." He sees an almost imperceptible nod, and continues. "Some people never have anything like this in their lives. Some people have it for one night. The luckiest ones, they have it for a lifetime. I'm not generally lucky, but I feel damn lucky to have known you."

She walks steadily on, while he paces behind her, waiting. Eventually, she sighs and turns to look at him. "We'll have to be careful. Like before, but even more so. But you're right, I tried to do the right thing, and that felt all wrong. I don't feel guilty, either. Loving you is a crazy thing to do, but it feels too right, God help me. So if you'll have me back, I'll come when I can."

He sucks in a deep, deep breath. "Thank the Lord."

And with that, she turns and walks on. He runs to catch up, and walks beside her, careful to leave a respectable gap. He sees her smile and begins to hum their love duet, from the second act.

* * *

He cannot sleep for hours, his mind a seething turmoil of possibilities. He tries to settle by rehearsing his role, imagining each scene one by one - but mistakes made in the past keep intruding, unwelcome visitors. He thinks of Paula; but that only makes him feel more aroused, more alert. By the time he dozes fitfully, light begins to creep through the curtains. After a couple more hours he finally gives up on the idea of sleep and makes coffee.

Broadway, by contrast, sleeps on happily through the early morning, deserted by the excited crowds, the grand entrances closed, restaurants empty; only the occasional coffee bar stirs with life. His breath quickens when he approaches Thirty-Ninth Street, the opera house slowly coming into view, its squat, Romanesque façade hemmed in by skyscrapers. He slows gradually to a halt, his heart pounding. He's walked past it before, even been inside as a spectator when he wanted to treat himself, but this is different. He's never felt like this before, not for years anyway. The surface of the street seems shiny, polished, the tram lines glinting in the sun like water. His mouth dry, he makes an attempt to swallow, only to produce a cough. He tries talking to himself, "Here it is - the old yellow brick brewery..." But he can't think of a reply, can't move; can't even think straight. He just stands there staring, frozen in his tracks, for an eternity. He cannot even cross the street.

"You're early. Taking it all in?" Someone jostles his arm. "Hey Ricky, you OK?" He turns. Freddy, dressed in a suit, stares at him curiously.

"I don't know. I ...er..."

"Jesus, Ricky, don't tell me you got stage fright?" Pat swallows; maybe that's what this is. He shrugs. "Christ, you pick your day, huh?"

"I didn't sleep last night."

"Huh. Suppose it's natural, buddy. Big day." Digging into his jacket pocket, he pulls Pat into a doorway. "Here, take a slug of this." Pat takes the flask gratefully and tips it up. The fiery grappa burns his tongue and throat but he nods gratefully, and then takes another hit. "That's enough for now. I might need some later. Come on." Propelled across and around the building by Freddy's formidable bulk, he gives in gratefully. They find a side entrance and wait for the others to arrive. Thereafter, the day quickly becomes a blur of preparations; navigating the dressing rooms and backstage layout, meeting the make-up assistants, trying out new costumes, and finally being fitted with a dress suit and bow tie for the publicity photographs. Meanwhile, various compromises are reached; their own small chorus will act and sing on stage, while the Metropolitan chorus adds power in the wings. Their small band of musicians reluctantly defers to the house orchestra, while the house director agrees to limit his input to a few important suggestions. Finally, they run through an extended dress rehearsal. Under the blinding lights and above the volume of the orchestra rising from the pit below, Pat feels like a mole emerging into the light under an express train. He has no sense of judgement, of how well he is singing; he suspects, badly. Afterwards, when the stage lights are off, he stands centre stage, looking out at the rows and rows of seats, the tiers rising above, the private boxes built for the original patrons; a sea of red and gold, waiting to engulf him.

But much to his surprise, he is not engulfed, one way or another. The first two nights pass with a feeling of anti-climax; ordinary, unexceptional, no bad mistakes, but the whole company seems to be trying too hard and nothing feels natural. The applause is polite but not extended.

On the morning of their final performance he wakes from a deep sleep, hearing a light tap on the door to his apartment. He knows who is there, though his heart still jumps as he opens the door; she brushes past him, leaning up and whispering in his ear, "I'm visiting my mother." He lifts her off her feet, elbowing the door shut, and carries her to the bedroom. They don't have much time, but they make the most of it.

In later years, Pat will often wonder if their passion that morning sparked a blaze; because that night is the performance of his life; of all their lives. Standing before the audience afterwards, drenched in the roars of applause, he feels content at last. His life seems to have a direction at last, to be set upon solid ground. He has a job and the skills to find work anywhere, within reason. He can boast that he has sung here, at the Met. No-one will ever be able to take that away from him. And soon, he will be a US citizen, just like Paula. But most of all, he has Paula...

As he sits in his dressing room after the performance, reluctantly returning to normality, he hears a loud rap on the door. It opens and a bald headed man smiles down at him. Pat swallows, nodding his head at the manager of the Metropolitan Opera chorus. The man flips a card onto his dressing table. "The money isn't great, but it's steady work and you'll learn a lot." Pat nods, as the door shuts. When my citizenship papers come through, Pat thinks, maybe I'll give that a go.

One task still remains; to collect photographs from a booth on Thirty-Sixth Street, his personal mementos of the greatest night of his life. Unlike the others, he feels in no hurry to do this; it seems a moment to savour. He leaves it for a week; he tells Freddy that he'll pick them up Monday, on his way to work. On the Sunday morning, much to his disappointment, Paula does not visit. He spends the day listening to his phonograph, reading a newspaper.

In the morning he collects the pictures, taking time to study each one, whistling in admiration. The photographer has captured their musical souls in black and white. Some he's already seen; enlarged as posters for their performances. There are four pictures of him on his own (two in costume, and two in his dress suit) plus two with Paula, four more with Freddy and the other leading players, and one of the whole cast. These, his personal copies, are all stamped "New York Metropolitan, September 1932. Ricky MacMahon as Alfredo in La Traviata." He shakes his head, unable to believe the evidence of his eyes.

Tucking the precious bundle under his arm, he takes a leisurely, contented stroll back to his room, thinking of how to broach the subject of joining the chorus with Freddy. He won't like losing him from the business, Pat knows that much. He wonders what Paula will think. She'd want him to do it, probably. Maybe they all had the same offer; but if so, Freddy hasn't mentioned it. He is almost home, turning into Cuylers Alley, when he hears her voice calling his name. His face cracks into a broad grin; is this his lucky day? He turns, only to discover a tear-streaked, anxious face.

"Thank God I caught you. Freddy mentioned you'd be in to work late this morning." Her voice sounds frantic, harsh with tension.

"What is it?"

She glances over her shoulder and pulls him into the alley, holding onto his arms. "Oh Pat, it's all over, I'm sorry." She looks him in the eye and bursts into tears, resting her head on his chest as she sobs.

"Jesus, Paula, you don't behave like it's over. Not for me, or for you. Will you be putting me through all that again?"

She wails a little, and then slowly stifles her sobs. "He's gonna find out, Pat, you gotta leave. You know what his friends will do to you."

"Wait a minute, Paula." He shakes her a little. "Tell me what's going on. We'll work something out."

She takes a deep breath. "It's my daughter. She knows, Pat. She knows about us. She followed me last time, and she's been talking to my mother. The only reason she hasn't told Freddy already is because I begged her to wait a couple of days, so I could get you to leave town for good."

"Come with me."

She wails again, "You know I can't do that." She says this forcefully, shaking her head, but her face looks stricken, uncertain.

"How long before they're old enough? Four years? Five?"

185

She shakes her head, "Please..." and sobs again.

He resists the urge to slap her and wraps his arms around her. "Listen, Paula. In four or five years they'll be fully-grown, and believe me they won't need you the same. I didn't need my mother at that age, and I'm damn sure you didn't either. Remember?" He rocks her from side to side, as her shaking subsides. "I'll meet you four years to the day, today, at noon outside the Met. If you don't turn up, I'll come back a year later, same time. Just bring yourself. I'll have everything ready, tickets to a new life, I promise. We'll just disappear. I've done it before, I can do it again, believe me." He kisses her hair. "You know you need this just as much as I do." He feels her sigh, and then her head moves, a slight nod. "Promise?"

She pushes him away, leaving her hands on his chest, and looks up into his eyes. "All right; if my kids feel grown up, I'll be there. But you have to leave, Pat. I know him. He'll explode. For a few days he'll want to kill you. And he's got a gun. And if he doesn't, his friends will. You know what they're like. It's a matter of honour for them."

"I could go up to Boston."

"No, they've got friends up there. Even among the Irish. If you stay in the States, you'll have to find a small town and keep your head down. His friends have got connections in all the cities. They'll put the word out for a singer who fixes marine engines."

"Jesus. Bang goes my singing career."

She starts to cry again, and he pulls her back into his arms. "Paula, it was worth every minute, I'd never have met you otherwise." He waits until she quietens down. "Listen, I still got my seaman's papers. I can go back as a junior engineer, work my way up to something in four or five years. One thing about the merchant marine, you can vanish into thin air real easy, go places they can't follow. It's easy enough to put money by, too - nothing to spend it on. It'll be fine. It's not so long to wait."

"It sounds almost bearable, put like that. I suppose it's better than Alfredo and Violetta ever had." With that, they hold each other for a long time, as if holding on to their promise to each other. Afterwards, he can't remember exactly how they said goodbye. In the long days and nights to come, his main regret is that he did not think to ask her back to his apartment, to make love one more time before he left.

*   *   *

He seems to be lost, almost floating, within a cloud; maybe its fog or mist, he can't really tell... he walks on, following a barely visible path. Despite the strangeness of his surroundings, he does not feel fear; what fills his mind is curiosity plus the anticipation of something that has a sense of the familiar, of safety, yet is largely unknown and exciting to him...

As the vapours swirl into his face, an aroma of hot, steaming food begins to tease his nose. Recognition prompts a flood of saliva onto his tongue; the mist clears. A laden plate awaits him at a table, piled with potato mashed with butter plus cabbage cooked with bacon and herbs; his favourite dish. Mary also appears, kicking his foot under the table, eager to tell him something. Somehow all the Hardy girls are there too, surrounding him.

The kicking dissolves into a persistent hand nudging at his ribs. Opening his eyes, the rising sun momentarily blinds him. Next to him, a match scratches as the lorry driver lights his cigarette; a stink of sweat and oil mingles with strong tobacco. Paddy winds down the window and, looking out, recognises a brick clock tower. He mutters his thanks at the driver, pushes the door open, shoulders his bag and jumps down. Digging into his trouser pocket, he feels a reassuring handful of coins; why not? He steps through the brick arch into the railway station and buys a ticket.

A line of carriages stands ready and waiting on the platform. Flopping into a seat by an open door, he sniffs the cold morning air and rubs his eyes. On the opposite platform, soldiers stand chatting, surrounded by kitbags. Durham Light Infantry, he thinks, for sure, feeling a pang of envy even after all this time. A succession of metallic squeals followed by a sudden juddering announces the arrival of the engine. Five minutes later, two mechanical howls precede a shrill blast from the conductor's whistle, commanding a collective slamming of doors. Paddy stands up, pulls his door to, and sits back to watch the world roll by. It's a slow journey, this; one to savour, once the town recedes and the flat flood plains gradually shift shape into low valleys, the route heading gradually upward, the engine puffing breathlessly. Glimpses of partially wooded slopes preface a long enclosed valley, he remembers, the line following the river erratically, the sides of the dale slowly rising, marked by lines of stone walls and scarred by quarries.

In some ways, he admits to himself, this place feels more like home than Ireland now. This dale has become his base each winter, when he sends long letters across the water using the Hardy address; in the summers, postcards from his travels. He hasn't been back to

Cork since the wedding, though he feels more ready now, less ashamed. Next spring, he tells himself. He digs into his breast pocket and pulls out a battered envelope. From it, he pulls out a grey booklet; his own Savings account and with a healthy balance, thanks to a summer of hard work. He marvels at the cover, shaking his head as he examines the name again, unable to resist a grin. Fons, or Paddy, as others call him, and as he now thinks of himself, has now officially become Patrick Reilly. He slips the book back into the envelope, checking that the other document, his baptismal certificate, is still in there. What had his mother written, when she sent it? "Give your thanks for the absent-mindedness of the blessed Father O'Connor, for leaving his blank certificates in an unlocked cupboard, and for the thoroughness of the Irish Free State army, in shelling the Four Courts and destroying the official records forever...the upshot of which is that you can use this like a birth certificate. PS I'm pleased you call yourself Reilly. My grandfather was also Patrick Reilly."

At the last small town, the head of the valley, several families board the train, the children chattering, excited at the prospect of a day out. At every village further up the dale, more and more people crowd aboard. Some carry heavy burdens, presumably on their way to market; others carry baskets, the contents carefully wrapped, carried as if both mysterious and precious. A few bring pets, carefully groomed, of all shapes and sizes. Of course, he thinks, I'm back early this year; it must be the show this weekend. As the train moves higher up the dale, it fills to bursting point with swaying people, the engine hooting in plaintive protest...

The crowd disgorges from the train at Stanhope. Paddy allows himself to be carried along in the flow, letting his tiredness and excitement melt into the carnival atmosphere. The masses sweep him along past terraced houses to the main street, then down "the butts" to a path along the river and through a gate into Castle Park. He knows the Hardy girls will turn up at the show, somewhere, sometime; this will be as fine a place as any to surprise them with his presence. In fact, it couldn't be bettered.

He munches on a pork pie while watching the sheepdog trials; after that, a wander through various market stalls, inspecting the wares, trying to resist the lure of the beer tent. He buys a bag of toffee apples, eating one of them while watching a group of acrobats on horseback. When the sun bursts from behind a bank of cloud and the day heats up, he can resist the beer tent no longer. He goes to buy a pint and sits just outside, on the shady side, keeping an eye out for Gilly and the girls. He sips the drink slowly, trying to make it last, fighting the urge to take a doze in the last of the summer heat...

He jerks awake abruptly, and yawns, scanning the crowds. Some instinct has alerted him, perhaps. A glimpse of red ribbons catches his eye; there they are. He watches the three girls moving as one, their arms interlocked; tallest and dark, smallest and fair, and the middle one with her reddish brown hair. Grace is well named, he thinks, her figure announcing that she is becoming a woman already, at 14. Maggie still seems much more of a girl, by comparison. He watches as they halt and debate with each other, deciding which way to go. Maggie seems to be holding her own in some battle of wills with her older sister, who eventually shrugs and gives way. June, the youngest, waits expectantly. A softer person, she seems happy to be led by her older sisters. He notes the direction they take, finishes his drink, and follows. He finds them outside a tent advertising "The *smallest* man and the *biggest* woman in the *whole wide world*". The girls are trying to sneak a glance inside through a rip in the fabric; without much success, judging by their faces. Paddy does his best to adopt a local accent, "Hey up lasses, pay thy way..."

Looks of shock turn to disbelief. June screams in delight while Maggie throws herself at him, leaping up onto his shoulders to hug him and dangle from his neck, kicking his legs with her feet. Grace watches patiently; he catches her eye as Maggie begins to voice their curiosity, "Paddy, where did you spring from? Did you have a good summer? How far did you get this time?" The others echo her questions.

"Far enough," Maggie lets go of him, so he turns to pick up June, who squirms and giggles. "Come here, you." While he's distracted with June, Grace pecks his cheek, very chastely, backs away, and sneaks a glance at Maggie's expression. Paddy hugs and kisses June, and then steps toward Grace, adopting a Weardale twang, "Call that a welcome, lass? Hast tha joined the ranters?" He gives her a hug, lifts her off her feet and swings her round.

"Paddy, stop it..." Quiet laughter and a deep flush reveal her pleasure; she darts another quick glance at Maggie.

"Which of you wants a toffee apple, or is that a silly question?" After they've devoured his treat, the girls take him to watch jugglers and then a dancing bear. His attention wanders; he notices Maggie dig her elbow into Grace, whispering in her sister's ear. Grace turns pink again. "What's up, Maggie?"

"Nothing, Paddy..."

"Come on, little Maggie, tell me the secret..." She shushes him in a stage whisper, but looks past him, pointing with her eyes. Paddy follows her gaze; a fresh-faced boy of about fifteen picks his way through the crowd, his eyes fixed on Grace. His pressed white shirt, striped tie and polished black shoes mark him out from the crowd.

He approaches Grace, smiling shyly at her, and nods his hello. She nods back, but looks down at the floor.

Maggie breaks the silence, "Hello, George."

"H-h-hello, M-Maggie." The boy stammers slowly and carefully, giving Paddy the impression of enormous effort. He continues to look at Grace, as if willing her to speak.

Maggie sighs in exasperation, "George, this is Paddy - the man who helps us in the winter times. Paddy, this is George Bonville."

The boy manages to tear his eyes away from Grace, examines Paddy with a mixture of curiosity and envy, and blushes. "P-p-pleased to m-m-meet you." He holds out a hand tentatively.

Paddy shakes it, careful not to crush the boy's soft hand. "Pleased to meet you too, George." The poor boy looks terrified, Paddy thinks.

George turns back to look at Grace and takes a deep breath; with immense effort, he manages to speak the next sentence with minimal stammer. "I'm having a birthday party next S-Saturday at the hall. My father said I can invite you and M-Maggie. Can you c-come?"

Grace blushes again and glances at Maggie, who nods enthusiastically. Grace allows herself a smile. "We – I'd like to, George." George grins and nods enthusiastically; Grace frowns, darting a glance at Paddy, "I'll have to ask my father, though."

A shadow of doubt crosses George's face; he nods and bites his lip, scanning both girls' faces carefully, trying to read their intentions. "All right... s-s-see you next Saturday, I hope." He nods at Paddy and walks away through the crowd, his gait upright, awkward and stiff. The two older girls wait until he is out of earshot and then dissolve into giggles together.

Paddy scratches his head and raises his eyebrows. Maggie cups her hand over his ear, using a stage whisper, "George really likes Grace."

Paddy grins, "Really?"

"She likes him back, too."

Grace whacks her on the arm. "No, I don't. You like him more than I do..."

"No I don't." Maggie turns to examine Paddy's expression; she reverts to her stage whisper, "Well, he's all right really. And we do like going to the Hall. They have their own ice cream and *everything*..."

Grace adds, "You should see the fancy carpets, Paddy..."

"I can imagine, just like the officers mess." He's said it before he realises what he's revealed. His heart skips a beat but the girls don't pick up on it, anyway. He glances around to see if anyone else is listening, just in case. "Come on girls; let's see if we can find your folks."

"Mum didn't come." Grace bites her lip. "She wasn't feeling very well today."

Maggie looks at Paddy. "*You know*. Not feeling like *herself*."

"I'm sorry to hear that. Let's find your dad, anyway."

"Come on, then." Maggie sets off, pauses, and looks back. "But he'll just get you to help him, you do realise that?" Paddy shrugs, she sighs. The three girls lead him back to the market area. He spots Gilly from a distance, on a stall selling oranges and lemons to a long queue; he must have brought those down from Newcastle that morning, Paddy thinks.

Their eyes meet; Gilly's face registers no surprise until he finishes serving his customer, then slowly cracks into a wry smile. "Hello, stranger. Good timing, lad; get yourself over here, I could do with a hand. And you, Grace, you go help your cousin Billy on the hardware stall." Maggie pokes a finger into his ribs meaningfully and shakes her head. She tries to pick up June, who wriggles away out of her grasp. Gilly winks at his daughter. "Aye, all right, Maggie, I can see you're busy. Look here Paddy, this one's easy. Here's the moneybox; the prices are marked up, clear and simple. I've organised a few stalls today; one of my jobs is to take over when they all have a break. There's a lass called Betty will take over here when she comes back from having her tea. Meanwhile I'll get on over to the cake stall and let Mrs Peart have her break. OK?"

"Fine, Gilly; is it all going well? And how are you?"

For once, Gilly doesn't know what to say; he looks at the floor, before giving Paddy a rueful smile. "Sorry, lad, I'm forgetting my manners. It's really good to see you, and I'm fine. It's a perfect day for the show. Too perfect, maybe; that's why I'm rushed off my feet. We'll chat tonight when it's all done and dusted." Maybe it isn't so great a day to arrive after all, Paddy thinks.

By the time they get back to the house that night, he feels ready for his bed; wherever that's going to be. Gilly, though, has other ideas. While the girls chatter their way upstairs, their father fishes a bottle out of its hiding place; he takes two fancy glasses from an old oak cabinet, cleaning them carefully with a tea towel before pouring two careful measures. "Here's to you, lad."

Paddy raises his glass, "Slange, a chara." The whiskey burns his throat. Smokey, he thinks; probably Scottish.

"So where did you get to, this year? I don't suppose you went back to Ireland, did you?"

"I did not, Gilly, but I did send lots of postcards while I was moving around. I did myself a bit of fruit picking in Kent, vegetables in Hampshire, then back up through the midlands, near Warwick.

Started gathering some hay there and ended up repairing some sheds and barns for a feller. Paid me well, so he did; even offered me a steady job, with a cottage too. I was tempted."

"I bet you were."

"Told me most of the young men there had gone to the cities." He examines his host, noticing the deepening lines on his face. "How's Violet?" He watches Gilly take a long sip of his drink as he considers his reply. "The girls told me she's not so good."

Gilly stares into the fire. "Did they now? Well, I suppose not. I've got used to it, I suppose."

"Used to what?"

"Oh, the silence; she stays in her room more and more, and says less and less. She has good days, but not so often now." Paddy sips his own drink and waits. "The girls don't know yet, but she's carrying a child again. That's probably why she's like this. But the pattern's worse this time, it started as soon as she knew." He knocks back the rest of his drink, pours another, and chews his lip. "I tried to be careful, Paddy. But sometimes that's the only time that she's like her old self, in the night." He glances at Paddy, who nods. "Can't be helped, can it, now? Another mouth to feed; but we had a good day at the fair today, and the businesses are doing well enough." He tops up Paddy's glass. "I was thinking you could help me with some of the buying again, this winter. And I can teach you the book keeping. You with your numbers, it'll come easy to you."

"Whatever you want me to do, Gilly. But I think I must take a trip to Ireland in the spring."

"Oh yes. That reminds me..." He goes back to the cabinet and reaches up. "These letters came for you, after you'd left." He frowns. "I didn't like to mention it in front of the girls. But I don't like the look of them, somehow. You might need that drink." He holds them out, gingerly.

Paddy takes them, and sees that there are three letters, all addressed to "Paddy Reilly, care of the Hardy family". One hand he recognises instantly, his mother; but the second is written by an unfamiliar hand, and the third has been typed. He sighs and opens the one from his mother first, carefully.

"*Dearest Fons, I'm sorry to tell you that I have been ill these last few months, sorry for myself too and for Sean. I didn't want you to see me like this so I hope you will forgive me not telling you before now, but when it comes to it I wanted you also to know that I have had a good life with Sean and no regrets on that score. He is a good man, like you. I know you feel bad about the wedding but please forget it. That was my fault as much as yours for wanting to see you in the uniform. Myself, I didn't have any notion it would* cause a Pandora's box to be opened. If only I had talked about it to Sean, it might have been prevented. Anyway we have both been pleased to hear about the English family and how you return there every year, it tells us they are good people of the earth, like the folk here. I suspect this letter will not reach you before you leave for your latest travels but if it does it would be good to see your face. You will always be welcome here with Sean and his brother. Know that I will always keep you in my heart, your loving mother, Alice."*

He feels a tightening in his chest while he considers her words. Aware of Gilly watching him, he clears his throat and tries to speak evenly. "This is from my mother. She's been ill." Then he tears open the second letter, his hands shaking.

"Dear Fons, there is no easy way to tell you this. Your mother died yesterday afternoon from the cancer. This will be a terrible shock and I am sorry you have had no warning. She found out about it four months ago. For a long time she wouldn't talk about it with me either and I'm betting she didn't mention it in her letters to you. I wanted her to tell you sooner, but she wouldn't until near the end, when she wrote you a letter, which I posted for her. We also did our best to see if the doctors in Cork city could help but they told us from the X rays it was already too late. So the local man did his best to help her and make her as comfortable as he could. That's all I can say. I'll delay the funeral as long as I can in case this letter finds you soon. If it's later, know you will always be welcome here with myself and Ernie. Sincerely, Sean Mahon."

He hears a flat voice; his own. "She's died." He picks up the envelope and looks at the postcode. "Last May, just after I left." The typed letter informs him that his mother has bequeathed him (Alfonsus Gilligan, also known as Patrick or Paddy Reilly) eighty Irish pounds, giving him instructions on how and where to collect it. It reassures him that the British Military Police have no jurisdiction in Ireland. He looks up, hearing movement, to see Gilly filling both glasses up to the top. They talk deep into the night; the next morning, unusually for him, he has absolutely no memory of what they discussed.

*   *   *

A gentle rain sweeps in from the west, banks of low grey clouds rolling slowly across the horizon like an army on the move. Fons, as he's become again here, lingers by the headstone, staring at the black letters. His body and mind still feel entirely numb, in a way that makes him pinch himself or surreptitiously thrust his finger into a hot cup of tea just to feel some reaction. He shuts his eyes. Through the pervading damp, faint smells of flowers and manure seep into his senses. His right hand, he remembers, still clutches the bunch of flowers picked in the garden at the Mahon farm. Sean told him his mother had planted these flowers. Through them, he finally senses a living connection to her. He has no idea what they're called, but he recognises their smell. He recalls memories of the cottage, of half-pint glasses filled with flowers in unexpected places. At last, he feels a sharp pang of longing and grief; an urge to cry, even if the tears don't flow. He lingers for a while, trying to fix the image of this grave in his mind before he leaves, but the effort seems to make the scene feel unreal again, as if he is watching himself in a film. The accumulated dampness finally begins to run down his neck. He replaces his cap, carefully places the flowers on the grave, and walks away.

The bus to Cork city groans as it climbs the hill, bumps and rattles over the crest. It seems to take an eternity to reach full speed on the down slope, only to slow with a sudden howl of protest, diverting down a lane to reach yet another village. Fons rubs his chin as he watches a great splash of water scythe into the hedge. There are few passengers; none of them are saying much. They look like this country feels, he thinks; poor, miserable and bedraggled. In Cork, he digs the scrap of paper out and makes his way to the address scrawled upon it. He finds a small flat, two floors above a draper's shop, half a mile from the city centre. The stairs leading up are bare wooden boards, with a musty smell of cats; the wallpaper has seen better days.

But as he knocks on the door he feels a pang of excitement, of energy, for the first time on this trip. And Mary's face, when her beaming smile greets him, seems well worth the journey. "Fons...God love you, you're a sight for sore eyes, you big handsome devil..."

"You too, Mary..." He stands back to survey her. "You're quite the woman about town, I'd say." She looks to him far prettier than she ever did as a girl; he admires her stylish dress, a luxuriant mock oriental pattern, with a matching top. They hug the shape of her figure perfectly; her body also seems far more self-assured as she moves forward to hug him.

"Am I now? I'm glad to hear it. But come in, we'll have some tea first." He watches her shut the door and turn to examine his face. "I was terribly sorry to hear about your mother, Fons." He takes a deep breath and nods. Much to his surprise, he feels a tear slowly trickle down his cheek. "It's not the way I wanted it, Fons, but I'm so glad you came back to see us again." He nods again. She reaches up and gently brushes the tear away, taking hold of his arm. "Come along now, this way." She sits him down and feeds him ham, potatoes and peas, followed by tea and biscuits, while he tells her about his visit to the Mahon farm.

"All in all, I suppose the place was what I expected. Physically, the house is a bit bigger than your parents' place, but not much. The land's similar, not so much clay maybe, better soil. The real difference is the Mahon house feels more like a museum, a shrine. Did you know the father died too?" She shakes her head. "It was last year, he caught the pneumonia. So Ernie and Sean have lost their mother, Pat, their father, and now Alice, all from that house. Sean wanted me to stay longer but I couldn't. They are nice fellers, and so keen for company, but they are like two old men. I felt I would suffocate." He feels enormous relief, putting these feelings into words. "But then, from what everyone told me, it's been a terrible struggle to keep their farm going."

Mary nods. "For Michael and my parents, too; did you visit?"

"Of course, I wanted to see our old cottage, but that was the worst sight of all. The roof is going; I suppose it'll fall apart, now that it's empty."

"Yes, that's the problem, Fons; you see them everywhere, places like that, with so many people leaving the country for work. Places empty, with no value, just falling apart. The farming surplus sent prices of food to rock-bottom; a surplus at home and the foreign markets in recession."

He sighs. "But you seem to be doing well."

She smiles. "Not as well as I might be, soon." He raises his eyebrows. "I'm moving to Dublin, Fons. I got myself a promotion, for the Grafton Street store. Cork is grand in its way, but in Dublin I can educate myself even better than here; there's so much going on there. And everything's better for women in the cities."

Fons frowns. "I'm sure it is. Sean and Ernie were telling me a few tales about Ernie's experiments with the matchmaker. A devil of a job, they say, around these parts, hunting for eligible females to pair off with all those bachelor farmers..."

"Away with you; that's precisely why I want to go to Dublin, to get away from all that nonsense. What about yourself, Fons?"

"I'm not fond of cities."

She pulls a face. "Not that, you lummock; have you not got a girl somewhere?"

He scratches his head. "Well, I must have, but she hasn't told me yet." He sees a look of concern on her face. "Don't you worry about me, Mary; I've met some girls here and there. Put it this way, when I was picking fruit down in Kent I had myself a full basket now and then. The girls down there had a bit of fun educating a shy young Irish lad; and I was not such a lummock as to want to spoil their enjoyment. But none of them was wanting anything too serious; least of all me. All in good time, I say. I think you and me are a bit alike in that way, Mary."

She gives him a searching look. "Maybe. But while we're thinking of the great temptations, have you heard from our Pat recently?"

"Not for a while, myself; we were both too busy running away, last time we met, remember? So we lost touch with each other. But I've got an address now from Sean – care of some shipping company. I'll write when I get back to England. Sean told me he was in America a while, but he didn't settle there."

"Well, you can write to me in Dublin and tell all me his news. And you can tell him I was asking after him."

Fons raises an eyebrow. "Is that water under the bridge, or a candle waiting for the dusk?"

"Never you mind, Fons Gilligan." She laughs and shakes her head, adopting a softer tone. "If you must know, it's a bit of both. I'm not one to bear grudges. More than that, I'm awfully curious to see what kind of man he's turned into. He might just have got better with time. You certainly have."

"Have I?"

"You've got yourself an air of calmness these days. You used to be so nervous."

"Well, I know I can survive and turn my hand to different things. I still miss the army, though, that was what I was best at."

"Well, let's hope they don't miss you enough to root you out."

"I think that's unlikely after all this time, Mary, and this is for why. When you write to me, you see, this feller Fons Gilligan only exists over here in Ireland. There's another feller across the water by the name of Paddy Reilly. It's him you'll have to be writing to, and he's never been anywhere near the British army." He winks and shows her his baptismal certificate.

* * *

Paddy wakes early, roused by the light of dawn. He pulls on some clothes, rakes out the ashes below the range and feeds logs into the fire, adding a small amount of coal to raise the temperature. Gilly appears; both men slip silently into their morning routine - washing, shaving, heating water for tea, preparing the breakfast, making sandwiches for everyone's lunch. Upstairs, they hear Grace waking the other girls. "Is it today that doctor is coming, Gilly?"

Gilly ignores him for a full half minute; Paddy waits, knowing how much the older man has worried about this day. Eventually, Gilly finishes cutting bread and utters an affirmative grunt. "Supposed to be here at eleven; don't say anything to the girls, will you?"

Fons nods and ignores the sharper than necessary tone. "Don't worry, I won't. Shall I walk down to the village with them this morning?"

"Better if you drive Grace down to the station; make sure she catches her train. You can see if there's any parcels waiting for me down there; I'm expecting some paint for Violet's brother. Maggie can look after June and Rose; it's no distance to the village school. When you get back I'll take the bairn to my sister. That way one of us is always here. I don't want any chance of Violet going wandering this morning. After that, you can take the car and do the rounds today. I'll have to be here all day, just in case. "

Fons nods. "How is she?"

"Same as ever." Gilly frowns; Paddy watches the deep lines etch into his face. "Three months now, she's not spoken to anyone, since Harriet was born. Even before that, she'd not really made any sense since Christmas." Paddy shakes his head. The likes of Violet's problems are something of a mystery to him. He remembers one boy from St Joseph's who didn't speak much, but that boy was obviously completely stupid. His early experiences with the Hardy family showed him that Violet is nothing like that; she has a case full of books in her room and has read them all. But he rarely sees Violet now; when he does, she avoids all eye contact or discussion even when he attempts to greet her. She rarely ventures out of her room, except when she visits the lavatory outside. And since she has a commode in her room, this happens only occasionally; usually, when no one is there to observe her.

"Is this doctor coming down from Newcastle?"

"Aye, a specialist; he's charging enough for it, too."

Paddy nods; time to change the subject. "You want me to go to Newcastle, Gilly?"

"I should think so, Paddy. The living in the dale's improved no end recently; building that reservoir at Burnhope brought work for a lot of families. The shops are busy at last." He scratches his head. "Added to that, I hear steel making is picking up at last."

"How does that help?"

Finally, Gilly allows him half a smile. "Some people make a living picking out fluorspar from the spoil heaps. They use it as a flux, apparently; whatever that is."

Paddy considers this. Certainly better to be here than in Ireland, he thinks, judging by Mary's letters. Good for this family, too. "So will Maggie be going to the grammar school with Grace next year?"

"Aye, as long as she passes her admission test." Gilly looks up from buttering the bread and raises an eyebrow. "I'd put my house on it. She's as bright as a button, that one." A clatter of feet half tumbles, half runs down the stairs. He puts his fingers to his lips. "Speak of the devil..."

Paddy's mood lightens as he drives up and down the dale that morning, kept busy collecting the orders. He begins to relax until a slight rattle begins to draw his attention. What is it, and where is it coming from? He doesn't want to go back and ask Gilly; that man has enough on his plate today. But it worries him - he knows how precious this car is. He forces himself to drive slowly, and stops to ask the opinion of the mechanic at the pump in Stanhope, just before the point where the road climbs up out of the valley, over the moors towards Newcastle. The man jacks the car up, and then rotates the wheel. Unloaded, it spins easily, but with a faint scraping noise. The man cocks his ear and nods at him. "Bearing's bit tewed. Owt else is in canny fettle, mind."

"How far will it go?"

The man shrugs, "Nowt's brak; a fair way."

"To Newcastle and back?"

"Oh aye, ah've heed varra warse."

However, the relief he feels soon begins to evaporate. The further he goes, the rattle from the wheel just keeps getting louder all the way to Newcastle, where an accompanying squeak develops. He stops to eat his lunch, only to discover he's forgotten his sandwiches. Driving through the city streets, the noise becomes ever louder; people begin to turn and stare as he drives past. So much so, he begins to have second thoughts. He cuts his foraging short, deciding to head back without visiting the leather shop or the candle maker. Half way back across the high moors, the wheel hub begins screeching in protest. He stops to have another look at it; nothing seems obvious. He grasps the hub, to see if he can wobble the wheel by hand. A second later, he whips his hand away, cursing, a bright red welt on his palm.

He waits half an hour for the hub to cool, and sets off again, listening carefully. Suddenly he hears a loud pop, and slews to a halt again. He can't believe his eyes. The car has a flat tyre on a different wheel. He digs out the tools from under his supplies and manages to fit the spare wheel, despite the pain of his burned hand. He drives on slowly, stopping to wait at the top of Crawleyside, the steep bank above Stanhope, to let the hub cool again; the brakes will certainly add friction and heat, going down the hill. By the time he gets down into the valley, darkness is falling; more important, the garage at the bottom is closed. After another wait for the wheel to cool off, he sets off to drive the last few miles. The bearing finally gives up the ghost with a loud crack in the village of Eastgate, locking the wheel. With some help from the locals, he manhandles the car onto a patch of ground next to the village shop and asks the owner to keep an eye on it. Then he sets off to walk the last three miles in the darkness, cursing his own misfortune.

The final half-mile is the worst, a steep walk up the side of the valley and a stumble along a dark, rutted lane. By the time Paddy slips the latch on the back door, his stomach is rumbling, his legs feel like jelly, and he can barely raise a smile, even for Grace. Sitting at the kitchen table reading her schoolbook, she glances up and beams a welcome. Then she frowns and mouths the word "Dad", pulls a face, and mimes a wagging finger. He understands this to mean that Gilly is not in one of his better moods. Oh no, he thinks, just what I need. She points upward. Through the ceiling, he hears a child sobbing and a stern male voice; he can't make out the words. On the table, he notices a packet wrapped in brown paper. Grace pushes it towards him; he flops down gratefully to devour his sandwiches. Grace gives him a sympathetic look and pours him a glass of milk.

When Gilly descends, he stares at Paddy in surprise. "I didn't hear the car."

Paddy feels heat in his cheeks; he wonders whether to break the news quickly, or in stages. "No, I walked. I had to leave the car in Eastgate."

"Why the hell did you do that?"

He looks Gilly in the eye. "The car broke down; I think the wheel bearing has gone." He is tempted to tell him about the mechanic, but decides to leave that part of the story untold.

"Jesus Christ, that's all I need." Gilly stares back at him for a long moment, walks over to the back door. He lifts the latch, stares out into the night for a moment, and turns back to Grace. "You can get yourself up to bed now, young lady." Grace starts to open her mouth, then thinks better of it. Paddy watches them both exit. He sighs to himself and waits at the table. Outside, he hears the stable door bang twice, three times, and then a long silence. He finishes his milk, and slumps forward on the table, his eyes shut, head resting on his arms. A beer would go down well right now, he thinks. A little walk down the hill into the village might revive me; or maybe not...

The scratch and whoosh of a match striking close by wakes him. He lifts his head and sees Gilly puffing on his pipe, hazel eyes narrowed but meeting his own gaze steadily. Paddy yawns and stretches, waiting for the older man to speak. "Come on then, Paddy lad, tell us what happened."

"The wheel started making a noise while I was getting the orders. I asked the fella at the pump below Crawleyside to take a look at it. He told me it was a wheel bearing but it wouldn't need fixing for a while. He said it would get me to Newcastle and back all right. He was wrong. It got much worse coming back, and the wheel seized up in Eastgate."

Gilly takes a couple more puffs on his pipe before replying. "I'll have a quiet word with Norman about that. The bearing must have had a bad crack, though. I did have one of those go before, but that one lasted three months before it got bad." He sighs, his face one of exhaustion rather than anger, now. "No use crying over spilt milk. We'll have to borrow one of my brother-in-law's ponies until it's fixed."

Paddy nods and watches Gilly examining his own right hand. Probably where he thumped the stable door, he thinks. He feels wary of speaking, though Gilly seems much calmer. Eventually he risks, "How was your day?"

"About the same as yours." Gilly takes another couple of puffs on his pipe, then adds, "That damn doctor arrived an hour late, demands his money first, and then only spends five minutes with Violet. Five minutes. Then he tells me there's nothing he can do unless I let him lock her up in his bloody madhouse. And even then he can't be sure that she'll ever come home again. I ask you, as if I would even think of doing that to Violet."

"Jesus."

"So I told him what to do with his specialist advice and his bloody special hospital for nervous diseases. You should've seen the look on his face. Trouble is he already had my money. Twenty guineas, Paddy, all for nothing; bloody quack."

"Sounds like your day was even worse than mine."

"Aye, lad I reckon it was. I did find out one thing, though. The midwife also called about Harriet's feeding. She told me I should get a goat for Harriet's milk. Violet's not feeding her, and cow's milk seems to upset the bairn. Easier to digest, goat's milk, apparently." He takes another deep puff on his pipe, but this provokes an extended fit of coughing. When it subsides, Gilly goes to the back door and spits into the yard.

"You all right, Gilly?"

"Smoke went a bit too far down, lad. Touch of miner's lung. Still, there's a drop of that whiskey left if you can stand it. Think I need a drop to loosen the phlegm."

"If you go twisting my arm again, Gilly, I'll have to force some down, just to keep you company, of course." The nightcap will help us both sleep, he thinks.

Sometime in the early hours he hears someone moving down the stairs, going out of the door. Gilly or one of the girls, needing to use the toilet, he thinks, and drifts back off into a dream. He finds himself moving through a field of barley, checking that the grain is ready to harvest, along with one of the army cooks from the Irish guards, who needs the grain to make illegal whiskey at the barracks.

It's all top secret, but very, very important. Some great mystery is about to be revealed to him; he hears a voice whispering to him, whispering secrets from the real world... he wakes to find Gilly standing over him, holding an oil lamp. "Wake up, Paddy."

He groans, "What is it?"

Gilly scratches his head and pulls a face. "It's Violet. I woke up and she'd gone. I've had a look outside but she's not out there using the toilet. She must have gone wandering."

"In the night?"

"Yes, maybe the doctor's visit upset her too."

Paddy swallows. "If he said anything to her, you mean?"

"Aye." He swings himself out of bed, reaching for his clothes. "Paddy, you wait here, in case the girls wake up or she finds her way back while I'm out. I'll take the dogs and find her." Paddy starts to dress while Gilly goes back upstairs, returning a few moments later with a thick blue coat under his arm. Paddy looks at the coat; it's a warm, windless night. Gilly scratches his head again and bites his lip. "She... I'd better warn you, Paddy...if she comes back, I don't think she took any clothes with her."

Paddy waits, sitting at the kitchen table with a candle, for a long time; he thinks of his own childhood, of his own running away, his own desperation to escape. He can't understand exactly why Violet might feel like that, but he can understand the sort of feelings that might be driving her to act in this way. He's seen the fear on her face often enough; in fact, he realises, the root of her problem seems to be that she is afraid of everything and everyone - to a degree that seems to paralyse her, mentally and physically. There is no logic to it, but that is the way she is. What astonishes him more is how Gilly tolerates it day after day, patiently accepting the way she is. Paddy can't understand why Gilly does not get angry with her, as other men surely would. He sits, thinking, until the candle burns down and he has to light another. He nods off a couple of times, sitting upright, before the jerk of his head wakes him again. The third time this happens, he senses a change. He feels a draught, hears someone breathing nearby. He blinks, and pushes the candle back, so that he can see around him.

By the half open door, Violet stands, watching him intently. She's entirely naked; her feet, hands and ankles streaked with mud. She shivers occasionally, her breathing shallow and rapid. Her pose seems provocative, making no effort to cover herself, but also fearful. He can't help but look at her body. She's still a very attractive woman, even after five children. He breasts are small but full, and her hips slim and shapely. There are streaks of grey in her dark hair, which falls almost to her waist. She has a large, prominent belly button, above a delicate mound of curls. He tears his eyes away, back to her face. He watches her swallow; one hand moves down to cover her pubic region, while the other lifts to play with the hair around her ear; half of her ashamed, the other half seeming to tease him. She even gives him a half smile and then looks away.

"Violet..." he stops, unsure what to tell her. What can he say?

"He won't send me away, will he?" Her voice is a whisper, though the unexpectedness of it cuts through him like thunder. After the shock, relief floods through him.

"No, Violet, he won't."

"The doctor said he would."

"He won't, Violet. You know Gilly; no doctor can tell him what to do. Ask him yourself when he gets back." She stares at him, as if examining the veracity in his face.

"Has he gone away?"

"No, no ... he's not here now, but he's only out looking for you." She looks away and nods, looking down, and her other hand moves to cover her breasts. Paddy is left wondering what to say once again. She looks up at him again, with that same half smile.

"Do you want to send me away?"

He sighs. "No, Violet, I don't." Then, something in her tone makes him blurt out, "But you should go upstairs. I mean, Gilly will be back soon... why don't you wait for him upstairs?" A wounded look crosses her face. She looks away again, rejected, and runs across the kitchen, padding quietly away and up the stairs without another word.

He sighs, and whispers to himself. "Jesus, Mr and Mrs Hardy, I thought I was the fella that trouble followed around. What on God's earth have you two done to deserve this?"

*   *   *

The half-light creeps through the flimsy curtain; he allows himself to continue dozing, hovering where sleep and wakefulness sit silently and comfortably together, like old friends. It's Sunday, he remembers, the spring bank holiday; the previous evening, Gilly declared that they should all have a day of rest together. He drifts back into his doze again, letting go of this memory, vaguely aware of the sound of the animals and birds greeting the dawn. This unaccustomed luxury, soaking himself in warmth and comfort, secure in his bed, reminds him of Sundays in Ireland at the Conlon farm. His sleeping self decides to start out on a fishing trip there, sneaking out of the farm to catch the sun rising over the river, watching the fish rise as he baits his rod. He waits patiently until he feels the nibble at the end of his rod. Just as he lands the fish, the fruit picking girls appear to watch him at work, making raucous jokes as he handles the slippery fish. He doesn't want to leave this dream, aware of its possibilities, with these girls. But in the real world, he can now hear movement in the kitchen next door. Reluctantly, he lets go of the dream as a tapping on the door drags him into wakefulness. He sits up, yawns, and rubs his eyes, "Alright, Gilly." The tapping repeats, a little louder, "Hello?"

A female voice calls, "Can I come in, Paddy? I've brought you some tea."

"Just a minute..." He feels a moment of panic as he checks and adjusts the blankets, aware of his erection, the last gift of the dream. As an afterthought, he leans out, finds his vest and pulls it over his head. "Come in."

The door swings wide to reveal Maggie, smiling shyly as she moves slowly and carefully forward, balancing cup and saucer, "I've made it how you like it." He conceals disappointment, having hoped the voice belonged to Grace; now a very beautiful girl, well named. Paddy cannot help but think about her sometimes when he is alone. Still far too young for him; though not that much younger, he remembers, than some of the fruit pickers. He expects that she will remain a fantasy, albeit a very enjoyable one; she adopts a reserve towards him, which he accepts as his lot. By contrast, Maggie follows him around whenever she can, smiling shyly, and blushing wildly when he dares to glance at her, comparing her with her sister. Her breasts are just beginning to develop and the rest of her body is still boyish.

He keeps his eyes on his tea, today. "Thanks a million, Maggie. What time is it?"

"It's half past seven; Dad's making breakfast. He said to tell you to get up now. He'll take us to Sunday school after breakfast. It's a beautiful day; he thinks it's going to be hot today."

"Is it? That'll be grand, won't it?"

"Dad says if it is, we can all go to the bathing pool when we get back. Are you coming?"

"The one at the hotel?"

"No, silly; the one in the river, down at Eastgate."

"Maybe, if it's warm enough."

"Softy... old lazybones..."

He grins and looks up. She is the only one brave enough to tease him like this. "Today, maybe I am, baby Margaret." She puts her tongue out and pulls a face.

It promises to be a fine, cloudless and windless day. After breakfast Paddy basks in the garden at the front of the house, which sits half way up the steep valley on a shoulder overlooking the village below. Facing the sun, looking over the narrow valley, the temperature steadily rises. When Gilly returns with the girls, he announces that he is making tea; usually, a signal that he wants to talk. Paddy goes inside and waits at the kitchen table. The older man pours hot water into the teapot, avoiding his eyes. "Do you still want to go fruit picking this year, Paddy?" The tone is casual, but he wears a frown on his face.

"Only if you can spare me, Gilly."

"Well, I've been doing some thinking, Paddy, about Violet." He places the teapot on the table, replaces the kettle, and clears his throat. "To tell you the truth, I'm thinking of moving again." He rubs his forehead. "For a number of reasons."

"What did you have in mind, Gilly?" Paddy watches him considering his next words.

"You and I both know Violet's not showing much sign of going back to her old self."

Paddy feels shocked by these words, at first. She still has occasional good days, doesn't she? Gilly's always so loyal to Violet, usually so quick to make excuses for her...

"It's not that I'm giving up hope, Paddy, it's not that."

He looks up, realising his emotion must have showed in his face. Gilly sees her every night, he thinks, as no one else sees her. "I don't think that, I'm just surprised..."

"... to hear me talk of it?" Gilly nods, as if to himself, "Well, yes, I don't talk of it much, but I do think on it; all the time, if the truth were known. Anyway, there's no point in wishing away your life. Do something about it, that's what my father always said to me."

"That sounds like good advice."

"It was. What Violet needs is a decent place where she can be left alone, but with us nearby. Somewhere that's easy for her family and mine to visit. I moved up here to Chesters because it would be a smaller place, easier to run. But she's never even managed the garden, and it's a long way up this hill. Then there's my business. I don't really need the land here or any of the animals any more. Violet's not going to miss any of that, it might even make her feel better, not having it there to worry about. Then there's the girls; we'd be far better in a village, near the railway station, for Grace and Maggie's schooling." He looks at Paddy, checking his expression.

"I can't be disagreeing with any of that, Gilly."

Gilly sighs, with relief and with guilt, it seems to Paddy. "You know the pub at Eastgate?"

"The Cross Keys?"

"Aye. It has a lot of rooms; even got a big sitting room on the first floor that catches the sun, with grand views out of the windows. Ideal for Violet; and be ideal for everyone to visit, too. The men would come for a pint, their wives would call in to see Violet. The railway station is just down the road. I've had my eye on it for a while. It has the Post Office on the premises too." He looks at Paddy again, directly. "When we moved here, the girls needed more looking after. You've helped make up for Violet, Paddy, until now. But now the girls are a bit older they're beginning to look after each other more. And a pub and post office would be something the girls can learn, and help with, when they're older."

"So you won't be needing me this summer, you mean?"

Gilly gives him a wry smile. "I'm hoping not; but I will need a barman in the winter."

Paddy shakes his head, "A barman? Christ, Gilly, that's a worse temptation than a sweetshop." The idea of being stuck inside all day doesn't appeal much to him, but he keeps quiet about that. "Is this pub about to be sold?"

"No, it's a letting. But guess what I heard yesterday? The present tenants are giving it up."

"Are they now? And when is that likely to be?"

"A couple of months; as soon as I heard about it, I went to see the owner and made her an offer. She's happy; she knows I can make it pay."

Paddy feels a stab of disappointment. Why hasn't Gilly asked him about this before now? He swallows that down, "Smart work, Gilly."

"Well, we should all go to the pool to celebrate; I'll try and persuade Violet to come with us. She started talking again when I told her about the pub, this morning."

A couple of hours later, Paddy watches most of the family cram into their tiny motor car, complete with a large picnic basket, blankets and towels. He has already volunteered to walk down, three miles along the riverbank. Maggie stands at his side, seizing his arm just as tightly as she seized the opportunity to have him to herself. Grace gifts him an enigmatic smile and looks to the heavens. Gilly winks at him; even Violet makes half a wave as the car moves off, the engine whining and groaning.

They descend the hill, Maggie chattering about wild strawberries and other plants that grow near the bathing pool. He has to admit, Maggie's hero worship softens the hurt of Gilly's news. Every time somewhere feels like home, he thinks, he has to leave. He's been here with the Hardy's eighteen months this time, he calculates; the longest time in one place since leaving Ireland. What next, after fruit picking? There's no work back in Ireland. Canada? He feels a thump against his side. "You're not listening, are you, Paddy?" He shakes his head. "I asked if you like poetry."

"Ah well, sometimes I do, but I don't know much. I didn't go in much for the schooling back in Ireland; the Christian brothers were a terrible lot."

"Who are they, Paddy?"

"They were the teachers, Maggie, but the only thing they taught me was what a strap felt like across your backside."

She looks at him curiously while she decides he's joking or not. "Our teachers don't do that. Would you like to hear some poetry? We're doing Wordsworth at the moment."

"Have you got the book with you?"

"No, silly," She slaps his arm again, more gently. "I can remember it. I can read a page three or four times and remember every word."

"Can you indeed, little Maggie?"

She looks hurt; "I'm not that little."

"You are compared to me." He pauses for a moment, adding with a tone of admiration, "but you are growing up fast, and I would say you'll be a very clever woman, Maggie; you could be a teacher yourself, I'd say."

"Could I?" She blushes a deep pink, "Really?"

"You can teach me about poetry, anyway."

She slaps his arm again and looks away. "Don't joke about it. That's just what I want to do, Paddy, to teach, when I... when I'm older." Her eyes return to examine his response.

He feels surprised at the strength of his own reaction. "I think you'll be a grand teacher, Maggie, honest to God you will. You have a real sharpness and honesty in you; I'm not joking." She watches his face for a few moments and then nods. They walk on in silence for a while. Paddy ponders the surge of protectiveness he has just felt, wondering if Mary Conlon felt like this towards him. His nagging feelings of embarrassment about Maggie's crush on him seem to have been washed away. When they reach the river, Maggie begins to recite. He doesn't know any of the poems, but they seem to fit the day; reflections of clouds within a blue sky float past on the river.

Another nudge disturbs his reverie. "What about you, Paddy?"

"Me? I couldn't do anything like that, I have no schooling."

She looks at him, her face intent. "Don't be so sure, Paddy. You're cleverer than you think, and dad says you're the most honest person he knows." He feels the heat in his own cheeks, now. "What do you want to be, Paddy?"

Again, he feels shocked by the perceptiveness of her questioning. This, he realises, I have been avoiding. He swallows the urge to lie, or to make a joke of it, feeling that he owes her the truth. "Well, Maggie, I'd really like to be a soldier. Look, I'll tell you a secret, but you mustn't tell anyone else. I was a soldier for a while... I was pretty good at it, but I made one big mistake and they threw me out. I was very young at the time."

She nods, her eyes studying him. She has unusual eyes, a dominant blue-green in the centre, ringed with brown. The colours seem to change with the light – or is it her mood? Today, they seem green. "You should try again, now that you're older."

He opens his mouth to tell her why that's impossible, but then shuts it. Better to keep all that to himself; and maybe, he thinks, it might be possible now, with his new identity, so many years later. It would have to be a different regiment, but why not? Why not indeed? He smiles. "I might just do that, Maggie; I might just give it a try."

The river, here in the high valley in summer, babbles along between natural stepping-stones, wide but not much more than ankle deep at this time of year. He and Maggie meander downstream between steep valley sides, the river bordered by woodland, stepping across streams adding to the river. When the railway bridge crossing the river comes into view, Maggie points just beyond it. He sees a natural deep water pool, just below a small waterfall, right by the bridge. In order to reinforce the bridge foundations, engineers have constructed rounded, gently sloping concrete banks on either side of the pool. Grace, June and Rose sun themselves on one of the banks while their parents and baby Harriet lie in the shade on the other. A shriek of welcome greets them; after which Paddy finds himself used first as a boat, and then as a lifeguard by the younger girls. The water's deep enough to dive into; after much persuasion, even Grace has a go.

This exercise seems to make the girls ravenous; they demand their picnic. Paddy watches Violet surrounded by all her daughters, something he has not seen since the day he met her. She seems confused at first, uncertain, but manages to smile shyly as she passes plates of food around. The girls all crowd around her, resting some part of their bodies against her feet and legs, apparently greedy for this physical contact with her, sneaking occasional glances at her face. Though the food is devoured all too soon, the girls continue to linger around her. She strokes the younger ones' hair, and then distributes some of her own sandwiches to the older girls. The scene has a dreamlike quality; none of the girls speak, unwilling to break the spell.

Paddy lies down and dozes in the afternoon heat. The sound of a distant whistle eventually disturbs him, and the rattling of a train across the bridge brings him back to reality. He sits up and sees Gilly nearby, still trying to doze. The girls are lying on the opposite bank, soaking up the sun. Violet and the baby are nowhere to be seen. He waits for a few minutes, then nudges Gilly. The older man's eyes spring open and stare at him. "What is it?"

Paddy gestures towards the girls. "I can't see Harriet, or Violet."

"Christ." Gilly sits up and looks around. He calls to the girls, "Where's your mother?"

The girls look puzzled. Grace shrugs her shoulders, "She was lying down with you."

"All right, we'll find her." He whispers to Paddy, "You look upstream, I'll look downstream. Meet you here in half an hour. Let's hope she's not got one of her ideas into her head."

Paddy retraces his earlier path along the bank. He hopes Violet hasn't gone into the woods, rather than along the river. It could all get very confusing if she returns to find us gone, he thinks. He hasn't gone far, when he sees something floating in the water, a flash of white. His heart lurches as he recognises the baby's shawl. He jumps off the bank, stumbles, and splashes out into the river. The shawl has caught on a sharp rock; it looks as if it has floated downstream. Please God, not that, he thinks, not that. Looking upstream, the river bends to the right. He picks up the shawl and wrings it dry, stumbles back to the bank and jogs rapidly upstream, scanning the pools and shadows. He stops, reckoning that he has come about a hundred yards. The shawl wouldn't be likely to go for more than three or four hundred yards in this river before getting caught, he thinks. He runs another hundred yards, and stops to look back, to double check again. He sets off again, and stops after fifty yards. He almost misses it, but something makes him stop and look back a second time. In the shadow of a small rowan tree, on the opposite bank, the child sits in the shallows, quite still, watching the water. Suddenly she leans forward and smacks the water, babbling to herself, almost overbalancing. Violet is nowhere to be seen.

He splashes across and picks Harriet up; she gurgles a welcome, clinging onto him, warming her cold wet little body. He hugs her, feeling his own tears of relief pricking his eyes, and makes his way back to the pool. Gilly takes the news very calmly; he bites his lip and whispers, "I'll go find her; if I don't return, take the girls home in an hour." Paddy sits back and watches the older girls play with Harriet while he waits. To all intents and purposes, he thinks, those girls are all her mothers, already. He wonders what to tell the girls; though none of them ask. Time passes; perhaps half an hour, before Gilly returns with Violet on his arm. He whispers into Paddy's ear, "Thought I'd left her, apparently. She said she was looking for me."

Paddy nods and bites his lip, seeing the uncertainty on the other man's face. He glances over at the girls. They whisper to each other, though none of them mention the incident, or ask what has happened, afterwards. There are some things, Paddy realises, that the girls do not want to know.

*   *   *

A memory strikes him as he strides down the rickety gangplank; 'Old Reliable', the last ship he left like this. He turns to look back and grins at the contrast. You may be just a dirty old tramp steamer, he thinks, but at least on you I'm second engineer. This time, he's made no attempt to draw his pay. If Paula isn't ready to come with him, he can slip back on board. If she is, no one will miss him for a few days. He carries a small haversack, a change of clothes, and his money belt; ideal for travelling light. He hesitates for a second, sucks a deep breath of air into his lungs, and steps onto the dock, back in Manhattan after four years at sea.

He pulls his cap down over his face as he nears the dock exit, but things seem to have changed since prohibition ended. One uniformed man lounges in a dilapidated booth, takes a cursory glance at his papers and waves him through. No black car; no thugs watching over their territory. No need any more, from what the skipper's told him. A surface of normality now hides the ILA's total control of the docks; Red Cat was swimming against *that* tide. He wonders about Freddy's business, minus all those bootleggers, and shakes his head. He'll be doing fine.

He treats himself to a late breakfast at a diner on Thirty-Ninth Street, partly to pass the time and partly to line his stomach for the long journey that he hopes lies ahead. He takes an extra coffee, resisting the urge to spin a line to the waitress about the chorus at the Met; he keeps his head down, blending into the background. At half past eleven he pays, buys a newspaper, and heads toward the opera house, his stomach churning. No need to be nervous yet, he tells himself. They can both be scared together, later... will she look different? The only pictures he has of her are those from La Traviata, dressed to the nines. Hopefully she won't be that conspicuous, he thinks, shaking his head. Maybe he can get her to wear some spectacles, make her look more ordinary...

He arrives twenty minutes early, walks around the block once, and settles down with his paper outside the front entrance, as if waiting to buy tickets. Glancing up and down the street over the top of his paper, he scans the same articles over and over, never quite taking it in. Each time he sees a woman walking alone, he examines her carefully, trying to make reality fit with his memory. Sometimes it's the body shape that fits, sometimes the hair, sometimes the walk. Each time his hopes rise like a balloon and then fall back to earth when he sees the mismatch, the otherness. One time, a doppelganger in dark glasses walks right past on the other side of Broadway. She seems to glance twice in his direction; he wonders if it could be her, watching out for him but still unsure what she wants. By the time he decides he should call out her name, it's too late.

He checks his watch, sees that it is still five to noon, and takes a deep breath. She was never early anyway, he tells himself. A well-dressed couple arrive in a taxi, laughing, bustling in to buy tickets. The man glances at him curiously as they emerge. Pat has an urge to tell him, I sang here once. Suddenly the sidewalks seem deserted, as if noon signals a curfew; then a rush of possible sightings has him turning back and forth like a revolving door. His hopes rise and plummet each time; gradually, his certainty begins to drain away. Another woman in dark glasses seems a dead ringer for Paula until he sees that she's wearing a mink coat. She walks right by, almost touching him, trailing a scent of French perfume. By ten past twelve, doubts are trying to creep into his head; he refuses to consider them, and forces himself to turn the page of his newspaper and read.

"Excuse me?" He turns around and sees a woman - the same attitude, the same smile, with that exact same hair. He stumbles forward a step in his eagerness.

"Paula..." He sees a blank expression, the nose too thin, the eyes not quite the same. He stops and swallows, watches her retreat a step. "Sorry, I... you look just like someone I know."

"Do I?" She smiles, her face colouring a little. "I'm sorry if I startled you. But I wondered, is there another entrance? One for the performers?" She has a trace of a foreign accent, German perhaps; she looks smart but not over-dressed. She meets his eyes, examining his expression.

He nods, "There is. I can show you if you like."

"That would be so very kind." Her accent both softens and slows the words. She smiles; her pencilled eyebrows lift, "Are you a singer?"

He clears his throat, unsure what to say. "I used to be." What the hell, he thinks. "I sang here once, a while ago."

"Ah... that's good. I thought you must be a singer." She stares at him expectantly, and then glances back and forward. "Which way is it?"

"Of course, sorry - this way." As he gestures, she lightly takes his arm so that he walks around the corner with her in step, the smell of lavender and violets teasing his senses. She's flirting with me, he thinks. He coughs again, and forces a smile, "How did you guess; that I can sing?"

She considers this as they walk. "You look like a singer. And I am new here, my first day today. You were waiting outside. To be honest, I hoped you might be waiting for me."

He doesn't reply, but nods. When they reach the stage entrance he tells her, "Good luck... you'll love it, it's a grand place to sing; heaven on earth, in fact."

She looks up at him, nods, and offers her hand, "Thank you, Mister...?" The softness of her voice contrasts with the formality of the gesture.

"MacMahon; Pat MacMahon."

She opens the door and then turns back, "My name is Vera. Perhaps I will see you again?"

He shrugs, "Perhaps." He catches a look of disappointment in her eye as she turns away. He watches the door shut, staring at it for a long moment, overwhelmed by the strangeness of the encounter, the possibilities of another life, on this day of all days. Then he hurries back around to the Broadway entrance, convinced that Paula will arrive at this very moment and decide that he hasn't turned up. But the sidewalk's still deserted, empty.

By half past twelve his doubts are taking form, shaping into real possibilities. Maybe she had an accident, or one of her kids is sick. Maybe she is sick. Maybe she just isn't ready yet. Maybe she's changed her mind, or met someone else. He waits outside the Metropolitan until one o'clock before returning to the diner for more coffee. He hasn't really thought this one through, he realises. What next? Go half way round the world and come back next year? Even for an Irishman, he thinks, that's crazy. I can't wait that long without knowing something; better to know. Even if she's changed her mind, she obviously hasn't told Freddy, or I'd be dead or in hospital already. I'd better take a look, sneak round and see if I can talk to her, just for a minute. At this time of day, after four years, it should be safe enough; though it still scares the shit out of me.

An hour later, standing outside the apartment, he checks the name on the door. His fear and anxiety started to rise when he entered little Italy; seeing the name "Manzini" does nothing to quell it. He hasn't felt this scared since he was back in Ireland. Alone in the hallway, he puts his ear against the door; nothing. He waits, listening intently. There - someone moving around inside. In the distance, on another floor, a door slams.

What the hell, he thinks, and knocks softly on the door. After a while, he knocks again, louder. He hears slow, soft footsteps from inside, and the door opens. He stares at the woman; older, rounded face, ash blond hair. A relative, he wonders? He hopes it's one of hers. "You selling something, or what?"

He swallows, "Is Mrs Manzini here?"

"I'm Mrs Manzini."

His mouth opens; he's not sure what to say. Are you sure, he thinks? She stares at him as if he's an idiot. "I mean... well, Paula?"

212

She blinks; a penny drops, behind the curtain of her disdain. Her face softens as she regards him, "Oh, I guess you mean his first wife." He nods, wondering if Freddy's divorced her. Please God, yes. "You don't know, do you?" He shakes his head. "You an old friend?"

"I am; I used to sing with her."

She sighs, "Look, I'm sorry. She had an accident." She looks down at the floor. "She got hit by a car. That's all I know; killed outright, as far as I know."

The floor opens up and swallows him. The sensation passes, although he wants it to continue. He hears his own voice, whimpering, "Oh no; please, no..."

"I'm sorry." She avoids his eyes, talking rapidly, "Freddy was real cut up by it, the kids too. I came as his housekeeper first, to look after the kids. And then, you know..." Automatically, he nods. Yes, he thinks, he's quite a catch, for you. "Who shall I say called?"

He stares at her for a long moment, "Just tell him... tell him Alfredo called." He watches her nod, before she shuts the door quickly, eager to get away from his pain.

Emerging onto the street, his mind is a whirl. It stinks, somehow; he knows that much. Stinks worse than anything that happened in Ireland... he has to find out more. At the headquarters of the 'Wobblies', he shows his marine workers card (the first time he's really used it) and asks for Johny Lewis. After a short wait he's ushered into a large, sparsely furnished office. The man behind the desk examines him, scratching his head, "Do I know you? You look vaguely familiar."

"We met a few years ago. I was with Red Cat; you let me stay while I found work."

He nods; "So, you out of work again?"

"No, nothing like that; been at sea four years now. I worked my way up to second Engineer. Look, Mr Lewis, I was real grateful to you and Cat for that start. How is she?"

The man leans back in the chair and squints up at him, "You have been away, haven't you? Well, they let her out of jail, anyway." His mouth twists into a rueful smile. "She got locked up for a while after the big strike in thirty-four, over on the west coast. I reckon she must've done a damn fine job for that to happen. She'll be okay now; though bored stiff, if anything. We're supposed to be winding the marine workers union down; orders of the Comintern."

"The what?"

"The international Communist Party." He winks. "Moscow." He shakes his head and shrugs. "International politics, I guess; God alone knows why. But I guess you didn't come here just to chew the fat, did you?"

Pat smiles and looks around for another chair; there isn't one. "I did not, Mr Lewis." He takes a deep breath. "You remember I started out working with Freddy Manzini?"

"Oh; yeah, now you come to mention it, I remember."

The tone sounds far less welcoming. "Listen, I was never that keen on Freddy, or what he stood for, but it was a job. And I did know his first wife, Paula." He has to stop and take a deep breath before he can continue. "I just heard today that she was killed in an accident. Do you happen to know anything about that?"

The other man blinks, walks over to the door, and shuts it. "Why do you want to know?"

"Let's just say I have a personal interest."

Lewis sits down, picks up a pencil, and taps the desk, thinking. "Okay, I'll tell you what I remember. It was a hit and run; big black car, at least two men, that's all the witnesses could say. Someone tossed a bottle of Canadian rye out the car as it sped away, so the police assumed it was a drunk driver. Freddy made a big show of his grief. His friends down here on the waterfront certainly put the word out for information. But neither they nor the cops ever heard anything or found the car. Which suggests to me the car was disappeared and the guys were from out of town. Or they weren't looking too hard."

Pat feels no surprise. "When exactly did this happen?"

"Let's see; it would be about this time of year; but three, maybe four years ago." He looks up and nods as the penny drops, his eyes narrowing. "And you left four years ago?"

Pat makes his way back to the boat in a daze, the words he's heard going round and round in his head but never making sense. In the tiny cabin he shares with the third engineer, he collapses on his bunk, curls up, and cries silently to himself, aware only of a gathering darkness. When the dim light of a new day rouses him, he sits up and discovers several paper bags, things he must have bought, on the other bunk. He can't remember doing this; but he finds bread, cheese, tinned meat, a pint of whiskey. He takes a pull of the whiskey. He thinks, I should have made my way to Freddy right away, faced him down. Instead, here I am skulking away in my little cabin, hiding away like the coward and failed soldier that I am. But what's the point? That bastard would only lie about it, pretend his innocence. What on earth is the point of facing him down, if not to kill him? Should I have sneaked up behind him and rearranged his brains for him, once and for all? Would that be, as Brendan said, tit for tat? I'd surely feel good about that, I surely would, but for maybe about half an hour. Then God only knows where it would lead me, one way or another I'd be joining Paula in the grave. Joining her where though, in heaven or in hell? I've never really believed in any of that nonsense; and I know one thing, she'd want me to live. I should be hanging on to that idea. She'd want me to be a coward, to stay here in my cabin until the ship leaves. Jesus Christ, it's probably too late to kill him now. That stupid crack about Alfredo will have put him on his guard. So he'll be looking over his shoulder. Well, let him carry on looking over his shoulder, the bastard, the rest of his days. Maybe I'll send him a card from Alfredo every now and then; he doesn't know I'm a coward. Let him feel exactly what it's like, to be looking over your shoulder every morning. Yes. But why, oh why, oh why, did they kill Paula? He takes another slug from the bottle and sighs. You know damned well, Patrick Mahon. That's the really hard part. The reason she died is, because you are such a fucking good coward that you got away. Freddy's friends looked all over New York and they couldn't find you, and they couldn't kill you. So they killed Paula instead, instead of you. Maybe she said something. Maybe Freddy guessed she wasn't planning to stay forever. Maybe his friends thought they were doing Freddy a favour. So why didn't we see that one coming? God almighty, why not?

*   *   *

Liverpool docks - he still hates the *idea* of England, but over the years Liverpool has become his second home. And he has to admit, it's the nearest place to Ireland in character as well as geography. This time he's signed off properly, drawn all of this pay. The gangplank wobbles precariously, as if the old tub feels furious at him for abandoning her. He steps onto English soil and looks back, feeling a sharp stab of anxiety, but he needs to do this. Since he left New York six months ago he hasn't stopped working; checking, adjusting, refitting, improving anything that moves above and below decks. He's not left the boat once. Better than drinking himself to death, he tells himself; but is it? The time has come to face the world again, to chance his arm, to see Dublin again one more time; and maybe see Mary. He owes her that. He won't risk Cork, not yet; but Dublin, from what he's heard, should be safe enough. Safer than New York, that's for sure.

His ferry arrives on a fine spring morning; he spends the day wandering the city. Late that afternoon, he finds and enters the largest department store on O'Connell Street. In the men's department he treats himself to a couple of shirts. He explores the rest of the store carefully, eventually approaching the perfume counter. He clears his throat, "I wonder if you could help me. I'm looking to buy something for a friend of mine."

She turns to face him, "Of course, how old is the lady...?" She stares at him, and bites her lip. "Pat? Holy mother of God, is that really you, Pat the singer?"

He grins at her like a Cheshire cat, savouring the moment. "Well, it might be. Though I think they'd be more likely to call me Pat the oilcan, these days. And as for your first question, the lady's older than the girl I knew, but any change that I can see has definitely been for the better. Then again, Fons did warn me about that."

"Get away with you." Her tone is scolding, though she colours and smiles. "I see you have not mislaid your silver tongue, either." She straightens her back and looks around. "Listen...I have enough perfume of my own at home, and I also have a position to keep up here. Will you meet me after work?" He nods. "There's a Lyons café just along the street. I'll meet you there in an hour, and then you can buy me some supper; how about that?"

"Thank you very much, Miss; I'm sure that will do fine." He doffs his cap, winks, and departs, shaking his head to himself. Later, while they eat, he puts it into words. "You look exactly the same in some ways, so different in others. How long has it been, anyway?"

"Fourteen years. A lot of water has flowed under our bridges, Pat. I was just a farm girl then, you were but a schoolboy soldier."

He grimaces, puts a finger to his lips; not entirely in jest. "So I was. But now, look at you. You're a woman of fashion, with your own career here in the city. And well you look on it."

"I'm happy enough. Dublin may not be London or New York, but it has good cinemas, the Gaiety theatre, and a great public library."

"Does the old Gaiety still put on opera?"

"Of course; though I must confess, I've never been. I use it for the plays and the ballet."

He raises an eyebrow, "I will have to put that right."

"I might allow you." She looks up, studying his face. "But... tell me, what are you doing here, Pat? Are you still on the boats? You haven't told me a thing about yourself, yet." She waits, and then adds, "Some things, I can see. You've filled out."

He nods, chews, and swallows; taking his time. "I suppose I've got the sea in my blood now, after all this time. I've worked my way up to second engineer; and if you saw the size of the average marine engine, you'd understand how I got these muscles. The pistons can be the size of a house, on the big ships; a horse, on the smaller ones."

"But what's it like? Don't you get lonely? And what about your singing?"

"It's a decent job; the pay's okay as long as you don't drink or gamble it away. The engineer is an officer, see, once you've served your time. As for the work, it's like looking after a great, hungry, powerful beast that keeps the ship moving. You get to know them and love them, these great beasts, like a farmer does with an animal that he depends on. And my job is to stop the beast from getting sick. As for lonely, that depends on the crew. But mostly, no, you don't get lonely; on a decent ship, you all look after each other, you all help each other out, and off duty you pass the time together. The singing comes in handy for passing the time, plus I'm teaching myself to play the squeezebox. A ship is a damned good place to forget your troubles, believe me. I take my phonograph, too, for the opera, but I don't find too many other sailors listening to that with me."

"Interesting, but..." She hesitates, and he sees the concern in her eyes. "You look exhausted, Pat. And it makes me wonder what those troubles are, that you want to forget."

Ouch, he thinks, that's the trouble with women; they can sniff out your pain. He sighs, "Oh, most of them you know about, Mary; no home, no country."

"There's something else."

He blinks back tears, tries to stifle the panic rising in his chest; pushes the remnants of his food away. "That's a long story; not now." He needs to change the subject, and grasps at his own nagging curiosity about the past. "What I'd like to know is, exactly what happened the night of the wedding party, in Cork? I mean, after we left?" Now, he sees pain on her face. She looks away, taking a deep breath. "It was pretty bad, I take it?"

"That's a long story too; you don't need to know, Pat. Not now, not here. Leave it alone."

He's shocked by her refusal; it feels retaliatory, as if her silence is intended to punish him for his inability to speak about Paula. *It's too raw, too painful, don't you understand?* He wants to shout this at her; but he feels frozen, a vast chasm opening up within the long silence that follows. Feeling an urge to escape, he stands up. This is going nowhere, he tells himself. "I'm sorry. I'll pay the bill." He picks up the slip of paper and takes it over to the till to give himself a moment. Maybe this whole thing was a really bad idea. On his return to the table, he helps her with her coat, tells her, "I'll find you a taxi."

She still looks troubled; but nods, bites her lip, and looks away. Outside, they stand awkwardly at the roadside, watching the traffic, the long silence ringing in his ears. He sees a cab, hails it, and they watch it slither to a halt. The driver winds down his window. "And where will you be going to?" She leans forward to give her address, opens the door and steps inside. I've done it again, he thinks, messed up her day. But at least it wasn't her life, this time.

He watches her hesitate, turn and look back at him, "Wait. Where are you staying, tonight?"

He has no idea; he tells her, "Just along the road."

She bites her lip and studies his face, "Some little cottage, maybe?"

He can't help but smile, "Maybe."

"There's a little pub at the end of my street. I've never been in there yet. Why don't you come with me and take me in there?" He feels torn between his urge to escape and an urge to atone for the pain he has caused her, today and in the past. Will it just make things worse, to go with her? "Come on, Pat. We can't part like this, not again."

He sighs, feeling his own fatigue; decides to give in to it, and to her; "Why not?" He sees the confusion on her face. "I mean, all right, I will come with you." In the taxi she takes hold of his arm, silently. He looks at her, trying to see her as the woman she is now without the girl from the past intruding. She's not really his type, any more; the wrong body shape. But she's not bad looking, either; if it came to a case of fun in a foreign port, she'd be fine. The real problem, he knows, she's not Paula. She seems deep in thought, makes no real attempt at conversation until the moment when he sets the drinks down in front of her.

"Let's start again, Pat. So what did you do today?"

"Oh, I inspected my old school - from the outside, anyway - and the cathedral. Then I took a look along the river, and then O'Connell Street. It hasn't changed much."

"They rebuilt the Four Courts at last."

"I saw that. I liked the way they left some of the bullet marks on the Post Office and other places. They'd never do that in America. We Irish wear our scars like beauty spots, so we do."

"Tell me about America."

He wonders; how do I begin? "Well, when I was there, it was prohibition...you know, no drinks, at least no legal bars..." Starting with the strangeness, the newness, he finds himself telling her the story. Not all of it, of course. Not the other women he knew, nor Freddy's gangster friends. But he tells her, as the hour passes, about New York, the people, the places, his work, the amateur opera company, the Metropolitan Opera house, and his love for Paula. He even tells how he left America in order to wait for her, and his final trip to New York. Somehow the past disappointments they share make it easier to tell her... "So there you have it, that's my long story."

"Oh Pat, that's terrible; I'd no idea. I must've hit a raw nerve, back in the café." He looks down at their empty glasses and nods. "Get me a whiskey, and I'll tell you about my raw nerve." He goes to the bar and returns with two doubles. She takes a sip, and then a deep breath. "The night of the wedding... you know it turned into a riot, don't you?"

"It was turning that way when we slipped out the back. We had to run for our lives. Someone took pot shots at us, as I remember. We were lucky to get away."

"Well, I'd say so too. How nobody was killed I'll never know. I think sixteen ended up in Cork hospital, everything from broken arms to cracked skulls. And some burns. Did you know the hall was burned to the ground?"

"I did not."

"Well, it was, and poor Sean ended up having to pay for a new one, by order of the court. Don't tell Fons any of this, by the way; he'll only blame himself." She takes a long sip of her drink, continues in a flat tone. "That wasn't the worst of it. It was just chaos, that night, even the women were fighting. Alice had some of her ribs broken. I remember some woman was hitting me with a stick; I tried to get away and ended up running into the woods. It seemed quiet enough after a while, so I thought I was safe..." He watches her face crumple, before she takes another deep breath, and continues, "...but I wasn't. Some man had seen me go in there, and when I started to move, he grabbed me." She looks at the floor, her voice straining with effort, pushing away the emotion. "You can guess the rest. He was so much stronger than me. There's nothing you can do. You feel so terrified, so helpless; and so ashamed, after." She swallows the rest of her whiskey. "There; I've never told a soul about that, before today."

He swallows, "Jesus. And there I was, feeling sorry for myself."

"You and me, both," She glances up at him. "What a pair. You won't be able to look at another woman for years. And now, men scare the living daylights out of me."

"Do they?" He wants to ask, even me?

"Any man who wants to get close to me, anyway. As soon as they touch me, I just panic. I can't cope with it." Her voice seems dead, expressionless; she lifts a face so full of pain that he looks away, feels a surge of guilt.

"I'm truly sorry."

"Can't be helped," She forces a smile. "I've got used to it." After a long pause, her voice comes alive again. "We can be friends, though, Pat the singer. I can cope with men that way - and I'm guessing that might be a relief to you right now. You might even come back and stay at the house; you've no cottage to go to tonight, have you?"

He laughs, "I might at that. Friends, Mary; a chara. That sounds pretty good to me."

"It's all we ever really were, Pat, when you think about it."

*   *   *

On the ferry back to Liverpool he settles into a corner, finally able to acknowledge the weariness in his bones. He reflects on his visit to the cathedral, remembering, beginning to doze; sliding into a dreaming memory...the voices of the choir echo around the cathedral, soaring up to the high oak beams under the roof. He's forgotten how amazing the sound is, in here. Looking out to the front, he notices that for some reason that Mary is conducting the choir. She looks every inch like a well-dressed schoolteacher. Yes, that must be it, he thinks, she must be our teacher now. He checks the faces around him. Yes, we are still boys. But wait a minute – the chorus from Freddy's opera company also seem to be here, all those Italian girls; suddenly, they're all singing the chorus of the Hebrew slaves together, rich harmonies of male and female voices echoing up to some musical heaven...at the end of the performance, the congregation bursts into lengthy applause. The noise dies slowly away; Pat notices that O'Brien has joined Mary. They seem to be arguing about something; every so often, they both glance up towards Pat, hiding in the roof. He feels convinced that they are arguing about him. He begins to make out occasional words, but they don't make sense. Perhaps O'Brien needs him to fight for the Republic again? Maybe he just wants to separate him from the New York choir, to rescue him before Freddy and his friends arrive? Are they watching him already, somewhere in the congregation?

He jerks awake, feeling a hand grasping his shoulder; a man sits next to him, frowning, "Ye are a sight for sore eyes, so ye are." The husky voice and unshaven face seem familiar. The shock of recognition hits him like a brick, along with a moment's panic. Is he following me?

"Brendan; Jesus Christ, what are you doing here?"

That familiar, dangerous grin creases his face. "I could be asking you the same, couldn't I? Well, no matter. We're both headed in the right direction; away from Ireland."

Pat stares back at him, thinking about Mary. Christ, was that you, you bastard? I'd put money on it. He swallows and drops his eyes, thinking hard. "Tell you what, Brendan, how about a drink for old time's sake?"

The other man nods, "I was hoping ye'd say that; I always did like ye, Pat. Once I'd decided not to shoot ye, that is." The lop-sided grin returns.

Crammed into the crowded bar, Pat sniffs his whiskey, trying to counter the stale sweat and bad breath of his companion; he thinks about Mary, again. "I'll tell ye where I'm going, Pat, I will. I'm going to fight for a Republic again." Brendan pauses, shakes his head in mock disbelief. "Not ours, though, this time; for the Spanish." He looks up at Pat's face and nods, a light in his eyes. "It's true, I swear it. I'm on my way to Paris, there's a bunch of us meeting there. Why don't ye come along, boyo? Be just like old times."

Pat bites his revulsion back; shrugs, shakes his head, "I was never such a good soldier, Brendan; you know that."

"I'd be looking after ye, Pat. Besides you're older now; tougher, too, by the looks of ye. And I'd a thought yourself, with your politics, would a' jumped at the chance." Within the persistent, hectoring tone, Pat can hear a note of desperate pleading, *come with me.* For one long moment, he is tempted to give in and go along, to give in to his tiredness, to lie down on a foreign field for another Republic...

He shakes his head, clearing the thought away, "Brendan, I got myself a trade, now - I'm an engineer in the merchant navy. And I got family..." The lie pops out without thinking; that's it, he thinks, that'll shut him up, "...a wife in America." In my heart it's true, he thinks.

Brendan shakes his head, sadly. "Ye got yourself caught in that trap? Jeez - I never thought ye'd do that, Pat. All the more reason to go to Spain, I'd say." He winks, but the urgency has vanished from his tone, "I did hear ye'd been in America."

"Did you now?" Pat curses, silently. "Who from?"

"Just one of the boys, Pat; someone who came back from there, they'd seen ye somewhere. He was involved in the liquor trade, if ye know what I mean. We still look after our own, you know, always. Ye remember that, if ye ever get in trouble."

Pat can't help but grimace inwardly; if only...another life, maybe if he'd taken Paula to Boston, perhaps? He sighs, "How about yourself, Brendan? What've you been up to?"

"This and that," Then, the mask abruptly drops, "but between ye and me, nothing worth a tinker's fart. I should'a done the same as ye, Pat - got myself over to America, instead of skulking back in Cork all this time. I swear to ye, Pat, I never felt so good as when I was with the boys. And that's the only thing I was ever good at, fighting. That's why I've jumped at the chance to do it again." He grins and downs his drink, the moment of revelation over. "I just hope the Spanish girls don't all have their legs tied together like our women."

This is the chance Pat has been waiting for. "You must have had a girl, now and then?"

He squints up at Pat, his expression incredulous. "Who'd have me, boyo? Christ, any decent woman would need a blindfold over her face before she'd be willing to touch me." He shuffles his feet, "I got my needs, like any other man, but I never got your face. So I take what I can get, if ye know what I mean."

Pat nods and thinks, yes, maybe I do. He takes a deep breath, "Let's get some fresh air, Brendan. Come back in half an hour."

Brendan nods, deep in thought himself; "Why not?"

The Irish sea rises and falls, lifting the ferry slowly up and down; at the stern, they stare back towards a distant green smudge in the half light of dusk. Officially, this part of the deck is off limits to passengers; but this is an Irish ferry. Brendan leans on the rail smoking a cigarette, his back turned invitingly. Pat glances around, sees no one; stares at the other man's back. One push, that would be it; justice for the Fitzgerald family, for sure, and for Mary, perhaps. Serve the bastard right. He's just another Freddy, Pat tells himself. With each draw the other man takes on his cigarette, Pat imagines it; one quick push, a cry, a muffled splash. That would be it. Elsewhere on the ship, nothing would be heard above the engine noise. Something holds him back - cowardice?

Brendan flips the cigarette away and turns to face him. Pat summons up his remaining courage. "Did you ever see that old girlfriend of mine down in Cork, Brendan? The one you liked, at my cottage?" He's tempted to add, the night of the wedding, but that would be too obvious.

Brendan's brows furrow, as if thinking hard, "I did not. Not after that wedding, anyway."

"What do you mean?"

Brendan scratches his head. "I don't suppose ye heard, did ye?"

"Heard what?" Pat forces his voice to remain casual, but his body feels tense, ready to spring, to explode.

"I don't remember much at all, from that time. They put me in the hospital, Pat, so they did. Split my head open, broke my arm and ribs. I fight the Black and Tans, then the Staters, for four years without a scratch, and then some stupid drunks put me in the hospital. Isn't that just the way of it? Still, we kept them busy while ye and your friend got away."

Pat stares at him, incredulous. Brendan isn't crafty enough to make this one up, is he? He decides that's unlikely; plus, it fits with what Mary told him. He scratches his head, examining Brendan's expression, "I had no idea." The other man shrugs, silent, looking at the floor, his face sheepish, embarrassed. Pat has never seen him act like this before; he must be telling the truth. Thank God, he thinks, that I *am* a coward. "Come on, Brendan, there won't be much whiskey where you're going; let me buy you another." He glances back at the wake of the ferry, now somewhat ashamed, and clears his throat. "It'll be a grand thing you'll be doing, fighting for someone else's Republic. I may not be joining you in the fighting, but I will sure as hell drink to your health and to your success."

"Now you're talking, boyo; lead the way."

*   *   *

Seagulls wheel around the boat as he steps up on deck,

deafening him with a cacophony of hungry screams. Not a bad run, he reflects; Durban and Cape Town. A tidier ship, this one, too. He sniffs the air repeatedly as he descends the gangplank and strolls along the quayside to collect his pay from the company office. Hello again, Liverpool. The city smells, he thinks, like an odd, unwashed friend. Like Brendan, maybe; he chuckles.

In a cheap lodging room he settles into a chair and takes out the letter he collected with his pay and reads it a second time; then writes out his reply:

"Dear Fons,

Good to hear from you again. You seemed so settled with that family, I was pretty surprised to hear you'd joined up again. I hope it goes better for you this time. Myself, I decided the army was a bad career move, especially when you join the wrong one. The merchant navy suits me better; tinkering with engines, lots of travel, loose discipline and, it seems to me, a lot less dangerous. If I use Liverpool as my home port for long enough, I can also get a British passport. That would be ironic, wouldn't it? Any port in a storm, as they say... I missed out on one in America and I'd rest much easier having one, especially when I go back to Dublin. The seaman's papers are all right for work but if there was any serious trouble they don't count for much. At the moment I feel stuck between three worlds; here in Liverpool, Ireland and America. For various reasons, it's better for me to be based here. It would be nice to lay down some roots again, somewhere, but where? I almost did in America, but that's another story that will have to wait till we meet.

I visited Mary as you suggested and that went well, she and I are going to be friends again. She's turned into a fine woman all right but friendship suits the both of us these days. It's no life being married to a sailor, anyway. We spend many long weeks away working without a break and then when we hit port it's far too easy to go wild with the booze and the wrong kind of girl. It's the same all over the world, for us. What do you Tommies get up to? Anything remotely similar?

Well, take care, a chara, Pat."

He stuffs the letter into an envelope, sighs and seals it, licking his lips. Dry as hell. Why not, he thinks? It's a long time since I really cut loose. He heads for the door.

Later that evening, Pat meanders from pub to pub with a group of Welsh sailors. In one pub they find a piano; one man hammers out the tunes while the rest sing a mixture of hymns and rugby songs. Most of the pub joins in and Pat winks at the barmaid, a pretty girl with dark red hair. She blushes, winks back, and gives him a smile.

Pat persuades the Welshmen to sing some Irish tunes, teaches them the drinking song from "La Traviata". He blows a kiss at the barmaid; she laughs, shakes her head, and gives him a long look. A man whispers in his ear; he sings a few military songs, finishing with "Lily Marlene." Elbowing his way to the bar, he waits his turn patiently.

"What can I get you?" She meets his eyes directly, a curious tone in her voice.

"I'll have a large Irish whiskey with a little promise in it, please."

"With what?"

"With a little promise that you'll let me walk you home tonight. That's what I'd like, anyway, if you have one."

She smiles, shakes her head, and wrinkles her nose, "I'll get you the whiskey." She hasn't said no; Pat grins to himself. When she returns she tilts her head and asks, "Anything else?"

He lifts the glass and examines it, "That looks full of promise to my eyes", and hands her the money. She laughs and shakes her head again; when she hands him the change, she whispers, "I finish in half an hour", and motions towards the back of the building with her eyes.

She emerges into the summer night with a raincoat on her arm; her body hesitates, her voice challenges him; "Who told you, anyway?"

"Who told me what?"

"My name; Lily."

"Ah, that would have been an inspired guess."

"I'm sure. And your name is?"

"Pat."

She sighs, "Well, Pat, maybe you can walk me home. Or we could go past a little jazz club I know; I'm starving." She steps forward and takes his arm. The club concerned hides in a large cellar where the food, a hearty stew, is surprisingly good. This sobers him up a little; a lone saxophonist wails a series of mournful tunes. She asks the usual things about him, weighing him up. She doesn't seem put off by the fact that he's a sailor. And she's far more attractive than most of his pick-ups. "So how long are you in Liverpool, Pat?"

"It's my home port; I always come back here."

"Do you now?"

"I do; to tell you the truth, I have to, if I want to get my hands on an English passport."

"Oh, next you'll be telling me you want to give up the sea and settle down."

He laughs, "No, I've no plans on that score. This life suits me fine." He watches her expression carefully, but she just nods, acceptingly, almost approvingly, he thinks.

"What about you? You like working in that pub?"

She sips her pink gin. "Yes, I do, tell you the truth. Gets me away from my family; from my father, that is. He's a holy terror, gives my mother a dreadful time. And knocks seven bells out of my brothers, if they don't do exactly what he says. I just wish I could leave home, rent my own place, rather than give my pay to him. I'd be gone like a shot."

"Has he ever hurt you?"

She shakes her head, and looks at him sideways, "Not yet. I keep my head down, and I've always been his favourite, being the eldest girl."

"Very wise, though it may not last."

She sighs, "When he finally realises I'm not a child anymore, there'll be hell to pay." She looks up. "Tell you the truth, I'm terrified of him, always have been." She drains her glass, but makes no move to stand up and looks at him meaningfully.

He smiles, "You don't seem in a hurry to leave."

She returns a wry smile. "You're easy to talk to. And I told you, home isn't the most enticing destination."

He's heard this before; and smiles to himself. Thank you, Lord, for what I am about to receive. "Well, you could always come back with me tonight. If he isn't waiting up for you, that is."

"He'll be full of beer and snoring by now." She takes his hand, "One more gin and I'll be in the right mood to consider your offer."

"In that case, both of us will be drinking to a little promise."

In one way, the ease with which she acquiesces surprises him; she is young, not yet twenty, and looks innocent on the surface. Yet beneath that, he can see she's self-sufficient; like him, she's had to look after herself for a long time. In his room, she hesitates initially, as if having second thoughts; then seems to let go of her doubts and clings to him with an unexpected passion until they are both spent. Her body is shapely, deliciously curved, and slightly plumper than he expected. Unlike Paula, he thinks, with a pang of guilt. Then a shock; he realises he has not thought of Paula all night. He swallows the bitter taste of whiskey lingering in his mouth, inhales the smell of her body - a sweet, sweet medicine. Puppy fat, he thinks, Lord help me, as he drifts off to sleep.

He feels the warmth of her long before he opens his eyes. When he does, he finds her eyes watching his face, anxious to catch his first reaction. He raises his eyebrows, "Hello there."

"Morning, dearie," Despite the light tone in her voice, she frowns a little, studying him.

"You look like you might have something on your mind, Lily."

"Oh, nothing," She purses her lips. "Well, I suppose I'd like to know if I'll see you again. After you walk me home, that is."

He grins at her, waits a moment, to tease her. "I think you might. Assuming you want to, that is. I don't go back to sea for another four days." She sighs, and cuddles into him like a child. On their last morning together, the same scene repeats itself. This time, she wants to know if she'll see him when he returns.

"If you want to," Why not, he thinks.

"I've been thinking about what you said, Pat, that first night."

"What was that?"

"About your passport; don't take this wrong, but there's an easy way to get your passport."

"And what would that be?"

"Hear me out before you decide." She looks away for a moment then looks him in the eye. "You could marry me; you'd get your passport straight away. I wouldn't hold you to it, Pat, honest I wouldn't. We could go our separate ways afterwards, whenever you want. Just help me get away from home. We could rent a house for a year; after that, if you decide to go, I'd take in a lodger. It would suit the both of us, don't you see? Promise me you'll think about it while you're away."

He laughs, shakes his head. "Jesus, you are a deep one." It sounds crazy, he thinks, but with a grain of sanity running through it. "I'll bear it in mind in Cape Town."

He walks her home; both deep in thought. So much so, the journey seems to take no time at all. As they turn into her street, she stops. "Oh Lord," she sighs, "the old bugger's taken a day off." Pat follows her eyes and sees a middle-aged barrel of a man scowling at them. As they watch, he begins to head their way, holding a stout walking stick in one hand.

"That's your father?"

"It is. He must know I didn't go home. Just let me do the talking, Pat, or he'll go for you."

The man marches towards them like an ex-soldier, grim faced. When he faces them both two yards away he bellows at Lily in a thick Scouse accent, while staring at Pat, "So is this the bastard you've been seeing then?" He lifts the stick and points it at Pat's chest, "Give me one good reason not to kill the bugger now."

"Dad, this is Pat; Pat, my father, Joseph Kelly. If you must have a reason, dad, I'm hoping to marry him." Mr Kelly opens his mouth and shuts it again. Pat starts to open his, feels a dig in the ribs from Lily, "He hasn't asked me yet, but I know he's thinking about it. Aren't you, Pat?"

Pat considers this while he clears his throat, and then nods, "I am; I am."

Mr Kelly looks from one to the other and back again, scratches his head. He growls, "You'd better be, son. Put it this way, it's a lot better to be a Kelly than to have the Kelly clan after you." He turns on his heels and walks back down the street. Pat feels a peck on the cheek from Lily, and watches her follow quietly behind her father. She's no fool, he thinks, I'll give her that.

*   *   *

The day dawns like any other; once the decision was made, as Lily had said, why hang around? But the result of this haste is that he hasn't even told his brothers, or Fons, or Mary. Not even his shipmates. Why not? They may not have been able to come, but why not tell them? He calls into a bar on his way and takes a double whiskey, sipping it slowly. Not so much Dutch courage, as a last chance to consider what he is about to do.

I'm marrying her for the passport, deep down, he thinks. And she's marrying me mainly for convenience too, to get her own house. Is that so wrong? Well, I'm not a churchgoer, and neither is she, so the religious stuff is not a problem. I'm not in love with her. Maybe that should be a problem, but frankly I'm not sure if I'll ever feel like that again after Paula. Not for a long time, and Lily has made it clear that she doesn't insist on permanence. Lily knows all about Paula, so I'm not deceiving her, and she's the person that matters in that regard. On the positive side, I do like Lily a lot; she has a lovely body, she's a smart, free-thinking girl. She certainly makes Liverpool something to look forward to. Can love grow out of that? Maybe; but the point is it doesn't have to. We can go our separate ways after a couple of years if it doesn't. I wonder, though, what does she really feel about me? That's the thing that puzzles me. She's never really said she loves me, only hinted at it; sometimes acted so, but maybe that's just her teasing? Or maybe it's something she has to do, to pretend to be in love, to persuade herself and her family of what she is doing. Does it matter? It must do, to her, surely. Does it matter to me? No, it probably doesn't. Maybe it should.

The thing that most niggles him is his failure to tell his brothers and Fons. There must be some shame within me about it all, he realises. Maybe I'll write and tell them if it goes well. He shrugs to himself and downs the last of the whiskey.

He sees Lily from a distance; she stands outside the entrance biting her lip, fiddling with a posy of flowers, dressed in a simple pale blue outfit. Her brother and his girlfriend, the witnesses, each touch her arm, reassuring her. He feels surprise that it is she who has the nerves on this day and smiles. The kindness of strangers, he thinks; then wonders for a moment why that phrase should pop into his head on his wedding day. Why not? He calls her name; she looks up with a cry of pleasure, detaches herself, and then steps forward to greet him with a shy hug. She whispers, "Thank God. I was worried you'd change your mind, Pat."

"Were you now? And why would that be?" She blushes, a bright pink. "Were you having second thoughts yourself?" She shakes her head and looks at the floor. Her reaction puzzles him for a moment. He notices the brother, glancing at his watch. "There was me thinking what a smart girl you are. I keep my promises, Lily. Come on, we'd better go in and tie the knot..." He can't resist leaning forward and whispering, for her ears alone, "...a sailor's knot, what we call an adjustable hitch." She laughs, slaps his arm, and then wraps her own around it, resting her head on his shoulder as they walk up the stone steps.

They emerge half an hour later into a burst of welcome sunshine. Both he and Lily seem subdued by the serious nature of the ceremony; not, he recalls, "a matter to be entered into lightly".

She nudges his arm, "Are you ready for the next part?"

"Your family? I suppose so; though I don't suppose we could just run away, could we?"

She squeezes his arm, "In some ways there's nothing I'd like better. I'm only doing this for my mother and her sisters. Don't worry; there won't be a lot of people, Pat. But my father will almost certainly embarrass us and everyone else. He'll insist on making a speech and he'll also get blind drunk, sooner or later. Just humour him, or he'll take it out on my mother."

"Why does she put up with it?"

"Oh, I wish I knew. She says she still loves him, it's just that he's never been the same since he got back from the trenches."

"Ah well, he's not alone there. Maybe you'd better find me a tin hat." They enter a dimly lit room above a pub called the Lord Nelson. Pat finds himself being examined by a small crowd, who break into a muted cheer of greetings. Lily leads him around the room patiently; he shakes hands and kisses cheeks while he tries to commit at least some of the names to memory. Trays of sandwiches and beer appear, making his stomach rumble. Whatever happens, he tells himself, at least there should be no repeat of the last wedding I was at...

An hour or two later, Joseph Kelly rises to his feet. He blows out his cheeks, sucks in a gulp of air like a whale breaking the surface. His eyes dart around the room, surveying his audience. "Me darling daughter, Lily...ain't she a gorgeous lass, a flower in bloom? Yes, me little flower... what has been plucked by her own sailor boy..." Joseph nods slyly, amidst a burst of ribald laughter. "I must thank her husband as he's a very decent feller. Not a Scouser I'm sorry to say, but at least he's from the old country. A skilled man too, an engineer;

but clearly not afraid to get his hands dirty..." He winks at the audience, producing a mixture of sniggers and embarrassed coughs. "But then he is a sailor too. And he's a lucky man as well as a decent one to be getting my Lily full in bloom as she is." More sniggers. "Anyway I have to welcome him to the Kelly family in my usual fashion." He belches loudly and pats his ample stomach. "I shall buy us both a pint of bitter and a large whiskey. A toast to Lily..." He frowns, as if trying to remember Pat's name, then shrugs and raises his glass high, "Cheers, everyone," he slurs, before draining the glass and falling back into his chair.

Watching his new wife undress later that night, Pat recalls the speech, the emphasis on the 'decent man'. He sees the fullness of Lily's breasts and the roundness of her stomach, a little plumper, it seems, each day. Oh Lord. The realisation hits him in the guts. She's pregnant, and not by me, for sure. The first thing they taught me on that liner, he remembers, when I was a young lad - how to use a sheath. Oh Lord. Me, a sailor; I've been caught with the oldest trick in the book.

*   *   *

Moving to the door, he pulls the window down and smells sea air, mixing with smoke from the engine. They pass endless lines of goods wagons filled with shipping cargos, waiting to be moved away from the port. The train rattles slowly to a halt, steam and smoke swirling along the platform. Lime Street station; the last time I was here in uniform, he thinks, I was in the Irish Guards. Releasing his grip on the doorway, he drops, skips briefly and then steps out in long even strides along the platform. Perhaps because of his uniform, the crowds pull apart out of his way. Now, what was it Pat had written? Turn right out of the station for a couple of hundred yards and take the third left. Then look out for a small hotel, the Queenstown; a quiet snug at the back. I wonder if he's changed much, after all this time?

He spots Pat sitting in a corner, a newspaper on his table, as soon as he enters; the face is the same, though he's filled out now, as you'd expect, now he's thirty. Their eyes meet; broad grins crack their faces simultaneously. He hurries across, stuffing his forage cap into a pocket. Pat hugs him warmly, something Fons is not altogether expecting; that dispels any lingering anxiety that he's felt about this meeting. "At least your uniform's a bit more in keeping, this time, Fons."

"And where would your uniform be, mister Second Engineer?"

Pat laughs, "We don't bother much with that nonsense, Fons. You might be lucky and catch me wearing a cap now and then; but only on deck, it's far too hot for that in the engine room. Right now, I told you, I'm between ships. What will you have?"

"Peace in our time; failing that, a pint of mild and bitter."

"I think you'll have to settle for the mild and bitter, myself. Strangely enough, I find myself in the curious position of agreeing with most of what that old bastard Winston Churchill says, these days." He turns and orders a round.

"Winston's well thought of in the army."

"And in the merchant navy, too, the old bulldog; but then, he was head of the Admiralty during the great slaughter. Mind you, I think he's right about the fascists. They won't be happy until they have another war. The British and French should have stopped them in Spain before they got too cocky. And handing over Czechoslovakia is just encouraging them. We might all be paying the price for that soon."

"You've changed your tune."

"Not so much deep down, Fons. But I have to make my living under the red duster, and I don't like fascists. A lot of Irish lads fought for the Republicans in Spain. Plus, I've met a few Jewish sailors who've been educating me about what's happening in Germany. That stinks. Not that I want to get involved personally, but I know which side I'd choose if I had to."

"We may not have much choice when it all kicks off." Fons, or Paddy as he now thinks of himself, points at his own insignia. "I certainly won't, and you may not have as much as you think. Remember the Lusitania."

"I do, I do." Pat takes a sip of his drink. "Did I tell you I got a British passport? No? Well, I have. But if a war comes, I'm thinking I'll sign on with an American shipping line; the pay and the food's better, and it'll be a whole lot safer. They'll stay out of it this time, I think. I see you got some stripes. What's your regiment?"

"Royal Warwickshires; I just happened to be passing through the midlands when I saw the recruiting office and couldn't resist. Took to it like a duck to water. I've done all the basic training before - though I couldn't tell them that, so of course I looked like God's gift to soldiery. I got the stripes for being good with the mortar bombs. Always had a knack with figures, remember? Somehow I can just look at the map and work out the elevation to make it drop in the right place."

"Jesus, I wouldn't like to be fighting you."

"Don't worry, I can't ever see that ever happening now, can you? So what's it like, being a grease monkey?"

"Hot. Down there in the engine room, most of the lads don't wear much; only what you need for protection. You sweat so much that you drink all day and sweat gallons - it can get to a hundred and fifty down there. The stokers just wear boots and shorts, especially in the tropics. You've no idea, Fons, what heat is until you've been in the boiler room in the tropics. And you're right about the grease; it gets filthy with oil and coal dust. Can take me an hour to clean up, when I've been fixing something. But it pays well. We see the world. We deliver the goods, Fons, anywhere and everywhere. That's us. Everyone thinks the British Empire was built by you soldier boys. The truth is, an ocean full of tramp steamers delivered the bullets for you boys, and then took all the gold back to London. And I keep one of the little beasts moving..."

After catching up on the present, they reminisce about Ireland; a safe subject. But he can feel his curiosity stirring about the time in between; so he takes the bull by the horns. "What happened to you in America, Pat? You never really told me anything about that in your letters."

His friend gazes at the floor for a long moment. "No, I did not. Tell you the truth, Fons, it pains me to think about it." He nods his head and waits, trying to give his friend some time. Pat glances up at him, rubbing his neck. "Did you ever feel crazy about a woman?"

He shrugs, "I don't suppose I ever did, not really."

"You would know if you had. Well, that was it. In fact, the two of us both felt that way about each other, Fons, but she was already married. It's a long story, and maybe some day I'll tell it all to you. But the worst of it was; she died."

"Jesus, Pat, that's awful."

He watches Pat fight back tears for a moment, suck in a deep breath, and bite his lower lip. "I would've settled out there if things had turned out better, Fons. But here I am in Liverpool, now. Who would've thought it? Me, settled in England."

He shakes his head, allows himself a wry smile, "You and another million Irish lads; come on, Pat, it's not so different over here. I've been all over this country, working on the land. You should visit those northern dales. They're not so different from the old country, and the people there too, they're just like the folks at home."

"Really?"

"They are."

"Tell you the truth, Fons, I don't feel at home here. Never have."

"Then why do you stay?"

"Good question. It's a mean little life I'm living here. " His friend forces a smile, stares at the floor again. "One day, I'll find myself a proper home. They say confession is good for the soul, don't they?"

"Some do; idiots like Brother Daniel, for instance."

Pat laughs, deep from his belly, "Trust you to spoil my big spiritual moment, Fons, remembering that feller. Still, you put him in the gutter where he belonged, last time we saw him."

"So I did. Go on, though."

"I told you I got a passport, but I didn't tell you how I got it, did I?"

"You did not, as I recall."

Pat adopts an all too innocent expression. "I married a girl for it. A young girl who told me she was desperate to get away from her family. Pretty, too - I thought she was a real honey. At first, I couldn't believe my luck, all things considered; a pretty girl to come home to, plus a passport." The opportunistic, boyish smile turns into a brief beam of triumph, and then vanishes. "But she turned out to be pregnant with another feller's child. Some married man. Maybe it's divine retribution for my sins." Mock bewilderment passes across Pat's face while he looks up to the ceiling; he turns to catch Paddy's eye again, serious once more. "It's not as bad as it sounds, Fons. No one's fooling anyone. Believe it or not, at the end of it, we're just good friends. I'll be renting her a house for a while and then we'll go our own separate ways."

Fons feels an urge to laugh but holds it back, aware that this has been an important confession for Pat. The whole thing sounds so absurd, yet so absolutely typical. Deep in his own belly, he feels the urge rooting, building and rising. "Jesus, Pat, you must be at one and exactly the same time both the luckiest and the unluckiest feller I've ever known. Don't you think?" His friend nods, returns a wry smile. "And I'm sorry to tell you this, but..." Fons starts to grin, suppressing his laughter as best he can, "this is just so bloody typical of the messes you get yourself into... so bloody typical..." For a moment, Pat looks affronted. Then, he nods his agreement at the exact moment that Fons starts to giggle uncontrollably. Pat's mouth opens in a quiet chuckle, just as Fons' chest explodes with laughter, unable to hold it back any longer. To his great relief, Pat's features also crack open and the two of them collapse into a long and extended fit of the giggles together.

* * *

He's not sure exactly why he's here, looking down into the water of the Liffey from the O'Connell bridge with Mary on his arm. He imagines a brief image of a man sinking into it, arm upraised, the blackness covering and swallowing him, and shivers; his past, or his future? This dark water feels like an embodiment of his mood. When he tries to relax, disappointments rise to the surface of his memory. After a long trip to the east via the Mediterranean, his ship required a refit. So did he, really; but not in Liverpool. His urge to get away, to escape the dingy Liverpool bars, to make sure he didn't run into Lily's father, had him by the throat. Fons was stuck in barracks; he'd fled here, to Mary, his other friend.

She nudges his arm, "Penny for your thoughts."

He forces a smile, "Oh, it's terrible strange being back here in the old country again. I have an urge to spit in the Liffey for luck."

"Well, go on then, why not?" He spits, emphatically, watching it fall and strike, tiny ripples widening and disappearing. "Now make yourself a wish."

"I will if you will; your turn, Mary, to spit in the water."

"It's not ladylike, Patrick."

"Ah well, you have to, to make the luck for your wish. Come on, one little spit won't damage your social standing. It's only the seagulls will see you." She giggles, leans forward, and turns away from him. He hears an equally emphatic spit, followed by more giggles. "Very good, I think you almost enjoyed that."

She nods, looking down in disbelief. "I did. After a day serving up perfume and lipstick to rich old biddies, that was perfect; truly liberating." She beams at him. "I shall have to do this again. What will you wish for, Pat, on this fine spring evening?"

He wonders: something to cheer me up? "I'm still working that one out. What about you?"

"Hmmm, let me see now. Last year it would have been a wish for the stupid trade war to end. Now it's over, I'm not sure."

"I wouldn't be wasting my wish on politics; how about something more personal?" She withdraws her arm, and looks away. Too sensitive by half, he thinks. "I'm sorry; I didn't mean it like that. It's just that I'd be saving my wish for what's going on in my own life. Maybe that makes me selfish, but there it is."

She turns back, wipes a tiny tear from her eye, and takes his hand. "We're all selfish, Pat. Until yesterday my wish would have been a visit from you. But since that's also been taken care of, I'll have to carry on thinking." She smiles, ruefully; examines his face. "And what on earth is going on in your life that makes you so touchy?"

He feels his own face redden with embarrassment. "That's a long story."

"I'm sure it is, but I'm all ears."

He sighs, "Let me sit and have a drink first, and then I'll tell you."

She nods, and gestures back towards the city, "Come along then."

Listening to himself telling her the story of Lily and her child, he wonders at his own naivety. How could he, a sailor, fall for that? He still can't believe that he didn't see it coming. To his great relief, she doesn't laugh. Whenever he looks up from the floor, he finds her shaking her head, frowning. When her eyes meet his, he hears a note of real sympathy. "Oh, Pat..." But as he goes on to explain what's happened since the marriage, he's gripped with a sudden fear that Mary, still having her religion, will find his actions repulsive. She seems to gather herself together, sitting upright and facing him, as if affronted, determined to hold to her beliefs. At the end, he waits for her to speak in judgement; she stays silent.

"Have I shocked you?"

She gives one shake of her head and smiles, "After what went on in Cork, Pat, I'm beyond shocking." She draws circles on the table with her finger.

"I was worrying what you would think - the sanctity of marriage, and all that."

She gives him a wry smile, "I'm not a schoolgirl anymore. Neither am I anyone else's conscience, for that matter. Do you really want to know what I think about it?" Away from her, he still thinks of her as a girl; but sitting with her now, he's conscious how she's changed. He suddenly realises that he does want to know, very much; he nods. "Are you sure?" He sees a glint in her eyes.

"I am. Come on, get it over with."

"Well, I think you did that girl a favour all right. God knows what her family and the church might have done to her. Taken her baby, put her in a madhouse. She might have ended up on the streets, or worse. I know what the fear of all that is like, Pat. I might have been with child after what happened to me that night in Fermoy."

"Jesus, of course; and you're right, they're a Catholic family."

"You got something out of it, too. You got your passport, a proper identity. And that's why you did it. You've not been cheated out of anything that was promised you, not really. You must have known she wasn't in love with you."

"When you put it like that, I did, you're right."

"So, what I think is, you should stop feeling so sorry for yourself, Patrick Mahon. It's a bit of a mess legally, but nothing that can't be fixed, and let's face it, you've been in far worse situations with the law, haven't you?" He feels as if he has been kicked and hugged at the same time. He swallows, and nods. "In fact, instead of beating yourself up about it, I think you should be proud of what you did. You helped that girl. You're a good man for doing that." She points at her glass, "And you can prove it by getting me another gin." Wise beyond her years, he thinks.

When he returns to the table, he lifts his glass. "Slainte," He takes a sip. "I got my wish, by the way; someone to cheer me up." She draws circles on the table again, biting her lip, the colour suffusing her cheeks. "What is it, Mary?"

"Oh, it's nothing."

"It doesn't look like nothing." She squirms in her seat. "Spit it out. I owe you some ears."

"It's not your ears I'm worried about." He squeezes her hand in reassurance, and she sighs; with her other hand, she takes a long sip from her glass, and bites her lip, before whispering, "I made a wish too. Do you want to know what it was?"

He tilts his head. "Of course I do."

"Remember when I told you about what happened to me? After the wedding?"

He swallows, his mouth suddenly dry, "Of course."

"I told you how I get with men. How I get the panic whenever I'm close to a man?" He nods and holds his breath. She looks him in the eyes, looks away. "Well, I don't get that with you, Pat. Never did, and never have. I suppose it's because we go back so far, before it happened."

"That makes sense." He exhales, slowly.

"Well, I'm a practical woman, Pat, far more than you might think. So when I hear how you helped another girl in trouble, you can't blame me..." She looks at him again. "Don't be shocked. But you must know what I wished for. I don't want to live a whole life without knowing... what it's like, with a man."

"You should have told me, before."

"You'd have run a mile." He admits to himself, maybe I would, then.

Now he tells her, with more sharpness than he intends, "Don't be stupid." He sighs and softens his voice. "Mary, it's not exactly the moon that you're wishing for, is it now? Even if you were not a beautiful and wise woman, what sort of friend would I be, not to help you? A man could not be more fortunate than to be asked."

*   *   *

Thirteen: 1939-41

She swims down through shoals of rainbow-coloured fish to explore the seabed, breathing water like a mermaid. Ever since her first sight of the sea (on a summer outing with the Methodist Sunday school) she's visited this place regularly. Peering through vast forests of swaying seaweed, she glimpses giant crabs and lobsters. She swims on, keeping well out of their reach; at the edge of the forest, strange blue sea cows munch sea grass. She notices an orderly line of footsteps heading away from the cows, heavy imprints made by boots. She swims over to inspect them; Paddy must have made these in his army boots, she decides. She should follow him and catch up with him; now that she has become a woman, perhaps he'll notice her. Something grabs her arm; she turns, fighting off panic... what kind of strange creature has hold of her?

"Maggie...wake up, it's Sunday; your turn to make the breakfast."

She hisses disapproval at her sister and turns over, "Go away; do it yourself if you're so hungry." Grace pokes her in the back repeatedly until she gives in.

The day seems a Sunday like any other, at first. Grace dresses Harriet, reminds Rose and then June to put on their Sunday best. After his own breakfast Gilly takes a tray up to their mother's room. He gives Maggie a wry smile and a shrug on his return, responding to her unspoken question. "Awake, but quiet as usual. Maybe you can take the little ones up to see her after Sunday school." Maggie nods. While their father takes the younger girls to Sunday school, Maggie washes glasses in the bar and Grace cleans the pewter mugs which hang from hooks driven into the ceiling beams. As Grace stretches up to replace one, Maggie glances enviously at her sister's black hair and hourglass figure. One day, she thinks, pulling a face to herself. She hears a tapping on the front door; her sister does not react.

"Gracie..." She catches her sister's eye and adds in a stage whisper, "It'll be *him* again." Grace sighs, pushes her hair back from her face, glances at Maggie; she stands on a stool and picks off another pewter mug. The tapping repeats, a little louder.

Maggie puts down her tea towel and goes to look out through the tiny window in the front door. A tall, gangly figure in a tweed jacket stands outside, his head jerking around nervously as he scans the building for signs of movement. She turns the enormous key and pulls the heavy old door ajar, "Why George, you know we're not open now."

"He...he...hello, Maggie; I kn...kn...know that." He blushes furiously with the effort, stares down at the ground, but doesn't move away. In fact his face lights up with a grin; he produces a small book from his pocket and waves it in front of her, "Poems, Maggie, f...f...for you." Maggie shakes her head in exasperation, inspects the book, and opens the door; she can't resist poetry.

Grace greets him with a pained smile, gives him a sideways look, "Well, since you're here, George, make yourself useful. Reach those mugs down for me with those long arms of yours."

He nods, looking pleased to be asked, though he avoids making a verbal reply. A busy silence then ensues; George's eyes never seem to leave Grace. He's like a faithful dog, thinks Maggie.

When Gilly looks in on his return, one eyebrow raises before he greets George; as he turns away, he winks at Maggie, "When is it you go back to university, George?"

"T...t...t...t..." He stops, takes a deep breath, tries a different tack. "A...a couple of weeks, Mr. Hardy." He glances at his watch. "H...h...have you got a radio, Mr Hardy?"

"Aye, in the back room."

"Th...th...there's something on at eleven o'clock. My f...f...father told me to listen."

Gilly shrugs as he leaves, "I'll give you a shout, assuming the damn thing's working today." At five to eleven, Gilly pops his head round the door. "All right George, come and help me tune it in; you can wave the aerial about while I find the signal."

Grace watches him leave, then flops into a chair and shuts her eyes in mock exhaustion. "He's such hard work. He never says a word to me."

"You know why *that* is. You have to make him talk. Ask him things."

"Why should I? The man's supposed to take the lead."

Maggie shakes her head, "You're as bad as he is. You don't even try." She gives her sister a rueful smile. "You might regret it one day; he's got lots of money. You could live in that big house with everything you want."

"Not *everything*. I want a man who makes me happy, who can make me laugh."

Maggie considers this idea. "I suppose so. Maybe George could, if you gave him a chance."

"I doubt it very much. Anyway, if you're so keen you can have him and his poetry books and his big house. Just keep practising your posh voice, Maggie, he'll notice you eventually." The sharp tone stings her into silence. In the past, she could always get the better of Grace; not any more. She wipes the last glass and escapes to the kitchen, where she looks up to see George balancing precariously as he drapes a wire along the clotheshorse that hangs from the ceiling.

"H...h...how's that?" The radio whines, hisses, crackles into life for a second.

"...The BBC...Prime Minister..." The signal lapses into a steady hiss.

"Double it up; the U-shape works best."

George does as he is told while Gilly fiddles with the dial; a voice fades in and out of earshot, repeatedly. "Cabinet room...the British Ambassador...a final note stating..."

"What is it, dad?" George shushes her.

Her father mutters, "The batteries are going. It's that old duffer, Chamberlain."

"... would exist between us...no such undertaking...this country is at war..." Maggie stares at her father, unsure whether to believe her ears. He shakes his head, sadly, chewing his lip as he listens, "...all my long struggle...has failed. I cannot believe...would have been more successful... honourable settlement...Hitler would not have it..."

Maggie turns and runs into the front of the pub, "Gracie, Gracie, we're at war."

Grace opens her eyes, "What did you say, Maggie?"

"We're at war. We just heard it on the radio."

"Who with?"

"Germany, I should think. Mr Hitler - that's Germany, isn't it?"

"Oh, Maggie, that's awful; just think. Paddy will have to go and fight them."

"I didn't say I was pleased about it." She feels her own throat swelling, and blinks her tears back. Losing Paddy? That would be unbearable.

Her sister's voice suddenly softens, "No, you didn't. I'm sorry, Maggie. But you're not the only one with a soft spot for Paddy. He *can* make me laugh."

Suddenly, Maggie feels very small and guilty. She blurts out, "You can have him then..." and instantly feels a stab of regret. "I mean, he's far too old for me at the moment."

"Oh thanks. That really nice of you, now that he's gone away, isn't it?" Her sister gives her a wry smile. "The whole thing is just bad news for both of us, anyway, Maggie. All the other men will go away, too." The two sisters stare at each other for a long moment then look away, thinking of their maiden aunts and the last war.

* * *

Paddy jerks awake with a start, throws out an arm to steady himself. A hoarse, exhausted refrain drifts into the lorry from somewhere nearby, "...he had ten thousand men; he marched them up and down the hill, and marched them up again..." The engine roars, jerking them all sideways, drowning out the singing voices. He blinks sleep away and stares around him. Three days without proper rest; his men slump against each other around the sides and sit back-to-back in the centre, heads nodding together as they try to catch forty winks. Behind them the road fills; they edge forward, part of a line of vehicles pushing through carts, trudging refugees and clusters of soldiers on foot. He shakes his head and mutters, "Bloody chaos, and no bloody wonder."

"What's that, Sarge?"

"Well, Corporal, I was just admiring the organisation of our glorious expeditionary force. You might think that in this day and age somebody might have understood the importance of radio communication."

The Corporal grins. "Oh, that would be against tradition, Sarge."

"And of course they probably wouldn't work, would they, army radios?"

The other man shakes his head and yawns, "What day is it, anyway?"

"Sunday, I think." He settles back and shuts his eyes for what seems like a brief moment.

Someone slaps his arm, "Aye, aye, Sarge; something's up."

Through the tarpaulin he glimpses men, women and children running into the fields. Aircraft, he thinks. He jerks to his feet and hammers on the forward partition to the cabin, "Stop, stop...everybody out, air raid..." Everything seems to move in slow motion; after an eternity, he's the last to climber down. He hears a steady drone somewhere above, though he can't locate the direction. He runs, following the others towards a hedgerow where he flops down beside the Lieutenant, who points into the distance.

"Over there, Sergeant. That must be Cassel hill. Our lads are dug in up there along that low ridge."

Following the direction of the pointing arm, he nods. Four aircraft peel slowly into a dive, in turn, screaming down with a wailing of sirens. He hears himself mutter, "Poor sods." Even at two or three miles distance, they see great spouts of earth flying up into the air. A second or so later they feel the shockwave in their bones and a muffled crump in their ears. After the silence that follows the last bombs the driver stands up, yawning.

The Lieutenant yanks him back down to the ground, "Not yet. They came this way; they might come back this way." Sure enough, a sudden roar of engines prompts shouts and screams all around them. Paddy kneels and raises his rifle as two aircraft flash past at low altitude, wings tilted almost vertically, allowing the rear gunners to shoot down at the vehicles below. He swings his rifle and fires a shot, more in frustration than in hope. He doesn't bother to shoot at the second pair; the Lieutenant gives him a wry smile.

"Where are we headed for, sir?"

"God knows, Paddy. Right now, everything seems to be shunted towards Dunkirk. Our original orders were for Arras, but the officer directing traffic at the last town told me Arras has fallen already. Jerry seems to have outflanked us."

"We've come all this way, sir, and yet we've done no fighting at all."

"Ours not to reason why, Paddy; between you and me, though, it's one hell of a cock-up. Dunkirk suggests to me that the battle's lost already." The further they go, the slower they move. They edge around a column of burned out and broken down vehicles, forced to detour into muddy fields where other vehicles have stuck in the morass. Everyone has to get out and push. In half a day, they travel ten miles. The Lieutenant calls him forward into the cab. "It's quicker to walk, Sergeant. We're sitting targets on this road; what do you think?"

"It certainly is, you're right about that, sir. But I'd give it just a bit longer; there might be a bottle neck up ahead, you never know." Now wedged between the driver and his officer, he shuts his eyes, drifting away until the sound of a door opening wrenches him back. He watches the Lieutenant climb down and salute a Major with a clipboard under his arm.

Paddy turns to the driver, "Where are we, Private Farrell?"

The other man yawns and points at a group of houses, "I reckon that's a place called Wormhout, Sarge; about halfway to Dunkirk, maybe."

He nods and rubs his eyes. The Lieutenant beckons him down, so he climbs out and salutes, conscious of the Major's eyes upon him. "Sergeant Reilly, this is Major Ridley. It seems the Major needs our mortar platoon."

He stiffens, "Sir."

"At ease, Reilly; you lads are just what we need. In case you haven't realised, the BEF is completely cut off, surrounded. The order is to evacuate as many men as possible. This road here is the escape corridor to Dunkirk. The Germans have started to probe the flanks with tanks. We've got anti-tank guns and infantry in place, but we need mortars to support the infantry." Paddy nods. "One other thing, my company mortar squad was bombed. They took a direct hit, but the gun itself seems undamaged. I need your best man to come with me and help some of our lads use it."

The Lieutenant interjects, "That would be you, Reilly."

He feels his face flush, "Sir."

The Lieutenant offers his hand, "Good luck, Paddy. See you back in England."

"You too, sir," The Major coughs, inclines his head. "I'll get my kit, sir." He barely has time to explain his departure, let alone wish each of the boys luck as he would like to do. The last thing he sees is the shock on the driver's face as he hears, "Push that truck off the road and set fire to it. We won't be driving out of here; we have to destroy everything the Germans could use."

He follows in the Major's wake. An hour later he inspects the abandoned mortar gun, positioned in a patch of scrub behind a rise barely the height of a man. He takes it apart slowly and reassembles it in front of his makeshift five-man squad; two red-faced cooks (Rafferty and Harding) a thin, bespectacled orderly (Jones) and two drivers (Atkinson and Redfearn). "Now then," he asks, "which of you can do what I just did?"

Atkinson volunteers; Paddy delegates him to teach the process to the others while he inspects the ground and makes a rough copy of the Colonel's field map. They have to defend flat, open land, partly cultivated with small patches of scrub and woodland dotted between the fields. Natural cover's in short supply; the anti-tank crews have grabbed the best places. He picks out two other firing positions for the mortar gun nearby, and two more toward the rear, marking key positions through which infantry are likely to advance. The trick is to zero the gun in on these places from each firing position in advance. The two cooks, he reasons, are used to hot metal; they can carry and fix the gun in place when they move. Jones and Redfearn can fetch ammunition and relay messages. Atkinson has the best eyesight; he can act as spotter. He makes them practise until darkness falls. On an improvised bed of straw, he plunges into a deep well of sleep.

A voice calls; he feels a boot nudging his arm, smells a mug of hot black tea, and opens his eyes to see Harding grinning at him. The cook, he thinks. There are some advantages to his new squad, he thinks. The light's already brightening; a constant low rumble, like thunder, contrasts with the muted birdsong. "Something's up, Sarge."

He nods, "The Jerries are probably trying to take that ridge, back at Cassel." If they had any sense, he thinks, they'd just by-pass it. "Or maybe it's the French, further away. Thanks for this, Harding." He slurps a mouthful of hot, sweet nectar.

"No problem; Redfearn and I found a farm nearby, sir, lovely people. Bring you some breakfast in ten minutes." Paddy salivates wildly at this idea.

Five hours later, the memory of that breakfast stubbornly competes for his attention against the distant rumble of guns and the sharper, intermittent crump of bombs. Then – is it his imagination?

Something else? Engine noise, perhaps a faint vibration in the ground? He shuffles forward on his belly, joins Atkinson on top of the rise. "Tanks?"

"Aye, Sarge, two or three; I think they're behind those woods."

"Infantry?"

"No sign of that, yet." He settles down on his stomach, next to Atkinson, determined to see the enemy himself. Something moves in the woods; branches? Bushes and then small trees begin to collapse; three tanks, swastikas clearly visible, burst out into the open, six hundred yards away. They rev their engines, moving forward in single file; after about two hundred yards, he hears a bang. A shell from one of the anti-tank guns flies out from his left, passing just in front of the turret of the lead tank. He's amazed how visible it is; the shell must have a tracer base to help the gunners follow its path. The trouble is the tank commander also sees where it came from. The turret rotates and the tank fires. He hears an explosion to his left, hears a whisper, "Short, fifty yards."

Another bang; this time the shell hits the front of the tank, but deflects up into the air like a rocket. The tank fires again, misses. Another bang, another hit; once again the armour deflects the round away. The duel between the tank and the gun crew continues for what feels like an unbearable length of time, perhaps six shots each, with no result; Paddy hears himself muttering, "Christ, come on... hit the bloody thing properly..." He wonders how the crews stand it. The other tanks begin to fire, prompting the other gun crews to join in. Firing from the side, they hit the tracks of the front two tanks, disabling them. The first tank explodes in flames; the other spins in a circle, helplessly, until the hatches open; the crew leap out and run for the woods. The third tank also wheels around and retreats with a throaty roar, firing as it moves, until it crashes back into wood. The surviving tank crew scramble after it as shots ring out; about half of them make it.

The resulting mood of elation drains away when they hear gun number one has been knocked out. Nothing else happens that day, or that night and even the following day, though the sounds of battle to the south first intensify, and then fade away. They enjoy this unexpected respite amidst a mood of grim determination. It's their turn next; the Germans know they're here, and will surely return in force. He sleeps fitfully, dreaming of burning tanks.

Wednesday dawns with a grey drizzle, overcast. The others moan about this until he points out that low cloud will keep the Luftwaffe grounded. As he drinks his tea, a runner hands him a message from Major Ridley. He reads it aloud to the others, "Unwanted guests sighted; large force assembling. Prepare to send best wishes to their scouting parties soon, Ridley."

Half an hour later, Paddy glances at the map one last time, mentally checks his calculation and makes a tiny adjustment to the firing angle. "OK, one round for correction." Jones carefully slides the fins of the bomb into the top of the barrel, releases it and steps back, slapping his hands over his ears. The bomb slides downwards out of sight with a metallic scrape. The gun fires with a deep, deafening "whump". The crew flinch collectively then look mightily relieved. No damage, it seems; their shared unspoken terror has been that the first bomb would go off in the barrel. Had the gun been damaged? Was it jinxed? Paddy waits, another round in his hands. He hears a distant crash, and then the voice of Private Atkinson, "Right on target; give them one more, Sarge." He drops a second round in, and steps back quickly. It fires again, perfectly. Nothing wrong with this gun, he decides; it wants revenge.

After their second bomb explodes, all hell breaks loose. Bullets whistle over their heads and German shells crash around them. At first, the German bombardment is guesswork - noisy, but not too dangerous. The Germans hold their tanks in reserve; while they bombard the British line, small groups of infantry, accompanied by heavy covering fire from the woods, push forward, trying to identify the British positions. Every ten or fifteen minutes Ridley sends a message to drop bombs on a certain position, trying to halt them in their tracks. But gradually the German spotters begin to identify British positions, to call down a rain of fire upon them.

"Come on boys, time to move." After fifteen minutes of crawling and crouching, they watch shells fall on the position they have just vacated. Soon after this, he hears a short whistle, like an approaching express train. He glances at Jones just before the sky cracks open above their heads. Hot shards of metal fly down into the ground around them; Jones opens his mouth in pain and terror. Paddy tries to shout, "Airburst, are you all right?" All he can hear is ringing in his ears. Jones looks at him, shows him a torn sleeve and points at the little trench they have just started. They both dive into it, digging frantically to deepen it before the next shell arrives.

After a mid-day lull, tanks join in; now, the fighting becomes intense, chaotic. Since the British guns are well hidden and dug in, the Germans fire smoke shells to mask the tanks advance. A fierce close quarter battle erupts when the tanks finally emerge from the smoke, closely followed by infantry. Their gun overheats; in his haste, Rafferty burns his hand as they dismantle it, though he makes light of it. "Cook's curse", he shouts, as they run, German mortar bombs falling around them. Redfearn disappears, though he catches up with them an hour later, unscathed. Setting the gun up in the third position, they fire all the ammunition to hand and move back towards their last ammunition store, bullets whistling around them. They set the gun up again, fire six times and make one last move, carrying what they have left, just as the last attack of the day ends. Atkinson disappears; whether he has been hit, captured, or ran away, Paddy has no idea.

Major Ridley visits him that night. "You've been a great help, Sergeant Reilly."

"Thank you, sir." He decides not to mention Atkinson. "The men you gave me have done their jobs well."

"I can see that, but we won't be able to hold these positions much longer. My anti-tank guns have no armour piercing shells left and our small arms ammunition is low. How many rounds have you left for your gun?"

"Eight shrapnel and some smoke bombs, sir."

"That many?" The Major scowls, his tone ironic; he rubs his chin. "Our orders were to hold as long as possible and then make a fighting retreat to Dunkirk. I'll tell you what we'll do. When I think the Germans are about to make their next push, we'll fire everything we've got at them. Should delay them a bit; they might even believe it's a counter-attack. While they're thinking about it, we'll pull back."

"What about the gun?"

"Smash it up the best you can. The French are setting up another perimeter closer to Dunkirk. They'll try and hold there until we get away from the port."

"Can I rejoin my unit, sir? Your boys can probably manage without me."

"Sorry, no." The Major gives him a steely look. "I'm not sure they can. Besides, the rest of your unit was moved north on Monday. They may have already left, if it's any comfort."

That night, nobody sleeps. When the attack doesn't come at dawn, sighs of relief and ironic complaints break the silence, "Trust the Krauts to have a lie-in."

"It's those jackboots, cookie, takes hours to get them on and off."

The sun climbs higher and higher. Fons can't believe it. Every hour, according to Major Ridley, another thousand men will get away. Finally, a distant clatter of tracked vehicles tells them to prepare. He waits by the gun, for what seems like another hour. At exactly fourteen minutes to twelve they hear a few shots, an exchange of rifle fire followed by the chatter of a lone machine gun. A single crash follows, and a small explosion echoes in the distance.

A hoarse voice cries out, "Smoke, Sarge; it's a smoke shell..." Paddy nods at the others. Jones and Hardy, grim-faced, drop bombs into the gun while he aims, dropping all his smoke bombs just in front of the German positions. Then he fires the other bombs into the German lines. Finally, he bashes the gun barrel with a hammer until it looks slightly out of shape.

"Right lads; as the saying goes, run like hell. Come on, boys."

At a loping run, they reach the road half an hour later, discovering a continuous line of abandoned vehicles. The rest of the day feels chaotic; a lethal, curiously haphazard game of hide and seek with German tanks and armoured scout vehicles, running from road to hedgerow, hedgerow to building, building to woodland. Bullets whistle around their ears three times, though no one is hit. The other men follow him automatically. By nightfall, he estimates they are about five miles from the coast; but also wonders if they're now behind the German advance. Stumbling across a ploughed field in single file, the pop and hiss of a flare illuminates the night. A voice with a heavy accent calls out to them, "Put down your weapons. Put hands onto your head."

Harding mutters, "Oh, shit."

"We'd better do what he says, boys." Paddy drops his rifle, and hears the others do the same with a chorus of expletives.

"Into the bloody bag we go."

"Step forward, one person only." He hesitates. "Venez, Venez..."

Paddy half steps, half skips towards the voice, and calls out over his shoulder, "Don't you be fretting boys; it's the Froggies, bless 'em." A ragged cheer greets his words.

*   *   *

Maggie leans forward, trying to pick out the words; "...*seem to belong to some ridiculous holiday world...*" Her sister, kneeling in the fireplace, carries on raking, metal scraping on metal.

Grace suddenly stops and sings out, "What's he going on about, dad?"

"Hush. Do be quiet, Gracie, I'm trying to listen..."

Grace ignores her, "Dad?"

Her father sucks on his pipe; his eyes narrow. He reaches up to increase the volume on the radio, now installed as a centrepiece in the bar of the pub. This brings in extra custom, especially since Paddy improved the reception during his last leave by running a wire up onto the roof. He listens for another moment, "...*left that innocent world to sail into the inferno...*" and turns to his daughters. "That's J B Priestly, talking about all the little boats that went over. Some paddle steamer called 'Gracie Fields' was sunk over there."

"What about the soldiers, Dad? Will Paddy be all right?"

"There's a good chance. According to Churchill, we lost thirty thousand men but we got three hundred thousand back. Bloody miracle if you ask me." Ten to one, she thinks, crossing her fingers.

"Anthony Eden was going on about it how wonderful it all was the other day, but it must have been hell on those beaches. And they left all their guns behind; doesn't sound so bloody marvellous when you think about that, does it? An army with no guns?"

At that moment the door opens. A red-faced man carrying a leather satchel shuffles in, looking around in embarrassment. Maggie watches her father stare at him coldly, before a look of horror crosses his face, "Oh Christ... Bert, what do you want?"

"Now, now, Gilly; I'm just doing my job."

"That's what I'm afraid of." Meanwhile, Bert clears his throat and reaches into his bag. "Girls..." Gilly swallows, and thinks again. "Never mind, you might as well stay." Bert looks at a slip of paper, hands it to him, and quietly makes his exit. Maggie knows what it is; a telegram. *One of those telegrams.*

"Open it, dad." She prays silently, watching the silent scream on her sister's face. Gilly rips it open, reads it, puffs out his cheeks, and blows a mouthful of air. She prays again.

"Missing; it says he's missing." He reads it again. "That's all it says." He tries to catch her eye, "I suppose it's better than the other kind." She runs upstairs, wanting to laugh or cry or both, but not in front of her father or her sister. They wouldn't understand. She flings herself onto the bed that she shares with Grace. She curls up, sniffling, examining her thoughts carefully until the feelings no longer overwhelm her. As long as he's alive, she decides, that's all that matters. Even if he's a prisoner and she never sees him again, just be alive, she thinks. It makes her realise she can't rely on anything, anymore. She may have to live without Paddy, whether she likes it or not. Their lives may go in different directions. After a while, she reaches out for one of the books of poetry and begins to read. A couple of hours later, she hears a light tapping on the door.

"Who is it?"

"It's me, Maggie. Can I come in?"

She sighs, "Oh, all right." The door opens, revealing her father smiling down on her. She thinks; how can he be so cheerful?

"Guess what?"

She scowls, "What?"

"We got another telegram. It was all a mistake. Come and see for yourself." Her throat constricts; she nods and slips her legs off the bed. She follows him down the stairs, through the kitchen, back into the bar, into a crowd of locals discussing the latest news about the war. Her father gestures towards a table by the window. A man in uniform turns his head; a familiar face grins. "Where've you been hiding all this time, Maggie?" The cuts and bruises all over his forehead, added to by dark rings under his eyes, give him a look of

Lazarus.

"Paddy...what...how...?" She feels her father squeeze her arm.

"I was somewhere between here and Dover when they reported me missing, Maggie. That's the British army for you. Pity I didn't beat the telegram, but the trains were just a little bit crowded, you know." As he cocks his head on one side she notices Grace settling herself next to him, holding on to his arm. Grace meets her eyes with a look that says, *he's mine now.*

"You're alive, Paddy. That's all that counts." She waits, uncertain of herself.

"That's right, it surely is." He grins. "Come and give Paddy a hug, then." Her relief mixes with all sorts of other emotions as he whispers in her ear, "How are you doing, Maggie? Did you leave that school behind you?" She nods, forces a smile.

She wants to tell him that she wanted to stay on to do her higher certificate so that she could train as a teacher; her father could not afford it, especially with the war and everything rationed. "Grace and I will help look after the pub and the post office counter, when Dad has to go out." She bites back the urge to tell him, that's nearly every day.

"Will you indeed? No wonder you look so grown up." She blushes; thinking, of course I am. "Is that strictly legal, Maggie?"

"Officially it's just Dad and Grace, but as long as one of them is there, I can help." She looks over at her father, who polishes a glass, studiously ignoring them.

"That's not all, Paddy," adds Grace, in a conspiratorial tone. "Maggie has a boyfriend." Maggie shakes her head, trying to tell her sister, no, please, no.

"Does she now? And who is the lucky feller?"

"She's seeing George, George Bonville." Maggie finds herself trapped; she can't really deny it, or admit that she's only stringing him along. That would make her sound mean and selfish. The truth is, she loves to go up to the big house to see how the other half live, to experience a little luxury. George's mother has also taken a shine to her; she passes on lots of lovely clothes, hardly used, which Maggie alters for her own use. She likes George; but mainly she feels a bit sorry for him, that's all. Suddenly, she realises that Paddy is staring at her, expecting her to speak. "I'm not really going out with him, Paddy. I only let him kiss me a few times." She blushes more deeply as she realises that the whole pub has gone quiet, listening.

"Ah well, that would be how it usually starts, Maggie."

She hears laughter; she wishes the ground could swallow her up, but she also makes a mental note not to give Grace any of the underwear that she has started to make from her latest gift, a fine silk dressing gown. Paddy turns to Grace with a sparkle in his eye, "What about you, Grace?"

Grace squeezes his arm and flutters her eyelids, "Ah well, I've been waiting for you to come home, Paddy."

Paddy beams and wraps his arm around her shoulder, "Well, thank the Lord I didn't get stuck in France." She hears loud chuckles and murmurs of approval from all round the bar. It dawns upon her; the returning soldier has become the centre of everyone's attention. How can she possibly compete? She gives her sister a daggers look; hears her father's voice, "Come here, Maggie, you can take a turn serving at the bar." She notes the tone of sympathy; he's rescuing her, deliberately. She feels both reluctant and relieved; she must leave them to it, but with some dignity intact.

*   *   *

He finds himself back in France; running, endlessly running. Shots whistle around him; every so often a voice cries out, "I'm hit". His companions fall away one by one as darkness falls. He staggers on, running through the ruins of the town. Somehow he knows that the last boat will sail from the harbour tonight. When he finally reaches it the queue at the mole seems hopelessly long, the boat already full. As he tries to push into the queue, French troops first laugh at him, push him away, then throw him in the water. He struggles back to the shore, gasping for air, shivering with the cold. A voice tells him to run to the dunes, to find the beach before the last small boats leave. His wet uniform feels heavier and heavier; somewhere, a sniper shoots at him as he runs up and down enormous dunes. Each time he reaches a crest he expects the sea, only to find another dune stretching in front of him. A bullet hits his back and knocks him over. It must be a ricochet, he thinks, as he gets up. He finds himself crossing a beach littered with bodies and abandoned kit; otherwise the shore seems completely deserted. He cries out, but no one answers. He runs into the water, wading out for what seems like miles and miles. He cries out in the cold and darkness, hoping for a boat, a companion, anything. A giant, rising wave breaks in front of him, as he hears a noise ...

Instantly awake, he blinks and opens his eyes, feeling the relief wash over him. Someone knocks on the door again, "Letter for you, Paddy." The female voice sounds incongruously cheerful. But then, everything that used to be normal seems strange. His mouth feels dry. On cue, the voice adds, "And a cup of tea."

"Come in, Maggie." He hauls himself half upright. "You're an angel." She pushes the door open, giving him a hesitant smile. She places the cup and saucer in his hands, retrieves an envelope from under her arm and places it on the bed. He slurps the tea, glancing at the handwriting.

"Dad says you can rest all you like for few days. Who's the letter from?"

"Looks like my friend Pat, the one in the merchant navy." She nods, blushes a little, and stares at the letter. She steps back and meets his eye, perhaps a little more distant than usual, but curious and attentive, eager to please once again. She seems to have forgiven me, he thinks. "I'll tell you what he says, later. But first, you can tell me what's been happening here. How is everyone; your mother, especially?" He sips his tea, more patiently.

She stands for a moment, pursing her lips, then tosses her head and sits down on the end of the bed. "Oh, you know... same as ever." She looks away, nibbling her lip.

"Ah, the thing is, Maggie, it's been a while since I stayed more than a few days. Not since before your dad took this pub. I know she has her own sitting room here, doesn't she?"

She frowns, as if in concentration. "Yes, it's a lovely room, she loves it in there. It has big windows that catch the sun, and she can watch the world going by." She forces a smile.

"Is that what she does?"

"I think so." She sighs and drops her eyes. "She doesn't come out much."

"What does *she* say about the move here?" Maggie lifts her head up and pushes her hair back, away from her face, while she considers the question.

"I think she likes it. She said so, when she first came." She glances at him, as if checking that he really wants to know, and then drops her eyes. "The problem is, she doesn't ever say much, these days. Not to anyone, not even to Dad. It's been like that ever since Harriet was born." She takes a deep breath. "Grace and I used to go in and see her every day, at first. We'd take her flowers or something from the woods and try to get her to talk. Or we'd take the little ones in to see her. The best we ever got was a yes, or no. Sometimes, if we were lucky, we got a smile out of her." She shakes her head.

"Sounds like hard work."

"It was..." She lets out an enormous sigh and scratches her head, while he waits. "Oh, Paddy, it was such hard work. Grace and I...we..." She fishes in her sleeve for a handkerchief, and blows her nose. "We gave up in the end. We started taking turns, rather than going together, but... gradually..." She shrugs her shoulders. "I suppose we go in about once a week, now."

"At least you tried, Maggie. And you still do. Not so often, but it must feel like banging your head against a brick wall. You can't go on doing that every single day."

"Dad does."

"He's married to her."

"I know. But I sometimes think... it must be *awful* for him."

"He's a good man, I'll give you that. Does she ever go wandering, here?"

"Not so much - maybe twice, this year. She has a commode in her room, you see. She doesn't need to go outside. And with the business, we usually lock the doors at night."

He grunts and thinks, those poor girls. "Do *you* like it here?"

"Yes. It's much easier for the schools and everything; closer to the shops. And the post office and pub are interesting. You get to know a lot more people."

"You wanted to be a teacher."

She tosses her head. "I still do." She flashes him a smile. "But I may have to work my way towards it, slowly. I'm not giving up hope just yet."

"Good for you, Maggie. I'm awful glad about that. It'd be a waste, if you did." She smiles again. A beautiful smile, he thinks, like all of them. "And your sisters?"

"What do you mean?"

"How are *they*? I mean, are they happy here, or not?"

She stares at him for a long moment, as if examining his intentions. "Oh, let me see. Grace loves it here, mostly. She's always complaining about the extra work, but she just loves being the centre of attention. In the pub, she has the men eating out of her hand; didn't you notice?" She gives him a wicked grin. Fons feels the heat in his cheeks.

"I did, so; couldn't miss it, could I, Maggie?"

Now, she blushes, too. "I suppose...the other thing, for Grace, you see, *she* didn't mind giving up school. She'd rather work and have money of her own. She likes the Post Office best. She'll be happy doing that, in the long run."

"And June...?"

"June likes school, though..." She hesitates.

"She's not as clever as you?"

She nods, and shrugs. "Not just that. You won't say anything to her, will you?"

"Of course not, Maggie; this is between just you and me."

"She's a bit of a baby. Likes to be looked after and told what to do. So even if she has to leave school, she won't mind. She'll be happy doing whatever dad tells her."

He laughs, "And the little ones?"

She gives a wry smile. "They're happy enough. You know ...what we've been talking about, with mum?" He nods. "They've never really known any different. Grace and I have brought them up, really, and Dad, of course. The sad thing is they've never really known her when she was well. But in a way, that makes it easier for them, now."

"I suppose it does." He looks in his tea, and finds it empty. "Maggie?"

She takes the cup and saucer from him, "Yes, Paddy?"

"I'm sorry if it hurts you, that I like Grace. But I can't help that. I like you too, but in a different way. In some ways, I feel closer to you, but more like a sister."

She forces a smile and looks away, blinking back tears. She starts to open her mouth, as if she has something more to say, but then nods abruptly, turns around and leaves the room. He watches the door for a long while, then sighs and picks up the letter.

"*Dear Paddy,*

With this opening line, I feel that I am talking to myself, and maybe I am too, but that is a curious state of affairs, how we have both changed, and yet not changed, isn't it? I wonder when you will be reading this letter? Hopefully not too far distant in the future, but nothing is very certain now, is it? The whole circumstance reminds me of Dublin in 1922, the way everyone is excited when maybe experience tells us we should all be horrified.

This last year has been far, far too interesting for me. We were steaming up the west coast of Africa, on the way back from Cape Town, heading for Liverpool, when this bloody war broke out. The skipper already some sort of sealed orders in his safe, so that shows there was no real surprise for the bosses of the shipping companies. From what the older blokes have been telling me, the Brits must have expected the Germans to send out the U-boats. Still, it was a big shock when we all docked and discovered that the Athenia had already been sunk just off the coast of Ireland. We all looked at each other, thinking, that's not so very far from here, is it?

It set me to thinking hard. Obviously nowhere can ever be completely safe, but since staying alive ranks high on my list of wishes I kept myself on the tropical routes after that, all the way down to Bombay and suchlike, and then the trade routes from there down through all those islands to Australia, avoiding the shooting gallery (as we now call the northern routes). Some beautiful places down there, believe me, but when it rains, my God, it makes a westerly in Cork look like a shower. Mind you, at least the rain is warm, which cannot be said for Cork, so I'll take the monsoon any day. And beautiful women, oh my goodness, if there was such a thing as a week of creation the good Lord must have spent at least six of the days working down there in the East Indies, that's all I can say. And before you tell me off for thinking this; me and Lily have now gone our separate ways, with no hard feelings on either side. That other feller is still married to his wife, but at least he now has the decency to pay for her and his child, so she'll be fine. She seems happy enough.

It's not all a picnic down there in the tropics, by the way. Some places you wouldn't care to go ashore for the stink of it, and you'd also be in danger of having your wallet lifted or your throat cut; or both, likely enough. These are the ports we hate, as there is nothing worse than being cooped up with nothing to do and nowhere to go. After that, Australia was a bit hot and dusty, but I did like New Zealand. Not too different from the old country, it seems to me, but with proper mountains. That's also a place where white people didn't look down on you for being Irish or for being a sailor, and there aren't too many places in this great Empire where that can be said.

After a lot of thought, I decided to sign on with an American shipping company so I am writing this as I head across the Pacific for San Francisco. As you might expect, the pay and the food are both much better than on British ships. I've heard that American oil tankers pay the best so I'll be looking into that when I finish my stint with this line (I'll be with this company for a few months at least). If you can write soon, send it to the company address below. If not, I'll let you know as soon as I change lines. I'll send my letters to your friends until I hear otherwise.

All the best to you; keep safe, a chara, Pat."

* * *

The Postmaster waits by the door, inspecting his watch, the chain dangling, while the last customer exits. Maggie watches the old lady clutch her savings book and postage stamps in one hand, pick up her stick in the other. She moves painfully, ignoring the postmaster; at the doorway, she stops, turns and waves, "Goodbye, dear, thank you so much."

"It's nothing; goodbye, Mrs Skinner." Maggie waves back; knowing that she has the rest of Saturday afternoon to herself, she also blows a kiss. She takes a pride in memorising her customers' names whenever possible, so that she can greet them personally, with a smile. It's something her father taught her; she takes a pride in her work. She has her independence at last and she wants to keep it. She tidies up her desk carefully, locks the drawers, and places the payment book prominently, ready for inspection.

"Are you going home this weekend, Margaret?"

A polite enquiry, she guesses, nothing more. "Not this weekend, Mr Gates. I shall telephone though, to see how they all are."

"Well, give my regards to your father."

"I will, of course." She likes Mr Gates; he's a shy man, a bit fussy, a chapel-goer, but with no harm in him and a self-effacing attitude. He's not good at conversations; his face turns pink whenever she does more than glance at him. She decides not to tell him about the dance.

Outside, the sun warms her face as she walks, listening to the birdsong from the trees that border the village green. She's very lucky, she reflects. Although the threat of invasion has receded, this war is going very, very badly. Even this far north, the industrial towns have been bombed regularly. She's heard terrible stories. For years Grace and she longed to go to London; that idea no longer appeals. Her jealousy of her sister has also faded, as the realisation dawned that her sister was needed at home, whereas she could leave if she could support herself. So, she has escaped. This place is both safe and familiar without stifling her; Middleton has a quiet charm like her own village, plus a variety of shops and a market, almost a town. Best of all, at the weekends a crowd of servicemen from airbases in lower Teesdale stream into the pubs. The dances here, and in Barnard Castle, attract a crowd of handsome boys in blue uniforms.

Back at her digs, she climbs the stairs to her room and picks out her dress for this evening; one she's made recently, stylish but comfortable, copied from a Joan Crawford film. She slides open the top drawer of her dressing table, pulls out the precious box, and opens it. She runs her hand over them again, still shaking her head, disbelieving. Silk stockings! She has only known the boy three weeks. Last weekend, he slipped these into her hands as if they were unimportant, an afterthought, as he left. She hadn't even unwrapped the gift until she got home.

She knows she should wear them again for him, tonight. But the gift raises a lot of questions in her mind, not least about him. He seems a shy boy, admittedly tall and athletic; an ice-hockey player, apparently. She could see that he needed Dutch courage before he approached her, but he danced well enough. A Flight Sergeant, a navigator, he must be clever; though he also seems polite and self-effacing, like most Canadians. He hadn't even tried to kiss her on the first night. She had found herself wondering if he really did find her attractive until this gift. It seems, somehow, out of character. Does he appreciate how difficult silk stockings are to find, let alone to buy, in England now? Is he really sweet on her, or is this a clever way of making her think so? He doesn't seem the type to try and buy a girl's affection. She sighs, and shuts the drawer.

For lunch, she discovers bread left out for her in the kitchen with a tiny portion of cheese. Her landlady has taken possession of her ration book. She decides to treat herself, boiling one of the eggs her father gave her last weekend. In the country, at least they can always find extra eggs. She takes one of her poetry books to sit and read by the river; to let go of her worries and breathe freely in the summer air while she can. When the warmth of the sun fades, she goes back to her digs.

She's almost ready to go out when footsteps rush up the stairs, making her pause, the lipstick in mid-air. She hears a light tap at the door, which instantly flings itself open. Her sister's voice exclaims, "Guess who, little sister? Dad gave me the whole night off – said I need to relax a bit. Ooh Mags, where did you get those?" She feels a rush of emotions; pleasure to see her sister and to have her company, tempered with a trace of annoyance - why tonight? Pleasure at her sister's jealousy, too; draining away with the thought that Grace doesn't need silk stockings to stand out in a crowd.

A pang of fear strikes her; the thought of being eclipsed. She hugs her sister to distract herself. "A boy gave me them - a Canadian flyer. God knows why."

She feels herself being squeezed, hears her sister chuckling, "Ooh, Mags, what on earth have you been up to?"

She feels her face flush. "It's nothing like that, Grace."

Her sister's round eyes examine her face; Grace beams, and hugs her again. "I know that, I was only teasing, silly." She leaves a pause, and then adds, with a hint of seriousness, "Mind you, if it was me, I'd be seriously tempted, if he's half decent."

"Get away with you." Her sister can still shock her; she has an earthiness that Maggie would envy if it didn't worry her so much. But at least she can tease her sister back about this. "Besides, I thought you liked Paddy."

Her sister sticks out a tongue. "Trust you to remind me of that." She studies the ground, and then looks up. "If you must know, I do, but he's not here. And he could be sent anywhere, couldn't he? Given this war, it's not a good time to pin your hopes on anyone. He... well, he could be away for years." She feels a pang of disapproval, but her sister's appeal sounds heartfelt.

"I suppose."

"Well, has this flyer got any friends? I hope so." Grace watches her face and smiles. "Don't worry, Mags, I'll be good tonight." The tone has reverted; light and teasing again. Dammit; it's so hard to tell when Grace is serious, and when she's not. She sighs, knowing that she has no choice but to give in to these circumstances; besides, a night with her sister should be fun.

"Of course he has. They come in a bus, the Canadians. They all get dropped off on the village green at seven, and taken back at midnight." She turns back to the mirror to finish her lipstick.

They sit on a bench on the far side of the green, watching the men pour off the bus. Most of them form groups and head straight for one of the three pubs in the village. Two other girls waiting nearby are quickly snapped up. A few of the men stare over at them; one or two wave, but none are brave enough to head in their direction. "Can you see him?"

"No, I can't." She can't see if the bus is empty because of the blackout blinds along the side windows. "Come on, we'll go and ask." He did warn her that he might not be able to come, though he said he'd leave a message at the Post office; maybe he didn't understand about half day closing.

The driver of the bus consults his clipboard. "James Martindale, you say? Sorry, honey; not on my list." He sees her disappointment, frowns. "Look, missy, maybe you could phone the office." He scribbles a number down. "This lady deals with the billeting, Miss Palmer."

"Will she be there?"

"She virtually lives there, except on Sundays." They crowd into the phone box together, a handful of coins at the ready. She picks up, asks for the number, pushes the coins in; the phone at the other end rings for a long time before a female voice answers.

"Yes, who is it?" The tone is one of exhausted irritation.

"Hello? Is that Miss Palmer?"

"Yes, who's that?"

"My name is Margaret Hardy, Miss Palmer." She's not sure what to say next.

"What do you want?"

"I...I was expecting my boyfriend, Miss Palmer. Flight Sergeant James Martindale. There was no message from him. I wondered...I mean, is he all right?"

She hears a deep sigh. "Hang on." After a pause, she hears a grunt, and another sigh. "Your boyfriend, you say?"

"Yes."

"Are you engaged?"

"No... no, we're not. Why?"

"Just that it's bad news, Miss Hardy; his aircraft didn't return, so he's officially missing, I'm afraid. I hope that's not too bad a shock for you." The tone of voice tells her, Miss Palmer has said this before, to others. She swallows, unable to speak. "I'll tell you what I tell all the girls that I speak to, Miss Hardy. Flying is a very, very dangerous job. If I were you, for your next boyfriend, I'd find yourself a soldier or a sailor." The phone clicks.

Her face crumples; she shuts her eyes. Her sister seems to know;

she takes hold of her hand. Maggie bites her lip, manages to blurt out, "He... his aircraft...it's missing."

"Oh, Mags, you poor thing; come on, we'd better go back to your digs and get you a cup of tea." But after a ration of tea and sympathy, Grace insists that they have to go back out, back to the dance. "You can't let it stop you living, Maggie. That way, the Germans will beat us. We have to go and have a good time with those other boys. God knows, they deserve it, don't they?" Maggie examines her sister's face. She sees a mixture of determination, concern and humour. Hidden depths, she thinks, my sister. She swallows, and nods.

*   *   *

Sergeant Reilly watches the other men enter the office and then depart. Some look stony-faced, others disappointed, a few triumphant. He waits; patient on the surface, turmoil within. His is the last name to be called; he wonders if this is a good or a bad sign.

He enters, stands to attention; "Sir."

"At ease," The officer, a Major, continues reading his file for about a minute, his face sharp and intent. Eventually he closes it, straightens up and looks at Paddy's face. "So...you are Sergeant Patrick Reilly, Royal Warwickshires?"

"Yes, sir."

The Major allows himself a smile and brings his hands up behind his head, leaning back to watch Paddy's reaction, "Not for much longer. Congratulations, you've passed the course."

Fons sucks air in, puffs out his cheeks, blows out a sigh of relief. He can't quite believe it; himself, an officer? Jesus wept! The thought hits him; I wish my mother had lived to hear of this. Abruptly, he remembers his manners; "Thank you, sir; what happens next?"

"All in good time, Reilly. There are a few things I need to discuss with you before we go any further." Don't count your chickens, he tells himself.

"The first thing is something I say to all of you who come up through the ranks. The army's changing because of the war. We want officers who can lead men because of their ability, whatever their background. You, for example, were selected for officer training because you showed leadership in France." He pauses, lights a cigarette. "But not everyone likes this policy. I have absolutely no doubt you'll find many officers who will look down on you and resent your presence. They won't accept you, especially when they see you in the officer's mess." He looks Paddy in the eye. "You especially, Reilly, since you're both working class *and* Irish. So the question is - how will you cope with that?"

"I wouldn't expect any different, sir. That's the way of the world, and I certainly won't get be getting a chip on my shoulder about it. I expect I'll have to work twice as hard with the men, too. It's not what they expect either."

The major grunts, "Took the words right out my mouth - all right, next point. You lost the whole of your platoon in France, didn't you?"

Fons stiffens, partly out of respect, "I did, sir. I got separated from them... "

"I know the facts, Sergeant. I just read your file."

"Sir."

"You know they were shot after they surrendered, I take it?"

"Yes, sir."

"The point is we can't send you back to the Warwickshires. You need a fresh start, and they don't need reminders of a bunch of ghosts. Bad for morale, I'm afraid." He stifles a surge of irritation on behalf of his platoon; though he can understand the rationale. A whole new start... I hope it's not the Irish Guards, he thinks. "Based on your aptitude tests, I'm going to recommend you for the Royal Signals."

He feels relief, and puzzlement. "Why is that, sir?"

"You have very good scores on mathematics and the use of symbols. And it says you've done some book keeping before you joined up. I would say that makes you ideal for codes and ciphers, wouldn't you?"

"I suppose it does, sir."

"Good man. Now, the next thing is a bit tricky."

"How do you mean, sir?"

"To put it bluntly, Sergeant, we know who you are." The form of words puzzles him for a second; then he feels paralysed, a deep red flush growing across his face in the silence that follows. The Major pushes a file across the desk, turning it so that he sees "Private Alphonsus Gilligan, Irish Guards" emblazoned across it. Fons clears his throat, though he doesn't know what to say. "Having said that, I am more concerned with the fact that this is wartime and that you, Sergeant, are a damned good soldier, than I am with ancient history. So I am going to write in this file that Private Gilligan settled in America and obtained citizenship there. If someone else recognises you in future, I suggest you tell them that you have a cousin by that name who left for America years ago. That should throw the bloodhounds off the scent, don't you think?"

Fons clears his throat again, "I hope so. Thank you, sir."

"Don't mention it. By the way, we never had this conversation, did we?"

"No sir, we did not."

"Finally, and not entirely unconnected with this, I'm

recommending you for an overseas posting. I take it you have no problems with that? Not married or anything?"

Fons gulps, and thinks of Grace. See the world and die, he thinks. "No, sir."

"Well, we'll get you sorted out with the Signals first; basic training and kit. Then you can have a week's leave. And then off you go."

Typical, he thinks. I finally get myself a girl, and they send me overseas.

* * *

Maggie sits, watching her father's silhouette while they drive slowly across the moors in the darkness, peering out at faint, all but blacked out, headlights. He seems older, his face more lined than she remembers. Or is he just exhausted? "How are you, dad?"

"Me?" He sounds astonished, and then his tone changes, betraying how pleased he is to be asked. "I'm fine, lass, don't you worry about me."

"I do, dad."

He nods and glances over at her, then squeezes her arm affectionately, "I know." So much remains unsaid, she thinks. He adds, "You're like your mother." The statement alarms her a little, though she knows he means it as a compliment. She waits a while and asks, "What do you mean?"

"Oh, you think a lot about other people; and you have her brains."

"Do I?"

"You know you do. You remember when Paddy first arrived? That winter?"

"Sort of, I was only a girl."

"Yes, but even then you were worried about him missing his mother."

"Was I; really?"

"You were, Maggie. I remember you telling me. There he is, a great lump of a young man, and you can understand that about him without a word being said. Your mother's like that too."

"Is she?"

He swallows, "Well, she was, when she was herself."

She sits, wishing she could remember more. She does have memories of sitting with her mother in the sunshine, sitting in her lap, feeling happy. She can also remember a time when her mother talked to her normally; but she can't remember anything that was said. She sighs. The journey passes through a comfortable silence until she asks, "How did you get the petrol, dad?"

"Old man Bonville; he owed me a favour."

"Well, thanks for picking me up. It's an awful bus journey."

He smiles. "I had to make sure you came. Paddy told us yesterday that he's been posted overseas. So this weekend may be the last we see of him for a few years, perhaps even until the war ends." Her heart lurches. God knows when that will be; let alone *how* it might end.

"Where's he going to?"

"He has no idea and he couldn't tell us anyway. He won't know until he gets there, Maggie. Did you know; they've made him an officer?"

"Really?"

"Aye, Second Lieutenant. He says they're promoting a lot from the ranks, these days. About time; they might win this war, if they're not careful."

"Let's hope so, dad." She tries to picture Paddy in an officer's uniform. Quite a catch, she thinks. Grace doesn't know how lucky she is. She smiles to herself, ruefully. Oh well, plenty more fish in the sea. Once, that thought would have shocked her, she realises. Has the war changed her, or is it just growing older, wiser? A bit of both, probably, she decides.

She and her father find Paddy chatting with a local lad, Bert; Grace serves behind the bar. Grace rushes out to hug her, whispers in her ear, "How are those dances; any news?"

"Nothing serious, Grace; just fun, like we said, remember?"

Paddy waits his turn patiently. "You look well on it, Maggie."

"Thanks." She smiles and carries her bag upstairs, returning to find that her father has taken over the bar. Grace has taken possession of Paddy, sitting next to him on the bench against the wall. I don't feel so envious now; now that he's leaving, she thinks. Bert, meanwhile, moves a sacking bag off the chair adjacent to his own, gesturing for her to sit next to him.

"Thanks, Bert. What's in the bag?"

He grins. "Oh, you know; a few rabbits."

"I wonder where those came from."

"Oh, you know..." He winks.

"I thought you'd been called up, anyway."

Bert looks embarrassed. "I was, Maggie, but the buggers said I had a weak heart. Must have been when I had the rheumatic fever as a child. They classed me as unfit for duty."

"Count yourself lucky, Bert."

"Funny kind of luck, Paddy... the military doctor said I might drop dead anytime without any warning. He seemed to think this could be quite confusing for the army if it happened in the middle of a battle. I can't see the difference, myself. I said to him, what does it matter whether it's a bullet that gets me or not? I can shoot as good as anyone in this dale." He points at the bag. "But they still wouldn't have me. I didn't know whether to laugh or cry." He delivers this in a deadpan style, ending with a crooked grin. She wonders if he's serious or not; he is a notorious joker.

"Did you really say that, Bert?"

"Of course I did, Maggie. What else could I say?"

"Thank you very much. You could have said that."

"I was insulted, Maggie, think about it."

She studies his face, decides he's telling the truth. As she opens her mouth, Bert mutters, "Oh Christ..." He leans across her, pushes the sacking bag under Paddy's bench. He puts his finger to his lips; Maggie hears the front door open and shut.

Grace calls out, "George... how are you? Come over here..." Bert covers his face in mock despair, winks at her. George pulls up a chair; he looks flustered but pleased.

"H... h...hello, everyone, I'll g... g... get a round in."

"You all right, George?"

"F...Fine, old chap, been chasing a damn poacher; nearly caught him too, at one point."

Bert looks up, a picture of innocence. "What would you have done, George, if you'd caught him?" He sips his drink.

"W...W...Would've shot the bugger." Bert chokes slightly, puts his drink down. "W... Well, maybe not, but given him a good scare."

Bert stares at him, shakes his head, "You should join the Home Guard, George." He turns to Maggie and adds, "George volunteered, you know; they turned him down, too."

"I'll d...d...do that when I'm q...q... qualified."

"I'll join you, George. We'd make a good team, you and me. Come on, I'll help you with the drinks."

George moves away; Bert winks, kicks the bag completely out of sight, and follows him. She and Paddy collapse with laughter.

That night, she cannot sleep. After an hour she slips out of her room to get a drink of water. She hears voices in the kitchen, talking; her father and Paddy, she realises. She hears Grace's name. She can't resist the temptation, puts her ear to the door.

"...the thing is, we're not really engaged, but she's promised to wait for me, Gilly, if she can. We'll just have to make do with writing to each other until I come back."

"Has she now...let's hope it's not a long war, then."

"Is that all right with you, Gilly?"

"Of course it is, lad; I'm glad she's got the sense. We'd better drink to your health."

She hears the sounds of a refill, a clink of glasses, and some soft laughter; the sound of Paddy, clearing his throat. "How are things with Violet, Gilly?"A long pause.

"The same as ever, mostly." Another pause. "Ach, I might as well tell you before you leave. Don't tell the girls, but she's with child again." Maggie bites her lip.

"I thought you looked a bit worried."

"Aye, I didn't think it were possible, at our age, to tell you the truth. Thought she'd stopped all that, you know..." She hears a deep sigh. "It was like last time, you know, she came to me in the middle of the night for a cuddle. First and only time for over a year, and bang, she's pregnant." Maggie moves away from the door, not wanting to hear any more. She pads upstairs silently, back to her room.

She feels panic and rage both rising within her. A voice whispers, "You'll have to come back home, to help Grace. You'll have to come back, and you'll never get away again..." She puts her hands over her ears, though she knows the voice is inside her head. She thinks, I wonder if this is how it all started for my mother, with a voice in her head...

*　　*　　*

Fourteen: 1942

He steps forward into the cacophony, standing in a narrow space between two giant metal columns, cocking his ear at the one on the left. Waves of vibration and heat hammer at his exposed skin; his senses feel as if he's sunbathing within a dark, roaring furnace. Wearing nothing but a pair of shorts, he mops his face with a rag. On the steam ships many of the stokers wear nothing at all; hides like tanned leather. He grins at the memory, then frowns and concentrates on the music of the giant beast - the deep, slow, throbbing pulse seems steady enough, but there - there it is again, a slight and intermittent tapping, as if somewhere inside the belly of this beast, a tiny creature is trying to get out. Something lands on his shoulder, twice; he turns. A grizzled, unshaven face mouths words at him. He half hears, half lip reads the question. Leaning down, he cups his hand around the other man's ear, shouting each word slowly and clearly. "Just a little gremlin in the works, but don't you worry, Jimmy, nothing too malevolent." The other man nods and grins.

Pat taps the metal skin affectionately, wipes his hand on the rag, and consults his watch. He points at the oilcan in Jimmy's hand, and then makes the shape of a circle with his hands. Jimmy nods. The two men make their way aft carefully, stepping over pipes and valves, climbing down a ladder into the deepest part of the engine room. Pat opens a steel hatch built into the floor and Jimmy descends into the tunnel below, holding his oilcan carefully. Pat passes down an electric torch, gives him the thumbs up, and closes the hatch. He stares at the hatch for a moment longer, shaking his head at the idea of being trapped down there, within the long tunnel enclosing the prop shaft, in the event of a torpedo strike. The bearings down there need constant attention or the whole shaft will seize up and render the ship's engine useless; Pat inspects them every watch, Jimmy oils them every hour. We make a good team, he thinks. He checks the cooling valves before getting himself a long drink of water plus a salt tablet, to counteract the sweat he's lost so far. He takes a second tablet with the water bottle for Jimmy, ready for when he emerges from the tunnel, and goes to wait by the hatch.

Two hours later, he pokes his head out above the deck and sucks in sweet morning air, swivelling his head to scan the horizon. The sun, emerging from a gold and silver trail across bright blue water, blinds him; he grimaces and looks down. Jimmy's red face and bleary eyes stare up at him, "We outta the bay yet, Pat?"

Pat shakes his head. "Chesapeake's a long bay, Jimmy, but we'll be out of her soon. Feel the swell. And smell that fresh air."

"Too fresh for my liking, I guess we're only just outta February.

Any wind to speak of?"

"Breezy, no more than that."

"C'mon then, let's sit out in the sun a while and cool off." The two half-dressed men clamber through the hatch onto the deck, carrying boots and a couple of layers of clothes which they gradually don as their body temperatures return to normal. "Seems an awful waste of time to me, going through that canal."

Pat grunts, "If it saves us getting fished, Jimmy, I wouldn't be complaining. They say the U-boats are down here already."

"This close to Virginia, with all the navy here?"

"That won't make too much difference to them Germans, Jimmy. Besides, *your* navy hasn't got much of a clue when it comes to fighting submarines."

"What d'ya mean?"

Pat hears the tone of upset pride, and holds up his hands. "I just mean they haven't got the experience, Jimmy. The Brits have been doing it for years." He watches Jimmy nod reluctantly. "We should be in convoys, see? In a group, with escorts, it's far safer. And there's a decent chance of sinking *them*, that way."

"I guess."

"It's a proven system, Jimmy. God knows why your navy won't use it. We're sitting ducks on our own. Anyone can see that."

"Well, if it happens..." A long, mournful blast of the ship's foghorn makes Jimmy cover his ears with his hands, his face grimacing, until it stops. "...I just hope we're not on watch."

"Too right; mind you, I don't think it'd make any difference, Jimmy. We never get de-gassed these days, so we'd go up like a bomb, anyway."

"Would we? Aw, Jesus, maybe I'll get outta tankers."

"I've been thinking the same, Jimmy, ever since Pearl Harbour." A further series of blasts on the foghorn ends this conversation. Pat stands up to pull on a thick sweater; he stumbles, almost falls, as the ship lurches almost to a halt. A loud metallic crash assaults their ears, the sound of giant cymbals being struck and then torn apart in metal jaws; then a horn blast and a piercing whistle.

"Christ, Pat, we been fished?"

Pat sprints to the port side, peering forward. "We hit something, Jimmy; Christ, we hit another ship..." He stares in disbelief. It's a fine, clear morning. How did that happen? "She's heavily loaded, low in the water, whoever she is."

He senses Jimmy's presence by his side, hears him whisper, "Jeez, Pat, we've damn near cut her in half." Their own engines suddenly roar at full power and Pat feels the tanker trying to pull back and away, while the metal hull of the other boat screams in pain.

"What's he doing, for Christ's sake? He'll open up the hole in her side..."

"Shit, you're right, look at that... Jeez, she's going down, and fast."

"I reckon she's an ore carrier, Jimmy; dead weight." The tanker backs away in a slow turn, giving them a perfect view of the other ship. Tiny figures emerge from hatches; some scurry across the deck, running to lifeboats, while others seem too shocked to move. The deck of the other ship seems to be slide forward towards them, as if making a bow for the performance, tilting slowly but surely down into the water.

"Jeez, they'll never get those boats away." The figures hack at ropes, frantically throw wooden rafts and hatches over the side. Pat hears the tanker's engines slow, pause, and then change again, rising to full power. "What the hell's the skipper doing, Pat? We gotta stay and help those guys. They'll freeze in that water."

Pat shakes his head in horror, "I don't believe this. He's running away from it, Jimmy. He's bloody running away." Within three minutes, the other ship vanishes beneath the placid waters of the bay. Pat and Jimmy remain transfixed, unable to tear their eyes away from the tiny figures moving amidst the detritus on the surface, which slowly recedes into the distance.

*   *   *

Wandering the streets of Aruba at dusk, Pat smells baked earth and sharp, fishy smells drifting up from the port. A sudden shrieking and laughing jerks his eyes upward. On the balcony of a large colonial house, three dark haired girls are waving and beckoning to him. A brothel, he thinks, though one girl looks uncannily like Paula. She lifts her blouse, giving him a brief vision of pointed breasts and nipples. It jolts him all the way down his spine; another girl makes obscene gestures with her fingers. She calls out to him, laughing. He tears his eyes away and sighs, forcing himself to walk on. The ghost of Paula often tortures him like this, especially in his dreams. Not always torture; sometimes he dreams that they are lying in bed again, in the morning, together at last... he shakes his head and tells himself to hurry; he's probably already late for the audition. His gut churns, though he knows this will only be a small provincial theatre company, nothing for him to worry about. He rounds the corner into the main street, expecting to see a ramshackle, wooden fronted theatre. Everything has changed, somehow. He finds himself staring up at the New York Metropolitan Opera house. They must have moved it here during the night. He feels his fear rising again, out of control. He's so much older now, out of practice; and all those years in the engine room have numbed his hearing... He forces himself to calm down, to breathe steadily, while he waits outside the front door. Perhaps they won't ask him to sing, this time. Maybe they want him as an engineer, to fix the generators and the heating pipes. He feels a hand on his shoulder...

"Pat, wake up... the skipper wants you on the bridge."

He hauls himself upright and groans, shaking his head, "Jesus, Matty, I just got off watch a couple of hours ago. Can't I ever get my head down?"

"Nothing personal, Pat; he's going through all the senior crew, one by one."

"Shit. And what's this all about?"

"Oh, you'll see. Some little birdie's been whispering in his ear, I reckon."

"Have they now? About time." As they emerge onto the deck in the half-light of dawn, an overpowering stink of crude oil hits the back of his throat. "Jesus, Matty, we got a leak?"

"Naw, Pat, can't you tell the difference? We're carrying kerosene, ain't we?" He sniffs, to emphasise the point. "Someone else has gone down, hereabouts. We spotted a big flash from the bridge, a ways ahead, couple of hours ago. And now we've been ploughing through this slick for half an hour. She must a' been a big one." Just like us, Pat thinks. Jesus, this is not good news; we're sailing right over someone's grave, probably right past a U-boat. We must be a sitting duck, following the same course. But then we have to, he realises, there's no other way. We'll be going through the straits by now.

On the bridge, he finds the Captain and the First Mate studying the charts. He waits, staring at Captain Parker. Little Napoleon, they call him; a small, wiry man, pug-faced, with sharp, nervous eyes. A former riverboat captain, Jimmy told him. He hears a cough from Matty; the Captain darts a look at him, his body twitching, bristling with nervous energy. "MacMahon; how's the engines holding up? The Chief tells me you've an ear for problems."

"Oh, they're fine, Captain, new enough. There's a bit of wear and tear developing in number two cylinder, but she'll do a few more trips before she needs a refit."

"Even at full speed?"

"Shouldn't make that much difference; it's a steady load on the engine, in these waters."

"Good. You see, our speed is the best thing in our favour. No U-boat can catch us, assuming he's not close enough to take a shot."

Big assumption, he thinks. "That's good to hear, Captain."

Parker studies his expression. "I thought I'd better spell the situation out to everyone. We - that is, the skippers of boats heading out - had a briefing from the navy before we left Virginia."

Pat can't resist, "The US navy?"

"Of course, MacMahon." He sighs, gives Pat a suspicious look. "It was depressing, for sure. They warned us of increasing U-boat activity along the coast and sea lanes, as a direct result of our declaration of war on Germany."

Pat can't help but respond to the tone of sufferance; Captain Parker had not wanted America to enter the war. "As you'd expect, surely." The captain gives him a sharp look.

"They also gave us very, very clear advice." He pauses for effect. "Which was, keep moving as quickly as possible along the coast and move in daylight, wherever possible." He stares, waiting for some reaction on Pat's face. "Which is why we couldn't afford to hang around a minute longer in Chesapeake Bay; I'd timed our run out to get as far down the coast as possible in daylight."

Pat considers this. "We could've picked them up and just waited another day."

"Not there we couldn't; we were far too close the mouth of the bay. Damn it, that freighter was holed up inside a breakwater, waiting to go upriver on the morning tide. She just pulled out into the channel and cut right across our bows. Misjudged our speed, I reckon. So the problem was all her own making. We radioed her position to the coastguard; that's as much as I'm obliged to do, in the current circumstances. I have orders to keep this ship moving."

Pat glances at the First Mate. His face is a mask; for a brief moment his eyes stray upward, glancing at the ceiling. Ah well, Pat thinks, no point in arguing. We all know what's going on here. "Did you ask the navy about using convoys, Captain?"

Captain Parker looks away, down at the charts. "Of course I did. There were twelve of us all asking the same thing; they gave us the usual bull. Good idea, it takes time, other priorities; you know the deal. Sounds like politics to me. Maybe the oil companies can sort it out; I hope so." Pat nods, turns to leave. "Wait a moment. Do you know how many wrecks we saw along the coast?"

"I heard we passed one or two, Captain."

"One or two? We saw wreckage from nine ships, MacMahon, between Cape Hatteras and the straits, most of them lying in shallow water. And did you smell the oil on your way up here?"

"I did, sir."

"That's the third slick we've passed through since we left Aruba." He pauses to let Pat consider these numbers. "So think about that in relation to my decision to let nothing delay us. You don't see what we see, down in that engine room." No, I don't, thinks Pat, biting his tongue. But I do have to go down in that bloody tunnel every time I go on watch. The first thing that happens in a torpedo strike is that all the ladders fall off. So even if we're not in the tunnel, all of us in the engine room are fucked. Kerosene, he remembers. We're all fucked, anyway. For the love of God, I've got to get off this ship as soon as I can. Or I will be meeting Paula soon, and not in my bloody dreams.

*   *   *

He glances at his watch again, feels the engine vibration through his gut. He shakes the watch - the minute hand hasn't moved for at least an hour, it seems. This is pointless, he thinks, as he holds it to his ear. I couldn't hear the damn thing ticking down here if it was beating like a bass drum. He sighs; decides to take the watch off, to stop torturing himself. He lays it carefully down on the table top alongside the water bottles and stares at it resentfully, as if it were the embodiment of the shipping company, Little Napoleon, and the German navy, all rolled into one. He feels a sudden urge to pick up one of his hammers and smash the watch.

This thought takes on a malevolence all of its own as the watch suddenly jumps an inch into the air. He steps back in shock, almost losing his balance, and staggers into the ladder just as both water bottles topple and fall off the their perch. A dull, distant boom; or was that his imagination? His first thought is, torpedo, but maybe it hasn't exploded properly; or a near miss, somehow? Jimmy, he remembers; he's in the tunnel... he rushes to the hatch and throws it open. He's supposed to lock Jimmy in down there, officially, but he can't do that. He sticks his head down and screams in frustration, "Jimmy, get a bloody move on..."

Surely he must have felt that? Torchlight approaches; Jimmy's face appears, streaked with grateful tears, "Jeez, Pat, thanks a million. I'll do the same for you, I swear." Pat scrambles up the exit ladder, noting its intactness, to see what's happening; the top hatch opens as he reaches it, Matty's face peering down.

"It's OK, Pat. The skipper told me to inform you, in case you felt it too; we think it must have been another tanker, I'd say about a mile astern. Something just went up in one big bang, maybe carrying aircraft fuel, something volatile. We felt a lot of vibration on the bridge. Skipper says, give those engines absolutely everything you got, now, flat out."

"OK." He licks his lips, "Matty?"

"Yes, Pat?"

"You got a spare rope ladder?"

"Sure, Pat. You want me to tie one up top, here, just in case?" He nods and tries to smile. His legs are shaking so hard, his knees almost give way under him when he climbs back down.

Four days later, his right leg still twitches with relief as he walks down the gangway to step back onto solid ground. He crosses himself automatically, then resists the urge to kiss the dock. He'll sign off later; right now, he needs a drink.

By the time he leaves the bar it's dusk. He weaves his way slowly and hopefully back the way he came through a haze of contented numbness. Where exactly am I, he thinks? The tankers berth is right next to the naval base, he tells himself. The streets seem vaguely familiar, so his confidence rises; he takes a short cut. After a quarter of a mile, he finds himself lost among a maze of high warehouses and naval stores, fences topped with barbed wire. The main problem is that stacks of empty pallets stand outside most of the gates, blocking his view ahead. The place seems pretty deserted, too; there's no one to ask. He scratches his head and turns back. He immediately spots a white uniform heading his way and stops to wait for the man. As he approaches the sailor keeps his head down, seemingly avoiding eye contact, pulling a cap over his face with one hand and holding the other behind his back. He feels a moment of puzzlement; hears more footsteps running up behind him. He senses danger and turns just in time to see another man swing a blow at his head. He ducks instinctively, hears a curse as the blow misses. He gives this man a solid push and tries to move away, feels a jerk on his arm; hears his coat sleeve rip and feels his body pulled around. The other sailor's cap has fallen off; he sees a scowling face, eyes widening. He raises one arm to fend off another blow, tries to grab the man's arm with the other. He feels a dull pain, a cudgel glancing off his shoulder, but he manages to grasp a wrist, stick out a leg, and push him over. Before he can feel any relief, the other man grabs him from behind, holding his arms in a vice-like grip. This man seems heavily built, much stronger; Pat can't get his arms free. The first attacker gets to his feet, muttering, "The bastard saw my face." He reaches into Pat's coat, takes his wallet, stuffs it into his own pocket, "Thanks, buddy."

"Brain him then; come on, otherwise, he'll recognise you." Pat tries to stamp on the feet of the man holding him, but finds himself first lifted up bodily and then forced down onto his knees. Jesus, these bastards could kill me, he thinks. He tries to bend double to move his head away, bracing himself. He hears the sound of a solid blow, hears a gasp, and another; a series of blows seem to rain down upon him, except that he cannot feel a thing. Must be the booze, he thinks. Abruptly, the arms pinning him fall away, releasing him. He looks up.

A long, crooked face filled with yellow stained teeth, on top of a giant's body, grins down at him, "Haway, bonny lad. Yarl reet?" Pat wonders what language this is. It seems vaguely familiar.

"Don't mind Dennis, mate, he's harmless; most of the time, anyway." This voice carries a strange clipped accent. Pat turns to see a fresh-faced, athletic man, kneeling on the back of one of his assailants, tying his hands together.

"He just can't speak his mother tongue, is all." This deep, rich voice belongs to a very swarthy, curly haired man who sits, grinning, on the other attacker; a fourth man hands him down another piece of rope. The American sailor struggles in vain as they tie him, then curses, "Fucking limeys, lay off; we was just having a private argument."

The athletic rescuer rolls the man over, looking down into his face. "Oh yes? We'll let the harbourmaster be the judge of that." He looks up and beckons, "Bernie, is this them?"

A small man with a bandaged head appears, taking a close look at both men. "That's them, Chief, certain of it."

The Chief nods, turns to Pat and offers his hand. "Chief Officer Frank Swainston, SS Dinsdale; I'm a Kiwi. The big Geordie lad is Dennis, our donkey man." He nods at the dark skinned man. "That's our Bosun, Billy Campbell; Windward Islands. Pete Carr, first mate and Scouser. Bernie here's our steward; poor lad is Welsh, God help him. He had the misfortune to meet these gentlemen earlier. We came down here to see if they were daft enough to try it again."

"Good job for me you did. Thanks, I owe you. They got my wallet, by the way."

"Oh, yes, let's see." The Chief fishes out five wallets from the assailant's pockets. "Caught red handed, boys." He glances at their contents, tossing one to Bernie. "Which is yours, mate?"

"My papers are inside; Patrick MacMahon, Engineer. Call me Pat, or Ricky."

He checks the wallets, throws one to Pat. "Well, Pat, if you want to say thanks, come and see our skipper tomorrow. We badly need a second engineer."

"You do? Maybe I will. What's she like, your ship?"

The chief grins. "No better Captain and no better crew under the red duster, mate."

The others all agree, without hesitation. "Canny buggers, the lot."

"Aye, even the skipper."

"We got no beefs, none of us, man."

"Any of you like music?"

"Us? You're speaking to the multinational hornpipe orchestra."

Pat grins. "And what kind of ship is she?"

The chief looks at the others and winks, "A freighter, old

steamship. She's a beaut, isn't she, boys? A real old beaut." The others shake with laughter. "Put it this way, Pat. She won't win any beauty contests, and she's showing her age, but she's a tough old cow who's got us here so far. We've all learned to love that about her."

* * *

He approaches the water warily, unable to believe his luck. The stream babbles a welcome, running around large circular stones before descending towards a darker, deeper pool. He kneels at the edge, reaches out and touches the cold, clear water; a silver flash jumps away in the corner of his eye; a fish, disturbed by his touch. The water sparkles like crystal clear glass, clean enough so that he wants to stick his head into it and drink his fill. He kneels down in the stream, feeling the shock of the cold water on his knees, and sticks his head in, blowing bubbles. He hears the sound of children shrieking with laughter. They have no idea what it feels like to be thirsty, he thinks. Mary and Michael have never been through the tropics, or across the equator. Somehow, he has stepped back in time and carried all his recent memories with him. He pulls out his head and grins at them, then cups his hands and begins to drink...he feels a sharp nudge on his shoulder, senses that the rhythmic shaking and rattling have slowed, markedly. He opens his eyes, only to be blinded by the intense white light entering the compartment through ragged, dirty curtains.

"I think we're here, Paddy. I can see a big town ahead, must be Peshawar. Looks like a God-forsaken hole alright..." His companion, a fresh-faced Royal Engineer subaltern from somewhere in Cheshire, leans through the curtains, his head out of the window. Paddy grunts and licks his cracked lips with a tongue that tastes like sandpaper. Next time I take a train in India, he thinks, I'll make damned sure I have plenty of water. Two days, this journey has taken. God knows how all those natives sitting on the roof have survived it. British officers have a whole compartment to themselves here in the front coach - they can stretch out and relax. The next few coaches are filled with other ranks and white civilians; nearly every seat is filled. Further down the train, he guesses that only the rich Indians have seats - everyone else is crammed into the corridors, onto the roof, hanging on with baskets of produce, bundles of clothes, and small children. He's never seen anything like it - another world. This is going to take some getting used to, he thinks.

He shades his eyes with his hand. The light is so intense here. He now understands exactly why the older officers wear sunglasses; though he wonders, what will a decent pair cost? The locomotive shrieks and blows a long sigh of steam while the carriage jerks and rattles across a maze of points; the steady squeal of metal on metal slows to a walking pace. He gazes outside, surveys a mess of dusty wooden shacks in the foreground and a jumble of larger, mud-coloured buildings reaching up to the skyline beyond. Lines of washing hang out to dry upon flat roofs; he spots a woman, beating a carpet. A strong whiff of sewage invades the compartment from the huts by the railway. What a life, he thinks.

The train enters a tunnel of shade at last; a station platform materialises out of the gloom. The whole of humanity has gathered there, a vast crowd of myriad colours, ages and dress styles, patiently held back by a line of uniformed Sikhs, arms linked, batons hanging from belts. He watches curiously, feeling in no hurry, making no effort to move even when his companion lifts two small cases down and hurries out into the corridor. He starts to open his mouth, but the young man has already gone. He shakes his head, stands up, sticks his own head out of the window; a little reconnaissance will do no harm.

On this part of the platform, the Sikhs have held their line, though a number of fruit and tea sellers have slipped through to join a flock of porters. The latter cluster around each door; every passenger emerges into a sea of beseeching faces. He observes that a curt nod is used to select the favoured beasts of burden; they dart forward to lift enormous leather trunks onto half-starved backs. If a face looks uncertain, then after the briefest of pauses someone will dart forward and simply grab the luggage from its owner. It seems to be assumed that white men (or women) cannot carry anything. He watches a fight break out between two porters, each trying to claim the same piece of luggage. He hears a roar from the other end of the platform; turns and sees the line of Sikhs parting there, allowing the crowd to surge forward and race for empty seats, battling with those still trying to force their way off the train. The British section remains calm; a world apart.

A woman appears, thrusting bananas up at him; he shakes his head. She shouts something at him with a questioning tone. He licks his lips, remembering the meal he'd been given on his arrival in India, and tells her, "Mango." She smiles and screeches at another woman, who runs over and hands him an enormous yellow fruit from her basket. So that's what they look like, he thinks. The first woman holds up two fingers; he gives her two rupees. She smiles and bows. He sits back down, pulls out his pocket knife, and attacks the fruit. Sweet fluids dribble down his hands and face while juicy slices of heaven slither down his throat. His only regret is that he is too thirsty to savour it properly; next time, he tells himself, I'll take my time.

By now, he is almost the last to depart. Stepping onto the platform, he spots an athletic young porter staring at the others with a look of disdain. At least he looks strong and healthy, Paddy thinks. He waves at him; the man smiles broadly, steps forward and lifts his trunk effortlessly. "Follow me, Sahib."

Paddy hesitates. "I want the Royal Signals HQ."

The porter turns and nods, his expression earnest. "I know, Sahib. I can see from your uniform. Come." Paddy grins, shakes his head to himself, and follows; so much for secrecy. The porter weaves through the chaos to the street outside and strides towards a bicycle rickshaw. He carefully loads the trunk into it. Paddy wonders whether some hierarchy exists among the porters.

"Tell me, why did you wait at the back?"

"I knew you would pick me, Sahib."

Paddy scratches his head, "How?"

"I just knew, Sahib, God willed it." The man smiles broadly and oscillates his head, something between a nod and a shake. He gestures at the man on the bicycle, "This is my brother. He will take you to your headquarters." Paddy reaches into his pocket, but the porter waves him away, "Pay my brother when you get there, Sahib."

One hour later, standing in a small office, he lifts his head slightly to catch any downward movement of air from a slowly rotating ceiling fan. He hears a cough, looks across to see a wry smile on the face of his new C.O. "Finding the heat difficult?"

"I'm grand, sir, just catching the breeze."

"Very sensible; I'm afraid this heat is par for the course in the summer. The rule is, stay indoors and don't move around during the day. No physical work at all, it's too exhausting. We do our PT first thing in the morning. After that, no sports allowed until the evening."

"Sports?"

"Yes; believe it or not we have some of the best facilities in India just down the road. There's even a swimming pool at the Colonial Club. Pesh is a major training area for mountain fighting, you see; sports are the one of best ways to get men fit. This whole area's a gathering point for units getting ready to fight the Japs. Part of our work entails training those units with the latest signals equipment and procedures. You'll work damned hard, but you'll find it's a decent posting."

"What will my job be, sir?"

"We'll decide that after you've settled in. What languages do you speak?"

He feels his cheeks burn. "None at all, sir, unless you count a smattering of Irish."

The colonel snorts, and shakes his head. "Not much use up here, Reilly. Well, we'll send you to learn some Urdu. See how you deal with that. Then you can have a couple of weeks at the camouflage school. We'll decide what to do with you after that. Looking at your record, I'm guessing you're not really a desk person, are you?"

"Probably not, sir."

"Well, off you go. After you've unpacked, get someone to take you to the mess and have a drink. I'll meet you there, later. Look around the facilities and relax while you acclimatise for a couple of days. Language training will start on Monday. Dinner's at seven, by the way."

The Signals compound, he discovers, consists of two not quite equal areas within a secure perimeter; the larger for the Royal Corps of Signals and the smaller part for the Indian Signals. Each has its own administrative HQ, mess, and accommodation for officers (bungalows) and other ranks (barracks). No barrier exists between these two areas; men seem to move freely between them. However, two heavily guarded buildings sit at the centre of the complex, covered by a mass of radio masts and aerials. The business end of the operation, he thinks.

After a shower and change of clothes, he strolls down to the officer's mess - a large square off-white building surrounded by mature gardens and shady trees. A Sikh sentry salutes him outside an arched stone entrance leading to a junction of three marble corridors. Taking the central one, his mouth drops open; was this once a palace? Above dark wood panelling, decorated with carved elephants, he admires the intricate geometry of the stucco ceiling. Passing through a second arch, he enters a marble themed bar, scattered with leather sofas; large French windows open onto a central courtyard, where enormous plane trees shade tables grouped around a fountain. A plume of water springs from the trunk of a half-man, half-elephant; Paddy shakes his head in disbelief.

"That's Ganesh, old chap. Some of our native friends might think that's blasphemy. I take it you're new here?" He turns to seek the voice's owner; that turns out to be a stocky red-faced Captain, sporting a monocle and nursing a long drink.

Paddy nods, "I am, sir."

"You don't happen to play polo, do you, old chap?"

Paddy laughs. "I can't say I've had that pleasure, sir, even if I had been able to bring a horse with me."

The other man allows a smile to play on his lips, nods, and looks him up and down, "Oh well, damned shame. We need some new blood." Giving him one final nod, the Captain turns away, taking his drink into a corner without introducing himself. Paddy watches him go.

The only other occupant, sitting at the bar, waves him over. Also a Captain, he smiles broadly and offers a hand, "I'm George

273

Melsonby; I see you already met Arnott Poulson."

"Pleased to meet you, sir; Paddy Reilly."

"You can drop the sir in here." He gives a conspiratorial wink, lowers his voice, "Call me Uncle George; it's my job to show new boys around. Poulson just marked your card, Paddy."

"How do you mean?"

"Oh, there are two types of officers these days. The pukka types; you know, pre-war Indian army, public schools and polo ponies, like Poulson." Paddy nods. "Then there's the rest of us; we play our polo on bicycles."

"That sounds a little bit interesting."

"It is. But don't play with the NCO team; they're bloody *dangerous*."

A white-coated steward sets two golden coloured drinks down next to Melsonby. Whiskey, Paddy thinks, with lots of ice; Melsonby pushes one towards him. "Mind you, the pukka types did have some foresight. This is the best stocked bar in India, bar none."

Paddy has a sip, and another. Irish, he thinks, and good stuff. I haven't had that in a long while. "Ah, now, I see what you mean. It is indeed. And what's the food like here?"

"Not bad. You'll find out; we're having dinner with the CO tonight. But if you want a real curry, get yourself an invite to the Indian officer's mess. That's also where the real action usually is. We can go over there after dinner, if that's not a problem for you."

"A problem; how do you mean?"

Melsonby lowers his voice, "Well, Poulson and his friends wouldn't be seen dead in there. It depends on your attitude." Paddy shrugs; Melsonby sighs. "The issue is, frankly, how much you look down on the natives." I must be tired, Paddy thinks.

"Ah, well, there's a curious thing..." He swirls the ice in his glass as he considers the rest of his reply, and then meets Melsonby's gaze firmly. "Between you and me, what I mean is, as an Irishman I'm pretty ignorant of these things. Except that, you know, over the years I've had a fair share of people looking down upon *me*. Maybe I *am* just a thick Irishman, but since I don't actually know any natives, I wouldn't really understand exactly why I should be looking down upon them."

Melsonby raises an eyebrow, nods, and gives a wry smile. "Nicely put. But you should be aware that not many people here share your ignorant wisdom."

Paddy shrugs and sips his drink. "What did you mean by real action, anyway?"

Melsonby beams at him and winks, "Girls, and very pretty ones, you'll see, later..." Paddy feels himself slowly relax while Melsonby chats easily about the war, about India, about the routine of life here. A breath of fresh air, he decides; a decent feller. The CO joins them for dinner, briefly, though he appears to regard this as an awkward duty. The conversation dries up; even Melsonby seems relieved when the CO leaves. "Shall we trot across the compound? It's almost cool, now."

Paddy wipes his brow, feeling a trickle of sweat run down his side. "Is it really?"

His companion chuckles, "For the time of year." Outside, he can smell incense and something that makes his mouth salivate, despite the meal he's just eaten. A faint breeze reaches them while they walk in the space between buildings; he hears the sound of jazz in the distance. As they approach, the Indian officer's mess looks slightly ramshackle, plain, unadorned. As they move closer, he sees it has a homely, welcoming feel; three flat roofed buildings surround an earthen courtyard on three sides, with makeshift awnings projecting out for shade. Wooden tables and chairs scatter themselves haphazardly within this space while music drifts out from open patio doors, competing with a hum of conversation. There aren't many white faces, but most of those seem to be female. All the women, he has to admit, look simply stunning. At first glance most seem very European, especially in their fashionable dress, but their skin...he's not sure if it's a trick of the light, but they almost look too healthy. More like Italian or Spanish women, he thinks, used to the heat. One or two have much darker skin. Born here, he wonders?

He feels a tug on his arm. "This way, Paddy; I know this chap, he's fairly new, like you."

Melsonby leads him to a table occupied by a small, muscular Indian officer and a rather elegant girl; they seem deep in conversation. "Hello, Vic. I hope you don't mind us barging in on you, but Lieutenant Reilly here has just arrived. I'm showing him round."

The Indian officer glances up; Paddy sees his eyes widen in surprise before he nods, pushes his chair back, and stands up to greet them. His accent is as impeccable as his manners. "Of course; Captain Melsonby, isn't it?" Paddy notices a brief nod of acknowledgement from the Captain, while the girl looks to the heavens. She's not best pleased, he thinks.

"Call me George, please."

"Of course," The man turns and gives Paddy a shy, welcoming smile. "I am Lieutenant Vikram Mittal; call me Vic. I've been here a month. This is an old friend of mine, Dorothy Sawyer. She's a nurse; just posted here too."

"Paddy Reilly, pleased to meet you both."

Melsonby catches the girl's eye, "I shall have to fall sick, tomorrow." Vic laughs; the girl smiles politely, looking down. You old charmer, Paddy thinks, glancing at Melsonby ruefully; mind you, it's not going to work tonight, by the look of her.

Vic gestures for them to sit down, turns to Paddy, "Have they told you your fate yet?"

"Not yet."

Melsonby interjects, "You know what our CO is like, Vic, by the book."

Vic grins and turns back to Paddy, "Well, everyone in Peshawar knows we have two main roles. You'll either be listening to the Japanese signals or you'll be training our own men. I don't suppose you speak Japanese, do you?" Paddy laughs at the idea, shakes his head.

"They're sending me to learn Urdu."

"In that case you can probably relax; you'll be on the training side. Much healthier, don't you think, George?"

"Better than being stuck in an office all day, absolutely."

"Exactly; do you play tennis, Paddy?"

"Not very well."

"No matter; when the weather gets a bit cooler, I'll give you some lessons."

"You're on. Let me get you a drink, Vic. George? What would you like, Dorothy?"

The girl smiles and gives him a half shrug, "Actually I'm very sorry but I will have to go now. I'm on duty in an hour. It was a pleasure to meet *you*, Lieutenant." She rises to her feet, leans over, and pats his hand, "See you again, I hope."

They all watch her leave; Vic informs Paddy, "She likes you, by the way."

"Does she?"

Melsonby snorts, "Come on, Paddy, you're not that stupid." He grins. "I told you they were beautiful, didn't I?"

"*She* certainly is."

Vic adds, "They nearly all are."

"Who?"

Melsonby sighs. "Anglos; it means Anglo-Indian girls, Paddy, mixed race. I'd better explain; this is one place they can come. They can't go to the English clubs; they're not really accepted by the Indians, either. But because this place is mixed, they can come here. Lucky for us, don't you think?"

* * *

"Ready?" He nods, settles himself into a crouching position, balancing on his toes, and watches carefully. Vikram pats the ball three times against the ground with his racket, shows it with a little flourish, and tosses it up. His swarthy, muscular body rises, stretching with poise and confidence as the racket swings in a wicked arc. He's taken a while to get the hang of this, to anticipate the power and spin that Vic imparts, not to mention the direction. After their first match he learned that Vic had been a junior regional champion. No surprise there; Vic had completely outplayed him. But give the man credit; he'd spent the next two meetings coaching Paddy, improving his basic technique and skills. As a result, Paddy's game has come on in leaps and bounds. Vic seems to admire his dogged determination to keep playing despite the inevitability of the result. Paddy guesses that most white officers, having been defeated convincingly, would never play with Vic a second time.

The first serve flashes past, but it's out. Paddy watches him patting the ball, and waits. Perhaps Vic also respects him because he doesn't mind losing. Well, that's not quite right, he thinks. I do mind losing, but I'm playing a long game. Tennis is new to me. Give me a year or so, then we'll see what happens. I was a damned good hurley player as a boy; I could hit the ball very accurately, which counts for a lot. And hitting a hurley ball with a thin stick is a damned sight harder than using this racket...

The second serve is well placed, but not quite so fast; Paddy manages to get his racket to it. He knocks it back, concentrating on accuracy rather than speed. The ball arcs back over the net, dropping at Vic's feet just as he rushes in towards the net, hoping for a volley. Vic manages to adjust his position and sends a half-volley over to the other side of the court. Another thing Paddy has is boundless energy. He'll chase anything, all day long. He's discovered the heat doesn't really bother him as long as he drinks enough water. So he runs after it, glancing at Vic's position on the court, and returns a lob towards the back of the court. Vic retreats, watches it bounce up to its zenith, and effortlessly hits an overhead, as if serving the ball again. Paddy dashes across the court again, only just reaching it, but he gets it back. This pattern repeats itself three more times. His own returns are never going to be winners, but he manages to drop the ball into areas where it's not so easy for Vic to hit a winner, too. He knows that if he can just keep the ball in play long enough, Vic will get impatient. That's his weakness. Paddy watches the ball loop just over the net at the side, and Vic stretches, trying to hit an outright winner. The ball whizzes past Paddy, well out of his reach; but just out of the court. He wipes his brow, trying to convey the impression that he is both relieved and surprised to win the point.

"Love-fifteen..." Vic's tone implies both surprise and respect; at the end of the match, he hears the same tone again. "Your game's really improving, Paddy. I'm not sure how you get some of those shots back, but you do. Your style's more like a badminton player, but it works for you."

"Ah well, you still won very easily, Vic."

"It didn't feel easy. You took a few games off me today, more than you've managed before." He glances at Paddy with a glint in his eye. "One day you might even take a set off me."

Paddy looks him in the eye and grins, "Give me another year and I might." He towels some of the sweat out of his hair. "Tell you what, I'll take you into our mess tonight and you can try some decent whiskey, Irish whiskey. If you want to, that is?"

Vic glances up at him. "Run the Pukka gauntlet, you mean? Why not? But you'll have to wait by the entrance and sign me in. They're very strict about that, you know. And you'll never play for their polo team again." Paddy laughs; Vic gives him a mischievous look. "Did you know that before the war, only your CO could sign outsiders into your mess?"

"No, but I rather like getting up their noses. They used to look down on the Irish the same way; some of them still do."

"What on earth is that about? You're all white British officers."

"That's complicated, Vic. Take a while to explain. A bit like Sikhs, Muslims and Hindus, I suppose. You can explain that to me, sometime. But the short answer is, we Irish are not really British any more. We fought for our independence, and we got it, in 1921."

"Good God. No wonder they hate you. You're a white Gandhi, come back to haunt them."

Paddy grins. "Maybe - but I'm in their army, fighting alongside them, same as you and the rest of the Indian army. It does the Pukka brigade no harm to be reminded of *that*."

Vic puts down his own towel and gives Paddy a thoughtful look. "Do you really want to get up their noses?"

"I'd like nothing better."

"Do you have any leave due to you?"

"About a week, I think."

"Excellent. So do I; I'm planning to use it to meet my wife in Mussoorie. That's a hill town in the foothills of the Himalayas; my father has a cottage there. He's a lawyer in Delhi, by the way. Come with me. If you come we can show you some of the real India." Paddy feels surprise, even shock. The offer's intriguing, and the more he considers it, immensely appealing; but why has Vic chosen him? Has he not got other friends? Paddy knows that he does; though he's also observed how Vic seems habitually rivalrous with his brother officers in the Indian Signals; not with him, presumably because they are so different. And like Paddy, Vic has no actual brothers, either. He senses that he and Vic just feel relaxed in each other's company, as if they have known each other for years. Like it was with Pat, he thinks.

"I'd love to, Vic, but you'll need to be with your wife."

"Oh no, she loves company, really. She always asks me to bring someone. You must understand; Indian families like to spend all their time together, in groups. She would hate it if we were alone all week."

"But I've never met her."

Vic sighs and gives him a hard stare. "Look, Paddy, let me put it this way. You are the first British officer I've ever known who doesn't treat me like a wog. That means a lot to me, and it will to my wife, too. So please accept my hospitality."

Paddy feels the heat in his cheeks. "In that case, I will, Vic, I will."

Vic glances about him, as if checking whether anyone's eavesdropping. "If you like, Paddy, I can ask Dorothy to come along too."

Paddy bursts out laughing. He loves the way that Vic can switch in one moment from utter seriousness to wicked humour. "For Christ's sake, Vic, no. I've told you before; I have a girl at home. Grace is her name; she'd scratch my eyes out, I tell you. I'll come; but no Dorothy, please."

*   *   *

He wakes early, throws off the blanket and immediately feels the coolness around him. It's the first time he's used anything other than a sheet since he arrived in India. He slips out of bed, pulls on some shorts and a vest, finds his camera and creeps out of his room; along the corridor, towards the steps that lead up to the flat roof. They'd arrived late the previous night, having taken the train to Dehradun, where Vic's wife and sister had met them in their father's car. Everyone had mentioned the view from the roof.

The dawn that greets him takes his breath away. The house stands a little way out of town on the side of a mountain, lush green vegetation falling away below into thickening layers of mist, curling languidly around the contours below, all the way down to the valley floor. On the horizon, the snow-white giants of the Himalayas rise above turquoise layers in the middle distance; the sky colours shift gradually from blood red splashed around the rising sun to a deep, dark blue above his head. A spectacular tropical chorus begins to grow and echo around him. He pulls his camera out of its case, frowning as a crumpled letter also falls out onto the floor. Ignoring this, he carefully takes four different views with the camera. These black and white snaps can never begin to capture the reality, but he wants some proof that he has actually been here, no matter how pale the imitation will be. How much do colour films cost, he wonders, out here? Well beyond a subaltern's pay, likely. He bends to pick up the letter, shakes his head, and sits down with it, a deeper frown etched upon his face. He starts to re-read it again, hoping that somehow the contents have changed. He doesn't hear the steps behind him.

"Wishing she was here?" Vic's voice makes him start slightly.

He sighs and scratches his head. "I'm afraid not." His friend looks puzzled. How to explain? He offers him the letter. "See for yourself."

Vic's eyes open wide; he takes the letter and reads it silently. At the end, he sniffs to himself, folds up the letter and passes it back. "I knew something was bothering you on the way here. We thought you might be ill."

"It arrived the morning before we left."

"Must've been a nasty shock."

"I suppose; though when I think about it, I talked her into the engagement at the last minute. And I could be here for years. So it shouldn't really be a surprise. I just hope the feller she's met is worth it." He forces a smile. "Anyway, it's nothing, really. No one's been killed, have they?"

"Just a nasty wound, Paddy, in the heart. Maybe a kick in the balls, too?" Paddy doesn't reply. "It's different for us. That would never happen here. You see, our families arrange our marriages. They choose someone who they think will suit us from a similar background; normally with a lot of planning and preparation. Everyone knows where they stand."

Paddy nods, "You seem to have done alright out of it."

Vic grins, "Yes, I think so too." He pauses, as if thinking hard. Paddy feels sure that he's going to mention Dorothy; to say I told you so, we should have invited her. "Are you interested in temples? Or waterfalls?" He feels relief, mixed with a little regret.

"Anything and everything; it's another world, for me. A very beautiful world, too."

"Right, well we shall have to keep you busy the next few days. The girls will make picnics, and we'll take you to our favourite places. You have a lot to see and taste. First thing is a cup of hot, sweet chai, Indian style."

Paddy smiles, and nods his head, "Some things seem to be universal, Vic."

*   *   *

Vic leads the way, the path climbing the mountain through the forest, followed by his wife Suhaila, his sister Roshni, and Paddy. The last full day, he thinks. He grins, feeling a deep satisfaction as he watches the two women ahead of him. They seem to float effortlessly from one step to another, two blazes of colour in their silk saris. The garments hide all of their bodies except their feet and a few inches of shapely calf above their thin sandals; he can't stop admiring the sensuous way they move. Suhaila means moonshine, apparently; she's beautiful, a round, wide-eyed face above a slim body (just as he would have expected, since Vic is a handsome devil too). Roshni means light, which Paddy thinks is also appropriate, in a different way. She's stouter, plainer; with a friendly, open nature, so attentive and easy to talk to. The light grows and then blinds him as they emerge onto a small plateau at the summit of the forested hill. They stand, shading their eyes and blinking, trying to take in the views back down into the valleys below. Roshni points into the distance, "Shame; we can't see the big mountains for the clouds today."

"Never mind, we came here to show Paddy the temple." All Paddy can see is a white, windowless building, the size of a small house. "That's it, Paddy. Not exactly the Taj Mahal, is it?"

"I wouldn't know. I suppose we'd call this a chapel back home."

"Wait till you see the statue inside; take your boots off and we'll show you." Inside the building, little light penetrates; the earthen floor feels surprisingly cool on his bare feet. The statue seems to emerge suddenly out of the dark shadows, as if alive, while his eyes adjust.

The stone looks very old, with signs of weathering, as if at some point in its life she has stood outside for a few centuries. Nonetheless, the images portrayed are clear and unmistakable; a beautiful bare-breasted woman sits astride a lion, whose paws pin a buffalo to the ground. The woman has six arms, two of which hold swords, the third a mace, and the fourth a spear. The other two stretch out as if offering peace. Despite her weaponry, the woman smiles and appears completely relaxed. Is she victorious, he thinks? Is that it? "What's her name, Roshni?"

"She is called Durga; she is the warrior aspect of the Divine Mother."

Looks a bit like my mother, Paddy thinks; after all, she rescued Pat. "A goddess?"

"Yes, of course. She's the one who defeats the evil that men cannot defeat; like selfishness, envy and prejudice. As women, Suhaila and I know that these things have to be confronted, but not with force." The two women kneel before the goddess with offerings of incense and flowers; Vic joins them, bowing his head to touch the floor. To Paddy, something about the scene seems uncomfortably familiar. Of course, he thinks; at home the Virgin Mary, here a warrior queen.

Sitting in the sun outside, he teases Vic, "She seemed very familiar to me."

Vic leans over to whispers in his ear, "Like Dorothy?"

"No, it's the Virgin Mary with balls." They both burst into laughter.

The two women, busy unpacking the picnic, look to the heavens. "Don't be so disrespectful, Vic; and don't encourage him, Paddy."

Vic whispers again, "Suhaila's favourite deity."

"I should hope so; powerful and beautiful." He turns to the women. "I'm sorry; she represents some wonderful ideas, and looks far more interesting than anything in *our* churches."

While they eat, he thinks back to the day before. Walking along the main street in the town, they'd come across a battered wooden sign, only recently torn down; *'NO DOGS OR INDIANS'*. He'd stopped to stare at it, astonished; Roshni had grabbed his sleeve and pulled him away from it. "Come along. You see, the British created these hill towns for themselves, to escape the summer heat. Those signs used to be commonplace here and in all the other hill towns. It's only since this war started they've come down. Because my brother fights for them, they can't ban him anymore."

Paddy had muttered, "Things are changing in England too, Roshni; ordinary men like me can now become officers."

She'd flashed him a smile. "It's also changed here because some Indians used to defy them. They would walk there every day, even if they had to pay the fine every day too."

Chewing on a chapatti, he wonders if she was referring to Gandhi and his followers. "What do you think will happen after the war, Roshni? Will you break away, like Ireland?"

A long silence follows; Vic speaks first. "My father thinks nothing will change, but my little sister thinks that we will break away. Myself, I believe there will be some kind of compromise. We Indians are very good at that."

Roshni purses her lips. "Actually, that's not what I think, Vikram. I think we should break away, but I don't think the British will allow it. Not after all this time. They'll find a way to delay and delay until we all give up or die of old age."

Paddy looks at Vic. "That's one way of forcing a compromise."

Roshni laughs, "Oh, please don't tell me I agree with my brother." She looks at Paddy. "What would an Irishman advise?"

"Hmmm, now you put me on the spot. I would say, think very hard. We got our freedom, but it was a disaster for our economy. I wouldn't worry about any of it now; not until this war's over. So, there's no hurry there."

She beams. "Good advice."

After another silence, Vic taps Paddy's shoulder. "We're all so glad you came, by the way."

"Are you? Well, thanks. But I should be thanking you, for bringing me here."

"You may not be, when we return."

"What do you mean?"

"They'll probably send you to Coventry, Paddy - your English officers. Maybe not all of them; people like Melsonby may be all right, but the rest will."

"Will they?"

"Yes. And they'll call you a wog-lover." Paddy sees the girls look away, embarrassed. He shrugs, and rubs his feet. It feels good to have his boots off, to let his feet cool.

"I've been called worse." He thinks about when he was cashiered, years ago, for wearing his uniform. "There's no end of stupid people in this world. I know that much, for sure."

Vic nods, staring at Paddy's feet. "Yes. We'll have to get you some Indian sandals before we go back." He sees the look on Paddy's face. "Not for public use, don't worry. For wearing when you're off duty. They're much more comfortable, especially in the heat; wear them like slippers."

Paddy shrugs and then thinks, why not? In for a penny, in for a pound.

*   *   *

Fifteen: 1942

His restless mind questions the path he's followed these last few months; sure, it would've been crazy not to get off that big tanker, but this ship? Captain MacGuire's opening speech comes back to taunt him; the middle-aged, schoolmasterly Scot had so impressed Pat with his frankness, he'd swallowed the bait. "The Chief Engineer, Harry Roberts, he's getting on a bit; but he knows this ship inside out. He'll be a great supervisor, though he's not so mobile now - you, as his second, will have to do the leg work on the engines. And the third engineer, John Oswald, now he's bright but just a young lad; he'll take a watch, but mainly he'll look after the electrics and deck work." He'd surely been warned how hard it would be; his mind replays his tour of inspection, his eyes darting around, trying to reassure himself that he's not jumping from the frying pan into the fire. When he opened the entrance hatch to the engine room, his eyes were drawn to those ancient welds attaching the ladder. How much vibration would they take before the ladder falls off, sealing him within the heat and noise below? Not much; even back in port, it had taken an effort to go down. He sighs and shuts the thought away, turns over in his bunk, drifts in and out of sleep.

How carefully he'd inspected the engines; but how well prepared they must have been, knowing he was coming. The levers and controls were all properly greased, the brass adjusters and gauges shiny and clean. A nine thousand ton coal-fired steamer, built sometime around the last war. She'd looked in reasonable shape, well cared for, on that day. The old cow's back to normal now though; dirty, surfaces thick with coal dust, and slow as hell after what he was used to. Steam engines, what was he thinking? Plus, of course, the massive drop in wages. What the hell, maybe his instincts were right? He feels happier among this crew. Another memory pops into his head; the first time he'd followed Frank Swainston down into the darkness of the forward hold, his curiosity growing. Frank's voice, his matter of fact tone; "We got lucky this time, Pat, the hold's full of flour. Billy and I cleared some space in the middle. See?" Frank flicks on a dim electric light. Pat stares at a mound of flour sacks resembling the crater of a volcano, the insides lined with old blankets. "It deadens the sound, see? Back in 1940, we had a really good bash and a sing-song one night. Skip told us this escort ship came tearing in all the way from the far side of the convoy, cut right through the middle, following his sonar, trying to locate us. They tore almighty strips off us when they found us. Said they could hear it for miles; and if they could, so could the U-boats. This is our muffle kit." Later, five of them sat within the crater of flour. "Let's go, boys,"

Frank brought his flute up to his mouth and launched into a sea shanty. Billy grinned, strummed his guitar, picking out the rhythm. Adbul (able seaman from Calcutta) frowned for a moment then began to tap out an irregular, exotic beat on the drums cradled within his bandy legs. Dennis picked up his spoons. Pat let them settle into the tune and then lifted up his squeezebox, drawing in the air...

Someone screams in the distance; a long, agonising shriek, seemingly endless, as if someone is being slowly torn apart. He opens his eyes and blinks; he's in his cabin, awake now, though the unearthly screaming continues. Who or what on earth is that? Oh Christ, he thinks, that sounds like a steam pipe's burst. He sits up; it must be Oswald's watch. Damn it, I hope the kid's OK; I'll have to fix it, anyway. Stumbling along the dark corridor, he meets someone coming the other way; a torch shines into his face. "Pat, thank God you're awake. We've got a big problem."

"Steam pipe blown, I'm guessing, Frank? Any pressure remaining?"

"None to speak of, it seems to be the main pipe. Young Oswald got scalded when it blew. He's not too bad, but he won't be able to use his hands for a day or two. At least he protected his face. What can we do?"

"Unless we can isolate the leak between a pair of stop valves and re-route, we'll have to shut the engines down and replace the section of pipe that blew."

"Shut everything down? Christ."

"Everything - every fire, every damn boiler; we should ask Harris first, though. He'll know where all the stop valves are."

"That might be a bit of a problem, Pat."

"How do you mean?"

"Well, you know he said he was feeling ill last night?" Pat grunts an acknowledgement. "I couldn't get an answer from his cabin, just now, so I just barged in. He's cold, lifeless. I reckon he's croaked it, Pat; must've had a heart attack."

"Jesus wept. Will young Oswald know anything about the stop valves?"

"No chance."

"Well, best go and tell the skipper we'll be shutting down; he'll have to signal the rest of the convoy. I'll get myself on to it."

"OK, mate." At the open hatch, a dense cloud of a steam vents up from below. He forces himself down the ladder, to focus on the job in hand for the sake of everyone aboard. If he can't fix this, he tells himself, we're probably all dead, one way or another. The place looks like a Turkish bath, thick with vapour, and sounds like a barn full of squealing pigs. He can't get anywhere near the blown pipe; the jets of scalding steam would poach him alive. So he can't get anywhere near the stop valves, wherever they are. He forces himself to be patient, focussing on what he can do, gradually cooling and dousing each of the fires in turn, three in each boiler, slowly enough to prevent damage and enable a quick re-start. He's just starting to think about the next stage when he hears Frank's voice in his ear, "Christ, Pat, can't you stop the sparks coming out of her?" The tone is strained, aggressive, badgering.

Pat refuses to turn around to acknowledge this stupidity. "What sparks? I've shut the bloody fires down in both boilers."

"Come up and see for yourself." He turns around, but Frank has already disappeared. Sod you, he thinks, I will go up and take myself a break. He checks his watch as he climbs the ladder. Two hours gone. Up on deck, he hears a noise; someone coughing. The cold night air shocks his skin, though it's bearable, a summer night. He stops to enjoy this sensation while his eyes adjust to the darkness. He makes out a group of men standing ready, fully dressed with lifejackets on, by one of the lifeboats. They seem to be standing almost on their tiptoes, ready to jump into it. He opens his mouth to ask what's going on, thinks better of it. One of the men points upward; Pat follows the line of his arm to the single smoke stack rising silently into the sky. As he watches, it belches an enormous mass of sparks upward. The sparks swirl on the breeze, spiralling upward, a great glowing cloud of red and orange light rising into the sky, a beacon of their distress. Jesus wept, it's a giant roman candle, he thinks. He feels a tap on his shoulder and hears the Captain's voice.

"Can you no stop that? We'll be visible for nigh on fifty miles."

Pat scratches his head. "Must be the soot in the flues off of the furnace, skipper; bit like a chimney fire on a bigger scale. They can't have been cleaned out properly last time she had a refit."

"Can you no stop it?"

"Nothing I can do with that, skipper; she'll burn out in an hour or two."

The captain takes out his pipe and fills it. "Well, you just carry on then, don't worry about it. I've got the men out by the boats, just in case." He sniffs, "How long will you be?"

"Another three hours or so."

"Need any help down there?"

Pat thinks carefully. "Send me a couple of strong lads to help me with the nuts and bolts."

The match flares; he glimpses the Captain's eyes watching his face. "I'll do that. Off you go then, laddie." It takes over a minute to get himself back down the ladder; half a minute to steel himself, another half minute to stop his legs shaking at the bottom. The screaming pigs have gone; replaced by the hissing of an unseen, giant snake. He takes a long drink of water with two salt tablets. His head keeps reminding him, fifty miles, fifty miles; there's bound to be a U-boat somewhere within fifty miles of us, and the convoy's left us behind by now. It's a clear night; we're a sitting duck. He knows these thoughts will echo through his head, a repeating siren, whenever he stops work. He feels exhausted already, before he starts.

Clouds of slowly cooling vapour hang in the air; every part of the room drips water. His wrench slips on the nuts; when he gets the nuts off, they slip out of his hands even when they don't burn his skin. Something large, shapeless and white looms up; "Howay, Pat."

He recognises the voice instantly. "Dennis, thank the Lord; give me a hand. You can send the other lad back; it's like working in the dark down here. I'd be forever showing him what to do."

"The other lad? Why, never mind that, bonny lad; give us that bloody spanner."

Pat wipes his brow, hands it over and points, "This one next." He watches the big Geordie loosen a nut that clearly hasn't moved for decades. "You done this before, Dennis?"

"Me Da built ships all his life, see? Me, well, I ganned in the yard a while; but why wud'aah built a thing when aah can tak' a ride on it, eh?" Pat grunts, feels his face smile; he feels surprise, that he can do so. The big lad works well; they each take turns and when necessary, put their backs together. Yet whenever he stops to watch Dennis, the thoughts return; a sitting duck on a clear night, a sitting duck on a clear night... it's easier, he decides, to work than to watch. The nuts slip out of his aching, painful fingers; Dennis has big hands but suffers the same problem. Better than getting blisters on your fingers, he tells himself. Sometimes Pat has to go down a level, under the gratings, to retrieve them. Down under the gratings, trapped, the water flooding in...images like this drive him on, working himself harder and faster despite his aching hands and wrists. His exhaustion makes him weak, his limbs screaming; Dennis does not complain. Replacing the section of steam pipe is the straightforward part – except that everything has to be improvised, cut to size, fitted in two sections with an extra joint. He feels sure that a torpedo will strike just when they have it fixed. To hell with that, he tells himself, glancing at the ladder. They couldn't get me before, on the bloody bridge, or above that poxy village. And the Staters didn't catch me and hang me either, did they? So sod the bloody Germans. They won't get me either. Just in case the new joints don't hold, he takes the precaution of fitting an extra stop valve protected by plates to deflect the steam; it all takes time. Sod them, they won't get me. By now, his thoughts bring back images from the bridge and the Fitzgerald farm. Blood and bodies; he sees them, floating in the water.

He starts talking to distract himself while Dennis works. "Dennis, you must've travelled about a bit, haven't you?" He hears a grunt of acknowledgement, a long pause while Dennis tightens a nut.

"Oh aye, Pat; aah've seen the inside of many a flootin' scuttle."

He wipes his brow, "You ever heard of a place called Weardale?"

"Way aye man, me granny was from Allendale."

"Where?"

"Next dale oop, man."

Pat works for a while in silence, then gives Dennis the tools, "So what's it like?"

"Canny as hell, man; God's oown country."

"How do you mean?"

"It's wild, man; unspoilt. Canny folk, an' all."

"How do you get there from Liverpool? I had a mate knows some people there, thought I might take a look sometime."

Dennis grunts with effort repeatedly, sighs as his foot slips. He takes a breath, rebalances himself, "Why, I'll tak y'there, Pat. S'on me way hame."

"Tighten it up, Dennis; hard as you can." Pat wipes his brow, glances at the big stoker. "After this one, that's it. We can light the boilers again."

Dennis's eyes light up; "Aah'll dee that, Pat; proper firebug, that's me."

"You go ahead, Dennis, thanks. I'll pop up top for a while." He emerges into a dim grey light. One or two men stand smoking, leaning against lifeboat davits; most of them sit with their backs against the superstructure. A few have curled up on the deck, asleep. He can hear a gentle slapping of the sea, uncannily calm, lapping against the ship; a sleeping beast, all her menace hidden away under the surface. The distant horizon seems flat, empty.

He feels a hand on his shoulder, "Any luck, laddie?"

"It's done, skipper; we'll be under way as soon as we get the pressure back up."

"Good lad." He rubs his chin. "When we dock, I'll be looking for a new Chief Engineer."

He remembers; Harry, poor old Harry, he thinks, "Of course."

"Mind you, if your repair gets us home and passes muster with the company inspectors, I might just be looking for a second engineer instead. Would that suit you, Mr MacMahon?"

It takes him a moment to puzzle this out. Christ, my own personal cabin, he thinks. "I guess it would, skipper."

She sweeps the wooden floor, wipes the tables, staring at the windows. Should she bother to clean them today? She decides not; watching her father laying the fire, she folds her arms and wonders what Paddy's doing at this moment, somewhere out there in India. Nothing too dangerous, she hopes. The back door slams; June, she thinks, always in a rush to see her friends in the village. But when she returns to the kitchen and glances out of the window, the pram has vanished from the place she had left it; the spot that catches the sun in the morning. She doesn't feel unduly alarmed; in this house, any of her sisters might have decided to take her. Normally they'd have told her or her father. She throws the cloth into the sink, opens the door into the bar, and calls out, "Dad; has someone taken Ellen for a walk?"

He shrugs, scratches his head, "Not that I know of." She walks to the front door, unlocks it and steps outside, ignoring a quizzical look from her father. Stepping out into the road, she looks right and left. Her heart stops for a second, her mouth drops open; what has she just seen? It was clear enough, but Oh Lord, how to tell Dad? Her mother pushing the pram, disappearing around the corner, but as naked as the day she was born. She can't have imagined it, surely?

She dashes back inside, "Dad," she hisses, to get his attention. Then she lowers her voice to a whisper; "I think Mum's taken Ellen down the road, but she hasn't got any clothes on..."

Her father's eyes widen, blink, stare back at her for a long moment; he grimaces with frustration. His voice matches the reluctance etched on his face, "I hope she's not headed for that bloody river again..." He sighs, seems to pull himself together, "Come on, Maggie."

He runs surprisingly quickly, pulling ahead of her despite her youth. They catch up with Violet on the road to the station, just before the bridge over the river. Her father grasps one of her mother's arms gently, holding his other arm out in front of her. "Violet... Violet..." Her mother stops, lifts her eyes to meet his for a brief moment, shakes her head from side to side. She turns to glance at Maggie, looks away again, darts an angry look at her husband. "Come on now, Violet, we need to get you home and dressed; you can't go out walking like this." After a few moments of mute, passive resistance, her mother seems to give in; they cover her nakedness up as best they can with Gilly's jacket, plus the apron that Maggie's been using.

Maggie reaches across the pram intending to pick Ellen up; she senses a blur of movement leap towards her, feels her body thrust backward so hard that she staggers and falls. The shock of this act freezes the moment in Maggie's memory; for days afterwards, she can't rid herself of this image; her mother's face jumping at her, teeth bared, cold hostility in her eyes, her voice hissing, "She's mine..."

*　　*　　*

She glances up to see a stranger standing patiently at the bar, waiting to be served. There's something different about *him*, Maggie thinks; not a local man, for sure. Dressed in thick working trousers and a thick sweater, a plain cap tucked under his arm; definitely not military, the hair's too long. But he stands plumb line straight, the same way Paddy does; more confidently, if anything. She works out the change, hands it over; turns towards him, "Well, what would you like?"

The blue eyes twinkle while they regard her, "Oh, all sorts of things; but a pint of your best beer will do for now." The voice shocks her. She realises why after she turns away; he has the same accent as Paddy, the way that the 'h' in things is almost (but not quite) silent. She finds herself blushing, almost dropping the glass while she fumbles with the pump.

She takes a moment to compose herself; looks back at him, "Are you Irish?"

"I was, I was, once upon a time; but tell me, is this tiny little place Eastgate?"

"It was, once upon a time." She smiles up at him. "They took the road signs down in 1940 and never put them back up. You're not a German spy, are you?" She means it as a joke; to her horror, the whole bar falls silent and turns, staring at the newcomer. He grins, much to her relief.

"I wasn't, not the last time I looked in the mirror. Why, do you think I look like one?" She shakes her head, blushing furiously; she can't help glancing at his fair hair, his blue eyes, blushing again. Out of the corner of her eye she sees a short, chubby red-faced man struggle to his feet, detach himself from the table in the corner, waddling towards them. She groans, inwardly.

"Where's tha uniform? Get tha self in th'army or get thee gone."

She flinches at the tone, the slurred voice, "Now, Billy..."

"We don't need to wear uniforms in the merchant navy; we just do our job." The stranger's voice is suddenly crystal clear, calm and resolute.

Billy scratches his head, muttering to himself. He starts to turn away and then turns back, "Bloody shirkers; get tha self a uniform." The stranger doesn't even blink.

"Tell you what; we could all do that, us seamen. You know something? We'd all get far better pay plus a spot of paid leave. The problem is, though, me and my mates are bringing in all the sugar to make your beer, the flour for your bread, the corned beef, the tinned milk, not to mention all the guns and ammunition to fight the war with, and all the fuel for your cars and tanks and planes. So you might just find yourself in a little spot of bother, without us." He takes a sip of his drink while he watches Billy's face. "Another thing, before you tell me all about these brave lads in uniform, I'll tell you something about life in the convoys. In a tanker ship, now, one torpedo can blow the whole ship sky high. Even when it doesn't, you'll be jumping into a layer of burning fuel. Then there's the ammunition ships; you surely do not want to be anywhere nearby when one of *those* gets hit. So if you're really lucky, and you're not carrying anything like that, you've nothing much to worry about. Just how to get up onto the deck in pitch darkness while the water comes in, how to get off the boat in three minutes flat, and then how to survive in ice-cold water; oh, and how to swim, or maybe row, a thousand miles." He takes another sip. "And when you get home, say after three or four weeks in a lifeboat, you know what? They'll dock your pay from the exact moment your ship went down. You bloody shirkers, they'll say; sitting in a lifeboat all that time."

He turns back towards Maggie and winks. "You were telling me about the village..."

"Was I?" She tries to ignore the sight of her father walking purposefully around the bar, a grim look on his face. "What would you like to know?" Behind the stranger, George Bonville rises to his feet, clutching his personal silver tankard.

"Well now; is there anywhere I could stay for a couple of days? I'll pay the going rate."

"Maybe - we can ask around." She watches her father escorting Billy out of the door. "I'm sure we'll find somewhere." George appears next to the stranger, looking at her for his cue.

"That would be grand." He nods at her and sips his drink, his face a picture of innocence.

Gilly returns to her side, rubs his hands and announces, "Good riddance; I've been wanting to turf him out for years." He catches the stranger's eye. "Sorry about that."

"No problem, we get nonsense from idiots like that all the time; occupational hazard."

"I'm the landlord here, Gilbert Hardy; call me Gilly."

"I guessed as much, to be honest. My name's Pat - Pat MacMahon; I'm a friend of Paddy Reilly's. He's told me a bit about this place."

She squeals with delight before she can stop herself, "I *knew* it."

"This is my daughter Maggie; and this is George Bonville. I imagine you enjoyed seeing Billy get his comeuppance too, George?"

"I...I did. He's a p...p...pain in the neck, let me buy you a drink, P...P...Pat."

"I wouldn't refuse any man *that* request, George."

As she reaches for the glasses, her father whispers in her ear. "I'll manage here on my own, Maggie, when you're finished serving these two. You go and look after the baby awhile, give Gracie a break. She'll do the bar tonight, with me. You can get the others their suppers and put the little ones to bed." Though she loves her baby sister Ellen, she feels a surge of disappointment; does her father think that scene was her fault? That she couldn't have handled Billy herself?

No, she tells herself; he just prefers having Grace in the bar at night. She's prettier and she uses it; that's good for business. Maggie hopes she can talk to Pat McMahon again later; she wants to hear what Paddy was like as a boy. "All right, Dad. But don't forget, he needs a place to stay."

"Does he? Well, go and ask your uncle first. That's decent, not far out of the village." After organising that successfully, she spends the next few hours with her younger sisters, acting as their mother would if she were well. She feeds the baby with a bottle of goat's milk; perhaps she should feel resentful about her role, but the bond that's grown between herself and Ellen prevents her feeling that way. She had to sacrifice her independence for this child and leave the Post Office at Middleton-in-Teesdale; initially she hated the idea, but the reality of caring for baby Ellen made her feel good and strong in a different way. Somehow she accepted it and moved on; she wonders, has she put all her love into this child to make that sacrifice seem worthwhile? Was it the knowledge that her mother, unlike with her other sisters, made absolutely no effort to care for this infant? Deep down, Maggie knew that someone had to take charge and love her as a mother would. No-one else was going to do it.

Later, after putting the little ones to bed, she sits in the garden at the back, thinking. Unlike herself, Grace *is* resentful; she's made that perfectly clear - for her, this baby is the last straw, just when she should be making her own life. Maggie does miss her life in Middleton, but she cannot feel resentment towards her baby sister; quite the converse, she feels a deep stirring of her own maternal feelings. Her mother remains aloof, silent, withdrawn; like a hollow husk of a person, going through the motions of life, as if devoid of inner experience. Maggie feels occasional urges to try to shake her out of it, but mostly she feels a terrible sorrow for her mother, coupled with an enormous relief that she can be different, that she's not crazy like her mother. That, for Maggie, would be the real terror. She could cope with anything else, but not that idea. Her love for

Ellen, for all her sisters, proves to herself that she's not going to turn out the same way.

"Penny for your thoughts," She looks up and sees those blue eyes watching her.

"Oh, nothing; just thinking about my baby sister," She shakes her head and frowns. "The kind of ordinary stuff that must seem terribly trivial..."

"It is not, it is not; believe me. It's grand; really, a great relief to see some normal life again. It's been a long time since I slept in a decent bed. Thanks for organising that, by the way." She shrugs. "Like you, we all look after each other on the boats; same as you and your sisters. We have to. Your shipmates will always look after you, no matter what."

"That must be a comfort."

"It is; it is. There's a bond among sailors. We'll pick up the enemy when we can, and we'll treat them just the same as ours. Early in the war, I heard tales about U-boats sinking a ship and then surfacing to make sure the survivors had water in their boats. They won't now; it's too risky, with the convoys. They'd be blown out of the water." He drops his voice. "I'll tell you one of my tales. One time early in the war we were down off the coast of Africa. There was a German ship stuck in a port there, interned for the duration of the war. Down on their luck, you might say, so we passed them a bottle of rum. Our Captain was furious, tore strips off us, consorting with the enemy. Until we told him what those German lads had told us."

"What was that?"

"They warned us where the U-boats would be, further down the coast. That helped us to sail round them; a small but very important diversion."

"Worth a bottle of rum, then..."

"Worth treating them as ordinary men, the same as us."

She nods. "I gather you can sing."

"A little bit. There's no piano here, by any chance?"

"No."

"In that case, I'll get my squeeze-box out. You'd better ask your father if he minds."

"He'll love it. I don't think we've had music in the pub since the war started. If word gets out, the place will fill up in no time."

She watches Paddy's friend sing and play for three consecutive nights before he leaves. She never does get the chance to ask him about Paddy as a boy, though the tunes and songs don't leave her mind; she hums them all to Ellen again and again over the coming weeks and months.

* * *

She wakes a little early; she feels rather than hears Grace slipping out of their shared bed into the semi- darkness. She stays put, dozing, enjoying the warmth under the covers until she hears her father moving around in the pub below. She glances at the cot in the corner of their room, sees that it's empty. On her way to the bathroom she hears Grace talking to the little ones in their room; she assumes Grace has Ellen with her. Only after she's dressed and gone down for breakfast does she realise Grace doesn't have her, and asks, "Is Ellen with June?"

Grace shakes her head. "Don't think so."

"Rose, have you had her?" Rose looks up, puzzled.

Grace inclines her head; her eyes meet Maggie's. "You don't think...?"

Maggie doesn't want to think that, but she takes a deep breath. "I'd better go and check." She exits the room as calmly as she can and runs up the stairs. In her head, she sees that image of her mother's face, leaping at her. She taps on the door of the room. "Mum?" She doesn't wait for a response that may never come; she pushes the door open, casting her eyes around the room. Everything looks normal; her mother's sitting room feels large and airy, its two bay windows overlooking the street outside. The curtains have been neatly drawn and fastened; the sun shines in obliquely, down onto polished floorboards. Her mother, awake and dressed, sits demurely, statuesque, upon a long sofa (on which she also sleeps) staring out at the view over the fields towards the river. Maggie sees no obvious sign of the baby. "Mum, have you seen Ellen?"

The head turns and regards her; there seems no warmth in the eyes, as there always used to be, even when she was silent. In fact, it feels to Maggie that she recognises that same look of cold hostility from the awful morning when her mother had pushed her over. Is she imagining it? Maybe; but she feels afraid of her mother now, for the first time in her life. A different expression passes across her mother's face; a smile of satisfaction, of triumph. Her mother turns away, back to the view. That facial expression alarms Maggie, nags at her instincts; so much so, she decides to go down and tell her father. She scampers back along the corridor, heart in her mouth, wondering what to say; she meets him half-way up the stairs already, his jaw set. He nods, "I'll talk to her, Maggie." Grace must have told him; she feels a flood of relief. She follows him back to the room, stands at the door with Grace, watching. Gilly stands between his wife and the window so that Violet cannot ignore him; he takes hold of her hands. "Where is she, Violet? Where's Ellen?" Violet swallows and then smiles, breathing deeply, as if in pride. "You're her mother, Violet; we know that. But I've told you, Maggie has to look after Ellen. Where is she?" Violet darts a hostile glance at Maggie and frowns; the head shakes in refusal. After a few seconds, that smile of triumph passes over her face again. Her father sighs, scratching his head; at this moment, Maggie sees her mother's eyes glance briefly at one corner of the room where the bedding is neatly piled.

Maggie walks over to it, her heart racing, and lifts blankets from the hand-made quilt, the one her grandmother made for her mother. She sees now that the quilt contains a small bundle. Lifting the edge, she sees a tiny hand first and gently unwraps the child. She looks asleep, but her lips and face are blue. She hears an intake of breath, next to her. "Oh Jesus, Violet, what have you done?" Her father's voice sounds cracked, broken.

"Wait." Maggie picks the child up, feels her warmth, and holds her, rocking her back and forth. Please God, she thinks, please God, patting the child's back. As if in answer to her prayer, she feels Ellen sigh. Did she imagine that? She dare not breathe herself, while she holds her finger under Ellen's nose and mouth. Yes, there it is. "She's all right, Dad, it's OK. She's breathing." She hears her father sobbing, muttering swearwords; she cannot bear to look at her mother.

She puts the baby back on her shoulder; behind her, she hears her father say, "No!" and hears muffled footsteps, an intake of breath; a half-grunt, a half-wail. She turns around to see Gilly holding her mother back, forcibly lifting her away, carrying her back to the sofa. His voice still sounds cracked, yet no longer broken. "Take Ellen out of here, Maggie, for some air. Grace, you look after the others. I'll have to stay and talk with your mother for a while. Go on, now."

She does as she's told, relieved to escape; the thought is already forming, echoing in her mind, "What on earth are we going to do now?"

*   *   *

Up here in Landi Kotal, the light has a peculiar jaundiced tinge, especially towards dusk. Maybe it's all the dust, he thinks, watching the wind creating swirls that play along the empty roadside winding back down the pass. He feels like a character in a Kipling novel, in this place, standing atop the wall of the old British fort positioned at the highest point of the Khyber pass. If he turns and looks the other way, he can about just about see Afghanistan; though there are far better views a few miles up the road. The hours pass so slowly here.

He takes out a cigarette, taps it a couple of times, sighs, and lights it. The tobacco smoke sears his throat but wakes him, keeps him alert. After eight weeks, the novelty of this place has completely worn off; this is my reward for 'being provocative', he thinks. He can understand the CO's point of view, though deep down he feels his commander has pandered to the pukka brigade, sending him up here to join the Indian troops guarding the fort and the pass. On the other hand, the CO's job is to ensure that everyone works together. How difficult is that, when half of my own men refuse to speak to me? He sighs. He really hadn't seen that whole business coming, the vehemence of the reaction towards him. He'd crossed a line, apparently. Befriending an Indian officer was possible; visiting his family was not. The look of disgust in so many eyes... as if he had just emerged from a shit pond. The really daft thing was, the ordinary ranks were if anything worse than the officers. Private Jones, the batman he'd shared with another junior officer, had refused to work for him; that act had brought the matter to the CO's attention. Now, he has to pay for his own bearer, an Indian trooper named Abdul Huq. No bad thing, as it turns out; he pays Abdul less than he was accustomed to giving Jones in tips, and Abdul gives far better service. He can sniff out the best curries from the local bazaar too, which cost next to nothing. That, though, is the only silver lining; the isolation and lack of facilities make Landi Kotal mind-numbing, compared to Pesh.

He sighs and glances up at the mass of aerials mounted on the circular dome of the central tower, relaying signals down to Pesh picked up from God knows where. This is what they're guarding; in reality, who on earth could attack that? The Japanese would never get agents this far unless they enlist Indian nationalists to do it for them; hardly likely. There seems no real threat to the pass itself; the military presence helps to maintain a semblance of law and order on the road. He fervently hopes his punishment will have a finite term. He crosses his fingers for a second, stubs out the cigarette on the wall, flicks it away. Almost time to do the rounds again.

Later, he yawns and checks his watch; a quarter to midnight, time for his last circuit. His escort, Rifleman Faqir Shah, strolls behind him at a respectful distance as they exit the gate. Eight sentry posts surround the outer perimeter of the fort; on the flatter ground nearer the road, the lights from the fort and nearby settlements guide them. The slow tapping of animal steps and neck bells echo from the road, though they can't see exactly where the animals are; a camel caravan, perhaps, going down to Pesh? Bit late to be out, but still. The first three sentries look as bored as he feels.

Away from the road, the night seems inky black, moonless, clouds sweeping down from the mountains. The ground feels more difficult underfoot; rocky, with patches of thorns. Paddy uses his torch to light the way, inspecting the barbed wire fence. Halfway round, he stops; small strips of cloth dangle from the top strand; he points this out to Faqir, whose eyes widen. Paddy unholsters his revolver; Faqir slips his rifle off his shoulders. He shines the torch all around; nothing. They pick their way forward silently, scanning the ground and the thorn bushes. This is ridiculous, he thinks, though his heart thumps away. The torch beam picks out the next sentry post; Paddy feels relief as he sees the sentry standing by the fence, peering out at something in the gloom beyond. He's about to make a joke when he sees the other figure, prone on the ground. If he didn't know better, Paddy would think this man was dead. No; just playing dead, frozen in the torchlight, caught in the act of crawling up behind the sentry; in one hand, the glint of a wickedly curled knife. Paddy swallows, takes a deep breath, shouts "Sowar, behind you..."

At this moment he hears two things; the sound of running feet to his right and the sound of Faqir Shah's voice from behind, shouting "Sahib!" He turns to shine his torch, catches a brief glimpse of another man dashing towards him brandishing a knife, before Faqir's rifle crashes out. The running man falls to the ground, howling in pain. He hears a shout from the sentry; swinging his torch around, he sees the previously prone figure leaping to his feet. Another shout behind him - he turns back to see Faqir turning and lifting his rifle, trying to fend off a third man leaping right on top of him. The sentry's rifle crashes out behind him, twice; he runs to help Faqir. This turns out to be wholly unnecessary; as he arrives, Faqir drops the rifle and grapples with the man briefly, plucking the knife out of his hand before plunging it into the owner's body once, twice, a third time.

The two Indian soldiers and Paddy stand together, back to back, until they feel sure there are no more intruders; by this time, the moans of the wounded attackers have faded into silence. They lay the bodies out together to inspect by torchlight.

"Jesus Christ." Paddy sees the faces of boys with wispy beards, perhaps no more than fifteen. No wonder Faqir overpowered the last one so easily, he thinks.

"Who are they, Faqir?"

"Pathans, Sahib. They probably wanted to take a rifle, so they could hold up traders to extract ransom money." He jerks his head at the sentry, "Lucky for him we came along."

"They're just boys, Faqir."

He shrugs. "It's how they live, Sahib. They need a gun." He grins wickedly, "And how they die, Sahib, without one."

"Will there be trouble with the Pathan chief?"

"No, Sahib. We'll pay some blood money to their families and that will be the end of it."

Paddy looks down. Stupid boys, he thinks; what a waste.

*　　*　　*

Vic leans back in his chair listening to the story with polite interest. "There's a war on, Paddy; they all knew that. Not that it made any difference, in this case. Anyway, we should be grateful to that Faqir Shah. He's probably got you back to Pesh quicker than usual, and I need someone to practice my tennis with. What will they do about your job, this time?"

"The CO's put me on training duty with Indian regiments until it all blows over. He seems to think it will eventually. Lucky for me, he looked in my file and discovered I can teach mortar gunnery as well as signals; useful for jungle and mountain fighting."

"Absolutely; no wonder you're so good at the lob shots."

"The best bit is I get to share Melsonby's bungalow; so I've come out of it quite well, really." He glances over at Dorothy. "How's the hospital, Dotty?"

She gives him an enigmatic smile. "Oh, just the usual; the acute ward is full of soldiers injured on your training exercises."

"What about the other wards?"

She raises her eyebrows and shrugs. "Oh, you know. I'm not supposed to tell you about those wards; bad for morale, apparently."

Paddy nods. "I was at Dunkirk, you know, I can guess. Do you work on those wards?" She meets his gaze for a long moment, gives a little nod. "In that case, you definitely deserve another gin. Must be tough, but I'm sure they think of *you* as some kind of angel..."

She laughs. "More like a devil, when I have to make them move or change their dressings. You should hear them cursing me. I know every bad word in five languages."

"Ungrateful bastards..." He turns to Vic, "Another whiskey?"

Vic yawns and shakes his head. "Sorry, no, got to be up very early. You two stay and enjoy yourselves." He stands up, giving Paddy an almost imperceptible wink. "You'll have to walk Dorothy home, but it's not far."

He suddenly realises, Vic has planned this; though he feels no resentment. Dorothy has found her way into his thoughts repeatedly, up at Landi Kotal; "My pleasure." He notices a look of anxiety changing to relief on her face; though she still looks a little anxious when he returns with the drinks. "What's the matter, Dorothy?"

"Are you sure you don't mind about this?"

"Of course not, why should I mind? I thought my chance had gone when they sent me up to Landi Kotal; I thought I'd never get back here. I imagined they'd send me off to Burma next." She stares at him for a long moment, nods; sips her drink slowly, before speaking.

"Vic said you were different to the other white officers; he thinks a lot of you. Perhaps he's right, but it's hard for girls like me. Do you realise how desperate we all are to go out with an officer? Our dream is always to marry one. Whether he's Indian or white, it doesn't matter to us. But usually they just use us and throw us away." She looks up, watching his reaction.

He takes a slow intake of breath, considers his next words carefully. "I'm not making any promises, Dorothy, but I'll treat you the same as any other girl. That's all I can say."

She laughs, "The same as any other girl? Not so special, then?"

"You know what I mean."

She tilts her head to one side, pursing her lips. "Actually I do, that sounds very good; maybe you are different." She takes a deep sigh, moves her chair closer, resting her hand on his forearm. Her touch feels like a jolt of electricity; he starts to open his mouth, but she continues, "I'm sorry, Paddy, I'm not normally so serious. I think it's because I'm jealous."

"My engagement's over, didn't Vic tell you?"

"Not that." She strokes his arm twice, causing more electricity. "I mean, jealous of your friendship with Vic; he's my friend, too, you see. He doesn't make friends easily, but he told me he thinks of you like a brother. You've no idea what a compliment that is, but it makes me jealous."

Looking at her, he suddenly sees a little girl inside the woman; he feels lost for words. She shakes her head, gives a shrill little laugh. "I must sound like a fool, but will you be my friend too, Paddy? Like you are with Vic? Will you promise me that?"

"I'll do my best, Dotty. I'll treat you the same as him or any other person I know." She beams up at him silently, slips her arm inside his, her mood visibly lightening. He feels the softness of her now, and smells her hair. Rose, mixed with something exotic, he thinks. The conversation lightens, becomes a humorous dance around their mutual likes and dislikes. For the rest of that evening, his body feels taught, alert, highly charged; especially where he can feel the touch of her skin. He becomes aware that his body, after all this time without a girl, simply aches for her. And yet, he remembers her words; he does not want to seem just like the others. When he walks her home through the shadows, he's careful to treat her respectfully.

"This is it. I live with my mother, above this shop." He looks up, sees two floors above a narrow, typical shuttered front.

"Well, goodnight, Dorothy." She turns, gives him a quick hug. The touch of her whole body, no matter how brief, jolts his spine, jerking his longing for her into life. Instinctively he reaches out and pulls her back to him, turning his own head to look down on her, intending to kiss her hair. But she turns her own head up, raises it, kissing his lips. Her first kiss is light, like a brush of wet petals; then, while he still savours this, he feels her mouth return and open, a long sweet sensation that he does not want to end. He releases her, feels her move away. He opens his eyes, sees her fumbling with her purse, extracting a key. He turns to leave, but feels a tug on his sleeve.

"Wait... I don't usually do this, not the first time..." She sighs, looks up at him. "I can tell you want me and I want you just as much; I'm sick of pretending otherwise. So come inside."

He returns to his own bed early the following morning, falls into a deep sleep. When he wakes with a start, he remembers; he goes over everything that happened in his mind, trying to savour the memory of her, again and again.

*   *   *

Sixteen: 1943

Holding the mug in one hand, he descends the ladder one step at a time; the sweet smell of hot cocoa mingles with an acrid stench of coal dust. Switching hands, he ducks and hurdles through the mass of pipes surrounding the rest area. At last, he places the mug in one of four circular recesses within the metal table, flips a folding seat down and flops into it; his back now resting against the steel plate of the hull. He watches the contents of the mug swill gently from side to side with the motion of the boat while he waits for the hot, sweet cocoa to cool. The weather's not bad, he thinks, though he wishes this was a glass of cold fruit juice; preferably the syrup from a can of peaches with ice. That's the problem with British ships; no ice, except in the cool box with the meat. And even if they have any, canned peaches would be far too much of a treat - cookie will be saving those for a special occasion. Up on deck, it's beginning to freeze. Soon, there'll be ice all over the deck, *salty* ice. Everyone up there wants cocoa, or sweet tea; something to warm their insides. Down here, of course, warming up is the last thing on your mind; he's explained this to the cook dozens of times, been met with the same indifferent shrug each time. What the hell, he thinks; it gives me an excuse to take a break.

He glances across at the two stokers steadily feeding the voracious fires, a bright glare reflecting off their sweaty, coal-blackened hides. He marvels at the ease of their movements, hour after hour. His own job can be physically tough at times, but for him it comes in fits and starts. It's not as constant, as brutally exhausting, as feeding those fires. The old cow's so heavily laden that she struggles to keep up with the convoy. As if reading his thoughts, the men pause and set down their shovels; at that precise moment, his vision seems to blur for a second. The ship seems to jump slightly; he feels the wall jump out and hit his back. One of the stokers staggers, caught off balance. His mate's arm reaches out to grab him, keeping him away from the fire. The air's suddenly cloudy, filled with soot and acrid dust from every surface. The mug of cocoa has somehow left its recess and begins to tip, its contents slapping over the side. He grabs at it instinctively, stops it toppling, wipes the hot fluid off his hand and curses. His ears prick up - yet above the roar of the engines, nothing can be heard. Paralysed with uncertainty, he physically shakes his head, forcing his brain to work. His eyes flicker first to the ladders, their escape route; they seem to be intact. In fact, everything else in the engine room looks intact; so, if that was a torpedo strike, maybe it didn't explode... take a deep breath, he tells himself, think. A vast emptiness grows in the pit of his stomach. Come on, work it out, do something... but what? Get out now, or wait for the order? Christ, he thinks, suddenly filled with the urge to piss his pants; we have to get out of here...

The others are already running for the ladders, unbidden. The engine room telegraph still hasn't moved from "full speed ahead"; the bell hasn't rung. That puzzles him, but by the time he reaches the base of the ladder, Jimmy's feet are already scrambling out of the hatch at the top, with the rest of them following as fast as they can. No one attempts to speak or make eye contact; they're all thinking the same thing. They have to get to their bunks fast, get some warm clothes on before she fills up with water; otherwise, they'll freeze to death out there. As Pat climbs, he becomes aware of a blockage ahead of him; something seems to be happening above him. He and the man above him stare upwards, muttering... please don't shut us down here, for pity's sake... when the water hits those fires, it turns to steam... God help us... hurry up, for the love of God...

After what seems an eternity, movement begins again. He sticks his head out of the hatch into the corridor above, greeted by a line of boots under a queue of dirty, sweaty bodies, with puzzled, suspicious faces staring down at him. All stuck, it seems, here in this corridor. Christ, what now? He feels a tap on his shoulder, turns to see Frank Swainston's face grinning down at him. What's he got to smile about, he thinks, the fucking eejit...

Frank's head looms suddenly closer, leans down over him. Pat flinches, instinctively; Frank cups his hands and shouts into his ear, "Take it easy, Pat. She's fine, *we* haven't been hit. It was a big shock wave from the next ship across. Maybe a torpedo hit her, but she just exploded. She must have been carrying a lot of TNT; I've never seen anything like it, Pat. Boom, lit up the whole sky and knocked us sideways like a giant fist. But it's not us, Pat - believe me. " Frank straightens up, watches his reaction. Pat stares back, wondering if he *can* believe this. Not again, he thinks, remembering the tanker. He feels all their eyes upon him, gauging his response. A hundred questions...how far away exactly, what sort of ship, has anyone spotted the U-boat? He forces himself to scratch his head, shrug and nod. Time for all that, later. Frank leans over him again, "Skipper says can you squeeze an extra knot out of her?" His eyes flicker downward.

Pat sighs, licks his lips, feels how dry and cracked they suddenly seem. He mouths "OK" to Frank, turns back and looks up at the other faces. He puts his thumbs up, pointedly; most of them glance away, sheepishly. He gestures 'come with me', points back down the ladder. One or two nod; he sees, rather than hears, a collective groan, and forces himself to descend.

Staring at the page, he tries to make sense of the words; his mind won't focus. "What's that you're reading, Pat?" He lays the book down in response, scratches his head and rubs his eyes.

"Celtic mythology, the adventures of Cuchalain and all his companions; but I'm not in the mood. The light's too dim in here."

Across the metal table, Frank grunts, "Sounds a bit heavy going, mate."

"When did you first take to the water, Frank?" A frown passes across Frank's face; was it that long ago, Pat wonders? Pat watches him close his own book and put it down before he speaks.

"Oh, that would be back in '32. I always wanted to go to sea. My dad and brothers, they run a sheep farm back in New Zealand; that line of work never appealed much to me. I always wanted to see the world." He gives Pat a sideways look. "What about you, Pat?"

"I was a farm boy too, back in Ireland. Bit like yourself, Frank, I guess. Truth is, back then, that was a bad time to be in Ireland, you know?" Frank nods. "So I started on the liners as a boy steward, back in the twenties. But I always liked fixing things. So I got some training with marine engines and worked my way up the ladder. Or down the ladder, maybe."

Frank grins, "You ever think about going back?"

"To the old country? Never."

"Why not?"

Pat sighs, examines his companion's face. "The short answer, there's no work for me there; never likely to be. We got our independence, sure, but then we got a trade war with the British for our trouble. After that we got the great depression, and now because of this war there's no trade at all. The place is cut off. No, I wouldn't mind a fresh start, but it won't be in Ireland."

"What about your family?"

"My parents are dead. I miss my brothers, but they're older, set in their ways. It's another world, Frank; the Catholic Church is everywhere, telling you what to do and what to think. I couldn't stand that, even if there was work there for me."

Frank nods, deep in thought. "You make New Zealand sound progressive, mate." He shakes his head and sniffs. "I just heard, though; my kid brother joined the army."

"Bloody fool."

"What, you think he'd a' been safer in the navy, with us?"

They both laugh. "Christ, no, Frank. I just... well..." He stops himself from saying too much. "I just know that I could have volunteered, but I'd have been a lousy soldier. In a real battle, I'd have run away at the first opportunity; yellow streak, a mile wide."

He feels a surprising flush of relief after admitting this; he looks up to check Frank's expression, sees a look of disbelief.

"You must be joking, Pat."

"I am not; I do know that about myself."

Frank looks puzzled, shakes his head. "Look, mate, remember the time you fixed that bloody steam pipe, on your first trip with us?" Pat nods. He could hardly forget *that* night. "Well, you were working down there to save the ship for five or six hours while the rest of were skulking up by the lifeboats."

"Dennis was down there with me."

Frank gives him a sideways look. "Christ, mate; that just proves my point. There we were, lit up like a bloody Christmas tree, inviting every U-boat within fifty miles to come and say hello. Did you know the skipper asked for volunteers to help you?" Pat shakes his head. "No? Well, Dennis was the only man on the ship fool enough to volunteer, including my good self. I couldn't have gone down there under those circumstances. You and he were the only ones daft enough to do it. Yellow streak? Christ, Pat, you and Dennis are the bravest men I know, bar none."

"Or maybe the stupidest, like you say. It was a job that had to be done."

"In Dennis's case I might allow that, mate, but not in yours."

He's thought of himself as a coward for so long that this alternative view puzzles him. Yet he has to admit, Frank has a point. Maybe he's older, wiser, and stronger, in some way. Maybe he doesn't need to hide himself away, crossing and re-crossing the water. Maybe he could make a fresh start on land somewhere; providing, of course, he can survive this bloody war.

* * *

He lies dozing in Paula's arms, somewhere safe, onshore. It must be Dublin; he can hear the cathedral bells ringing out. The room also seems familiar; slowly, he realises that he has become a teacher at his old school, that he now occupies the house, the very room, where Mr O'Brien first introduced him to Caruso's voice. Paula has become his wife and sleeps beside him. Somehow, he knows this is a dream; most important, he must not wake himself up, or her presence will vanish. He lies, holding on to her precious presence, holding on to sleep, for as long as he can. Caruso's voice suddenly fills the room, the sheer power of his voice bringing back all his astonishment, his disbelief at such perfection, long ago. The man was alive, then. Like Paula... with this thought, Pat reaches out and finds her presence has slipped away; he's returned to his narrow bunk in the middle of the ocean. He sighs, rubs the sleep out of his eyes.

Up on deck, the air's cold and fresh, not quite freezing. The light seems diffuse, uniformly grey; he peers outwards, looking for the horizon, sees nothing. Fog, he realises, a real pea-souper. Up here, the engine noise has shrunk to a quiet background rumble; the ship rises and falls gently in a moderate swell. From every direction, he hears plaintive whistles; all the ships in the convoy call out to each other, a lumbering school of blinded whales. He scratches his head; how on earth does everyone hold their position, in this?

On the bridge, the Captain grunts a welcome; though neither he, nor the first mate, turn to look at him. They peer into the blankness of the forward port and starboard quarters with fierce concentration. Slowly, Pat's eyes begin to make sense of shifting shapes in the foreground, where the fog and the water meet, perhaps forty or fifty yards from the ship. "Anything I can do to help?"

After a pause, the Captain growls, "While you're here, laddie, just you keep a lookout for anything out there. Keep your eyes peeled for a fog buoy. The ship up ahead of us in the line has recently become a mite slower; even slower than us. We come up on her every half hour and have to back off." He glances at his watch; "Should be due to appear in the next five minutes or so." He frowns, "You've got your turn on duty in a couple of hours, so don't overdo it." After a while, Pat's eyes begin to play tricks on him. He thinks he sees something but when he looks again, or the ship moves closer, he sees nothing. Frank often complains of sore eyes, he thinks.

"There she is, skipper." The first mate points a finger, "Ten degrees to port, more or less." Pat can't see a thing. The skipper grunts, shifting his attention. Slowly, a strange yellow shape materialises, drifting in and out of the fog. The buoy leaves a small wake behind it; he can't see the towline that pulls it. A small jet of water spouts up whenever it hits a wave. How on earth do they see that at night, he wonders?

"Signal three quarter speed." Pat listens to the engines slow; after a minute or so they all watch the buoy pull away, ahead of them, back into the fog. The Captain stares at his watch for what seems to Pat a very long time, before he grunts again. "Signal full speed ahead." He looks over at Pat. "It's not the ship in front I'm worried about; it's the bugger behind us. He got so close he cut our fog buoys loose twice last night. Lucky for us we had an extra spare." Pat swallows, remembering the collision in Chesapeake Bay. The first mate adds, "Don't worry, Pat, we'll bill him when we get to port." Pat shakes his head, decides to leave them to it.

Back on deck, he takes a slow circuit of the ship before lighting a cigarette; one of his rare luxuries, a cigarette in daylight, out in the fresh air. He can't do this at night – the glow can be seen five miles away. But in this fog, he thinks, what the hell. He hears their own engines slowing again, shakes his head. Must be something going wrong up ahead, slowing them up; problem is, everyone further back in the line risks hitting the ship in front. He stares down at their wake; and beyond, into the fog. He can't see anything, though his ears prick up, alert. He takes a last drag of the cigarette and flips it away; there it is again, he thinks, a distinct low rumble of diesel engines. One of the new liberty ships, probably. For a second he imagines a shape moving closer, low in the water, astern and slightly away to port. He tries to focus his eyes; there it is again, that noise. He grunts with frustration when he hears the ship's own engines coming back up to full speed, drowning it out. And then, a low dark shape appears for a fleeting moment in a small patch of clarity before it vanishes back into the fog; he can't believe what he's seen. It seemed to be slowing, dropping away behind, he thinks; thank the Lord for small mercies. He bounds back up to the bridge, taking the steps two at a time.

"What's your hurry, Chief Engineer?" The skipper's comment reminds him that up here, he's out of place, out of his depth.

"I think I just saw a U-boat, skipper."

"Are you sure?"

"Pretty sure, Skipper. I heard the engines distinctly; diesel engines. Then I saw something low in the water, on the surface. Just a glimpse, but I'm damn sure it had a periscope."

The skipper nods. "He's probably trying to tag along with the convoy while he calls his mates. Don't worry; he won't attack at the moment. In any case, he'll have to dive when the fog starts to clear and then we'll leave him behind. I shouldn't worry about him, laddie, it's his friends that will be waiting up ahead, that's what worries me."

"Shouldn't we signal the escorts?"

The captain shrugs, "Not possible until the fog clears. Visual signals only allowed; absolute radio silence out here, no exceptions." Pat's next watch feels like the longest of his career. Except perhaps, the one after that, when the fog has cleared...

*   *   *

Someone very, very heavy is sitting on his head. Every time his heart beats, someone hits the back of his skull with a rubber hammer wrapped up in a cloth. Plus, it's dark, pitch black. Mind you, he can't remember getting drunk; so why, he asks himself, have I got such a devil of a hangover? Turn over; go back to sleep, he tells himself. He tries to turn over, moves his right arm, but it jabs him with a sharp stab of pain; his left leg also complains vociferously, aching as if the bones are bruised all the way down. The bunk feels so cold, too. It smells of metal; or is that the smell of blood? Christ, he realises, I'm lying on the floor. He hears men shouting in the distance, feels an overwhelming weariness mix with relief as he drifts back into nothingness.

He rises to the surface again, gasping for air. Is this a dream? He's lying on the floor again. That's not a dream. How on earth did I fall out of my bunk? Nothing's moving - there's obviously no storm. He tries to lift his head; an acute pain splits his skull in two. He can hear someone else moaning, here in his cabin. How can that be? Something strange is happening out there, he thinks. Thank God it's not my watch. Maybe I should get up and see, anyway. He moves his body a little. His right arm hurts like hell but it still works. His hands feel up and down. All present and correct, he thinks, and drifts off back to sleep again.

Now he's under the water again; in this recurring nightmare, he's somehow attached to the ship, his clothes snagged on one of the metal hooks. This time it seems terrifyingly real; he's being dragged down as the ship slips under the water, struggling to think, to realise what's happening, trying to get free, wriggling with all his might... finally, just as the pressure rises in his ears, he kicks off his boots, pushes himself out of his pants, and kicks for the surface. He's gagging for breath, desperate for air. Can he hold out, or will he succumb and give up, allowing himself to breathe water into his lungs? What awaits him on the surface? Burning oil? Ice upon a frozen sea? An aircraft, dropping bombs to finish him off? Or what he dreads most, nothingness - nothing but an empty, lonely ocean? He breathes, feeling the cold floor with his face. It's tilting, he realises. Christ, we're sinking. I have to get up. Meanwhile, someone seems to be trying to prise the back of his head open with a can opener. He slowly brings his hands up and feels his face and head. There's an enormous lump on the back of his head; wetness runs down his face, a cut on his eyebrow? The effort he expends, pushing himself into a half sitting position, holding on to his head to stop it falling off his shoulders, exhausts him. He can't move any further. It's hopeless, he thinks; I'll never make it. I'm going to die here in this cabin. Wait a minute. With his left hand, he pulls open the door of the cabinet under his bunk. His rum bottle rolls out. Half full, he thinks. He feels for his wallet and the envelope that contains his savings, and brushes them out onto the floor. Not much use to me now. Where is it? He feels the oilskin wrapping under his hand. There they are; the photographs of Paula. He pulls the package out, clutches it to his chest with both hands. Then the realisation hits him; it's dark, he can't even look at them, one last time. He bursts into tears, consumed with self-pity.

He surfaces again. Footsteps hurry along the corridor, a glimmer of torch light flashes for a moment, under his door. A door opens; the next cabin, he hears someone rummaging. That must be Frank rescuing his personal stuff, grabbing extra clothes; silly sod, get off while you can. His own door opens, pushes his useless legs aside. A blinding light sears through his eyes and brain like two red-hot needles, "Christ, mate, what are you doing? Get up, we're sinking."

Pat shuts his eyes. "Can't do it, Frank; leave me the torch."

"What?"

"Leave me the torch, so I can look at my pictures."

"Oh, Christ," He feels hands exploring his head. "No bloody way, mate." The package is wrenched out of his hands. "See? You're coming with me." He opens his eyes, sees Frank undo his top button, stuff the precious package inside his greatcoat. He groans, feels himself lifted up onto the bunk. "Come on, get these boots on." Frank guides his feet into the boots; he pushes, obediently. He feels like a child, having his shoelaces tied.

"Frank, do my laces for me." He giggles for a brief moment, flinches at the pain in his ribs.

"Bloody Irish, you'd die laughing, wouldn't you? Now your coat, that's it. At least you have the sense to sleep with most of your bloody clothes on. Come on, mate; we've got about ten minutes to get up on deck, I reckon." Frank pulls him upwards and ducks under his left arm to support him while Pat tries to stand up. My Caruso collection, he thinks...

Next thing he knows, he's sitting in a lifeboat. The intense pain in his head is now a dull ache; it's daylight. The horizon looks empty, whenever the swell bobs them high enough to see it. Each time they hit a crest, he stares again at the horizon; no smoke, anywhere. He looks around the boat, recognising faces. It seems pretty full. That's a good sign, he thinks, as long as we're not the only boat, and as long as we've got some food and water...

He feels a nudge beside him, turns to see Frank's face, "Feeling any better?"

"A little; thanks, Frank. I don't know how you did it, but thanks."

"I owed you one. Besides, I might need your help, mate, after the war."

"The chance would be a fine thing."

"Aye, it would. But I'm serious, Pat." He lowers his voice. "I got an idea."

Pat blinks, "Now? Here, in the middle of the Atlantic?"

"No, you Irish half-wit; I've been meaning to ask you about it for weeks. You know my folks are farmers, back in New Zealand?" The expression is so intense, so serious, that Pat wonders what will come next. "Ever had New Zealand lamb, Pat?"

"I wouldn't mind some now."

"It's the best there is, mate. Point is we've got so many sheep the stuff is dirt cheap back home. Sometimes they have to throw it away."

"So what; you want me to give you a recipe for Irish stew?"

Frank can't help but grin, "Later. I was talking to the crew of one of those Liberty ships. Told me their ship had an enormous refrigerated hold, piled full of steaks for the Yank army. What will happen to all those ships, after the war? After the troops go home? Put two and two together, Pat, and sometimes it makes a lot more than four."

"I think I might see what you're getting at."

"You want a fresh start, after the war, Pat? The two of us could run a couple of those ships and my family can organise the meat supply. We can ship it anywhere once the war's over." It doesn't sound that crazy, he thinks, staring at the man who's saved his life.

"You'll need money. And mine went down with the ship."

"Ah. That reminds me." Frank passes over the oilskin package.

"What's inside this is precious to me, Frank, but not to anyone else."

"I gathered that, mate. But I also found these, next to your boots." With a flourish, Frank hands over a wallet and an envelope.

"God love you, you crazy Kiwi. I owe you one, all right. If we survive this bloody war, you've got yourself a partnership. But we're not out of these particular woods yet, are we?"

"No, though we did get a signal off, Pat. Maybe someone heard it..."

"Anyone else go down?"

"I think so. Maybe the escorts are busy elsewhere."

They lapse into silence, staring at the empty horizon.

* * *

Paddy's back in France with his old platoon, back in the lorry, driving down French country lanes. Somehow they're completely and utterly lost, cut off from the rest of the army; stranger still, the roads are eerily empty. There are also no animals in the fields, which worries him even more. Where have they all gone? They stop at cottages and farmhouses to ask the way; no one answers, the houses and fields seem abandoned. He feels panic rising in his chest, the fear that they will drive around in this landscape, lost and trapped here forever. The worst thing is the Lieutenant doesn't seem to be bothered by any of it. Maybe I should take over, he wonders; after all, I'm an officer too, now. Then he realises, with another stab of panic, they're all dead; I'm driving around France with a lorry full of ghosts. With this thought, he's suddenly sinking into a mass grave along with the others. They don't seem to mind at all; he watches them lying down to rest, making themselves comfortable. But I'm not ready, he realises. He wants to get out, to run away, but his body feels utterly paralysed. Someone shovels dirt onto his face; he can't brush it off, he can't breathe. He's suffocating, trying to move, to breathe, to kick, to scream...he really is gasping for breath, choking back the tears. The light comes on. Dorothy stands over him, rubbing her eyes, looking down at him with a mixture of fear and concern, "It's all right, Paddy, another nightmare."

He feels a deep flush of shame. "I'm sorry, Dotty, really sorry. I don't know why..."

"Hush, hush, my darling; just relax for a minute." She sits back down on the bed next to him, folds her arms around him, hugging him like a child. He chokes back a sob and gives in to her. No one has done this for him since his mother; it feels wonderful, painful and soothing all at the same time, like lancing a boil. The tension drains out of him, washed away by the warmth and smell of her body. Why, he wonders, are the nightmares getting worse? They should be getting better.

"Tell me about it, Paddy." He loves that slight sing-song accent.

He shrugs, "No, I can't."

"You must; tell me now, or I'll go back to Peshawar tomorrow."

"You wouldn't."

"I will, I mean it." He can hear the steel in her voice; she doesn't sound like that often.

He sighs, "All right." He thinks for a minute, collects his thoughts; clears his throat. "It's usually about Dunkirk; fighting our way there, to the beaches, swimming in the water. Things I saw there, what happened to...to the ones who didn't make it. I'm back there, re-living it with them."

"I guessed that, Paddy. Most of the men in the hospital have similar nightmares."

"Do they?"

"Oh, yes, in different ways. What does it all mean to you?"

He shakes his head. "It doesn't mean anything, it's just a nightmare."

"Oh yes it does, Paddy. Why do you think you have these dreams?"

"Christ, Dotty, how the fuck should I know?"

"Come on Paddy, you're not stupid. Answer my question."

He stares at her for a long time; she doesn't back down. He sighs again, "I suppose at the time that you're fighting, you don't have time to be frightened. I think it's all the fear that I should have had, back then." He shakes his head, "You don't think you're brave at the time, you just do your job. There are moments when the fear hits you, but you get on with it. Afterwards, you wonder how the hell you did it." He sighs again, stares at the floor. "What bothers me now is that it's getting worse and worse. It makes me feel that deep down, I'm really a coward, because I have all of this fear stored up inside me and it won't go away, even now when I'm fine. Why won't it stop?"

She pulls him close again, stroking his hair. "It's probably a bit more complicated than that. Tell me about this dream tonight."

"It was a childish nightmare about ghosts. Do I have to?" She continues to stroke his hair. "I was lost in France with a lorry full of ghosts; my platoon. Then they buried me alive with them." She says nothing. He expects her to press him for more details; instead, she kisses his cheek once more and pushes him away. One way to get my attention, he thinks.

"It sounds like several things to me, Paddy. You knew these men. You are sad for them; in fact you are grieving for them. They were friends and comrades. Some of them you loved; they all died for you, in some sense; didn't they?"

"Christ, yes."

"You're grieving for them and you were re-living it with them, the men who didn't make it, as if you were in their shoes. You feel you could have been in their shoes. Perhaps you think you should have been in their shoes. Why were you so lucky?"

"Christ knows." He takes a deep breath. "You're right, though, that's bothered me for years. I lost my whole platoon back there in France. I was the lucky one, all right."

"So when you have these dreams it's like you're visiting their graves, trying to tell them how sorry you are; sorry that they died and also guilty because you were lucky and they were not." Jesus, he thinks. Why is it women can see these things so clearly? He nods. "Come. Come on up to the roof." She leads him by the hand, up to the darkness on the roof, where the sky seems to be filled with a million bright stars. He opens his mouth but she puts her fingers on his lips, points upwards, and pulls him down to the floor. They lie back and stare at the sky in silence, holding hands, for half an hour. He reflects on the stars, the enormity of the world, the strange path that has led him to this place and this woman. He feels a whole gamut of emotions and wonders why, at other times, he cannot feel his emotions at all. Something about men, he thinks, that makes it a real struggle; whereas women seem to be able to sense their feelings at will.

Out of the blue, her voice tells him, "You know, one thing this war does is make you appreciate what you have. Even if we only ever have this one week together like this, this is more than many people have. People are dying everywhere. Even out of those who live, many never feel like this in a whole lifetime. So I would never regret coming here with you." He rolls onto his side and stares at her for a long time, before the kissing begins.

*　　*　　*

"*Dear Paddy,*

Thanks for sending us your latest news. Dad asked me to write back to you as he is not so good with letters. We were all very pleased and happy to hear that you are still safe and well after all this time. India sounds very exciting; we're all very envious of all that heat after the bitterly cold winter we had here. I read your letter out to the girls. Even with all the rationing here they weren't sure about all that strange food that you describe. You know how fussy they are! But the fruit sounds wonderful to me. And somehow I can't imagine what it's like to be too hot.

More important, I hope you weren't too hurt by Grace's letter. She thought it was best to be honest now rather than leave things unsaid; I hope you understand that. It might have been different if you were here, who knows? Grace is not very good at explaining things but I think she just believed she wasn't right for you.

Anyway I am now back at home helping to look after little Ellen. She is an absolute darling and a delight. I was sorry to give up the job in Middleton as I enjoyed the freedom there, but that can't be helped. Hopefully I'll get back to it when the girls are all a bit older. The sad news is that my mum's condition got so much worse that my dad reluctantly accepted the doctor's advice; so they took her into that special hospital. It's a long way to go, but we visit when we can.

We also had a visit from your old friend Pat, the one in the merchant navy. He came into the pub asking after you; I could tell straight away that he spoke just like you. He said you'd told him to come to Weardale; he knew you were probably overseas but he wanted to come anyway. He stayed in the village and did us a great favour by singing and playing in the pub a couple of nights. Dad was very pleased; it went down very well and brought in extra customers. "We'll meet again" and lots of other songs! Hopefully it won't be too long before you'll both be back and you can join in too, next time!

Love from Maggie and all the Hardy family."

He folds the letter, puts it in his pocket and looks across the table at Dorothy. A deep pool of shade surrounds them under an enormous tree full of bright pink blossoms. The faint breeze flutters around them, just enough to cool the skin, causing tiny pink petals to dance in the air while they float down to settle like confetti upon her hair. On the opposite hillside, out in the intense midday light, the red sandstone remains of an ancient mogul castle shimmers in the air like a mirage in the desert. She looks radiant, he thinks; she's his mirage, in the desert of war.

"What does it say?"

"Oh, just news from home; to be honest, it seems like another world. You've no idea how cold, wet and miserable it can be in England. And with the bombing, you really know you're at war, not like here. Apparently the food rationing is very bad too; much worse than here."

"Well, Paddy, here we are in the safest part of India. But there is a famine in Bengal, you know. They say it's terrible there." Paddy thinks of Ireland, the famines there.

He sighs, "What I mean is, Dotty, I just can't believe how lucky I am to be sat here right now with you. Just look at this." He gestures up at the tree, sweeps his arm towards the view. She nods and shrugs. A small girl appears, grinning from ear to ear, and carefully sets two glasses of fresh mango juice in front of them. Dorothy speaks to her in her own language, and she runs away, giggling. He takes a sip. "Here we are in heaven, while the rest of the world is in hell, or fighting to avoid it. I can't make any sense of it."

"Do you believe in a God?"

"I do not. The people that spouted that stuff in Ireland put me off it. A bundle of hypocrites, they were. It's not for me."

"Then why *should* it make any sense?"

He scratches his head. "I suppose I believe in fairness, in justice. That's what I want to see in life. That's what we're fighting for, and we're all supposed to be in this together, aren't we?"

She frowns. "You are feeling bad again, because you are not sharing all the suffering going on in the world around us. Is that it?"

"That's about the gist of it. One minute I feel wonderful because I'm in this wonderful paradise with you, and the next I feel awful for the same reason. I feel like I should be fighting the Germans or the Japs, not sitting here enjoying myself." He takes a deep breath. "I've been thinking of asking for a transfer to the action." She stares at him in disbelief for a second, and then looks away. He watches her frown again, the sign that she's thinking hard. Eventually she looks up, gives him a brittle smile; brushes an unseen tear from her cheek. She moves her chair around to sit next to him, leaning her body against his.

"I won't argue with you, Paddy. This is our last day here and I want us both to enjoy every moment we have, especially if you do go away to fight again. But please listen to what I say."

"Of course I will, Dotty."

"What you're doing in Pesh is very important; the soldiers you are training need teachers they can believe in. Vic told me that they really respect you; did you know they call you 'The Englishman who never swears'? Every other white teacher swears at them, calls them bad names." He bites his lip, smiles. "Secondly, you're right; there is far too much suffering in this world. In our religion we recognise that but we hope the next life will be better. I'm not sure I really believe that, maybe I just have one life. But I do think that it is our duty to enjoy the gifts that come our way. You haven't had an easy life, but now you tell me you've never felt so happy. Well, we must both cherish this gift and not throw it away. Otherwise it's disrespectful to all the suffering ones, who cannot have what we have. If you *were* suffering now, you would want your friends *not* to suffer."

He thinks of Ireland, of Gilly and Violet, "I see what you're getting at."

"Good." She puts both her arms around his waist. "Lastly, I want to ask you something for me. I have had a hard life too, and I have never known such a beautiful man as you. We have only had a short time together. I could not bear the thought of your body being broken like those in the hospital. Let me have another year of your life before you go. The war will not end soon. Please."

Christ, he thinks; how can I say no? He lifts his mango juice. "A year it is, Dotty."

*　　*　　*

The other girls surround her, Maggie realises, as they once used to surround their mother, whenever they had the opportunity to do so. She forgets they're there, sometimes. She wonders when her father will next take her, with June and Grace, to visit the asylum. Her mother has also been asking to see the little ones. Her father feels uncertain about this, perhaps thinking they have enough to cope with. Will a visit to that palace of gloom only cause them more distress? Who knows? It certainly leaves her and her father exhausted, wrung out like clothes through a mangle. In any case, the asylum is twenty miles away; petrol's difficult to find. She sighs; the empty sitting room upstairs will need cleaning again. She usually reserves that job for herself.

She looks down at Rose, on her knees scrubbing the kitchen floor. Now a gawky fourteen year old, desperate to be grown up, Rose is the most willing to help her; the one who never needs to be chivvied and harried. Maybe it's because she looks more like me, she thinks. June sits opposite her at the table, reading her book. June's reached the age where she too can help in the post office and bar; she considers that quite enough work, thank you very much. Grace and I were always looking after her, Maggie thinks; but then June is always so good-natured, so good-humoured, she gets away with it. She just forgets to volunteer and smiles in that disarming way...

A half-hearted wail from her left reminds her of Ellen's presence; now a chubby faced toddler, Ellen struggles with her sister, hanging on determinedly to a red crayon. Harriet frowns while she gently and patiently pries it out of her hands. "Come on, Ellen, you need a blue one now..." The drawing paper that forms their battleground rises into the air, sandwiched between competing elbows; tears begin to form in Ellen's eyes. Maggie purses her lips. Harriet's trying to be helpful again; she's very good at entertaining Ellen, at giving Maggie a break from her. But she always tries to instruct Ellen, as if there was a right and a wrong way of doing things...

"Ettie, let her do it her way. She doesn't understand."

Harriet frowns even harder for a moment, releases the crayon. "But she's colouring the sky *red*. It's silly." She tries one last appeal, "I was only trying to show her."

"I know, Ettie; but it's her drawing. Why don't you do one yourself and *show* her?" Harriet considers this, nods, and picks up another crayon. Maggie finishes the list she was making for the shopping and watches for a minute. She picks up her stool and moves away from the table into the centre of the room to give herself space. Taking the precious packet out of her apron pocket, she pulls out one of the stockings. Since America entered the war, even the Canadian flyers can't get hold of stockings; nylon and silk production have been reserved for the war effort. Somehow, she's kept this pair intact. She hasn't worn them for a long time; but tomorrow, her father's promised to let her go to the dance. She needs to check them; she carefully pulls each of them over her legs and fastens them to her suspender belt, enjoying the smooth sensation. She sits on the edge of the stool, skirt raised, stretching out her long legs in turn, checking for faults. None at all, she thinks, proudly, admiring the effect, stretching and looking again.

She becomes aware of a silence, looks around the kitchen. Her audience stares at her, a variety of expressions etched on their faces. Ellen simply looks curious, puzzled. Harriet wears a smirk on her face; is that amusement at the general craziness of the adult world, or her sister in particular? By contrast, June wears a thunderous look of envy and astonishment that almost shouts, where did you get those? From the floor, Rose gazes up with a mixture of envy and hero worship; one day, her face pleads, let me be like you. Maggie feels her face burn; she stands up, brushing her skirt flat. She looks defiantly around her, challenging them to say something. No one says a word; they all look away. She goes upstairs to remove the stockings.

When she returns from the shopping she takes her father a sandwich. The war's aged him, she thinks, looking at his receding hairline, the lines on his face. He used to look so young.

"Thanks, Maggie, you're an angel."

"Where's Gracie, dad?"

"I gave her the afternoon off; don't you worry, lass, she'll be back by half past six. Then I'll be able to take you over to the dance."

"She gone off with that lad again?" He nods. "Looks a bit serious to me, Dad." She smiles, "I was wrong about that one." He chews on his sandwich, giving her a quizzical look.

"Were you? He's a decent lad, though. Good family. They've a nice farm up there. But you've got more sense."

"What do you mean?"

"Oh, I mean that you shouldn't get too attached at your age. Wait for the right person, I say. At least have the sense to wait until the end of this war. She's always been impatient, our Grace."

"You don't think...?" He takes another bite, before he answers.

"It's not what I think, that matters. I've heard them talking, Maggie. He'll be called up, likely, next year. I'd say there'll be wedding bells before he goes. I'd put money on it." Maggie's mouth drops open. Her first thought is, what will Paddy think? She wonders how upset he was, when he got that letter; now, someone else has replaced him. Perhaps that's why Grace didn't say anything to me; she thinks I'll disapprove. Do I? Well, she really should have been more honest with Paddy. On the other hand David's a good man, she can see that, and handsome with it. But why rush? Then again, it's Grace's life, not hers.

"Penny for your thoughts."

"Oh, you know. You're right, Dad, about the war."

He munches and nods, then tips his head and points with his eyes to a table by the window. "That Irishman's back, asked about a place to stay again." She looks over, sees Pat in the corner reading a book. His right arm rests in a sling. "He seems a bit subdued to me. Why don't you go over, Maggie, and ask him if he'll do some singing while he's here. He filled the pub last time."

"Good idea, Dad." She takes off her apron and walks over, noticing that Pat's face looks thinner, drawn, as if he's been ill. His clothes also hang loosely upon his frame; he's lost a fair bit of weight, she thinks. He hears her footsteps, looks up; gives her half a smile. "Hello stranger."

"Hello yourself; I was wondering where you and your sister would be."

"What's that you're reading?"

"Oh, it's just a tuppenny dreadful, light and easy to read." He shows her the cover, a garish image of a circus scene; a couple on a trapeze, high above two lions.

"Any good?"

"Not really."

He does seem to have lost his sparkle, she thinks. "Well, I'm glad to see you back. We never did have that conversation about you and Paddy, back in Ireland."

Panic seems to cross his face, for an instant. "Ah, I remember now, our childhood."

"What on earth did you think I meant?"

"Oh, nothing, but that childhood business might be a long old story, I warn you." His voice seems flat, toneless; so unlike what she remembers of him.

She stares down at him; something's definitely wrong. "What happened to your arm, Pat?"

He grimaces, "Ah well, I feel out of bed." Seeing the disbelief on her face, he gives her a rueful smile. "It's true. And no, I wasn't drunk at the time; in fact, I was asleep."

"How on earth...?"

At last he gives her a full smile, a sort of lop-sided grin. "The German navy threw me out of my bed. Don't ask me to go into all the details, Maggie. It is Maggie, isn't it?" She nods. "I got a bang on the head too, you see. Don't remember too much about it. Just that we had to get into our lifeboats in a hurry. And we spent quite a while in them before we got picked up. They told me to go somewhere for a rest, you see, when we got back to Liverpool. So here I am; I've nowhere else to go. You can't get to Ireland very easily, these days. I hope that's alright with you." He looks up at her, frowning, as if he really worries that it might not be.

She feels a rush of sympathy for him, for his modesty, his obvious loneliness. "Of course that's alright. You're Paddy's best friend. Besides, the last time you were here, you filled up the pub for us. My dad just sent me over to ask you to sing again."

He looks away, embarrassed, "Maybe in a couple of days." He lifts the sling, by way of explanation. "Someone else would have to accompany me."

She comes to a snap decision. "Come with me to the dance tonight, in Middleton. It's always a good night. You look as if you need some fun." He looks up at her, open-mouthed. "What's the matter? Are you going to turn me down, Pat the singer?"

He shakes his head, glancing down at the floor. "Do I look like a madman? No, it's just I won't be doing much dancing, with one arm and a gammy leg. Normally, I'm not bad. But at the moment, you'll be bored witless."

"No I won't. You can tell me all about Ireland. And when I want a bit of fun, I can take a dance with one of the Canadian aircrew. They bus them up to the dance from their bases."

He glances up at her, rubbing his chin. "Do they now? The boys in blue; and I'm to be your chaperone? Well, there's a new role for me. I suppose it sounds like a fair exchange. I get the pleasure of your company, without spoiling all of your fun."

"Exactly."

*　　*　　*

He follows in her wake, flexing his arm occasionally, trying to rid it of the stiffness. It still aches; the muscles have shrunk but it's mostly healed as far as he can see. The leg too is loosening up, getting stronger by the day. Reading his thoughts, she tosses the question over her shoulder, "How's that leg of yours?"

"Seems fine, Maggie. If I get any pain, I'll let you know. I started off with little strolls, been building it up step by step. I did a good few miles yesterday, up that stream next to the pub."

"Did you get up to Rookhope?"

He grunts, "Maybe; where exactly is that?"

She laughs. "The stream's called Rookhope burn; Rookhope is the village it comes down from. My aunt lives up there."

"Ah well, that would be where I turned around." For a girl, she walks at a decent pace, he thinks. They follow the river at first, crossing it twice on footbridges, walking through meadows filled with buttercups and rich green grass. The sun begins to peek through a flock of billowing cotton wool clouds. "It might be a bit warm later."

"Let's hope so."

"Was your father OK about this?"

"Don't worry, Pat; he quite likes you. And he trusts both of us; I often go for walks when I get some time to myself. Especially in the summer, it can be glorious in the dale. I take a book of poetry and sit and look at the views." She speaks in a matter of fact way, as if she were his nurse.

Well, that's how it started, he thinks. I was at low ebb, for sure, when I arrived. He wishes she'd slow down just a bit. Well, she probably just wants to keep a bit of distance, he thinks, to avoid giving me the wrong impression; I must seem like an old man to her. "Thanks for looking after me, by the way."

"Oh, I have my motives. After all, I get to escape from behind the bar, and in return we get you to sing now and then, which I also enjoy. So I win, both ways."

"Fons always did say you were the smartest."

"Did he? Tell me, why do you call him Fons?"

He grins to himself behind her back. "Ah well, it's just an Irish nickname, is all."

She seems to accept this; she stops at a narrow exit through a stone wall, points to a settlement ahead. "That's Westgate, the other end of the park."

He looks around, bemused. "What park would that be?"

She laughs. "Didn't you see all the deer, and the wild boar?"

He tries to puzzle this one out. "With the little people on their backs, you mean?"

She smiles, tilts her head sideways. "Maybe; you're on the right track. We're standing in the royal hunting park of the Norman Prince Bishops, between the east gate and the west gate."

"I see; but if someone like you or me took a deer, they'd a' cut off our hands, wouldn't they?"

She laughs, "Or worse." She tilts her head sideways. "You seem more like your old self, today." She stands there watching him with her blue-green eyes, expectantly.

He shrugs, nods, and looks at the floor. "It's surely done me good, coming here."

She pauses, deep in thought; asks, "What happened in that lifeboat, Pat?" Oh Christ, he thinks, why did she have to remind him of that? I just stopped dreaming about it.

He sighs. "Nothing much; that was the problem, nothing happened. We sat in that boat for two weeks while nothing happened except wind and rain, while we ran out of food and finished our water. You've no idea how long that two weeks felt. Then they picked up what was left of us."

"What was left of you?" Her tone is incredulous, uncomprehending. He realises, she really has no idea what it might be like. He holds his forehead, pinching it, searching for words that won't sound too brutal.

"Well, when a torpedo hits a ship, everything inside tends to fall apart - the ship sort of jumps up in the air, for a moment. Even if you're not close to the explosion, you get thrown around. Some of the lads were injured much, much worse than me... burns, internal injuries, that sort of thing. Even if we had a doctor..." he shrugs. "They just died in that boat, Maggie. They died, one by one. All the lads that didn't have the strength left in them."

"Oh Pat, that must have been awful. Watching them die." He gestures with his hand; enough, no more. She reaches out and squeezes his hand, resting her hand in his for a long moment. "Come on then, Pat. We've got a fair way to go, just yet." She turns away, squeezes through the gate. He follows, breathing in the air, smelling the life, the wild garlic from the riverbank. Let's hope so, he thinks; I'm growing fond of this girl and she doesn't seem to mind.

Something about her, she has a healing touch for the soul. Well, don't make a fool of yourself, he thinks. In the village, she leads him along a small lane onto a footpath past an old watermill; the path begins to climb a wooded gorge, past a series of tumbling waterfalls. He removes his sweater, tying it round his waist. The clouds have mostly blown away, revealing a bright blue sky through the branches and dazzling reflections of sun on water. He studies her hips, legs and ankles, moving effortlessly up the path. Correction, he thinks, she's not really a girl, she's a woman; a young woman, for sure, but one who knows her own mind. *Like Paula.*

The thought causes his chest to tighten for a moment, adds to his breathlessness. "Were you an athlete, by any chance?" She stops, turns, rewards him with that wide, half-embarrassed grin.

"I did a bit of running at school. Why, am I going too fast for you?"

He laughs, "Well, that depends on how far you're taking me up this path." He pauses, considers his own words, the unwitting innuendo; he feels his face heat up and looks away. "I mean, does it level out again soon?" He looks up to see her waiting, half turned toward him, her expression serious, as if she's thinking hard about his words; a wry smile appears.

"This is the steepest part." She turns away, "This stream is called Middlehope burn."

"Where does it lead? Middlehope?"

"Yes, but it's not a village."

"What is it, then?"

"Wait and see." She turns and skips away. He follows, sighing in exasperation. This is what you get for trying to keep up with *her*, he thinks. At the top of the gorge, the path and the stream meander up a twisting valley through steep sided hills, passing a variety of disused, roofless buildings. Storehouses, he thinks. Is that a kiln? They come to a place where the stream tumbles out of the ground below a small, flat plateau. Climbing onto this, he looks down into a round hole, carved out of the rock, and sees the stream running through a deep pool below. He scratches his head, and sits down next to it. She sits opposite, watching him, her arms hugging her knees.

"Fancy a swim, Pat?"

"Sure, it's warm enough in the sun all right; but that water will be as cold as the North Sea. And I didn't bring my costume. Would all this be part of some old mine workings?"

"That's right. This is an old hushing, where they'd separate the lead ore from the rock. You can see two or three mine entrances a bit higher up; the whole dale's full of them. In the old days, most of the men went down the mines while their wives worked the land."

"Sounds like a hard life."

"It was. Imagine coming up here through the snow and ice in winter, carrying all your food for a fortnight plus all your tools. And paid a pittance, too, dad says."

"I'd sooner take my chances crossing the water."

"Have you always been a sailor, Pat?"

He wonders how much he should tell her. "I prefer to think of myself as an engineer. I didn't always go to sea; I sort of drifted into the merchant navy when I left America."

"Did you like America?"

He looks up, sees genuine curiosity. "I did, I did."

"So why did you leave?"

"Oh, that's a long story, Maggie; when I know you a bit better, maybe."

She studies his face. "Tell me, what will you do after the war?"

"Now that is a good question. I'm not sure, is the honest answer. Maybe something back on dry land, maybe find a new life, somewhere. I have an idea or two."

She puts her hand on his arm. "Well, come back here before you go."

"Are you flirting with me, Maggie Hardy?" Her face flushes pink; she smiles, looks away.

"Not yet; but I might, when the war's over." Might she? Jesus Christ, he thinks.

He blurts out, "Why on earth would you be flirting with an old man like me?"

Her eyes stare back at him. "You're not *that* old, Pat. Besides, take a look around you. Look at the other men in these parts. By comparison, you're a decent catch. More important, I *like* you. You're well educated, so I can talk to you about anything. And you also make me laugh. But I'm not flirting yet; I don't want anything serious until this war is over."

There's a moment here, for Pat, before she looks away; he sees the same cool intelligence in Maggie's eyes that he remembers in Paula's. He feels the same sense of shock and disbelief that such a beautiful woman is choosing *him*. He feels dizzy with it; he takes a deep breath to steady himself. "Wild horses won't keep me away... at least..." The U-boats might, he remembers. "I was going to ask your father to look after one or two things for me, anyway; until the war's over. Then you can be sure I'll be back." He glances at her, throws a pebble into the black pool, watches the ripples spread. He needs time to get used to this idea, so he does. He lies down in the sun and stretches. "Why don't you read me some poetry?"

*   *   *

Seventeen: 1944

"You don't really need this, Grace, with your long lashes; you hair's almost black, anyway."

Her sister's face breaks into a wry smile tinged with anxiety. "Indulge me, Maggie; I do want to look my absolute best, today. I'd like to surprise David a *little* bit."

"Don't crowd me, I need the light." Shaking her head with exasperation, Maggie glares at her younger sisters. The circle around Grace expands, inch by grudging inch. Maggie can feel their critical eyes fixed on the tip of her finest paintbrush, studying her technique. "He knows you're the most beautiful girl in the dale already, Grace."

"Only if you like dark haired girls; if you like them fair, June's going to win that one. And strange as it may seem to you, Maggie, some men prefer redheads." The younger girls exchange glances with one another, as if checking shades and preferences. A giggle erupts from June and spreads around the circle; Maggie frowns.

"I'm not a redhead. At least, not like Rose." Rose colours a deep pink, but squeals in delight.

Grace waves her hand, airily, "Oh, call it auburn if you must, Maggie. A lot of men like it."

"I suppose; keep still now." She applies the finishing touches to her sister's long lashes and then steps back. "There; you can show her the mirror, June."

June steps forward; Grace turns her head from side to side, examining her reflection. After a pause, she beams at her sisters. "You haven't lost your touch, Mags; and by the way, thanks *so much* for the stockings. That's the best wedding present any girl could get, these days. It'll certainly give David a *lovely* surprise when he sees me in those..." She raises half an eyebrow; assumes an innocent expression. The three eldest sisters clasp each other and begin to giggle; the outer three observe in mute fascination.

Maggie whispers in Grace's ear, "I hope that's not the only thing that will surprise him."

Grace adopts a shocked expression, "Maggie! I don't know *what* you mean."

Maggie smiles and shakes her head; she feels a pang of envy for Grace's acting ability. Sometimes she resents her flippancy too, especially when Grace uses it to push her away or to put her in her place as the younger sister. "You know exactly what I mean, Grace. Not that my opinion would make a blind bit of difference. For what it's worth, I hope you'll be very happy together."

Grace nods, squeezes her sister's arm, and looks away. "Thanks."

"You're sure about him?"

Grace meets her eye: an expression of puzzlement dissolves into determination. "Oh, yes, absolutely." She grins and gives a mock salute.

Maggie sighs in exasperation; the thought occurs to her, *my mother should have asked that question, not me.* "I'm sorry. It's not my place, but I wish..." The others suddenly seem to have taken a step back, away from her, as if anticipating what she is about to say; have they actually stepped back, or is it just the sudden sense of emptiness she perceives in the room? "I wish our mother could be here today, Grace. She'd be so proud of you."

After a long silence, Grace sniffs loudly and shakes her head, as if to shake away her sense of loss. "Dad wanted to bring her out for the day, you know. He told me."

"I know, Grace. The doctors said she wasn't well enough."

"Well, the point is that he tried his best to get her here; and he *will* be here to give me away. That's enough for me, Maggie - for all of us; it'll have to be." She flickers her gaze at little Ellen for a moment. "So let's all enjoy the day, shall we; all six of us?" Ellen nods up at her, her little eyes round with wonder. For a long moment they all move together again, the inner and outer circle uniting to touch and hold each other, a ritual of solidarity and comfort before they face the world.

A loud rap on the door makes them all jump. "How long will you be?"

"We're finished, Dad, come in."

Their father enters, waving two slips of paper. "Telegrams... I assume this one's about the wedding." He hands one to Grace, and waits. "Well?"

She tears it open, reads it; shakes her head. "It's from Paddy in India. *Someone* must have told him the date." She glances pointedly at Maggie. "It says 'Congratulations and best wishes, Paddy. The groom is a lucky sod.' Typical Paddy don't you think; short and to the point?"

Maggie laughs, "No bitterness there, then, eh, Dad?"

"Not too much; this one's for you, Maggie. Don't worry, it's not war office." She takes it with trepidation. It wouldn't be war office anyway, she thinks, with him being a civilian; it would probably come from a shipping company. She tears it open carefully, her hands shaking; she scans quickly to the end, sees his name as the sender, and gasps with relief. "What is it, lass?"

She reads it again before she speaks. "It's from Pat; it says, 'Gerry saw us off, stop; short swim this time, stop. See you when I can, Pat, stop."

After a long pause, Harriet asks, "What does he mean, Maggie?"

"I think it means he was torpedoed again but they were rescued very quickly."

She feels her Grace's arms enclosing her, hugging her, hears her sister whisper, "Which makes it an especially good day for both of us." Grace's voice raises for her father's benefit. "I think Maggie and I should both have a gin and tonic to celebrate, don't you think, Dad?

* * *

Standing before the mirror in the early evening light, he notices how much his tanned face and body contrast with the white shaving foam. I've almost gone native, he thinks. He glances out of the open bathroom door into the spacious bungalow, remembers Abdul Huq sitting patiently by the front doorstep, awaiting his next instruction, having pressed his uniform. Well, not really. He sighs and scrapes his chin, wondering what Gilly Hardy would make of all this luxury. Would he be shocked or even surprised? Probably not; Gilly has a keen sense of history, of how the powerful exploit the poor, even in England. He's also worked like hell so that his own family escape that fate. What would Grace think? The lovely Grace; married by now to a local farming boy. She would think he's got above himself, for sure. Maggie, on the other hand, well, she'd probably be envious. She'd happily live at Hagtop Hall, she'd told him that herself...

The real question, though; what would all the Hardy girls think of Dorothy? He still hasn't mentioned her in his letters home. He can just imagine their polite, puzzled reaction; the question on their lips, "A black girl?" In fact, she's not much darker than him now, of course; but that's what they would think and say, like everyone else in England. Or Ireland, for that matter, dammit. This bothers him, because he's very fond of Dorothy. Not crazy about her, as she seems to be about him, but increasingly comfortable with her - and uneasy without her, come to that. He washes the foam from his face, takes another look at himself. If this carries on in a few years he'll have to make a decision, one way or the other. He's not ready to get married yet; but she might come back with him anyway, after the war, if he asks her. He hears the front door open, Melsonby's footsteps advancing down the hall. He calls out, "Evening, Uncle."

A face peers round the edge of the door, "Oh, evening, Paddy; no tennis tonight?"

"Vic's wife's in town. Plus, he's suddenly less keen since I started taking sets off him. Is it cooling down out there yet? I've just finished in here, by the way."

"A little; are you eating with your friends tonight?"

"I am, Uncle, I am. Would you like to join us?"

"Thanks, but I need a quiet night in; busy day, tomorrow. Can I send your bearer out to get me something again?"

"Of course, I'll let him know." He nods at Melsonby, informs Abdul, and heads for his room, aiming to catch a short nap before he gets dressed again for dinner. Thoughts of Dorothy keep him awake; his girl now, in every sense. Memories of their physical intimacy, anticipation of more tonight, keep him too aroused to sleep. He can't believe his good fortune, though it can't last forever; eventually, this war will end. Then what? He shuts his eyes, tries to still his brain, relax, and look forward to the evening...

"We have an announcement; we're celebrating." Vic darts a look at his wife, smiles sheepishly. "In about six months a new tennis champion will be born." Paddy and Dorothy glance at each other; Dorothy raises her eyebrow, gives him a little shake of the head, as if to reassure him that she has no plans in that direction.

She can't resist a little tease for Vic, though, "What if it's a girl?"

"She'll be a champion too, don't worry; but Suhaila's absolutely sure it's a boy."

His wife smiles, shrugs at the others, "I just know."

Paddy hears pride and satisfaction in her voice; he rises to his feet to raise his glass, "Well, congratulations and well done to the both of you. You'll be great parents, either way; here's health and happiness to your child. Hopefully, he'll have most of his growing up in peacetime."

Vic pats his wife's hand, "Let's hope so." He too gets to his feet, "To the future..."

Dorothy raises her glass, darts a quick glance at Paddy, reaching across the table to grasp Suhaila's hand. "I envy you. He will bring you so much joy...and your future now has a shape..."

"A much larger shape," quips Vic.

Dorothy waves her finger at him, "Hush, Vic."

"Yes, Sister..."

She looks to the ceiling, ignores him, "...and a map, something to guide you..."

"I think I know what you mean, Dotty; the war makes everything uncertain. I feel like I'm living in a bubble that has to burst sometime..." Paddy says the words without thinking; he sees hurt cross her face before she looks away. "I don't mean that personally, I mean for *all* of us. We're all here for the foreseeable future, and that could be years. But after it, everything will change."

Dorothy meets his gaze, her face flushed. "Except for Suhaila; her world is changing *now*."

"Exactly, that's what I meant; we don't have that."

"Is that what you want; change?" Her words shock him with their directness.

He swallows; tastes anxiety in his mouth, "No, it isn't. Far from it - right now, I don't want *anything* to change." He watches her take a deep breath, nod and sit back, apparently satisfied.

Vic exchanges a meaningful glance with Suhaila and clears his throat. "Things are changing, slowly; at least we know we're going to win this war now. The Germans are being pushed back in Italy *and* the east. When we finally land in the west, they'll be fighting on three fronts. Once that happens they won't last long. The Japs are running out of steam too, with the Americans pushing back across the Pacific. Their air force is virtually gone; that's always the turning point."

"They're still managing to attack us down at Imphal."

"It won't last. That supply line is impossible in the long run."

"Tell that to the Chindits."

"Look, the Japs only chance of taking India was to persuade the Indian army to change sides; there was never any chance of that. When Gandhi finally demanded independence and the British locked him and the rest of Congress up, who sorted out all the trouble? The Indian army."

Paddy scratches his head, "I've never really understood that feller."

Vic laughs, "Gandhi? What's the great mystery? He's a wily old fox but he's also an impossible idealist who thinks non-violence will always win the day. In fact, as long as the British keep the support of the Indian army they can just ignore the Congress party."

Dorothy leans forward again, shaking her head, "I'm not so sure. In the long run, after the war, maybe Gandhi will be proved right." Vic looks astonished; contradicted by a woman.

Before Vic can bite back, Paddy prompts, "What do you mean, Dotty?"

"Look, before the war most Indian people thought the Congress party had spent too much time in the sun, that independence was an impossible dream. But then the Governor-General declared war without even asking us about it; suddenly, the word independence had a real meaning, because ordinary people never want a war that they don't understand. But now there was also a problem for Congress. Fight the decision to go to war, and you risk joining the enemy, like Chandra Bose. Or be patient, like Gandhi; and wait until the war ends."

Vic bites his lip, then laughs, "To see which side will win, I suppose?"

"Maybe," she shrugs, "or maybe you really believe in peace, so you just don't want to join either side. So you ask for your independence politely, first. But when Mr Cripps makes it clear that there's absolutely nothing on offer, you can demand it; though without the threat of violence."

"But violence happened anyway; so the whole Congress party was locked up."

"Of course; but now, the Indian people can all see what is happening. And they see that most of the violence is done by the British. Suddenly independence is something that most of them want, even if they know they can't have it, and they don't even want to fight for it; not yet. But now it's *in their minds* as a real possibility. *That* is what is new. Talk to the shopkeepers in the bazaar."

"When the war ends, the army will still be the key; and Gandhi will still be in prison."

"Not for long."

Paddy clears his throat, "She has a point, Vic; when I was a boy in Ireland, we never thought of ourselves as a separate country. Anyone who did was a little soft in the head. But that all slowly changed after the authorities started cracking down and killing people. And once the people all turned against them, they couldn't govern."

Vic stares at him. "We're a long way from that. The whole protest died down after a few months; and Congress is now out of sight, out of mind."

Dorothy shrugs, "I'm sure that's right for you, Vic, and the rest of the army. You're busy with the war. And even for ordinary people, that kind of protest can't last - they have to eat. But there was a lot of killing, and people don't forget these things. I think Paddy's right; things will have to change after the war, one way or another." She smiles, disarmingly. "After all, what are you soldiers going to do when you all come home?"

Vic blinks and then yawns, as if bored with the conversation. "What will be, will be."

Paddy laughs, "There you go again, Vic. Falling back on your traditional fatalism."

"Why not? It's the best thing my father taught me. It helps him cope with the legal system, and it helps everyone else cope with the war. How else should we do that?"

Paddy swallows, thinking about his platoon, back in France. "I understand that, but we still have choices." He glances at Dorothy, "I thought about asking for a transfer for a while, but Dotty talked me out of it." Vic sits up sharply, frowns, and nods his understanding.

Suhaila looks puzzled; she glances at Dorothy, who looks away. "Why on earth would you want a transfer, Paddy?" Paddy feels a sharp kick from Dorothy under the table.

"Oh, nothing, just a stupid idea; anyway, I decided not to. I'm just saying we do have choices, even if we don't take them. And you will have choices, after the war."

Vic exhales slowly, looking thoughtful. "Well, if I can't stay in the army I'll probably choose to study law and join my father's practice; he would love that." His wife takes hold of his arm; he turns and smiles at her. "So would Suhaila."

His wife raises her eyebrows, "So will your son, husband."

Vic glances at Paddy, smiles, shrugs his shoulders. "This is what women are for, Paddy. To save us from ourselves; don't you agree?"

*   *   *

She steps off the path and slips between the new growth, young rowan and beech with the occasional oak, following a faint animal trail. Are there still deer in these woods, she wonders? She stops at the edge of a clearing; dappled sunshine glowing on the green leaves above, splattering colour across a thick carpet of bluebells. She feels an arm slip gently around her waist and rests her own on top of it, feeling the strength in his. She whispers, "I wanted to show you this." She senses acknowledgement but he remains silent; perhaps the sight has taken his breath away. She likes that about him; he's good with words, but he also knows when they're not necessary. She leans her head back onto his shoulder; in response, he turns his body a little to make her more comfortable. "There are wild strawberries further on, near the bathing pool. If you can stay until the autumn, I know a place where we can pick hazelnuts."

He whispers, "Now I know where the Garden of Eden really was."

"It feels like that today, doesn't it?"

"It surely does, Maggie; you've no idea how much, after nine months at sea." She considers his statement; nine months? Is that how long it's been? Time enough to grow a baby, as Grace is now doing. She feels her own desire rising within her, despite (or is it because of?) the thought of babies. He must be thinking of that, too. The reference to Adam and Eve is plain enough. Not once has he tried to pressure or persuade her, either with words or with his body. *He doesn't need to*, she admits to herself, with a shock of realisation; all he has to do is wait. She wonders whether to ask him, how long is he staying, this time? She decides not; she doesn't want to know, not yet.

"Come on, Pat, let's go to the pool."

"Are you going to swim?"

She looks up, sees blue sky and no cloud. "I should think so if it stays like this."

"How long have we got?"

"Most of the afternoon." She feels him unhook his arm and steps away.

At the pool she carefully chooses a spot where shade and sunlight meet; "Here." She watches him unroll a blanket onto the flat concrete bank; he sits upon it cross-legged, examines his surroundings, looking up the bridge. "How often do the trains come past?"

"They don't, not anymore; this is the branch line to an old mine. You can hear the main line from here, but you can't see it."

"Thank Christ for that. I thought we'd have the world watching us swim." He grins, squinting up at her. "My costume is not exactly the height of fashion, I warn you. Just some old shorts I use in the engine room."

"How on earth; I mean, how did you manage to save them...?"

"I was wearing them at the time. With some other clothes on top, thank the Lord. I'd just come off watch." She nods, decides not to ask any more. He's told her about the nightmares and that's enough; today, she wants to make him forget the war.

She takes her own costume out, drapes it against her body as seductively as she can. "What do you think? I copied it from one in a Betty Grable film."

"Thinking doesn't come into it, Maggie; it's more like drooling while a load of steam blows out of my ears and nose."

She flips the costume at his head; "Get away with you. You'd better turn around, now."

He shrugs, "Can't I just shut my eyes? Then at least I can imagine what's in front of me..." For a second he pauses, looks up at her with a wicked grin, and then turns away.

She watches him while she undresses. He sits perfectly still, making no effort to sneak a look behind him. "I'm sure you've seen lots of girls before, at your age."

"Not one like you, Maggie."

She blushes with pleasure, "I bet you say that to all the girls."

"I do, I do." He pauses. "But this time, I really mean it."

She shakes her head in exasperation; does he, really? "I've finished, your turn."

He turns around, looks her up and down; gives a low wolf whistle. "You, my dear, make Betty Grable look like an auld harridan. Honest to God, you do." He stands up, turns his back again, and looks over his shoulder at her. "You turn around, now."

She turns her back; "I'm serious, Pat. You must have had other women; I mean, you must have been in love before..." Once the words are out of her mouth, the implications of her comment take her breath away; she sneaks a look at him over her shoulder, to see what he makes of it.

He's stepped out of his shoes; he stands stock still, looking down, caught in the middle of unbuttoning his shirt, deep in thought. His voice drops to a baritone. "In love? Only once, a while ago, when I was in America." He slowly pulls the shirt over his head, revealing a white back, slim but muscular. "The trouble was, she was already married; truth is, Maggie, I took a long while to get over her." He sighs, throws the shirt down. "It's past now." He fumbles with his trousers.

She turns away, thinking long and hard during the silence that follows. At least this shows he *can* be serious. He obviously felt pretty deeply about this woman; the thought of her still upsets him. "What about the others, the girls in every port? Isn't that what you sailors often say?"

She hears a laugh, senses his presence standing behind her. She glances over her shoulder and turns around. He wears a pair of faded navy blue shorts, patchy with old oil stains, the pockets torn, plus a sheepish expression. He shrugs, "I did warn you."

She shakes her head, "I'll make you some proper ones; but answer my question."

"You have no need to worry, Maggie. I'm no innocent, like any sailor, but when I like someone, that's it. Honest to God."

"Promise?"

"Cross my heart." She can see he means it; she reaches up, kisses him softly on the lips. Then, before he can grasp hold of her, she slips around him, steps away and dives into the pool.

Later, they cuddle together while they lie in the sun, warming up after the cold shock of the pool. Lying in his arms, she thinks again about what he said; she can't really find much fault with it. In fact, she can't find many faults with him. She feels so safe with him; it just feels right, in so many ways. One thing, she wonders if he feels the same desire as her; although part of her admires his self-control, another part of her wishes he wasn't quite so restrained. She sighs, begins to drift off into a doze. His voice wakes her, whispering in her ear, "What about you, Maggie?"

"What do you mean?"

"Ever been in love?"

She opens her eyes, examines his face, checking that he's not teasing her. "Not really. I might have fallen for one of the Canadian airmen if I'd had more time, but he didn't come back from a mission. It felt like a warning, really. That's why I decided to wait until the war ended."

He grunts, "Sensible girl."

She sniffs, "Maybe; how much longer do you think it will last?"

"At least a year, maybe two; the tide has turned, for sure. The Yanks have made the difference; you should see the amount of weapons we're shipping over."

"I suppose that's not *so* long; but it's still *too* long."

He strokes her hair. "I can wait."

"Can you?" She stares at his blue eyes, his hair beginning to lighten in the sun, the smile lines under his eyes. "The trouble is, Pat, I'm not sure that I can."

She watches him blink with surprise, meet her gaze. "Well, just give me the word, Maggie, anytime." He blushes, "What I mean is, I'm crazy about you, if you hadn't realised that yet."

She feels relief flooding through her. "Are you really?"

"Of course I am. Isn't it obvious?"

She considers this statement carefully; her father has certainly made comments, so maybe it is obvious to others. She places her finger on his lips. "All right, I feel the same. So I'm not sure I want to wait any longer, now. But not here, not today - it's too public here. Anyone could come along; but I know places we can go another day."

He nods, pulls her close, kisses her hair. "Somewhere special?"

"Yes; but Pat..." she hesitates, searches for the right words, "I don't want to get pregnant."

"Don't worry about that, Maggie. I - well, it's the first thing we learn on the boats; how to use the rubber things, that is."

"Good. But how did you know...I mean, to bring it?"

"Ah well, Maggie, you know what they say. Hope springs eternal."

She giggles and cuddles into him. "It certainly does; I can feel it springing, now."

* * *

Somewhere in the distance, an aeroplane drones across the sky. In the Atlantic, that would be a menacing sound; the cry would be, is that one of ours? Here, the noise slowly fades away within a gentle whistling wind that blows down from the flat tops of the moors, interrupted only by the sounds of curlews calling to each other. He's not even tempted to lift his head up above the curtain of grass surrounding them, hiding them away from the world. Who cares what happens out there? This is what's important; this soft bed of heather and drying grasses, this warm sunshine playing upon their bodies, this soft skin against his head, these arms entwined around him. She suddenly sighs and moves, her hand creeping up his back, stroking his hair.

"I thought you were asleep."

"I was for a while; you, too. But I'd rather be awake; it seems silly to sleep this time away."

"I know what you mean; though God knows, I haven't felt so rested in years. It was almost worth getting sunk again to get back here."

"Don't say that, Pat." She squeezes his shoulder.

"Why not?"

"Tempting fate, I suppose; twice is quite enough, don't you think?"

"I would have come back anyway, soon enough; don't you worry yourself about that."

She makes a long, protracted, contented noise. He tries to fix everything about her in his memory, especially the scent of her hair. He's going to need his memory of their time together to keep him sane, soon enough.

"There's some truth in it, though."

"In what, Maggie?"

"Oh, you know; when you sent that telegram, it shocked me. Made me realise I could lose you. It made me question the idea of waiting."

He grunts, waits for her to continue. When she doesn't, he feels uneasy. What is she telling him? Did she feel pressured by that telegram? Has he taken advantage of her, like all the fighting men do, on the last night before they leave for the front? He blurts out, "Honest, Maggie, I didn't intend that; I was just telling you I was coming ..."

"Oh, Pat," She turns to face him, smiling, framing his face in her hands. "I know that. I thought about us for a long time, you know. If anyone influenced me, it was my sister." He stares at the grave expression on her face, half reassured, half puzzled. "My sister Grace; she's always been impatient. I used to think that was foolish, but it isn't, not always. She could see how I felt about you. She whispered something wise in my ear, that day." She watches his face, smiles again. *Better to have loved and lost, than never to have loved at all.*"

He nods, "Perhaps; though it can be bloody painful, believe me."

He watches her forehead furrow, "You mean the American girl? What was her name?"

"Paula."

"Well, would you rather you'd never met her?"

"Of course not..." The vehemence of his own reaction surprises him.

"Well, there you are. Your telegram woke me up. It made me think hard about the reality of this war, Pat, one way or another. I decided that if you hadn't been rescued, I would have regretted waiting for the rest of my life."

He swallows. Sometimes, women could be so much more logical than men, in that way; certain women, anyway. "You're quite special,

Maggie. You know that?"

Her smile broadens; she snuggles back into his chest, "Of course, it comes from all the poetry I read."

"Does it now? And how do you work that one out?"

"Oh, it wasn't just my sister. Haven't you ever read Andrew Marvell?"

He rubs his chin. "The name's familiar, but I can't place it."

"*But at my back I always hear time's winged chariot, hurrying near...*" She pauses, frowns, and then continues, "*Now let us sport us while we may, and now like amorous birds of prey, rather at once our time devour, than languish in his slow-chapt power...*"

"Sounds like powerful stuff."

"There's a lot more to it; it's written for his shy girlfriend."

He laughs and stretches out. "Well, I should thank Mr Marvell for that, and thank Paddy for telling me to come here." He takes a deep breath and sniffs the heather. "You know, when I was younger I hated the English, for what they did in Ireland." Her eyes blink at him, uncertain. "They burned down peoples' homes, Maggie, things like that. And then there was a civil war; the place was a mess. That's why I left. All I'm saying is that I don't feel that way anymore." He wants to tell her more, to tell her everything; but the look on her face warns him not to do that. There's too much to tell; he feels trapped by the past, caught in its net, gazing out at her. Too many secrets, he thinks.

She still looks puzzled. "Did they burn your home down, Pat?"

The question shocks him, with its simplicity and directness. "No, but they would have burned our farm if they'd known about my brother. He fought against them."

She takes a sharp intake of breath; "Did he survive?"

He suddenly feels a sharp longing for his brothers, and his home. "He did, Maggie, thank God. My two brothers are still running that farm, back in Ireland."

"Maybe you can take me to visit, after the war."

"Maybe I can." He tries to smile, to reassure her, though the doubts swirl in his mind. The image of introducing Maggie to Carr, to Brendan, and to Mary, pops into his head. What would he show her? The road past the Fitzgerald farm? The bridge across the Blackwater? How ironic, if they captured him with an Englishwoman...

"What is it, Pat? Is there something else? What did they do to *you*?"

He turns away from her; what can he say? He takes a deep breath, thinks about her question. "I suppose, well...did Fons ever tell you about the shooting on the bridge? When we were boys?"

"No. I told you, he didn't talk about his childhood."

"Well there was a fight... some British soldiers got themselves shot. We were caught in the middle of it. One of the soldiers grabbed me, held me in front of him. I really thought I was going to be killed; and I nearly was, too. Luckily for me, someone shot that damned soldier instead. But there was blood everywhere."

"That's awful. How old were you, Pat?"

"About thirteen, I think." He feels relief flood through him. "I never told anyone about that, before." He laughs. "I nearly pissed myself."

"I'm not surprised you didn't like the English."

He turns back to face her. "Look, the point is that's all gone now; my shipmates are mostly English. I want to look forwards, not back. Maggie, I feel alive again for the first time in years. The last few years I've only been existing; not really living. Partly, you know, the war; everyone's just trying to survive. We used to have sing-songs on the SS Dinsdale; since we lost that ship, Frank and I haven't the heart, not like we used to. I haven't sung in public for years, but singing in your dad's pub made me feel alive again. You make me feel alive again. This place makes me feel alive."

"I'm glad. After the war, I'll take you to the Lake District. It's lovely there."

"Maybe I'll take you to New Zealand."

"New Zealand?"

"It's really beautiful there, Maggie. Like England, but with bigger mountains and lakes. I have a shipmate who has a great idea for a business there. He wants me to be a partner. We could have a great life there together, after the war."

She looks a little sceptical, but she doesn't object; he feels elated. If she really does love me, she'll come with me, he thinks.

*   *   *

The jeep roars up the last rise and swerves off the road onto a small, circular plateau, where it skids to a halt. A lorry follows more sedately, coasting to a halt next to the jeep; a group of turbaned soldiers descend athletically from the back and immediately begin to erect a large tent.

In the cab of the lorry, Paddy stares for a while at the snow-covered peaks of Afghanistan spread across the horizon in front of him. They call this place Big Ben, because of the view. He's been here before when he was stationed in Landi Kotal; it still takes his breath away. Technically it's in Afghanistan, but only by half a mile or so. He puts on his cap, adjusts his sunglasses, steps down from the lorry and gives a sharp salute.

"At ease, Reilly." The C.O. yawns, steps out of the jeep, stares into the distance along the ribbon of road meandering up the pass.

He points out a group of tiny figures about a mile away, leading camels in their direction, "There they are." He turns and points at a couple of chairs, around which the tent is being erected, "Come and sit down while we wait. Did you bring some money?"

"Yes, sir, as you suggested."

"Good, but I wanted to have a chat with you while we're here." Aha, thinks Paddy; maybe he's going to send me back to Landi Kotal, after all. "Nothing to worry about, old chap; just thought we could combine business with pleasure." Catch me off guard, you mean, he thinks. "Melsonby told me you did some book keeping; is that true?"

Paddy tries to appear relaxed; he crosses his legs as they both sit. "I can add up a column of numbers all right, Colonel. I worked for a feller with a small business; he showed me how to do his books." The Colonel seems to suppress a smile for a moment; he leans back in his chair as if he finds the situation amusing. "Though I did wonder why you wanted me to buy some carpets."

The Colonel gives Paddy a shrewd smile. "Actually, Reilly, it's a bit of a reward for you; you can sell these for three times the price, back in England. Probably four times, in Ireland."

"In that case, thank you, sir. Do you think we'll all be here much longer? I mean, the war seems to be going pretty well now."

"Oh, I think we'll be here a while yet, Reilly." The Colonel considers his words, and sighs. "The war in Europe won't last much longer, from what I can see. If the German leaders had any sense they'd surrender now, but in any case they won't last another year, surrounded on all sides. Next spring will see a big push." He frowns. "The Japanese are a different kettle of fish. All that ocean and all those islands; our armies are having to hop from one to another, fighting hard for every damned atoll. They'll fight to the last man, it's in their culture. When we invade Japan itself, it'll be a bloodbath. We're still recruiting hard, and we'll be training them until it's all over."

"Will you stay here, sir? After the war, I mean?"

"Good God, no; we won't be needed here. Probably won't be wanted, either."

"But what about the frontier; isn't that why we are up here in the first place?"

The Colonel gives him a rueful smile. "Of course; but the Indian army is now so large they won't need us after the war. Neither will our government. You ought to be thinking about that, Reilly; I am. Put it this way, that's why I'm sending all these carpets home."

"Aha. That's what I call foresight...very wise, sir. Anything else I should know?"

The Colonel gives him a long look and nods. "All right, since you asked. Once this war's over, we'll have to let the Congress party leaders out of jail. No excuse to lock them up, and then the genie will be out of the bottle. They'll demand independence, and after all the fighting, they'll probably get it. Our government will be too exhausted to resist. We'll be kicked out of India, in my view. So I don't think it will be easy to stay even for those who want to. And it may also be very difficult for those that worked for us."

Paddy thinks of Vic's father, the lawyer. "Like it was in Ireland, you mean. A lot of the Anglo-Irish gentry had their homes burned."

"Exactly; I wouldn't count on staying on. And your friends may have a tough time."

"I wasn't planning anything like that, Colonel. But thanks for the warning." He looks up. "Would you mind if I passed your thoughts on? Privately, as my own opinions?"

"Fine; but you're right, best to keep my name out of it." He leans back in his chair. "I must say I had my doubts about you at first, Reilly. Especially when you went out of your way to provoke the polo set. I thought you might have a large chip on your shoulder." Paddy feels his face reddening, but he stays silent. "Although reports from the training school said you were very easy to work with, so I kept you. And since then, your soldiers seem to get consistently high marks. We do notice these things." Paddy exhales, feeling relief. "And you've been more *discreet*." Paddy looks up, noticing the emphasis on the last word. He's leading up to something, he thinks, and waits. "Why is that, by the way?"

Paddy feels his face redden again. "I...well, I don't like a fuss of any kind, sir. It all shocked me, everyone's reaction. Normally I just like to get my job done without any fuss."

"I thought so." The Colonel raises an eyebrow, and lowers his voice. "Between you and me, Reilly, I don't care what you do in your own time as long as you're discreet. I don't care if you decide to marry the girl and stay with your Indian friends, after the war, as long as you keep your plans to yourself. Do I make myself clear?"

"Very clear, sir, thank you, sir." In other words, thinks Paddy, don't ever bring Dorothy to the British mess. Or even mention her name, there.

"Between you and me, are you thinking of marrying her?"

Oh Christ, Paddy thinks, is that why he put me in with Melsonby; to keep an eye on me? He swallows, thinking hard. What the hell, he thinks, no point in lying. "No, sir, but I'm quite fond of her. I have been thinking of asking her to go back with me, after the war."

The Colonel frowns. "Well, in my time out here I've known a few officers who did that; all I can say is that it usually didn't work. You remember what it was like for you after you stayed with your friend? Well, it's ten times worse for the girls, back in England. And they hate the climate; most of them come back to India. Sometimes the man comes back with them, but then that's pretty difficult, too. Think about it hard, that's my advice; but enjoy what you have now." He reaches out and pats Paddy on the arm, in a fatherly way. "If the truth were told, half these polo types are in the same boat, you know." Paddy snorts, suppressing a smirk.

"That's very interesting, sir, but no concern of mine." At least he's not in trouble again.

The Colonel raises his eyebrow, nods sagely; Paddy allows himself a smile. "Exactly right, Lieutenant, I like your attitude. Although now that we have a clear understanding, I think I'm going to call you Captain Reilly from now on, in recognition of your exemplary record as a trainer. And as such, I will put you in charge of the accounts for the training kit. The rank is on an acting basis for now, mind you. Until I'm sure you can handle the responsibility."

Promotion; I'll be damned... he feels a rush of elation, tempered suddenly by a vision of Dorothy's face. Would she be upset by all this talk? Maybe, he thinks, but she knows what the score is. He's often asked her to go to the British mess with him, but she refuses. It would only make trouble for him, she insists. He puffs out his cheeks with relief, feels a massive grin forming on his face. "That's grand sir, thank you."

"You've earned it." Paddy glances around, discovers that the tent is now fully erect with the front open, where two men are setting up a tea-maker. "When these carpet-wallahs arrive, by the way, drink some tea with them first. Don't be in a hurry. Let them show you their wares and when you've chosen, haggle as much as you can."

Paddy laughs, "I know the score that way, sir. Dorothy taught me how to haggle."

The eyebrows lift, "I'm sure she's been *very* educational, Reilly."

When the caravan arrives, Paddy stands to one side at first, as if part of the escort. He watches the Colonel drink tea and view an unending series of large, brightly coloured carpets. He takes some tea over to a trader who seems to specialise in smaller pieces. They drink their tea together, watching the negotiations. The man seems to sense his intention; he silently lays out his wares. Paddy tries to feign reluctance, but the man merely grins and waits. So he shrugs and inspects the pile of rugs. He picks out two red patterned rugs, one multi-coloured floral design, and another with what looks like a hanging basket above a vase of flowers in a glorious mix of bright colours. They are all thick, made with luxuriant wool.

The man regards him with a serious expression. "Very good

choice, Sahib; are you a believer, Sahib?"

Paddy frowns; "What do you mean?"

"Who is your God, Sahib? What do you believe?"

Paddy thinks hard; he doesn't want to offend the man. "Well, I believe that we are all equal under God, and the God we all worship is the same God, even if we use a different language."

The man grins at him. "Very well," he points at the red ones, "these rugs, Sahib, are Turkmen, antique, fifty years old. This floral one is Persian, lambs' wool, very new. And the mihrab, Sahib, this is Afghan, maybe twenty years."

Paddy shrugs; "Age is no concern to me..."

An hour later, the Colonel and he compare their buys. "You did well, Reilly. Not just the price, but the fact he sold you a mihrab at all; he must have liked you."

Paddy scratches his chin. "What exactly is a mihrab, sir?"

"You don't know?" The colonel slaps his own thigh and chuckles. "I thought you'd bought it for one of your friends." He puts his hand on Paddy's shoulder. "You've just bought yourself a Muslim prayer rug, Captain; or, in certain mystical tales, a flying carpet. Whatever you do, don't let Chaplain find you kneeling on it; I'd never hear the end of it."

* * *

The ball sails high up in the air, seeming to hang for an eternity while he waits underneath it, positioning himself. A drip of sweat runs into his eye as he stares upward; his vision blurs. He decides to let the ball bounce, takes a couple of steps back; quickly wipes his brow. His shirt and shorts feel soaked through; soon it will be too hot to play, even in the evening. It's almost dark now, and he's completely exhausted. The ball finally bounces at his feet, a few inches behind the baseline. His mind suddenly registers this fact, almost in disbelief. He calls "Out," drops his racket, and bends forward to catch his breath, resting his hands on his knees.

Vic slumps into a seated position at the other end of the court; after a moment, he lies flat on his back, gasping like a stranded fish. "Are you sure?"

Paddy grins, savouring the moment. "Don't you believe me?"

A long silence follows. Struggling with his pride, Paddy thinks. Eventually Vic sits up, forces a half-smile. "So, you've finally beaten me. Well, I suppose it had to happen one day."

"Nearly three years, it took me; worth waiting for, though."

"Should I be grateful for that? Your game gets better, while mine gets worse." Vic gets to his feet, scowling. "I was going to make this our last game, but I can't spend the whole summer waiting for revenge."

"You may have to, Vic, if it doesn't cool down; unless we can get up to Murree for a weekend." He watches Vic's face, resists the urge to tease his friend some more. "Don't worry, Vic, you'll get your revenge soon enough." Vic walks over to the net, loosens it and gathers up his kit in silence. "Come on, Vic, we can shower and cool off at the clubhouse. Then I'll buy you a couple of beers before you go, to make up for your sleepless nights with the baby. Relax you a bit."

Vic shoots him another sulky look, but then seems to think better of it. "All right, but I can't stay more than an hour tonight..." Exactly one hour later, Vic stares at his glass pensively, as if wishing it would refill itself. "Just one more, and then I have to go." He shakes his head, as if trying to shake off his negative mood. "Have you heard the latest rumour?"

"Which one?"

"About the war in Europe; the Germans are going to surrender."

"That's not a rumour, Vic; it's a stone cold certainty. Berlin is surrounded and the only other army they have left is in Italy; it's only a matter of time."

"But what will happen after that, do you think? Will it affect you, here?"

"Not according to our C.O.; we'll be here until the Japs are beaten."

"That could be a while yet."

"A year or two, probably; don't worry, you'll have time enough for your revenge."

Vic manages a smile. "I hope so. But I suppose I'm finally beginning to think about my life after the war."

"Good God, Vikram; what's brought this about?"

Vic picks up his glass, swills the ice around, takes a slow sip. "If you must know, Suhaila's pregnant again. Which in itself is a good thing, but it will bring more pressure from my family to make plans. I'd like to stay in the army, but I can't rely on that. Whereas I don't want to be a lawyer, but everyone else wants that, and I *can* rely on it."

"Tough choice; I see where your fatalism comes from. Maybe you need a third option. Especially if everything changes, like it did in Ireland."

"Oh, not that again; India is not Ireland. Personally, I'm sure we'll end up like Canada. Besides, even if we don't, they'll still need lawyers. The worst they can do is kick my father out of his bungalow in the civil lines, and there are other places to live. We own other properties, you know. My father rents them out. Don't worry about us."

"Okay, Vic." He holds up his hands. "But I do worry..." he hesitates, feeling foolish.

A slow smile dawns upon Vic's face. "About Dorothy? Are you worried about her too?"

"Of course; what would it be like for her, if everything changed?"

Vic shrugs, "Why should it be any different? Look, she has a good career as a nurse. It may even be better for her. Someone will have to run the hospitals without the British matrons and doctors. If all the British go, all this nonsense about Anglo girls will probably go with them."

"You really think so? I'm not so sure. I've been thinking of asking her if she wants to come to England with me, after the war."

"Do you really want to marry her, Paddy?" Vic grins. "Because that's the only way she'll go back with you. I've known her a long time, since college. She's a proud girl."

Paddy sighs; "It's probably the only way she *could* go back with me, come to that."

"If that's what you want, then ask her. But you'd better be sure it's what you want, first. Because wherever you live it will be very, very difficult for both of you."

"I know that."

"And for your children..."

He bites his lip; he hadn't really thought about children. He feels himself blush while Vic stares at him; he nods, reluctantly. "I suppose so."

Vic shakes his head sympathetically. "Listen, Paddy. She doesn't need to be rescued; she's a very clever girl and also beautiful. Girls like her will always survive." Vic shuts his eyes as if thinking hard, glances sideways at his friend. "Look, maybe I shouldn't say this, but one of the problems is that these girls all dream of marrying an English officer. You need to be sure that she really loves you and not just what you represent here." The words feel like a kick in the stomach; Paddy's always taken her affection for granted, never questioned it. It's an insult to Dorothy.

"That's not fair, Vic. You've seen the way she is with me; you're her friend, dammit."

Vic raises his hands, palms upward. "I know she's very fond of you, she likes you very much. But dreams are powerful. Listen, she had an English father who died a long time ago, before he could take her to England. I know that as a girl she felt cheated by that. Now you come along."

Paddy swallows; his mouth feels dry. He takes a sip of his drink, tries to grasp what that might mean. "I suppose it might play a part."

"She might think she can cope with England, but who knows?

She'd be terribly homesick for her mother's family, and she's used to a good life here. Everything would be different for her. They probably won't let her work in England. The food, the climate, the way she'll be treated. All I'm saying is, you have to be sure about how *both* of you feel. Whatever you do, don't marry her out of some kind of misplaced sympathy."

"Christ, I'm not that stupid."

"Of course, I'm sorry. Please don't take offence. Just think it over very carefully. From what you say, you have plenty of time to do that."

* * *

Eighteen: 1945

The stone gateposts stand forlorn, stripped of their decorated wrought iron gates (long since removed for the war effort). The little car putters through and follows a winding drive to the main house - also a monument to better days; a patchwork of cracked roof tiles crowns the crumbling bricks and windows flaked with stubborn, olive green remnants of paint. Yet at ground level, a parade of blooming rose bushes erupts in splashes of colour. The gardens look beautifully kept, she thinks; but that's what the male patients do, when they're well enough. Occupational therapy, they call it; even when he's mad, a northeast man will keep a tidy garden. She wonders if her mother has ever worked in these gardens, since she too has a passion for flowers; or would she be set to work knitting, for the soldiers?

They coast to a stop; her father turns to her, scratching his head. "Sorry, but I can't come in with you today, Maggie. The shop's so short on hardware; I've been told of places in Darlington, with it being a railway town." His eyes give her a knowing glance, slide away.

She reaches out and squeezes his hand, "I know, Dad. Besides, we've discussed this before; you visited mum on your own last time. And the way she is now, there's no need for more than one person." What she really means is *she never talks to us, anyway*. She's said it more bluntly to her sister; *why share the suffering, better we should just take turns*. "You leave it to me today, go and see what you can find for the shop." She gives him her best smile and steps out, steeling herself for the ordeal ahead.

A smell of disinfectant assaults her nostrils as she hurries along the gloomy corridor. I suppose it's too much work to open all the blackout blinds, she thinks, but a few more wouldn't hurt. Occasionally a whiff of urine, or worse, escapes from somewhere nearby; she raises the bunch of sweet peas to her nose as a posy, a defence against the madness. At the large double doors she glances up to the sign, "Females – long stay"; the voice in her head whispers, *that means for life.* Her heart hammers too fast; she forces herself to wait for a minute outside, to breathe slowly and calmly, telling herself not to be so stupid. It's always worst at this point, on the threshold. One awful day, will she end up in a place like this, just like her mother? At least mum has company now, Maggie tells herself; the staff finally persuaded her father that Violet might be less withdrawn if surrounded by others, so he stopped paying for a separate room. Not that it seems to have changed her, one way or the other.

She knocks on the door softly and waits. She hears the lock turn; the door opens, revealing a round pink face above a starched uniform. "Oh, Miss Hardy, isn't it? Is your father not with you?"

"Not right now, Matron; he'll be coming later." She resists the urge to make excuses.

"That's a shame; Violet seems a little better this last week." She looks Maggie up and down, "Still, you'd better come in. This way, dear, follow me. I'll bring her through to the visitor's room; you sit down and wait in there." The bay windows look out over the gardens; she reaches up to open an upper window, sucking fresh air into her lungs. Will they allow her to take her mother outside? Not without her father, she supposes. Somewhere in the distance she hears a steady thumping noise and raised voices. Behind her, the door opens; she watches the matron guide her mother to a chair. Violet looks thin, emaciated, with the expression of a startled rabbit; seemingly terrified, but at least her eyes dart up to meet Maggie's gaze. That's something, at least.

Maggie swallows; "Hello, Mum."

She sees a smirk cross her mother's face, hears a whispered reply, "Don't call me that, Ettie." She almost jumps back in surprise; she hasn't heard her mother's voice for nearly two years. The meaning doesn't immediately register; what had she said? Does she think I'm her sister?

The matron glances from one to the other, then shrugs and she turns away; "I'll bring you some tea in a little while; you must have a lot to catch up on."

Violet watches her go and stares at something in the garden; Maggie wonders whether or not to humour her mother. How to keep her talking? She clears her throat; "Dad - I mean Gilly - sent these for you." She steps closer, puts the bunch of sweet peas into her mother's hands. Her mother smiles shyly, like a schoolgirl. She sniffs at the flowers hesitantly at first, then catches the scent and inhales as if her life depended on it. Maggie hasn't seen her mother smile for years; she feels some of the dead weight lifting from her stomach, some of the dread evaporating. She steps back and watches her mother for a long moment, wary of breaking the spell. Yet there's one piece of news she's bursting to tell; she can't resist. "Have they told you, Mum; the war's over? The Germans have surrendered."

Her mother looks up, her eyes wide, "Did they?" She sniffs the flowers again, whispers, "He was wounded, you know; that's when he started to grow flowers, while he was recuperating." This is news to Maggie, though she nods eagerly; in this, the longest conversation she's had with her mother for years, she doesn't care if it makes sense or not. "Where is my Gilly; is he all right?"

Maggie nods; her words tumble out in relief, "He's fine, Mum; he would have come today but he had to go into Darlington to get some supplies for the shop." At the mention of the town, Violet looks around the room curiously and blinks, as if suddenly realising where she is. She stands up, moves to the window, her gaze scanning the grounds intently. A look of immense sadness crosses her face; she lapses into silence. "He'll be coming to say hello before we go, Mum."

Violet gives her a sidelong glance, nibbles at her lip, shaking her head to herself; seemingly deep in thought. She sniffs the flowers. "Can you ask him something for me, Ettie?"

Maggie hesitates, and then nods, "Of course."

Her mother's whisper becomes so faint she can hardly make out the words; "Ask him to bring the little ones to see me, please... I miss them terribly... make him bring them, he'll listen to you." Her mother turns to face her, stares into Maggie's eyes with an imploring look; then, to Maggie's horror, she drops onto her knees, "You must bring them, I beg you, please..."

Maggie swallows, avoiding her mother's eyes, her face burning. How can she promise that? Her father might allow it, but he'll take some persuading; so it's not within her power to promise it. She doesn't know what to say; biting her own lip, she shuts her eyes, trying to think, paralysed by her own uncertainty. "I'll ask him, Mum; but it would be better if you ask him yourself when he comes to pick me up. If you ask him yourself, he'll see how much better you are."

When she opens her eyes, the moment seems to have passed; Violet has returned to her chair, staring out of the window. Whatever Maggie says or does during the next hour and a half, she's met with the same blank silence and that vacant stare into the far, far distance. It feels as if a thick steel shutter has dropped behind her mother's eyes; a bomb-proof shutter, shielding Violet from any further communication, from the possibilities of further disappointment and hurt.

When her father reappears, Maggie makes one final effort. "We've been talking today, Dad. Mum seemed a lot better." She sees a tiny flicker of eye movement in her mother's face, presses on. "The first half hour I was here, Mum seemed back to her old self. Maybe the company on the ward is finally working. The matron said she's been better, too."

She hears her father take a deep breath; he moves forward, crouches by his wife, squeezing her hand gently, "How are you, love?" He talks to her gently about his own day, with humour and patience, but Violet remains statuesque, indifferent to him; for Maggie the look of hope and frustration on her father's face feels almost too much to bear.

"I guess it must have tired her out, Dad, that first half hour." She watches her father's face work, struggling with emotion. How cruel that he should have missed this opportunity; for another ten minutes Maggie observes, willing her mother to respond. She ponders her own actions; should I have been more positive, gone out on a limb to give her mother hope? If I had, would mum have carried on talking? She shakes herself; tells herself to let it go. "Tell you what, Dad. I'll go and get some fresh air. You have some time on your own with Mum; I'll see you back at the car." She leaves the building feeling despondent, wracked with guilt over her cautious response. I can be bold, sometimes, she tells herself. She looks back; in there, I feel like a frightened rabbit. Well, probably that's how my mother feels, too.

*   *   *

She jerks awake as the car stops, opens her eyes to see a tractor and trailer standing outside the Cross Keys. Her father waves his hand, "Looks like Billy Swinburne's tractor, he's a bit early; still, I suppose we're in for a busy night." Of course, she remembers; it's all over, at last. She wishes Pat were here to celebrate too; but at least he'll be safe, now.

As they step inside the kitchen door Grace appears, hands on hips, "Dad, thank goodness."

"What is it, Grace?"

"It's Billy; he's brought his Italian POW's in for a drink, to celebrate the end of the war. I've served them all once, but he wants to get them another round. Is that all right?"

Gilly scratches his head, "I suppose so; didn't they change sides, the Italians?"

"That's what Billy says. He said they all seemed really happy when he told them and all very rude about Hitler, too; says they're all good lads, hard workers."

"All right then; let's face it, Grace, we're going to run out of beer tonight, however we play it. I'll draw the line at German POW's; otherwise, the local lads will all take their business elsewhere. The Italians are a different matter; nobody minds them. Look, I'll take over in the bar now. You and Maggie can sort the girls out."

Grace gives Maggie an unusually long hug, whispering in her ear, "I bet you're missing Pat as much as I miss David."

"You can say that again. Do you know where David is?"

"Somewhere in Italy, believe it or not."

"I wondered why you didn't want to serve those boys. Where's your baby?"

"Oh, June and the others took him out in the pram; with him being a boy, they were all fussing him. They should be back soon."

"How is it up there on that farm, without David?"

"Oh, it's difficult; I don't really get on with his mother, you know. Occasionally she can be a help, but she's always criticising.

Little Daniel helps take my mind off it. Mind you, he's hard work too; though he's a good feeder, and sleeps a lot, too, so I can't complain." She shrugs, "It's not so bad, but I wish David were home."

"At least they're all safe now."

"Yes," Grace sighs. "David's brother Richard came home a couple of days ago. He was wounded in Normandy, got his discharge on medical grounds."

"What's he like?"

"Bit of a queer fish, Maggie. I was quite looking forward to it, but he's nothing like David - quite surly, in fact. I suppose I should feel sorry for him, with his bad leg, but when I try to talk to him he snaps at me. His mother did tell me that he and David used to fight like cat and dog. Always did, apparently."

"Is he staying long?"

"It's his home too; the problem is both of them want to take over the farm from their father. That's the root of it, and it won't get resolved until David comes home."

"That sounds like hard work, Grace..." A burst of singing erupts from the bar, an Italian chorus; Maggie gives a wry smile, "I wonder what they're singing..."

"Pat would know; and he'd make a better job of it." Grace sighs, "Still, we must make an effort tonight." She gives her sister a wicked grin. "I suppose our George will turn up again?"

Maggie shakes her head and laughs, "I'd put money on it, probably with a poetry book. He knows about Pat, but he never gives up."

"What's he up to now?"

"He qualified as a lawyer, though he won't practice because of his stammer. He's got some ministry job, going round checking the farms, clipboard in hand."

"Bert?"

"He'll turn up too, if he's not busy poaching."

Grace gives her sister a wink, "Oh well, there's always the Italian boys. I have to admit, some of them are rather dishy."

"They are, aren't they? I suppose that'll the highlight of our VE night, won't it?"

*   *   *

The couples move in slow circles around each other, like the hands of a clock. He wonders how many others around him are wishing that time did not exist, that this feeling could go on forever, of holding and being held. Her perfume mixes with the scent of spring blossoms in the air; he breathes her into him, savouring the effect on himself; putting him 'in the mood' while they dance to 'Moonlight serenade'. Among those seated at the surrounding tables, he detects a slightly forced atmosphere of gaiety. Out here in India, 'Victory in Europe' only holds out the promise of a peace yet to be arrived at. Who knows what lies in wait on this side of the world? He brushes the thought aside, breathes her in again. As the music hits the final note, she clings to him and whispers, "Another dance; I don't want tonight to end."

"Neither do I, Dotty. To be honest, I never do, with you; despite my dancing."

She steps back and looks up at him, checking his expression, snuggles back into him as another slow tune starts up, "I never know when you're serious or not."

"That's the Irish for you, Dotty; neither do we, half the time."

He feels a gentle kick. "That explains a lot of things; more than you realise, Paddy."

"Ah, you got me right, there; but at least I know what I want, right now."

"I can tell that. Fortunately for you, I probably feel the same way."

"Only probably?"

"I've got to find some way of keeping you on your toes. Speaking of which..." He feels her pull away, wave at someone behind him; he turns, sees Vic and Suhaila waving farewell.

He gives a wave, scratches his head; "Back to the married quarters already?"

"She's anxious about her pregnancy."

He watches them depart, arm in arm. "Is anything wrong?"

She purses her lips; "No more than usual," and holds him close again. "Put it this way, I'm glad I'm in my shoes and not in hers."

"I'm very glad to hear it; but also a tiny bit curious about your first comment."

"Oh, you know; how quickly they've become an old married couple. It doesn't really suit Vic very much, does it? He's not his usual self, is he?"

He has to laugh. "You're damn right, Dotty; I hadn't really thought about it, but it fits him like a pair of one legged pants on a horse."

She reaches up and whispers in his ear, "Well, I have a little theory about it, but you must keep it to yourself."

He pats her back. "Ah, you know me, Dotty, the very soul of discretion."

"You know what Vic's like, his opinions. Must be right at least ninety per cent of the time."

"If you're lucky..."

"And if you're male. Imagine what it's like for Suhaila;

personally, I think the only way she can get his attention or influence him is by being ill."

"Jesus, I can see that. It fits perfectly; clever girl, Dotty. Bit sad, though; and Vic certainly seems a bit cheesed off, now you point it out." He can't help also thinking, is that because of the marriage? Does something like that happen to every couple?

She seems to read his mind; "Don't worry, Paddy, you're not like him. You don't try to take over everything; that's very unusual, for a man. It's what I love about you."

"I know my limitations; that's all."

"Don't be silly, you probably just had a strong mother."

"I suppose I did; though I lost her, for a while."

She looks up at him. "Maybe that's why you're so cautious." She sighs.

"Am I?"

"In some ways; sometimes, you know, you're the exact opposite of Vic. Too patient." She puts her head on his shoulder. "Look, I just want to enjoy tonight; in fact, I want to enjoy every moment of our time together from now on. Don't you realise, Paddy, tonight is the beginning of the end? Of the war, I mean." He nods instantly at the truth of it; the idea troubles him a little. The music stops again; she grasps his shirt with both hands and whispers, "Kiss me, then; all night long." He needs no second invitation.

*   *   *

Pat feels - literally - on top of the world. But even here, on top of the mountain, the wind doesn't really whistle in his ears; rather, it creates a noise like canvas flapping in the distance. On the far side of the lake, the early afternoon sun sparkles; on the nearer half, the shadow of a cloud passes across the water. He gazes back down the path, humming the chorus of the Hebrew slaves.

Maggie picks her way up the steep slope, one hand holding a small picnic basket, the other balanced on her hip. She looks up, smiles at him in a way that makes him glow with pride, and brushes her hair back in that characteristic gesture of hers. Her hair glints red in the sun, glowing with health and vitality. He pulls out the blanket from his rucksack, lays it out and sits down; starts to sing, despite his own shortness of breath. She flops down in front of him wordlessly and rests her head against his chest. This is a song she knows, but she seems content just to listen and hum along, today. When he finishes, neither of them moves. Pat certainly feels perfectly contented, his arms wrapped about her, breathing in the smell of her hair. He has no wish to break this spell.

"I told you, didn't I, you'd like it here."

He nods, blows in her ear. "It has a few features in common with paradise, I'll give you that." He breathes her in again, nibbles her earlobe gently. "Mind you, with you for company I'd happily go along with Dante and enjoy the other place."

"Get away with you." Her tone of voice belies the message.

"I would, I would." He thinks for a moment; "What about you, Maggie? I mean, do you still feel the same way about me; now that the war's ended?"

She gives him a scornful look. "Of course I do; isn't it obvious?"

"I was hoping so; but how on this earth did you organise all of this?"

"It was Grace's idea. She misses David as much as I missed you; but I think she finds the in-laws really difficult. Organising this gave her a good excuse to go back home while we're here. And George told me about this farm; it belongs to some old friend of his father."

"What about your father?"

"He didn't like it but we talked him round. He likes you; and I'm almost twenty-one now."

"Old woman;" he feels the elbow hit his ribs, "not that I can talk." He sits back and breathes her in again, letting that deep feeling of contentment spread right through his body. "Look, I really do want us to be together, you know, now that it's over." He feels her take his hand and squeeze it. "I didn't ask before, because I wanted to make sure I was coming back."

He feels her sit up, turn her head. "Is this a proposal, Pat?"

He grunts and nods, to himself as much as to her. "I suppose it is, Maggie. A bit off the record, just yet, until I sort out a few things."

"Like a ring, for instance."

He chuckles, "That'll be one little essential, for sure, Maggie."

She sighs and leans back again; "Well, when you get yourself organised, I might just be ready to accept."

"Oh, I'm organised; I've got plans, don't you worry."

"I'm very glad to hear it. Maybe you could tell me about them, sometime."

He squeezes her waist, "All in good time." She digs him in the ribs with her elbow. He chuckles. "Would that be a little sign of curiosity? Tell you what, when you pour me some tea out of that thermos, I'll tell it all." Now it's her turn to tease him, by not moving; neither of them, it seems, want to rush this day. They watch a man in a rowing boat doing a spot of fishing down on the lake; he drifts motionless for a long time before his rod jerks into movement. As if in response, Maggie reaches for the basket. Pat watches her pour the tea; he sighs contentedly and clears his throat. "I've told you about my friend Frank, from New Zealand?"

"The man who saved your life?"

"That's him; we've stuck together since '42, him and I, and one or two others. He plays the flute, you see. The music brought us together; he's become my best mate."

"I'd like to meet him."

"You will, Maggie; I was planning to ask him to be best man." He notices a hint of a frown on her face. "I know what you're thinking - Paddy will be disappointed. But I can't have them both, can I?" She blushes, nods. "Anyway, to get back to the matter in hand - Frank's a Chief Officer right now, but he could skipper a ship anytime he wants. I'm Chief Engineer; between us we can run a ship;" he pauses a moment, "or ships."

Maggie tilts her head to one side, staring back at him. "This sounds interesting."

"I hope so. Another thing to consider is that his family have sheep farms in New Zealand; big ones, and they know other farmers. There's a surplus of meat there, and we have the connections to get hold of it."

He watches her take a deep breath, nod. "Go on..."

"Did you know the American army here in Europe eats mountains of beef steak?" He grins at the look of astonishment on her face. "Some of those liberty ships have enormous refrigerated holds. They built a whole fleet of ships to feed their army; most are now heading for the Pacific." He pauses to let this sink in. "Frank and I have saved our money, and his father knows a banker. Once Japan surrenders, we aim to buy one or two of those ships. They'll be surplus once the fighting's over. Europe is starving, and you know what good quality lamb costs. Frank's checked it all out. We'll have to work hard at first, Maggie, but it'll be our own work. In the long run, well, we'll never be poor, put it that way."

He watches her shake her head in disbelief; she inhales, blows air out of her cheeks, lifting her eyes to meet his again. "You're serious, aren't you?"

"Never more so..."

"It sounds... well, like a wonderful opportunity." She bites her lip. "I remember you talked once... about going to New Zealand; is this what you meant?"

"It is." He watches her brow furrowing.

"Would we have to live out there?"

He nods, watching her face, "I'm afraid so, Maggie. You can't run a business from the other side of the world." She looks down at the floor, biting her lip. "It's a beautiful country, Maggie. Not too different from this, except the mountains are bigger."

"Isn't there any way we could stay here, Pat? I mean, for a few years, anyway? It's little Ellen, mainly, but the others... and my father...they all rely on me."

"I know, Maggie; too much, in some ways, though that's the way it is. Listen - we wouldn't be going immediately. Nothing will happen until the Japanese are defeated, and that'll probably take another year at least. Frank and I are just going to do short runs, stay close to England, till then. He's got a girl in London, so that suits us both. I reckon we've got probably between one to two years to make all our preparations. Your sisters will all be a little bit older, and they're stronger than you think. They'll find a way to cope without you; your father, too. We could even take little Ellen with us, if that's what you want."

"Oh, Pat..." she shakes her head, her eyes misty. "That's a lovely idea but I know my father wouldn't want that." She sniffs, trying to smile. "I'm sorry... well; it's a difficult idea to swallow, in more ways than one. It's just so far away... it makes me think I'd never see any of them again."

"That's not how it would be, Maggie; the travel's not as difficult as you think, believe me. If the business goes as planned, you'll be able to come back every so often."

"Would we; how often?"

He shrugs. "I don't know...every couple of years, if things go well."

She takes a deep breath, settles back against him, apparently satisfied with this answer. She wipes her eyes and sniffs again. She talks, as if thinking aloud. "I suppose I'll have to talk to Grace first. She's the most likely to understand. June probably could do more, but she'll find it all difficult, emotionally. She'll hate the idea of me going away; they all will. I suppose it won't be so bad if they have a year or two to prepare themselves." She takes a deep sigh. "It's Dad I feel most sorry for. I'm not sure how he'll react."

Pat squeezes the top of her shoulders, massaging her collar bones as he talks. "He'll want what's best for you; and that's the main reason for going out there, Maggie. I have zero prospects in Ireland, and after this little war my guess is that England will be bankrupt too, with far more sailors than it'll need in peacetime. We can build a new life out there for ourselves and for our children, better than we could ever have here. Your father will understand that better than anyone."

She sits silent, for a long time. He begins to relax, thinking that she has understood, at last. She speaks, finally, in a deceptively soft voice. "Would you still propose if I told you that I couldn't be uprooted, that I didn't want to leave?"

He feels shocked, uncertain; he didn't anticipate this at all. He thinks hard, lets the silence grow. Eventually, he lets out a long groan. "Please, please don't put me in that position. I suppose I'd marry you anyway, but you'd be making me give up a chance to really make something decent of our future. It wouldn't be the best way to start a marriage, now would it?"

She nods, "No, I can see that. But you have to realise how difficult the whole thing would be for me, Pat."

"I do, Maggie, I do; but we'll make it work, and in the long run you won't regret it."

She sighs again, "I hope not; look, I'll try to start preparing myself, first. That's the first step. See if I can get *my* head around the idea. Then I'll work out what to do about Ellen and the others. I'll try my best. It may not work out as easily as you think - I might have to follow you out there after six months. Who knows? But I will do my best." He feels a flood of relief, wraps his arms back around her. "One other thing, Pat; let's not talk about this anymore while we're here. We'll just try and enjoy our time together now. The future can wait a while longer."

He pulls her backwards to the ground, turns her over; begins to kiss her. After a little token resistance, she begins to respond.

*   *   *

Maggie rocks carefully from side to side; Ellen, lying slumped over her shoulder, grumbles quietly as her little body relaxes, her eyelids drifting together. She sees her own closeness with Ellen mirrored across the kitchen table, where Grace feeds her baby. "What does it feel like?"

Grace looks up, gives her a quizzical look, "Feeling broody, are you?"

"Not particularly, just curious."

Her sister gives a half smile, as if she doesn't believe her. "Oh, I like it. It hurt a bit at first, but you get used to it. There's something lovely about it. You'll be fine." She flashes her sister a grin. "Look at the two of us, anyway. Who'd have thought it, a few years ago? I know she's not yours, but you'd never guess it."

"Don't remind me." She feels a stab of guilt; what will happen to Ellen, if she leaves? "I still don't really know what to do."

"Have you talked to Dad yet?"

"No; you're the only person I've told. I'm waiting for the right moment. You know what Dad's like; you have to catch him in the right mood. And he's feeling bad at the moment because we didn't visit Mum last week."

Grace looks up, sharply, "Why not?"

"No petrol; apparently he didn't get the right number of coupons. I offered to go on the buses but June wasn't feeling well either, so in the end I couldn't."

Grace gives a deep sigh, moves the baby from one breast to the other. "That's unfortunate. I missed my visit too, the week before."

Maggie feels her heart sink. "Oh, dear, does Dad know about that?"

"No, probably better not to tell him." Grace frowns, her voice suddenly serious. "Maggie, I didn't know what to do. I got as far as Stanhope and discovered most of my money was gone. I had to borrow the fare to get home, so I went to see May, and spent the afternoon there. I was too ashamed to tell her the full story. The thing is I think David's brother must have taken it out of my purse. He disappeared off to the pub in Westgate that day, came back late after a skin full."

"Oh, Grace." Maggie's tone of voice expresses her disgust.

"I know; but I couldn't say a thing, his mother would just take his side. She always does. If I say anything about him, she jumps down my throat." Grace frowns, "To be honest, the last few weeks have been hell. He lies about the house, leering at me, taking every chance he has to stir his mother up against me - which doesn't take a lot."

"That really is terrible. Have you heard anything from David?"

"I had a letter." Her face brightens, "He sounds fine, but he's no idea when he'll get home. It can't be too long, surely?" She laughs, a little bitterly. "Otherwise, I'll be asking Dad if I can move back in here."

"It's not that bad, is it?"

"It is. You know, we've both been left holding the baby. It would be so much easier for me if David were here, in all sorts of ways, for me and for the baby. And for you too - I can't even ask David about Ellen until he's been back a while."

"I know that."

"And you could do with Pat being here a while longer, next time, to help *you* out. He should be the one talking to Dad about New Zealand."

"I hadn't thought of that; I suppose that would be more traditional, really." Her father might expect that, Maggie thinks.

"How long is he away for?"

"It's supposed to be a short trip, this time; the trouble is they never know exactly how long it'll be. I'm not sure I can wait indefinitely."

"I know how you feel." Grace detaches a sleepy baby from her breast, adjusts her blouse, lifts Daniel and pats his back. "Have you heard from Paddy recently?"

"I have, actually. He sounds in good form; still quite happy out there, by the sound of him."

"Has he forgiven me yet?"

"Oh, yes; he was never one to bear a grudge, Grace. Besides, he's got himself a girl over there. Sounds quite keen on her; they go away together whenever he has leave."

"Thank goodness for that." Maggie frowns; Grace adds, hastily, "I mean, that will be good for *him*. It's about time he had something that lasted." She gives her sister a wicked grin.

Maggie blushes and shrugs, "I suppose you're right, but he's very mysterious about this girl. It makes me wonder if she's a married woman."

"Really? That would be a turn up for the books... I hope they won't send him to the front, if it's the general's wife... "

"Oh Grace, don't say such things..." Her sister catches her eye; they both start to giggle at the same moment.

*   *   *

She watches her father moving around the side room that serves as the post office, sweeping the floor rhythmically while he whistles 'It's a long way to Tipperary...' He seems in a good mood today, she thinks; perhaps I'll try and talk to him, later. She finishes unlocking the drawers and fishes out everything she needs; various forms, postage stamps, and ledgers. When she looks up, her father's watching her, leaning on his brush. "Did you hear the news on the radio this morning?"

She gives him a rueful smile. "You know I didn't, Dad, I was walking Rose to the station while June looked after Ellen." It must be good news, she thinks. "Go on, what did I miss?"

"We've dropped some kind of new bomb on Japan, some kind of secret weapon. They sounded quite excited about it. Seem to think it'll shorten the war."

"Do they? That would be good." She thinks for a moment. "Did they say anything about it? Is it like those V2 rockets, do you think?"

"More like about twenty of those in one go, perhaps; they said there was an enormous dust cloud over the place where it exploded. It sounded like some new type of explosive. Point is, if they've got lots of these things, the Japanese won't stand a chance."

"Poor devils; I mean, the people on the ground."

"Yes, but a short war's better that way, than a long war. I was thinking of Paddy."

"I know you were, Dad." It occurs to her, that if this does shorten the war, she'll have less time to prepare herself, and everyone else. She tries to swallow, feels a knot of anxiety. "Dad; there's something I need to..."

At that moment, the telephone rings; they look at each other, warily. It's been quite a while since anyone in the village had bad news. "Better pick it up, Maggie."

She nods, lifts the receiver, "Hello; Eastgate Post Office here."

"Hello, Maggie." She recognises the voice; Amy, the operator at the exchange in Stanhope. "That Irish sailor your family knows, who sings, is his name Pat MacMahon?"

Maggie sighs, imagining the gossip. That's village life for you, she thinks. "Yes, that's him, Amy." She has a sudden terrifying thought – not now surely, not in peacetime – though she knows, it does happen, sometimes. She swallows her fear, and waits.

"Is he there, by any chance?"

She exhales, feels the relief flooding through her. "No, I'm afraid not, he's away at sea at the moment. He left about a month ago."

"Will he be coming back any time soon?" She stifles an urge to tell Amy to mind her own business; the exchange girls listen in to all sorts of things. She makes her voice sound casual.

"I expect we'll see him again, but I don't know when."

"Can you take a message for him? Give it to him when you next see him?"

"I suppose so." She remembers his brothers, in Ireland; she knows Pat has been meaning to contact them. "Is it family?"

"Yes, it is; hold the line and I'll connect you. It's sounds as if it might be important."

"All right," Maggie hears a click; the line goes silent. She mouths the word 'Pat' to her father; he nods and shrugs, a slight frown of concern on his face. Long distance calls are rare; they don't often bring good news. She hears another click, and a voice with an accent speaks.

"Hello, can you take a message for Pat MacMahon? Is that the place where he goes to stay, up in the hills?" Maggie feels puzzled; the voice is female and the accent, though thick, is not Irish.

"Yes, this is the post office and pub at Eastgate; Pat stays here sometimes. He sings in our pub, but he's away at sea right now." Who is this woman, anyway?

"Would you take a message for him? In case you see him before I do?"

She stifles her curiosity, keeping her voice neutral. "Yes, we can do that."

"Just tell him Lily wants a divorce. I need his agreement."

She listens to the words but can't make sense of them. "Pardon; who am I speaking to?"

"I'm Lily; Pat's wife. Tell him I want to re-marry, properly, so I need a divorce."

Maggie drops the phone; she hears herself give a little cry of pain and steps back as if the phone were a snake that has reared up and bit her. She stands, frozen in shock; she watches her father pick up the phone and repeat the conversation almost word for word. He bites his lip, shakes his head, and carefully replaces the receiver. Then he puts his arm around her, leads her into the kitchen, and sits her down. She watches him go into the bar and return with a large brandy, which he sets in front of her. "I'm sorry, lass. I'd never have let him in the house, if I'd known."

She buries her head in her arms and begins to sob. She'd always known he had secrets, parts of his life he didn't like to talk about, but this? It doesn't make any sense. It doesn't fit with the Pat *she* knows.

* * *

He's been trying to get through to Delhi for hours. The lines are jammed; it takes a couple of minutes just to speak to the local operator, if he's lucky. The sweat trickles down his neck; he leans back, tilting his face towards the electric fan that slowly rotates above his desk. This part of the job, he hates. Today, it's literally giving him a headache, adding to a growing knot of anxiety that settled in his stomach a couple of days ago. He feels an urge to throw the telephone through the window just as Vic's head pops into view, grinning at him. "Paddy, you have to come with me. We're taking our photographs now, with *all* the officers and men."

He listens to the silence on the telephone for a moment longer, "Right now?"

Vic nods, "Now; the war's over, remember?"

"Oh, is it? I was wondering why I've spent the last two days trying to cancel all the equipment orders I put in last month. Not to mention undoing all my training arrangements for the next couple of months." He remarks into the mouthpiece, pointedly, "But no one seems to be answering their phones, anywhere."

Vic shrugs; "We're not even *trying* to use our telephones. Give it a day or two."

Paddy hangs up the receiver and wipes his brow. "That doesn't fit with *my* orders. But then, my orders seem to be bloody impossible to carry out, so you're probably right." He stands up and grabs his cap. "Christ, I could do with a break anyway; just to have some space to think."

They walk in silence towards the Indian half of the compound; Paddy feels a comforting arm slip across his shoulders. "I know it must be hard for you, Paddy. It's come as a shock to all of us. We thought another year, at least; and now... who knows..."

He swallows, feels his stomach tighten a notch. He grunts his assent, not trusting his voice to speak, squeezes his friend's shoulder. They walk on; Vic's arm a tangible reminder of his attachment to this place, this country. Eventually he clears his throat and speaks, husky with emotion, "That's just it; I've really enjoyed my time here. In a curious way, I feel quite at home."

Vic squeezes his shoulder in response, "Strange as it may seem, I know what you mean. Suhaila talks about the army as my alternative family; for me it always felt like that. A family in which I could breathe - I always felt so stifled, at home." Paddy nods and bites his lip; like brothers, he thinks; that's what he's telling me. "And this war has brought us, both our armies, together into one family. Well, most of us; the ones that we're bringing together for these photographs, anyway. Men like you, who have lived and worked with us, together."

"I wondered whether this was official or not." Nearing the Indian mess, they pick their way through clusters of men and officers.

"It is for us, Paddy; these are our official photographs, for posterity. But we are inviting selected British soldiers to join us as our guests, one last time, before the family breaks up." The knot in his gut tightens; he feels as if he is hanging on a rope above a chasm of loss.

He sniffs, fighting back a surge of emotion. "Ah now, it's a job well done when soldiers make themselves redundant; so they say, anyway." He spots a familiar face; right now, he needs to distract himself from these emotions - standing with Vic isn't going to help. "Tell you what Vic; I'll have a chat with Melsonby until you're ready for us." Vic flashes him a sideways look and nods.

Years later, whenever he picks up these particular photographs they will never fail to bring a surge of affection into his chest. He, Melsonby, and the other British soldiers are surrounded by a sea of grinning Indian officers and men; marked out not just by their complexion, but by garlands of flowers hung around their necks over chests that seem to burst with pride.

Back at his desk an hour later, Paddy stares at the phone, glances at his watch; he's no further forward. Voices approach; more distractions, preparations for the party to end all parties, he wonders? A familiar voice calls out, "Come on, Reilly."

"What is it now, sir?"

"Photographs; the Colonel commands our presence."

In the courtyard, he plonks himself down at the end of the front row of chairs and glances along at the others, checking their appearance. It's cooler now; he sees open collars, normal battledress, just like him. Relief at this helps him to settle back, just for a moment. "Come on, chaps, give us a smile; that's it." He hears the click of the camera; too late, he thinks, even if he felt like smiling. He hopes this is the last photograph of the day; no garlands, here.

"I have a few announcements." He looks up again, sees the

Colonel standing where the photographer had been. "First, I'm afraid I have no definite plans or dates to give anyone yet; but as I'm sure you've realised by now, as a result of the Japanese surrender most of our work here becomes unnecessary. And before you ask, I have no idea what an atomic bomb is or how it works; so don't ask me about that, either. But in regard of our work here, the general principle is that the majority of the training staff will be sent home first, then the signals intelligence staff. The latter will go in stages; about half of you will probably remain here for a while." He looks up and smiles, "I expect a variety of reactions to this news." Paddy hears polite laughter, excited muttering. "Some of you will be sent to Germany as part of the army of occupation; you'll all be given the chance to apply for rapid demobilisation if that's what you prefer. Knowing the army as I do, gentlemen, I would advise that you don't rely on this having any impact at all on the outcome. But whatever happens, good luck to you all. I would like to thank all of you for your hard work and say what a pleasure it has been to serve with you; with no exceptions." He hears a collective murmur of approval. "Finally, on to more pressing matters; as you all know, today has been designated VJ day. As such, I am now commanding you to stop work immediately - apart from the unfortunate duty officer, who drew the short straw." He holds his hand up as a ragged cheer breaks out, "Lots of sympathy for Lieutenant Hanratty, I see; anyway, this is an exceptional evening. As such, we have agreed that the British Officers mess will have an open door policy this evening. You'll still have to sign people in, but bring anyone you like, females included; I mean *anyone*."

A voice calls out, "How many guests, sir?"

"You can't sell tickets, Lieutenant. But let's say a maximum of four per member." He glances around. "That's it, then; off you go."

Paddy sits in his chair, feeling relief; at last, he can abandon his fruitless efforts to contact Delhi. He feels a tap on his shoulder; "Coming to the bar, sir, to celebrate?"

He turns, sees a group of eager young faces. "Sure, but not right away; see you in about half an hour." He tries to make himself relax; waits patiently for the small crowd around the Colonel to shrink, the knot of anxiety in his stomach tightening until his turn arrives. "I was wondering if there was any chance of switching roles, sir, so I can stay on a bit. I was expecting I'd be here a while longer; banking on it, in fact."

The Colonel pulls a face, stares at the floor. "Weren't we all? I'm really sorry, Reilly, but there's no chance of that. I have to give priority to officers who've been here longest. And that won't be you, will it?" His tone is sympathetic, but unbending, as he lifts his eyes. Oh Christ, Paddy thinks; that's going to spoil the party tonight.

She stops in her tracks when she sees him, perhaps surprised that he's come to meet her outside the hospital. Or perhaps, he thinks, looking at her eyes, she's simply as exhausted as I am.

He waves, hurries forward, "I managed to get hold of a jeep tonight, Dotty; but I couldn't get through on the phone to tell you."

She nods, "I know; everything's been impossible the last couple of days. I couldn't get off sooner. At least I managed to change out of my uniform, so I don't need to go home first. Some of the girls have done a bunk, you know; it's been crazy." She puts her arm upon his, but does not lean in to kiss him, as she usually does.

"This way...I had a hell of a day, too. Everything's being dismantled; it feels awful. I'm probably going to get roaring drunk tonight."

She looks at him suspiciously, "You sound as if you already are."

"I had to have a couple with my Lieutenants before I left; by the way, the British mess is having an open night tonight. I'd like to take you there, just for once." She considers this, shrugs. "Shall I take you there?"

"Why? Do you want to show me to your British friends before you go?"

Dammit, he thinks; "It's not that, at all. I just thought, for once..."

"I'd want to be at their beck and call? No thanks."

He curses under his breath; he wants to tell her, even if it weren't open night, I'd want to take you, to tell them all to sod off, to show them who I care about, now that the war's over; the army will get rid of me soon enough, anyway. But what will that sound like to her ears, at this particular moment in time? Who knows?

After a long silence, she adds, "Do you know anything yet?"

"Nothing certain, Dotty."

"I know you'll be going home soon, Paddy; there's no use pretending."

"I suppose not, Dotty." He gives her a sideways look as he drives. She looks calm enough. "If you must know, I did ask if I could transfer and stay on here, but the C.O. told me it was impossible. He's a decent type; I think he would've helped if he could."

She bites her lip and nods. "Thank you for that." She turns away and wipes her eyes. "I'm sorry, Paddy. I'm a bit fragile, as you can imagine."

"I know; I feel the same."

"Do you? Do you really?" Her tone is full of doubt.

He puts his foot on the brake; the jeep screeches to a halt. He turns to face her. "Of course I do. All day, I've felt in a panic. Time is suddenly running out and I don't know how to stop it. It's been like sitting on a bomb; it's driving me crazy." She nods, but won't look him in the eyes. "I thought I had another year, Dotty."

She looks up at him with dark, tearful eyes. "I know, but that's gone, now; all we can do is to enjoy the time we do have, however short. Remember what I told you in Mussourie; some people have much less time together, some people have *no* time like this." She leans on his chest, puts her arms around him, and seems to summon up her strength. Eventually, she whispers, "Now you can take me to the Indian mess, because for once I am the one who is going to get roaring drunk."

She becomes, that evening, a fountain of gaiety; he marvels at this, at her strength of will, to be able to do this. He knew she had a brain on her, a quiet competence and determination, but he has never seen her shine quite like this before; the life and soul of the party. He makes no attempt to compete - as if he could - he sits back and tries to complement her mood with his own quiet, dry, Irish wit. He moderates his own drinking too, out of concern that he may have to carry her home. In doing so, he remains sober enough to reflect how easily they work together in a social situation, how compatible they seem. It finally dawns upon him that this is exactly the kind of woman he wants to have by his side when he does get home, whatever anyone else thinks. He feels a strong urge to propose to her while they are dancing; he resists this, deciding instead to wait until they are alone in her room. He rehearses his speech in the back of a rickshaw taxi. Outside her apartment, she suddenly turns, biting her lip, "Do you want to come up?"

He starts to laugh, then sees that she's not joking. "Of course I do, Dotty. Why on earth do you ask me that tonight?"

She gives him a brittle smile, "It could be the last time, you know. So I don't want to spoil it all with some kind of scene; I'd rather end it here and now, standing here, with good memories." She takes a deep breath; "So if you come up you must promise not to try to talk about us. You can come to bed with me and hold me as usual, but when you go in the morning you have to pretend it's a normal day. Those are my conditions." He scratches his head, unable to comprehend her meaning. Why's she saying this? Is she just too exhausted?

He has no choice, really, but to agree. Eventually, he shrugs. "I won't make a scene, that's the last thing I want." She waits; staring at him, insistently. "All right, then, I agree."

She puts her finger on his lips, signifying silence. "Come on then." He follows her up the stairs, still trying to make sense of her words. What dreadful scene is she imagining? Can he ask her to marry him, without breaking his word to her? Or should he just leave the proposal for another day? In other circumstances, maybe; but the way things are, he may not even get another chance...

He waits for her in the bed, placing a new sheath under his pillow where he can reach it easily. She blows out the candle, turns her back to him as she climbs in; her signal that she is exhausted, she only wishes to sleep. Yet she also reaches behind her and guides his hands around her body; "Just hold me now; I may wake you up later." He does as she asks; though his own desire for her rises, smelling her hair and cupping her breasts in his hands for what seems an eternity. He feels pinned down between conflicting expectations, his and hers; unable to move physically, unable to make a decision. Finally he drifts away into sleep.

He finds himself back on a bridge in Fermoy, a small boy pinned down by a large adult body lying on top of him. He can only watch, helpless, while his closest friend is dragged away from him, about to disappear completely, to God knows where...

He jerks awake again, his body throwing him back into the present with a spasm of panic. He wonders how much time has elapsed, listens to his own breathing slow while he tries to calm his mind. Her breathing, too, seems irregular. "You awake?"

After a pause, she sighs and whispers, "Yes."

He swallows, "Can I say one thing?"

"What is it?"

"I don't want to say goodbye in the morning. I don't want to say goodbye at all. I want you to come to England with me. I'll marry you, if that's you want."

She lies perfectly still, unmoving, for a minute, saying nothing. He begins to feel tiny movements, interruptions to her breathing, and muffled noises in the pillow. Christ, he thinks, she's crying. His instinct tells him not to say anything more; for a moment, he begins to hope that they are tears of joy. The noises slowly subside. "I knew this would happen; I told you, no talking."

"Christ, Dorothy, I just proposed to you."

She moves away from him, sits at the edge of the bed. "I've thought about this for a long time, Paddy. I made this decision and promised myself I would stick to it. I judge people by their actions, not their words; and by *how* they act. If you had asked me last year, or even six months ago, I would have said yes. And I also decided then, that if you asked me at the last minute I would say no. It was the only way that I could judge whether you loved me *enough*. You see, this feels like you are just feeling sorry for me."

He sits up. "Christ, Dotty, this wasn't *meant* to be the last minute. I thought we had a year yet." She does not respond, so he adds, "I have been thinking about it for a long time, too."

"But you never *did* anything about it, Paddy, until the last minute." Oh Christ, he thinks, holding his head in his hands. She's not going to listen, whatever I say.

He makes one last effort. "Look, Dorothy, please don't do this. I really do care about you, but I'm not very good at this. Before I met you I'd never really known a woman before. I had no idea how special you are and I took you for granted, at first. I'm sorry. But that's why I was so slow making up my mind. Please, please believe me."

"Now you are making me angry. You were engaged to someone else, Paddy. You are a handsome English officer more than thirty years old, so don't pretend you are some kind of innocent. Now either you can be silent or you can go, I will tolerate no more of this scene."

He bites back a curse and throws himself back down, turning his back on her. The bed moves as she lies down, too. Their physical separation lasts about a minute; he simply can't bear such rage and bitterness, the idea of feeling this way about her. He turns over and holds her again. They seem to lie for hours, unable to sleep, trapped in their own separate thoughts. Then, at some point in the restless dark eternity of that night, she turns over, kisses his chest once; a small crack in the dam. Instantly aroused, he responds by caressing her breasts; the dam weakens, begins to split. She slowly scratches his back, raking it up and down twice. His own longing and rage erupt; he grasps her hair, falls upon her and crushes her body while she devours him, yet also tries to wrestle him away. Both their bodies are swept away in an angry, animal passion, a feast of desire; filling their bellies before the famine. He seems to float above their bodies, mentally marrying his soul with hers, looking down while he pins her flesh to the earth. His sense of a spiritual coupling slowly rises, soaring into something ecstatic; finally, their flesh explodes in a frenzy of need, followed by sweet pain as the sensation of unity fades. Even as he lies there recovering his breath he feels her fingers gently trace a seal over his lips; reminding him of his promise.

He can't stand this craziness any longer; he swings himself away and dresses quietly in the dark. He plants two final kisses on damp eyes, silently leaves her room and descends the stairs to walk back to his bungalow.

There, in the wreckage of the living room, he finds scattered bottles and glasses; plus a loudly snoring Melsonby lying on the couch. He toasts the man's unconscious body with some remnants while he watches a new dawn rise.

* * *

Something's going on in the kitchen, judging by the noise and laughter; probably, Grace has come to visit, or one of her aunts. She rubs her eyes; she actually managed a decent amount of sleep last night, for the first time in weeks. She notices how light it is, feels her heart leap into her mouth - she's slept in, what about the little ones? Then she remembers, relaxes again. It's Saturday, her birthday; June volunteered to sort them all out today. She sits up in bed, looks around and sees the photographs lying scattered on the floor where they fell out of her hands. She cried herself to sleep looking at them last night; perhaps that had helped, a little. She slips out of bed, gathers them up carefully and slides them back into the oilskin envelope, placing the one of Paula at the bottom of the pile. She had thought her rival was only a ghost; now, she's not quite so sure. Her hope and her logic keep trying to convince her that Lily isn't a threat in terms of Pat's affections; after all, she wants to divorce him. Is this woman the real reason Pat was so insistent on living in New Zealand, to get away from her? Now, there might be no need. She still feels hurt and angry at the deception, but she might be willing to forgive him as long as he has not been stringing her along, two-timing her. Something tells her that, for all his faults, Pat wouldn't do that. That is certainly what she needs to know. She goes to the bathroom, dresses, and goes downstairs.

The muffled voices cease when she opens the door and steps into the kitchen; she stares at a row of grinning faces, all turned towards her – she almost jumps when a chorus of excited voices wish her happy birthday. Her father, his sisters, and two of her mother's sisters lean against the walls; her own younger sisters cluster around the kitchen table. They suddenly part to reveal a cake, then converge upon her, "We saved up our eggs, Maggie..."

"Dad thought you could do with cheering up, sis..."

"Ellen helped me bake it; well, she licked the bowl, anyway..."

She opens her arms, allows them to hug her in turn, feeling Ellen tugging at her skirt until she bends to pick her up. Then it's her aunts' turn, finally her father. She finds herself sniffling, unable to speak. He whispers in her ear, "Just wanted you to know that we're all thinking of you."

The day passes in a warm blur of shared affection. The girls present her with gifts; a crayon picture from Ellen, a bag of sweets from Harriet, a hat knitted by Rose, and some face powder from June. The aunts insist on taking her shopping, all the way to Bishop Auckland on the train, to choose herself a new coat for the winter. She's treated to lunch there in the Lyons café. Only later, back at her home, does she wonder, where's Grace? Her father scowls, when she asks. "All I can say is, she promised she'd come. She can't be relied on, that girl."

His tone is flat, as if someone has drained the energy out of him.

Something's wrong. "What's the matter, Dad?"

"Oh it's nothing, I'll tell you tomorrow."

"Tell me now, Dad." She surprises herself, the firmness in her tone.

He gives her a rueful look, shrugs. "The damned hospital rang to tell me not to visit tomorrow. They had to sedate her today; they don't want her excited again tomorrow." For once, he drops his pretence; he clenches his fists, looks up at the heavens and exhales a sound somewhere between a groan and a whimper. "You know, I've been hoping and hoping she'll have another good day; just one more, but on a day when I visit her. Ever since that day she was so much better, I've been hoping; just one day, one bloody day when I can talk to her again. You've no idea how much I'd give for that, Maggie."

"Oh, Dad," She moves toward him, to comfort him, but he holds up his hand.

"Sorry, lass; I shouldn't burden you with my troubles, not today." He stares at her for a moment, a look of respect. "You've enough of your own. I'd best open the bar before someone breaks the door down; I'm best keeping busy when I'm feeling like this." Before she can object, he's gone; she sits, brooding a while, before going into the garden to join her sisters. Grace finally arrives after supper; she and Maggie retreat to the kitchen.

"I'm really sorry, Mags." She pushes a small parcel wrapped in fancy paper across the table.

Maggie studies her sister's face; the haunted, exhausted look, the dark rims under her eyes. She gives a wry smile, "You look like I feel."

"You've no idea." When Grace looks up her eyes flare with anger. "I meant to come this morning but David's parents had to go to a wedding. So Richard chose today to be ill; I had to stay with him. He made out it was something serious, at first, so I couldn't get away this morning."

"You make it sound like he was faking it."

"I'm damned sure he was, Maggie."

"Really; why do say that?"

"Well, he made a dramatic recovery once I'd put Daniel down for his afternoon nap." She sighs, "Keep this to yourself; Maggie. But suddenly, as soon as Daniel's down, he's following me around and telling me how much better he feels and it's all due to me. Telling me how lovely I look, trying to get me to sit next to him, and telling me how lonely it must be for me without David." She shakes her head, "He gives me the creeps."

"How awful; what did you do?"

"I told him that I was married to his brother and even if I wasn't, he's the last man on earth I'd be attracted to. That shut him up for a while. Then he started saying he'd just been trying to be nice to me and I'd got it all wrong. Told me that I'd misunderstood him, and suddenly he felt ill again and went back to bed."

"Thank goodness for that. What on earth would David say?"

"That's the problem, Maggie, if David ever heard any of this, he'd kill Richard; it would cause the most unholy row. That's why you mustn't breathe a word to anyone."

Maggie shakes her head, slowly, and bites her lip. "Have you heard anything from David yet? About coming home?"

"No, he's stuck in Germany at the moment. He has no idea when he'll get home leave, or anything. Tell you the truth; I'm sick to the teeth of David's family. I've decided to ask Dad if I can move back here until David returns."

"When?"

"No time like the present." She points at the parcel, "Go on, open it, while I go and ask him." Maggie looks down and blushes; she'd quite forgotten. She opens it carefully, trying to preserve the paper, and discovers a blue cashmere scarf. She feels the softness, rubbing it against her cheeks. She detects a faint smell of expensive perfume; otherwise it seems pristine. Where in the world did it come from? For that matter, where in the world is Pat right now?

The door opens; Grace breezes back in, her face neutral. Her eyes fix on the scarf. "Well?"

"It's lovely, just my colour; where on earth did you get it?"

"David sent a few things. Black market, I should think; probably traded for cigarettes - that's what they do, I'm told."

"It's lovely. It'll go nicely with my new coat." She tilts her head. "Any luck with Dad?"

Grace shakes her head briefly; purses her lips and shrugs. "Not today. He seems to think Mum might suddenly get better and need her room again. Also, that Paddy might be back any moment too. Basically, he told me *my* place was to be there for David when *he* gets home."

"Maybe if you try and explain things..."

"God, no, Mags; you know Dad, he'd be worse than David. It would just be war between families, rather than within one. No, I'll just have to be a bit more patient with Dad. He'll come round in time; he usually does; especially if *you* have a word in his ear."

"Of course I will." She feels a flush of guilt; if Grace hadn't missed her birthday this morning, maybe her father wouldn't have been so tough with her. Poor Grace, her timing was awful... maybe I should have warned her... but she gave me no time to think about it...

* * *

Vikram strides across the wet dew of the lawn, his wide smile signalling the warmth and sense of mischief lying at the heart of their friendship. The expression falters at the last moment as the two men regard each other at close quarters, each trying to fix the memory of this farewell into their brains. "So, this is it."

"Afraid so, Vic; it's rather snuck up on us, hasn't it? You'll have to say goodbye to Mussoorie for me; not to mention Suhaila, little Anjou and the new Mittal. Ranjan, isn't it?"

Vic nods, "They'll miss their Nunky Paddy." He shrugs, "As will I. Suhaila sent this for you. I think it's her curry masala; about a year's supply, I'd say." He hands over a parcel wrapped in brown paper, pulls out a cardboard folder from his tunic. "These are for you, too. I had them taken last time I was at home."

Paddy opens the folder carefully, revealing two large black and white portraits; one of the whole Mittal family, the other of Vic in uniform, inscribed 'See you again.' He sniffs, blinking to prevent his tears. "I hope so, Vic, though God only knows when that will be." He turns, places the parcel into the top of his kitbag, and pulls out a bottle wrapped in brown paper. "I managed to wheedle a bottle of Irish out of our mess steward." Vic's wide grin tells him that he's chosen well. "And I want Anjou to have my tennis racket."

Vic nods; his gaze flickers sideways as the whine of a jeep ascending the hill disturbs the early morning calm. "Did you manage to see her at all?"

Paddy shakes his head, pulls a face. "She wouldn't answer my calls; when I did manage to get through, they invariably told me she was too busy. I tried going up to the hospital in person but they told me she wasn't at work that day; when I went to her apartment her mother told me she wouldn't speak to me."

"You could write to her from England."

"What's the point? She won't answer, will she? It's crazy, Vic, I just don't understand it. It doesn't make sense; she always said she was crazy about me."

He feels Vic squeezing his arm; "I did warn you about her pride."

He meets Vic's gaze, "So you did."

He feels another squeeze; "But I don't think it's just that, Paddy. You know what she said about you not caring enough?" Paddy bites his lip and nods. "Well, maybe it's the other way round. However you look at it, you asked her; you were the one who was prepared to take the risk, and she said no. Perhaps in reality she was the one who did not love you enough." Outside on the road, a vehicle pulls up and honks its horn.

For the last few days, Paddy has been fighting an urge to go

AWOL, to force Dorothy to speak to him by attempting to remain in India, to show her that he would be willing to do this for her. The idea has been torturing him; it seems to be the only thing he can do, yet is so patently self-destructive in every other way. Why repeat his past catastrophe? How could he outrun the army again here? They'd throw the book at him, this time. Nonetheless, the urge had been growing stronger as the last possible opportunity approaches; the notion he must do this, to show her how he feels. Vic's words kill this idea, once and for all. "Maybe;" he sighs, "perhaps you're right."

"You shouldn't worry about her future, Paddy; if she needs help, I'll look after her." Behind him, Paddy hears Abdul Huq's footsteps, carrying his kitbag to the vehicle.

The two friends embrace; the half-forgotten words tumble out of his mouth, "Beannacht de, a chara." After a pause, Paddy adds, "That means God bless you, friend, in Irish."

Vic slaps his back, "Go with God." He steps back and salutes, wheels around and marches back across the lawn the way he has come; the horn sounds again, impatiently.

At the airport, he and three companions devour a healthy breakfast before being driven onto a hot, dusty runway. At one end, a Stirling bomber sits, engines idling, apparently waiting for them. They climb into the belly of the beast; a Flight Sergeant hands them each a flying jacket. "You'll need these; it's cold up there and there's no heating back here." He points at mattresses and blankets, scattered on the floor. "Make yourselves as comfortable as you can."

"How long's the flight?"

"Christ, didn't they tell you? Three days." He laughs at the expressions on their faces. "Don't worry; we'll do it in three legs. First leg about seven hours, today, to Persia." He gestures to the rear. "If you want a look outside, go to the rear turret. There's a bucket there, too, by the way, if you need it." The engines begin to roar, drowning out the possibility of further conversation.

The view from the rear turret is spectacular; he and another officer each use up a whole film on the mountains of Afghanistan. By then, they're both shivering uncontrollably in their tropical uniforms; metallic surfaces are beginning to freeze. There's nothing to do but join the others, wrap themselves in blankets and curl up on the mattresses, listening to the steady deafening throb of the engines, trapped in their own thoughts.

In this enforced solitude he can't escape the emotional shock, the reality of his separation from the woman he loves, from his best friend, and the place he's grown to love. He turns his back to the others; since everyone is deaf and shivering, he can sob his heart out in total privacy. For a long while he lies there, feeling just like a child again; bereft of his mother, alone in a freezing cottage. He begins to think about everything that's happened, trying to work out what he can learn from it all. He curses himself as an idiot, a total fool, for not realising exactly what he felt about Dorothy sooner; for not acting before. The depth of feeling had been new to him, granted; but hadn't she often tried to tell him that he might never have this again? And because he clearly hadn't understood, she'd decided he was some kind of Lothario, probably. How wrong she was, he thinks; just a bloody stupid fool. He suspects himself to be a hypocrite too; so proud of himself because he'd befriended an Indian officer, and yet so blind to the way he'd taken Dorothy for granted. Deep down, hadn't he treated her with far less respect than Grace; using her for so long without even becoming engaged? In the end, hadn't he buckled under to all that pressure from the pukka brigade? Certainly from the Colonel; keep everything discreet, which really meant silent, invisible? Out of sight and out of mind, even out of his *own* mind; Christ, he hadn't even talked it over with her until it was too late. His shame feels almost more painful than his loss. He can't get her words out of his head; *I would have said yes.* He forces himself into memories, trying to blot out the painful present, and slips into a doze.

It's an autumn day in Ireland; he's dawdling across the bridge, hearing the bells, still tasting the apples in his mouth. Someone pushes him down onto the cobbles and falls on him. He hears a shot ring out, followed by shouting. But the voices are not Irish; from the far end of the bridge he hears the sound of the bazaar in Peshawar, the merchants' and the beggars' cries, and then the rhythmic calls of the Sikh tug of war team as they steadily haul their opponents in. He twists his head around to see Melsonby and the Colonel sitting on him, pinning him down; behind them, officers on horses wielding polo sticks cheer and applaud. He looks ahead, sees someone being dragged away from him, caught in the grip of a soldier with a rifle. It's not Pat, but a beautiful brown skinned girl who reaches her arms out to him in mute appeal. Yet what shocks him most is the identity of the soldier who holds her, grinning at him in the triumph of possession.

He jerks awake, his mind full of horror at the implications of his dream. Is that why Vic put doubts in my mind? Were they lovers when they were young students? Was that the basis of their original friendship? Did Vic want her back now, as his mistress? *If she needs help, I'll look after her.* And what about Dorothy; was that the real reason she would not take the risk? Because she knew she had Vic to fall back on? Christ, he thinks; I really don't want to know.

*   *   *

Nineteen: 1945-46

She follows the banks of the winding stream up the little ravine towards Rookhope; a route that she has walked for much of her life, whenever she visits her aunt. Somehow, she finds herself in unfamiliar territory. At first, she tells herself she's imagining it; but the further she goes, the less she recognises. Somewhere along the way she must have taken a wrong turn. How could this have happened? She finds herself searching for landmarks in a scarred, deserted wasteland, the valley filled with acrid smells of burned waste and smelted metal. Blackened remains of wooden buildings stand half-collapsed, as if recently torched. This is how the approaches to Slit Vein and Middlehope mines must have looked fifty years ago; after the big mines closed, their assets stripped. Has she somehow been transported back in time?

As if this problem were not enough, the deep shadows on the hillside steadily lengthen while the gloom in the narrow valley deepens. It must be late afternoon, nearly dusk; she has no torch, no means of lighting a fire. For some reason, despite the wintry conditions, she's dressed for a summer's day. The frost crunches beneath her shoes; she treads carefully, avoiding patches of ice that might cause her to slip and tumble down the bank. Under a layer of ice the stream still babbles softly. It dawns upon her, now; what am I doing? How could I be so stupid? She stops, a sinking feeling growing in her gut. Why am I heading upstream? How idiotic... this path will peter out on an open, exposed moor... she turns around, heads downstream; she needs to get warm, to find the nearest settlement. She stumbles back downhill, filled with an increasing foreboding, for what seems an eternity. Her exhaustion grows, welling up, threatening to overwhelm her. She longs to lie down and sleep, to give in. At last, in the distance she hears the sound of a church bell. Stumbling down the path through a dark, wooded ravine, she emerges onto a road and sees the spire silhouetted against the moon. The bell has stopped; the church gates stand open. Although the churchyard looks deserted, somehow she knows that a funeral service has just finished.

In the moonlight, she sees three freshly dug graves. She runs to the first, drops to her knees and begins to claw at the earth with her hands. She digs and digs, reaching down into the cold earth with numb hands until finally, she grasps something. The shock and terror she feels tell her that she is holding a hand. She pulls at it, and suddenly the hand comes alive and begins to flail about within the earth. Soon, the body begins to move purposefully, reaching upward and fighting its way out of the grave. Coughing and spluttering, spitting earth out of his mouth, Paddy emerges from the ground, smart in his army uniform. He seems unfazed by his ordeal; embraces her, "I'm fine," he tells her, "Don't worry about me."

She turns to the next grave and starts to dig once again. Paddy kneels beside her and helps; they must go deeper this time, which takes much longer. She feels a face in the earth, though the body does not come to life quickly, as Paddy did. They scrape the earth away and uncover the face; Maggie sobs in recognition, kisses his face, tastes the earth, panic and nausea rising in her throat. Suddenly the body wakes; Pat now rises from the earth, resplendent in a brown suit. He smiles at her and winks, "You were just in time, darlin'; thanks a million."

The three of them stand up; she turns to examine the third grave. The two men shake their heads, sadly. Each man takes one of her arms and gently but firmly they drag her away, out of the churchyard. She screams at them to go back, to rescue whoever is in the last grave; they shrug and shake their heads, silently telling her that it's far too late for that. She tries to break free of their grip; they're far too strong for her...

She jerks awake with a start, finds herself safe in her bed; the grip of strong hands on her arms fades into nothing. The night is silent and still except for Ellen's steady breathing. She slips out of bed, drawn to the window by the strong moonlight. Relief flows through her when she sees that the ground outside is still covered by autumn leaves, not by frost. But her deep sense of foreboding remains even as the memory of the dream fades.

* * *

The noise of the compartment door penetrates his doze, calling him back from memories of hornpipes and reels played inside a ship's hold. He opens one eye; an elderly couple hesitate at the door with bags of shopping, uncertain how this tall, sleeping man will react to being woken. He shakes himself upright, waves them in. "Come on in," he tells them, "I could do with the company."

The woman rewards Pat with a shy smile; the man nods at his kitbag. "Have you come far?"

"Oh, just up from London docks today; before that, a little trip around the Med."

The man nods knowingly, "Aye, I was in the navy during the last war - safest place to be, as it turned out, in the end. For us, I mean - Royal Navy. Not for you merchant boys."

Pat smiles at this, an acknowledgement that he rarely hears; the train jerks, squeals, and begins to move. "Where are we now? I'm headed for Eastgate."

"We've just left Bishop. You've a few stops yet; the wife and I are just going to Wolsingham. We live next to the station; it's a handy train for us, for the market."

"I'm sure it is; and I bet you can't get much in Wolsingham these days."

"Too right," the man sighs; he gets out his pipe and starts to clean it. Pat interprets this as an end to the conversation; he stares out of the window at the autumn colours, lit up by the evening sun, while the train meanders up the valley. It does remind him of Cork - with a few more trees, maybe. That will have to be next on his list; a trip to Ireland to see his brothers, perhaps for one last time. Cork seems a lifetime or two away now; God knows how much his brothers have aged. Even his own hair's thinning at the temples, just as theirs was when he last saw them. Sean's letters have become infrequent, filled with names that have dropped out of his memory. No mention of women, other than those who have emigrated; two old bachelor brothers, stuck on a farm. He shakes his head, knowing he couldn't have stood that life, for sure. What had seemed a disaster had fired him out of Ireland like a cannonball into all sorts of messes and scrapes; but he's glad it happened, even so. How far would he have got without it, he wonders? Teaching music in Dublin, most likely; and here? He glances at the old couple, their black clothes a throwback to Victorian fashions. The place has the same timeless quality as Cork, somehow. Fons led me here, he thinks. My God, Fons has been my guiding light, twice; first through his mother, now through the Hardy family. Perhaps with Mary too, come to that? The best thing I ever did in this life was to befriend that little dark haired boy back in that awful place. Why? I suppose he was the rebel that I wished to be, back then; and we both needed a friend. Well, Fons has repaid me ten times over for anything I ever did for him. With luck, I should be able to thank him, soon. Maybe I'll put that in my wedding speech, he thinks; that would be appropriate.

He studies the scenery again; could I settle here, in this part of England? He feels his body shiver. Even with Maggie by my side, I'm not sure how long I could stand it. It would stifle me; too much like Ireland. If I went back to sea, living here, I'd have to be away all the time or I'd end up paid a pittance, doing short runs on some little tramp steamer. A lot of sailors will be out of work soon, now the war's over. And what work might there be for me on land, when all those soldiers come home? Bar work for Gilly, if I'm lucky? No, we'll have to leave; my opportunity with Frank will never be bettered. In my life, progress always seems to involve taking that leap forward into the dark, having faith in an uncertain future. I just have to convince Maggie of that; there'll be plenty of opportunity for her, too. She's a smart girl.

Dusk is falling as he steps down onto the tiny platform at Eastgate from an empty carriage. The air feels cool; already a hint of winter in the air. Above him, the shaded near side of the valley rises in a wild dark mass of pine forest, waiting to swallow the darkness. He shivers despite the familiar blast of heat, the smells of coal and oil, as he passes the engine. The station-master takes his ticket, gestures him through; he ignores Pat's greeting. A little unusual, in this place; they all know him. But Pat's spirits are rising anyway; he climbs the steps up to the road, crosses the bridge over the babbling River Wear, looking ahead to the village. He can feel the slight bulge in his breast pocket where the diamond engagement ring sits, ready and waiting. He hasn't planned his speech; he'll wait for the right moment, play it by ear.

Whistling as he strides along the deserted street, his boots scatter a few loose stones; he sniffs wood smoke, and coal, anticipates an open fire and a pint of best. Hopefully, Maggie will be serving in the bar. He crosses water one last time, the tiny stream of Rookhope burn, glancing up at the battered wooden sign hanging on its chain above the pub door. That needs a coat of paint, he thinks; maybe I can do that while I'm here. Pushing through the door, he registers a slight pang of disappointment; he sees Gilly alone behind the bar, two or three of the local farmers around the fire. They turn and stare at him curiously, as if he is some kind of circus freak; this is not so unusual, but he also detects an exchange of glances, the raising of eyebrows. He tries to ignore this, drops his kitbag and gives a broad beam of greeting, extending his hand across the bar; "Evening, Gilly; it's good to see you again."

Gilly gives him a hard, curious look, as if he were a drunken stranger who's just collapsed on the floor. He ignores the proffered hand, picks up a glass and polishes it. Pat feels his face flush; his confidence drains away, replaced by a deep sense of unease. Gilly glances again at the outstretched arm, seems to consider his words carefully, "I can't say the same; and I'll not be serving you either, you're not welcome here. Not now, not ever."

Pat drops his arm back to his side, blinks and swallows; his mouth and throat suddenly dry. Is Maggie pregnant, he wonders; though he took great care, and even if she was, surely Gilly would not humiliate her in this way? Has his Irish past somehow caught up with him? He forces himself to think, to speak calmly; "Is there a problem, Mr Hardy? What...what have I done?"

"You shouldn't need me to tell thee that, lad." The tone is that of a headmaster, making an announcement to the assembly; Gilly's eyes bore into him with a look of disgust, sending a shiver down Pat's spine. Pat doesn't respond, his thoughts racing, exploring the possibilities. He feels a flush of heat in his face as he remembers; the shame and humiliation burn in his throat and chest. It must be Lily; how could he be so stupid, he thinks, to leave it so long? Gilly's voice confirms his fear, "But since you asked, it's about time you took yourself back to Liverpool to that wife of yours, and left my daughter alone. Do I make myself clear?"

Pat nods, bites his lip; he's got to say something, though he knows better than to confront Gilly too hard in front of an audience. Truth is, he's been avoiding the issue with Lily; firstly, she's Catholic, he's no idea if she'll even give him a divorce. So he couldn't promise that. Secondly, he hasn't docked in Liverpool since VE day; there hasn't been a chance to see her. He sighs, clears his throat; "It's not as bad as it seems, Mr Hardy, I haven't seen Lily since 1940. I only married her to stop her family throwing her out; she was pregnant with another man's child ..." One of the farmers bursts out laughing; the others chuckle. Pat feels his face burn, forces himself to continue, "...Last time I saw her, the father of her child was supporting them both; I've no real tie to her."

Gilly shakes his head, though Pat detects a slight shift in his expression. "I'm not interested in your excuses, lad. Just get you back to Liverpool and deal with your own responsibilities." He jerks his head at the door. Pat picks up the kitbag, wondering for a second if Maggie might be listening at the door; he needs to see her, to explain. Maybe he'll come back tomorrow; watch out for her, wait until Gilly goes out? He has to get word to her somehow.

Please God, it can't just end like this, in a chorus of humiliating laughter...he turns away from Gilly, giving the farmers an angry stare.

They turn away their faces away, towards the fire, though the youngest of them smirks; laughing boy, thinks Pat. He's sorely tempted to call the lad outside, to vent his frustration upon him; but he looks too much like a bull, short but very wide. He turns away, walks to the door, grasps the handle; behind him, another door opens, "Wait; I thought I heard raised voices." Her voice, thank the Lord; he turns, sees Maggie wrapping a shawl around her shoulders, a grim look on her face.

"He was just leaving." Pat's eyes shift from one to the other, watching the battle of wills.

"Not before I talk to him, Dad. He owes me an explanation, if nothing else; and I want to hear it with my own ears." Gilly looks for a moment as if he might explode, then thinks better of it.

"Take him outside, then; he's not welcome in here."

"Right, then," Maggie walks over, a gleam of satisfaction in her eye, takes Pat's arm and steers him out of the door. Pat feels an enormous rush of relief; though as soon as they're outside, she drops his arm and steps away from him, her hand raised. "Don't get the wrong idea; I'm just as mad with you as he is. But I want to make my own decisions."

Pat nods; he whispers, "I'm so, so sorry, Maggie." He starts to open his mouth again; then, his instinct tells him to let her speak first.

"Who is this *Lily*, anyway? You never mentioned her."

"I did not." He tries to gather his thoughts; he can't stop himself squirming with shame, at his own stupidity. He blurts out, "She's not that important to me."

"You married her, for Christ's sake."

He swallows the lump in his throat with difficulty, gives up trying to think. "We married before the war. We were...we were just helping each other out, Maggie. She was pregnant and her family were going to throw her out, put her on the street or worse. I got a British passport out of it."

Her voice rises, incredulous with horror, "You have a child?"

He shakes his head and groans, tries to reach out to her, but she steps away, down the side of the building. "Wait, wait; I do not, Maggie, the child wasn't mine. It was some married feller she knew, I swear it. Her family would've put her on the street and the Church would've taken the baby away from her. That's why I helped her. You can ask her yourself."

"But you married her, anyway."

"I did, but it was never going to work out between us; we both knew that. When I got back from sea I found the married feller was looking after her and the baby; he must have money. So Lily and I parted with no hard feelings. I haven't seen her since 1940. I swear on my mother's grave." He takes a deep breath. "I should have told you; but she's Catholic, you see. I wasn't sure whether she'd give me a divorce." He looks up from the floor; she's moved further into the shadows.

Her voice, when it comes, seems full of derision. "You fool, you stupid fool; and I thought you were the mature man." Much to his surprise, her remark gives him hope. Scorn is better than disgust, he thinks.

He takes a deep breath. "I didn't know what to do, Maggie."

"What, were you going to marry me illegally?"

"I don't know. No, I wouldn't have done that. I was going to see her next time I was in Liverpool, Maggie, I just haven't had the chance."

"Well, you'd better go and do that now. I don't want to see you ever again unless and until you have those divorce papers in your hand." The absoluteness of this demand shocks him, though something in her tone of voice has changed; she sounds less anxious, as if she believes him. He gulps at the implications, but he's in no position to argue. She needs time to get over her anger; and in any case, he'd better see if that particular bridge *can* be crossed, in the meantime. "Go on, off you go." The voice is now chiding, not without warmth; he feels like a child being ordered to go to the shops. He hears her footsteps disappearing, heading away to the back door.

He walks back over the stream in silence, stops to consider his options. He'll have to go back into Stanhope for the night. That's either a long walk, or back to the station and wait a while for the train on its return journey. I'll be living on the bloody railway now, he thinks.

* * *

The post office door bangs open; she feels an icy blast of air as a figure wrapped in a thick duffle coat backs in, clutching an enormous parcel, the mailbag under one arm. He places them on the counter, stamps his feet, rubs and blows on his hands, "Christ, it's cold out there; I thought it was a passing shower but it's settling already. It'll be a bitter winter if this keeps up."

Maggie nods absent-mindedly at her father; a thought occurs to her, "Will you manage to visit her today, Dad? With the snow on the roads, I mean."

"Not if this keeps up; I couldn't risk getting stuck." He scowls. "If it's not one thing, it's another; shame. She looked awful last time I was there, like a scarecrow."

Maggie frowns, shakes her head in sympathy, points at a steaming mug on the counter. "I made you some tea while you were out."

"You're an angel; has anyone been in?" She shrugs, lifts the book she's reading as her answer. He cradles the tea, warming his hands; she senses him watching her while he sips it. He can probably see how tired she looks, with those black rims under her eyes. He must also know how miserable she feels. She pushes the hair back from her face with her hand, "I must look a mess."

He shakes his head, smiling ruefully, "Never." He sets the mug down and tips the mailbag out onto the counter; Maggie returns her attention to John Keats. She likes the way he sounds, but wishes he wouldn't use such obscure language.

"Two for you here, Maggie," The letters land on the counter in front of her as she looks up; one is from Paddy, she can tell from the envelope. The other has a foreign stamp, though the hand is familiar. She feels her heart racing, glances across at her father; he feigns disinterest and tells her, "I'll just go and bring some more coal in."

She watches him go, then rips the envelope open.

"My dearest Maggie,

I miss you badly, every day. I'm also terribly, terribly sorry and hope against hope that you will be able to forgive my stupidity soon.

I am writing to you from Cork where I have come to visit my two brothers Sean and Ernie and see the family farm again. It seems to me that things have not changed at all here since I left, apart from them having less hair – they're both a few years older than me. Ireland's neutrality didn't make much difference because the place was virtually cut off during the 'emergency' (as they call it here). The U-boats didn't much bother whose boats they sank, neutral or not. As a result, Ireland makes Weardale look like the land of plenty.

I've come here from Liverpool, where I set the divorce in motion, which in itself took several weeks. By the way, you have no idea how terrified I was on that journey down, thinking that Lily might refuse on religious grounds. When I arrived she asked if I'd got her message - I said no, and then nearly fell over with relief when she explained what her message was. I suppose I deserved that, and I hope you feel I've had my punishment.

The whole process was like finding your way through a coal mine in the blackout, what with agreeing the best way to proceed with Lily and her feller Desmond, writing out a long, detailed, and partly embellished story of the marriage, finding certificates, obtaining photographs, witnesses and their statements, and finally concocting a scene of confrontation and confession which the lawyer told us we must do, and writing an account of suchlike. Apparently we have to pretend it's not something we both agree on, or they won't let us divorce. How daft is that? Fortunately we seem to have a fairly competent lawyer who has organised all this for us (but even sharing the cost with Desmond I reckon six month's pay will go up in smoke). Lily has agreed to be the guilty party. She wanted me to take the blame - they would have paid for everything if I'd agreed - but I wanted you and your father to see the truth in the divorce papers, at the end of the day. I'd also better warn you the process will not be quick, I think the general intention is that one party or the other will die of old age and thus save the court the trouble. With a lot of luck I should get the decree nisi sometime in January. I hope having this decree in your hand will be enough for you to allow me to see you again, since it will take another six months for the decree absolute, though that is automatic.

I am longing to hear your voice, so I will try to phone you when I get back to Liverpool sometime next week. By the way, Frank has taken a ship bound for New Zealand and will be trying to set things in motion when he arrives. He'll let me know when the wheels are turning.

Apologies again; I hope your father may also forgive me, in time.

All my love, Pat."

She re-reads it several times, trying to decipher every nuance. Her initial relief (that her faith in him was justified) gradually mixes with frustration at the time scale she has created for herself; plus a growing curiosity. Why hasn't he talked *more* about his home? *Why* does it all take so long? Should she allow him to come back *before* he gets the first decree? How on earth is she going to talk her father round? She sighs and rubs her forehead. She's sure of one thing. His absence, plus the fear that she might have driven him away forever, has helped to clarify her feelings; she doesn't want to lose him. She sighs and opens the letter from Paddy in an effort to distract herself, just as her father returns.

"Dear Maggie,

I hope you, Gilly and all the girls are well and enjoying the peace. I have gone from the heat of India to the cold ruins of Berlin; since most of my kit was tropical this was an unpleasant shock to say the least. I was expecting to come home and be demobilised but no such luck. Everything here is in ruins and the people are starving, mostly living in cellars. This makes for a thriving black market and I spend most of my time checking the contents of our stores; everything in it has a tendency to develop legs and walk out of the door unless it is nailed down. (My CO in India had mentioned in his report about me that I was good at ordering and managing supplies. Unfortunately, someone must have read it.) I can't believe it, after all this time the British army has turned me into a desk wallah! As you may recall, I joined the army to avoid that.

On the positive side Berlin is a very interesting place to be, what with French, American and Russians soldiers all wandering around, mixed up with Germans of various types, refugees, displaced persons (who can be from anywhere) and deserters from various armies. It's safe enough as most of the ardent Nazis were either killed off, are prisoners, or on the run.

Hope to get some home leave soon, Paddy."

She looks up to find Gilly waiting; she hands the letter to him. His face relaxes as he reads, giving off little grunts to show his amusement. He shrugs and hands it back, "Typical damned army. Be nice to see him back, though, wouldn't it?"

"Of course it would, Dad," she thinks a moment; "but I don't understand why you won't let Grace use the spare room in the meantime."

He gives her a thoughtful look. "Has she been on to you again?"

"No, I haven't seen her this week." She avoids his eyes, wondering how much she can divulge. "Look, Dad, that brother of David's has come back and he's awful to Grace."

"I know that, Maggie; I know all about it."

She looks up, astonished. "You do?"

"Yes, I hear all sorts of things, some from David's father. The big problem in that family is that the mother favoured Richard, the first-born, always has; spoilt him rotten. David's a much nicer lad. His father tries to balance things out, but the two lads always fought. Richard's trying to drive Grace out, thinking that David will go where she goes. But the father tells me Richard's no use as a farmer; David, on the other hand, could run the place. So Grace has to stick it out. Once David's back, Richard will go, in time. Mark my words."

She can see the sense in it, though she feels uneasy; "She's pretty miserable."

"Aren't we all; what with one thing and another?" The frustration and weariness in his voice, so rarely expressed, shocks her. "Whatever's next, Maggie?"

She bites her lip; a part of her thinks that things will have to be said sometime, and now is as good a time as any. "You might as well read this too; it's from Pat."

He grunts. "I guessed it was." He reads the second letter silently, his face giving nothing away; he folds it up and hands it back to her. He frowns, considers his words carefully. "I'm glad he's sorting it out; but if I were you I'd think very hard about it, and what it tells you about him."

"What do you mean, Dad?"

He sighs, scratches his head. "His character; put it this way, he's not like Paddy. Paddy's honest and straightforward. If your life depended on someone doing something for you, you'd ask Paddy to do it. This friend of his - well, we've discovered a lot of things we didn't know. He's certainly not straightforward and his honesty is open to question." She starts to open her mouth; he holds up his hand. "Don't get me wrong, I liked him well enough at first. He's clearly no fool and he can be a great feller to have around. But will he make you happy in the long run? Would he go out of his way for you or anyone else? I'm not sure, Maggie. He strikes me as a bit of a loner. It's a queer life, you know, on those boats for months on end. He's used to it, but you'd also be sitting at home on your own for just as long; probably spending most of your life waiting for him to come back. You really need to think about that."

"I have, Dad. I've thought about nothing else these last few weeks; the one thing I'm certain of is that I do love him." Stony-faced, he shakes his head from side to side slowly and walks out of the room, banging the door as he goes.

*　　*　　*

Avoiding the patches of solid ice, he picks his way carefully along the street in semi-darkness, mounds of rubble looming above him on either side, towards the single intact building in the area. His eyes flicker about him, shifting his attention from frozen ground to deep shadows and back; you can't be too careful, when you're alone in this town. He hears a wailing saxophone from the American club, a distant hum of conversation. This might even be worth the effort, he thinks. The lights of a distant vehicle swing into view, illuminating his path; he relaxes, rubbing his hands in anticipation. Outside the front door, a gum-chewing sentry stares at his uniform, nods, and jerks his head towards a staircase at the side, "Visitors, that way."

Paddy grins at him, gives him a salute for good measure, and takes the stairs two at a time. Pushing a heavy door open, he finds a bored looking girl filing her nails behind a desk. She stops, briefly inspects her work, and glances up; "You gotta pass?" After a second glance, she adds, "Sir?"

"Lieutenant Wise said he would arrange it for me; he told me to ask for him."

The girl gives him a curious look, "That would be the Canadian officer, sir? Ok, one moment;" she glances at his uniform again, "are you Captain Reilly?"

"That I am."

The girl picks up a telephone, dials; "Hey, Mabel? You know that Canadian Lieutenant? Can you tell him Captain Reilly's arrived? Yeah, he's in with the Major, I think." She replaces the phone, fishes an envelope out from a drawer. "This is your pass, sir;" she lowers her voice, using a conspiratorial tone, "you can use that one for a week."

Paddy nods, tries to look impressed. "I'll make sure it's put to good use." He looks around the lobby; notices a leather couch, a table and a large thermos.

"Take a seat, Captain, and help yourself..." She lingers over the last phrase; Paddy smiles, takes a good look at her, but decides that hot coffee is the greater attraction. He's midway through his second cup when a slim, fair-haired officer appears with a very attractive girl on his arm.

"Evening, Paddy. I'd like you to meet Gisela."

"Evening, Graham; pleased to meet you, Gisela." The girl blushes; offers a delicate hand, giving him a shy smile when he wraps both hands around hers.

"Good evening, Captain." German, he thinks, by the accent.

He feels Graham's hand on his shoulder. "I've brought you both here as a bit of treat for helping me with my work; so you two just follow me and relax. I've got some influence here." He leads them through a door, down some stairs, along a long corridor towards a growing noise of jazz; eventually, they enter a crowded ballroom where a whispered conversation with the head waiter brings them a reserved table alongside the band.

"I'm impressed, Graham. How do you manage all this?"

Graham taps his nose. "I'll explain later. First, let's eat; steak or turkey?"

Paddy feels the saliva forming at the thought, "Steak."

The girl smiles, "Same for me."

"That makes three of us; oh, and some wine. Make it one red, one white." The waiter nods and heads for the bar.

"I'd better introduce you properly; Paddy, this is Gisela Muller. You should know that she was a member of the German resistance, part of the plot to kill off Hitler."

"Really? In that case, I'm very honoured to meet you, Gisela."

"I'm the lucky one; believe me, just to be here. But I was only a courier; Graham makes it sound far too ...too much."

"How on earth did you get involved?"

"It was through the church at first... the Lutherans." She shrugs, "When they start persecuting very, very good people...it makes your mind up." She frowns.

Graham reaches across, squeezes her hand. "Of course; and Gisela, Paddy here is the man who helped me to set up my house. He told me where I could get my whiskey supply."

Paddy shrugs, "All I did was point you in the direction of Zeigler. The man had been sniffing around my staff for weeks, trying to find a way to get his hands on my stores. It was pretty obvious he was a black marketer."

"Ah yes, Paddy, but that was a crucial step for me. Once I'd identified our Mr Zeigler, all I had to do next was catch him red handed." Graham nods at the waiter, who pours out wine and then disappears again. "That's good stuff, by the way."

Paddy lifts an eyebrow, "So, did you catch him?"

"Of course I did; he wasn't exactly a criminal mastermind."

"What happened to him?" Paddy sips his wine.

"Nothing much; I agreed to let him continue his business as long as he supplied me with all the whiskey I need." Paddy chokes a little, takes a second look at Graham's boyish face. "Don't worry, Paddy, it's all in a good cause. Let me explain. I've set up a house where we exchange a glass or two of whiskey for useful information. Gisela here helps me to assess the information and the informants. I wanted to try something a bit different; my boss was a bit sceptical, but it's exceeded all our expectations, an absolute roaring success so far. We've got far more useful stuff than all the cloak and dagger boys have ever managed. Everyone's very appreciative, including our American friends."

Paddy grins, "At last; someone's discovered the meaning of military intelligence."

"Exactly; that's why I wanted to thank you both tonight. You see, this place has the best food in Berlin. Speaking of which, here it comes." Paddy has already smelt the food approaching; he doesn't turn around, preferring to watch Gisela's eyes widening in disbelief as a large plate is deposited in front of her. The steak extends most of the way across it, thicker than he has ever seen; the other half of the plate piled high with fried potatoes and vegetables. "If there's any other way I can thank you, Paddy, you just let me know..."

He takes a long sip of wine. "I'll consider that carefully while I do my best with this..."

*   *   *

That plateful of food still lingers in his memory two weeks later. As they hand in their coats at the British officers club, he's tempted to describe the experience to his companion, though he realises this might be a little cruel, given the fact that his American pass has now expired. Maybe he should have chatted up the American receptionist, he muses; but then, this Polish girl on his arm emits a natural warmth and enthusiasm that makes him feel far more comfortable. She lives in a camp for displaced persons, having been brought to Germany as forced labour; it's no wonder, he thinks, that anything resembling normality is such a wonder and novelty to her. She clings to his arm, bouncing gently up and down on the balls of her feet as she gazes around the wood panelled dining room, festooned with ribbons and streamers. "My goodness...there will be a party tonight...later?"

"There will, Anna; one hell of a party. That's the reason I brought you here tonight, I thought you could do with a little bit of fun." She shivers with excitement, squeezes his arm.

"It's wonderful; I don't know how to thank you." I do, he thinks; but he shrugs and smiles. She looks down at her dress, a practical grey outfit, and blushes, "I feel so out of place here."

"Nonsense; you're fine. The other officers are all giving me envious looks. There'll be dancing later; I can show you off then. First, we'll eat."

She seems reluctant to sit, to let go of his arm. "Are you sure?"

She's scared; like a child, he realises. "Of course, Anna; look, wait a minute." He moves the chairs together, rather than facing each other across the table. "There; sit down. Look, you helped me organise the supplies for your camp. I wanted to thank you; and besides, I like you."

She beams at him; "Thank you, Paddy." Yet she glances around nervously, lowers her voice. "I'm sorry, sometimes all the uniforms... it scares me." She lifts her eyes and forces another smile. "Not you, I feel safe with you." Poor kid, he thinks; God knows what happened to her.

"Right then, have a look at this menu. Three courses; you choose one for each course. I can't vouch for the quality, but there'll be a decent helping."

Her eyes widen with anticipation, "Oh my God; what a treat." She bites her lip, blushes, glances at the tables around her. "Can we have something to drink, too?"

"Anna, we'll have as much beer as you like; or wine if you prefer. It's New Year's Eve; everyone here will be celebrating the end of 1945."

"I will, too..." Anna proves herself to have a remarkable capacity for alcohol; on the dance floor, her enthusiasm more than compensates for her lack of finesse. When the music slows just before midnight, she moves closer, clinging to him in a way that makes him think safety may not be her only consideration; she has a wonderful giggle, infectious, he thinks. A slightly slurred whisper announces, "You must be married, Paddy."

"Am I? I wish someone had told me about it."

The giggle, again; "You must have a girlfriend."

"I'm a terrible slow starter, Anna; I only just got started last week, before I met you."

Her body shivers; "Oh...I don't believe you". She quivers a little more, settles against him. "But I don't really mind."

She's the first girl that's made him feel real desire since Dorothy, he realises. The dance ends; the musicians put their instruments down, someone begins a countdown. The floor slowly empties a little; he sees two figures waving at him from the other side of the room. It's Graham and Gisela, gesturing at him to join them. He turns to speak to Anna but a roar of approval bursts over them as the count reaches its climax; streamers fly above their heads, the remaining couples bend to hug and kiss. Anna pulls his head down and they, too, are kissing; a long kiss that seems to be full of promises. Out of the corner of his eye, he notices Graham entwined with Gisela; he'd wondered about that. Eventually, he tears his lips away from her mouth.

"Come on, Anna, this way."

Her voice, suddenly plaintive; "It's not over yet, is it?"

He chuckles, "No, Cinderella, not yet; just seen some friends." He leads her through the crowd. Graham has somehow captured a table and four chairs; not only that, but after the introductions he produces champagne and brandy out of a picnic basket (courtesy of Herr Zeigler, he assures them). Anna has never tasted either. She assures him they both taste wonderful; though after a few minutes, she whispers in his ear, "This is good, but does he have any Polish vodka?"

Before he can ask, he feels a tap on his shoulder, "Captain Reilly, sir?" He turns, sees an orderly from his unit. "The CO would like to see you, sir, urgently."

"Oh Christ, can't it wait?"

"Apparently not, sir; he's next door, in the dining room. It won't take a minute."

Paddy excuses himself and follows the orderly, a little unsteadily.

In the dining room, his CO looks a little worse for wear, too. "Ah, there you are, Reilly; been looking for you. I've a little Christmas present for you. Bit late, old chap, sorry about that; meant to give it you yesterday." He flourishes an envelope, waving it in the air.

Paddy blinks, trying to read what's written on the cover. "What is it, sir?"

"Two weeks home leave. See for yourself." Paddy tears open the envelope, unable to believe his ears. "Probably means your demobilisation is on its way too. You'll probably be reassigned once you're back in England. Your leave started, by the way, at midnight."

"Tonight; how do I get home, sir?"

"Oh yes; you'll find some other papers in there. There's an aircraft leaving this morning, heading for one of the northern airfields. You should just about make it if you hurry; you'll have to find a driver to take you. Better get going."

Paddy stares at him, totally astonished. "Thank you, sir, ever so much."

"Not my idea, Reilly. In fact I was hoping to keep you; you're a bloody useful chap. But someone up there likes you. Any road, thanks for all your good work. Much appreciated." He looks up, gives Paddy a sheepish smile. "Off you go, now". His heart is suddenly pounding at the idea that, after all this time, he's going home. He jumps to attention, gives his best salute, feeling a wide grin bursting out on his face.

Waiting in the belly of the bomber, swaddled in three layers of clothes, he thinks first about Anna. What will become of her, in the years to come? Graham and Gisela would look after her, in the short term; he'd asked them to. Anna had been upset about his leaving, naturally. Gisela had comforted her, insisted that Anna should stay with her, that night. It was a good job he'd run into them; otherwise, it would have been *very* difficult to leave Anna behind. In fact, part of him wished the CO had not found him till morning. The engines throb and roar; he feels movement. He thinks I'm ready to go home now; I've had enough of the army. I've seen enough of the world. I'd just like a normal steady life, a job and a home. I'm not completely over Dorothy - maybe I never will be – but I'm ready to try again. Anna proved that to me. Yes, a normal job and a home, someone to share it with. I'll settle for that.

*   *   *

"You're like a bear with a sore head, Dad."

"Is it any wonder, lass?" He rubs his forehead with both hands. "New Year is the one night that the customers all buy *me* a drink."

"You didn't have to accept them all."

"Bad manners if I don't."

"Nonsense, Dad, you could have said you'd have one later, put the money in the till." She points at his cup, "There's your tea, anyway."

As she walks away the phone rings; she turns, hopefully, to listen. "Eastgate Post Office... yes, speaking," he frowns, closes his eyes, as if attempting to shut the world out. "Good morning, Sister... Happy New Year, I was going to..." He pauses, as if interrupted. "Yes; one moment, I understand. Yes, I was planning to visit today. There's a bit of snow, but nothing like last week." He opens his eyes, suddenly alert, "How? I mean, when did this happen?" Maggie watches him bite his lip, as if restraining himself; "I know, I know; but why didn't you let me know sooner?" His eyes glance at his daughter, flicker upward to the ceiling. "I can see that, Sister. If you've had a couple of days off, fair enough, but someone..." He sighs, seems to restrain himself again. He hates listening to excuses, thinks Maggie. "Yes, I'll come. But can you tell me exactly what's wrong with her.... no, I mean her *physical* illness. Is it flu?" After a pause, he shakes his head. "All right, put him on." He waits for a few seconds, mouths the word 'doctor' at his daughter. He straightens up, "Yes?" She watches the blood drain out of his face; he swallows. "It's what? Yes, I thought that's what you said." He shuts his eyes again, listening with a fierce concentration. Eventually, he mutters, "All right, I'll come as soon as I can." He replaces the receiver and sucks in a deep breath.

So this is it, she thinks; "It's Mum, isn't it?"

He nods, staring at the telephone as if it were a snake. "She's been taken ill; it's pneumonia, Maggie." For a long moment he looks crushed, a beaten man; then he pulls himself together and meets her eyes. "It's pretty serious; but he's sent someone over to the big hospital in Darlington to get some new drug that might help." He thinks for a moment. "She's pretty tough, Maggie. She survived the flu in 1921 and that killed a lot of fit young men, believe me."

"I'll come with you if you like. We can shut the pub today, after last night."

He sighs, scratches his head. "No, I'll go on my own today. The roads will be tricky and I don't want us both stuck out there; but thanks for the offer." He bites his lip, considering something. "You'd better concentrate on the Post Office; don't worry about the pub. Oh, and don't tell the others, Maggie, just yet. Just make out I went a bit early today."

She goes to embrace him, watches him fight back his tears before he hurries out of the door.

For the rest of the day she keeps one ear listening out for the telephone; though in the afternoon, she leaves the Post Office to June. She distracts herself making scones; sits with Ellie on her knee, helping her to make pastry men. The phone remains silent; perhaps no news is good news, she hopes. Darkness has fallen when she hears heavy footsteps approach the back door. She looks up expectantly, thinking it will be her father. But rather than being flung open, she hears a double rap on the door. She sighs, wondering who it can be; unkindly, perhaps, she hopes it's not George. She gets up, carefully places Ellie on a chair, and opens the door.

She sees a deeply tanned face with abundant smile lines under an officer's cap; it regards her with a mixture of curiosity and disbelief. The posture conveys both alertness and relaxation; the face does seem familiar, but the maturity and confidence seem new. She recognises the voice first, and then the smile. "Don't you recognise me, Maggie?"

She leaps to embrace him, her face flushing with embarrassment, her heart jumping with delight at the same time. "Thank God you're back, Paddy." She hangs on his neck, lost for words.

"I have to admit I didn't know it was you either, just for a moment." She feels his arms around her, giving her a hug; not quite the bear hug of old, a little more careful. Relief floods through her. "You've grown up so much, Maggie...I mean, it has been four years, you know. You've grown more beautiful; like your mother."

She chokes up for a second, tears springing to her eyes. She hangs onto him a little longer, sniffing and rubbing her eyes, before stepping back to take a second look. "That's a lovely thing to say, Paddy." She gives him a wry smile. "Time hasn't done you any harm either, from what I can see. If this is a sample, you've become quite the handsome charmer too."

Now he blushes, though his face cracks into that wide grin; "Well, are you going to keep me standing out here in the cold, or invite me in? I should say Happy New Year, too."

"Happy New Year," she takes his arm, pulls him inside. "This is little Ellie." Paddy bends down onto one knee, trying to make eye contact. Ellie studiously avoids his eyes, concentrating on the pastry leg that she is trying to mould into shape.

He shrugs, "Typical Hardy girl. Shy at first; later, she'll be like a typhoon."

"Where did you spring from, anyway? You gave us no warning."

"I came from Berlin at very short notice; no notice at all, in fact. We flew into a place called Croft this morning; I caught the train from there. Not many trains running today, though." He looks around, "Where's your father? How is he, anyway; and the other girls?"

"I'll get them down in a minute, they're all upstairs. But I need to tell you, first..."

The back door opens again; they both turn to see Gilly, haggard and exhausted. For a long moment he looks in puzzlement at Paddy, blinks, and gives a nod of approval. He looks at Maggie and swallows, readying himself to speak. But the words won't come; every time he opens his mouth and starts to move his lips, he chokes.

She walks to the door, pulls him inside, leads him to the table. "Dad, take your time. Here, give me your coat." She gently pulls his coat off, hangs it up. "Is it bad?"

Gilly nods; allowing his head to sink onto his arms, he emits a series of choking noises; eventually, he gets the words out, "My Vi...your mother..." Little Ellie stares at him, frowns and pushes a pastry man towards him. "...we've lost her, Maggie; the pneumonia killed her. Didn't even get there in time; God almighty, I just wanted... to hold her hand... once...one more time."

Silence descends. Paddy steps over and lays his hand on Gilly's shoulder; a quiet sobbing begins. Maggie suddenly feels nothing, or almost nothing; a vast, cold emptiness surrounds her.

*   *   *

When was he last in a proper church, he wonders? Was it as long ago as his mother's funeral? She must have been about the same age as Violet; he would have been just a little older than Maggie. This English church seems much plainer, more practical, than the ones in Ireland; it does contain Christian symbols but he has to look for them, rather than finding them decorating every surface. The austerity suits his taste; instinctively, he feels more comfortable here.

The idea of a service that he can actually understand appeals to him, too. The only problem today is the temperature; despite liberally scattered paraffin heaters, the heat vanishes without trace into these ancient stones. The whole village seems to be tightly wrapped, shivering together.

He glances to his left; from his position at the end of the front row he can see all of the immediate family. Gilly stands next to him with his head down, his eyes closed, trying to shut out this awful reality; he looks like a condemned prisoner, awaiting execution. Despite this, Paddy feels very privileged, in an odd sort of way, to have the task of supporting him today. He can sense curious eyes examining his back. On the other side of Gilly, Maggie looks tense, distracted; she keeps turning to look back at the entrance, no doubt hoping that Pat might still turn up.

Paddy has sent carefully worded telegrams to Ireland and left messages in Liverpool with Lily and the lawyer; with no result. Paddy hopes that Pat hasn't gone back to sea; a day or two late might be tolerated, but a matter of weeks might become something of a last straw, as far as Gilly's concerned. Paddy has been working hard enough on Gilly, trying to persuade him that his friend has some amount of good in him. Privately, Paddy can't help but think his friend is an idiot, indeed a *bloody eejit* of the first order. He's a clever man, practical in most ways; so why has he been so careless? Then again, suddenly it seems obvious to him; the war, of course, that little distraction - plus, like himself with Dorothy, the situation probably sneaked up behind Pat and by the time he realised it, events were suddenly out of control. He sighs, hoping Pat doesn't make the same mistake he has...he has a bad feeling about it all, though, it has too many echoes of the Conlon family and Mary. He looks towards Maggie again, her figure silhouetted against the light from one of the windows.

If he had someone like Maggie... the thought shocks him a little, but not so much as it might have a few years ago. She's not his sister, though that is how it sometimes used to seem; then again, at one time she had a crush on him. No, perhaps his discomfort is more to do with the feeling that maybe, deep down, he's not sure if he wants Pat to sort things out, if he's honest. He's not entirely confident that Pat will make Maggie happy, judging him on his past record. His eyes flicker past her, to the pews on the other side. Grace, holding her baby, absorbed by the child; that's a lucky man too, whoever and wherever he is, he thinks.

Next to Maggie, June looks anxious, uncertain of her role. Her eyes dart rapidly around, searching, as if she is lost. For a moment her eyes meet his. She swallows and gives him just a hint of a smile, just enough to acknowledge him; he nods and gives her a little shrug in reply. As if reassured, she takes a deep breath and turns to face the front, standing as tall as she can. She has a quiet pride, he thinks. She too has turned into a lovely girl, but one who keeps to herself more than her sisters; she blends more into the background. Next to the aisle stands Rose, still a gawky teenager, keeping her head down, staring at the floor, her expression blank. She's probably avoiding looking at the coffin, placed at the front on a stand, in full view. On the other side of the aisle, next to Grace, ten year old Harriet looks confused and slightly puzzled. She holds on to one of her Aunt Ettie's arms; the other enfolds her protectively. She's only ever known her mother as a silent, living ghost. Another aunt, May, nurses little Ellie in her arms. Ellie looks about her, wide-eyed, sucking her thumb, while May rocks her to and fro.

Paddy hears movement, the shuffling of feet plus a general clearing of throats. A white robed clergyman makes his appearance. He walks to the coffin, touches it with his hand, and then turns to face the congregation. "Dearly beloved..."

Paddy does his best to listen to the words, though his attention constantly wanders. Even in plain English, his critical faculties baulk at the ideas; eternal life after death, but only for those who accept Christ? The actual Son of God; how does that work? And how can His suffering make up for *our* misdeeds? It all sounds slightly outlandish to him, requiring outrageous leaps of faith and logic. Deep down, it feels more important for him to focus upon Gilly; his emotional struggle is obvious. Paddy listens carefully when Gilly's breathing turns rapid and shallow at the beginning of the service, but it gradually settles. He watches how warily Gilly observes the service, perhaps terrified that the vicar will make him go to the front to speak about Violet.

When it comes to the eulogy, the vicar begins by emphasising Violet's energy and generosity of character as a young woman; this provokes a chorus of sobbing from the aunts. Gilly, too, finally gives in to his grief. Paddy and Maggie both put their arms about him, simultaneously; he can feel the older man's chest heaving while he weeps, silently. At the end of the service, six pallbearers step forward, including one brother-in-law resplendent in an officer's uniform from the Great War. He catches Paddy's eye and nods as he slowly passes, the coffin on his shoulder. Filing out of the pew, they all follow very slowly. Gilly's legs are shaking so badly that he has to lean on Paddy to keep his balance. The ground is frosty, rock hard, treacherous. Paddy can't help thinking, I'm bloody glad I didn't have to dig that hole.

The family slowly gathers around the grave. The lowering of the coffin seems to take an eternity; it requires extreme care not to slip and follow it down. This also applies to the act of adding a handful of earth; Paddy keeps a tight grip on Gilly's arm at this point, mindful of what his grieving mind might do to his body. The repeating thump of earth on wood causes the babies to whimper with fright and then cry out with cold. Grace whispers to her father, "I'll take Daniel back now, Dad; in fact I think we should all go back and warm up now." Gilly nods, a look of relief crossing his face. As he moves away from the grave, the sisters and aunts sense the moment, surrounding and embracing him. Grace and Maggie have both been crying; the other girls look shocked but thoughtful, more concerned for their father. They and the aunts escort him away, leaving Paddy and the men to thank the vicar.

* * *

She leans down, whispers in her sister's ear, "Grace... can you give me a hand getting the bar ready? Rose will look after Daniel..."

"Of course," she gives Maggie a wry smile, stands, hands the child to Rose; "I'm glad you asked. It'll be just like old times."

Maggie leads the way. "I'll warn you it's a bit of a mess. Dad keeps saying said he'll clean up, but his mind hasn't been on it."

"I'm not surprised." Grace looks around the bar. "Was it as much of a shock to you and him as it was to me? Let's start with the glasses. You wash, I'll dry."

"Fine," Maggie shakes her head, trying to clear her mind and get the lump out of her throat so that she can speak. "Of course it was; but with hindsight, maybe it shouldn't have been."

"What do you mean?"

She bites her lip, feeling her face flush, "Oh, you know how thin she was. I mean, always naturally thin, anyway. We'd all noticed her losing weight since last summer, hadn't we?" She looks up, sees Grace nod. After a long pause, she continues. "Well, it turns out she only weighed five stones." Maggie watches for her sister's reaction, sees astonishment.

"Good Lord."

She feels relief that her sister hasn't reacted with disbelief or fury. "The winter clothes hid it, of course. This all came out when Dad tackled the doctor in charge of the ward; he said her weight had left her body very weak and made it far more likely for flu to become pneumonia."

"So why didn't the staff try and feed her up?"

"Oh Grace, they'd been trying, apparently; but as the doctor pointed out, rationing doesn't help. Everyone's underfed, anyway. And sometimes the patients steal food from each other, or give it away. They can't watch everyone but they know sometimes that went on. But they didn't want to force feed her except as a last resort. They might have done that, if they'd known exactly how low her weight was, but they didn't realise until it was too late." She thinks for a minute, "You know, the whole story makes me feel completely helpless, rather than angry."

Grace grunts, "Still, I bet Dad played hell about that."

"He did; but apparently this doctor got on his high horse and claimed the staff had been warning us she was in poor health for some time."

"Had they?"

"I suppose so; in their own way. Looking back, they'd been saying Mum was not so good. We always assumed that meant she wasn't talking to anyone. No one said anything about her weight or her not eating." Maggie can feel a headache brewing, rubs her brow. She puts the last glass on the counter, leans against it, holding her head in her hands. "It's no use, all this, I hate it; passing blame back and forward. It's all too late; we can't go back and change it."

Grace nods, puts her tea towel down, moves to embrace her. Her sister's voice whispers in her ear, "I know, Maggie. It's awful; but we'll end up blaming ourselves anyway."

"Will we?"

"Of course we will." She feels her sister rubbing her back. "What will we say to ourselves? Lots of things about what we did and didn't do. Why didn't we visit more often? Why didn't we notice her losing weight? Why didn't we find a way to make her happy? Why didn't we take the little ones in more often?"

She feels her own tears coming at last, "You're right, Grace. That's the worst thing - knowing all the things we didn't do. It's been a terrible year, you know. We've missed so many visits, both of us, and Dad, because of our troubles with Pat, and David's brother, and the weather."

"I know, I've been thinking about that. Our minds haven't been thinking about Mum, any of us, even Dad; not for a long time."

"No." Maggie puts her head down, allows herself to cry for a minute. When her sobbing slows, she feels Grace giving her a gentle shake.

"We're the lucky ones, Mags; that's what we have to tell ourselves. The little ones have never really known her; at least we have some good memories of her."

"I suppose."

"Listen, I can remember sitting watching her baking a cake, with you on her knee. Then we both got to lick out the bowl in turn. Can you remember that? I think it was your birthday." After a moment, the scene surfaces in her mind, the taste of eggs and butter dominating her senses.

"Yes, I do. I don't have many memories of her, but that's one. And I do have a strong impression of someone very loving, very affectionate, when I was small. That must be her." She wipes her eyes, "Thanks, Grace. I wish...I mean, you know, I'm sorry Dad's being so stubborn."

Grace shuts her eyes, biting her lip. "You no idea..." Maggie sees tears spring into her sister's eyes; Grace turns away, hiding her expression.

"What's the matter, Grace?"

For fully half a minute her sister struggles to bring herself under control; she speaks over her shoulder eventually, in a hoarse whisper. "Look, I know it's a difficult time for Dad, and how sensitive he'll be about mum's room. But I'd happily share with you. I could really be a help here."

"I know that, Grace; so does he." The idea of sharing a room again has not occurred to her, before this moment. She's not sure what she thinks about that. "Give him a week or two, we'll ask him together. He just has this idea in his head that you have to stay at the farm for David's sake."

"I know, he's told me, but it's not worth it. Christ, Maggie, I really can't stand living there a moment longer. It's a madhouse. The mother's at me all the time; I'm not even sure it'll get any better when David comes home. The father tells me she was like that with David too. Some comfort that is; she blames me for things that Richard does, sometimes deliberately, and then thinks the sun shines out of his arse. If only she knew."

The bitterness in her voice prompts Maggie; "Knew what?"

Grace shakes her head, keeping her back turned, "Nothing."

"It's obviously not nothing," she squeezes Grace's arm, "come on."

"All right," Grace turns, looks her in the eye, "but you must keep this to yourself." Maggie nods. "He's obsessed with me, Maggie. He keeps pestering me... not in front of his parents, obviously. When they're not there, he tells me he's crazy about me, that I married the wrong brother. He won't stop. He seems to think I'm only pretending that I can't stand him; it scares me."

"Has he tried anything? I mean..."

"You mean; has he tried to force himself on me? Well, yes, a couple of times, half-heartedly. I fought him off easily enough, but only because he let me. He's a big man. The first time it happened, I thought that would be it; it'll stop now. But it didn't... look, he's trying to wear me down, I think, by sheer bloody persistence. That'll never happen. But please, Maggie, don't tell anyone. It would cause an unholy row and no one would believe me. Just help me talk Dad round so I can get out of there."

"Oh God, Grace, of course I will."

Grace embraces her again, whispers, "Thank you; now let's change the subject." She wipes her eyes, careful not to smear her make up. Maggie watches her sister's face set itself back into that familiar mixture of eagerness and determination. She sighs; it doesn't feel like they've finished this conversation, really, but she's also aware of the tasks ahead of them.

"All right, Grace - better get on, they'll be bringing the food in soon. If you wipe the tables, I'll sweep the floor."

*   *   *

Twenty: 1946

Her dream, whatever it was, shatters like glass; she feels a sudden rush of air through the window, hears a muffled crash as something heavy falls over down in the garden. She lies still for a couple of minutes, surrounded by darkness, calming herself; listens to the wind howling, the beginnings of a gale whistling over the top from Allendale. For the first time in a long while she wishes Grace was here, sharing her bed and room; even with her baby. Until recently, having a room to herself felt such a privilege, but now... it just feels empty. She understands, emotionally, exactly why Grace wants to return home; she too longs for whispered conversations and shared confidences. The thought comforts her; she drifts into a doze, imagines Grace's presence in the room. She slips into long forgotten memories; a child feeling her cradle rock as a soft voice sings a quiet lullaby. She wakes again when these sensations fade away, sharpening into a sense of loss, of real emptiness. God knows, she thinks, but having Grace back at home would make things much easier; she could plan her own future, too. She pushes back the blankets, leans down and fumbles under the bed, feeling for the torch and the envelope.

Sitting up again, she re-examines the photographs of Pat. Slightly younger, looking very theatrical in his operatic costume; he looks as pleased as Punch. She studies the faces of the others; they too look uniformly happy and proud. Otherwise, they give no further clues about his past life. That opaqueness bothers her; then again, he is Paddy's best friend. And she does love him, for better or for worse; that can't be changed now. She's never really doubted that he loves her, either. Until tonight, she only dreamed of sharing this room with *him*. Despite everything, she feels sure it will happen one day; he's out there somewhere, hopefully on his way here by now, with the papers that her father needs to see. Will that be enough? Not immediately, her instinct tells her, it'll take some time. But surely, Dad will have to forgive him in the end?

She also worries, how will the loss of her mother affect her father? Will it make him more difficult? For herself, it's made her more aware of how much she wants Pat to be here. What about New Zealand? Surely that could be delayed a year or so? She needs some time to get herself and everyone else prepared for that. If Grace did move back in, that would make everything so much easier. As soon as Grace stepped back in the house, Maggie would feel that her other sisters could at least cope with the idea. She could then break the news of their plans and start preparing; they could organise a marriage just before they left. She would still worry about her father, of course. But with Paddy also back on the scene, her father would cope a lot better. The main uncertainty revolves around David; Grace has had enough of his family, but will she be able to persuade David to join her here, rather than return to the farm? Perhaps by then, their father will decide to allow the young couple to use her mother's room...

She sighs, crosses her fingers. In a curious way, perhaps everything is finally falling into place at last. This is how she, and everyone else she knows, have always envisaged the end of the war; that in the end, everything would be sorted out neatly so that they could all resume their lives and settle down to a happy and peaceful future. After all the disruption of the last six years, that wasn't too much to ask, was it? Including a better future for her and Pat, in New Zealand? Why not? She feels slightly guilty about this thought, so soon after her mother's funeral; but it's time she allowed herself to think positively about it. It would be quite an adventure, that's for sure. It would make the most wonderful honeymoon, a voyage around the world. They could face any challenges together, too, knowing how much they loved each other. She kisses the tips of her fingers, and transfers the kiss to the picture. Wherever you are, Pat, sense that, and come back soon.

A minute or two elapses; she tries to imagine a new town, home, and friends. She slips the photographs back into the envelope; replaces everything under the bed, switches the torch off. She sings a lullaby to herself, thinking of her mother, as she drifts back to sleep.

* * *

The inspector checks the ticket, glancing at him curiously before punching it and handing it back to him with an approving nod. One of the benefits of wearing a suit, Pat thinks, apart from impressing the legal profession; let's hope that Gilly also appreciates the gesture. His new outfit is intended to demonstrate his respect for his prospective father-in-law, though Pat suspects that Maggie and the girls will appreciate it far more. He watches the falling snow through the window, chewing his lip thoughtfully; feels the bundle of papers in his inside pocket. He sighs, extracts a letter, and re-reads it.
"*Dear Pat,*

It was just grand to have you back in the old house one last time, for sure, even if might indeed be the first and last time you visit us here. We keep ourselves to ourselves far too much these days and having the company was a wondrous tonic for both of us. Hearing you sing was something the both of us will never forget. Since you left, we've played that gramophone you donated every night. This little ritual has become a grand way of settling ourselves down after the work of the day is done. It works much better than kneeling down and praying ever did, I can tell you. Ernie's been scouring the local markets for some more recordings (you can pick them up very reasonably this way, even if they have a few scratches). I did say 'the last visit' advisably because despite our great care to be discreet your visit has somehow become public knowledge in these parts, to the extent that the parish priest was asking after you. Gossip's a terrible thing in these rural parts, I'm afraid. The point is, although the Fitzgeralds have moved on up to Dublin we did see in the newspaper that one of them has become a TD, so they are not without influence if they happen to get a sniff of the gossip. As it happens, I did some thinking on my feet, and told the priest that you had emigrated to America years ago and that you had been only been able to visit us because you were over in Europe as part of the American army. That seemed like a good way of throwing him and anyone else off the scent. Plus, I've been told by one of the boys that, legally speaking, the yanks would never give up one of their own soldiers no matter what he might be accused of in the past.

Having said all that, there's a lad on the farm next door who has said he would look after our stock for a couple of days if we needed him to, so that we would be able to meet you in Cork or some other city before you leave for New Zealand. Ernie and I would jump at the chance to do that.

Well, I hope it all goes well with you and your English sweetheart.

Your loving brothers, Sean and Ernie."

He folds it up, replaces it, frowning. After all these years, he thinks, that damned night still haunts me. I still suffer from nightmares, though the content has changed; less about endless pursuit, more of being trapped on a sinking ship. The letter's an unwelcome reminder that he's still a fugitive. He allows himself a rueful smile; the other side of the world should suffice.

The train slows almost to a halt as it begins to climb a long gradient; at the top, it stops for almost half an hour before lurching cautiously forward again. This is going to be a long journey, he thinks. Well, I'm too late for the funeral anyway; the ferries and the lawyers have seen to that. Forty-eight hours later, he steps off the bus wearily opposite the Cross Keys. That faded sign, thickly encrusted in snow and icicles, somehow clings onto its perch above the door. He walks carefully across the icy road to the Post Office entrance, removes his coat and combs his hair. His suit looks pretty rumpled now, but it will have to do. He swallows, pushes the door open.

June looks up at him from behind the counter. Her look of surprise gives way to a wry but welcoming smile, causing intense relief to flood through him. She looks him up and down, "Well, you're a sight for sore eyes. How on earth did you get here? The trains have all stopped running."

"I know, June; I was on the last one across the Pennines. Had to stay a night in Darlington, even then I had a devil of a job getting up the dale. It took me a day and a half." She nods and then frowns, biting her lip, as if she wants to ask him a question. "I was awful sorry to hear about your mother, June. I came as soon as I could."

She nods again, seemingly relieved that he knows. "Yes, thanks. Dad's taken it very hard." She looks up and meets his gaze. "I'll go and get Maggie, shall I? She'll know what to do."

He nods, "She will, June." At least, let's hope so, he thinks. His wait lasts half a minute, though it seems like days. Suddenly she's there, rushing into his arms again, her head against his chest, her tears wetting his shirt.

"Oh, Pat..."

"I know, I know, Maggie; it'll be fine, now." He waits until her sobbing subsides. "I'm sorry I didn't get here for the funeral, Maggie. I didn't get the message until it was too late. I came as soon as I could; I was telling June, it took me two days."

She nods, sniffs, "The other thing... is it..."

"It's all done, Maggie, I have the decree nisi. I brought the papers to show to your father."

She squeezes him tight. "Good; in that case, I might let you kiss me again." Before he can react, she steps away from him, "But first, we have to talk to my father. Are you ready?"

"As ready as I'll ever be." He reaches into his breast pocket; pulls out the thick brown envelope, gives a little shrug of his shoulders.

"Come on, then," Maggie squeezes his hand, pulls him after her. He follows her out through the door into the hallway and up the stairs; outside her mother's sitting room, Maggie knocks softly on the door before she enters and pulls him after her, still holding his hand.

Gilly sits on the sofa, statuesque. His red rimmed eyes stare out of the window, his face gaunt, darkened by shadows. His head slowly turns and regards them, blankly at first. Pat feels Maggie release his hand, as if signalling him to speak. He clears his throat, "I'm terrible sorry for your loss, Mr Hardy; I'm also sorry that I never really knew Maggie's mother. If she was anything like your daughters, I can understand how much you loved her."

Gilly blinks; his eyes seem to swim into focus, regarding Pat's expression. He nods, turns away, licks his lips. After a long silence, he turns back, "You don't give up, do you?"

"I would never give up on Maggie, Mr Hardy." Pat waits until he sees a tiny movement, an acknowledgement; he adds, "I've done what you asked, sir; sorted out those responsibilities." He steps forward, holds out the envelope. At first Gilly doesn't react; his eyes flicker towards a small coffee table. Pat places the envelope on the table, steps back again. "All I can say is that I hope to give her the love and care that she deserves, Mr Hardy. And my prospects are quite good."

Maggie raises a hand, warning him not to say any more, but as far as he's concerned he's finished anyway. *Short, and to the point*, that's what Sean had advised.

"They'd better be." *Don't rise if he baits you, keep your peace.* Pat nods, says nothing. "Well, I can't say I approve, but Maggie has a mind of her own and I won't stand in her way - even if I could." Gilly turns to stare out of the window; Pat exchanges glances with Maggie, who blushes furiously. *I won't stand in her way.* Grudgingly as they are given, the words sound magical to Pat. They suggest that Maggie would have defied her father anyway; that Gilly knows this. Pat feels as if he's suddenly floating, his tension released at last, until Gilly's voice brings him back down to earth. "All right, lad, you leave me in peace now. Let me have a few moments with my daughter."

Down in the kitchen, the range feels cool; he busies himself topping up the fire with coal and boiling up water for tea. When Maggie reappears, he waits for her to speak first.

"Well, that's one hurdle overcome."

"It is so. Were you as surprised as I was?"

"Not really; he's had lots of time to cool off since he threw you out. And he just told me something interesting."

"What was that?"

"Apparently my mother's parents didn't approve of him at first; that probably helped him give you another chance, although he's still not very happy about it." She sighs. "He's got an awful nose for things; there's something else, he says. Is there anything else, Pat? Or anyone else?"

She looks directly into his eyes; Pat feels distinctly uncomfortable, the heat burning in his face, but he meets her gaze. "No other women, only...you know, New Zealand. Look, Maggie, there's only been Paula and you...the only women I ever loved. I had other girls before I met her, but none of them meant much." He's still conscious of heat in his face; knows he has to say more, about something. "Except for Mary, I suppose; that's Paddy's foster sister. She and I were sweet once, when we were kids. You can ask Paddy about her; she was like a sister to him. We both write to her as a friend, but neither of us have seen her since before the war." She continues to stare at him, her eyes steady. For a long moment, he stares back and considers telling her about the Fitzgerald farm. But his instincts scream at him, no; how could she understand all of that? Gilly would just be proved right about him, in her eyes.

Eventually, she nods. "I'll ask Paddy about her; but you're right, he's not going to like it when he finds out about New Zealand."

"We'll have to tell him some time - and the sooner the better, Maggie. He needs some warning too, just like the girls. Especially after your mother..."

"I know, Pat; you have to be patient. First I have to persuade him to let Grace come home."

"Grace?" Now, he feels confused.

"Yes, don't you see? How much easier it would be?" It dawns upon him, how that would free Maggie from her role. "That's the next step, Pat; it's what Grace wants, too. We just need to give Dad a little time to grieve and I'm sure he'll agree to it. When he comes out of my mum's room and gets back into his routine; that will be the time to ask him. Then once Grace is here, we can tell him about New Zealand." He stares at her, shaking his head in admiration.

"Jesus, you two girls have got everything sorted, haven't you?"

She smiles, "I hope so – but all in good time, Pat."

*   *   *

Maggie gives Harriet one last hug as she leaves for school, starts to make a shopping list, and stops to consider June's suggestion to clean up the bar in the hope that they can reopen the pub soon. Little Ellen sits at the table, drawing a picture that looks suspiciously like a funeral to Maggie's eyes. She shakes her head, ruffles the child's hair.

As if on cue, the latch on the door lifts, the door swings open. Gilly's face still looks exhausted, though now she can see life in his eyes. Wordlessly, he steps over, picks Ellen up and cuddles her, rubbing his unshaven cheek against her face until she cries, "That tickles, Daddy... Daddy, stop it." He gives his youngest a rueful smile and puts her down again, then gives Maggie a peck on the cheek. "You used to like that too." She nods, wipes a tear away.

"I'll get you some tea, Dad." In her memory, someone watches and smiles while she shrieks with laughter in her father's arms; she takes a deep breath and fills the kettle.

"Where is everyone?"

"Rose and Harriet have gone to school. June's doing the post office."

"Rose too? So the trains are running again?"

"Yes, Dad, it's thawing at last." She turns; sees him staring out of the window, nodding.

"So it is; well, it thawed me out, anyway. What about Paddy? Where's he got to?"

"He had to go back to Catterick, Dad, to sort out his

demobilisation; I did tell you."

He scratches his head; "How long ago?"

"About a week."

"A week? Christ, what about the shop; have they any stock left?"

"It's all right, Dad. Paddy sorted it out before he left and Pat's done what he can since. Plus, he'll sing in the bar when we reopen. If you want him to, that is."

He frowns, "I suppose so; we do need to get things started again." He gives his daughter a grim smile, "Where's he got himself to, anyway?"

"I put him with Uncle Willie again, since they know him already. He was at the hotel, but it was costing a fortune."

"I read those divorce papers, by the way. Seems to back up what he told us; it still worries me, though, what else he might be hiding."

"I've talked to Paddy, Dad. He says not."

"Paddy's loyal to a fault, Maggie; we'll see."

She sighs; still, he's come a long way, she thinks. Maybe she should strike while the iron is hot. "Are you going to open the pub, Dad? Get back to normal?"

"It's about time."

"Well, we need to think about the arrangements. Paddy will be back soon. You could do with some help, and so could I. And we need the extra space." She takes a deep breath while he considers this. "If Grace and I could share mum's room with the little ones, the other girls can shuffle round and Paddy can have a proper room."

"What? That's not extra space, Maggie...that's a crowd. Talk about a full house..." But Maggie sees his expression is one of surprise, not anger; she waits, holds her tongue. "You really want to go back to sharing a room?"

"Right now, I do, Dad. I really do."

"All right, I'll think about it; Grace has made it clear that she's not bothered about the farm. She knows the score on that." He looks up at her, his eyes narrowing. "But don't think you're pulling the wool over *my* eyes. You and Grace have cooked this up because it suits you both; she gets away from her mad in-laws and you can also prepare the girls for your leaving the nest." Maggie's mouth drops open. "I thought as much. I'm not stupid, Maggie, I can see what's on the cards; you and Mr McMahon will be thinking of getting married. Well, I can't stop you; the last thing I want is for you to run away and do it. And maybe a house full is what the other girls need right now; maybe it's what we all need. So I'll give it some serious thought. Meanwhile, get me that tea and then I'll see what we need for the bar and the shop."

*   *   *

Somehow, things have got mixed up in time; he's back in Ireland at the farm with Mary - not as a boy, but as an officer in uniform. His friend's in trouble again; someone needs to smuggle him out of the country. Fons feels totally confused about this; because of his uniform, he's not sure whether he should be helping Pat to escape or helping the authorities to catch him. He tells Mary about his dilemma; she smiles, tells him to do neither, to find Pat a better place to hide so that he can stay with her on the farm. Fons feels immense relief; he knows this is the perfect solution. But when he goes to the window, he sees Pat outside talking with a woman; both dressed for travelling, bags at the ready, waiting by the horse and trap. He assumes the woman must be his mother until she turns to wave farewell; with a shock he sees that the woman is Violet Hardy, looking young and perfectly well... he hears Mary crying out, tugging on his arm...

"I think this is your station, sir." He opens his eyes, pushes his cap up to find a young ticket inspector grinning wryly down at him. A quick glance out of the window confirms that the man is right; Paddy mutters his thanks, stumbles to his feet and lifts his kitbag down from the rack. "Sorry, sir, there are no porters at this station." The man's eyes seem to sparkle with delight.

Paddy recognises this as an example of officer baiting, common now as the war recedes; he feels no resentment. "That's OK; my batman's hiding in here somewhere, lost his ticket." He keeps his face deadpan, observes a second of confusion followed by a wry smile.

"If I'd known, I'd have let you both sleep, sir. Good evening."

A short walk later, he pushes open the front door of the pub and steps inside, relieved that the place looks open for business. Gilly turns, rising from his position by the fire, having banked it up for the evening. Before either can open their mouths, cries of delight distract them both; Maggie and June both fall upon him, hugging him fiercely. "How on earth ...did you get leave again?"

"Ah, no; I deserted." June looks shocked; he quickly adds, "Only joking; to be honest, the place is so full of returning soldiers they're glad to get rid of us. I got a weekend pass this time."

Maggie whispers, "Pat's back too; he'll be in later to sing." He nods, turns back to inspect Gilly; he looks drawn, his hair thinner, greyer. Paddy has an urge to embrace him, but the older man keeps his distance, facing him and fishing for his pipe, something he often does to distract himself.

"Glad to see the place is up and running again, Gilly."

Gilly coughs an acknowledgement, manages half a smile, "It won't be for long, Paddy, unless I can get more beer soon. Bit of a shortage, apparently. All these damn thirsty soldiers..." He sucks on the pipe, gives Maggie a meaningful glance. "Speaking of which, get the lad a cup of tea. June and I will finish this." Watching him, Paddy feels a surge of relief. Back to his normal self.

He follows Maggie into the kitchen. She seems distracted, deep in thought; worried, he wonders? He clears his throat, "Your Dad seems a lot better."

"Maybe - who knows? It's hard for him."

"What happened with him and Pat?"

"On the surface, nothing too drastic; Pat brought his divorce papers and Dad seems to have accepted him again. Though I still feel like piggy in the middle. Dad seems convinced Pat has other secrets; he sent me in here to quiz you about that, I think." She flashes him a quick smile, "Not just for the tea, if you hadn't realised."

Oh, Lord, he thinks. "As far as I know, there's no other woman in his life, Maggie. And I would tell you if there was. Are *you* worried?"

"Well, I want to believe him but he didn't look too comfortable when I asked him. He did mention an old flame called Mary."

"Mary Conlon?" Her expression tells him the surname means nothing to her. "They were both sweet on each other before Pat went across the water. She was like a sister to me; I stayed with her family when my Ma was on the boats. That's how Pat met her, but then my Ma got Pat *his* first job on the boats, and he never came back. So that little romance fizzled out *years* ago."

Maggie examines his face. "Does he still see her?"

Paddy scratches his head, "He didn't see her for years; I think just before the war he visited her in Dublin a couple of times. Just as a friend, he told me."

"Are you sure of that?"

"I think I'd know, Maggie; she writes to me pretty often. She'd have said something. And it was impossible to get to Dublin, you know, during the war. They stopped all the ferries."

"He's just been over to Ireland."

"I know; he wrote me a long letter from Liverpool. But there was no mention of Dublin, Maggie; all he talked about was how much he missed *you*." He watches her consider every word. "You can forget *that* worry, believe me. Besides, he'd have to be mad..." He feels the heat in his cheeks, shrugs.

She gives him a long hug, "Thank you, Paddy."

The feel of her against him sends a surge of desire through his body. It's been too long, he thinks; he wonders, for a moment, how Dorothy might have coped with this place, this situation. God knows; she would have helped me cope, though, that's for sure.

She steps back, "There's something else you might do for me,

Paddy."

"Ah. Now, what would that be, Maggie?"

"Remember I mentioned Pat's plans - New Zealand and all that?"

Paddy nods, "Is anything decided yet?"

"It is in Pat's mind, Paddy; he's dead set on it. Always was. The problem is, with the whole business of his divorce I haven't dared tell anyone about it, apart from you and Grace. When we first talked about it, it seemed a long way ahead, with lots of time to prepare." Oh God, he thinks, just like Dorothy and I... "Now, he's impatient... but Dad and the girls will hate the idea."

"I can imagine. What about you, though, Maggie?"

"I have to go with him, Paddy; I love him. But I need time to prepare. Grace wants to move back in, which would make it easier for the girls. Once that happens, I can start preparing them... and myself. Maybe I can follow him out after six months."

"What can I do?"

"Talk to Pat for me, Paddy. He'll listen to you; he's pressuring me to go soon, within the next six months; and he wants me to tell everyone now. He doesn't seem to understand." She sighs. "I think he and Dad set each other off. And that just makes Pat more impatient to get away. Just try and get him to see my point of view."

He scratches his head. "I'll do my best." It occurs to him, at that moment, that he's not really the best person to be the go-between; a task he neither wants, nor feels very confident about. "But I warn you, he's not the best listener in the world. Once he gets an idea fixed in his head, it's pretty damned hard to budge."

Three hours later, Paddy examines his friend's face carefully, looking for traces of the boy that he knew back in Ireland. Instinctively, he feels that he has to connect with that person before anything important can be said. He feels at a disadvantage, wearing his uniform. On seeing him for the first time in six years, Pat didn't hide his reaction to it. Maybe it's not just the uniform; all this time as an officer has made him more restrained, more circumspect in his action. Pat has changed, too. He looks older, for a start. Behind his affable exterior, Paddy can sense the underlying tension. It must have been hell on those boats, constantly waiting for a torpedo, he thinks.

"Penny for your thoughts, Captain..."

"Oh, I was thinking about the war; what it was like for you on those boats."

"You can't imagine. Well, maybe you can. You were at Dunkirk, weren't you?"

"I was."

"Well, it would be a bit like your journey back; except that it went on a wee bit longer."

Paddy laughs; "I'm not sure I could've done *that* for six years."

"You got used to it in the end. On the other hand, I'd have run a mile from a serious battle."

"We did; that was our problem. Still, we both got back in one piece, Pat."

"So we did."

"We both lost a few mates along the way, though. That was the worst part, wasn't it?" Paddy draws a circle with his finger. "Fortunately I had a girl in India who helped me through that."

"You too; that's how I got to know Maggie, you know? I was at a terrible low ebb, you see; after a few weeks in a lifeboat. She sorted me out." Pat looks down at the floor, shakes his head. "That must sound awful ungrateful; it's you I have to thank for meeting her in the first place."

Paddy shrugs, "She's a grand girl. They all are."

"She is that; and I've seen the way you look at them, Paddy. You didn't just come back here for the beer, now did you?" He looks up to see his friend grinning at him. "I thought so."

Pat always did treat him as the junior partner, he remembers; it feels uncomfortable, now. Is this the right moment? "You mentioned New Zealand in your letter. Is that still your plan?"

Pat glances around, checks that no one else is within earshot. "It is *our* plan." He gives Paddy a sideways look. "It's our chance for a fresh start, a new life. Maggie's spent enough of her life looking after her family, missing out on a career for herself. Out there, we'll have our own business and she'll have a chance to be a teacher, if that's what she wants. They need teachers out there. So it's not just for me, Paddy; it's for her, too."

He raises his hands. "Maybe, but she needs time…"

"I know, she needs time to organise for Grace to come home; then she'll be free. I hope that Grace being here won't be difficult for you, Paddy." That grin again; he can feel his irritation rising. "As soon as that's organised, Maggie and I can sort things out."

Paddy feels bemused; this, he did not expect; Pat seems to believe that the thing holding Maggie back is guilt, rather than affection for her family. He tries again, "Have you considered settling in England?"

Pat lifts his eyes to the ceiling, "Of course I have; that might suit Maggie in the short-term, but longer term, it would be a disaster. There'll be nothing here for me. The peacetime fleets will be half the size they are now; I'll be lucky to have any work at all. There's no real choice, Paddy. I'll never have another chance like this one."

He scratches his head, tries another tack. "OK, but Maggie can't just up sticks and leave her family just like that, especially now."

"There's never an ideal time, Paddy, I know that. Christ, you're worse than her father; but then I suppose you are the golden boy in his eyes."

"What? Come on, Pat, don't be so bloody stupid." The words are out of his mouth before he knows it. His tone of voice, too, sounds disconcertingly officer-like.

"I might have known you'd take his side. Here you are, just back from the British army, telling me how to run my life. Or is it that you're jealous? Is that it? Either way, just stay out of it."

"You'll lose her, if you push her too hard." He mutters this comment at Pat's back as his friend walks out of the front door. At the bar Gilly turns, raises his eyebrows. How loud were our voices, he wonders? Fortunately, Maggie's nowhere to be seen. That went well, didn't it?

He decides to take a little stroll; like Pat, to cool off. When he returns, a smiling Maggie beckons him into the kitchen. He decides not to mention his failed diplomacy. She catches his arm, whispers in his ear, "Dad just said that I can tell Grace she can move in next weekend. That's OK with you, I take it?"

"Of course it is, Maggie." He sighs with relief. "Just make sure Pat knows I gave it my seal of approval."

* * *

"Where do we start, Dad?" She stands on the threshold of her mother's room, wary of the task she's set herself.

"It looks clean enough, Maggie. You've been up here often enough."

"That's not the issue." She sighs, "Do you want to move the furniture around?"

Her father shakes his head, "That's up to you and Grace. We'll sort the beds out later; we just need to sort out your mother's stuff, today." He scratches his head.

"Shall I start with her clothes?"

A look of relief crosses his face. "You and the girls help yourself to anything that fits. And whatever you can alter, put in the big trunk in the hallway for now."

She realises, he wants to be told what to do. "All right, Dad. You should go through the writing desk and all her personal things. Keep most of it; there may be things that you want to give to us or to her sisters. But really, you should think about all that for a while."

He nods, meets her eye, "I will." He looks away. "I'll go for some boxes from the cellar." They work in silence while the afternoon shadows lengthen outside. By the time they finish, a rosy sunset casts its glow through the large window while the sun dips below the line of hills to the west.

Maggie leans on the window frame with her hands, shakes her head; "Beautiful view, Dad."

"It's one of the reasons I took the pub; this room, I mean."

She imagines her parents together, inspecting the room. She's careful not to turn her head to look at him as she speaks. "You should have been in here together, Dad."

His voice thickens but remains calm, "Don't I know it, lass. That was my hope, if she'd got better." She can almost sense his shrug. "Some things just aren't meant to be. No matter how much we wish for them." It seems so unfair. She has had some difficult moments, but nothing like that. All those years he must have spent, waiting and hoping - her poor father. How would she bear something like that? She feels a cold sensation growing, all the way down into the base of her spine. It feels as if two icy hands have grasped her waist, from the inside of her body, filling her with fear and dread. The intensity of this sensation seems to petrify her both emotionally and physically; she and time both seem to freeze. At last, a spasm of icy shivers erupts, travelling up her spine through her neck into her brain. She gasps and the involuntary movement suddenly frees her, so that she moves away from the window. She turns to see her father watching her. "You all right, Maggie?"

She shivers again. She nods, stiffly, hoping this odd feeling is nothing to do with her mother's ghost. "I'm just cold, Dad. Can we go downstairs?"

She sees doubt in his face; he bends down to pick up a box. "Alright; we could do with burning a fire in here to dry it out." She follows him out, suddenly grateful to leave.

She sits at the table nearest to the fire, warming her hands; Pat arrives and joins her. He seems in a good humour again; he hugs her with a grin and greets Gilly with a broad smile. "Shall I sing for my supper again, Mr Hardy?"

Gilly offers him a wry smile in return. "No real need tonight, Pat; there's never that many in, midweek. But don't let me stop you, if you feel so inclined."

"We'll play it by ear, then, shall we?"

This also produces a smile, followed by a thoughtful look. "Speaking of which, maybe you should be telling me about these prospects of yours. Between Paddy and yourself, I'm curious as to what each of you have planned. Will you be staying in the navy?"

Maggie places a warning hand on Pat's sleeve, hoping to restrain him. He glances at her, turns to her father, "I suppose so." Maggie breathes a sigh of relief; but Pat catches her eye, smiles, and adds

"After a fashion."

"How do you mean?" Maggie tugs on the sleeve, urgently. Pat looks at her and winks.

"I had some good news today." He turns back to Gilly; "I have a friend with his master's licence, Mr Hardy. As you know I'm an engineer. Between us we have the knowledge to run a ship, or ships; we plan to do that."

"Sounds interesting; so what was the good news?"

"My friend has been promised the finance to buy a couple of refrigerated ships. They're virtually ours, it seems. Surplus to US army requirements, now the war's over."

"Really?" Gilly looks stunned; then, thoughtful. "Must have cost a pretty penny; I hope you know what you're doing, Pat. Not much call for fridges in this climate." Maggie tugs Pat's arm again, watches him bite his lip, stay silent. "What are you planning to transport, anyway?"

Pat gives her a helpless shrug. "Meat, people in Europe need meat, Mr Hardy."

"I can't disagree with that. But meat's an expensive cargo, Pat; how on earth will you find the money to fill a ship with meat?" Maggie can't help but admire her father's logic; though she also fears his persistence, wearing down Pat's already weak resolve.

"We'll manage."

Gilly laughs out loud; "That's not prospects, that's bankruptcy. You need to *know* that you can do it." She tugs his sleeve again, one last time.

Pat blushes, rubs his head. "We know we can."

"How do you know?" Pat picks up her hand and squeezes it, gives her a quick glance.

"My friend's father also knows most of the meat farmers in New Zealand, Mr Hardy. There's a surplus of lamb over there. We have a deal with those farmers; they'll provide the meat at New Zealand cost but we'll pay them *after* the sale and share the profits."

Gilly nods; "A bit like a cooperative. That could work, all right." He gives Maggie a long look. "But I don't see how..." He stops, swallows, sucks his lip. "You'll have to go out there, won't you, to live?" Pat nods, slowly; Maggie feels her face heat up. "When were you planning on telling me this, Maggie? The day before you left?" She shakes her head, too choked up to reply. "I knew there was something else you were keeping from me." He looks pale suddenly; older than ever.

"It won't be immediate, Mr Hardy. We have a few months to prepare the girls."

"A few months?" Gilly doesn't bother to disguise the scorn in his voice. He looks at Maggie, "I suppose your mind is made up?" Maggie sniffles, avoids his eyes; gives a quick nod.

"Well, I just wish you had both thought to ask me about it before it was all cut and dried. I would have told you, Pat McMahon, that Maggie is the most giving of all my daughters; you probably know that already. But that makes her the most connected, too, with all of us. She'll find it very hard in a strange land away from all her connections; if you're not careful, part of her will wither and die. Maybe the best part of her; you should really think about that." He looks at Maggie and raises his voice, "And so should you."

Suddenly, Maggie feels absolutely terrified at the reality of it; the prospect of leaving everything she knows and loves. Pat's arm envelopes her, but somehow that makes no difference to how she feels. His words sound perfectly logical, but his tone of voice suddenly seems too loud, too hollow, tinged with vanity. "Don't you worry, I'll take good care of her, Mr Hardy. I grant you it won't be easy, but she'll be gaining a better life, a fresh start with the chance to do all the things she's not able to here. She can be a teacher, out there..."

As the two men face each other, Maggie feels like a prize they are fighting over. She feels torn, bruised and despoiled; as if they have wrenched her back and forth, fought over her while they trod upon her. So, she feels relief when the front door bursts open and another man steps in, rubbing his hands against the cold, wiping his boots. Constable Burns isn't a regular; though when he has business higher in the dale he often calls in for a drink before he heads back down to Stanhope. At least this will stop them arguing, she thinks. Gilly turns towards him, clears his throat, "Good evening, Harry. What'll it be?"

The Constable holds his hand up in polite refusal; his face looks far, far too serious, with a hint of embarrassment. "Sorry, Gilly, I'm here on business; it's bad news, I'm afraid." Gilly blinks, his eyes puzzled and wary. Maggie wonders what it is now; some petrol coupons or farm goods gone astray, a forged ration book?

When the Constable speaks again, his words make no sense to Maggie. "I'm afraid it's your eldest, Gilly; it's about Grace. We found her in the old quarry up above the farm. I'm afraid she's killed herself. I'm terribly sorry." Maggie stands up, tries to puzzle out the meaning. She experiences a curious dizzy sensation while the words seem to fall slowly into place, and then a sudden shock as she hits the floor.

*　　*　　*

She tosses and turns, smothered by a black cloak of exhaustion and despair, entombed by her grief in restless dreams. She finds herself wandering the moors again, searching for a path back to safety. She feels utterly lost, yet has a curious sense of familiarity with this landscape; somehow, she knows she has been to this place before. Here in this wasteland, the deep shadows on the hillside steadily lengthen, darkness approaching. She picks her way down the deserted valley, filled with an increasing foreboding, dreading what must await her at the church.

Stumbling out of the wooded ravine towards the pealing bells, she sees the church spire silhouetted against a full moon. The gates stand open; out of the corner of her eye, she glimpses the last of the mourners skulking away back to the village while she hurries into the churchyard. She runs to the newly-dug grave, drops to her knees, begins to claw at the earth with her hands. She digs and digs, reaching down into the cold earth with deadening hands until finally she feels something move. Overcoming her shock and terror, she pushes her fingers down; other fingers reach up, touching her own. She tries to grasp the hand, feels the fingers reaching for her; she's about to call out to her sister when two strong faceless men take hold of her arms and pull her away from the grave, losing her grip. She struggles and pleads, crying and begging; they ignore her and slowly but firmly drag her away out of the churchyard. She screams at them to let her go back, to rescue Grace, wriggling to break free of their grip, but the two of them together have far too much strength. She sees both sympathy and concern on their faces; yet Pat and Paddy act like robots, implacable and irresistible, as if she were the crazy one.

She falls out of the dream, wakes to find herself gasping a lungful of air, as if breaking the surface after a deep dive. It's been like this for days, now. Sleep eludes her completely, wriggles out of her grasp, or transforms into nightmare as soon as she captures it. Her body feels drained, exhausted, emptied of rest; her mind feels constantly alert, afraid. She feels split in two; as if she were both the quarry, constantly hunted, while she also hunts for sleep. She lies there and listens to the sound of Ellen's steady breathing.

As soon as Grace walks silent and smiling into the room, she feels enormous relief; after all that, the last few days must have been a bad dream. Grace pauses and waits by the door, as if choosing to stand apart and watch over her. The two sisters communicate wordlessly, every glance and nuance of expression effortlessly understood. Grace tells her *everything will be alright, don't worry about the future, it will take care of itself.*

"I've missed you; even when we fought, I always knew you would be there. I'm so glad we're going to share a room again. It's a lovely room, isn't it?"

Of course it is; mum will be pleased that we are using it. You must rest and gather all of your strength. Maggie feels her hair being stroked from the far side of the room. She luxuriates in this feeling, savouring it, as she used to do when Grace or her mother poured bowls of hot water upon her hair while she stood in the bath in front of the kitchen range. After a while, she wonders how Grace can possibly do this. She wants to thank Grace for coming back, for making everything possible once again. She turns her head and opens her eyes. For a moment she sees a figure in the shadows, watching her, in a room that's suddenly smaller; she's back in her own room. She blinks, and Grace vanishes back into the night. In her place Maggie hears Ellen breathing; life.

* * *

The simple austerity of this rural church strikes him first, reminding him of the one near his home; where that damned priest had so angered him, preaching against the Republican movement. As they walk together down the aisle he can feel Maggie's weight leaning and pressing against him, a physical expression of her need for comfort; this is where she wishes to be married, later this year. They enter the front pew next to Gilly and Fons, who both turn to examine Maggie with concerned eyes, directing faint nods in his direction. June squeezes in behind him; the younger girls and the aunts move into the space across the aisle. Pat has felt the eyes of the villagers watching their faces curiously while the family procession passed; twice, he realises, in such a short space of time. No wonder the girls all seem so shocked, he thinks, completely paralysed in disbelief. Maggie cannot speak about Grace without dissolving into tears. The other sisters also avoid speaking about her openly; though they gather together sometimes, to whisper in corners. Somehow Gilly holds himself together, keeping his words simple, focussing his actions on practical tasks. For Pat, this confirms his own view of Gilly as a tough old buzzard; Fons seems amazed at his resilience. Either way, it seems to be his anger that currently holds him together. Gilly's furious; the police had blandly assumed suicide and spread a rumour to this effect about, even before the inquest. As it turned out, the coroner had ruled Grace's death as 'misadventure'.

Pat listens to the rain pattering down outside the church window, punctuated by the occasional cough. The place needs an organ, he thinks; some source of music to console or lift the spirits, though the latter would need a miracle in these circumstances. The sound of more feet shuffling down the aisle causes all the heads to turn; following the collective gaze, Pat sees a young, dazed looking private soldier, his features set in a grim mask, eyes staring fixedly to the front as if on some ghastly parade. That must be David, he thinks; poor bastard. They finally sent him home from Italy, too late to do anything but grieve. An older couple follow closely behind, the woman clutching a small child. The man glances over at the Hardy family with sympathy in his eyes and nods; the woman keeps her eyes fixed ahead, holding the child in a way that provides her with a shield against the stares of the Hardy family. A tall, ungainly man with an exaggerated limp and prominent, darting eyes brings up the rear. He too avoids eye contact, half-turning his body away. Rather than joining his brother and parents behind the aunts, he shuffles into the next row behind them and moves across to the far side, as if the Hardy family have some contagious disease. That'll be the man who started those rumours, Pat thinks; rumours that Grace had killed herself because she was depressed and crazy like her mother. Whatever happened, so the rumour went, it must all be due to something odd in the Hardy family, surely?

In his own mind, Pat has formed a very favourable impression of Maggie's family, especially the aunts and uncles. They've all rallied around Gilly and the girls; especially the couple that he stays with, Violet's brother and his wife. Glancing around, he hasn't quite sorted out who all the others are, but clearly Gilly's and Violet's clans both look after their own. He's observed various aunts delivering home-baked food over the last week or so, despite rationing. Since Gilly and the girls have no appetite, he and Paddy have been hard pressed to eat it all. Somehow they have all produced more today, for the English version of a wake. The aunts have also kept the Post office open while he and Paddy helped Gilly in the bar. All this support has left him thinking that when he and Maggie go to New Zealand, she's not indispensable. Of course the family will miss her; but as an outsider, he can see simple facts. The family's not poor, and has a plethora of helpful relatives. He can't help but compare to Irish families, to the famines and forced exiles, and feel that Maggie will leave something stable and viable behind. It seems self-evident to him, they'll cope.

A nervous cough drags his attention back to the front of the church, to the man in a white cassock standing by the coffin. Compared to priests in Ireland he seems oddly hesitant, unsure of himself. The service also seems awkward, the eulogy truncated, as if the man feels that he cannot refer to the tragedy except in the most general of terms. He claims to have known Grace since childhood and makes much of her loving nature and her sense of fun, referring to Daniel as "the gift she left behind". Yet when he finishes, Pat thinks that he's not learned anything new about her.

Standing at the graveside during the final ritual, Pat stares into the distance over the heads of the others, watching villagers drifting out of the exit gate. He sees the limping man shuffle away without a backward glance; not even towards his brother, his parents, or his nephew. As if in response to his absence, Grace's husband finally breaks down and sobs uncontrollably. The girls cry silently; Gilly adopts a soldier's posture, standing stiffly at attention, staring directly into the cold wind and rain, as if daring fate to test him yet again. Pat cannot help but admire; he thinks *the old buzzard certainly has guts.*

Maggie leans upon him, silent, throughout the short walk back to the Cross Keys. There, she sparks back into life, helping her aunts finish preparing the food. Behind the bar, Gilly pulls a beer for him and Fons, then waves them away. "Let me do this; I need something to do, today." They retreat into a corner, watching June and Rose attempting to comfort David.

"Nobody can make any sense of it, can they?"

"I'm not surprised, Fons. The both of us have seen a lot of senseless deaths in this war; like everyone else, we thought that would be stopping now." Pat examines his friend's face. "You were engaged to her once, weren't you?"

"I was." He looks down and shakes his head, "One of those things that happened just before the soldier went away." He looks up, gives a wry smile. "There was a few of us in that boat, out in India; not many of them lasted."

"Did you love her?"

Fons gives him a sharp look, his eyes narrow. He looks away, considers, and then sighs, "I thought so at the time; though I wouldn't say that now, Pat. But she was still a lovely girl; a bit like Maggie, but quieter, deeper maybe."

"It must be tough for you, anyway."

"Tougher for him," Pat glances across at David; sees that Maggie has joined him.

"I'm sure it is; what a homecoming." She and David seem to be talking earnestly.

"I'm glad the poor beggar didn't have to endure the inquest; that was a bit of a shambles, Pat. Fraught would be the word."

"Was it? In that case I'm glad Gilly kept Maggie away." Pat waits for Fons to tell more.

"So am I." Fons takes a slow sip of his beer, considering his words carefully. "I suppose it is human nature to want to blame someone else. From what Gilly told me, the mother-in-law told the coroner that she thought Grace had killed herself because she was miserable away from home and Gilly wouldn't let her go back."

"Jesus, that's a bit harsh; and it doesn't quite fit, does it? Gilly had already told her she *could* come back. And as far as Maggie knew, she was really looking forward to it."

Fons nods, "Yes; Gilly made that point in no uncertain terms when he got his chance. He also made it pretty clear that he thought it was the in-laws that were making her miserable. He told the coroner that the brother and mother had driven Grace to despair. So we had the two families blaming each other, to start with, and on top of that we had the police assuming she'd killed herself because she was crazy like her mother."

"Sounds like a hell of a mess."

"It was; but I suppose in a small place like this, the police know all the families, and make assumptions. Mind you, it was obvious the police had talked to David's family first."

"So what did the coroner say?"

"He was very logical about it. He pointed out there was no note, nothing to indicate any *intent* to kill herself. He said he couldn't rule out that her mind may have been disturbed, but since everyone agreed she was a devoted mother, that made suicide unlikely. She probably went for a walk by the quarry because she wanted to have some peace and quiet; very diplomatic assumption, I thought. He felt it was most likely a tragic accident. In other words, she went for a walk to enjoy the view, got too close to the edge, then slipped and fell."

"Is that likely, Fons? You knew her pretty well."

"It's possible, though she wasn't such a great walker as Maggie. But she had reason enough to get out of the house." He frowns, biting his lip. "It's uncanny, though, Pat. Violet did something similar at another one of those old quarries, soon after I first arrived. She got stuck on a ledge; I helped her down. She used to get pretty strange when her babies were born, you know. I think that was the start of all her problems."

"You think Grace having a baby..."

Fons shrugs, "I've no idea, Pat. It might just be coincidence. Don't mention it to the girls, anyway; it would only worry them." He frowns. "I shouldn't really have told you. I promised Violet not to tell a soul."

Pat nods. He looks at the floor, wondering about Maggie; how will she react to having children? He remembers how she is with Ellen, shakes his head. You can forget that, he tells himself. As if on cue, he hears Maggie's voice, "Well, what are you two plotting? How to escape from this crazy family?" He looks up; her face looks so fragile, on the edge of tears.

"We'd be the crazy ones to do that, now wouldn't we, Pat?"

"We surely would." He stands up, gestures for her to sit between them. "Come and sit between your two favourite men." He watches her blush and whispers, "You can count on the both of us." She nods, blinks back a tear. "I think you need a gin; and your Pa should have some whisky. I've got a bottle of Irish in my bag I brought from Liverpool. He needs it more than I do."

Fons gives him an approving nod, "That he does."

When he returns with the gin, Fons asks, "You're not sleeping, are you, Maggie?"

She shakes her head, "Not much, Paddy."

"Bad dreams?"

"Sometimes; plus, I keep remembering things we did together, Grace and I."

Fons nods his head, slowly. "My Indian girl would have said you were just trying to keep her alive in your head." He blushes; "Dorothy. She was half-Indian, to be exact."

"You never told us that before, Paddy," Maggie stares at him, astonished.

He pulls a face, "I didn't know how you'd react."

Maggie drops her gaze, takes a deep breath. "Well, she sounds like a wise woman." She nudges Pat, "Don't you think so?"

Pat shrugs, thinks of girls in foreign ports and the sailors who jumped ship for them. "She probably had other attractions, too." He watches the colour deepen in Fons' face and grins.

Maggie forces a smile, for the first time in weeks, "I bet she was beautiful, Paddy."

"She was; wise and beautiful, and more."

Maggie stares at Fons; "What would she have said about guilt, Paddy?"

"What sort of guilt?"

She sniffs, takes a deep breath, "When Mum died, Grace pointed out how we all keep thinking of things we could have done to change things, to stop it happening. Like visiting more often, taking the little ones." She takes a large swallow of her drink. "With Grace, well...I keep blaming myself... for... all sorts of things." Her face twists in distress, before she struggles on. "Mostly, for not talking Dad round much earlier; if I'd done that, she'd be here today."

Pat shakes his head, "You don't know that, Maggie."

She puts her head in her hands. "I do."

Fons lifts his hands in a pacifying gesture, "Maggie, I'll answer your question. Dorothy would have said that Grace would never, ever want you to torture yourself in that way. What's done is done; you can't undo it. Grace of all people would want you to move on."

She looks from one man to the other, "Far easier said, than done."

The two men exchange glances. Pat shrugs; to his surprise, Fons stands up abruptly and walks away. Pat turns to see what Maggie makes of this; he sees puzzlement followed by a rueful, embarrassed look. "What is it?"

She hisses, "I think he's bringing George. Oh Lord, he is." She musters an effort to force a smile, whispers in his ear, "George was sweet on both of us."

Pat turns and sees a man wearing a very expensive suit; remembers his stammer. Fons pushes George forward, "Maggie, I don't suppose your father's told you much... about the inquest, I mean." He's gone into officer mode, thinks Pat; funny, I can't get used to the idea of Fons ordering everyone about. "George was there in the court; tell Maggie what the coroner decided, George, and why." Not such a bad idea, Pat thinks; Fons might be right about this. Yet when he looks at Maggie he sees her face turning very pale.

George's explanation takes an eternity, due to his stammer, though he makes a good summary. That should help, Pat thinks. It seems to work, initially; Maggie looks calmer, more matter of fact. She thinks for a moment, asks, "Who found her?"

"The... the police, I suppose."

"Are you sure? How did they know where to look?"

"I'm n...n...not sure, Maggie. I got the impression the T...Turnbulls had been worried about her. She'd gone for a walk w...while the p...p...parents were out. When she didn't come back for the baby they phoned the p...p...police."

"The parents had been out?"

"Yes, they'd been gone all morning."

"Oh, God," Maggie chokes the words out, before her head sinks into her hands. "I'll bet it was Richard that told them where to look."

Pat has to think who Richard is for a second; the image of the limping man, half turned away, jumps into his mind; the man who couldn't bear to look at them. Fons' jaw tightens, while George's large brow twitches and furrows. Instinctively, Pat leans forward, wraps his arm around Maggie, whispers in her ear, "Why is that so important, Maggie?"

She shakes her head, turns and hides herself against his chest, sobbing, as if sheltering from a hailstorm of pain. He listens as if to an aria; he hears a tone of pure anguish. After a while some whimpers begin to break through, adding a quality of desperate pleading. She tries to speak, but chokes. He makes out two words, "Not here..."

"Come on, then," he lifts her up, carefully walks her out through the kitchen, enfolding and shielding her as if the blizzard was real rather than emotional. Heads turn, glance in their direction; not with surprise, more with relief, it seems to him. When they reach the hallway he takes a deep breath, waits for her breathing to slow, and gives her a gentle squeeze. "Now, Maggie, there's just us. Tell me what's going on."

"Oh, Pat - I promised...I promised not to tell a soul."

"Promised who, Maggie?"

"Grace. I promised Grace, but I should have told my father. She'd be home now, and safe."

"Told him what, Maggie?"

He waits while she sobs again, her voice choking, "Richard... the brother... he was nasty to her at first, Pat. Dad knew about that; but later... he was trying... you know..."

"...to get fresh with her?"

"Yes, that's it," he hears relief in her voice; "Grace had begun to be frightened of him. She said he had got a bit obsessed about her, but..." she chokes, for a long moment.

"But what, Maggie...?"

"Grace said he was very clever about it; he never did anything in front of his parents. The mother would have taken Richard's side, anyway, and it would have caused an unholy row with David; and with my father. It still would, and we don't know..."

"Christ, the calculating bastard..." As Pat's burst of rage subsides, he feels a certainty about this man; like the bastard who hurt Mary. It's happened again, he thinks, only worse. Then it hits him; dammit, it's Paula, all over again. "Are you the only one she told?"

"I think so."

"You can't keep quiet, Maggie."

She rests her head on his shoulders, "I know." After a long pause, he hears a greater firmness in her voice. "But we can't tell my father, not yet; he'd kill him, I know he would. We need to find out exactly how they found the body."

"We should go to the police."

"They'll just think I'm crazy, like my mum - and like my sister, in their eyes."

"Don't say that."

The anguish returns to her voice; "But it's true, Pat. They will; we both know that."

"What about George; isn't he a lawyer?"

"He's never practised, you know..." a brief pause before her tone of scepticism vanishes; "You're right; he'll know what to do, at the very least. He's no fool, you know; his family also have a lot of influence in this dale. If anyone can get the police to listen, George can."

"Come on, then. No time like the present."

Her head falls back into her hands; "Can you do it for me, Pat? I just can't face them right now; I feel too ashamed. Tell George to be discreet – he'll understand why. You can tell Paddy as well, but make sure he doesn't breathe a word of this to my father. I'll sit on the stairs for a while." She looks up, manages a weak smile. "When you come back, Pat, bring me another gin."

*　*　*

Padding silently across the floor, she pulls back the curtains. By the window, the cold floorboards make her feet pucker upward while she squints at the rose pink light growing above the hills. Stepping backward onto the rug, she continues to stare out at the horizon. Grace should be looking at this with me, she thinks. I don't want to be alone in this room, not now. Perhaps I should ask June to share it with me. She's always kept herself a little too apart. Or maybe the truth is that Grace and I tended to leave her out once we got a bit older; we never let her catch up. Yes, she thinks, that's what I'll do; it'll help us both. Then Paddy can have a decent room until he decides what he's doing. At this simple thought of the future, she feels her gut tighten; not yet, she thinks, I can't think about all that now. Out in the hall, she hesitates outside the door of her old room. "June?" She hears a muffled groan, pushes the door ajar, looks in, "Time to get up; Harriet's back to school today."

In the half-light a tousled head emerges from under the covers. "I know; Rose can take her, I'll do the post office." She can't make out her sister's expression.

She hesitates for a moment, and then sighs, "Can I ask you something?"

June sits up, her face suddenly alert. "What is it? Are you all right, Maggie?"

The look of concern that she sees touches Maggie so much, she has to blink back her tears; she moves into the room, sits on the bed. "I was thinking about the rooms, June." She wonders how to put it, so that it will not seem like an order, "I..."

"Do you want your old room back, Maggie?" She feels June reach out and take her hand; the voice drops to a whisper. "It must feel awfully strange in there, now."

She swallows back a tear, feels relief flooding through her. "It does a bit, June. It's a lovely room but it feels too big for me on my own. I was wondering if you would like to share it with me."

"Me? Are you sure?" June seems stunned, taken aback.

"Quite sure, June; I know you have your own room now..."

"No, Maggie, that's not it, I'd love to share a room with you; I'm just not sure about *that* one. It's not haunted, is it?"

Maggie stares at her expression for a moment, then laughs. "No, June, it's not haunted. You can feel traces of Mum in there, but not in a bad way. I've never felt scared in there." Then, she remembers, "Well, only once. And that was the day Grace died; I felt very odd... as if I had a premonition, somehow."

"You and her always were very close, Maggie." She hears a small note of envy.

"I suppose." She sniffs back another tear; "So how about it?"

June narrows her eyes, bites her lip, "As long as we can put Ellen in with Harriet - it's about time Harry pulled her weight."

Maggie blinks, looks at her sister with new respect. "That's a damned good idea, June."

Suddenly June's hugging her, thanking her, excited at the prospect. Maggie feels waves of comfort emanating from her sister; it washes over her, sends relief tingling up and down her spine. Who would have thought it, she tells herself, that June would be the one to understand her feelings so clearly? The moment lodges in her mind; she comes back to it, again and again, that day.

"Penny for your thoughts, Maggie...?"

She looks up, shakes herself out of her daydream. "What? Oh, nothing. " She watches one of his eyebrows raise. "I was just thinking about our June; she's got hidden depths, you know."

Pat nods, "That she has; she's not your baby sister anymore." He frowns for a moment, as if considering something, pulls a letter out of his pocket. "She spotted this for me in the lunchtime mailbag; got it a day early, thanks to her."

She bites her lip, "What is it... the decree absolute?"

He pulls a face, "Not yet, but *that* shouldn't be long now." He looks up, his face eager, boyish. "It's from Frank's father in New Zealand. Everything's going according to plan." She nods and looks away. Her instinct tells her, don't discuss this now; she walks to the kitchen window, stares out at the trees. "I thought you'd want to know."

She takes a deep breath, tries to ignore the tone of irritation in his voice. "I do, Pat, but not right now. Tell me later; I've just got too much else to worry about."

"I know you've got a lot on your plate, I'm sorry. But this is something to look forward to, Maggie, not to worry about. For once in my life, things seem to be working out."

The comment brings an aftershock, a slap in the face. What does he mean, *for once in my life*? Haven't we spent the last eighteen months working something out? And some things are most definitely *not* working out, *can't he see that*? She stifles her own irritation. "I'm very glad about that, Pat." Then, she can't stop herself adding, "But I really can't think about it all now." She hears a grunt of frustration; turns, to see him rubbing his forehead with his hand.

He seems to think for an awfully long time before he resorts to a quiet pleading tone. "We have to think about it sometime soon, Maggie. I have to leave England within the next six months, preferably sooner. If you want us to be married here, we'll need to set a date pretty soon."

"Don't rush me, Pat. I really need some time to think about everything."

He stares at her, his eyes widening, "How much time do you need? Christ, it took us over a year just to tell your father; and your sisters still don't know."

"Whose fault was that?"

His face colours; he looks away, shaking his head. "OK, OK; but you know damned well what I mean. I'm just pointing out that we do have *some* time limits."

"*You* have time limits." She sees his face blanch; she adds, "With everything that's happened here recently, I can't just up sticks and go right now; you must see that."

He takes a deep breath, takes hold of her hand. "Maggie, I know how hard it is for you, but there never will be an easy time to go. There's always going to be some reason to put it off. Believe me, I know; I know the pain of leaving home. But sometimes you just have to trust your instincts and take that leap into the unknown."

She pulls her hand back, turns away, "That's just it, Pat. My instincts are screaming at me not to go." She turns back to face him, sees horror in his face.

"You can't mean that; it's just grief talking."

"I wish it were, Pat; maybe it is, but I don't think so."

"Christ, Maggie, don't do this to me."

"I told you not to rush me. When we first talked about this, we talked about a year or two, Pat; and my mother and Grace were both alive then."

"You really don't want to go, do you?"

And in that long moment, watching his eyes examine her face, it seems quite clear to her that she doesn't; she feels completely foolish for having gone along with the idea for so long. She feels the heat in her face but shakes her head emphatically from side to side, too terrified to speak the words aloud.

"Christ; then why have we been wasting all this time? Look; I've committed myself now, Maggie. I thought we'd agreed; that it was just a matter of when, not if." She hears his irritation peak and then watches it evaporate from him, his posture slowly slumping as his hopes also escape, as if through a myriad of tiny puncture holes...

"Oh, Pat, please don't go... not now; give me some more time."

Suddenly, his voice sounds resigned, defeated. "I can't." His eyes give her a long and wary stare so that she feels, for the first time, that he's viewing her now as a foolish young girl. "No, I can't. Frank and his family are relying on me to go; I've committed myself and my life savings. More important, I've given him my word. I'm not going back on my word, not even for you, Maggie." He shakes his head, draws in a lungful of air, his face devoid of expression. "The hard thing is; I'm sorry, I couldn't live here with your family. For lots of reasons; there's no work here, I'd feel stifled, and I'd end up resenting them too much. And even if we lived down at the coast somewhere, I don't want to go back to working for someone else. No, I'm going, whatever you decide. I want you to marry me and come with me; but that's your choice."

She feels hot tears running down her face; surely he can't be that cruel? Why can't he understand? "I can't go with you. I can't leave my family now, Pat - maybe in a couple of years, but not now. I'll gladly marry you if you stay."

She watches in disbelief while he shakes his head sadly, walks to the door. "I think I'd better go to my brothers in Ireland. There's no point in us torturing ourselves by me staying here any longer. You know where you can reach me, if you change your mind." She stands there, stunned into silence. The door shuts, quietly; after a few seconds the thought begins to burrow into her gut... has Pat, too, gone from her life? Part of her wants to run after him; another part feels so hurt, so betrayed, so furious that he can't or won't understand her feelings. Perhaps she can't really be that important to him? Was her father right, all along? She stands frozen, paralysed by doubt.

* * *

Holding himself together with a steely resolve, he strides back to his lodgings, focussing on the practicalities, planning out his course of action. Approaching the lane to the farmhouse, he meets his hosts (a quiet, middle-aged couple) heading in the opposite direction. He nods his greeting and stops, as if to pass the time of day.

"Now then, Pat; forgotten something?"

He forces a rueful smile, "Not this time, Willie; but I need to thank you for your hospitality. I'm afraid something's come up back in Ireland, so I have to be off today."

They both nod sagely, a hint of curiosity in their eyes, but refrain from asking more. Probably, Pat thinks, out of relief; relief that this particular crisis does not involve them, this time. Maggie's aunt picks something out of her purse; for a second Pat thinks he is being treated to a few pence, like a child. "You'd better take this back, then."

He recognises his ration card, gives another wry smile, "Thanks, for your cooking especially, Marjorie." She blushes, shakes her head; her husband winks at him, gives a farewell handshake and slap on the back.

Back at the house he gathers together clothes and possessions, packs them carefully into his kitbag. This extra journey will eat into his remaining money, though that can't be helped. He can compensate by organising a way to work his passage. Right now, it feels uncannily like this particular ship is sinking; as if he has suddenly been given an hour to get ready for the lifeboat, to prepare himself. Yet, in another way, he feels that this crisis has been brewing, inevitable; ever since Maggie's father found out about his marriage, this boat has been heading for the rocks, despite all his efforts. The very place seems to have turned on him, creating a bizarre mix of circumstances that have combined to drive him out, exactly as America did - even down to the most peculiar of echoes; the deaths of Paula and Grace. He takes a deep breath and forces himself to sit down, to stop and think, untangle his guts. The urge to hurry away, to run, feels tangible within his body.

Has he been too hasty? He forces himself to re-examine the conversation; maybe he has, maybe he should have waited longer after her sister's death before trying to press her. How much longer could he have waited? He has to tell Frank *something*. She could have gone on avoiding the issue for ever; delaying, procrastinating, while time ran out. He had to make some preparations, to know what was possible, or likely. Better to know where he stood; even if it was on the opposite side of the fence. He sighs. If he stayed around now, knowing this, just hoping for her to change her mind, the situation would drive him crazy. There's more of a chance that she'll change her mind when she's confronted by the reality of his absence. This, he realises, is the logic of his own action. *That* is what I am hoping for. Well, I've been in a lifeboat before, he tells himself, in the middle of a cold bleak ocean. Here we go again; except the ocean's in my head, this time.

Walking back down the lane toward the road, he watches a battered little car slow, turn up the lane and head toward him; Gilly, he thinks? For a brief moment he hopes that Maggie may have changed her mind; then he sees the cropped dark hair over the wheel. As the car coasts to a halt, Fons stares out at him, his expression wary. "I thought you might appreciate a lift into town."

"I suppose Maggie told you?" Fons grunts, gives him a slow,

resigned looking nod. Do his eyes also twinkle with amusement? "Is this to say goodbye or to escort me off the premises?"

Fons leans across, pushes the door open. "Get in, you great lummock."

Pat scratches his head, reluctantly offers a wry smile. He swings his kitbag onto the rear seat and flops aboard, trying to appear casual. "Take it away, Captain Reilly."

Fons waits until they reach the main road before he speaks again, this time in a more serious, urgent tone; "She sent me to ask you to stay, if you must know."

Pat chews his lip for a while. "Does that mean she'll come with me?"

Fons shrugs, "Maybe, eventually - probably, I'd say, if you give her enough time. You'd have to ask her that yourself."

"Eventually? Five years, or maybe ten?" Fons ignores the question, stares at the road ahead with an apparent grim concentration; Pat sighs and looks away. "I can't hang around, Fons; I have to help get this thing up and running. I have to be in Auckland within six months."

After another pause, Fons resumes, his tone a curious mix of impatience and resignation; "Try to see it from her point of view, Pat. Her sisters have lost their mother and one sister already; if she goes, they lose another sister. She can't do that to them."

"There's no easy road out of home, Fons, we both know that."

Now, he hears a hint of cold anger; "It's not the same, Pat." And then, as if mustering his will, Fons reverts again to a patient, pleading voice. "She's lost her mother and her sister. Try to remember what it was like for you, when you lost your mother."

Pat thinks about this for a long time; his ideas seem to loop up around over terrible similarities but then spiral down over equally difficult differences, never reaching a conclusion. "You're right, it's not the same. We're all different, Fons, I grant you. But it seems to me there's a lot of family here, lots of others who would help her father and her sisters."

"By the same token, lots of others she'd miss."

They both lapse into a sullen silence until the turn for the railway station comes into view, prompting Pat to make some kind of peace. "Thanks for trying, Fons. Look, let me explain it to you; it's pretty straightforward. I need to make a decent life for myself while I still can. I've messed it up before now and messed about going nowhere for years, so this feels like my last chance. I have to do it. Maybe for her it comes down to a blunt choice between me and her family. I thought she'd already made her choice, but she hadn't."

Fons nods, "Maybe, but..."

"No buts, Fons, I've had my fill of those."

Once again, the silence hangs between them like a wraith. He watches Fons clench and slowly unclench his fists on the wheel; they coast to a stop outside the ticket office. After another long pause, Fons gives him a sideways glance, triggering simultaneous shrugs that signal an uneasy truce, an end to discussion. Pat shakes his head, climbs out of the car and gives his friend an awkward embrace. He didn't want to part like this, from Fons; why did he have to take sides, dammit? "I had been hoping to see a bit more of you this time, to do a bit of catching up at last."

"Me too; well, take care of yourself, Pat the singer."

"And you, Alfonsus; if I were you, I'd get yourself off to college on one of those army scholarships; take advantage of it while you can."

Fons blinks, his expression puzzled, "Those what?"

"Christ, Fons, don't you read the papers?" He sees an expression of annoyance, raises his hands. "OK, sorry. It's just a bit of a sore point with all of us in the merchant navy. You people in the forces get campaign medals plus all sorts of extra help now that the war's over; we're getting nothing. We'll be damn lucky if we keep our jobs, since we won't be shipping all those bombs and tanks anymore." Fons nods, gives him a rueful grimace of acknowledgement. "I was reading about some scheme to send officers with enough war service back to college; you ought to look into it."

His friend rubs his chin, thrusts out a hand, "I will. Good luck to you, Pat."

"A chara," He feels his hand grasped and crushed; an impish grin crossing Fons' face. Pat buys his ticket, gives a last wave and walks slowly away, wondering if he'll ever see Fons again.

"Wait, wait..." He hears the call, turns back to see his friend jogging towards him, waving an oilskin envelope that seems to have appeared from nowhere. "Maggie told me I had to give you these if I couldn't persuade you to stay."

It hurts, the idea that she doesn't want to keep them. He wonders; is she calling my bluff? He sighs; probably not, it'll be like the ration card, just her sense of correct behaviour. He bites his lip, considers carefully. He needs to leave something here as a bridge, as a reminder that she can still choose to come. He shakes his head, waves Fons away. "Tell her to keep them, Fons, to remember me by; I have no use for old photographs, too much baggage already."

"Are you sure?" He's not, really; but he can't admit that, so he nods curtly and then turns his back, walking quickly away.

*　　*　　*

It feels strange to be out of uniform. Not that his demob suit is bad; in fact, he's very pleased with it, never having owned a smart suit before. So pleased, in fact, he's wearing it today - though as he approaches the Cross Keys, he feels rather over-dressed. Today is the first truly warm day of the year, the bright sun highlighting the daffodils sprouting along the roadside verge. He pushes through the front door, puts down his bag; glances around the bar. No other customers in here; a mop and bucket stand near the door. He resists the temptation to help himself and rings the bell, the one that normally signals last orders; nothing happens, so he sits down and takes out his paper to read. After a while, he tries again. Footsteps approach; he raises his paper to hide his face.

"Can I help you... is that *you*, George?" Maggie's voice sounds flustered. He lowers the paper, putting on his most innocent expression. She stares at him for a second before her hands reach up to her face, half-stifling a shriek of delight, "Oh my goodness, *Paddy*..." she looks him up and down, shaking her head, "...is this the new you, then?"

"I suppose it is; I'm now officially a civilian. Do you like it?"

"Of course I do. It was just the surprise... where did you get the suit?"

"Fitted by Montague Burton, in Leeds; should come in handy when I go for job interviews. The only problem is, everyone else demobbed round here has got one similar."

She nods, "Well, I hope you've still got your uniform, too, for special occasions. Tell me what you've been up to, Paddy."

"Me? Not a lot, Maggie. Filling in a whole bunch of forms and arguing over back pay, the usual rigmarole." He pauses, wondering whether to tell her yet, or wait until he knows for sure. What the hell, he thinks. "You know how you wanted to be a teacher, Maggie? I remember you once telling me I could do it once, a long time ago."

"Did I?"

"You did. Turns out it's not so far-fetched, after all; the demob advisors seem to think all the training I did in India plus my gunnery maths is pretty relevant. They've encouraged me to apply for one of these officer education grants, to train as a teacher."

"Oh, Paddy, that's marvellous." She frowns and sticks out her tongue. "But I'm jealous."

"Don't be; the idea of going back to college is a bit daunting at my age." He sits back, taking a long look at her pale and exhausted face. "Strangely enough, it was Pat who told me about the grants, you know; that was the last thing he said to me."

"Have you heard from him since?"

He shakes his head, slowly, "To be honest, I only wrote to him myself last week. What about you?"

"Yes, I've had a few letters." Her tone of voice conveys resignation. "Nothing's changed, though; he keeps begging me to go out there with him, in the nicest possible ways - but nothing about staying here with me. Just ignores that idea completely."

"I'm sorry to hear that, Maggie. He's an idiot – an eejit, as we say back home. If it's any consolation, I was pretty mad with him too, that day. I felt like I'd not even had time to say hello and then he was away again." He wishes he could tell her more, about the time Pat had left Ireland; he has a suspicion there's a pattern here, connected also with America, and with Pat's desire to make a fresh start. "I did try to persuade him to think again, to give it more time; but it's one of his faults, you know. Once he gets an idea in his head he doesn't listen much to anyone else."

"So I've discovered." She shakes her head, "Why didn't you warn me, Paddy?"

He almost chokes, "Me? I was in India. In any case, you wouldn't have listened."

"Probably not," She stares out of the window as if to signify, enough of that; then looks back at him. "We had one piece of good news recently, by the way."

"What's that?"

"Richard Turnbull has left the dale; seems to have gone for good, too."

"Really; how do you know that?"

"It's what he told his parents; his mother was very upset, apparently, but David is back at home and running the farm now."

"Do you think Richard was afraid the case would be reopened?"

"There was never a chance of that, according to George. He did look into it but there just wasn't any hard evidence to justify it. Mind you, George did discover that Constable Burns went to school with Richard; he felt that explained why Richard's story was never really questioned. When George tried to talk to the Inspector about it, the police just closed ranks."

"So there was a cock-up, then."

"Maybe; we'll never know for sure."

"Oh, I think we know, Maggie." He shrugs. "There are ways and means of doing things. It strikes me that someone has probably had a word in our Dicky's ear."

"But who would...?"

"Maybe George did, Maggie; maybe the Inspector."

"George isn't like that."

"Like what? Look, all anyone had to say was this; *I know what really happened, Richard. Word gets around quickly in these parts; Grace had a lot of people who cared about her. Just you think long and hard about that, Richard."* He lets her digest this, and adds, "I would've told him that myself, by the way, if I'd had the chance."

She looks up, blinks back the tears. "That makes me feel a little better." She reaches across and squeezes his hand. "I'm so glad you're back, Paddy."

She looks so vulnerable, he wants to take her in his arms and comfort her. And not just as a friend, either. In fact, part of him feels far too much desire; but instinctively, he knows he has to hold himself back, to be patient. He has to wait until she's recovered some of her strength, so that he's not exploiting her; they have to be, in some emotional sense, equals. And the thing with Pat has to be over; at least in her head, if not her heart.

*   *   *

She tosses and turns for what seems like hours. Lying in the darkness, the sound of June's steady breathing initially reassures but finally frustrates her; a sign of the rest she craves but cannot obtain. She admits defeat, slips quietly out of her bed, reaches down for the oilskin envelope. The remnants of moonlight penetrating the curtains guide her to the door; after that, she feels her way downstairs to the kitchen, lights a candle. From there, she slips through into the bar so that she can sit and warm herself beside the glowing embers of the fire. A smell of animals and farmyards lingers in the air; the end of the lambing season is nigh and several farmers have been in that night, supping a well-earned reward for their labours.

She sighs and opens the envelope, pulling out the photographs one by one. The soft light of the candle does nothing to lessen the impact of the images or reduce the pain they cause, burning through her as if a white hot iron has been carefully placed upon her skin and then pushed inward with ever-increasing force. Each time she does this, she hopes that the feeling will lessen, but it never does. Why does she do this to herself? She's not really sure, but this ritual has become a compulsion; something to do during the restless hours of her early mornings, at least making the time pass more quickly - lancing the pain out of her by night, so that she can get through the daylight hours without constantly thinking about him, without dissolving into tears.

He looks so young in these photographs; the man she knows now is no less handsome, just a little craggier. But why, oh why did he have to be so inflexible? And what on earth was wrong with this place, here, that he found so abhorrent? She bites her lip, feeling the soreness where she last drew blood, working on it. He looks so smart, so proud of himself, too; she knows that the theatre concerned, or rather opera house, is quite famous. This puzzles her; why didn't he want these photographs back?

At first she had been pleased, relieved that she at least had something personal to remember him by; she has no other pictures of him. But now she's realising that this memento comes with a cost. Not that she wants to forget him, but what she is doing now...she's using them to test her resolve, she realises. And to force herself to reconsider that terrible decision repeatedly, to make sure that she has made the right choice. Is she punishing herself; if so, for what? To force herself to go with him; that won't work, will it?

"Too much baggage," Those were his words, according to Paddy. He can't have meant it literally, she thinks... so perhaps he also found these photographs painful. Of course, she realises; he, too, must have gazed at these pictures repeatedly, feeling the same agony of loss, in the years after Paula's death. Probably he did the same as she's doing now, but gazing at *her* picture, instead. What else had he said, to her? That his operatic dreams were over, his hearing dulled by years in the engine room... her refusal to accompany him must have aggravated those earlier losses. She suddenly sees the photographs as a terrible, terrible symbol of broken dreams; for both of them. Perhaps no good can come of them, for him, after the manner of Paula's death. She knows one thing – she cannot allow herself to go on torturing herself in this way. Yet if she returns the photographs to him, he'll take this as a signal that she no longer wants him to return to her; she can't close that last hope off. She gathers the photographs up and pushes them carefully back into the envelope. She steels herself for a moment and places it carefully, almost reverentially, upon the glowing embers.

The tears stream silently down her face as the oilskin slowly browns and then wrinkles before suddenly bursting into flame, the noise exploding in the otherwise silent night. She resists the urge to thrust her hand into the fire to try to rescue one image, or maybe just to burn the offending hand; meanwhile her tears flow faster, as if in hope that they will pool upon the hearth and extinguish the fire. After ten minutes she sniffs and wipes her eyes, picks up the poker and rakes the pile of ashes, as if to remove any traces of her action from prying eyes.

She knows that she has taken a step forward out of her passivity. If Pat decides to stay, he'll understand. If he leaves her behind, then by this action she has at least decided that she will have to put his memory behind her and get on with her life.

*   *   *

Dublin hasn't really changed so much as weathered a little more. Even the big stores in Grafton street look a little dilapidated, the paint flaking on the most exposed surfaces of the window-frames. They have rationing here too; all the usual austerity, and more. The *emergency*, they call it here, whispering the word reverentially, as if still astounded that the country remained untouched by bombs (apart from the odd raider who missed Belfast and lost his way entirely). Every time they use the word, he wants to shout at them; *it was a fucking war - they sank just as many Irish boats, even with their flag of neutrality, you eejits...* Still, he tells himself, we Irish will always invent new phrases now and again.

He stands outside the store for quarter of an hour, enjoying the warm spring evening; the women who lock the doors and roll down the shutters give him curious looks. The clicking of high heels alerts him; he turns to see a well-dressed attractive woman stop in her tracks. His shock of recognition reflects in her expression, too; a face carefully made up, yet fresh and healthy nonetheless, above an ample body turning a little stocky. She swallows, gives him a nervous smile, glances up and down the street.

"You got my message?" though it's obvious, he thinks, she has.

She nods, frowns; "You obviously didn't get my last letter, did you, Pat?"

He shrugs, "Oh, I've been in transit, here and there, Mary."

She gives him a nervous smile, "Come along then, let's find somewhere quiet." She takes another glance around, examines his face. "Look, I'm happy to see you; just a bit surprised. Come on, I'll explain when we find somewhere private." He takes her arm, allows himself to be led into a nearby hotel bar, where they settle into a quiet corner away from any potential audience.

"So what's the mystery, Mary?"

"I had some feller asking after you a couple of months ago, Pat. Using your real name, he was, too." His mouth suddenly feels dry; he takes a sip of his drink, swallows carefully.

"Was he a Guard, or what?"

"He was some kind of private detective. He knew about us, somehow, back in Cork; he gave me his card."

"So what did you say?"

"I told him I hadn't seen you for years, not since I left Cork."

He exhales a long sigh of relief. "Thanks."

She squeezes his hand, looking tearful; "That's not all, Pat. He didn't seem to believe me; told me someone of your description had visited me just before the war. He must have been asking around. And he...he seemed to know a lot about me."

"What do you mean, Mary?"

She bites her lip, takes a long sip of her own drink. "You know what this country's like, Pat. A single woman like me can't afford to have a private life."

He nods, half of him pleased that she has a private life; the other half sensing her anxiety. "He's blackmailing you?"

She nods, her face blushing furiously, "I have a friend, Pat, a married friend; but if my employer and my landlord hear about it, I'd lose everything I've worked for all these years."

He can hear the fear in her voice; he feels his own fury, rising. "Jesus, I'll kill the bastard."

She stares at him, open-mouthed, for a moment; then shakes her head, gives him a rueful grin. "No you won't, Pat. That was the cause of the problem in the first place, if you remember."

He can't help but laugh; he shakes his head in admiration, "They say women have no sense of humour."

"*They* say a lot of stupid things. But the point is, Pat, I'll have to tell him *something*. He made it perfectly clear that if he finds out I've seen you and tell him nothing he'll carry out his threat. I wrote to you to tell you not to visit, and to send your letters via my brother in Cork."

At least it's a private detective, he thinks. But Mary's right, he can't allow her to become a victim because of his mistakes. He picks up her hand, gives it a squeeze. "Don't you worry, Mary, the timing isn't so bad. Thank the Lord, and all that." He looks up, watching her eyes. "The reason I came to see you is that I'm going to New Zealand in a week's time; a new start. I'm starting a business out there with one of my ship-mates."

He sees hurt in her eyes first; then resignation, finally a puzzled expression, "On your own? I mean, what about that English girl?"

Pat shrugs, makes an effort to keep his tone factual. "She seems to have decided not to go with me." He hasn't quite given up hope, yet, though he can hear the lack of it in his own voice.

"Is that why ... I mean...are you asking me, Pat?" Her question hangs in the air, his own thoughts matching the surprise that he hears in her voice. He finds himself blushing in confusion. This wasn't really in his plans; on the other hand, he doesn't want to belittle her, by rejecting the notion out of hand... and if Maggie sticks to her guns, well, the way he's reacted to Mary today makes the idea a lot less crazy than it sounds.

"Would you come if I did?"

She stares at him, takes a deep breath. "If you'd asked me that question twenty years ago, Pat, I'd have gone like a shot. Maybe again just before the war, when you came to see me, I'd have gone then. Sure, you're just a tiny, tiny bit slow, all the same." She looks away, shakes her head to herself, meeting his eyes again. "Not now, Pat. You're only asking me because the English girl won't go." Her gaze is steady, accusing; he can't deny this, so he stays silent. She sighs, "I've played second fiddle all my life, in one way or another. But with this friend of mine..." She blushes again, looks away. "I know I'm the one he really wants, Pat, even if he can't have me as his wife." Once again, she reaches for his hand, as if to reassure him. "So thanks for asking, but no. I've too much to keep me here."

He laughs; even to himself, his laughter sounds forced, a way of covering the confusion he feels... he scratches his head, forces a smile. "For your sake, I'm very glad to hear that, Mary." He rubs his chin, gives her another rueful smile. "But put it this way, if that bloody detective does mess up your life then you let me know and I'll send the fare and I'll also have a job waiting for you in New Zealand, no strings attached."

"You'd owe me that much."

"I would; hopefully it won't come to that." He thinks for a moment. "Listen, what you should tell the feller is this. Wait until next week and then ring him. Tell him I was here, but only for a day; that I'm now an American citizen, was over the water as part the American army but now on my way back to Boston. That's all I told you; say it was few days ago, you tried to ring before but got no answer. That should keep him happy and get him off your back. It'll sound plausible, don't worry; my brothers have put the same story about in Cork. Meanwhile I'll be on a boat going halfway round the world in the other direction. Look, they can only arrest me here on Irish soil. And they'd somehow have to separate me from my passport in order to do that."

She sighs, "Then you shouldn't hang around, Pat."

"One more drink and we'd better say farewell; I'll catch the night ferry back to Liverpool."

"Make it a double, in that case."

Waiting in the queue for the ferry, looking back on the conversation, it seems a fitting and memorable way to say farewell to Ireland and especially to Mary. He can leave feeling satisfied that all the important things have been said; there's no unfinished business left behind. Well, almost, he thinks, feeling his anxiety grow while he waits to present his passport at what looks like a fairly decent impersonation of a border check. Before the war, the procedure here was minimal; now, there's even a symbolic space in the centre of a long building, creating a significant gap between two sets of officials; an expression of the bad feeling between the two nations, he assumes.

He shows his ticket, hands his passport over for inspection. The younger of two Guards inspects it, passes it to his senior. The older man studies him, comparing him to the photograph. "Engineer, eh?" Pat nods. "What brings you to Ireland, sir?"

Pat notices the younger man watching him while glancing

repeatedly at some kind of list in his hand. He clears his throat, speaks in his best BBC voice. "I've been to visit an old navy friend, as it happens. We were on the same ship for three years out in the North Atlantic."

"Really?" The older man folds the passport shut, seems about to hand it back; but the younger one nudges him, shows him something written on the paper. Pat feels his heartbeat increasing but pretends not to notice; he holds out his hand expectantly. "I'm sorry sir, we'll have to ask you to stand to one side and wait a moment; just a routine check, I assure you, nothing to worry about." The older man smiles blandly at him; the younger one hurries away as if his role is to consult with higher authority. What about? Who with? Pat moves to one side, feels the hairs rising on the nape of his neck; heat surges through his face as he notices other passengers staring at him, whispering. He begins to sweat.

After five minutes, he remembers the passport. He waits until the next passenger moves away, asks, "Could I please have my passport back?"

Pat sees that bland smile again; "Your passport? Sorry sir, my colleague took it to make sure he has your right name." Pat swallows a feeling of deep unease, his panic beginning to rise. The bastards have done it, he thinks; they've separated me from my passport.

He has to fight back, he realises, before this goes too far. He allows himself a little irritation;

"Name; what's my damned name got to do with it? Dammit, I have to get back to my ship now."

"Perhaps there's a message for you, sir; it could be as simple as that. He's just gone to check why your name is on our list." Reluctantly, he stands aside again. Soon, the queue thins. He checks his watch; ten minutes. He has to get aboard this ferry; he can't let them stall him until it leaves. On the far side of the room, the British official glances across, yawns, leans back in his chair. Pat thinks about making a run, but that's no good without the passport.

Boredom, he thinks, of course; I'll give him a cure for his boredom. He takes a deep breath, as if about to sing, steps up to the desk, projecting his voice across the room. "Look, old chap, I'm Chief Engineer on one of His Majesty's ships and I have to be back in Liverpool in the morning. You can either give me my passport now or I will ask one of my countrymen over there..." (He points at the British official, who suddenly looks very alert) "to phone my skipper immediately. You will then personally have to explain to the British Admiralty and also to your own government exactly why you intend to prevent my ship from sailing."

The Guard shifts uncomfortably on his feet, glances towards a door. At the far end of the room, the British officials stands up, stretches his arms, begins to saunter in their direction. The Guard presses a button on the desk. Pat sees a face appear at the door; the older Guard sighs, waves his young colleague back in. Pat hears a whispered, "Can't get through," sees a slight shrug.

"Your passport, sir," The sleight of hand is such that Pat wonders if the older man had it all the time; he grasps it, resists a slightly crazy urge to tell the man where to go using his best Cork accent. "Thanks, old chap."

As he heads across to the British desk, he hears the older guard muttering to his colleague, "Some sort of eejit drew up that list; Churchill's got more Irish blood than he has."

The British official gives him a knowing look, glances at his passport. "What ship would that be, sir, if you don't mind me asking?"

Pat lifts his eyebrows a little, reverts to his normal speech. "To tell you the truth, now, I'm in the merchant navy."

"Oh, I thought you might be, sir." He hands it back and whispers, "By your cap."

*   *   *

Motes of dust float gently in the bright sunshine that penetrates the room, slanting down to the polished floorboards. On these sunny May mornings, the steep-sided dale traps the hot sun even here in the bar. Smells of farm and stale tobacco linger in the musty air. Paddy opens both windows, aiming to air the place out while he checks the stock and brings bottles in from the storeroom. He'd rather be out in the fresh air, but the battered car seats are in danger of falling apart; Gilly has decided to patch them up using cord and upholstery needles.

He's halfway finished when he hears a knock at the pub door. His urge to shout, "We're shut, use the Post Office entrance..." competes with feelings of boredom and curiosity... the locals surely know that, or would just go round the back for a family visit. So who could it be?

Pushing the front door half open, the sight of two men dressed in dark but patched and well-worn suits above working boots disappoints him; so obviously the clothes of farming men. The faces seem vaguely familiar too, though he can't quite place them. They both clutch their caps, regarding him intently. Both are losing their hair; one seems older and more portly, the other thinner, sharper faced. He shrugs, "Sorry lads, you're a bit early. You know the licensing laws."

The slimmer man nods, though the face breaks out into a knowing smile as he looks Paddy up and down, as if mentally checking against a memory... when he speaks, his voice and the accent provide the final clues; "Ah well, you see, it's not a drink that we're after. Maybe you'll remember us, Fons, when I say I'm glad to see you out of that bloody bearskin..."

"Christ, it's Sean... and Ernie too, isn't it?" He hears the surprise in his own voice; feels pleasure also within his tone of welcome, offers his hand.

"It is, Fons it is. It is us, indeed." The two brothers slap his back; hands are pumped while Paddy glances up and down the road; Pat, however, is nowhere to be seen. The relief at this observation comes tinged with guilt.

"You've got yourselves a long way from home." He remembers his manners, steps back, pulls the door wide open. "Come in, and have yourselves a seat. I'll get us some tea for now; we can have a glass later." The two brothers shuffle through the door, their curiosity evident as they stare about them, taking in the tables and chairs, the fireplace, the pewter mugs hanging from the beams, positioned in places chosen by their owners.

"It's a grand little pub all right."

"Well, not so little, Ernie, but grand all the same," corrects Sean.

Paddy's curiosity, previously shocked into silence, begins to clamour; he blurts out, "Will Pat be coming along soon, Sean?"

The two brothers glance at each other, conferring wordlessly; Sean acts as spokesperson. "He will not, Fons, I'm sorry to say; well, not unless we send for him. He's in Liverpool, at the seaman's mission." Sean seems to consider his next words carefully, clearing his throat before he continues. "He asked us to act as intermediaries, Fons. I suppose he fears that Mr Hardy has no time for him, that he might listen more to us, being more of the same generation, with our farming background."

Paddy rubs his chin, "It makes sense, when you put it like that. Look, sit yourselves down. I'll bring you that tea, then I'll find Gilly; Mr Hardy, that is." Out the back of the pub, the car looks empty until he spots a boot poking out of a half open door. He moves closer; Gilly lies on his back, grunting as he forces a long, thick needle through battered leather. His eyes flicker towards Paddy, then back to his work. "We've got visitors, Gilly; or maybe I should say matchmakers."

Gilly grunts, continuing to sew, "What on earth are you blathering about, Paddy?"

"It's an ancient Irish profession, the matchmaker, Gilly; I gather it's had a bit of a revival in recent years due to a lack of eligible females..." Gilly's forehead puckers; the eyes flicker at him again. Paddy grins, "...though that's hardly the problem in this case."

"I thought you'd left the world of codes and ciphers behind, Paddy; spit it out, lad."

"We've got visitors who've come all the way from Ireland, Gilly; Pat's two brothers, Sean and Ernie. They're decent fellers, both of them, good farming lads. I think they've come to lobby on his behalf." Gilly turns and stares, leaving the upholstery needle half inserted.

"Have they now?"

"They have; I'd take it as a sign of respect for you, Gilly, from Pat; and from his brothers, come to that. It's a hell of a long way for them to come."

Gilly considers this, sits up. He scratches his head, "I suppose it is; better if Pat had come with them, though."

"The brothers say they can send for him if we want to."

Gilly grunts and sighs, "Actually I suppose it's not so daft. I got my father to speak to Violet's father to smooth my path." He scratches his head, "Well, we'd better hear what they have to say. Though it's Maggie they really need to talk to."

"I'm sure that'll be the next stage, Gilly; that's the usual procedure."

"All right, you'd better warn Maggie first; then, you can introduce me..." Paddy, known to the brothers as Fons, feels a whole mix of emotions as the two sides come together; it feels as if his past, present and future are all about to collide like runaway trucks while he is forced to sit and watch. The scene reminds him a little of his own unexpected appearance in the middle of a blizzard; except that the Irish farmers, uncertain of their welcome, have been brought here by an emotional rather than a physical storm. He observes Gilly readying himself, steeling himself to be fair and courteous, to listen to the message that Pat has given them to bring; just as Paddy has to steel himself to accept the outcome, whatever that might be. And the future; well, just as he was beginning to hope that the field was clear, that he might have a real chance with Maggie, why, that very hope might now be dashed in front of his eyes. The four men eye each other like wary bulls.

"Shall I get you a tea, Gilly?" Paddy utters the words without thinking; then realises, yes, it's not really his place to eavesdrop on this.

"I never say no to tea, Paddy; bring us a pot, while you're at it." When he returns, the atmosphere has changed. The three of them are discussing the price of cattle and dairy produce on either side of the Irish Sea; discovering common threads. He sets the tray down and turns to go, but Gilly grasps his arm, "Sit yourself down, Paddy. I feel outnumbered. Besides, you can vouch for both families." The two brothers glance at each other; they nod with apparent approval. Gilly pours the tea, and clears his throat. "Best get down to business, then. First thing I'd like to say is that I have nothing against your brother. In fact, I liked him very much when he first arrived; we fell out because he'd not told my daughter that he was already married." Paddy watches the brothers nod and swallow. They obviously know the story; they say nothing. "Naturally, I told him to go at that point. To be fair to him, he did go away and sort out himself a legal divorce. When he came back, well, I never had the same trust in him; but that's his fault, not mine. The main point is, if Maggie had gone ahead and married him, I would have given them my blessing."

The brothers seem surprised by this statement; Ernie raises a hand, though Sean speaks first. "Divorce is not something we see back home, Mr Hardy... but Pat knows his first marriage was a big mistake."

"He also seemed to think you had advised your daughter not to marry him, Mr Hardy." Ernie speaks in a plain, matter of fact tone.

Gilly shrugs, "I did tell her that I thought she might find it difficult married to a sailor, especially if he was away for long periods. That's the sort of advice any parent would give to his child; but that's all it was, advice." He turns to Paddy. "You'd better explain what sort of people we are, Paddy. That even if I wanted to stop Maggie doing something, she'd never let me."

Paddy nods, slowly, "That's right, Sean, Ernie. She makes her own mind up."

"Do you have any doubts about Pat's ability to support your daughter, Mr Hardy?"

Gilly purses his lips. "Not really. Look, this thing in New Zealand is a risk, but he's got qualifications and a trade; that's more than I ever had. No, you're barking up the wrong tree; you need to talk to Maggie. Though if you want my opinion of what went wrong, I'll tell you."

The brothers glance at each other again. "Go on; we'd appreciate that."

"My daughter's a very loving girl and very attached to all of her family. Even if everything had been fine here, she would have found it difficult to go to New Zealand. The idea of leaving after the death of their mother and sister was unbearable... for herself, and for her sisters."

"We should have said earlier, Mr Hardy, we're terrible sorry for your family's loss."

Gilly swallows, takes a deep breath; "Your brother never understood that; he was far too impatient. He should have stayed and supported her if he really wanted her. However long he would have had to wait."

Sean nods, his eyebrows slowly raise; a half nod suggests that he agrees. "Maybe he should. He had his reasons for being impatient, is all I can say to that." Sean gives Paddy the briefest of knowing glances, tugs his ear, turns back to Gilly. "Mainly, Mr Hardy, he's given his word already to a man who saved his life, the one in New Zealand. He feels he can't let him down." Paddy only half hears these words; Sean has conveyed a private signal, *you know the reason I mean.* Is Pat still worried about his past catching up with him? Are the Fitzgerald family on his trail again, he wonders? He hears a scrape, sees Sean push back his chair and stand, offering his hand to Gilly. "Thanks for your honesty, Mr Hardy; you are right, I think, now we should talk to your daughter." Ernie follows suit.

For Paddy, the certainty of Pat's departure brings a deep rush of elation; followed in equal measure by shame that he should feel that way about his friend. Especially if the risk from the authorities is real; oh, Lord. He feels a deep and growing sense of unease. What should he do if Maggie decides to go with Pat, after all? Say nothing, or tell her? He'd be damned, either way...

* * *

She feels her father's hand resting in the small of her back, half supporting her and half pushing her towards the table where two men now rise to their feet, glancing awkwardly at her, as if this were a dance hall and they were the only men in town. All this is so unexpected, without warning; she has barely had time to put on her newest blouse, brush her hair; add some lipstick.

"This is my daughter, Maggie." The two men blush, nod and smile all at the same time. "This is Sean and that is Ernie, Maggie; Pat's brothers."

"Pleased to meet you, I'm sure." She hesitates for a moment; if Pat were here, she'd probably embrace them. Though it seems far too formal, she sticks out her hand.

Each of the men takes her hand and gives it a careful squeeze, with minimal movement, as if handling a bone china cup; they mumble, "Grand to meet you too."

"I'll leave you to it, then." She turns and watches her father exit, in two minds whether to ask him to stay.

"Please sit down, Miss Hardy. May we call you Maggie?" She turns back. The younger of the two gestures at a chair. Sean, she remembers; he seems to have relaxed a bit. She sits and the men also sink down, their chairs creaking a little while they settle. She looks at their faces; neither has a strong resemblance to Pat; they could be strangers, with no connection at all. "Pat has asked us to come and talk to you, Maggie, to explain his position to you and to your father." Sean seems to address his first words to the table top, but lifts his eyes to meet hers at last. "The first thing Ernie and I want to say is that we are terrible sorry for your loss. We lost our own mother when we were about your age, and that was bad enough; but to lose a sister too, that must be a most dreadful thing." With this word, she hears a tangible connection to Pat and Paddy; the almost silent 'h' in 'thing'. That same accent, that same tone of voice...

She swallows, blinks back a tear. "It was. *It is*," she corrects. They both nod and stare down at the table. "How old was Pat when you lost your mother?"

The two men exchange glances. "He'd be about eleven or twelve, was he not, Ernie?"

Ernie nods, "That's right. He took it hard, but that's how he got his education, Maggie. The church helped my father get him to a school in Dublin after she died. He was a bright lad, you see."

"It was for the singing, too, Ernie."

"So it was; but the point is, that's how he got to be an Engineer."

"Was it? I thought he'd learned all that in America." She feels embarrassed for contradicting them; hastily she adds, "I'm sorry, he's never told me much about Ireland."

She observes another exchange of glances before Sean takes over again, frowning, seeming to choose his words carefully. "What Ernie means is that without his schooling he'd not have been able to become an Engineer, Maggie. He enjoyed the science, so he did; that's all Ernie's saying."

She nods, feeling more curious about Pat's schooldays. How long was he at this Dublin school? Did he sit his science exams, get any qualifications? Why did he decide to leave? Pat has always implied that he ran away to sea out of boredom; it doesn't quite fit... "Your father tells us that if you do decide to go with Pat, you'd go with his blessing." She feels confused; why such an abrupt change of subject? It probably shows in her face, because Sean persists, "Is that true, Maggie?"

She thinks about her father; a reluctant blessing, probably, if the truth were told. But the fact that he would give it makes it harder for her to leave him and the girls. "If that's what I decide, yes." At this point in time, she tells herself, she still has a choice. She has clung to this idea, despite everything. The nature of the choice, she abhors.

"I know that my brother truly believes that you will be happier in the long run if you go with him, Maggie; he knows it will be terrible for you at first, but he cares deeply about you and wants to marry you. If you love him the way he loves you, maybe he's right."

The logic seems undeniable. The words form in her mind; *yes, of course I love him the same way; all right, I will go with him*. She hears herself saying these words in her head, though not out loud.

Not yet. Maybe, if Pat himself were here, she might say them; but not to his brothers, in this way. It doesn't feel right, somehow; she looks up and sees them watching her, waiting for an answer. She struggles to put it into words. There's something about this situation that feels unfair, as if all these men are blaming her, making it her responsibility. Even her father has abandoned her. What would Grace have said, she wonders? Grace was always so sharp, so logical, when men tried to push her around. Suddenly, she hears her sister's voice. "I do love him, but I'm not the only one with choices here. He has a choice, too, you know."

The Irish brothers glance at each other; Sean looks distinctly uncomfortable, Ernie shrugs and scratches his head. "I assume Pat has told you his reasons for going now, Maggie? That he gave a solemn promise to his friend, to the one who saved his life?"

She hears her own voice again, faltering at first but gaining in confidence. "He said something about that; perhaps not very clearly, but since then he's told me in his letters. So yes, I understand that. But I have my own reasons for staying, just as strong as his. Has he even explained things to his friend? Has he asked his friend about a delay?"

Another exchange of glances; both men shrug. "You'd have to ask him about that, Maggie; we don't know."

Ernie's previous statement suddenly hits her; "You said *now*, Ernie? Going *now*? What does that mean, exactly?" Ernie looks at his feet.

"He's leaving next week, Maggie, from Liverpool." His face colours, "He did say if that was too soon for you, he'd come here to say goodbye and give you the fare to follow on later." Maggie puts her head in her hands, lost for words. The men wait for her to speak, once again pushing the responsibility back to her. She thinks for a long time.

"Tell me, Ernie, how many times has Pat been back to visit you since he left Ireland?"

The two brothers slump back in their chairs, staring down at their boots, "A few times."

"Not many, I grant you; but it's been impossible during the emergency."

"Before that?"

"Not many... but he had his reasons, Maggie."

Maggie sighs, "He always has his reasons, Sean. Look, all this time I've been thinking it was something personal with my father. Talking to you, it sounds like he's been the same about Ireland." The brothers exchange another glance; as if they want to agree with her but daren't, out of loyalty to Pat. Abruptly, she makes her mind up.

"Look, you'd better just tell Pat that I can't go for at least a year. If he really wants to marry me, he should write to his friend and explain that to him - then come back here and talk to me himself."

Sean bites his lip and nods. "You're sure about that?"

"As sure as I'll ever be," Though as soon as she says it, the doubts begin to clamour.

"I'll pass your message on, but from what he told us I wouldn't hold out much hope. I'm really sorry, but I think you and Pat will both have to accept that circumstances have combined to split you up. That's a terrible shame, but there it is." Her hope seems to scream as it dies, staring at the honesty in Sean's face.

"There's one other thing, Maggie." Nothing else of any importance, she thinks, staring at him blankly. "He did tell us about some photographs he left with you..."

"...the American ones, from the opera place..." She looks from one face to another, a feeling of horror growing in her gut.

"He'd like them back, Maggie, if you're not going with him." Sean gives her a sheepish smile. "We'd both like to see them too, before he goes."

She swallows, unable to speak. How on earth can she explain this? She has a vivid image of the envelope turning brown, crinkling slowly, smoking; she feels the hot blood flushing in her face. Eventually, she stammers; "I... er...I'm afraid I ... I lost them."

Looks of blank incomprehension turn to incredulity; her face continues to burn. She knows how obvious it must be that she's lying, but what can she say? If she told the truth, what would *that* say about her? "You lost them?"

"Yes." She tries to think, blurts out, "On one of my walks; they must have fallen out of my bag."

They scratch their heads, looking embarrassed; "A walk?"

"I think so. I mean I think that's how I lost them. I've been over the route twice already, but I'll go and look again. They were in a waterproof envelope."

More glances exchanged; she feels that she's just confirmed all their worst fears about her. They probably think she just wants to keep them to spite Pat; there are lots of girls like that, she knows. She has an urge to run out of the room and hide; though she has to endure some awkward farewells first, which suddenly feel just as uncomfortable and awkward as their introduction. The brothers appear totally deflated; they have failed. Worse than that, their overriding memory will be, at best, her carelessness. As she watches them walk away, from an upstairs window, she imagines their comments about her...

She knows it's over with Pat, now. Her best hope of seeing him again would have been to produce the photographs for his brothers to see but then not to hand them over; to insist that she would only give them to Pat and no one else, to insist that they must speak together one more time in order to make a decision together. Nothing else was ever going to work, she now realises. And he might have listened to her, if she had only got him here.

Now, it's all too late. She lies on the bed, buries her face in her arms.

*   *   *

Epilogue: Autumn 1946

Reaching into the locker to check that he has emptied it, Pat finds himself slipping back in time. His brain tells him that something important is missing; automatically, he thrusts his hand into his breast pocket, feels for his wallet and the thick envelope containing his papers and personal letters. He frowns, stares down at the small pile of books and magazines on top of his kitbag, feeling a moment of panic. Where is the precious oilskin envelope? He bends to look inside the locker; a long moment of puzzled confusion precedes a flush of raw emotions that surge through him. Hurt, frustration and annoyance blend with embarrassment at his continuing stupidity.

"Bloody fool," he tells himself; narrowly avoiding cracking his head as he straightens up in the tiny cabin. He sighs, takes a deep breath. He'll never really understand what happened to those damned pictures; he feels sure that Maggie would never have been so careless with them, but neither can he accept that she would keep them just to spite him. She just wasn't like that. Perhaps one day, he might write to Fons to ask whether he knows. No, he tells himself; you have to let it all go. Leave it all behind; make a clean break, start a new slate. Perhaps it's all better this way; safer for him, the way things turned out. He collects his meagre possessions, makes his way up on deck.

To port, he can see the inlet to the bay; to starboard, the buildings of Auckland rise in front of him behind the harbour. Gulls wheel and cry above his head as he steps onto the gangplank. He pauses, the moment reminding him of New York, the time when he stepped off the liner as a young man, making his first new start. He gives himself a wry smile, tells himself he's not yet forty and mutters, "Third time lucky…"

He touches the wooden rail one last time and steps forward, whistling the chorus of the Hebrew slaves. It'll be good to see Frank again, he tells himself.

*   *   *

As the slope steepens, the bushy heather seems to rise up, reaching out for his face. Settling into a rhythm, he tracks left and then right, executing regular hairpins, as the mountain regiments were trained to do in India. He feels his heart rate steadily increasing while he sucks air deep into his lungs, the sweat rising out of his exposed brow and running down inside his shirt. He likes this feeling, that his body is still fine-tuned, capable of maximum effort. The sensations remind him of the long, exhausting march to Dunkirk, across the beaches to the harbour; and of misty days, hiking up into the Boggeragh mountains. This day has its own characteristics, too; a crisp fine autumn morning, the first chill in the air; a scent that takes him back to Ireland as a boy, to the smell of apples in someone else's orchard...

He stops and glances behind, down the slope, watching Maggie climbing steadily, a little slower but, he has to admit, with equal stamina. She glances up and pauses momentarily, reaching up to brush her hair back with that characteristic gesture of hers, triggered by the discovery that she is being observed. Does she do it to get the hair out of her eyes or to enable the watcher to see her face? He makes a mental note to ask her, later. Along with a million other things, he thinks. It feels like the right day, today. Before breakfast, he had gone on a little fishing trip; asking Gilly how long he thought it would take Maggie, before she got over Pat...

"No time and forever, lad." Half a smile crosses her father's lined face. "Look, that'll take care of itself. She's capable of loving more than one person. People often ask me how I've managed bringing up all these girls; but in one way it's easy, living in a house of females, surrounded by all their love. She may be hurting, but it's like damning a stream, Paddy. It'll find a way round."

*   *   *

By the time she reaches the top, she finds him already half-sitting, half-reclining on a mound of heather, sucking on a new, unlit pipe that her father has recently presented him. The pose looks relaxed, yet self-conscious and aware. How on earth has he got his breath back already? He watches her approaching out of the corner of his eyes, pats the heather beside him.

She leans forward, hands on knees, sucks in air. "In a hurry, are we?"

He laughs but shakes his head, "No more than usual; I knew you'd catch me." She watches him stare out, soaking up the view across the valley to the moors on the other side, glancing up and down the valley, shaking his head in admiration. Boyish enthusiasm for the simple things in life, plus his willingness to change his plans at the drop of a hat; he certainly has qualities she admires and envies. She flops down beside him. "It helps get a better perspective on life, up here."

She nods, still catching her breath. "You're turning into quite a philosopher."

He chuckles. "I hope I am, otherwise I'll never be any good as a teacher, will I?"

She resorts to a more serious tone, "How *is* your course going?"

"It's fine." He removes the unlit pipe, tucks it into his pocket. He catches her eye, gives her a sly grin. "In fact it's a piece of cake, compared to the army. The only thing that worries me is the teaching

441

practice. A bunch of kids can't be worse than a platoon of highland infantry, can they?"

"I hope not." She turns away, feeling a slight pang of envy. She turns back and adds "You've changed, for the better. It used to be hard work, talking to you."

"I learned a lot in India; about the need to keep talking, and the importance of making decisions together." She looks away, thinking of Pat... "Sorry, we're both a bit sore about that, aren't we?" She looks up and sees that for once, he looks very serious. The Indian girl, she realises. That must have been just as hurtful for him. He picks up her hand and holds it; she squeezes his hand to acknowledge his comment. "But that doesn't mean I want to become a priest." Their eyes meet; she smiles, blushing at the implication. He leans towards her and kisses her softly on the lips. "Is that all right with you?"

She feels a rush of confused emotions; shock, anxiety, guilt and pleasure... yes, pleasure. She hears herself making noises to express her astonishment; "Oh....oh, Paddy, I never knew you felt that way. About me, I mean."

"Didn't you?"

"No, honestly; I know you like me as a person, but I never thought you liked me... in that way..."

"Why on earth did you think that?"

"Well, from when... you know, from when I had a crush on you."

He smiles, "But you were just a girl then, Maggie."

"I suppose I was."

She feels her hand being squeezed again; "And I was just a boy. Well, not anymore; and now you do know how I feel, so I'll repeat my question. Is that alright with you, Maggie?"

She hears a clamour of voices within her head; feels a bubbling of feelings in her chest. She lets them settle, smiles at him. "I think it is, Paddy. In fact, I think it's more than all right."

He leans in to kiss her again, carefully, as if he realises that she needs time to work all this out. It suddenly strikes her, how different he seems from that young man she had a crush on. He has grown up, too; in fact, he seems to have developed all sorts of qualities while he was away. If anything, she feels a little in awe of him. Can't have that, she thinks...

* * *

Author's plea

A polite request; every author writes to be read… if you enjoyed this book, please tell other people about it; either by word of mouth or by reviewing it on websites such as Amazon. Even better, use it as a gift for people with similar tastes…

Acknowledgements

For everyone who helped, heartfelt thanks; to my wife Sheila, who encourages and supports my scribbling, to Helen and Lee at Cornerstones for polishing my meagre skills, to all of my ex-patients for teaching me about life, and to everyone who recorded (or collected) accounts of experiences during the turbulent era of this novel. Particular thanks are due to my wonderful aunts and others who directly shared experiences with me and thus gave the work its sense of time and place; and to Eileen Clifford for ensuring that the Cork way of speaking was not too wide of the mark.

Some events depicted in the book (such as the acquisition of rifles from British soldiers in Fermoy by the Volunteers) are real; others are based on a general pattern of events at the time (such as the raid on the Fitzgerald farm).

Inevitably, some people will have lived through very similar events. This book may rouse painful memories but it is intended as a mark of respect for that generation.

Makri press

Small independent publishers are an increasingly important source of tasteful literature... Makri press is proud to be part of this trend; a small independent publisher aiming to bring a few brilliant books to the world...

Makri press aims to publish stories in which the past comes alive, sits up, and begins a conversation; teases and seduces you, slaps you in the face and walks out... hopefully you, the reader, will follow...

"An idea, like a ghost, must be spoken to a little before it will explain itself" *(Charles Dickens)*

http://makripress.com/

email: makripress@btinternet.com

Ian next book, "The Soul Trader", is in preparation. You can read more about it on the Makri press website or on Ian's own blog at:

http://scribblingian.wordpress.com/